Cat lifted her face first, a shy smile playing on her lips. Subtly, she pulled her shoulders back, an action that caused her breasts to thrust forward, swelling just slightly out of her bodice.

"Jesus, Cat," I said. A little laugh escaped me.

"What?" she stumbled to stand straight and came to me. "Is it too much? Too little? What?"

"Isn't that a little obvious?"

"Well, it's not you I'm trying to impress," she said and turned away to recheck her box of clothes.

"Well, any gentleman you encounter will be. Impressed, that is."

"But will the king?" she cried, exasperated. "I want him to look at me and to see that I'm different! That I'm not just another maid-in-waiting."

"What do you want from him, Cat?" I asked. "He's already getting married."

"Whoever said I needed marriage?"

"Wait a minute. Are you trying to tell me that this whole act is so that you can be a mistress to the king? A fat, aging man with an ego the size of France and a temper the size of the Roman Empire?"

"I don't know!" she huffed. "Maybe I just want someone to notice me!"

Getting noticed was one thing. But what about the consequences? Manipulating the king of England could open a whole Pandora's box of repercussions.

OTHER BOOKS YOU MAY ENJOY

COURTED

INCLUDES *Gilt & Tarnish* BY

KATHERINE LONGSHORE

speak

An Imprint of Penguin Group (USA)

Gilt

SPEAK
Published by the Penguin Group
Penguin Group (USA) LLC
375 Hudson Street
New York, New York 10014

USA * Canada * UK * Ireland * Australia
New Zealand * India * South Africa * China

penguin.com
A Penguin Random House Company

First published in the United States of America by Viking,
a member of Penguin Group (USA) Inc., 2012
Omnibus edition published by Speak, an imprint of Penguin Group (USA) Inc., 2014

THE LIBRARY OF CONGRESS HAS CATALOGED THE VIKING EDITION AS FOLLOWS:
Longshore, Katherine.
Gilt / by Katherine Longshore
p. cm.
Summary: In 1539, Kitty Tylney and her best friend Cat Howard—the audacious, self-proclaimed
"Queen of Misrule"—both servants to the Duchess of Norfolk, move to the court of King Henry
VIII, who fancies Cat, and when Cat becomes queen Kitty must learn to navigate the complexities
and dangers of the royal court.
ISBN 978-0-670-01399-9 (hardcover)
1. Catharine Howard, Queen, consort of Henry VIII, King of England, d. 1542—Juvenile fiction.
[1. Catharine Howard, Queen, consort of Henry VIII, King of England, d. 1542—Fiction.
2. Kings, queens, rulers, etc.—Fiction. 3. Court and courtiers—Fiction.
4. Henry VIII, King of England, 1491–1547—Fiction.
5. Great Britain—History—Henry VIII, 1509–1547—Fiction.]
I. Title.
PZ7.L864Gi 2012 [Fic]—dc23 2011028214

Speak ISBN 978-0-14-751368-7

Printed in the United States of America

1 3 5 7 9 10 8 6 4 2

For my dad, who never let me feel unloved

Gilt

1539

"You're not going to steal anything."

I left the question—*Are you?*—off the end of the sentence. But Cat heard it anyway.

"Of course not." She paused to look at me, shadows eclipsing half her face, blue eyes glittering in the moonlight from the tall, narrow windows of the upper gallery. "I could be flogged. Or pilloried. Or have a hand cut off."

A drunken roar of laughter vented up through the beams of the great hall below us.

"Or executed," I muttered.

"We're just going to look. They can't hang us for that," she said, pulling me into a room congested with luxury. Arras tapestries mantled the walls, depicting knights on horseback charging to distant crusades. A silver goblet sat on a table by the fire between two chairs that were cushioned in velvet and tassled in gold.

"Consider it inventory," Cat explained, trailing her finger along the gold thread in a tapestry. "We're doing the duchess a favor."

"Right," I said. "Explain to me how Agnes Howard, née Tylney, the Dowager Duchess of Norfolk, most esteemed noblewoman in England, will think it a favor when she discovers two of her protégées riffling through her clothes."

"The duchess has gowns and furs and rings and pendants that she only wears on state occasions, and God knows we haven't had one of those since Queen Jane died. Someone has to appreciate her things."

"Without her realizing it."

"She's downstairs," Cat said. "Feasting with the duke. Nothing interrupts her when her stepson comes to visit. They closet themselves away and scheme until dawn."

She sat and laid her childlike hands over the lions' heads on the arms of the chair.

"Not like our wobbly old stools," she said, caressing the golden mane.

"Or splintery benches," I agreed, risking a seat in the other chair. I stretched my ragged slippers toward the fire.

Few had access to the duchess's chambers. Close to two hundred nieces, nephews, cousins, and staff lived at Norfolk House. Only select family members and the duchess's most trusted servants were allowed into her apartments. The rest of us did our best to stay out of her way. I stared up at the ceiling and wondered how it felt to have people care enough about you to avoid your presence.

"I could get used to this," Cat murmured. "Like being at court. Like a throne."

"Just like old times," I said, resting my head against the heraldic images carved on the back of the chair.

Cat laughed.

"You still remember that?" she said. "How we used to play that we were at court?"

"Used to?" I said. "We never stopped."

The game had just changed—from little girls playing princesses to a more grown-up and complicated hierarchy of status and favor.

Cat leaped up and mashed her face close to mine, a mischievous smile flickering over it.

"Onward," she said, widening her eyes. She spun around and marched to the next door. The door to the duchess's most private place: her bedchamber.

I pulled myself from the chair and stepped forward, the thrill of what we were about to do making my fingers tingle.

Cat stood to attention like the duchess's steward, staring straight ahead, eyes blank and unemotional. Even drawn up, she stood a full head shorter than me, and I slouched self-consciously to redress the balance.

She flicked the latch—the sound loud as a cannon shot—and pushed the door open with a grunt and a flourish. The room beyond lay draped in moonlight.

"After you."

Cat kept up her gallant pantomime until I came abreast of her. Then she threw back her auburn curls and danced through the door ahead of me.

"Glass in the windows!" she crowed, pressing her nose to the glazing. Our room had nothing but leaky shutters that

remained closed in the worst weather, forcing us to live out the winters in Gothic gloom.

Outside, the twisted and massacred topiary shambled to the banks of the Thames. Slightly downriver on the opposite bank, the abbey and palace of Westminster glowed ghostly, their hollows etched in shadow.

The heavy bed loomed like a giant, crouching toad in the center of the room, shrouded in velvet and redolent of sleep. The duchess had a down mattress and two real pillows and I desperately wanted to know what it felt like to lay my head on one of them.

Cat skipped right past the bed and into the narrow robing chamber, so I followed. The windowless room reeked of cedar and silk. I stood in the doorway, stunned by the number of chests and the potential opulence they might contain. But Cat threw them open, one by one, turfing out bell sleeves lined with fur, bodices trimmed with pearls, overskirts shot through with gold thread.

"Look at this!" she hooted, and held up the steel cage of an undergarment. "The duchess wears a corset! To lift those sagging, pendulous breasts!"

"And to trim her thickening middle," I reminded her.

Cat cackled and dove into another chest.

"This would look stunning on you," she said, pulling out a French hood, its buckram crown covered in deep green velvet, edged with a twisted tissue of gold and studded with pearls. "Bring out the color of your eyes."

My eyes were my best feature. That is, they were the one thing about my appearance that I liked, sea green and edged with gold, like the hood.

Cat tossed the hood at me and I snatched it out of the air, not wanting it to fall to the floor. I wrestled my straw-like hair into the black velvet veil and fitted the jeweled coronet over my head.

"Then again," Cat said, holding up a pink brocade bodice fronted by a crimson velvet stomacher, "perhaps your eyes are not something you want to call attention to."

"What do you mean?" I asked, my self-image purling away like leaves on the river.

She scrutinized me, head cocked to one side, the red-breasted gown completing the look of a robin about to catch a worm.

"Your eyes are too knowing," she said. "Men will think you see more than they wish you to understand. They want to surprise you. You look at them and they want to slink away."

"Thanks," I grumbled, pulling the hood over my face. "Better?"

But I wondered if my eyes were the reason no boy had ever visited me at our midnight parties. Or if it was some other lamentable feature—my hair, my height, or my face itself.

"What are friends for?" Cat smoothed her hair beneath a red velvet caul networked with gold braid and pearls that the duchess had probably worn for a royal coronation. "I tell you these things so you can attend to them in the future. You should practice looking more demure. Less judgmental."

Cat was a firm believer in practice. She had invented the way she walked, smiled, laid her fingers on a man's arm—even the way she turned her face to catch the light. She wasn't a stunning beauty, a brilliant musician, or a quick wit, but she could get a man's attention merely by entering the room.

And I was the perfect mirror. I helped her refine every performance—echoing and casting back at her all the things I couldn't be myself. She took me with her everywhere. We complemented each other. Completed each other. I was the Kitty to her Cat.

Being a reflection was better than being nothing at all.

"Why doesn't she do anything with this stuff?" Cat asked, pulling on crimson brocade sleeves lined with pink silk and trimmed with ermine. Their heavy bells dipped in the pool of the rosy train at her feet. Other people's clothes always looked ridiculously large on Cat.

"Maybe she doesn't want to wear it out," I said, swirling an overskirt the color of goldenrod. I thought of my own gowns, already worn out by two sisters I never saw and barely knew. Castoffs that fulfilled family duty, if not affection. The livery of the unloved.

"Humph." Cat dropped the duchess's gown to the floor, revealing her own frayed kirtle. Pink. The color brought out the roses in Cat's cheeks, and she insisted we all wear it every Tuesday and Saturday, despite the fact that it made me look sallow. "When I am rich and well-married, I shall wear something different every day, then give all my castoffs to the poor."

"The poor hardly have need of pearl-encrusted gable hoods."

"Oh, I'll take the pearls off first," she said. "And nothing could ever compel me to wear a gable, the most eye-gougingly ugly fashion accessory ever created."

"Well, that's all right, then," I muttered, but she didn't hear me. Something by the head of the duchess's bed had caught her eye and she crept out of the robing chamber to get a closer look.

It was a gilt coffer of wood and leather, covered in tiny romantic illustrations—*Tristan and Iseult* and *Orlando Innamorato*.

"No, Cat," I warned.

She ignored me and reached out cautiously, as though afraid it might scream like a magical box in a fairy story. But it opened silently, the leather and metal smooth beneath her fingers.

Cat let out a sigh that was half giggle, half moan.

"Come here," she said, her voice rich with awe.

"I really don't think we should be looking in there."

"Oh, come on," she coaxed. "I know you want to."

And she was right.

Tumbled within the smooth-sided box were pearls, rubies, emeralds. A diamond the size of a wren's egg dangled from a thick enameled collar. Cat stroked a gold letter *A* from which swung a single teardrop pearl.

"It's a good thing it's not a C," she said. "Or I might have to go back on my promise not to steal anything."

Coins sifted to the silk lining at the bottom of the box, gold sovereigns and angels, silver groats and pennies. Among them

9

lay papers folded and creased, the wax that once sealed them broken, smudged, or completely missing.

Cat picked up a roll of lace. It was a narrow series of white embroidery squares worked on white linen, the threads of the fabric cut and drawn out to leave behind nothing but air.

"Isn't this yours?" she asked. "Unoriginal. But pretty."

Ever since the dissolution of the monasteries, nun-made lace was hard to come by, and importing it from Italy was expensive. So the duchess had set all the girls on a program of learning how to make reticella and cutwork. Unfortunately, most failed miserably at the tiny stitches and intricate, repetitive knots. I surprised myself—and Cat—by excelling at it. It was the only thing I could do better than she.

"The duchess requisitioned it," I said. Not my best work. The pattern twisted crookedly, pulling the squares into oblongs.

I picked up a corner, and it unwound like a startled snake. A heavy iron key dropped to the floor. The sound reverberated through the quiet room, and we both stiffened, mirror images of horror.

"No one heard." Cat recovered quickly. She snatched the lace from me, wrenching it further out of kilter. She scooped up the key and paused, examining it.

"What's the matter?" I asked.

"Look at the scrollwork," she said, an edge of disgust creeping into her voice. "It matches the lock to our room."

The maidens' chamber was a dormitory crammed with

wooden plank beds, pallets on the floor, and twenty unwanted daughters. Cat and I had laid our heads on the same piece of timber in that room for eight years.

"Why is it in there?" I asked, pointing at the coffer, the money, and jewels.

"Because we are part of her fortune," Cat said, wrapping the key in the lace and stuffing it beneath a slurry of papers and coins. "We're a host of servants she never has to pay. Not to mention wardships and perhaps even a percentage of a dowry when we're sold into marriage."

She closed the lid and laid a finger on the engraving there. Sir Gawain bowed his head before the raised ax of the Green Knight, Lady Bertilak voluptuous and partially clothed in the background.

"Perhaps it's time we left," Cat said. "I no longer feel like playing dress-up. In fact"—she pointed at Lady Bertilak—"*un*dressing is a much more appealing prospect."

"Francis?" I asked, though I needn't have. He had shared our bed repeatedly for more than a year.

"Mmmm," she hummed through a seductive smile.

I turned back to the robing chamber. The cedar chests gaped like the mouths of benighted fish. Hoods and kirtles, sleeves and lacings lay strewn all over the floor. A single loose pearl scrolled out in front of me as I moved to put them away.

"I don't remember where they all go!" I smoothed a velvet hood and placed it on top of the bulging corset.

"It doesn't matter," Cat said, stuffing a fur-lined muff on top of a green silk sleeve.

"She'll know someone's been in here." I knew my voice was edged with panic, but I couldn't stop it. I matched a pair of sleeves to a bodice and laid them carefully on top of a similarly colored skirt.

"We'll blame it on a servant," Cat retorted, whipping the sleeves out from under my hands. "Or that weasely Mary Lascelles. The duchess probably never checks on this stuff anyway." She crumpled each sleeve into a different chest.

"Why wouldn't she?"

Cat whirled on me.

"When you have this much money and this much power, you don't have to check on anything. You can have two chairs in your withdrawing room, gowns you'll never wear, and jewels you can't even count, and it's there because you *believe* it's there. Because it always has been and it always will be, and there's nothing anybody can do to change that."

She slammed the lid on the last chest, a reverberating bang that shuddered the floor beneath us, quenching the current of voices and laughter from the great hall. Then she laughed, grabbed my hand, and ran.

We fled back along the narrow, stuffy, unused upper gallery at the back of Norfolk House to the tightly packed living quarters of the lesser members of the household. And straight into Alice Restwold.

Whip-thin, blonde, and blandly pretty, Alice collected

secrets the way the rest of us collected ribbons. Joan Bulmer stood behind her, eyes wide and lips pressed together, her expression one of permanent confusion caused by eavesdropping on partial conversations.

"Where have you been?" Alice asked in a scandalized whisper. "The duchess was looking for you."

2

"Nowhere." Cat pushed past them into the maidens' chamber.

Alice's nose twitched beneath her particularly ugly magenta gable hood. She had married the previous summer and as a result could no longer wear her hair loose. However, her husband had left for Calais within weeks of their marriage and never returned, relegating Alice and her hood to the maidens' chamber. Cat called her a "once-again virgin."

"What did she want?" I asked.

"We don't know," Joan reported, tugging off her own hood, more orange than pink, though Cat didn't mention it. Joan's husband was also long absent and easily forgettable, her hood the only reminder he existed. "But when she asked about you, Mary Lascelles answered, 'Look in the company of Francis Dereham, for they are always together.'"

"That little . . ." Cat puffed up like her namesake, ready to spit.

"But Francis was right there in the room," Alice cut in, obviously not wanting the best part of the story to be told without her.

"Behind the duchess's chair!" Joan brayed, mirth shaking

her coif loose. Her unruly frizz of dark hair flew about her head like bees around a hive.

"Well, obviously what my *step*grandmother doesn't know can't hurt her."

As we talked, the room filled and crowded. The beds fitted together on the floor like a puzzle. A girl could walk between them, but not if another stood in the way. Our roommates climbed up on beds, had mock disagreements and danced aside, giggling and pushing. Gowns came off, hung on wooden pegs hammered into chinks between the stones in the walls. Cedar chests scraped the floors, pulled from beneath the beds and stirring the two-week-old rushes that moldered on the floor—no woven matting for us, just dried marsh-grass and herbs, loosely strewn. Chests opened to accept sleeves, hoods, shifts, and kirtles. Farthingales, their willow cane hoops creaking and clacking together like teeth, were shaken out and piled in the corner. Bedmates brushed and braided each other's hair in preparation for sleep.

Or not. At this moment, sleep was the last thing on most of the girls' minds.

"I shall be queen tonight," Cat said. No one disputed her. No one ever did. Cat ruled the maidens' chamber.

She sat enthroned on our bed, a coronet fashioned from yellow embroidery silk on her hair. Her nightdress, worn to the point of near transparency, slipped from one shoulder. I sat beside her, reflecting majesty. Elevated by proximity.

After dark, after the duchess and the dusty and decayed

members of the household had gone to bed, the doors of the maidens' chamber were thrown open and the room was invaded by boys. Each had received a personal invitation. Some were gentleman pensioners, dressed in the livery of the Duke of Norfolk. One, Lord William Howard, was the duchess's married son. Two were related to the duchess's steward, who, in turn, was related to the duchess herself. None were anything less patrician than the younger sons of landed gentry, making their way in a world that favored the firstborn.

The room was barely large enough to contain the girls who slept there. When boys entered, mayhem ensued.

"Ah, the Queen of Misrule," Francis Dereham declared as he strode up to our bed.

"Do you not bow before your sovereign?" Cat asked.

Francis cocked an eyebrow, and then extravagantly lowered his head over his bent knee.

"You may rise," Cat pronounced.

"My head?" he asked, straightening. "Or my . . ." His voice trailed off and he indicated his codpiece. I stifled a giggle.

"I brought wine." Francis produced a leather jug with a flourish. "Gascon. I bribed the wine steward."

The other men followed suit, and each deposited his pilfered offering at the foot of Cat's bed, like pilgrims at a shrine: marzipan that inspired Joan Bulmer to squeal, new apples from an orchard in Kent, spiced wafers so thin and crisp they dissolved with one snap of the teeth.

Cat bestowed on Francis a benedictory kiss that quickly became more heated. Cat and Francis could kiss forever. Their clandestine meetings in the chapel or unused galleries often concluded with their mouths puffy and red, their hair disheveled and clothing askew. Over Francis's ear, Cat gave me The Look. I would not rest my head on my own timber pillow that night.

Bedmates swapped and bickered and jostled for occupation. Four in a bed was not uncommon: half sitting, half lying, limbs cast out in the aisles.

The wine moved quickly, everyone taking a drink or two and passing it on. The sweetness overpowered the sharp tang of grape skins and soothed the burn of alcohol in my throat. I gazed hopefully about the room, though I knew none of the boys was there for me.

Joan pulled Edward Waldegrave, bearer of marzipan, to his feet, and hummed an almain, slightly off-key. Another girl giggled, but joined in, her gentleman offering a baritone harmony. They danced between the beds, tripping over feet and discarded clothing.

Alice perched precariously on the edge of her bed, as if ready to bolt the moment Joan and Edward returned for the rest of the evening's festivities.

"Come, Alice," I said to her. "Let's start something a little more lively."

I interrupted the monotonous hum with my own version of a galliard tune and coaxed Alice into a volta. My height put me

in the right position to play the man, but when I tried the first lift, I nearly dropped her.

The boys heckled and jeered, grabbing their girls to demonstrate proper form. Edward clasped Joan around the waist, and despite the fact that they probably weighed the same, lifted her up and buried his face between her unbound breasts, making her giggle uncontrollably. They collapsed together on the nearest bed, a tangle of limbs and laughter.

Suddenly the door banged open and the duchess herself stood framed by torches behind her, looking for all the world like an avenging angel come to hammer the light of righteousness into us.

"Out!" the duchess shrieked. Her long gray hair spilled from her head in wicked wisps. Her fur-trimmed velvet dressing gown churned with wrath. Her dark eyes scoured the room from furrowed sockets.

The men scampered to attention, straightening doublets and hunting for shoes. Girls bolted to their feet, arms held like breastplates over the thin fabric of their nightclothes. Francis looked bewildered as he tried to focus on his patroness.

"Francis Dereham," she spat at him. "You disappoint me."

Francis cringed. His chivalrous demeanor had always endeared him to the duchess.

"How dare you abuse my good nature and tarnish my name!" she shouted. She swept into the room, pushing and clouting as she went. The men hastened out the door like whipped dogs, shielding their faces and whimpering apologies.

Francis ducked a blind swipe of her bejeweled hand, but didn't fail to bow before fleeing down the stairs.

The duchess reached Cat, wrestled her to her feet, and then knocked her to the floor with a backhanded slap.

Cat sprawled in the rushes spitting lavender.

"Where do you think you are?" the duchess ranted. "The court of Henry the Eighth?"

She grabbed Joan, frozen nearby, and slapped her, too, for good measure.

"You think you can dissemble and cozen me? That I won't notice corruption and debauchery in my own household?"

Cat propped herself up on an elbow and laid a hand on her cheek. A red mark bloomed beneath it, a ring-shaped welt on her jawbone. She turned wide, brimming eyes to the duchess, who stopped screaming.

Joan knelt by Cat's side, but Cat took no notice. She stared only at the duchess.

A single drop welled in Cat's eye and spilled out over her fingers.

This was something we practiced together. I acted as Cat's mirror as she perfected ways to encourage emotional responses in her audience. *Tears bring sympathy,* she told me. Now I found that she was right. Cat's tears caused the duchess to pause and look about the room like someone who has forgotten her purpose.

"You know I would do nothing to vex you, *grandmère,*" Cat said, her voice high and sweet, as if laced with honey.

The duchess appeared to be considering whether or not the pretty, delicate girl weeping at her feet was really capable of deception.

"And yet you invite men to a room meant for virginal maids," the duchess countered. I suppressed a snort of laughter. Cat hung her head, a picture of abject remorse.

"Which one came to your bed?" the duchess continued. "Francis Dereham? I've treated him as a favorite, but he doesn't befit you. You are a Howard. You are meant for better things."

"Yes, *grandmère*." Cat knew very little French, but exercised it liberally around the duchess. It made an impression.

"I never want to see you with him again," the duchess said, brushing her skirts as if to remove the detritus of scandal. "If I see the two of you together again, even kneeling in prayer, I will have both of you thrown out of this house so quickly you will never return to polite society."

Cat's face was hidden from the duchess by a shower of hair, but I saw it harden, the jaw clench and the eyes kindle and spark. Then it smoothed to an image of gratitude and she looked up at the old woman.

"Yes, *grandmère*."

"Who let them in?" the duchess said. "Who suggested this bedchamber farce?"

She scanned all of our faces, her own drawn down with age and anger like a melting candle.

"Joan?" she asked. But Joan just gaped at her.

"Alice?" But Alice never parted with information without something in return.

"Kitty?" She turned her trenchant gaze on me, but capitulated immediately. "I should know better," she scowled. "Loyal to the grave, that one."

She turned wearily, her shoulders hunched.

"This is best forgotten." The duchess waved away our stares. "From tonight onward, a curfew will be set, and the door to this chamber will be locked. There will be no repeat performance. Go to bed. All of you."

She parted the torchbearers like the Red Sea and hauled them down the gallery in her wake. Girls crept to their beds, thankful to have escaped the duchess's ire. Only Joan, Alice, and I remained standing.

Cat rose from the debris on the floor.

"Forgotten?" she said. "I'm unlikely to forget any of it. I'll make her life miserable."

"Cat," I warned.

"You can wipe that sanctimonious look right off your face, Kitty Tylney."

I kept silent. When Cat's anger gathered momentum, it was best to stand back and stay quiet, for fear of getting flayed alive by words or fingernails.

"Besides," she sneered, "I wasn't talking about the duchess. I was talking about Mary Lascelles."

Mary was one of the few girls even less connected than I

was, her only family a bully of a brother who had dumped her unceremoniously in the duchess's lap when he decided Mary needed "elevating." I looked at Mary's bed. Her bedmate sat in the middle of it, shocked by our stares. Mary was nowhere to be seen.

"You mean you didn't see her? She was right behind the duchess! Smirking away as if she deserved a medal. She'll be sleeping on the duchess's floor tonight, not because she's favored but because she's afraid of retaliation. She'd better never set foot in this room again."

Despite the annoyance I felt toward Mary for informing on us, I felt a little sorry for her, too. The remainder of her life in Norfolk House would be miserable. The punishment for snitching was to be shunned by all the girls. She would be pinched in chapel and thumped at dinner. Mary would be black and blue by the end of the week. And for the rest of her days.

"Did you hear the duchess?" Cat returned to her rant. "*Just where do you think you are, the court of Henry the Eighth?* As if I'd confuse this dreary, boring, hypocritical place with the dazzling circle the king has around him."

"What do you think she meant?" Joan asked.

Cat sighed and enunciated slowly as if speaking to the village idiot.

"Joan, at court people are always making secret assignations. It's *de rigueur*. It's expected. The duchess finds it morally reprehensible."

"If the king allows it, why doesn't she?" I wondered.

"Because she's a *Howard*. Ha! She's not even that. She's a *Tylney*." Cat spat the name as she would a bitter seed.

I willed myself not to react. My side of the family was so far removed from the duchess that our name—Tylney—felt like the only indication we were related at all. If the duchess was inferior, what did that make me?

"She's not even my real grandmother," Cat said. "Just some grasper who saw a hole in the Howard family and filled it."

We waited while Cat's anger spun itself out.

"One day she'll be sorry. One day she'll have to scrape and bow to me."

I failed to picture a time when the highest noblewoman in the country would fall so low as to look up to Catherine Howard, forgotten daughter of the forgotten third son of the man who had once been Duke of Norfolk. But I said nothing.

"I'll find a way to see Francis. She can't keep us apart."

"We could get them in through the window," I suggested.

"He tried that, remember?" Cat shot me a withering glare that brought heat surging to my cheeks.

True. The spring before, in a fit of romantic valor, Francis had attempted to scale the outside wall to the second-floor window with a rose between his teeth, but proved unequal to the task.

"Could we bribe one of the servants to unlock the door?" Joan asked, looking for approval.

"I don't trust any of them," Cat said.

We lapsed into silence, waiting for her to speak. Cat always thought of a solution.

"We'll just have to steal the key," she announced.

"Simple," I muttered, unsure if I wanted her to hear. Cat didn't take criticism well.

"It is, actually." Cat stared hard at me. "The steward has his own set of keys. The duchess's copy isn't used. She'll never know it's gone."

"It's brilliant, Cat," I said. "But who's going to do it?"

Whoever it was would have to be very well connected or very brave—or very stupid.

"Why, Kitty," Cat said. "You are."

3

WORDS CAN KILL. AS SURELY AS SWORD OR AX OR DAGGER. THEY CAN prostrate the subject and render the speaker voiceless. Words may not fracture bone, but they can wound with devastating precision.

"Me?"

"She'll never know," Cat said.

"She'll never know because I'll never do it." I couldn't let Cat convince me. It was suicide. And I was the last person who should be doing it. Tall, gawky, slightly clumsy, I was a questionable covert agent.

"But Kitty, don't you see? You are the perfect candidate."

"How so?"

"You have no suitor," she said with a sticky smile.

"Thanks for reminding me." My sarcasm fell flat. "But how does that help?"

"You have no motive. No one will suspect you."

She had a point. I had no reason to keep the midnight revelries going. No reason except it alleviated the boredom of the day-to-day existence in Lambeth. It gave us a taste of what real court life might be, with the wine and delicacies stolen from the duchess's kitchen. With whispered songs and barefoot dancing across the lavender-and-rosemary-strewn floor. Even if my only partner was Alice.

If I stole the key and got caught, I could be sent home, a god-forsaken hole on the far side of nowhere. My parents had leapt at the chance to disencumber themselves of their unwanted youngest daughter when I was eight. Cat discovered me on my first day, crying alone in the garden and told me they weren't worth my tears. I'd never looked back.

"Also," Cat continued, "you have little family and no one who really wants you. You have no motive, but you have every-thing to lose."

The words cut like thin blades. Cat understood the grief and terror lodged deep within me. She knew my fear that ulti-mately, the rest of the world would treat me as my parents had and abandon me to my own inept facilities.

If I didn't steal the key, I would forfeit my place at Cat's side, as forsaken and friendless as if I had gone home. Because Cat's favor was everything at Norfolk House—more important than money, men, or family influence. She was the one who set the standard, guided the aimless, and judged the unworthy.

But stealing?

"I can't." I hadn't the breath to speak louder than a whisper.

Cat narrowed her eyes.

"Can't? Or won't?"

Refusing Cat was like refusing the king. No one did it. No one knew where it could lead. To disfavor? Or beheading? But

the panic-inducing thought of returning to the frigid bosom of my family forced me to risk it.

"Won't."

Cat stiffened into silence, and I felt the breath quake in my chest.

"Joan?" Cat said sweetly.

Surely I couldn't get off that lightly? Joan couldn't say no to anyone.

"Joan, darling, you'd do anything for me, wouldn't you?"

"Of course, Cat," Joan said, her glance flicking from me to Cat and back again. Jittery. She could feel it, too. The same disquiet that wouldn't leave my limbs.

"Anything for the good of all the girls here, right?" Cat said.

She aimed all her words directly at me. I knew that she wouldn't ask Joan to steal from the duchess's coffer.

"Of course, Cat," Joan repeated. "You girls are my family."

I wanted to close my ears to her toadying. Didn't she know when to be quiet?

Cat linked her arm with Joan's. They were almost the same height, but where Cat was all curves, like a perfectly proportioned miniature, Joan was round, almost doughy.

"And without our family of girls, what are we?" Cat asked me.

I squirmed. She no longer expected an answer. She expected submission. And with a hopeless surge of self-loathing, I knew she would get it.

Joan stared, open-mouthed, unable to participate in this

one-sided conversation. Alice remained silent and invisible.

"Nobody," Cat said. I hated her at that moment, with a white-hot rage. I hated her almost as much as I hated myself. "Unwanted and unloved."

Misery swept through me, scouring away all resistance. I sank down onto the bed, a glacial emptiness yawning in my heart. She was right. Without the girls, without Cat, I was . . .

"Nothing."

Four days later, a black pawn from Alice's chess set lay wrapped in the piece of lace in the wood-and-leather coffer. I tucked it beneath the papers and jewels of the duchess's shifting wealth. The key lay in Cat's smooth, open palm, a pale pink ribbon dangling from it.

"Oh, Cat!" Joan cried. "You got it!"

"Aren't you clever?" one of the other girls murmured.

"We'll have wine and dancing again!"

"And boys!"

News traveled quickly in Norfolk House. The maidens' chamber was full, in the middle of the day. It was a wonder the entire household didn't grind to a halt with no one to tend the duchess's fire or fetch her spiced wine.

Cat smiled. I waited for her to say it was me. I hadn't wanted to do it. I hadn't wanted any part of it. The least I could get was the credit.

She opened her mouth, and all around her quieted.

"Tonight," she said.

The cheer that arose rattled the shutters on the windows.

I couldn't breathe, stifled by Cat's treachery, and by Joan's willingness to accept it. Only Alice observed me through low-ered lashes, pity or contempt on her lips. My heart contracted with the realization that I probably deserved both.

The dancing and cheering stirred the dust and mites from the reeking rushes littering the floor, and nettled my eyes to tears.

I stumbled from the room. No one noticed. They were too busy congratulating Cat, who lapped it all up.

The top two stairs complained bitterly at the weight of the wretchedness I carried with me. I moved to the far left of the stairwell and crept unheard down the more secure runners near the wall. Cat had taught me that little trick when we were ten and raided the buttery at night.

I slipped through the oak gallery, which ran the full length of the house. Autumn sunlight fell heavily on the carved pan-eling, the duchess's allegiances spelled out in oak. I passed an ancient pomegranate carved in 1509 for King Henry's first queen, Catherine of Aragon. A Tudor rose carved for Henry himself. A falcon—abraded and indistinct—for Cat's cousin, Anne Boleyn, the king's ill-fated second wife. The third, Jane Seymour, hadn't lived long enough for the duchess to change any of the panels for her, having died quickly after giving birth to England's only prince.

The door at the end of the gallery squeaked a little when I opened it and I paused, breath held, before escaping into the garden.

Finally, my lungs functioned again. The sun angled over

the haphazardly shaped hedges. One may have been a griffin, another, a lion. The duchess wanted to keep up with social trends, but had no interest in paying a decent gardener, so the shrubbery grew wild and bizarre. Few people ventured outside, anyway. The duchess cultivated a very *indoor* household, so I often had the outdoors to myself. In the house, I was always surrounded by others, their noise and odors tangible. Outside, I could breathe.

I quickly passed through the garden and exited the grounds. The duchess forbade us to go out alone. She warned us of the murderers, scavengers, and vagrants who hid in the woods. Highwaymen waiting to prey on vulnerable young girls. The only things she didn't mention were harpies, trolls, and the descendants of Gog the giant.

I never went far—just through the narrow apple orchard on the southeastern edge of the duchess's garden, up a slight rise to the wooded area the duchess called the "park." Because Lambeth consisted primarily of marsh and mansions, the duchess coveted the little forest, owned by some long-feuding neighbor who was never willing to sell.

An arch between two oaks led into a clearing made by a huge fallen beech. The tree itself created a sort of bench, albeit one with arse-poking branches at regular intervals. It was the one, magical place where I could be alone. Not even Cat knew about it. My trips to the forest were my secret.

I hoisted myself onto the tree, gathering my skirts around me to avoid snagging. I held myself still, listening to the night-loving forest dwellers rising from their beds, and watching the

sky above me transfigure from white to gold. The trees exhaled the tired scent of autumn. All quieted, and my head sang with the silence.

My seething anger left me, replaced by a dull, familiar ache. Cat served herself well. It was remiss of me to expect anything different. Befriending me was one of the few selfless things she'd ever done. She'd found me, homesick and melancholy, saved me a place next to her at dinner, made room for me in her bed. Gave me my name. That first night, she'd wrapped an arm around me and said, "So, Kitty, would you like to come to court?" and the next day we entered the palace of her imagination, playing a game that never really ended.

Cat was still queen.

I sighed and lay back on the tree. It wasn't comfortable. Prickly. Awkward. But it allowed me full view of the crumbling leaves and the sky.

A squawk shattered the stillness. Three ravens, grumbling and croaking, bolted from the branches of a tree far to my right and flapped blackly across my view.

The sight of them felt like an omen. A chill crept over my skin like a million tiny feet, and I sat up. A noise froze me. Like an animal, large and clumsy. Or so big it didn't require stealth. It crashed through the underbrush, through the carpets of fallen leaves crusty from the lack of summer rains. Distant, but approaching quickly.

I pressed my hands against the rough bark of the fallen tree. My fingernails dug into it until flakes came off beneath them. I

couldn't decide if I should run or stay still. My limbs made the choice for me. I couldn't move. I hoped whatever it was would think me part of the forest itself.

I strained to look between the spindles and barrels of the bare tree trunks, feeling grievously exposed. A whip of white on the far side of a scramble of hawthorn caught my eye. A flash of gold.

The crashing stopped, cut off by a cry of anguish and replaced by a hungered grunting. It had caught whatever prey it chased.

And then something that sounded like laughter. Not the ravens. More like a man.

My skirt tore with a hoarse whisper as I slid from my bench. I ignored it and crept forward to the low, hedgelike hawthorn. The leaves were just beginning to fall, the berries blood-red against them. I hid, camouflaged in my moss-green gown and heavy brown sleeves, silently thanking Cat for making Wednesday green.

The leaves and branches obscured my vision. I saw one figure. Two. Movement. Leaves. Cobwebs. I used one hand to pry open an eyelet.

Not far away, a man fell to the ground in a patch of dappled late-day sun. He didn't live at Norfolk House, but obviously came from privilege, judging by the gold braid on his doublet. He was long and lean with blond hair, dark eyes, a straight nose, and a jutting jaw. His beauty was surprising, down near the forest duff.

He held himself up on his hands. His hose slipped down to reveal pale buttocks glowing in the fading light. Something swathed in dirty white writhed beneath him. A woman.

He crushed his face to hers, and a growl escaped him.

"I know you want this."

For one startling instant of intense clarity, I felt the woman's pain, the man's lust. My heart kicked me in the chest. Pummeled me. Screamed at me to flee. But my stomach sank right down to the roots beneath me and locked me where I knelt.

Two more men stood beyond, grimacing like the disembodied heads of traitors on London Bridge.

One looked down, his head bent at the angle of a supplicant. He watched the spectacle, one foot planted firmly on the woman's left wrist.

Her right hand dug spasmodically at the earth.

The other man was really a boy. Not much older than me. A swag of rich golden hair framed a round face and wide-set brown eyes. He stared out into the forest.

And found me.

He squinted. Bewilderment clouded his features. Then comprehension cleared them.

I recovered my feet and ran. Crashes and snaps echoed in my wake. Thin fingers of tree limbs yanked at my skirts and wrists. My legs leadened. My breath came in choking gasps. It was like fleeing pursuit in a nightmare, but knowing I couldn't wake.

I strained to hear a shout of alarm. A cry to give chase. I heard none. Just an exultant howl of satisfaction.

I reached the arch of the oak trees, crossed into the light of civilization. I ran back to the house with the visions I had seen streaming out behind me like a veil, twisting and unwrapping but never tearing completely free.

5

I CROUCHED IN THE HEDGES BEHIND THE BRICK MONSTROSITY THAT was Norfolk House and disgorged every morsel that had passed my lips that day. I shook like someone with the sweating sickness. If only I had the sweat, which left its victims delusional and babbling, dead within hours. I would prefer anything to the image engraved behind my eyelids, the image of that poor woman, contorted by pain and humiliation. The sound of the man's voice vibrated beneath my temples.

I sat back and wrapped my arms around my knees to stop the quaking. The moisture from the earth soaked through my skirts, and the night air cooled around me. I should have flown at the men in a rage, frightening them off like a harpy. I should have picked the woman up off the ground, tended her bruises. Offered her bread and wine in the duchess's kitchen. I should have stopped them.

I had done none of those things. I had done nothing. Fear had swaddled me in cowardice. Too weak, too pathetic to help, I was as much to blame as the man who held her down. As culpable as the boy who stood watch. Who saw me.

Why hadn't he called out? Why didn't they give chase and

hunt me down? Why was I not now weeping somewhere on the forest floor like that poor peasant?

I rolled forward onto my knees and retched again. Nothing but bile and self-loathing spilled from my mouth.

The man who had abused her looked prosperous, well fed, sure of himself. The richness of his clothes and the arrogance of his manner characterized someone who expected life to hand him everything he wanted, and if it didn't, he would take it.

I thought about what he had said. Had she, at some point, wanted him? She hadn't appeared to anymore, her face screwed up against his words, her arm pinned down by his crony. No one wanted that.

I hoisted myself off of the ground, brushed the soil from my hands and knees, and staggered back to the house. The duchess was right. It was wiser to stay closeted indoors.

I might never leave the house again.

The twilight filtered into the oak gallery, shadows like bars running the length of the paneling.

My skirt hissed along the floor, carried somehow by my trembling limbs. I reached the corridor to the back stairs, and a creak above me took my balance. I fell back, one foot caught on a stray bit of hem, my left hand grasping wildly for support. Anne Boleyn's falcon caught me.

"Kitty, if you grow any taller and more awkward, you'll need your own usher to keep you upright," Cat laughed, skipping down the last of the stairs and twirling me, stumbling, into the darkened gallery. "Still, as long as he's handsome . . ."

"Cat," I interrupted, and stopped the giddy dance, "I have to tell you something."

"Oh, but Kitty," she said coyly, "it can't be nearly as important as what I've got to tell you."

"No," I said. Meaning, no, don't tell me. No, don't speak over me. Don't tell me your news is more important than this.

"*Exactement,*" she started toward the north wing of the house. "Let's find Joan and Alice. They have to hear this, too."

She turned when I didn't follow and looked at me critically.

"You're filthy," she said. "You spend far too much time out in that garden. And you really shouldn't go out there alone."

"I've done something horrible," I blurted.

"So have I!" Cat cackled, pulling me through the back stairs corridor and into the servants' vestibule. I crawled after her, mind ablaze with agony.

"I've dumped the contents of every pot in the maidens' chamber into the one under the duchess's bed!"

When I didn't respond, Cat huffed in irritation, waiting in the doorway to the front vestibule.

"It's Mary Lascelles's job to empty it!" she cried. "She'll never get down the stairs without spilling, the silly cow. But she brought it on herself. Fools find their own misery."

She brought it on herself. She wanted it.

"And I rubbed rancid fat in her pallet while I was there," Cat whispered as we walked into the main withdrawing room, clustered with girls and women sewing. "Her bed will be full of maggots by week's end."

"Cat!" I gasped, one final desperate attempt to get her attention.

Cat's aunt, the Countess of Bridgewater, looked up. A pale woman, she wore pale clothes and engaged in pale activities. But she observed—and reported—everything.

"Hush!" Cat hissed. "Do you want everyone to know what I'm up to?"

She sauntered to the far corner of the room, swishing her skirts. I watched her go. She seemed so sure the world contained no greater wickedness than the perfidy of Mary Lascelles.

She was right about one thing. I shouldn't have been out in the forest alone. I should have stayed in the house, cloaked in the drama of stolen keys and sloshing chamber pots.

That night, after the party, Cat sent Francis from the bed early. She curled against me, breath sultry from kisses.

"Now, tell me," she whispered. "Tell me everything."

My throat closed with the enormity of it. Cat knew. As if my own thoughts were hers.

"You're upset," she said.

I nodded, still unable to speak.

"Over something that happened today."

I nodded again.

"Something you wished to tell me earlier."

A sigh escaped and I started to cry.

"It's the key, isn't it?" she said.

But I couldn't stop crying. I couldn't tell her she was wrong.

"I had to let them believe it was me," she whispered. "In case

someone blabs. I can't let you get thrown out, Kitty. You're like a sister. Better than my real sisters. You're a sister of my soul. What would I do without you?"

My head flooded with *ifs*. If she hadn't taken credit. If she had just stolen the key herself. If she had never opened the coffer to discover it. Terror and anger and blame welled up in me and I caught them in a gossamer bubble before it all escaped and ruined our friendship.

I couldn't spew it on Cat. Not the vitriol and spite. It wasn't her fault.

Fools find their own misery.

I certainly had.

I<small>N THE DAYS THAT FOLLOWED,</small> I <small>STUMBLED THROUGH THE HOUSE IN A</small> swamp of wretchedness. I did my chores, followed orders, smiled when it was expected. I couldn't enjoy the midnight parties anymore. The presence of men made me want to creep out of my very bones. Even when the men didn't come, I couldn't sleep, and when I did, nightmares bruised me. I thrashed so much, Cat threatened to move to another bed.

But time acted as a purge, and as the days grew cold and frost crept across the grass, I slowly came back to myself. Thinner, paler, bitter and inadequate, but extant.

As the winter drew on, the rains came. The walls of disused rooms ran with damp, and the rushes on the floors turned black within a week. The bed curtains hung limp and took on the vinegar smell of mold. The fire in the maidens' chamber wasn't lit, so at night we drew warmth from each other and sought out other rooms during the day.

When boredom overcame us, we went to what we called the tapestry room. The walls were lined with detailed hangings, bought at a discount from the estates of traitors, their coats of arms carefully picked out and covered with the Howard crest. The cold and colorless Countess of Bridgewater held court by the fireplace, but the bright designs and heavy fabrics gave the illusion of warmth, no matter where we sat.

Joan and Cat claimed a corner as far from the countess as possible. Joan sewed ribbons of silver tissue onto the duchess's blue velvet bodice. And Cat was repairing the hem of the duchess's widest farthingale—endless tiny stitches of eye-straining sameness.

"Damn the desperate canes on this thing," she muttered. I grinned. I had a reprieve from mending. The duchess had requisitioned another piece of lace from me, and I worked knots of white by the feeble light from the window.

"Shut up, Kitty Tylney," Cat muttered.

Alice slipped through the door and dipped a curtsey to the older ladies. None of them acknowledged her. Alice smiled.

"Alice," I said when she pulled a stool closer to us, "they didn't even see you."

"Exactly," Alice said. And smiled again.

Cat turned to me and raised an eyebrow. I knew what it meant. Cat would have thrown a fit if she'd walked into a room unnoticed. But Alice? Alice seemed pleased.

"What news do you have today, Alice?" Joan asked, sucking the end of a piece of silk to a point in order to thread her needle.

Alice leaned forward and we all leaned with her.

"The Lady of Cleves is on her way."

The Lady of Cleves was the king's wife-to-be. A German princess from an unknown duchy, she'd been chosen by Thomas Cromwell, the king's chief councilor. Not by the king himself, this time.

As one, we all sat back.

"Is she bringing her own household?" Cat asked, poking at the fabric with her needle, but not making any stitches.

"She travels with German ladies, but I believe the king wants to fill her apartments with English nobility."

We took a moment of silence to digest this.

"Imagine," Joan crooned. "All those gorgeous dresses. Velvets and brocades and delicious silks." She ran her hand down her thigh as though stroking a well-clad lover.

"Think of the parties," I said. "Masques and banquets and dancing." So much more than the midnight feasts in the maidens' chamber.

"Think of all the gossip," Alice said.

"Think of all the *men*." Cat's eyes shone. "There must be ten of them to every woman in the court. All with money. And power."

"Is that what you're looking for in a man?" I asked. "What about poor Francis?"

"He does possess many qualities I admire," Cat said. "High cheekbones. A chin dimple. An air of rakish danger."

"But no wealth or power."

"And to tell you the truth," Cat whispered, "his codpiece gives no indication of his actual anatomy. The sword is no match for the scabbard, if you catch my meaning."

"So you want to go to court to find a rich duke or earl with a big pizzle!" Joan laughed.

"And for the dresses and the gossip and the parties," Cat said. "I want it *all*."

"Do you think there's really a possibility we'll ever to get to court?" I asked. Our dream of going to court seemed just that—a dream. The only way to get a position was by petition from a patron or family member. A man. My father was unlikely to come through for me. But all our games couldn't have been practice for nothing.

"I have to. Or my life will be wasted." Cat echoed my own thoughts.

"If anyone gets there, you will, Cat," Joan sighed. "The rest of us have no connections."

Cat was a Howard. It was the appellation of the richest, most ambitious and pugnacious family in the kingdom. Unfortunately, it was all Cat got from her father, a negligent wastrel who had died virtually unmourned in March, leaving his third wife and ten children without a penny. Cat might have come from the gauche side of the family, but in our world, a name could be worth more than currency. The rest of us had nothing but our dreams.

"Speak for yourself, Joan," Alice said. "My husband has a position with Lord Maltravers."

I caught Joan's eye and then rolled my gaze to the ceiling. If Alice's husband didn't care that she existed, I doubted Lord Maltravers would. I also suspected that his opinion held little sway. Joan giggled.

"But there's more," Alice said, ignoring us. "The Duke of Norfolk is coming to visit."

The dowager duchess's stepson.

The most powerful and influential nobleman in the country.

"He's looking for girls to place in the new queen's household as maids of honor." Alice paused to let her words sink in. "He's looking for girls from here."

"So is he going to check our teeth and test our sure-footedness like hunting horses?" I asked as we hurried down the stairs for dinner with the duke. A masterful cleaning campaign by the duchess had brightened even the darkest corners of the stairwell.

"No, but he might give us all a good ride to break us in," Cat said, waggling her eyebrows and leering at me.

"Oh, Catherine, don't be disgusting," Alice sniffed. "He must be at least sixty."

"That doesn't stop him from dragging his mistress with him everywhere he goes," Cat said, slowing as we neared the great hall.

"I feel sorry for his wife," Joan said, slightly out of breath. "Out there in the country all alone."

"Sympathy," Cat scolded, "gets you nowhere. The English court is beautiful and cutthroat, and anyone going there has to be both. Or at least act as if she is."

"Well, I'll never get there, then," I said. Cutthroat I wasn't.

Cat stopped just outside the door of the hall and put an arm around me. Another Tuesday, and her pink gown made her skin glow. She hadn't let the rest of us choose our best gowns, not even on this occasion.

"Oh, Kitty," she said. "None of us is beautiful."

Alice snorted, and Joan looked aghast. I wanted to pinch Cat.

"We're not. We're decidedly average. It's what we do with it that counts. We have to be clever. Make yourself vital to someone's happiness, and suddenly you're the most beautiful creature in the world, and he will fall madly in love with you."

I didn't think I could ever make myself that vital to anyone. So far no boy had given me so much as a second glance. I suspected cleverness alone wouldn't merit a first glance, let alone a second, so Cat's falsely fortifying words fell hollow all around me.

We stepped gracefully and demurely into the great hall, into the shadows ever present there. No amount of candles could fill that cavernous space with light, and in the duchess's mind, even the duke's visit didn't merit additional illumination. The stone walls were covered in tapestries depicting tales of chivalry. Ladies, retainers, and ushers lurked in the shadows, the duchess's servants and dogs weaving in and out between them.

The girls craned their necks to seek out fresh faces in the duke's employ.

"That one," Alice said. She nodded ever so slightly toward a boy, almost a man, who stood at the back of the hall, near the linenfold paneling that hid the servants' entrance from view. He appeared to be a gentleman usher, lean, but not gangly, with a mop of sandy hair that fell over one eye. He shook his head to remove it and looked back at us.

The rustle of girls turning from his gaze attracted the attention of the duchess, who sat in an armchair on the low dais near the fireplace. She beckoned imperiously from the high table, and we approached cautiously.

Thomas Howard, Duke of Norfolk, sat next to her. He was four years older than his stepmother, our patroness. Yet where the duchess held her age aloft like a flag of truce, the Duke covered his with a veneer of athletic bellicosity. He had a hooked nose that dominated his small face and eyes that gave the impression of seeing into your very soul. And what he saw never pleased him.

I avoided his gaze, afraid to see the curl of his lip at my appearance and height.

"He's looking at you," Joan whispered. "No, amend that. He's *staring* at you."

All feeling left my face and my lips grew numb.

"The duke?" Could he really be considering *me*?

"No, he's watching Cat," Joan said blithely. "I meant the new boy. The good-looking one. He's watching you."

The blood rushed back to my cheeks and I met his eye. His

mouth turned up crookedly. On the verge of laughter. I looked away.

We curtseyed then waited on the duke and dowager duchess throughout the long, tedious dinner. The dowager duchess ordered variations of every kind of meat and fowl when the duke came to visit, as if to remind him of her importance to the Howard family. We carried platters, weaving in and out between benches and trestle tables at which most of the rest of the Howard clan sat, unwilling to miss an important gathering. Everyone wanted a place at court.

"The Lady of Cleves knows no English," the duke was saying as I brought forward a wide wooden platter of venison. "Nor any French nor Latin. She will need clever girls in her household."

"To help her adjust," the duchess agreed.

"To make her path smooth," the duke said.

I studiously avoided looking at the duke's new usher. It was a great honor to be a maid-in-waiting, or a lady-in-waiting, to the queen. Noblewomen climbed over and clawed each other to get a place. With the help of male relatives, of course. My only hope was the duke. And he certainly wouldn't help me if I were caught flirting over his shoulder at dinner.

"If we are not careful," the duke continued, spearing a piece of venison with his knife and beginning to gnaw upon it immediately, "the new men appointed to nobility by the king will

take over the court and run it like a brothel, salting the queen's apartments with the freshest and most desirable female flesh. We must take the opportunity to bring truly loyal blood to court."

"We have the Lady Rochford," the duchess said.

The misfortune-plagued Jane Boleyn. Once married to George Boleyn, brother to the king's second wife, Anne. Court gossip said that Jane was instrumental in getting Queen Anne beheaded by accusing her of adultery. And incest. George was executed, too.

I turned to take the platter to one of the lower tables, but the duke reached for my sleeve. I stopped, hardly daring to breathe.

"We need a girl," the duke said. "Virginity is temptation, and temptation will bring promotion to the house of Howard."

I felt sick. I didn't dare to look into his ferrety little eyes. The duke despised the idea of the queen's household being a "brothel," except when it was he who stocked it with whores of his own choosing.

Not bothering with a knife this time, he pulled a fatty piece of thigh meat from the bone with his thumb and forefinger and dismissed me without once looking at my face.

"That one," I heard him say, and I turned back to see him pointing with a lazy flick of his greasy finger. He indicated the girl with the pink cheeks and shining eyes, the glossy auburn curls and perfect curves. The girl who could make a man shud-

der with desire by throwing her hair carelessly over her shoulder. I left the platter on a side table and slipped invisibly back to my place amongst the unchosen.

"Catherine Howard," the dowager duchess called. "How would you like to go to court?"

"You could be a little bit happy for me," Cat said.

"I am happy for you," I said, stretching a smile across my face.

Knowing that I wouldn't be picked to go to court and actually not being picked were two different things. Before the duke chose Cat, at least I had hope, if only a thin sliver of it. And not until the candles guttered and the duke fell asleep in his chair had hope left me completely. He only needed one girl, and that girl was Cat.

"No, you're not," she said. "Not really. You're disappointed that you weren't picked, and that makes you feel guilty."

It could be unnerving, Cat's ability to read my thoughts. But often, it was like being wrapped in a heavy winter cloak to shut out a storm. Comforting to know I wasn't alone.

"Also, you're going to miss me." Cat crept over to put an arm around me. "We've never been apart. I don't know what I'll do without you. But don't worry, I shall find a way to get you to court, too."

"Now who's being silly?" I managed before my throat closed

again. Because she was right. It wasn't just jealousy that I felt. It was bereavement, as well.

"I will," she said. "I promise. Just you wait and see."

Her childish voice made her enthusiasm all the more appealing and lit again the hope that she was right. Because court was the only place either of us really wanted to be. If anyone could find a way to get me there, Cat Howard could.

I squeezed her back. "I'm very glad you will be there, ready to show me how it's done."

"Well, I will have no such mentor," she said. "So I have to get this right before I leave."

We were practicing her curtsey, just as we had every day since the duke's visit. Cat's skirts whispered against the rushes as she bent once more, her tiny frame curving over her knees, hair veiling her features.

"It looks perfect, Cat."

"No, Kitty," she said to her knees, and then stood up and repositioned herself near the door. "Watch this part. Pretend to be the king and tell me to rise when the time is right."

She walked with measured steps from the door to me, her head bent. No one looked the king in the eye until he spoke. No one turned away from him. All these things we had practiced into oblivion.

When Cat came within three feet of me, she fell again into a curtsey and remained there, the picture of humility. I considered making her wait, but figured she would only want to practice it again.

"You may rise, Mistress Howard." I affected a booming tenor.

Cat lifted her face first, a shy smile playing on her lips. She met my eyes briefly and then looked down again, her lashes brushing her cheeks. Subtly, she pulled her shoulders back, an action that caused her breasts to thrust forward, swelling just slightly out of her bodice.

"Jesus, Cat," I said. A little laugh escaped me.

"What?" she stumbled to stand straight and came to me. "Is it too much? Too little? What?"

"Isn't that a little obvious?"

"Obvious that I'm doing it on purpose?"

"No," I acquiesced. "Not so much. Maybe just to me."

"Well, it's not you I'm trying to impress," she said and turned away to recheck her box of clothes.

"Well, any gentleman you encounter will be. Impressed, that is."

"But will the king?" she cried, exasperated. "I want him to look at me and to see that I'm different! That I'm not just another maid-in-waiting."

"What do you want from him, Cat?" I asked. "He's already getting married."

"Whoever said I needed marriage?"

"Wait a minute. Are you trying to tell me that this whole act is so that you can be a mistress to the king? A fat, aging man with an ego the size of France and a temper the size of the Roman Empire?"

"I don't know!" she huffed. "Maybe I just want someone to notice me!"

"Well, *that* will certainly get you noticed," I gestured dismissively at her breasts.

"Don't you see, Kitty?" she said. "This is my chance. My ruin of a family has finally come through for me, and I don't want to bungle it. I could get *anything* if I have the king's attention. At court, that's all that matters. Getting into his favor. And staying there."

Getting noticed was one thing. But what about the consequences? Manipulating the king of England could open a whole Pandora's box of repercussions.

"Besides," Cat said with a wicked grin. "I'm just displaying my assets."

"No, Cat," I said, blinking my eyes bemusedly like Joan, "I think your ass is something else entirely."

Cat threw her head back and laughed. Crisis averted.

"At court, with the king's favor, I could get anyone," Cat declared. "A lord. A viscount."

"You could enamor an earl or bewitch a baron," I added, though a cold shiver ran to my stomach, a fear that when she became a famous lady, she would forget me.

"Bedevil a duke," she said. "Shame Charles Brandon's already taken."

"The Duke of Suffolk?" I asked. "But he's over fifty years old!"

"That didn't stop him from marrying Catherine Willoughby," Cat said.

"Hasn't he been married four times? And Catherine is younger than his children."

Cat smoothed the gowns at the top of her cedar chest. A bit ragged. Worn at the elbows. But presentable enough.

"Rumor has it he's great in bed," she said.

"He'd have to be."

"Imagine having a title of my own!" Cat crowed, slamming the lid of the chest. "I just want to *be* somebody."

"You will be."

"I don't want to marry some lame old fat man and die in secluded anonymity in the country. I've lived in the shadow of the Duke of Norfolk my entire life, just as my father did. Father was a nobody, and so am I, but when I go to court I could become a countess or at least a lady. Not plain Catherine Howard."

"You'd never be plain."

"Oh, Kitty, they shan't know what hit them. I will dance more than anyone and laugh more than anyone and eat the best foods and drink the best wines and make everyone laugh and love me. I will exhaust them."

"You certainly will," I said with a grin. I could picture it.

"I will be queen!" she cried.

My shock stifled any reply.

"Oh, Kitty," she said, whisking at me with her hand, "I mean the Queen of Misrule. I wouldn't *poison* her for pity's sake."

I looked over my shoulder to see if anyone was listening, but the maidens' chamber was empty. Everyone else was off performing the duchess's daily tasks—simpering, sewing, tending to imaginary aches and misgivings. Even speaking of poisoning royalty could lose Cat her head. And me mine, for hearing it. Keeping treason secret is treason itself.

"Cat," I warned. "You can't say things like that. Especially not at court."

"Then I shall have to come over every day and tell them to you. I shall have to tell you all about the horrible old lecherous men and the wonderful *young* lecherous men, and the bitchy girls who hate me because all the men lust after me."

I laughed. But her humor didn't dispel the creeping disquiet her other words had instilled in me.

"But Kitty," she said, her eyes widening with a sudden anxiety. "What will I do when we are at Hampton Court? Or Windsor? And too far away? Oh, Kitty, whom will I talk to then?"

Her eyes brimmed, and I wondered for a flash if the tears were real or conjured for my benefit. But I quelled the thought.

"You will just have to send me a letter."

Cat made a face and sat on the chest, arms crossed and pouting.

"Ugh," she said. "Writing is so tedious. Besides, if there's one thing I do know about court gossip, it's that you never, ever put anything on paper. At least nothing you don't want everyone else to know."

57

"You'll just have to save it all up, then." I sat beside her. "And tell me everything when you come back to visit." I reached out to stroke her hair. I knew she wouldn't come back. She knew I knew.

"Oh, Kitty," she cried. "Who will brush my hair?"

And in that sentence, she summed it all up. It's not everyone you let touch your hair. You can't trust just anyone to make you look your best when you have no mirror.

"You'll just have to wear a gable hood."

Cat mumbled a laugh and leaned into me. Just for a moment. Then she stood and walked quickly to the door.

"Come, Kitty," she said. "You must help me. Before anything else I have to do this one thing."

I followed her down the stairs, but paused before leaving the house. At sunset, the topiary animals cast leering shadows across the paths and the knot garden appeared to harbor wraiths and specters. Cat grabbed my hand and pulled me forward, marching like a nurse with a recalcitrant child.

A dark shape twisted from behind a tree. It moved swiftly, silently, and before I could scream, it reached for Cat. Wicked panic slashed through me, visions converging of men in black. I wrenched my hand from Cat's grip and she let out a little shriek. Then she scowled and twitched her shoulder from the grasp of Francis Dereham. I pressed my lower lip against my teeth with my knuckles, the pain sharper than the fear that burned my throat.

"Why didn't you tell me?" Francis asked, twisting his

empty hands together. I had never seen him so pitiful before. Cat liked her men confident and a little arrogant. Francis normally fit the bill perfectly, from his self-assurance in his anatomy to his swaggering air as a self-proclaimed pirate. But there in the garden he looked like a lost little boy, crying for his mother.

"Why do you think I'm wandering the gardens?" she admonished. "I asked you to meet me, remember?"

Francis looked at me. I shifted from one foot to the other. I had spent several nights in bed with the two of them, but this was by far more uncomfortable.

"Don't look at Kitty," Cat snapped. "She's no use in this matter."

Francis turned his eyes back to her. I wanted to sink into the mud.

"What about—?" Francis started to ask, but Cat cut him off.

"I'm going to court and there's an end to it."

She thrust out a hip and laid a hand upon it, the gesture of someone impatiently giving the appearance of waiting. She raised an eyebrow.

Francis glanced at me again, his misery contagious. He licked his lips.

"But you are my wife," he whispered.

A shock went through me, but before I could say anything, Cat slapped Francis with the quickness and ferocity of a striking snake. Francis flinched.

"Don't you dare say that to me again, Francis Dereham!"

Cat hissed. "I never want those words to pass your lips. Ever. To anyone. Do you understand me?"

Francis remained silent.

"We were not married in a church," Cat continued. "There were no witnesses. We never signed a contract. *We are not married.*"

"In my eyes we are," Francis said. "I love you. I have known you as a man knows his wife. If you leave me, I will go to sea to find my fortune, and when I come back, I will be able to grant you anything your heart desires."

"You can do what you like," Cat said. "But I am going to court. And I will not wait for you."

Shadows fell across Francis's face. I had always thought him a bit of a peacock, but he looked broken in the fading light. Cat could be hard and pitiless with her enemies, but I was shocked to see her treat someone she loved with such flinty disregard.

Francis reached for his belt and brought up a small velvet bag.

"Here," he said, handing it to Cat, "take this."

She peered inside, then back at him, her mouth open.

"There must be a hundred pounds in here," she whispered. "Where did you get this?"

"I've been saving it. For the day you and I might live together." His voice broke. "I give it to you for safe keeping."

"No, Francis," Cat said, her voice a warning.

"I will not ask for anything from you," he said. "I . . . I release you. If I do not return, the money is yours. If you are . . . taken when I come back, this money is all I will ask for."

It was perhaps the most honorable statement I'd ever heard him utter. Cat narrowed her eyes, obviously thinking the same thing and not trusting it.

"Fine," she said, and pocketed the velvet bag. It sounded a muffled clink.

"Will you leave me with a kiss?" Francis asked.

"No," Cat said, but held out her hand. He seized it with both of his, as if he would take it with him.

"Come, Kitty"—Cat drew away from his grasp—"or we will be late."

She walked back to the house, her head up and spine straight. She banged through the great oak door and disappeared into the gloom of the entrance hall. Only I looked back to see Francis watching her.

Cat started talking as soon as the door obscured the light behind me.

"That didn't happen," she said, her hand in her pocket jingling Francis's gold angels. The cold stone walls echoed the sound back to her, and she stopped.

"You're married?" I asked. "Without permission?" We weren't allowed to choose our own husbands. It was beyond imagining. Our families considered it contemptible. Despicable.

Cat placed a hand on either side of my jaw and pulled me

down until our noses touched. The fading light from the high, dirty windows barely illuminated her face, making her appear almost translucent against the dark.

"I am *not* married," she whispered, her words brushing against my lips like a kiss. "There was no ceremony. There was no priest. I am not his wife. And no one will hear any differently. Ever."

Even if they hadn't married in a church, an *agreement* could make any subsequent marriage invalid. If a rich and powerful husband found out about it, he could have the marriage annulled, and Cat would be out in the streets with no money, no man, and a tattered reputation. Not even her family would take her in after that, for fear of being tainted. A rich and powerful man could make life very uncomfortable for anyone who knew about her past and didn't mention it beforehand.

"I am untarnished," Cat continued. "Virginal. Innocent. I can make a good match at court. I can meet a man who will give me the kind of life my father wasted. A man who can throw a hundred pounds away on a single doublet, not present it to me like it's a fortune."

We stood there, suspended, locked by eyes and words and secrets. I could neither nod nor speak. Her gaze shifted from one of my eyes to the other. Searching. For hope. For acknowledgment.

"I need your help, Kitty. Please. Make sure no one from this household ever breathes a word of my life here. It's your duty.

To our friendship. To our sisterhood. The men of my past must vanish."

She let go and I swallowed.

"What men?" I whispered.

"Good girl."

1540

9

CAT LEFT FOR GREENWICH AND NEVER CAME TO VISIT. FRANCIS DISAP-peared, leaving behind the odor of thwarted love and a note to the duchess that rendered her silent with vexation. The midnight parties slowed and stagnated and then stopped alto-gether. And the rain and slush kept us indoors, cold and damp, compressed by the weather and our own lethargy.

When I couldn't stand the walls closing in on me anymore, I closed my eyes, counted to five, and stepped outside into the wide, wet world. I kept to the paths and remained in sight of the house, counting hedges between myself and safety.

I liked to watch the river flow, sluggish and churning when the tide came in, fast and raucous when it raced the tide to the sea. Even in fog, the air felt cleaner and sweeter than the air inside the house, where sides of beef charred on spits and men and dogs urinated in the corners of the great hall. I liked to look downriver to the great old palace of Westminster and imagine what life was like for Cat at court. Westminster—which the king avoided in preference for more modern palaces like Hampton Court—seemed to reflect my own state, abandoned and unloved.

In February, my father sent a message to the duchess that his scheming to get me married had so far come to naught. None of the men he'd contacted were interested. The duchess let me read the letter, addressed to her. It didn't include an inquiry after my health or a desire to be remembered to me. I meant as little to him as an aging carthorse or piece of bogland.

Joan found me sitting on the riverbank, staring into the water with my eyes open wide, trying not to let the tears fall.

"Bad news?" she asked, standing behind me.

"I'm going to rot here." Like the damp tapestries on the walls. Like the filthy rushes. Like the tattered cuffs and hems of my slowly decomposing gowns.

"Don't be such a melancholy Madge," Joan said, and nudged me in the back with her knee.

I turned my head to look at her.

"Why don't you sit down?" I asked.

"Because you're sitting on a mucky riverbank," Joan said reasonably. "You can get away with it in that sludge-colored kirtle. But I'm in blue. For Friday." She said the last with an emphasis that couldn't be denied.

"Oh," I said. Without Cat, I could wear whatever I wanted, whenever I wanted. No one said a word. I realized that only Joan kept up with the color roster.

"Do you think we'll ever go to court?" Joan asked, her eyes on Westminster.

Cat had promised. But I hadn't heard from her. And she hadn't promised Joan.

"I don't see how."

"Maybe we'll marry rich, important men, and we'll go to court with them?"

"Right now it's unlikely I'll marry *any* man," I said and turned back to face the empty palace. I neglected to mention that she was already married. And William Bulmer never went anywhere near court. Or Joan.

"Everyone who's anyone is at court," Joan mused. "All those banquets and parties and beautiful gowns."

"And not always being stuck in the same place," I agreed. "Dancing and masques and *movement*."

"Don't forget boredom and backbiting and intrigue," a voice behind us said.

My heart nearly throttled me.

We both looked around to see sandy brown hair flopping over grayish blue eyes and a freckled face lit up by a delightedly crooked grin. The duke's new usher. Staring at me again.

"How dare you spy on us like that!" I struggled not to return the smile and leapt to my feet to face him. Joan squeaked and wedged herself behind me.

"I hardly spied on you," he said. "I merely approached to ask directions."

"You sneaked up on us," I insisted. "We didn't hear you at all."

"Is it my fault I have a light step?" He failed to look remotely innocent.

"And what did you learn from listening to girls' gossip?" I asked. Joan remained mute.

"I learned that girls are as desperate to go to court as men are."

He wasn't even going to deny listening to our conversation.

"And who are you to be spreading gossip about the court?" I pursued. "You don't even know whom you're talking to."

"You could be anyone," he said, nodding sagely.

"Exactly."

Then I realized that the reverse was also true. I was standing in the garden speaking with an absolute stranger. He could be a molester or a spy, come to gather tidbits of scandal. A prickling flush crept up my neck.

"Allow me to take pity on you," he said, and bowed.

"No need to take pity on me," I bristled. "The onus is on you, entering the garden unannounced and interrupting a private conversation."

I looked him full in the face. We stood the same height. But that didn't seem to intimidate him. It was only when he looked in my eyes that he faltered and looked back down at the ground. I remembered Cat's criticism of me. *Your eyes are too knowing. You look at men and they want to slink away.*

"Forgive me, Mistress Tylney," he said quietly. "I forgot we had not been introduced."

He knew my name. Joan wrung my hand like a kerchief. I squeezed back once before I pulled away.

"After the banquet the duke attended, I made discreet inquiries," he said. "I know you are Katherine but prefer Kitty. You are distantly related to the dowager duchess and have been here for longer than most of her servants can remember."

He bowed before me. "I am William Gibbon, gentleman usher and general dogsbody for the Duke of Norfolk."

William Gibbon. I pressed the name into my memory like a late summer bloom into the leaves of a book.

He had narrow shoulders for a man, or perhaps it was just the cut of his doublet, not the extra-wide shoulders preferred by the king and those who wished to be like him. But they balanced lean, muscular calves and thighs. My gaze traveled up his legs. He straightened and I blushed from the thoughts that flitted through my mind.

"You are well met, Master Gibbon." I made my voice sweet and cast my eyes down in an imitation of Cat's flirtation practice from so long before.

"I am entrusted with a message for the dowager duchess and regret that I must deliver it quickly."

"Regret?" I asked, risking a glance at his face. It showed relief. At what, I wondered, amazed at a retainer who had yet to learn the art of hiding all emotion.

"I would much rather stay out here with you two lovely ladies." His smile lit the garden more than the piddling winter sun. I nodded stupidly, the word *lovely* ringing brightly in my mind.

"We shall accompany you," Joan said, nudging me with her elbow. Joan, ever the matchmaker. I'd forgotten she existed.

"I'm glad you're no longer angry," William said. "It was never my intention to offend you."

The reason for his relief came clear. And he surprised me again because he spoke so honestly.

"How is the duke?" I asked in an attempt to make conversation as he fell into step with us.

"Bellicose. Impatient. Slippery."

"You certainly tell what you see," I said, taken aback. No one at court or in the Dowager duchess's household ever talked about anyone except in the most glowing terms. Or in secret.

"The Duke of Norfolk is my employer. I must tolerate his moods so that I don't lose my position, but he knows I am not a crouching lickspittle. He says he is grateful for my honesty and knows I will follow any order he gives me without question."

"What if it's something you don't want to do?" I asked.

"My loyalty is to the duke."

I stopped in the chilled and begrimed entrance to Norfolk House. "That doesn't answer my question."

"Do you have no one in your life that you feel loyalty to?"

I thought of Cat. My loyalty to her had turned me into a thief, a liar, and an enforcer of secrets.

"Your family?" William prompted.

"My family does not inspire loyalty," I said wryly.

"Perhaps one day your husband," William suggested.

"Not if he's someone my parents select," I retorted, my voice higher and harsher than I had intended. It echoed peevishly off the dirty windows. We slowed as we neared the duchess's withdrawing room from which light and warmth crept over the stone floor.

"You prefer to make your own choices?" he asked. He turned to appraise me. My height. My hair. My eyes.

"Yes," I said without thinking at all. "I do."

"That's good," he said. "I like a woman who knows her own wants." I felt a spark begin to glow in my chest.

"Master Gibbon." The duchess's voice, like sand on paper, swept into the gallery. The heat and color of the room assailed us—fire and candlelight, tapestries, carpets, and the duchess herself decked in crimson and jewels. She saw me and Joan standing in the doorway and shooed us away. William strode to her place by the fire without a hint of good-bye.

"Charming," I said, my voice laced with sarcasm. But I loitered in the entranceway in the hopes of seeing him exit.

"Handsome," Joan added.

"I suppose."

"Oh, admit it, Kitty! He's handsome. He likes you."

I shrugged, but her words blew on the spark that kindled into something like happiness.

"And in service to the duke," Joan continued.

"Joan," I said. "I'm never going to get a chance to choose my own husband, so why should I even bother?"

I wondered, though, if my parents would accept a "contemptible" personal choice if only to get me off their hands.

If they couldn't find me a match, maybe I should find one for myself.

"You sound so bitter."

"I suppose I am," I said. "I mean, if a man marries someone who doesn't please him, he can find a mistress who will. He needn't stay at home with a woman he finds repulsive. He can go to court or to Ireland or go out to work. But the women have to stay home no matter what. Sewing and needlework and making clothes and seeing to the food and nothing else. Boring."

"But Kitty, men have to fight in wars, too. That's fearful."

"Yes," I said, grudgingly. But somehow the life surrounding war seemed much more interesting than sitting around and waiting for a man to return from it.

"And Kitty." Joan's thoughts dawned slowly across her face. "That's all we do here. Sewing and needlework and all the rest."

"Yes, Joan. That's how I know it's boring."

"You *do* sound like Cat sometimes, you know."

"I suppose someone has to talk sense when she's gone."

"Well," said Joan, putting an arm around my shoulder and whispering in my ear as if divulging a delightful secret. "If Cat were here now to talk sense to you, she would say that your marriage will happen one way or another, so why not indulge yourself now?"

Why not indeed?

I could do worse than a gentleman usher to a duke. And my father certainly hadn't done any better on my behalf. Could it really be possible? To make my own choice?

"A little flirtation never hurt anyone," Joan finished. "But desperation does. Don't let him find you waiting for him."

I didn't.

But I hoped the duke would need to communicate with the dowager duchess more often in the future.

Bᴜᴛ ᴛʜᴇ ᴅᴜᴄʜᴇss's ɴᴇxᴛ ᴄᴀʟʟᴇʀ ᴡᴀsɴ'ᴛ Wɪʟʟɪᴀᴍ Gɪʙʙᴏɴ.

It was Francis Dereham.

He came trailing a cloak of mystery and bitterness. Creases fanned the corners of his eyes and he walked with a newly rolling gait, as if he had spent much of his time on a ship's deck, squinting into the wind. But he hadn't been gone long enough to get very far, which left me wondering where he had acquired his counterfeit swagger.

If we hadn't seen his arrival ourselves, we would have heard it shortly after, for the shrieks echoed from the duchess's withdrawing room and bowstrung the nerves of the entire household.

"You leave here without word or warning and expect to return to your old position? Do you wish to make a fool of me, sir?"

Joan and I dawdled at the stairs, dropping and refolding our embroidery. Alice was nowhere to be seen.

"Heartbroken!" the duchess cried in response to Francis's murmur. "Don't be daft! You may have been a favorite of mine, but this is unforgivable."

More murmurs. Sonorous. Sensuous. Persuasive.

We took a step nearer to the closed door.

"Eavesdropping wenches!" The steward's bark from the top of the stairs frightened Joan into dropping her embroidery again.

"Out!" He surged down the stairs and smacked her with the back of his hand when she bent to retrieve the fabric and thread. I sprang to help her, dodging blows, and began to giggle.

"We'll never compete with Alice," Joan panted as we raced through the Oak Gallery in a bid to escape. "She probably knows the whole story already."

"We'll just have to find Francis himself," I said. "Catch him before he leaves."

"You go right ahead, Kitty." Joan rubbed her backside. "I'll wait to hear from you."

I sneaked through the south door that led through the back courtyard to the kitchens, knowing I could pass through them to the vestibule and the chapel beyond. Another trick Cat had taught me as a child. We had stolen sugar from the cook on feast days and devoured it behind the duchess's screen by the altar. Later, Cat had made use of the same passageways and pew for stealing kisses.

I sat in the chapel with my head bowed, winter sun diagramming angels in the southern window.

"Kitty!"

Francis slid down the polished bench until his hip touched mine. A jolting reminder of when we used to share a bed.

"Returning to the scene of your crimes?" I asked.

"Love is never a crime, Kitty," he said sadly. "I had to come here, to where she first kissed me."

"I thought you might."

"Everything here reminds me of her."

I knew that well.

"She never loved me, Kitty," he said, his face fallen into crags formed by sunlight and shadow. "And now she treats me like a stranger."

"You saw her?" I asked. "You went to court?"

"I did," he said. Only Francis would walk unannounced into court to speak with his ex-lover.

"How is she?"

"Fat and happy," he said. "Exactly where she wants to be. She's surrounded by jewels and great ladies and has no need for the likes of me. She has found someone new."

His voice broke, and I looked for tears in his eyes but saw only jealousy.

"Really?" I asked. "Who?"

"A little weasel in the king's privy chamber. Handsome and cocksure and full of the king's good graces."

Power. At least one of Cat's criteria fulfilled. As she'd said, the king's favor meant everything.

"What's his name?"

"Culpepper. Thomas Culpepper."

Francis spat the name in the hush of the chapel and slammed himself to his feet.

"At least I got my hundred pounds." He grimaced.

"Where will you go? Back to sea?" I asked, hoping he would tell me where he'd really been.

"Hardly." He laughed. "Piracy doesn't suit me. And I doubt the duchess would tolerate my absence a second time."

"You got your position back?" *Even after all that shouting?* I added silently.

"The duchess is like putty in my hands."

"I'm surprised she played into them. I suppose I should say welcome home, then."

"Not exactly. She's none too pleased with me. Doesn't want to see my face. I'm leaving my goods and coffers here, but she's exiled me to the Horsham estate."

"Good luck." I reached out to shake his hand.

"Oh, I won't be there long, Kitty."

He took my hand and kissed it—a bit wetly—winked at me, and swept from the chapel with a flourish, a swashbuckler in his own mind if nowhere else.

I wondered about Francis's rival, Thomas Culpepper. He'd have to be pretty seductive to win Cat's attention over the barons and earls and dukes.

"She'd never have stuck with him anyway." A rasping voice startled me as I made to leave the chapel myself. Mary Lascelles, her mouth twisted in disapproval, blocked my way. Her blue eyes swam in the pale pool of her face.

"Oh?" I took a step back. Mary always stood too close.

"He's beneath her. He's beneath her *family*."

"Are those your words? Or your brother's?" I had a feeling he shared his opinions freely.

"My brother doesn't know any of this!" Mary cried. "If he did, he would take me away. He would punish me just for being here."

For a moment, I felt sorry for her. Until her next words erased all sympathy.

"Cat believes you're beneath her, too, you know."

"I don't see that it's your business," I replied sharply, brazening out the pain she inflicted.

"But *she's* the one not worth the Howard name. She may imagine she's royalty, but she acts just like a common slut."

"Oh, shut up, Mary," I said. "I don't want to hear your venom. She's not the one emptying chamber pots and sleeping on the floor."

"Even the highest will be brought low," Mary intoned.

I laughed. "Perhaps you ought to tell the king that."

"I just think," she said, "that if she continues as she has begun, she shall come to nothing."

"I don't care what you think," I said, and walked away.

"And if you depend on her," she said, her voice rising to reach me, "you will be nothing, too!"

Francis departed and the rain returned. Cat sent no word from court. I began to suspect that she couldn't wield the influence to get me there, and her promises were for naught. Doubt nibbled at the back of my mind that perhaps, to a certain extent, Mary Lascelles was right. I wondered if I was actually beneath Cat, or at least beneath her notice.

I turned sixteen in the middle of Lent. Joan wished me the best and Alice smirked and we had no meat or cheese and the day swirled away like effluent in the river.

I spent that afternoon outside, alone. I felt that the water of the Thames itself flowed in my veins, toilsome and murky. The colors of the river and the sky melded perfectly, running together on the far side and seeming to drip across Westminster like an unfinished painting. I stared at the palace, lost in imagining the riot of color and intrigue behind those dreary gray walls.

"Much more beautiful up close."

I startled, slipping on the slick clay of the riverbank, and fell headlong into the mud. My heart beat an erratic rhythm of fear until I looked up and it nearly stopped at the sight of William Gibbon.

"Let me help you," he said, extending a hand. Amusement lit the one blue eye that remained unhidden by his sandy hair.

"I can manage," I said, ignoring the hand. And the eye. And the freckles. And the enticingly crooked smile.

I hauled myself from the mire. "You know, you really must stop sneaking up on a person." I tried to give him a withering glare. Unfortunately, it didn't work. He looked at my dress and burst out laughing.

The entire front of my bodice and skirt had changed from blue to a saddle brown. The thick clay coated the fabric so thoroughly that the piping and embroidery didn't show.

"I don't see what's so funny," I said, my embarrassment making me pettish.

"My apologies," he said, his sincerity marred by a twitching at the corners of his mouth.

I wiped at the mud ineffectively. William coughed. If he started laughing again, I thought I might smack him.

"It's a lovely color on you, Kitty," he said.

Lovely color. It was a horrible color. Reminiscent of bodily functions. In spite of myself, laughter burbled in my chest.

"I look frightful," I admonished him. "Mud is a color flattering to no one." I caught a smile creeping across my own lips.

"Monks' habits are often that very brown."

"We don't see many monks around here, anymore," I

reminded him. Not since King Henry had shut down all the religious houses. "Besides, I don't think I'd be accepted into a monastery."

"Oh, really?" he asked with a grin. "Skeletons in your cupboard?"

"Wouldn't you like to know?"

"Actually," he said, "I find secrets get in the way." And suddenly his expression opened. Vulnerable. I could read everything he was thinking. He looked shy. And hopeful.

"That's good," I said. "Because I have none." None of my own, anyway. I looked away to hide the hope my own face reflected.

Westminster Palace stared back at me from its empty eye sockets. I remembered what William had said before I fell into the mud.

"Is it really more beautiful up close?" I asked. From Lambeth, it didn't look beautiful at all.

"I didn't mean Westminster," he said quietly. I felt his gaze on my face and couldn't move. Could hardly think. "I meant you."

I turned so quickly I nearly fell again, but William caught me with an arm around my waist, turning my insides liquid. His touch warmed my entire body and made me feel I could run the joust against the king himself. And yet I hesitated even to carry my own weight for fear he would let go.

"Watch your step," he breathed into me.

My thoughts spun like leaves on the wind, whisked high

and giddy with no direction or destination. I nodded, struggling not to laugh out loud at the joy of it. I looked up to see the laughter mirrored on his face. But he wasn't laughing *at* me. I bit my lip to stop myself from kissing him right there. The movement drew his eyes to my mouth. To the rest of me. I felt the flush return to my face when he looked me in the eyes again.

"Perhaps the monks will take me," he whispered.

"What?" I gasped. I took a step backward, onto the dry, rocky path. "One moment with me and you're ready to join a monastery?"

"I believe I already wear the color of their robes." He indicated a line of mud that ran up the length of his body. Were we really that close? I quavered at the thought. Deliciously.

"The duke will have my ear for this," he said with a laugh. As though he didn't really care.

"The duchess will have our hides if she sees us both and jumps to conclusions," I added. Because even she would be forced to ask about two bodies coated in mud.

"Then she shouldn't see us together."

My heart sank. He couldn't go yet.

But instead of leaving me and going to the house alone, he offered me his arm and led me in the opposite direction.

We walked past Lambeth Palace, the residence of Thomas Cranmer, Archbishop of Canterbury. Just ahead of us, the landscape opened and fell away, the path rising above it, almost like a bridge. The river stretched to our left, gray-green and rippled.

Lambeth marsh lay flooded to our right. I could see forever. No strangers lurking behind trees.

East, down the river, London town splayed on the horizon. It looked black and grimy, choked and swarming.

"Is the city very frightening?" I asked.

"My father used to take me when I was younger," William said. "We still have a little house there. Near Cheapside. I remember watching a tournament from the window."

"You *are* a gentleman, then," I said. Surely good enough for my parents.

"The tenants give us a little money," he said, the crooked grin growing sad. "But personally, I'd rather be here. Outside, with the sky and the river."

"And the mud."

"That, too."

"Not at court?" I asked.

"I suppose I prefer a quieter life." He made a face. "At court, there is so little time, so little room to move. Everything is dictated by someone else's desires, telling you what to do, what to think, what to want."

My elation flickered for a moment, caught like a fly against glass. Could I choose a man who wouldn't be at court—who would take me far away from everything I'd ever dreamt about? Away from Cat?

"I can see you're not convinced," he said with a wry smile.

There on the riverbank, the possibilities seemed so distant, the ultimate choice so remote. That I could go to court. That

I could choose a man I wanted. That William would even ask.

"Convince me." I smiled back. In the meantime, the least I could do was flirt a little. And put those years of practice with Cat to use.

"It may take time." He took a step closer. So close we nearly touched again. "And persuasion requires frequent contact."

"Oh?" my voice barely a whisper. "How frequent?"

"I will be returning often."

"Is there much news to share between the duke and the dowager duchess?"

"Apparently so," he said. "I'll show you spring as it comes. I'll show you why I'd prefer to be here. With you."

I smiled, my words lost on lips ready to kiss him.

"When the weather clears," he added, blushing as if he could read my mind. "And the mud dries."

We returned to Norfolk House, the narrow path necessitating close proximity. Our knuckles brushed once, sending a flash of sensation up my arm. William spoke of his family home in the country, his face animated with delight. And I listened, bewitched by the cadence of his voice.

When we arrived at the garden, he bowed and turned to the grand entrance at the front of the house. I watched for a moment and then ran around to the kitchen, startling the cooks and scullery maids and setting up a racket amongst the dogs. I literally tripped up the back stairs to the maidens' chamber, banging my shins and leaving gobbets of mud on

the risers, but I didn't care. I was too caught up in my own jubilance.

He wants to see me again. One thought pivoted, so I could see it from all sides. *He wants to see me again.*

Happy birthday.

And he did. Twice more in March and on the first of April, William arrived with messages and walked with me in the gardens. Even in the rain.

I couldn't sit with him inside because the duchess hectored him until he returned to court. But he wanted to be outdoors, anyway, so he could convince me of its merit, unaware that it was something I already knew. Something I feared. But over the course of his persuasions, I found myself, slowly, becoming comfortable with the world outside the walls.

He always caught me unawares. I never had time to dress up or even tidy my hair. And he liked me anyway. The more he came, the more I wanted to be with him. Not just walking. I yearned to hold his hand, to feel his skin against mine. To have him kiss me.

I remembered how his arms had felt wrapped around me.

I wished we still had the midnight parties, so I could invite him.

I wished more than ever for Cat to be with me. To offer advice and assurance.

Then, after Easter, as if conjured by my inclination, she returned.

On a day we all felt fractious and at odds, she blew into the house in Lambeth like Zephyrus, bringing summer and light. She wore an azure gown, the bodice studded with pearls and edged with satin rosettes. Her sleeves flowed about her arms like a sunset, orange silk slashed with yellow.

She spun once on her own, her skirts belling around her in a rustle of luxury, before we descended on her.

"How did you get here?" I threw my arms around her.

"Where did you get this?" Joan nearly bowled us over onto the hearth as she joined the embrace.

"Why didn't you tell us you were coming?" Alice sounded vexed that she didn't know in advance.

"I wanted it to be a surprise," Cat sang, causing the Countess of Bridgewater to grouse and shuffle. "I want all of April—all the rest of our lives!—to be one brilliant surprise after another."

She flung herself at me in a swirl of skirts that propelled us into the tapestry of Solomon and the Queen of Sheba.

"I can't tell you how happy I am to see you," she whispered.

I was about to tell her the same. Tell her I needed her advice. But she leapt from the wall as if pinched and pulled me with her.

"Come!" she said. "All of you."

She led us up through the gloomy entranceway and into the oak gallery where our voices and footsteps echoed.

"So what's it really like?" I asked. "Living at court?"

"It's actually hard work," Cat said. "I have to help the queen dress and plait her hair. Not to mention sewing for the poor and providing entertainment for the king."

"They have no servants?" I asked.

"Kitty, we *are* the servants." She navigated the stairs as if she'd never been gone. "The queen can't be attended by common peasants. The worst part is when the older ladies think they can order me around. Like my stepmother, even though all she did was marry my scattergoods of a father. She thinks she can play *ma mère* now that we live in the same household. I may just be a maid of honor, and she one of the 'great ladies,' but I'm there to serve the queen, by the Mass, not Margaret Jennings."

"She is a Howard now."

"Margaret Howard. *Lady* Howard. I don't care."

"Do you get along with the other girls our age?" I asked, waiting to hear I'd been replaced.

"Like who?" Cat paused at the top of the stairs. "Mary Fitzroy the Duchess of Richmond? She's actually a Howard, daughter of the Duke of Norfolk. Wouldn't she be a fine confidante, tattling every word I utter? Then there's Katherine Carey, Mary Boleyn's daughter, and possibly the king's, though he won't admit to it. I don't blame him: the whey-faced ninny thinks marrying Francis Knollys is the epitome of courtly delight."

Cat dropped names and dispensed sentences with such

worldly abandon that I began to feel hopelessly provincial.

"Is it true the king might be her father?" Alice asked.

"Aren't you always on the lookout for gossip?" Cat said.

"If she was, surely he would claim her, like he did the Duke of Richmond," Joan said.

"But she's a *girl*," Alice argued. "Only boys are worthy of a king's acknowledgment."

"There's no way of knowing for sure," Cat cut in. "Her mother was Mary Boleyn. I mean, the king of France called Mary his English mare when she served over there because he'd ridden her so many times!"

We dissolved into giggles that silenced when she pushed open the door to the maidens' chamber. The room had been completely transformed.

Swathes of fabric lay across several of the beds. Yellow damask. Green velvet. Silk an incredibly pale blue like the center of a snowdrift. Four different pinks, from a magenta brocade to a rose-colored satin. The layers of cloth carried the exotic odors of foreign lands and spices from the holds of ships.

"What's it all for?" Joan asked, her voice hoarse with awe. "New gowns?"

And even I heard the unasked question: *For us?*

"Isn't it gorgeous?" Cat said, stepping into the room and whirling in a dizzy spin. "Can you believe the dried-up old bat finally broke down and got me something nice?"

"It must have cost a fortune," Joan breathed, but disappointment washed her face.

"And it's all for me!" Cat grinned. "Not a hand-me-down. Not something cut from someone else's leftovers. Mine. Made especially to fit me."

I couldn't quench a spark of envy. Cat and I had always been the same. The same age. Both unwanted daughters. Both wearing castoff clothing. And suddenly she was away at court, meeting new people, wearing new gowns. I was beneath her, just like Mary Lascelles said. A sickly petulance overtook me.

"Jesus, Cat," I muttered. "How many times can you put *me* and *mine* into one breath?"

Joan squeaked. Cat fixed me with a glare like a rapier thrust. I felt it pierce me. My envy mingled with anger and shame. I wanted to take back what I had said. I wanted to say more.

She approached me with a swagger like a lioness ready to pounce.

"I am the face of Norfolk House at court. The duchess can't have anyone believe her house or her family is shabby. I represent the entire Howard family. I *need* new clothes. Do you deny me that?"

"Of course not," I said. "No one is happier than I am that you're finally getting all you deserve. Beautiful clothes. Jewelry. A man you love."

She stopped moving. Stopped breathing. Then snapped, "Get out," over her shoulder, and Joan and Alice disappeared as quickly as dandelion fluff on the wind.

"Who told you?" she asked, her voice more deadly than ever. "No one knows."

"Francis," I whispered, my voice a paroxysm of nerves.

"Francis *Dereham?*" she asked.

"Yes," I said. "He saw you at court. Then he came here to get his old job back. I spoke with him."

"*Francis?*" she repeated, and her eyes opened wide, radiating surprise, or possibly fear. "He's here?"

"No, the duchess sent him to Horsham," I said, confused and shaken. "He said you were in love. That you sent him away."

"I told *no one.*" Her voice rose to a shout. "What did he say about me?"

"He said you loved a man named Thomas Culpepper," I said.

Cat began to giggle. The giggles came in little puffs at first. Then in a surge, like bubbles from the bottom of a pond. And suddenly, she was giggling so high and so hard that she couldn't catch her breath and had to bend over, hands on her knees, eyes streaming.

This wasn't the Cat I knew. The Cat who whispered dreams in my ear at night. The Cat who sneaked around Norfolk House, kissing and canoodling with Francis in the chapel. This Cat jumped from one extreme to another. This Cat didn't like me. This Cat was frightening.

"Cul-Cul-Culpepper?" she gasped.

"That's what he said!"

"Silly Kitty." She took a stinging swipe at my cheek.

"Culpepper is in the past. Culpepper is no one. He was just a . . . nothing." Her eyes unfocused a little, "Though so *seductive*."

She shook her head as if to clear it.

"No, Kitty, I have a better catch now. I have everything I want right here."

She opened her tiny hand and showed me her empty palm. Then she snapped her fingers shut like a coffer.

"It's all I'll ever want, Kitty," she said. "It's all I'll ever need."

Cat stayed, the epicenter of a whirlwind of fabrics and fittings, ribbons and pearls. She and I reached a truce that hinged on us both keeping silent regarding Francis, Culpepper, and her mysterious new man. And William. I wasn't ready to share my unblemished feelings for him. And I wasn't sure she would approve. We'd never had secrets from each other before, and it felt odd and strained. The awkward tension made me mute on all but the most mundane subjects.

Fortunately, the duchess embarked on a campaign of cleanliness and enlisted the assistance of everyone in the house, thus preventing the possibility of long, private conversations. The stairs were swept and washed with lye. All the gold plate gleamed in the buffet of the great hall. The dogs were banished to the kitchens and courtyards. Even we were doused in cold water—our hair scrubbed with lavender—and left out to dry in our camisoles in the weak spring sunshine.

The steward began to lose his corpulence because he had no time to eat. He had to be fitted for a new doublet, the duchess muttering over the expense of velvet.

Cat sat in the tapestry room as if holding court, sewing

embellishments from twisted gold tissue to her new bodices. Occasionally, she begged the duchess to release us from drudgery in order to assist her. As we did, she would regale us with tales of court like a traveling minstrel, and we hung on every word.

The duchess tried to keep it a secret, but we all knew the reason for the uproar.

The king.

Sometimes, it was a good thing to have Alice around.

"But why would he be coming here?" Joan asked, hunched over tiny stitches of silver on silver in the drab light from the window.

"He has to visit the nobility," Alice said. "They expect it."

"It's the same reason he has a progress," Cat agreed. "He has to get out and engage with the lords and dukes. Be seen by the people. And see his country."

"But why is it a secret?" Joan pursued. "If he wanted to be seen by the people, wouldn't he be telling everybody? So the peasants know he's coming and can see him? And besides, we're right across the river from him. It's not like he's never seen Lambeth before."

"Well, this visit isn't exactly like a progress," Cat conceded, and frowned.

"But it is a great honor," I added.

"Of course!" Joan dropped her stitching. "Oh, I didn't mean anything else by it. I just don't know why he would want to come *here*."

"Are we that boring, Joan?" I asked.

"The duchess is a great noblewoman," Alice sniffed. "Of course he would want to come here."

"Right." Joan sounded unconvinced, and looked up to ask another question, but was interrupted by a commotion outside.

Horses and carts and men in livery filled the courtyard. Everyone seemed to be shouting orders, and no one seemed to be heeding them.

"The duke," Joan said.

I stood and brushed my skirts. Perhaps in the chaos I could at least catch a glimpse of William, if not a word with him.

"Where are you off to?" Cat asked.

"Nowhere," I said, feeling the word a betrayal to both Cat and William.

"Kitty's going to see the boy who works for the duke," Alice said. "The one who brings the messages. William Gibbon."

My cheeks flared.

"You have a boy, Kitty?" Cat asked, hurt in her voice. "You didn't tell me."

"He's handsome," Alice said.

"He likes her," Joan grinned.

"He stops by to say hello when he delivers a message sometimes," I said. "That's all."

It was the truth. So far. I just wished it were more.

"I think Kitty has a secret lover," Alice said. She stretched out the last word like a sticky sweet.

"He's not a lover," I said quickly, the heat on my neck refus-

ing to fade. He was the closest I'd ever had. The only one I'd ever wanted.

"Then you won't mind if *I* talk to him?" Alice said.

"Do what you like!" I cried, all bitter nonchalance. Confusion tied my tongue and baffled the truth.

"But, Alice, you're married," Joan protested. I could have hugged her.

"So are you," Alice said. "And that doesn't stop you from prancing about with Edward Waldegrave."

"But you can't take Kitty's boy," Joan said.

"Kitty says she doesn't care," Alice said.

My heart threatened to spill from my sleeve and all over the floor, I cared so much.

"Well, that's all right then," Cat interjected. "Because I have my eye on someone for you anyway, Kitty Tylney."

We all stopped and stared at her.

"Don't think I've forgotten my promise to get you to court," she said.

Joan gasped, a look of uncensored hope gilding her features.

"And when you get there, you'll have your pick of some of the most eligible men in the country," she continued.

Joan sighed, a mournful note of envy.

"But I don't . . ." I said. "I'm not . . ."

I didn't want anyone else.

"It's true, you're nobody," Cat said quickly. "But there are plenty to choose from even at your level. The king likes to keep young men around him. His privy councilors have become so

old, but some of his gentlemen pensioners and yeomen of the chamber are really quite luscious."

Like Thomas Culpepper, I thought, but carefully didn't mention it.

"One in particular," she said. "A yeoman. Looks like a lion, with this gorgeous golden hair. You would kill for it." She reached up and smoothed down a shock of my own hair that had escaped my plait. I felt it fly away again when she was done.

"He would be good for you," she said, quietly, in my ear only.

I nodded and smiled. But I didn't want Cat's choice. I wanted my own.

Perhaps I didn't want to go to court after all.

"The king's barge!" A cry went up from the garden.

The galleries filled with the sound of running slippers and pounding boots. I had never seen the elder members of the household move so quickly. Even the duchess exerted herself enough for pink to rise beneath the white lead on her cheeks.

We fell into line outside the great door of the house, a welcoming committee of flouncing skirts and adjusting doublets. The duke's men waited at the landing. I could see William's head amongst them.

The duke had insinuated himself and supplanted the dowager duchess as head of Norfolk House. He'd marched through the rooms and galleries, sniffing out the ugly and inconstant with his powerful nose. He tolerated no idling. And no flirting. I hadn't seen William for three days.

"There it is!" Alice whispered. We all craned our necks to look. The royal barge appeared, painted in scarlet and gold, with detailed filigree and intricate designs. The canopy of cloth of gold was embroidered with the initials of the king. H and R. *Henricus Rex.*

On the king's barge were select retainers. This was to be a

private party. An intimate meal with only the king's beloved friends. All two hundred of us.

The king faced us, his clothes and hair and beard a riot of red and gold. He looked like a giant standing there, one foot resting on a cushion as if he had just conquered it.

"He never ages," Joan whispered.

But even at a distance, I could see a slight stoop to his shoulders, the swell of his chest and belly. He was no longer the lean knight who had escorted Queen Anne Boleyn to London when we were children. He was something else now. Weighted.

"In line!" the duchess snapped as she strode past us, black and gold damask rustling, jewels winking on every surface. The Duke of Norfolk kept pace with her, his little bowlegs scissoring in his black hose.

The barge landed, and we all sank into deep bows and curtseys. We were supposed to stay that way, crouched on the muddy path, until the king exited the barge and waved us all up.

Cat had told us that the king suffered from an ulcer in his leg, brought on by an old jousting injury. He had trouble getting around, and sometimes his temper was incredibly short. The entire court would walk on eggshells, wondering who would be thrown out of the chamber for sitting or smiling or breathing. I knew what the duchess was like when she had one of her migraine headaches. I tried to imagine that kind of power and pain in a king.

Still, it took him forever to get out of that damn boat. My own knees began to ache from the stupid curtsey, and my thoughts ran to treason.

"Norfolk!" the king cried, his voice surprisingly high for someone so large. It made him more human.

We took our cue to stand, and I was able to look at the king from beneath my lowered brow. Dressed all in crimson and fur, he blocked out the sun, which created a halo behind him. I wondered briefly how many animals had to die to construct his ermine cape. He towered over the duke. And he was *wide*. It couldn't all be fat, because he wasn't round, just prodigious. And intimidating. He stood with his feet planted far apart and his hands on his hips, like Colossus straddling the entrance to Rhodes.

He finished listening to the flattery of the duke and dowager duchess and strode toward the house. We all sank to the ground again. I curtseyed gratefully, not wanting him to see or notice me. He was too big, too beautiful, with his gold-trimmed clothing and neatly cut beard and fingers burdened by heavy rings.

But he stopped in front of me. I trembled, unable even to look at his shoes.

"Mistress Howard," he said. Of course it wasn't me. It was Cat. "I believe I have seen you at court."

"Yes, Your Majesty," Cat said, and rose. "I wait on Her Majesty the Queen."

"And how do you like it?" he asked.

"I like it well, Your Majesty. She is a good mistress, and you are a good master."

"Loyalty is a virtue," the king said.

"Your will is mine, Your Majesty."

"I like that in a woman," the king murmured.

Cat's skirts rustled, and out of the corner of my eye, I saw her sink back into a curtsey.

"Come, Mistress Howard," the king said, his voice quick and hearty. "You shall sit by me this evening."

I couldn't help but smile, wondering what the duchess's face looked like. Little Miss Nobody usurping her place at the high table. Cat rose and I remained in my curtsey, watching her satin slippers practically skipping down the path.

The duchess laid on a banquet of epic proportions for the king, even though in theory, he was "just stopping in for a bite to eat." Venison, spit-roasted pig, a boar's head, pike, sturgeon, rabbit, and lamb. Peacock, pheasant, duck. The very best wine, not the vinegary, watery stuff she usually served.

Because we weren't important, Joan, Alice, and I served the far end of the room, not even able to sit down. Others enjoyed the privilege of serving the king, and then the dishes were passed down the tables. We got the worst cuts of meat, and little of the sweets and marzipan, but it was still like Christmas and Easter all at once.

Cleaning and decorating had rendered the hall almost

unrecognizable. The scratched benches, ancient wooden trenchers, and dogs were all gone. The floor gleamed from repeated scrubbings, as did the tables. The king sat in a brand new chair, on a velvet cushion, the back carved in elaborate designs of stags and Tudor roses.

"Just look at the fabrics he's wearing," Joan sighed.

"Look at all the gold," Alice said.

From a distance, the king's eyes appeared to recede into the fat of his face, giving him a mean and piggy look. Cat looked like a doll beside him.

"What do you think of his men?" I asked, glancing about the room at the few courtiers he had brought with him. None of them looked to be Cat's type. They didn't appear dashing or dangerous. They didn't have sexy smiles or chin dimples or shapely calves. But they must have had influence, to accompany the king for such a private party. Power and riches. But could she give up looks?

"The two men behind him are passable," Joan said, dragging her eyes from the king's furs.

I had to squint a little to see them properly. One had stringy black hair but broad shoulders. He stood in a good imitation of the king's stance. The other man was older and indifferently handsome.

"Well, they're not too bad, I suppose," I said. Perhaps it was the second man Cat was interested in, but she paid no attention to either of them.

She seemed perfectly content to wait on the king, to smile at

his comments, to speak rarely. For the king didn't really seem to want to converse as much as impress. I couldn't hear what he said, but he did most of the talking. How could Cat bear it? She hated being around people who talked about themselves more than about her.

But then again, he *was* the king.

"I wonder what he's saying," I said.

"Whatever it is, it must be riveting," Alice said. "Look at Cat's face."

Cat watched the king talk as if it were the most fascinating thing in the world. She looked . . . *avid*.

"She has to look that way," I said. "If she looked bored, he would cut off her head."

Alice puckered, and Joan gagged on her wine.

"I didn't mean it," I whispered hastily. "It was a joke. It just slipped out."

"Jokes like that could lose you *your* head, Kitty," Alice muttered. "You must watch your tongue."

I nodded, voiceless.

Joan sighed, leaning back against the wall. "Cat has all the luck."

"She certainly does," Alice said. "She has the family connections, the looks, and now the clothes, too. Is it any wonder the king noticed her today? Her duckies are practically bursting out of that bodice."

"Now who's making inappropriate remarks?" I asked.

Alice made a face, and Joan giggled into her hand.

"I desire a dance!" the king cried, and clapped his hands. "Mistress Howard tells me that she and her friends here in Lambeth love to dance."

The duchess called for more musicians, and the servants scurried to remove the trestle tables and benches. The king had brought no ladies with him at all, so even the lowliest among us had a chance for a partner. Trust Cat to open every window of opportunity for us all.

One of the king's retainers took Cat's hand and she accepted impassively. Joan giggled at the invitation of Edward Waldegrave. Alice partnered the other courtier, but I kept my eyes on Cat. The man opposite her was tall. A little old perhaps. Blandly good-looking, with a narrow face that stretched into a pointy wedge-shaped beard. Cat smiled at him once but paid him little notice.

"I don't see what you find so interesting about Anthony Denny."

I turned to see that William Gibbon stood before me. I blushed.

"I didn't see you."

"It appears your attention was elsewhere." He held out his hand and we began the galliard.

"I was just . . ." I couldn't finish without giving away Cat's secret, so I stuttered into silence.

"I've been out on business for the duke," he said, rescuing me. "And have returned just in time."

I smiled. The galliard was athletic and inhibited conversation. But when the music stopped, William led me aside into the shadows so we could watch—and whisper—unimpeded. He held my hand lightly, his touch like summer—like the shape and feel and scent of a plum—intoxicating.

"You dance well," he said.

"Practice." I laughed. Thinking of late nights in the maidens' chamber made me feel warm. "Late night dances with Alice. Though I usually play the boy's part."

"Really?" he asked. "Why?"

I looked at him to see if I could detect a trace of guile, but saw none.

"It's impossible for someone like Alice to lift me," I said simply, and indicated my height. "I'd probably crush her."

"Funny," he said, slipping an arm around my waist. "I had no problem at all."

"You are a bit taller than she is," I said, but my voice caught slightly. "I'm huge compared to her."

"I think you're just right," he whispered.

I sensed every place his body touched mine. One hand on my hip. His arm along my back. Chest just touching my side. His right knee lost in my skirts.

"Kitty," William said, his mouth so close to my ear I could have kissed him with a turn of my head. "Kitty, I think I . . ."

He paused and I turned. So close. He raised his other hand to stroke a wisp of hair from my forehead. I felt lost in the lightness of his touch.

Then the musicians fell silent, breaking the spell, and we

looked back to the room. The king had risen and made his way slowly to the empty floor.

"A pavane!" he called. A slow, stately dance, one that wouldn't trouble his leg.

He turned and held his hand out to Cat. She curtseyed, and when she rose, a triumphant smile lit her face. She didn't like slow dances. But her countenance reflected no boredom or irritation. Far from it. She looked . . . radiant.

She no longer looked detached. No, she watched the king with every step she made. In the light, in the dance, beneath her gaze, his features lost twenty years.

The king and Cat only had eyes for each other.

I felt as if I had been struck by lightning. I stared, prostrate with the knowledge of who had replaced Culpepper in Cat's affections.

15

"I, Catherine, take thee, Henry, to be my wedded husband," Cat said solemnly.

The king told everyone he had been unable to consummate his marriage to Anne of Cleves. Her body repulsed him. His conscience pricked him.

"To have and to hold from this day forward . . ."

Anne had been engaged before. To the Duke of Lorraine. The ambassadors from the Duchy of Cleves were unable to produce the proper paperwork proving the contract was null and void.

"For richer, for poorer . . ."

A betrothal was as good as a marriage, legally binding. King Henry balked at bigamy. When it suited him. Queen Anne could be lost in translation and become the King's beloved "sister," no harm done.

"In sickness and in health . . ."

I saw the appeal of losing status rather than losing your head, but who would willingly accept being superseded by a little girl? Seeing one of your *maids* crowned queen while you sat by and smiled and pretended not to understand?

"To be bonny and buxom in bed and at board, till death do us part *are you listening to me?*"

The sharpness of the words startled me away from the open window in the maidens' chamber. The sun was out, carrying waves of the scent of the fresh June leaves in the apple orchard.

"Of course I am, Cat," I lied. I'd heard the words so many times already I could have said them myself.

"This is my *wedding*," Cat snapped. "I have to get it right. It has to be perfect."

"It will be," I assured her. Not that any of us would be there to see it. We weren't invited. We didn't even know what day it would be.

"What does it mean?" asked Joan, who lolled on her bed, rummaging through Cat's new cast-offs. Every day brought a new gown, a new jewel, a new bauble. Cat, festooned with attention, dripping with royal favor, passed on the least of her wardrobe to the rest of us. The poor.

"Bonny and buxom?" Joan grinned and hefted her own breasts to illustrate.

"No!" Cat said. "Bonny means cheerful. And buxom, obedient."

Henry wouldn't say that part. No man was expected to owe cheer and obedience to his wife. So it might as well have been breasts.

"What will happen to Queen Anne?" I asked.

"He's giving her Richmond Palace," Cat said. "And bucketloads of money. And don't call her that. She'll be the Lady Anne soon."

She'd be able to live on her own. Without having to answer to anyone. But she'd be alone. I wondered if the trade-off would be worth it.

"It's her own fault, really," Cat added. "She rejected him."

"No, she didn't, she married him. He's rejecting her."

"No, I mean before she married him. She was in Rochester and he disguised himself as a traveler. Rode hard from Greenwich to meet her. I mean, how romantic can you get? He couldn't wait to see her, to kiss her for the first time. But when he got there, she pushed him away."

"But if he was disguised, how did she know it was him?"

"Well, everyone else did."

"But she'd never seen him before," I said. It seemed unjust that she was vilified for a natural reaction. A strange old man comes up and tries to kiss you, who wouldn't push him away?

"That didn't matter to him. You see, he still thinks of himself as the handsomest man in Christendom. The golden hero. The statuesque godlike figure of classical art and mythology. The man she rejected was a dilapidated, fat, smelly old man. After that, whenever he was with her, that's how he felt."

"But I make him feel like the Greek god," she finished. "And as long as he sees himself that way through my eyes, he'll be happy. And once I get that crown on my head, I will give him no reason to feel any differently."

"I hope you're right," I said.

"Of course I'm right," she replied, laughing. "I'm always right. I was right about us going to court, wasn't I? When I'm

queen, I shall bring you to be my favored guest. You shall supplant the greatest ladies of the kingdom in status and in my affection."

When she's queen. Cat Howard.

"Cat," I whispered. "You're going to be queen."

"I know," she said, her eyes alight, an edge of awe creeping into her confidence.

"You're going to be the Queen of England!"

I threw my arms around her and danced her up and down the room, our laughter echoing up the long gallery. Joan sat still on the bed, smiling, rubbing the raised velvet brocade on her new skirt.

"And you'll really take me with you?" I asked when we caught our breath.

"I promised, didn't I?" she said. "When I left, didn't I tell you I'd find a way to get you to court? For us to be there, just like we always dreamed?"

"Well, you certainly found it," I said.

She grinned.

"And we'll do just what we always said. We'll eat too much and dance all night and flirt with *all* the boys," she paused. "At least you will."

"I'll flirt," I said to soothe, though I didn't mean with all the boys. Just one. "But we'll both dance."

AT THE END OF JUNE, ANNE OF CLEVES MOVED TO RICHMOND WITH
her furs and her head intact. Cat moved back to court.
Throughout the spring, Norfolk House had been in a contin-
ual furor. If we weren't planning a dinner for the king, we were
cleaning up from one—usually both at once. Now, the absence
of Cat and the king was like the space of a missing tooth. I kept
probing it to see if it was real.

Even more painful was the fact that William returned
only infrequently. And I waited as impatiently as the duchess
for news from her stepson at court. He came once, mid-July,
on what felt like the hottest day of that hot, dry summer. The
duke and dowager duchess sequestered themselves in the cool
cave of the downstairs withdrawing room. And William coaxed
me outside, where the sun had bleached the topiary and cast a
diamond reflection off the river.

"Why don't we venture outside the walls?" William said. "I
spotted a little grove of trees on a rise just south of here . . ."

He trailed off, watching me. In my mind, I knew those men
no longer lurked in the shadows beyond the apple orchard. But
in my heart I felt them waiting outside the gates.

"You don't like the park?" he asked.

I hadn't set foot in the woods since that evil afternoon the autumn before.

"Actually, it's one of my favorite places," I blurted. The quiet. The birdsong. The ever-changing, myriad shades of green.

"But?"

I couldn't tell him. Because I'd done nothing. Nothing to help. Nothing to hinder. I'd run. I'd saved myself. And still I didn't feel safe. I never felt safe.

Except with William. I managed a smile and moved toward the gates.

"Don't." He laid a hand on my shoulder. "Don't do something just to make me happy. This isn't only about me. It's about both of us."

Freckles dusted his knuckles like they did his nose. His nails were short and even a little grubby. William didn't spend all his time indoors drinking wine and flirting. He worked. I liked that.

He took his hand back, ducked his head, his hair concealing his embarrassment. I loved that his face told me at least as much as his words, and sometimes more.

"When I was little," I told him, "I used to pretend that the arch in the oak trees was a gateway to the fairy world. I could walk through there and be in the forest where the leaves changed the color of the light and the bluebells formed a carpet more luxurious than anything produced by man. I always felt it was there that I truly belonged because no

one expected anything of me. No one told me what to do or what I wanted or who I was. No one told me I wasn't good enough."

I took his hand from where he held it behind his back and smiled.

"A magical gateway." He sounded dubious.

I nodded. It was my turn to feel embarrassed.

"That is something I must experience for myself." He began to run up through the orchard, pulling me with him. Elation and terror mixed within me. The sun illuminated the arch like a golden door, and when we reached it, William swept me up into his arms to carry me through.

The light patterned through the leaves like stained glass. William set me down but didn't take his hands from my waist. The fairies must surely have lived there, for I forgot, in an instant, all that had happened in that forest.

"This will be our special place," he said, his gaze so keen I lost sight of the sun itself. "No one here will tell you that you aren't good enough." The dappled sunlight played across his features, chasing the emotions that sped from elation to confusion to determination. He leaned forward and pressed his lips against mine.

For one startled moment, I stared directly into both of his gray-blue eyes, then I closed my own and kissed him back. A kiss that dissolved with spice and sweetness on the tongue.

My arms ached to wrap around him, but I didn't know how.

His waist? His neck? Could I run my fingers through his hair? In the end, I stood still, arms straight at my sides and fingers splayed.

William stepped back and looked at me, blinking surprise.

"I'm sorry," he said.

"I'm not." Something about him drew the truth out of me.

"I have no prospects. I'm nobody. I have nothing to offer you."

"Neither have I. I have no family connections. I will bring no dowry. We're equals." The word ignited something in me. We were the same. The wonder of it made me smile.

But William didn't. Deep in the shadows of that shrouded wood, the expression that crossed his face combined anxiety with a half dose of despair. But his eyes still held hope. Just a shred of it.

"I am dependent upon the duke," he said. "My loyalty to him is based solely on need. The need to make the right connections."

I nodded. The sunlit warmth had fled from my body, and I shivered. I was not the right connection.

"He knows this," William continued. "And doesn't let me forget it. That my choices are not entirely my own. But you're related to the dowager duchess?"

"Distantly," I said. "Very, very distantly."

"He couldn't say no," William said quietly.

To what? I wanted to ask, but held my tongue. I didn't trust myself to speak.

"When I first saw you, at that banquet, I couldn't take my eyes off you," he said.

I remembered. With a blush.

"You were so different from the others."

So much taller. So much more awkward.

"So much more real." William took my hands in his. "You didn't preen or simper or bat your eyes. You didn't wear cream to make your skin pale or paint your cheeks. You wore a plain gown."

I had to.

"You didn't flirt with the duke when you served him."

Ew.

"In fact, it appeared you couldn't get away from him quickly enough. Despite the fact that he could get you to court."

Maybe that's why the duke didn't pick me.

"I liked you before I even knew you, Kitty," he said, and stepped closer still. "But getting to know you has made me like you even more."

When he kissed me again, my arms went around his neck of their own accord. My hand reached for his hair and buried itself in the thick, textured luxury of it. My tongue found his, and I lost myself in the brilliantly faceted sunlight and shadow of his touch.

17

I slipped in through the front door of the house, one hand to lips that felt green and renascent, like spring itself. The entrance hall dozed, languid, in the afternoon heat, buzzing with the hum of a single fly.

And voices. From the duchess's little withdrawing room.

I tried to slip past, but was caught by the sound of my name.

"Katherine?" the duchess said. "You try telling that snip of a girl what to do. I've tried for years now, and she still does whatever pleases her."

A shot of fear passed through me that someone had seen me with William. That the duchess disapproved not of my choice but of me making it.

"Perhaps that is why she is so headstrong," came the duke's voice. "She has never been punished for it."

"Are you trying to tell me how to run my own household, sir?" the duchess cried.

"I would never do such a thing, my lady. Though others might wish to if they discover the laxity of your control. Especially in the past."

"No one will ever learn Katherine's secrets."

Secrets? I had none. At least none the duchess knew. Or so I thought.

"Which is exactly why we must fill her chambers with those allegiant to the house of Howard. And one in particular who will be willing to tell us everything. What is said and by whom. Who is in favor and who is out. When they consummate the marriage. How often and how vigorously."

I realized which Catherine they discussed. And why.

"We will need to know every detail of her monthly courses," the duchess agreed.

"God forbid that she have them," the duke interrupted. "For what we really need is a Howard heir in the royal cradle."

The duchess murmured her agreement. I started to creep away, having no desire to be privy to the rest of their conversation. But the duke's next words stopped me.

"We will need help. Someone close to her. Someone we can trust, but whom she must trust as well. A sister?"

The duchess let out a condescending laugh.

"She hates her sisters," she said. "No, it will have to be someone closer than that."

"Someone loyal," the duke reminded her.

"I know just the person," the duchess said. "Loyal to the grave."

It was what the duchess had called me, many months before. *Loyal to the grave.* Closer than a sister. When Cat fulfilled her promise to bring me to court, would I be expected to tell all her secrets to the duke?

On July 28, Thomas Cromwell, who had engineered the marriage to Anne of Cleves, lost his head for his singular lack of judgment.

Cat married King Henry the same day.

Cat followed instructions and appointed great ladies to her household. She kept Jane Boleyn, the Lady Rochford, widowed sister-in-law to the first Queen Anne. And she selected several candidates from amongst her family members. Cat's half-sister Lady Isabel Baynton, thirty years older and infinitely more tiresome, and Cat's stepmother, Lady Howard, retained the positions they'd had in Anne of Cleves's household. Cat's aunt, the pale Countess of Bridgewater, and Lady Arundel, another half-sister, rounded out the Howard retinue.

And then Cat appointed the dowager duchess herself.

Cat finally had them all where she wanted them. She wielded more power than her stepmother. More influence than her aunt. More status than her grandmother. Cat had won. Finally.

But she didn't have us. As the long, hot summer stretched on, we received no word. The duchess packed up her house. Dismissed her servants.

Wrote letters to the parents of the girls in her care.

We waited as the summer scorched the earth. Into the dry autumn when the leaves dropped from sheer exhaustion. The wheat withered in the fields before it could be harvested. Cows and sheep and men and women battled starvation.

Joan started to cry.

"Don't worry, Joan," I said, barely able to console myself. "She promised, remember?"

"No, Kitty!" Joan cried. "She promised *you*."

I froze, one hand on her shoulder. Had Cat only promised me? And how much was that promise worth?

"I was there, remember? In the maidens' chamber. The day she was practicing her vows. She said she would make *you* her greatest lady. Her greatest friend. She didn't promise me anything. She didn't even look at me."

"Of course she meant all of us," I said helplessly.

"You can't really think that," Alice said. Quiet as ever.

"We've always been together," I said.

"It's always just been the two of you," Alice said. "Kitty and Cat. And me and Joan on the side. You were always the important one."

Not important enough.

"But I might have certain benefactors working in my favor," Alice announced.

"In *your* favor?" Joan said, petulance generating a shrill falsetto.

"Well, yes," Alice said. "My husband does work for Lord Maltravers."

I looked at Joan and mouthed *Lord Maltravers* with simpering, pinched lips. She smiled weakly.

"I even wrote a letter to Cat," Joan sighed. "I reminded her of our friendship. Of our history together."

A sudden fear clenched me.

History. Joan knew all Cat's history.

"And you put this down on paper?" I asked, barely able to form the question. A piece of paper could take on a life of its own. In the right hands, it could bring down a queen.

"It was pretty sickly," Joan admitted. "*Remember the love my heart has always borne towards you.* That sort of thing."

"And that's all?" I asked.

"Of course." She nodded, her face blank and guileless.

The other girls dispersed to the bosoms of their unloving families. Mary Lascelles cried piteously over the punishment of having to return to her brother's keeping. But whatever Joan had written must have jarred Cat's memory, because the summons came. For all three of us.

I had my chance to go to court. To be someone different. Someone important. Someone desired. Someone beloved of the queen.

19

Windsor Castle appeared above the goldening red ash of the surrounding forest, the gray stone glowing white against the painfully blue October sky. This was a true castle, not a modern approximation of one. Not like the duchess's house of brick and spit-shine. This was a castle built for defense with thick slit-windowed towers and crenellated walls.

"There it is!" Joan yelped. We had already traveled many long, boring hours and now she leaned over her horse's neck, as if hoping it would get her there sooner.

I found myself leaning forward, too. My horse danced sideways slightly, caught up in my excitement. The castle on the hill looked so far away.

"Let's race," I said.

"Most unladylike," Alice muttered. She rode primly in her dark brown riding habit, eyes straight ahead, completely unaware of the smudge of dirt across the side of her nose.

"Last one there tends the duchess's bunions!" I shouted, an old joke from when we were children.

My horse leapt forward when I dug in my heels. She seemed as keen as I was to enter the magical realm of chivalry presented by such an enchanted scene.

"Katherine Tylney!" Alice cried.

"We're not ladies!" I shouted back to her. "We're chamberers!"

Joan's laughter undulated over the warm-cold ripples of sunlight and shadow and I knew that she followed. Alice couldn't be far behind.

Our horses kicked up dust on the dry road and over the cracked-earth gardens and pigpens. We slowed as the road narrowed between rows of tall, half-timbered buildings—the kind occupied by merchants and town leaders, sellers of fabrics and slippers and lace to the court, all eager and bustling because the king was in town.

Suddenly the right side of the road opened out and up the hill to a great stone gate, looming above the rest of the houses. Protection. Defense.

We stopped. Almost as one.

"Here we are," I said quietly.

"We made it," Joan agreed.

Alice only nodded, all confidence drained from her face.

The guards at the gate recognized our escort and allowed us through. The air cooled considerably as we passed beneath the arch, heavy and dark. Then we came blinking into a wide, gaping courtyard, studded with knots of gem-colored courtiers.

We dismounted, and stable boys scurried to lead our horses away. I felt bereft at the loss of my palfrey's bulk and warmth. I pressed the anxiety beneath my stomacher.

To our left rose a perfectly rounded hill, topped by an ancient tower, thick and heavyset like an old man's chest. To our right,

the castle wall enclosed the quadrangle and all the activity that spun within it. And directly ahead, a looming gray residence studded with towers squinted at us through narrow windows.

The entrance yawned wide, ready to swallow us whole.

"This way," our escort said with a noise halfway between a laugh and a cough.

I realized we had stopped again, the three of us open mouthed and gawping. My skin burned with embarrassment. We giggled nervously and started forward again.

"*This* way," the guard repeated, and indicated the western wing of the building, the door hidden behind the tennis court—the servants' entrance, illustrating the fact that indeed, we were not ladies, or anything remotely akin. We were chamberers, and therefore not entitled to the same privileges. No matter what Cat had promised.

The courtiers looked up and ogled as we passed. One, a yeoman in scarlet Tudor livery, faced the others, and I admired his broad back, clipped narrow at the waist by a shiny black belt. He had gorgeous golden hair that I would have given my left hand for. The thought tugged a memory. *Hair you'd kill for.* Was this the man Cat had in mind for me?

He turned as we walked through the narrow space between the building and the tennis court, and I stumbled over the cobbles. His brown eyes widened, round face slack with surprise. And recognition. He'd seen me before.

In the forest.

Joan muttered a curse when I tripped over her in a scramble to escape. She looked up and saw the man staring.

"He's delicious," she breathed, looking at my red face. "And he's staring right at you!"

"We can't stop," I hissed, and urged her toward the building.

We slipped in through the narrow doors. Not the kitchen entrance, but certainly not the state entrance. After a stuffy vestibule, the building opened up to a giant room with a massive staircase.

This was obviously the place to be and to be seen. And it was crowded, so therefore also a good place to hide. Women clustered together like peacocks at a spill of grain. They were dressed in bodices of rich damask, with matching overskirts and complementary colors in their kirtles. Their sleeves were puffed and slashed to reveal vivid silks beneath, looking a bit like bread ballooning from the heat of the oven. Gowns of velvet trimmed with gold braid. Hoods decked in pearls. And all sorts of dazzling adornments—chokers and collars and pendants of gold, brooches the size of my hand, studded with gems, rings like jeweled knuckles.

I risked a glance at my own clothes. My Wednesday green dress was smudged with mud from the road. The tear in the skirt was coming open, like a secret dying to be let out. My face was likely splotchy, my eyes probably wild, my hands trembling.

I looked behind me, afraid of being followed.

"Watch where you're stepping!"

I turned to see that I had almost trod upon the bejeweled slipper of a small, compact woman. Her sleek chestnut hair peeked out from beneath a French hood the color of the sky just before nightfall. Her gown was of the same color velvet, simple, without the dazzling chaos of brocade, the sleeves a lighter blue shot with silver. She had wide-set eyes the color of wheat, like a cat's, and they looked up at me critically. I was yet again reminded of my great height and ungainliness.

"Excuse me," I said, and curtseyed. I assumed, from her dress, that her status would be higher than mine. I assumed everyone's would be. Surely the presence of this woman would offer some protection.

"Nicely done," she said, and smiled. It changed her appearance dramatically. Her pale face brightened and her pointed chin smoothed. From seeming somber and somewhat world-weary, she became a coy beauty. I couldn't help but smile back. Her gaze did not stray to my unsuitable attire.

"I am Jane Boleyn, Lady Rochford," she said. Her eyes never left mine, gauging my reaction. And I could imagine the many she got when she introduced herself. People likely recoiled in horror at her intimacy with the infamous Anne Boleyn. People

would pity her widowhood. Her dependence on the Duke of Norfolk. Not something I would wish on anyone.

I didn't look away, and smiled more broadly, determined to judge her on her own merits and not the gossip surrounding her. Determined I wouldn't mention Anne Boleyn or the painful past.

"I am Katherine Tylney," I said quietly, and curtseyed again.

"New chamberer to the queen," she said.

"And these are Joan Bulmer and Alice Restwold." Joan stared openly. Alice's mouth sliced into a smile.

"I believe you are called Kitty," Jane said to me. "You may call me Jane when we are in private company, but Lady Rochford when you speak to or of me in the public of the court."

"Of course," I said, a little nonplussed. No lady, especially not one so great as a viscountess, had ever asked me to call her by her first name. It seemed misplaced. Odd.

"The queen awaits you," Jane said, slipping her arm through mine, "but I must take you first to St. George's Hall to meet the king."

I risked a glance over my shoulder. The man with the blond mane was nowhere to be seen. Jane's arm pulled mine slightly.

"I believe you have met the king already?" she asked, probably assuming I felt nervous entering the royal presence. "I was under the impression that you lived at Norfolk House in Lambeth, and he visited there."

She tactfully did not refer to the fact that Cat was not queen

then. That, in fact, there had been another queen altogether at the time.

"I have never spoken to the king," I said.

"Well, it will be unusual if you get a chance to speak with him today," Jane said. "We will enter, you will be introduced, and we will leave. The king is a busy man and rarely takes any particular interest in the queen's household."

"Oh," I said, unable to think of anything else. I figured it would be churlish to say *good*.

She drew us up the broad staircase, whispers and a few snickers following us as we traveled. And then we stepped into a riot of color and sound. Great, painted wooden beams curved across the vaulted ceiling high above us. Embroidered tapestries cloaked the walls, sewn of pure gold and silk, embellished with pearls and sparkling stones. Courtiers milled about, bedecked in diamonds and bound in gold braid. A man could spend a year's wages on a single item of clothing. Each of them glittered. Each of them wore a dagger *and* a rapier. Beautiful and deadly.

Everything smelled of sweat and dust, breath and lavender.

"Sir Anthony Denny"—Jane pointed to a man in a pale green doublet trimmed with yellow velvet—"the king's Chief Gentleman of the Privy Chamber." I remembered him from the first banquet the duchess gave for the king.

"Thomas Wriothesley," she said, pronouncing it Riz-ley. Jane's lively face took on a fixed smile as she nodded to the man next to Denny. He was dressed in black, the slashes in his

sleeves revealing chevrons the color of blood. "Stay away from him if you can. He's like a ferret. Small, hungry, and with very sharp teeth. Most likely, you'll never come in contact."

Wriothesley caught me staring, scanned my face, my clothes, and my companions. I could *see* his mind ticking off items and columns as he did so.

A man who looked like a younger Duke of Norfolk, resplendent in orange and brown, stood to one side of the room. He was engaged in conversation with a bigger, broad-shouldered man who sported a mighty beard and scanned the room with keen eyes that lit only on the women.

"The Earl of Surrey, Henry Howard," Jane said, following my gaze. "And Charles Brandon, Duke of Suffolk."

"Is the Duke of Norfolk here?" I asked, a squeak in my voice. I scanned the room for the possibility of William.

"He's at his estate in Kenninghall," Jane said.

But not before a figure caught my eye. A figure and face I knew. A gasp became trammeled in my throat, ensnared by panic.

"Lady Rochford?" I said, trying to keep from choking on my own breath. "Who is that?"

Jane craned her neck to see around the broad shoulders of the Duke of Suffolk, and then smiled.

"The new girls always spot him right away," she said.

He was tall and lithe. The blue of his doublet matched the silk that winked from his slashed yellow sleeves. He had chiseled cheekbones and a straight, jutting jaw. His dark eyes danced, assessing those around him. Handsome. But repulsive. I knew him well, because he haunted my nightmares.

This was the rapist from the woods.

I struggled to remain composed, my muscles poised for flight, my heart pounding to escape.

"That, my dear, is the king's usher, Thomas Culpepper. A bit of a gallant, if you ask me, playing fast and loose with the affections of a dozen girls at once."

Thomas Culpepper. He had once been the object of Cat's affections. He was still at court, free and whole and unscarred.

"And never far from his company is Edmund Standebanke," she added. "One of the yeomen of the chamber."

A lion's mane of hair inclined as its bearer whispered into Culpepper's ear.

"Kitty!" A girlish cry nearly dropped me to my knees. "Joan! Alice! I'm so glad you're here!"

We turned to see Cat scampering the length of the great hall, dukes, duchesses, and courtiers scattering, bowing, and curtseying in her wake. Everyone watched her progress to see whom she considered important enough to greet with such ecstasy. The sleeves of her crimson gown billowed, tucked in at the wrists by gold-embroidered cuffs. A series of pearl-and-ruby ropes hung around her neck, anchored by a gold pendant enameled with a brilliant crowned rose.

Jane pinched my sleeve and I followed her into a curtsey of my own. It felt so strange making obeisance to my best friend.

"Oh, stand up for pity's sake," she cried, and threw her arms around me.

"Kitty," she said, and then whispered in my ear, "finally, someone I can talk to!"

She hugged Joan and Alice in turn. Around us, the murmur of whispers sounded like the hiss of disturbed geese.

"Joan, thank you for the kind note you sent," Cat said, a slim, cold edge to her voice.

"Your Majesty," Joan said, a blush turning the entire top half of her body pink.

"And Alice, always a pleasure." Cat gave a tight smile. "How fares my uncle?"

"I do not know, Your Majesty," Alice said, her eyes darting in confusion. "Lady Rochford says he is in Kenninghall."

"I swear you've grown," Cat said, ignoring her and turning back to me. "Soon you'll be too tall for any man save the king, and I'm afraid he's already taken."

The women around us tittered behind their hands, and I smiled weakly, accepting the butt end of the joke. I kept my eyes on her. I had the protection of the queen. No one could harm me. Cat would be my shield. From the laughter. From Culpepper.

"Come meet my husband." Cat giggled. She dragged me by the hand to the dais at the front of the room. The king sat in a velvet-laden chair beneath a cloth-of-gold canopy. Cat ran up the shallow steps to him, and he shifted his weight gracelessly to look at us.

"Who are your acquaintances, my love?" he asked. He must have seen us a hundred times at Norfolk House, and yet he hadn't noticed us once. Now, with Cat's introduction, I felt overly conspicuous and uncomfortable.

Not to mention the fact that he had his arm around her, his huge, meaty hand resting precariously close to her breast.

"Your Majesty," Cat replied. "This is no mere acquaintance, but my best friend, Mistress Katherine Tylney. We are more like sisters than my own sisters, for we grew up together."

"Ahh, Mistress Tylney," the king said. "A pleasure to meet you."

Since he had spoken to me, I was allowed to rise, but found that I couldn't.

"Thank you, Your Majesty," I said, curtseying to the floor again, my voice barely a whisper. Cat laughed.

"This is Kitty's first royal audience," she said. "I think you intimidate her."

"Ah, no," the king said, and I looked up to see him smiling in mock horror. "Surely I inspire awe and not fear?"

"No, Your Majesty," I said. He looked shocked and I realized my mistake. "I mean, yes, Your Majesty."

Cat laughed, and the king chuckled. He moved his arm around her waist and stroked her hip, a smile flickering across his face. He looked besotted. Smitten. Lustful. I gagged on my embarrassment.

"I shall go to my apartments," Cat told him, gently extricating herself from his grasp.

"Much to catch up on with your friends," the king said, and smiled again. Like an indulgent grandfather. Cat flashed him a grin and slipped through the hall, pulling me behind her, beckoning Alice and Joan to follow.

"Your Majesty." A short, stocky woman with a rather masculine face approached Cat and curtseyed.

"I don't need you, Lady Howard," Cat said, airily. So this was Cat's stepmother.

"As you wish," the woman said, seeing that Cat held fast to my hand. Her face twisted out of a grimace that I could read clearly. A Howard, passed over in favor of the prosaic, the homely, the minion?

Cat turned to the other women who had hastened to her side. The dowager duchess, resplendent and ravenesque in silver and black. The Countess of Bridgewater, drab as a sparrow, bland brown eyes receding into the shadow of her bland brown hair. And Lady Baynton, Cat's half-sister Isabel, pinched features and disapproving lips making a mockery of her swanlike neck and graceful bearing.

"I don't need any of you."

A look of venomous jealousy crossed the face of Lady Baynton. The others were shocked rigid by the dismissal. No one had pretended interest in Cat when she lived in Lambeth but everyone seemed keen on her company at court. The ladies quickly smoothed their faces to compliant smiles for the queen. But Lady Howard couldn't rid herself of the expression that suggested she smelled something repugnant when she looked at the rest of us.

"Ignore the Coven," Cat whispered to me and proceeded out the door. "They bark, but they don't bite."

I turned. The ladies clustered, hissing whispers and angling their necks. The men stood in their knots of color, making negotiations and preparations and telling secrets. And Thomas Culpepper dazzled in his inky wickedness like a beacon. Watching.

21

THAT NIGHT, CAT DISMISSED ALL OF HER LADIES—ALL OF THE DUCH-
esses and marchionesses, the daughters and wives of nobility.
She even excused Joan and Alice. She abandoned her giant
feather tester bed and crept onto my little straw pallet with me,
her shoulder pressing against mine.

"Just like old times, Kitty."

"But now we're living the dream."

"I'm glad you came," Cat said. "I need you here."

"Where else would I go?" I asked with a laugh, the double
meaning hanging in the air. I'd go where Cat asked. No one else
wanted me.

"I need loyal friends, Kitty. It's a nest of vipers out there."

"The Coven doesn't seem very friendly," I agreed.

"They're all right," she said. "They're Howards. Just looking for advancement. But the rest. The Seymours and the
Wriothesleys and the Cromwells. All looking for a crack into
which they can wedge a fingernail. To chip off the gilt."

I shivered.

"Cat," I said. "Even the Howards aren't trustworthy."

I told her of the conversation I'd overheard between the duke
and dowager duchess.

"You should just forget you ever heard it," Cat said.

"But how?" I asked. I had fretted over it for weeks, wondering who would betray her. Who would nestle into the duke's pocket and whisper in his ear.

"I already have the king. That's all they care about. When I came to court, they hoped I would look pretty and spread my legs in return for family advancement."

"Cat, that's so vulgar."

"Vulgar, but the truth. But I've gone beyond their wildest dreams. I don't just have the king's interest—I have his *heart*. No one can touch me."

But I couldn't shake the anxiety I felt at the duke's involvement. He frightened me with his sheer feline scheming, his false front of inflated aristocracy hiding a heart of pure unprincipled deviousness.

"They didn't reckon on me charming the king so much he'd want to leave his wife for me," Cat continued. "Not just a mistress. More like my cousin Anne Boleyn than her sister Mary."

"That's dangerous talk, Cat." It seemed a jinx.

"All talk is dangerous. Every word you speak can be turned around and turned against you. You can express your love for the king and someone else will say you've imagined his death, a hanging offense."

"Aren't you afraid?" I asked, thinking of the secrets, the lies, the gossip.

"Afraid?" she echoed. "Afraid of the king? Why, Kitty Tylney, how dare you doubt my husband?"

Cat proved her statement that all words could be turned to

mean something else. Something that implied wrongdoing by the speaker.

"Afraid of the court," I said, speaking generally but thinking of Thomas Culpepper. Knowing now that the face had a name.

"I am queen," she said, turning onto her side. "The court should be afraid of me."

I smiled and turned too, our backs stretched the length of each other like conjoined twins. Cat would protect me.

"You always wanted to be queen," I murmured.

"The Queen of Misrule," she replied, her voice almost lost in the luxurious darkness of the room.

We quickly fell into the routine of Cat's household. Alice, Joan and I were "chamberers," a few steps below the ladies, but a step above the common servants. It was our job to check the huge feather tester bed for knives and poison. We made sure the fires kept burning and the rush mats stayed fresh. We slept in Cat's bedchamber each night on our straw pallets on the floor.

Within the citylike structure that was Windsor Palace, Cat had her own little warren of apartments. An audience chamber, profoundly more grand than the duchess's, where she held public interviews and where her privy council asked her opinion on state matters, much to her amusement. A withdrawing room, bedizened with gilt and tapestries, where she sewed quietly with the Coven and listened to music. And her bedchamber, with its bulky four-poster bed festooned with heavy curtains.

She even had a garderobe for her own private use—no more chamber pots for Cat. She got to sit on a velvet cushioned bench in a tiny chamber closed off by its own little door. It was quite possibly the only privacy she ever got.

The king had his own suite of rooms above the north wharf overlooking the river. His Groom of the Stool (the man who accompanied the king to his own garderobe, therefore ensuring the king never had any privacy at all), Sir Thomas Heneage, came to Cat's rooms with news every evening at six. The king himself visited frequently. I found another place to sleep on those evenings.

Culpepper stayed in the king's rooms, a royal favorite. He was always surrounded by a gang of young men, Edmund Standebanke among them. Fortunately, the queen's ladies remained apart, in her apartments. A completely separate household. Most of the time.

When I could stand it no more, I found a quiet moment to ask Cat. Obliquely.

"What of the king's favorite, Thomas Culpepper?" I asked.

She looked at me sharply. Not forgetting that I had once connected his name to hers. The Coven shifted by the fire.

"What about him?" she asked, focusing again on her sewing.

"He seems . . . dangerous," I said lamely.

"Oh, Kitty," she said, her voice pitched low, "he is dangerous."

"What do you mean?" I asked, my limbs tensed as if ready for flight.

"He is as handsome as the day is long and cunning as a fox."

"I was wondering"—I licked my lips, my mouth suddenly dry—"why he remains in the king's chambers. If he's . . . dangerous."

"Oh, he's only dangerous to innocent girls," Cat said with a grin. "He would eat you for breakfast."

Isabel Baynton tittered.

"Diverting as that may sound," Cat continued, "I couldn't let it happen."

"Oh," I said, horrified. "I'm not interested."

"Good," she said, with a snap of the shirt she sewed for the king. "Because I have my eye on someone else for you, Kitty."

I recalled her saying this before.

"Who is it?" I had hoped she would give up her matchmaking. "It's not some lame, old, fat man, I hope."

As one, the Coven sucked in a breath, drawing all the air from the room.

Cat stared at me, dumbstruck. She hesitated for a fraction of a moment and recovered herself, a blush barely touching her cheeks. Mine flamed in response. The old joke struck too close to home.

"No, Kitty," she said. "Nothing like that."

"I'm sorry—" I began.

"No need for apologies."

But I saw there was a need. Cat went back to her tiny stitches. Her forehead puckered and she bent closer to the fine fabric. The bitterness of anger radiated from her.

"The king told me how much he misses her attention to detail," she said. "The first Queen Catherine. She made all his shirts. Even after he tried to divorce her."

I didn't have time to respond, because Alice and Joan dashed into the room together, setting the Coven to clucking.

"Cat, you'll never guess what," Joan said, flouncing to the floor at Cat's feet.

"A ghost from your past." Alice spoke over her, rushing to get the news out first, and tripped over her own skirts, almost landing in my lap.

Joan giggled. But Cat threw her sewing to the floor and stood, eyes sparking dangerously.

"Do you not make obeisance to your queen?" she asked.

"Of course." Alice curtseyed and Joan leapt to do the same. Cat let them stay down longer than absolutely necessary before she sat again and motioned for them to rise.

"And don't call me Cat. The king thinks it sounds too harsh and feral. He prefers *Catherine*. Or better yet, Your Majesty."

"Yes, Your Majesty," they said in unison, curtseying again.

"Much better. Now what is your news? You mention a ghost, but there is nothing in my past that could possibly haunt me."

Her voice remained calm, but the pointedness of the words drove them home.

Joan bit her lip and glanced at Alice.

"It's nothing, really," Alice said, the wind of her gossip removed from her sails.

"It's obviously not nothing, Alice," Cat retorted.

"It's Mary Lascelles."

Cat's hands stilled in her lap. "Mary Lascelles?"

"Yes, she was once chamberer to the duchess," Alice said.

"And now she has petitioned to be a member of your household here," Joan added, still slightly aglow with the news. "She was sent by her brother."

"A horrible man," Alice said. "Apparently she gets her holier-

than-thou attitude from him. He considers it his duty to infect all society with saintliness."

"Well, we shall have none of that." Cat managed a weak air of mischief. "Make sure she is sent away promptly."

I released a breath I hadn't known I held. Cat's temper had lit like straw but extinguished quickly. And it would be easy enough to rid herself of the tattling Mary Lascelles.

"And empty handed," I added.

"No," Cat said, stopping Alice before she carried the message. "Send her home to her brother with a chamber pot. For old times' sake."

Fools find their own misery.

I N December, the court moved en masse to Hampton Court Palace. Built by Cardinal Wolsey, sacrificed to the king, it sprawled along the banks of the Thames, blocked out in lines and angles, squared against the semicircular curve of the river. The turrets and gates, the buildings and towers glowed in the winter sun, embellished with red and white and gold. I had lived half my life across the river from a royal palace, and spent two months in another, but had never seen anything so majestic.

It seemed the entire country came with us, preparing for the Christmas season. Parties and banquets were never-ending and the rooms and halls and galleries perpetually rang with music and laughter, the pounding of feet, the whispers of expensive fabric and the rattle of gold and pearls.

Cat's true raison d'être as queen was to fill the court with as much pleasure as possible, planning a seemingly endless succession of feasting and dancing. Former queens had helped the poor, changed the king's views on religion, or begged for mercy for rebellious commoners. Cat enabled him, in his decrepit old age, to enjoy life again.

She dressed in a new gown every day, discarding them just

as she had said she would. She pushed her ladies to do the same, bringing some to the brink of bankruptcy. Queen Jane had insisted every lady dress modestly, her control reaching all the way to the number of pearls on a bodice. Queen Catherine Howard insisted that they dress for a party every day. That every lady at court wear a French hood, eradicating the ugly gable. And that everyone make merry. Or at least give the impression of it.

Christmas hit us like a snowstorm, and Cat was deluged by a blizzard of gifts, including a brilliant brooch, glittering with diamonds and rubies, edged with pearls. Cat counted them all.

"Thirty-three diamonds," she declared. "And sixty rubies."

And a sable muffler edged with rubies and pearls. And a square gold brooch containing twenty-seven table diamonds. And hoods of velvet and cuffs of fur and goblets and plates of gold. Enough to make the faint-hearted edgy and unnerved, but Cat accepted it all and asked for more.

On Twelfth Night, she received a collar fashioned from links of gold and enameled Tudor roses, flashing at the throat with diamonds arranged to form the letter *C*.

"You finally got your name in jewels," I said, lifting it to help her put it on. Remembering her threat to steal the duchess's *A* long before.

Cat pulled the collar from my hands and studied it.

"Do you know what the ancients believed?" she asked. "That diamonds are supposed to shine brightly before the innocent

and darken in the face of guilt. I wonder if the king is testing me."

"That's a myth, Cat," I said, reaching again to fix the jewels around her neck. "Diamonds symbolize constancy. Fidelity. Commitment. It's a beautiful gift. And one you deserve."

"It's not enough. He doesn't give me what I really want."

"What do you want?" What more could she possibly ask for?

"I want him to have me crowned!"

"He will."

"He never crowned her," she said. "Anne of Cleves."

"You told me he knew from the beginning he would get rid of her."

"That's what I mean!" She turned on me, speaking urgently. "If only he had me crowned, I would feel secure. I would never need or want another thing."

"He loves you, Cat," I said. More than that. He thought the sun shone out of her. "Why are you so concerned about this?"

"Because my entire family is breathing down my neck about it!" she cried. "Every twenty seconds the duchess mentions it or my stepmother makes a pointed comment or the duke is whispering in my ear about it."

"The duke is here?" I asked. I hadn't seen him, so rushed was I with Cat's preparations. But if the duke was in attendance, William might be, too. I hadn't seen him for three months.

"Of course he is," Cat snapped. "The whole world is here."

I hurried to finish getting her ready, suddenly desperate to get away. My fingers faltered and I held my breath, hoping

she wouldn't mock my desire to see William. Or, God forbid, remember her pledge to find me someone else.

"All they ever want is more, more, more," she said, oblivious. "As if I haven't given them enough already. Every wretched member of the family has a position at court. Everyone I know wants a piece of me. A piece of what I have. What a bunch of leeches."

"I suppose it's because court is the place to be," I said quietly.

"Oh, Kitty!" Cat threw her new jeweled brooch with its thirty-three diamonds and sixty rubies onto the bed and grabbed both of my hands. "I didn't mean you! You and I will always be Cat and Kitty."

She threw her arms around me in a hug like someone drowning. "No matter what, don't ever leave me. Promise me that."

My thoughts ran briefly to William. To a place in the country. To quiet and forest and open spaces.

"I need you, Kitty," Cat whispered.

"I know, Cat," I said. "I promise."

As a chamberer, I was not invited to the festivities, much to the delight of the Coven. They swept past me in the gallery that separated Cat's apartments from the king's, clucking and warbling, with barely a glance in my direction.

The gallery, empty of people, filled with shadows cast by the swiftly setting sun and the lowering fire that barely warmed the queen's audience chamber. Instead of following the gallery to the king's processional route, past the chapel and down to the great hall, I took the back galleries, through the rapidly emptying rooms, down to the clock court.

I craned my neck to look up at the carvings inside the gateway, brilliant yellow, white and red even in the dim light. Tudor roses proclaimed their dominance. More subtly, the paint beginning to age, the letters H and A entwined. HA HA. Painted for Anne Boleyn. Ha, ha, indeed. I slipped out from under those ill-omened designs to view the windows of the great hall.

I felt rather than heard the rumble of six hundred voices. Imagined the riot of color of everyone's finery. The aching beauty of the tapestries on the walls and the gilded ceiling. The smell of sweat and smoke and roasted flesh, the cacophony of overindulgence and exaggerated laughter.

"Wishing you were inside?"

I turned to see William striding across the courtyard. The sight of him stilled me and set my heart to racing all at once. He broke into a run and caught me before I could move to meet him. His arms around me felt like a blanket made of daylight—bright and solid and safe.

"Hmmm," I said, my cheek pressed against his shoulder. "A crowded hall where everyone ignores me or some time alone with you? Difficult decision."

"I'll wait while you make it," he said. He stepped away from me, hands behind his back as if at attention, waiting for orders.

"Perhaps I'll just see what they're serving." I turned as if to go, laughing.

"You can't get away that easily." He pulled me back and kissed me lightly. I closed my eyes and felt his lips on mine, his breath a sigh within me, his touch dancing between imagination and reality. The entire length of him fit with me perfectly.

"I'd never try," I murmured against his lips.

With unspoken agreement, we turned and walked beneath the king's great clock that tolled the hour and described the minutes, seconds, and phases of the moon. It displayed the astrological constellations and even predicted the running of the tides. Gold and blue, larger than the windows, it gleamed like a beacon of the enlightened prince who ran the country.

William held my hand, his thumb tracing circles around my knuckles as we walked without the need for words through the base court, beneath the empty eyes of the royal apartments and the rooms of the courtiers housed there, through the final gate and out into the garden and down to the Thames, flowing cold beneath the first glittering star of the evening. And I finally felt, for the first time in my life, that I belonged.

William stopped above the riverbank and drew his cloak around us both. Motionless, we watched the darkness fall.

"The duke is to be sent to Scotland," William said after a sudden breath. He wouldn't meet my eye. The Scottish borders were the very edge of civilization. The Scots were constantly encroaching, pillaging in violent disputes over land and authority. The Borders were dangerous. And very far away.

"Do you have to go with him?" I tried to keep my voice light, almost a tease. But the pain leaked through.

"I depend on him," William said quietly. "Not just for my livelihood but for my reputation. I may not agree with him. But I have to do as he asks."

"And what I want doesn't matter?" The words were out before I could stop them.

His body went rigid and he pulled away. He ran his fingers down my arms and clasped my hands in his, but when he looked at me, his face was cast in shadow.

"What do you want, Kitty?"

It was on the tip of my tongue to say one word. *You.* But I denied myself even that simple truth. I had made Cat a promise.

"I want the possibility of seeing you. No matter how busy we are. I want you here. At court."

"But even you don't want to be at court. Not really."

I balked. I had told him the truth—or part of it—and he denied me my own thoughts in the matter.

"We've been dreaming about it since we were little girls," I said. "It's all I ever wanted."

"Is it?" he asked. "Or is it what Cat wanted? Because I think you need to know the difference."

"Are you telling me I don't know my own mind?"

"I'm telling you that Cat's desires seem to eclipse your own. Her need for clothes and jewels and furs and fashion. That's all she cares about. Getting the crown and not thinking of what goes along with it."

"That is not all she cares about," I argued. "She cares about friends and family and . . ." I couldn't think of anything else. Truth be told, I didn't actually believe she cared about her family. But I had to defend her. I would be no one if it weren't for Catherine Howard. I would be hiding in corners and swishing out chamber pots like Mary Lascelles.

"No, Kitty," William said. "*You* care about those things. And more. You are not like her. She wants you to be her shadow. You can only truly be yourself if you cut her off."

"Cat cares about me!" I cried.

"No, she doesn't. Cat cares about Cat."

"How dare you?" I said, suddenly breathless with anger. "You don't even *know* her!"

"I know many like her," William said. His hands remained stiff at his sides, his profile turned to me. "She's just like her uncle. Ambitious and court-blind, seeing only the surface and not what lies beneath."

"And yet you stay with the duke. No matter where he goes."

"I have no choice."

The breach between our bodies was no more than a hand's breadth, but I couldn't find the words to bridge it.

"Neither have I."

"Yes, you do," he said urgently. "You need to get away. You don't belong here. You don't want to be like her—mercenary and artificial."

Before I knew what I was doing, I slapped him. The resonant sting in my hand surprised me and I clutched it back to my chest, nursing the hurt in my heart.

"You can leave court if you wish," I snapped. "But I won't go with you." Not that he'd asked.

I bit down on my tongue, relished the metallic taste on it. The punishment for lying was to cut the tongue, was it not? But the lie had to be brazened out, so I straightened my spine, and my gaze didn't waver from his.

He broke down first. His head sagged and he stepped aside, a weak gesture telling me I had clear passage.

"You shouldn't be with people who tell you what you want." William's sadness imbued his words. "What to think or feel or do. Like Cat does."

"Don't you see?" I croaked, my voice barely a whisper. "That's exactly what you're doing."

I couldn't feel my feet as I walked away, and my knees didn't bend properly. I felt like a wooden toy, inflexible and heartless. I left my own heart, crushed, on the riverbank at William's feet.

The duke left for Scotland at the end of January.

William didn't come to see me before he left. And I didn't say good-bye.

1541

25

"THAT'S GOOD," CAT SAID ABSENTLY WHEN I TOLD HER WHAT HAD HAP-
pened. We were making endless circumambulations of the
upstairs gallery, cloistered by the rain, dogged by the Coven,
who kept a meager distance.

I had suffered days of solitary anguish before I mentioned it.
I waited until I couldn't bear it by myself any longer. And in the
end, I didn't tell her everything. Not what William said about
her. Not what I felt about him. I only told her that we'd argued
and that I probably wouldn't see him again, the rupture in my
heart growing with each word.

"Good?" I managed to reply. "The only boy who has ever
noticed me?" And I'd lost him. Not just lost—discarded.

"Oh, no, Kitty," Cat stopped, causing the tide of ladies
behind her to eddy and retreat. "Not the only boy. There is
another."

I blinked at her, stunned.

"He is one of the king's yeomen of the chamber," she said. "A
tall young stud. Mounds of golden hair. Looks a bit like a lion."

"Standebanke," I said, the word jagged in my throat.

"You've noticed him, then." Cat smirked.

"No, Cat," I pleaded, saw-toothed memories from the forest flashing behind my eyes, "He's not . . ."

"You think you can do better?" She finally looked at me, her blue eyes flinty. "You think you can get a Knyvet or a Neville or a Percy?" She thought I wanted nobility.

"It's not that."

"Is it still that Gibbon boy?" she asked. "Ha. I say good riddance to him. Or did you fancy yourself in love?"

"I don't know," I said. Cat's tone was so contemptuous. So bitter.

"Well, I'm here to tell you, Mistress Tylney, that there is no such thing. Not in this court, not in this life. But if you must continue your infatuation, just get him back and have both. It never hurt a girl to have two men at once."

"I can't, Cat." A shudder ran through me.

"Then don't. Give up Gibbon for all I care."

She didn't. I could see that. Didn't care that my heart was breaking over something I'd ruined. Or that she was pushing me into a relationship with a rapist's sidekick.

"It's not William," I said. I needed Cat to understand.

"Good. Because Standebanke is yours. He's *asked* about you. I shall set up a clandestine meeting for you personally." Cat positively glowed with mischief. Cat the matchmaker. The Queen of Misrule.

"Your Majesty."

We turned to find that Jane Boleyn had broken free of the pool of ladies behind us.

"What is it?" Cat snapped, her light mood changed in an instant. "Can't you see I'm speaking with Mistress Tylney?"

"Yes, Your Majesty." Jane lowered her eyes. "That is exactly the subject I wish to broach."

"Have you been eavesdropping on my private conversations?" Cat asked, her eyes aslant with suspicion.

"No, Your Majesty," Jane said and glanced once over her shoulder. Jane never spoke unless she knew who was listening. The Coven gaggled a few yards away. The other ladies and maids whispered at the far end of the gallery, hesitating by the door of the chapel as if unprepared for holiness.

Jane lowered her voice and spoke with her head bowed. We had to lean close to hear her. "I come to give fair warning to prevent ill feeling in the future. It is my job to keep your path smooth and your life comfortable, and I do my best to fulfill my function."

Cat snorted with derision and turned back down the gallery.

"And what do you wish to warn me about?" she said.

"There are ladies who feel supplanted in the queen's favor. Ladies who feel they deserve to be in the queen's company more than a mere chamberer. They think affection should be dictated by status. That you, Kitty, are good for nothing but stoking the fires, changing the rushes, and fetching wine."

"You mean," I said, "as a servant."

They thought I should be treated no better than Mary Lascelles back in Lambeth. I tasted the sour tang of inferiority.

"That's exactly what she means," Cat said. "That because

159

you're not blood-related, you're not worthy. Because you're not the daughter of an earl or the wife of a knight or the widow of a duke."

"Do you think this, Jane?" I asked.

"No!" Jane said, "I see that the queen is naturally attracted to others who share similar interests. You enjoy entertainments. Music. Excitement."

Her own eyes lit up at the words. I felt a rush of pity for a grown woman who craved the company and pastimes of girls. A thirty-five-year-old who wished to be a teenager again. But she understood the way the court operated. She had served five queens. She was a survivor, and wanted us to be, too.

"Well, then, it's no wonder the others are resentful," Cat replied. "They've lived for so long in stuffy decorum that they can't imagine a court full of sunshine and gaiety. They want life to be boring."

The worst epithet Cat could attach to someone. *Boring*. More damning than *badly dressed*.

"They may be boring," Jane said. "But they are also powerful. Enough that they could make life very uncomfortable for you. They would find ways to purge your household of people they found undesirable."

"What do you suggest, Jane?" I asked.

"Perhaps the queen might spend more time in the company of other ladies."

Cat let out an exasperated sigh.

"And if she fell pregnant . . ." Jane let the sentence hang. But

I knew what she meant. If Cat were to have a boy, she would be invincible. She could have everything she wished, and no one would think to question it.

"It is so difficult for a monarch to depend on a single child to succeed him," Jane finished.

King Henry especially. His father had ended the bloody years of civil war, establishing the Tudor reign. Both father and son had ensured their throne by executing any other possible claimants. Henry VIII would not want his lineage to expire.

Cat twisted her rings as if trying to wrench her fingers off, and her mouth settled into a rigid seam of ill humor. I recognized the signs of a major tantrum building.

"He has two daughters," I said, trying to sound like that could be the end of it. "Two healthy, intelligent daughters."

Jane laughed. "I think we all know how well women are regarded in this court. Would these men *ever* accept a queen to rule over them?"

I had to shake my head. The idea was ludicrous. The dukes would undermine the pious, earnest Lady Mary. The earls and marquesses would tear the beautiful little Elizabeth apart.

"Listen!" Cat exploded. "There's not much I can do about a pregnancy! I just wish everyone would shut up about it. No matter how many times he can't get it up, it will be all my fault if we don't have children. I *know*."

Jane glanced about as if the four horsemen were upon her, dragging the Apocalypse.

"You cannot speak so, Your Majesty," she whispered hur-

riedly. Everyone knew that George Boleyn hadn't been beheaded for incest with his sister, no matter what the official record said. His execution traced its origin back to a public statement about the king's impotence.

Cat glared at Jane.

"Thank you for airing your concerns, Lady Rochford," she said. "But I believe I shall return to my rooms, for I am feeling rather fatigued. Your presence is no longer required. I feel the need for the company of more *distinguished* ladies."

Jane curtseyed without comment, the Coven clucking as they passed her. I watched the other women amass behind Cat's skirts, struggling to keep up with the haste that carried her back to her rooms.

"Words will be her undoing," Jane said quietly when she stood again, her face white.

I shuddered at the foreboding in her voice.

"She will not be undone," I said, more to convince myself than her.

"That will be our commission," Jane said. "To prevent it. To ensure that the rumor mill doesn't grind her for grain. To *guarantee* she bears a son."

26

But there would be no guarantees.

In February, the king's ulcer closed over, and infection spread a fever throughout his great frame. He couldn't walk, couldn't stand, couldn't govern. He refused to see Cat. Refused her presence in his apartments. So we remained sequestered in her rooms, bound by the murmurs of the Coven.

Gossip was their life's blood. Especially when it came to the king and his health. Under normal circumstances, every cough, every limp, every bowel movement was scrutinized by the entire court. This illness had them all buzzing like flies around a corpse.

It was treason to mention it. Treason even to think it. But the king's death would change everything. And the Howards hoped it would mean a Howard regency until the toddler Prince Edward came of age.

The king feared his death with a palpable madness caused by a loathing of limitation. He brought to mind a furious, demonic bear, pent up and confined within his own flesh like the caged animals of the Tower menagerie. We could hear his raging all the way down the long gallery from his apartments.

Could gauge the power of his anger by the force of the explosion of courtiers from his room. Every man moved tentatively about the palace, afraid one false step would bring wrath like a fireball upon him.

The women just stayed away.

With each day, Cat grew more irritable, more jumpy. She couldn't eat and retired early, sparking rumors that she was pregnant. That she had miscarried. That the king planned to take back Anne of Cleves.

Cat tolerated only my presence, ignoring all others or else snapping at them. The entire populace of the court seemed poised for flight—ready to flee the royal circle out of sheer, desperate self-preservation.

But the outside world remained oblivious to the seismic disruptions at Hampton Court and pursued, unheeding, its own agenda.

And suddenly, my parents found me a husband. Apparently, being the best friend of the Queen of England had perks that some people just could not deny.

Lord Graves lived close by my parents in the far end of nowhere. Through marriage, his land would be ensured to Tylney heirs. I shuddered at the thought of producing them.

My fate was written and sealed with wax. Sold like a parcel of land or a breeding mare.

The physical person of my intended appeared in late February, entertained by the dowager duchess herself in her private rooms. My parents still considered the duchess my guardian and had appealed to her to secure the match.

She did so with pleasure.

I was bestowed with the dubious honor of waiting upon them both. I wore a "new" gown, pieced together from Cat's discards, the rust-colored skirts skimming the tops of my slippers with no train and the bodice gaping obscenely if I didn't keep my shoulders thrown back like a soldier.

"My lord," I said, curtseying deeply and keeping my head bowed. Not out of respect, but because I didn't think I could look on his wrinkling, pox-marked face without crying. I couldn't even repeat his given name for fear it would make the whole thing real.

"Young Katherine," he said, and I heard an edge of lechery in his voice. He was practically drooling. "Rise and look on me."

I stood and looked.

And I saw my future unravel before me. The pits the smallpox had left glowed pink and shiny against his pale, papery skin. His jowls sagged as he gazed at me unsmiling. If anything, he looked bored.

"Turn," he said.

I turned.

This was how it was going to be. His orders. My obedience. The rest of my life, a vast expanse of mirthlessness and drudgery.

He reached for me. My skin tried to creep away, and I forced myself very still in order not to flinch.

"We shall marry in the summer," he said, gazing expectantly

at my flat chest and thin hips. As if he thought they might ripen in the sun in time for our wedding night.

"I expect the queen will be sad to see you go," the duchess said. I detected a trace of a smile in her voice.

"I had rather hoped Katherine's influence would find me a place at court myself."

"Kitty is a chamberer," the duchess rebuked him.

He wasn't fazed. "But beloved of the queen." He licked his lips.

I couldn't decide which was worse, leaving Cat to live on the Graves estate or having to see him every day at court. At least my position necessitated that we wouldn't share a bed.

"That will do."

Dismissed.

I hurried from the room, fighting down the bitter acid that rose in my mouth. I couldn't imagine being touched by him. Being kissed by him. I allowed one tear to escape. For myself. For my future. For what I could have had with William, if things had been different.

I ran straight to the queen's apartments. Looking for protection.

"Cat," I said, sitting down beside her on the bench beneath the window in her withdrawing room. "I need your help."

The Coven—sans duchess—erupted in a twittering dither in the corner.

"How many times do I have to tell you?" Cat seethed. "You have to call me Your Majesty!"

"Yes, Your Majesty," I said quickly, impatient to enlist her aid.

"And where have you been?"

"The dowager duchess called for me."

"So you, too, are prepared to spread rumors about me?" she hissed. "Groveling to the great ladies who secretly loathe you?"

The attack caught me off-guard and I shrank back.

"I don't know what you're talking about."

"You left me alone!" she retorted, causing another flutter amongst the Coven. Cat lowered her voice, "Abandoned in my time of need."

What about my time of need? I wanted to ask. I met her eye. The words formed at the back of my throat. She looked back at me, unflinching. But somewhere, in the back of her gaze, I saw fear.

"What is the matter, Your Majesty?" I whispered.

I heard the Coven creak and twist to hear what she said next, but her words fit only into my ear.

"I can't do it," she said. "I can't. I can't be brave in the face of his illness. I can't stand up to their pushing and gossip. I can't be the generous queen, giving alms to the poor. The poor make me cringe. I can't be noble. We weren't taught how to be queens, Kitty! We were taught how to be . . . property."

"We were taught how to be wives," I said.

"Same thing," she muttered. "Oh, Kitty, if I am so high, why do I feel so low? I am nothing more than the youngest daughter of an insignificant branch of the Howard family tree."

"That's what you *were*, Cat," I said. "But look at you now. You're Queen of England. You can do anything."

"Nothing queenly."

"So do something queenly."

"But I hate the poor. I don't care about religion. Politics bore me stiff."

"What about prisoners? You could save people's lives."

Like mine.

A spark flashed in her eyes, like a candle lighting right behind them.

"Thomas Wyatt is in the Tower again," she said. "You're right. What better thing to be known for than rescuing Anne Boleyn's former lover?"

I could think of many, but again held my tongue.

"What did he do?" I asked.

"What does it matter?" Cat said. "It will be a coup. He was one of Cromwell's men. That faction will love me. I'll get a reputation for a soft heart. For being a romantic. It's perfect.

"Oh, Kitty," she hugged me. "You are the best friend a queen could ever have."

The Coven shifted again in the corner. Gathering like pikemen prepared for conflict. Their attention flustered me, but I knew it was the right moment. To ask for help while Cat was in a generous mood.

But before I could open my mouth, she leapt to her feet.

"I must prepare my defense of Wyatt so I can present it to the king at exactly the right moment. I must look absolutely perfect."

She leaned in to whisper to me.

"I'll make the Coven happy, too." She turned to the room. "Lady Howard, Lady Baynton, Countess, I need to choose a very special gown. Attend me."

"You can help me practice later." Cat winked and left me, dumbstruck, by the window. Just as she was about to pass through the door in a cloud of women and silk, she paused and turned back.

"Kitty." My name itself an afterthought. "There was something you wanted to tell me."

The Coven waited, poised. Listening. Lady Howard narrowed her eyes.

"I'm to be married," I said weakly.

Cat smiled, her mouth pulled up on both sides like a marionette, her eyes untouched.

"Congratulations."

27

THE KING RECOVERED TO A COLLECTIVE SIGH—RELIEF FOR SOME, REGRET for others—from the court. The question of my marriage got lost in the scramble to return the court to normal. And the renewed requests from the king for Cat's company.

"Mistress Tylney, you will accompany me to the king's chambers," Cat said one evening in early March. She had been bathed and dressed, her hair bejeweled and her cleavage perfumed, and there was nothing else to be done. "I shall have supper there."

"Of course, Your Majesty," I said. At her suggestion, I wore a deep blue hand-me-down of Cat's, lengthened with a piece of silk the color of the winter moon.

"You look lovely," she whispered to me with a quirk of a smile.

A group of us moved through the palace in step with each other, walking when Cat walked, stopping when Cat stopped. Like a flock of birds, taking cues from a single source, whirling and diving in perfect harmony.

We made our way through the queen's apartments and out to the gallery. Courtiers and ladies, servants and messengers bowed to her as she passed, her smile widening with every step. She paused to speak with a viscount here, an earl there, just briefly, never engaging in a real conversation. But the number of people flocking the gallery made the short journey excruciatingly long.

We stopped at the door of the king's apartments and one of the ladies knocked. An usher opened the door, sweeping aside with a low bow.

"Your Majesty," he said.

"Master Culpepper," Cat answered, emotionless.

He stood and grinned at Cat as if she was a delicious sweetmeat, and she arched an eyebrow at him. The blood from my feet swirled in my ears. I wobbled. I reached out blindly and grasped an arm, a sleeve, to steady myself. The arm of the queen.

"Mistress Tylney, you do forget yourself," Cat snapped. She shook my hand off and glared at me. "You are excused."

Murmurs vibrated through the cluster of ladies behind us and one of the Coven sniggered.

"I beg your pardon, Your Majesty," I said, growing hot under their stares and whispers.

Cat leaned close to me, "Edmund Standebanke is off duty tonight. He waits for you in the clock court. You didn't think I'd forget, did you?"

She winked at me from beneath her lowered brow and gave me a push.

"Happy birthday."

171

Even I had taken no notice of the day. Trust Cat to remember. And to find a suitably Cat-like gift, dubious as it was.

I turned away from the ladies and the light of the king's apartments. Away from the gaze of the court. I couldn't flee. Cat would expect a full report. My feet took me back along the dim galleries, down the stairs and through Anne Boleyn's gateway. And there, under the timepiece, a man stood waiting. For me.

The other girls had all noticed Standebanke and commented on his golden good looks. Like a classical hero, he excelled at sports and games and physical tasks. He wore the king's livery well, tight in all the right places, sleeves flowing, chest and shoulders broad. The red hose, cut with the black lining, emphasized what were surely muscled thighs. Joan called him "swoony."

But all I could see was the monster from the forest.

I quickly scanned the courtyard. Dozens of courtiers, clustered in groups. He couldn't hurt me. He wouldn't dare. I was a favorite of the queen.

"Good evening," he said, and nodded a tiny bow. He was taller than I—though the extra inch or two could have been his hair.

"Good evening," I echoed, and dipped slightly.

"Mistress Tylney?" he asked.

I nodded, too afraid to speak.

"Would you care to walk in the garden?" he asked, holding out an arm.

"It's getting dark," I said, refusing the walk. Refusing the arm.

"And you are afraid of the dark?" he asked. He sounded sympathetic, understanding. I would have laughed had I not been so petrified.

"Yes," I said, surprised I told the truth.

"No need to be afraid with me," he said and patted the sword that hung at his side. "I am one of the king's own guard. I can handle the rats and owls that inhabit the gardens at night." Again he held out his arm.

"It is not the rats and owls I am afraid of," I said, and took up the courage to look him in the eyes. My arms remained firmly at my sides, and I struggled to release the fists I clenched.

He lowered his arm and leaned closer to me. I held tightly to my bones, which felt ready to fly apart.

"I knew it was you," he said quietly, his deep voice a rumbling purr. "I wanted to meet you. I wanted to tell you . . . the truth."

I looked upward. Watched the slow spinning of the clock. Waited.

"It wasn't me."

I snapped my head around to look at him.

"It was you," I said quietly, my fear coming out as vehemence. "I saw you. Standing there. Doing nothing."

"That's right!" his voice cracked. "Doing *nothing*. Kitty, James Millard was there, standing on her arm. He thought it was

sport. He laughed at me. Spited me. We fought and he's been thrown from court and I say good riddance to him. But . . ."

His words had come out in a rush like the Thames below London Bridge, spilling and dangerous. But now he slowed and looked at me, his eyes full of sentiment, making him look too young to be a king's guard.

"But what?" I asked. I studied his face for traces of deception. The high cheekbones, the strong chin just showing a beard, the full mouth. His eyes begged me to believe him.

"Culpepper. No one can refuse him. He's brash and daring and ever so brilliant." Edmund sounded almost fawning, then hardened. "But manipulative. And cruel.

"You've seen his cruelty, Kitty." He looked me full in the face. "Imagine it turned on you."

I had. In my dreams. Every night.

"But you watched," I said. "You did nothing to stop him."

"So did you," he replied.

I felt the words like a slap. The kind that wakes you from a faint. Because of course he was right.

"I was afraid," I admitted.

"So was I."

"How can you be his friend?" I asked.

"How can I not be?" Edmund said. "Surely, you of all people understand. A friend with that kind of power."

"Don't you compare him to Cat," I spat at him. "She's nothing like him." But felt a vibration of truth. I stilled it.

"Of course not," he agreed.

I swallowed. I remembered that night. I remembered that no one gave chase when I ran. When he saw me.

"You didn't tell him," I said. "That I was there."

He smiled then.

"I couldn't do that."

I took his arm. I understood.

28

Cat returned, flushed and irritable, sometime after midnight. She snarled and squawked until we roused ourselves to attend her needs and do her bidding. Then she dismissed everyone else. Alice and Joan settled onto their pallets and the Coven bickered their way out the door.

"I've been sent away," she moaned. "Fetch me cloths and a warm stone."

Her courses. Cat suffered terribly from her monthly battle with womanhood. She used to retreat beneath the covers of our bed for a full day, sometimes two, groaning and twisting the blankets like a winding cloth. The duchess once offered to have her bled, but Cat had barked, "I'm bleeding quite enough already, thank you very much!" and that ended the discussion.

"Join me, Kitty."

The thick tester mattress of the best goose down was covered by fine-spun linen, beaten to skinlike softness. Real feather pillows cushioned our heads, and mounds of velvets and furs cocooned us with warmth. Cat curled up on herself, rigid with pain. Tentatively, I reached out to stroke her hair, as I used to in Lambeth. Her muscles unwound and she heaved a sigh the size of the king himself.

"So did you have a good time with the delectable Edmund?" Cat asked, the question laced with petulance.

"I suppose."

"Well? What did you do?"

"We . . . talked."

"You talked. You have a young, gorgeous, virile man at your disposal and what do you do? You *talk*."

Cat raised herself up onto an elbow, rested her head upon her hand and peered at me.

"But don't you think he's divine? All that gorgeous hair. I know you want to run your hands through it."

I considered running my hands through Edmund's hair. But my fingers remembered William's. Besides, I didn't know how much I trusted Edmund.

"Should you really be saying these things?" I asked.

"It's only you, Kitty," Cat said. "If I can't say them to you, who can I say them to? Everyone else in this viper's den will go running to the king if I so much as fart in their direction."

I stifled my chuckle, but Cat giggled out loud. Joan, fast asleep, tittered and muttered something about marzipan, which made us laugh even harder.

"But you have the king," I said.

"I have a husband who thinks a quick peck on the cheek is foreplay. I have to coo with pleasure when I'm really gritting my

teeth and wishing for it all to end. I'm trapped. I've made my own snare and I'm stuck fast in it."

There was no comfort I could give her and no option out. Except one.

"What about Francis?" I asked.

"Francis?" she said, surprise and condescension mixing with equal parts. "He wasn't really that much better. Just quicker."

"No, Cat," I said. "What if you were precontracted to him? He said you were married. What if he were to come back and claim you as his wife? Then your marriage to the king would be invalid and you could get an annulment. Francis would take you back. I'm sure of it." Even if the rest of the world shunned her.

"The king wouldn't let it be that easy," Cat said, her voice as small as the hope she harbored.

"He did it with Anne of Cleves."

"He's too involved with me. You've seen. He paws me all the time. He says I make him feel like he's young again. He wasn't able to . . . you know, with Anne at all. That's how they got the annulment. But we've consummated the marriage. I can never be free."

We lapsed back into silence. I watched the fire flicker light across the ceiling. It was decorated in bas-relief, gilded lovers' knots curling around Cat's emblem of a crowned rose. The petals of one had already begun to crack, painted before it had dried sufficiently.

"Kitty," she said, suddenly urgent, "you can't tell anyone

that I've said this. That I'm unhappy. That I want other men. Not the king, not my uncle, not even Alice or Joan."

"I would never betray you, Cat, you know that."

"Swear." She clutched my arm tightly. "Swear you will never speak out against me. No matter what."

"There's nothing to speak of," I said, uncomfortable. It wasn't a question or even a request. It was a command.

Sweat shimmered on her upper lip. "Swear it."

"I swear," I said. "I will never betray you. None of us will. We're a coterie. A circle that can't be broken. We'll make it through."

"An unbroken circle," she echoed.

She turned to me, her face flushed with emotion and the heat of the stones pressed to her lower back.

"But you're the only one," she said. "The only one who loves me, aren't you, Kitty? Truly. My sister of the soul." She grimaced and shifted position.

"Everyone loves you," I argued. "You're queen."

"But do they love me enough to believe in me?" she asked.

"What is there to believe?"

"That I am faithful. That I am untarnished. That the king is the one and only man in my life. That I deserve the crown."

"No one will question you," I assured her. "No one will believe any ridiculous tittle-tattle from your past."

"The queen a promiscuous little slut when she lived with her grandmother?" Cat asked in mock horror. "Preposterous!"

"Impossible!" I joined in.

"Unthinkable!"

"Absurd!"

We clutched each other, giggling, our breath growing more hysterical as we perched precariously between guilt and rumor.

"I'll just have to live vicariously through you," Cat said finally, a smile on her face, but none in her voice.

"I'll do my best to make it pleasant for us both," I said. But when I thought about making it pleasant, the face that manifested before me had a crooked grin and sandy hair.

"Then move a little faster with Standebanke," Cat said. She kissed my cheek and rolled over, falling quickly into sleep. Safe in the knowledge that her bidding would be done.

It was very late in the night—or very early in the morning—when I realized why Cat's words kept me awake. Until she married the king, we had all lived vicariously through her. Any girl would think we still were—her gorgeous gowns and furs and jewels, the luscious dishes and divine entertainments. And yet, Cat had given up any hope of love. Or even lust. She was already bound to the life we all knew would claim us eventually. The dullness of the marriage bed. Compensating with accessories.

Cat made her inaugural trip through London with the king at her side. Other queens had journeyed alone, to be admired on their own behalf. But the king insisted they travel together.

Their barge shot the roaring waters beneath London Bridge to the accompaniment of gunfire from the Tower. The north wind whipped us downriver, past Lambeth and Norfolk House, and the sound of the cannons followed us all the way to Greenwich.

Cat chose this as the perfect moment to exercise her influence as queen and plead for clemency. After careful consideration, the king granted Thomas Wyatt his freedom. The condition was that Wyatt leave his mistress and return to his wife, whom he'd left twenty years prior. He almost refused.

Greenwich Palace crouched on a riverbank between the Thames and the deer park. The king's gardens created an illusion of space and openness, while the rooms within the palace felt cramped and crowded. The lesser nobles had to find accommodation outside the grounds. But my position as chamberer allowed me to stay within Cat's rooms. Protected.

I took comfort in the knowledge that my fiancé's pleas for

placement were ignored. The king's illness had prevented him from attending to business. And Cat focused all of her energies on more parties. But I knew I lived on borrowed time.

To celebrate the end of winter and Lent, Cat planned the most personal entertainment of her royal career.

"It's going to be the best masque ever presented before the king," she declared.

She was determined that we would all participate. Cat took the lead role, but the younger ladies would dance, the chamberers provide background, and the Coven play elaborately costumed goddesses. Everyone was made happy.

Cat wanted the entire production to be a surprise for the king, so she dismissed the deviser of court revels and planned it all herself. She designed the costumes and sets. She cribbed the music from other sources and dispensed with all but the most basic script. We spent hours sewing filmy shawls from seemingly inexhaustible supplies of multicolored silks. We decorated hanging set pieces with badges embroidered with gold thread. Perhaps it wouldn't be the most elaborately staged masque in court history, but it would be hers.

Cat made us practice again and again and again. Two days before show time, we were all thoroughly sick of the whole thing.

She was insatiable. Manic. As if her life depended on pleasing the king with this one ostentatious evening.

Not that she needed to. He still caressed and fondled her

at every opportunity. He sat her next to him at every banquet. Gave in to her every whim and desire. She didn't insist on piety, like Catherine of Aragon. She didn't argue about religion or get insanely jealous like Anne Boleyn. Her presence didn't destroy his vanity, as Anne of Cleves's did. All Cat wanted was pretty things. All the time.

She got them. And she made sure we had them, too.

"I have a surprise for all of you," she said, dragging me, Joan, and Alice into her robing chamber the night of the masque.

"Your Majesty!" the Countess of Bridgewater honked. "Your ladies are ready to help you prepare for the banquet."

"My *ladies* will have to wait!" Cat called as she kicked the door closed on the surprised faces of the Coven.

Joan giggled and bounced on her toes. She only needed to clap her hands to look like an expectant five-year-old.

"What is it?" Joan said, and then she did clap.

Cat glided to a cedar chest and opened it carefully. It exuded a scent of resin and lavender so pungent it made my eyes water. Cat reached in, pulled something out and shook it loose. An underskirt of rich blue velvet. Joan let out a little moan.

"This is for you, Joan," Cat said, and smiled. She looked younger. Almost shy.

We all knew it was one of Cat's cast-offs. But the quality of the fabric should have designated it for one of the great ladies of the court. Cat swiftly reached into the chest again and pulled

out an overskirt of light watchet blue shot with gold thread and handed it to Joan as well.

"And this," she said, and continued with a velvet bodice of the same color, and sleeves with fur cuffs, and flowing oversleeves trimmed with the same fur. Joan sank to the floor in ecstasy, surrounded by fabrics and gold embroidery, and the sound that came from her was something between a hum and a sob. When she looked back up at Cat, a single tear had run down her cheek and into the corner of her mouth. She poked at it with the tip of her tongue.

"Thank you," she whimpered.

"It's nothing," Cat said with a shrug, and went back to the chest to remove similar clothing for Alice, only in the russets and browns that made her look healthy and cheerful. Alice stood dumbly and nodded.

My wardrobe was all in green. The kirtle was the color of sea foam, the overskirt and bodice brocade the color of pine.

"Green makes your eyes magical," Cat whispered. "Just remember to keep them in check."

We dressed quickly. The Coven would have clucked themselves to death, because Cat tightened our stays and tied on our sleeves. She helped Joan and Alice tie their hair into French hoods of velvet trimmed in pearls, and plaited my hair elaborately. She flounced our skirts and smoothed the creases from our sleeves, then stepped back to inspect her work.

"And now for the gilding."

She strung a gold chain around Joan's neck, weighted with

a gold pendant enameled in blue. A square brooch decorated with pearls and a single ruby was attached to Alice's bodice. And for me, a delicate collar of little green-and-white enameled daisies.

"These are for loan only," she advised us. "But the gowns are yours to keep."

"Thank you, Your Majesty," Alice murmured, and we all followed her into curtseys.

"Oh, get up," Cat said brusquely, but a delighted smile lit her face. She looked at us critically for a moment. "Just one more detail."

She opened a small silver coffer and removed precious unguents and pastes.

"Alice is pale enough," she said, smearing a little white on my face. "But you spend too much time outside."

"I like it outside."

Cat hmphed and moved on to Joan. She applied a little crimson to Alice's cheeks and cleavage and closed the coffer with a snap.

"Done," she said with a smile. "More beautiful than my jewels."

Joan giggled, and Alice's blush competed with her makeup.

"Go forth and conquer," Cat pronounced. "Dazzle every male in Hampton Court."

We dressed Cat in a gown of crimson and gold so fine it almost hurt the eyes. Joan brought a hood trimmed with pearls and rubies, but Cat shook her head.

"Tonight, I want to be different," she said.

She pulled out an elegant caul fashioned of gold gauze and studded with diamonds where the networked bands intersected. We parted her hair in the middle, and Joan carefully gathered the auburn curls into a loose knot and bound them in the net of the caul. Alice secured it all with a series of clasps fashioned of gold and rubies that ran from Cat's forehead to the nape of her neck and I attached similar, smaller ornaments to the coils of hair just above her ears. She bowed her head for me to fasten the gold and diamond collar the king had given her for Twelfth Night around her neck.

The Coven hissed to each other when we finally made our way out of the chamber, but dropped into placid curtseys and murmured plaintive flattery as we neared. Cat swept past them out the door, and they struggled into their queue of precedence and preferment, the dowager duchess taking the lead. Alice, Joan, and I took our place at the back of the throng, safe in the knowledge that we were the queen's true favorites.

For the banquet, Cat had ordered the cooks to outdo themselves: a peacock stuffed with game hens, roasted, then the feathers all reattached so it looked like a living bird; venison and boar, caught by the king and his men in the woods nearby; fish of every color, size and description; sculptures of sugar paste, glittering in the candlelight; wine imported from Gascony.

The great hall buzzed like a giant, polychromatic beehive.

Everyone was decked in their best, hoping to be seen, hoping to be noticed. Waiting for that one glance from the king that could launch a brilliant career. Cat and the king took their place on the dais at the far end of the hall, the gold canopy of estate over their heads. The highest-ranking courtiers sat near them. The rest of the hall milled with earls and lords, cardinals and ambassadors, fawning and filling themselves.

And despite Cat's pronouncement in her bedroom, attention remained fixed firmly on her. She drank it in like the watered wine in the golden goblet in front of her. I searched my heart for the green bile of jealousy but couldn't find it. I didn't want to be in her position.

But I didn't want to be in my position, either. The eyes of three men found me in that crowded hall, amongst the bejeweled women, the platters of delicacies, and the gossip that vied for their attention.

William Gibbon stood in attendance on the Duke of Norfolk.

"The duke is back?" I asked Alice.

"Yes, of course," she said as if this were common knowledge. "He was at Westminster. Didn't you know?"

I shook my head, unable to draw my gaze from the face I'd pictured a thousand times since Christmas.

William took in my new gown. The enameled daisy-chain collar. My hair carefully smoothed and pinned. My face whitened and powdered. I felt overdressed and naked all at once.

His eyes met mine, and pain froze the crooked smile before he looked away.

Edmund Standebanke stood behind the king, jesting with the other men. He wasn't in the king's livery but wore a doublet in a burnt orange color called lion-tawny and sleeves of bright yellow. He practically glowed. His eyes lifted. Searched the room. Lit up when he saw me. And stayed.

Thomas Culpepper, standing next to him, followed his gaze. Briefly, his attention twitched from my face to my hair to my clothes. He turned, whispered something to Edmund, and walked away. Edmund's smile faltered briefly. Almost imperceptibly. He shrugged and returned to the shadows at the back of the dais on which the king sat.

I found some shadows myself, remembering William's words about how he liked me plain and unadorned as I was in Lambeth. Wondering what he thought of me dressed in finery, the very image of all he held in contempt. Wondering what Thomas Culpepper could possibly have said to Edmund. Wondering what I was doing there at all.

When the feasting was done and the tables moved away, Cat had some servants drop the fabric set pieces from the minstrel's gallery. An awed murmur threaded the room, and then hushed as the music started.

The masque was based on the story of Persephone. Cat entered from behind the set pieces, her hair still bound in gold, but now with a cloth-of-gold tunic wrapped over her gown. The diamond *C* glittered and flashed at her throat.

Jane Boleyn, dressed in pale blue and green, acted the part of her mother, Demeter. They danced together between several ladies dressed all in white who held aloft bright yellow scarves to symbolize sunshine. The Coven watched from a high platform meant to be Olympus, frozen smiles on faces stiff with white paste.

But then Persephone was stolen by the dark lord Hades and pulled down to the underworld. Alice and I and some of the less pretty maids, covered in black scarves, plucked at Cat's sleeves as she shied away. We moved about, sylphlike, portraying the restive dead.

Persephone's cries, comforted by no one, rang out in the haunting sounds of a vielle, the musician drawing the bow across the strings in long, wailing notes. Men dressed in black patrolled the hall, extinguishing torches to achieve a more sepulchral gloom.

The masked man playing the lord of the dead hovered over her, touching her hair and her dress, and she grew more and more despondent and more and more lethargic as he sucked the life from her. It was almost as if she could change the hue of her gown, and it grew dull and lifeless, too.

"Enough!"

The shout startled all of us and we dropped our hands. Joan let out a little shriek. The musicians stopped playing the dirge of the underworld, and we all spun to look at the king.

He stood on the dais, his pendulous jowls purple with rage.

"You dare to compare my court to hell?" he bellowed, "My lady, you dare to compare me to Hades?"

Cat trembled, but stood up straight. She lowered her eyes.

"No, my lord," she said, barely audible.

"That is exactly what you do!" he shouted. The entire assembly muttered and shook.

"No, my lord," she repeated, and then looked him straight in the eye. "My lord, if you allow me to continue, you will understand my true motives for choosing this fable as the story of my masque."

She smiled then, a hauntingly provocative smile. One that promised a certain amount of wickedness.

"I have changed the story somewhat, my lord." She spoke as though it were only the two of them in the room, though a thousand eyes observed them. "Hoping to reflect how I felt when I came to live with you."

I heard the king's labored breathing from across the room. The surrounding silence magnified it until it seemed to be the breath of God himself.

"Go on," he muttered. He winced as he sat, and his face tumbled into crevasses of old age and overindulgence.

Cat nodded to the man playing the lord of the underworld and I just glimpsed something in her face, in her eyes. I had seen it before. It was the look she got when she saw something she liked, something she wanted. Like a crimson gown or a fur muff or a hood trimmed with gold and pearls. But more than that, it was the look she got when she knew she could get a man

to fall in love with her. To want her as he had never wanted anyone else. The look that led to ruin.

It disappeared a sliver of a moment after it began, and I wondered if I had actually seen it at all. And I realized that I had no idea who the man disguised as Hades actually was. He had never come to our rehearsals but had practiced separately with Cat while we were otherwise engaged—embroidering costumes or practicing songs and music.

An unusually full mask obscured his face, showing only his eyes, not his nose and lips like the traditional half-mask. His black cloak and shiny black boots hid the rest of him completely, and he faded directly into the darkness.

But his eyes sprung a memory somewhere, one that trembled fearfully before falling back down into the impenetrable depths of my mind.

"Kitty!"

Joan pushed me forward. I stumbled over my long black cloak and almost fell. Cat shot me an icy look.

I continued the performance without looking at her or the man who played Hades. I knew that he handed her a pomegranate, and that she lifted it to her lips to eat.

But here, Cat changed the classical story. In the myth, Persephone eats six pomegranate seeds, thus condemning herself to six months of the year in the underworld. Her mother, Demeter, goddess of the seasons and the harvest, mourns for her for these six months, creating winter.

But in Cat's version, Persephone refused even a single pome-

granate seed. She was halted in her attempt to take a bite by a beautiful vision: Edmund Standebanke dressed all in gold, a false red beard on his chin and a crown upon his head. All he needed was a placard reading *Henricus Rex*.

The king laughed and clapped his hands like a child at the sight of his double, and some of us breathed a sigh of relief. He could have erupted at the sight of a mere yeoman portraying him. Better, however, than a nobleman with pretentions to the crown.

Edmund reached out and plucked the pomegranate from Cat's hand. He lifted her up, her tunic and sleeves radiant again as she stepped out of the shadows and unveiled her natural incandescence.

The man playing Hades shook his fist at them and then sank to his knees, defeated.

Cat turned to the pretend king and he bowed deeply to her. The light of the candles created a halo of sparkles over her head, and she spoke.

"And so it is always summer with my lord, even when the days are short and the rain ever-present," she said.

The king rose again, applauding, immediately followed by all of the courtiers. All of us players bowed or curtseyed deeply to the king, except Cat, who stood and glowed with the adulation.

"Music!" the king shouted as he stepped from the dais and the players struck up a stately pavane.

And the king danced with his wife, firmly assured that it would always be summer and he would always be young and handsome, as long as he was with her.

A very clever piece of propaganda.

But when the pavane was finished, the king strode back to the dais, the merest of limps betraying his infirmity.

And the queen stayed on to dance the galliard with Hades, still dressed in black, but now without his mask.

Thomas Culpepper.

The king cheered and applauded and drank copious amounts of wine. He laughed with the Duke of Norfolk and remained completely oblivious to his wife and his usher making eyes at each other under the guise of dancing for His Majesty's pleasure.

I had to be wrong. I watched them dance, their bodies moving as if anticipating the other's actions even before they were made. I closed my thoughts to the possibility that Cat would consider adultery. Treason. I watched them until the dance ended and Cat practically sat in the king's lap, laughter on her face, delighted with herself.

I wished for something to hold onto. Something solid. I remembered another dance, holding William's hand, whispering, his mouth so close to mine. I looked to where he had stood behind the duke, but he was no longer there. I scanned the room and saw his sandy hair shining over the greasy, grizzled heads of the older courtiers. Headed my way.

My fingers grew numb. My lips as well. I couldn't think what I would say to him. How to apologize.

A dozen steps away, he slowed. Hesitated. Looked at me. No smile. He took two more steps, broke eye contact, and bowed.

To Alice Restwold.

He guided her to the middle of the Great Hall with one hand firmly on the small of her back. She turned and smiled up at him, chin tilted, eyes reflecting the bravura of the painted ceiling.

I crawled into the deepest shadow I could find and watched alone. I watched them dance, their bodies mirroring each other. I watched them move together as the music changed for the next dance. I watched him kiss her hand.

"We can't have the queen's favorite hiding in the corner, now, can we?"

The voice was smooth and rich like burnished mahogany. But the face set me back like an onslaught. Handsome. Angular. Rapacious.

"Master Culpepper."

"You know me."

I edged closer to the crush of courtiers making negotiations and assignations in the candlelight.

"You are hard to miss."

Culpepper's smile was at once charming and disarming. It erased any hint of debauchery from his features. And yet, I knew what he was.

"That makes two of us," he said. "You look ravishing this evening, Mistress Tylney. Shall we dance?"

"No." I didn't want to be near him, much less dance with him.

He staggered backward, dramatically clasping his doublet where his heart should have been. Several nearby ladies tittered, and he winked at them conspiratorially.

"You wound me, Mistress Tylney," he said. "Perhaps you are too proud for the likes of me, a lowly gentleman usher to the king."

"I am no such thing!"

"Then dance with me."

"No." I wished he would go away. Disappear. Prey upon someone else.

"One dance. I promise." He sidled closer, slipped an arm behind my back. Fear rent every shred of breath from me so I couldn't even scream.

"I'm afraid this dance is mine, Thomas."

Culpepper turned his charming smile to Edmund, and I felt faint at my deliverance.

"Edmund, you always get the most *delicious* girls," Culpepper said, the word overripe in his mouth.

"No, Thomas," Edmund said. "You've tasted the very best, I'm sure."

Culpepper trailed his gaze along my body once more, his tongue just visible beneath his upper lip, sucking on his teeth.

Then he turned without another word and walked away.

"You look a little nervous," Edmund whispered, and took my hand.

"He terrifies me," I admitted, willing to ignore his implication that I wasn't one of the very best.

"You want protection," he said, and pulled me deeper into the shadows instead of onto the dance floor.

I did want to be protected. From Culpepper. From Cat. From the future. From heartache.

Edmund wrapped his arms around me, the press of his muscles tight against me. He lowered his head and breathed in, as if drinking the scent of my neck, my hair.

I rested my face on his chest, the fur of velvet and scratch of gold embroidery, the sure, steady, unadulterated beat of his heart.

"You're right," I whispered. "I want you to protect me."

He ran his hands up the back of my bodice, fingers catching on the laces, pressing into my ribs, up to my throat. He pulled away, my face cupped in his hands, held me with his eyes.

"The only person I can't protect you from is me, kitten," he said.

He didn't exactly make me feel safe. Not protected, really. But *wanted*, definitely. That thought urged me forward and I pressed myself into him. He breathed again, a smothered moan, but didn't kiss me.

"Not here," he said. "Not now."

He pulled away from me. I was dumbstruck, not sure of what

to think. I watched him weave through the crowd. Few noticed his passing, despite his bulk and good looks. A yeoman of the chamber didn't merit interest amongst nobility.

He returned to his position behind the king's dais.

Where William stood in attendance upon the Duke of Norfolk. Watching me, pain and betrayal scrawled across his features.

IGNORANCE IS BLISS.

Or so they say. But I didn't find it so.

I ignored the presence of the duke and his entourage. The pain that threatened to smother me when I thought of William. The way I felt when I imagined Edmund's breath buried in my hair.

I ignored Culpepper and the memory of Cat's smile. I ignored the biting fear that arose in me whenever I thought back to that evening in the autumn woods. I couldn't eradicate the vibrant nightmares that hunted me in the dark, but I could ignore them in the light of day.

Turning one's back on knowledge is not the same as the lack of it, so bliss eluded me.

So did sleep. And comfort.

Because the court began to move. From Greenwich to Rochester, Rochester to Sittingbourne, and back to Greenwich. King and court were like a restless beast, unable to settle down, pacing back and forth behind bars. The mood caught everyone. Waiting.

Summer approached rapidly, the threatening cliff-fall of my marriage with it. But then, without my asking, Cat blocked Lord Graves's request to come to court. Had him held at bay.

"My reasons are entirely selfish," she said when I tried to thank her.

"What, you want me all to yourself?" I asked.

"But of course," she said, and waggled her eyebrows.

She was carefully composing a note at her little writing desk. Dipping the quill in the ink before scratching a word or two. Slowly. Painfully.

"What is the status between you and Edmund Standebanke?" she asked.

"I'm not sure," I said. I hadn't seen Edmund in several days, except in passing.

"Perhaps he thinks you're not interested," Cat said.

"Maybe *he's* not interested."

"Of course he's interested," Cat said. "You're young. You're beautiful."

I snorted. We both knew I wasn't beautiful. I wished she wouldn't keep reminding me.

"You're a favorite of the queen."

"That's probably the pinnacle of my desirability," I said. It was easier to put myself down than build up hope only to have it crushed. "Besides, I'm betrothed to another."

"All the more reason for something to happen with Edmund

now," Cat said. "Have a little fun before you succumb to Lord Poxy."

Cat's pet name for Lord Graves. Trust Cat to focus on the positive.

"Is it that William person?" Cat asked. "Are you still pining away for the gentleman usher of a mere duke?"

"William is no longer fond of me," I said, the truth pressed like a thumb to a bruise.

"Well, then, something has to change," she said. "You can't have two men lose interest unless you're doing something horrendous. Speaking out of turn or expressing too many opinions. You could make a little more of an effort with your dress, as well."

I glanced down. The midnight-blue gown she had given me earlier in the year had begun to wear at the hem and cuffs, and there was a stain on the bodice that couldn't be removed by water or rubbing. Cat didn't seem to understand that I actually had to work for her and couldn't wear my best gowns at all times for fear of ruining them.

"Perhaps you don't take enough baths." She wrinkled her nose.

"I don't smell!" I cried.

"Then you hold too tight to your favors," she said. "You have to give men a taste to keep them around. Sniffing about like dogs when the smell of fresh meat is on the snout of their leader."

"I am not fresh meat." I shrank from her comparison.

"Well, the loss of Gibbon might not be your fault, you know," she added sincerely, giving me a look of pure pity. "It could be Alice. She's managed to hook her claws into him somehow."

I thought of the two of them dancing after the masque. Alice's claws twisted in my own heart.

"Do you think he likes her?" I asked, barely a whisper.

Cat sighed and folded her note.

"Go to Edmund," she said. "Go and ride him for all he's worth. I know you want to."

I wasn't sure what I wanted. I had to admit to myself the possibility Cat was right. But I didn't know if I wanted to admit it to her.

"Such a suggestion coming from the divine mouth."

"Only the king is God's representative on earth," she corrected me.

"So you must be the devil's," I teased.

"If the devil spurs you to make Edmund Standebanke feel like he's never felt in his life, then yes, I am."

She reached into her pocket and pulled out a little gold ring.

"Take these to Jane Boleyn," she said, pressing ring and note into my hand.

Jane, because she was one of the "Great Ladies" of the household, had her own rooms in the palace. And her own servants.

I studied the piece of jewelry. A simple, gold cramp-ring.

"Is Jane unwell?" I asked.

"Lady Rochford is fine," Cat replied. "I'm just returning it to her."

I turned to go.

"Oh, and Kitty?" Cat called. "Would you ask her when I shall have the thing she promised me?"

"What thing?" I wondered what Jane and Cat could possibly be trading back and forth. Cat despaired of Jane's fashion sense.

"She'll know."

31

THE WARREN OF ROOMS AT GREENWICH WAS STILL UNFAMILIAR TO ME,
and I made several wrong turns, cursing a court that couldn't
stay put. Hampton Court I understood, blocked out as it was
in great squares. Windsor was a distant memory. And the other
places we'd visited, I couldn't keep straight.

I found Jane in an ill-lit room with north-facing windows,
the smudge of fogged daylight barely penetrating the gloom. I
stepped in quietly, caught her staring at the distant trees. She
held a chain of pearls that seemed illuminated internally. From
them hung a gold pendant.

"Jane?" I asked. I wondered if this was the thing Cat wanted.

Her hands moved, deft as hawk's wings, to cover and conceal the necklace in her sleeve. Then she looked up and saw me
watching.

"Kitty," she said, and the pearls slid like water from her fingers, tumbling to the floor.

"Here," I picked it up. Smooth and heavy. The pendant a let-
ter *A*, a single teardrop pearl suspended from the center bar.
Like the one in the duchess's coffer back in Lambeth. A for
Agnes Tylney. I frowned.

"It is mine," Jane said, sounding defensive. "It was given to me."

"By the duchess?" I asked.

"No," she said quietly. "By Anne. Anne Boleyn."

"Oh." No wonder she kept it hidden. No wonder the duchess never wore her copy of it.

"People say I hated her," Jane said. "That I was jealous. But she was my friend. For a while. And the Boleyns?" Her face twisted into an uncomfortable smile. "They always stuck together. Except for one."

"Like the Howards," I replied.

"Oh, no," she said as she gently put the necklace into the pocket that hung from her waist. "The Howards will cut you off as soon as look at you. Every last one of them."

I shivered at the coldness in her voice, her eyes as dead as river stones. I felt suddenly desperate to get away.

"The queen asked me to deliver these," I said, and handed over the note and the ring. "And asked about something you promised her?"

"I didn't promise it," Jane said quickly. "But tell her it will be delivered. Eventually."

I knew Cat would not be happy with that answer. Immediate gratification usually wasn't soon enough for her. And I would bear the brunt of her irritation.

I pushed my way back through the darkening rooms, trying to figure out a way to reorder Jane's words to the best outcome. Not looking where I was going, I tripped over a stool and cursed.

"Language, kitten."

Edmund's words triggered a rush of memory of my conversation with Cat about him. And his presence, warm and masculine, one hand on my arm in support, liquefied me.

"Are you all right?" he asked.

I realized I was trembling. Just a little.

"I'm fine," I said, trying to recover some semblance of courtly poise. I stepped back. The raised carvings of the wood paneling pressed into my shoulder blades. Tudor roses. Falcons.

Edmund moved with me. Hard oak behind me. Velvet, muscle, and bone to the fore.

"I think you're more than fine," he said quietly, his voice resonating through my body.

"What gives you that idea?" I asked.

"Your eyes," he said, and tucked a strand of hair back into my hood. "They say more than your words." His finger traced the line of my jaw to my lower lip and tugged lightly.

"Oh? What are they telling you?" But I knew. I just wasn't sure I agreed with them entirely.

"That you want to be kissed."

I pressed my lips into a line, and he laughed.

"I see your mouth doesn't agree."

I lowered my eyes. They said too much. Just as Cat had told me.

He drew his finger beneath my chin, forcing me to look at him again, and put his mouth on mine. I had expected the kiss to be like William's, soft and bright, like a smile made for

two. But Edmund's kiss tasted of smoke and felt like a mad rush, like shooting the waters of the Thames beneath London Bridge. Thrilling and dangerous. Part of me wanted to run. A small part.

He pulled away, his lips just inches from mine, a devilish smile playing on them.

"Now I see your mouth and your eyes want the same thing."

"And what is that?" My attempt at playful flirtation wavered at the expression on his face. He looked intently into my eyes for half a breath, then focused covetously on my lips.

"More."

I couldn't disagree. His kiss made me giddy, disoriented, out of control. I moved to close the gap between our mouths. His smile widened.

The sound of footsteps stopped me just before the point of contact, and we stood motionless, Edmund's breath cooling my lips.

"Forgive us!" Alice's voice echoed down the gallery and then she strolled into my field of vision. Followed by William Gibbon. "We appear to have waylaid a private *tête à tête*."

William said nothing, just stared straight ahead. Edmund stepped back and pulled at the bottom of his doublet. The action caught my eye and when I looked up at him, he grinned. He thought I was looking at his codpiece. I frowned at him, which only made him grin more broadly. Until he saw me glance at William again. Then his eyes narrowed.

"Or perhaps it was a *bouche à bouche*." Alice continued. She

grabbed William's arm proprietarily. "Please don't let us disturb you." She wore the dress Cat had given her, the russet bodice making her eyes sparkle and her cheeks glow. And at that moment, I was more jealous of Alice Restwold than I had ever been of Catherine Howard. The state of my stained and frayed gown suddenly sat heavy upon me.

"It is no disturbance," I said, unable to look at William at all. "I must return to the queen's apartments."

I hurried off, uncaring if they had heard my mumbled words or even noticed my consternation. Let William have Alice if he so chose. If he wanted a girl like her, he was more stupid than I had thought. Alice liked nothing better than a tight ass and association with the duke. All she wanted was to lord her knowledge and conquest over everyone else. Let her. I pushed past them, my eyes on the floor, hoping to hide my face, ravaged by stifled tears and embarrassment. I heard Alice titter again, and their footsteps as they ambled in the opposite direction.

I looked back.

Edmund stood where I had left him, watching. He smiled, turned on his heel, and walked away. As if he had been waiting for me to look.

As if he had known I would.

32

NEWS CAME OF UNREST IN THE NORTH. ONCE AGAIN. YEARS BEFORE, during the time of Queen Jane, some of the northern bishops and lords had committed treason by instigating the Pilgrimage of Grace. It was a backlash against the king's religious policies when he made himself the head of the church, breaking with the Pope in Rome and dissolving the monasteries.

The pilgrimage accomplished nothing, except the mass execution of the rebels. And a general, nagging distrust.

So now, the king decided to put an end to all of it. To make his presence—*his* Grace—known to everyone. He, and the entire court, would travel north. To York, the city of his grandfather, Edward IV. A great progress. Proof of power.

The court flew into a whirlwind of activity. The progress would begin in summer, and it seemed the king planned to move most of the palace as well as courtiers, guards, bearers, archers, and horsemen. Armor, arms, pikes, and cannon. It was like an invasion, albeit one dressed up as ceremony.

Cat ordered dozens of new clothes, all to be packed away and carried hundreds of miles so she could be beautiful and resplendent every day of the journey. Gowns made of cloth of silver that shone like a pond in the summer sun. Bodices of crimson velvet trimmed with gold. Silk sleeves every color of the rainbow. The king called for the same, his doublets and caps fashioned from cloth of gold. We packed their furs, jewels, hoods, trims, and bindings—everything that made the king and queen things of beauty.

Their wardrobes would awe the ignorant common people of the country we passed through. How could the uneducated peasants not believe that the king and queen were God's very representatives on earth?

An army of servants packed the king's most beautiful tapestries, stripping the walls of Hampton Court, Greenwich, Whitehall, and Westminster. All manner of gold and silver utensils, plates, jugs, and accoutrements were carefully laid in cedar boxes to be used throughout the journey.

Saddles, litters, and carts were requisitioned, decorated, or made from scratch to transport all the people and materials the court would be carrying. The king commandeered five thousand horses, carts carried two hundred tents to house us all, and we were to be accompanied by a thousand armed soldiers to keep us safe.

But the more days I lived, the less safe I felt.

In May, the duchess came grinning with a note from Lord Poxy, claiming what was rightfully his.

I took it to Cat immediately.

She read it carefully, one word at a time, and handed it back to me.

"What can I do?" I asked.

"I suppose it's your duty to marry him."

"But . . ." I scrambled to contradict her. "But what about the progress? What about you?"

"You mean, what about Edmund, don't you?"

"No," I countered. Though it was true I preferred him to Lord Poxy.

"You've kissed him, right?" she asked. "Anything else?"

"No, Cat."

"Why not?"

"I don't think I love him."

"I've told you before that love doesn't matter."

"Cat," I said. "I am not going to have sex with that man." Maybe.

"And defy a direct order from your queen?"

"I don't want to get pregnant."

"There are ways to meddle with a man and not get pregnant," Cat replied. "You *need* Edmund Standebanke's attention."

"Why?"

"Because he travels with a pack."

"Like a dog," I said, unable to shake myself of the image she had conjured weeks before—the men of the court sniffing about like animals.

"Exactly. It's easier to conceal something in a pack. It's difficult to keep secrets when you run rogue."

I got a sinking feeling. I thought of the pack in which Edmund Standebanke ran. I thought of the bellwether of

that group—the alpha male whom all the rest followed. *Culpepper*.

"Conceal what?" I asked.

"Never you mind," she said, then added, "Help me out of my bodice and sleeves. I'm ready for bed."

"I think you should be careful," I whispered.

"Oh, you do, do you?" she asked. "You, who have never felt the pleasure of a man, think I should be careful? I'm not surprised."

I bristled at her condemnation of me. But I couldn't let her get away with it. I couldn't let her destroy herself.

"Cat," I began. "It's dangerous—"

"Oh, God's blood, Kitty, I'm only flirting. Everybody does it. Queens and kings and courtiers. It's *expected*."

"Then you don't need me to cover for you."

"Why, in the French court, apparently, they have open affairs all the time!" It was as if I hadn't even spoken.

"The *men* do, Cat," I said. "Not the queen."

"Shut up, Kitty," she said. "Just shut up about it. I hate being queen. All the stupid responsibilities. I'm having a little fun for once. And because I'm queen no one can do a thing about it."

"But Cat," I pleaded.

"Listen," she turned to me. "It comes down to this. You can marry Lord Poxy. Go off and live on the Poxy estate and have twelve Poxy children. Or you can stay at court. Entertain Standebanke. And maybe have a little fun. You choose. And I will ensure your choice comes to fruition."

"It's hardly a choice, Cat."

"Good," she smiled. "Then I'll make it for you. I know which one you really want. We don't have room in the entourage for one more. And I need my dearest friend to come with me. Lord Poxy will just have to wait to get his hands on you."

33

THE KING ELIMINATED POTENTIAL TROUBLEMAKERS BEFORE OUR DEPARture. Prisoners long held in the Tower. Anyone who carried a drop of non-Tudor royal blood posed a threat, as a standard around which rebels could rally.

Margaret Pole, the Countess of Salisbury, was charged with treason. She was daughter to Richard III's brother, sixty-seven years old and frail. She refused to plead guilty or lay her head on the block. It took the inept executioner ten or more strokes of the ax to dispatch her.

On that sorry note, it began to rain. The roads quickly clogged with mud and became impassable and we were forced to remain immobile in Greenwich, looking dejectedly northward, for three entire weeks.

There was no flirting. No lover's meetings. No men. Just dreary boredom.

The Duke of Norfolk took his trusted servants and braved the rain and muck, securing great houses and deer parks for the king's use. Rumor was he would meet back up with the court in Lincoln. I watched Alice for signs of distress, but she dared not show them to me. I didn't know how, but the pain of William's absence was greater than that of his presence. Even though he'd chosen Alice over me.

We listlessly played music or repeated old gossip or embroidered tapestries or tried on each other's clothes, leaving kirtles and sleeves and bodices strewn about the chambers, too lethargic to pick them up again.

"Why don't we just call it a day?" Joan moaned, staring out the window at the waterlogged hills and swollen Thames.

"We can't call it a day, it's been a month," I said.

"The king has to go," Alice said importantly. "He has to get to York."

"But why?" Joan said. "I'm so sick of the rain and the mud already and we haven't even left yet!"

"And your comfort is so important to the king," I snapped.

"It's not just me!" Joan said. "Everyone's complaining."

"You're just complaining the loudest."

"No," Joan said, sticking out her tongue. "You are."

"Me?"

"Yes, you're complaining about me complaining!"

We stared at each other for a moment and then burst into laughter.

"Oh, really," Alice sniffed. "It wasn't that funny."

But the laughter bubbled up unbidden. Joan and I clung to each other and giggled helplessly, our hair coming unbound and our faces red and splotchy.

"There's really nothing to laugh about," Alice said.

I considered the rain, the prospect of the long uncomfortable, muddy journey ahead of us, and the executions that had so recently taken place. Alice's perfidy.

"No," I concluded, "I suppose you're right."

"At least it's stopped raining," Joan said to the window.

"For now," I grumbled.

"What sour faces my maids have!" Cat swept into the room, the hem of her rose-petal pink skirts skimming the floor. We all sank into curtseys and she laughed.

"Why so glum?" she asked.

"The rain."

"The mud."

"The boredom."

"Need we say more?" I asked.

"Well, I have thought of something we can do to alleviate the last item," Cat said, hugging herself and bouncing on her toes.

"What is it?" we asked in unison and she giggled.

"Hide-and-seek."

We stared at her in silence.

"We can play in the castle galleries," she said. "There must be loads of secret hiding places in the vacated rooms and courtyards."

Hide-and-seek wasn't my favorite game. My discomfort in enclosed spaces gave me an animalistic fear of being found. As

a child, I would hold my breath for so long I saw spots before my eyes. And when I wasn't near fainting, I was bored out of my mind.

"We do need something to cheer us up," Joan said hesitantly.

"Of course we do," Cat said. "And here's the best part. We'll get the king's men to do the seeking.

"Come," Cat commanded, and ran down the gallery toward the king's apartments, her skirts belling behind her.

"Send him away," came a voice from behind the door when I knocked. "No more suits. We must get to Lincoln. We must get to York." The king trailed into grumbles.

"I do not look for favor," Cat called from the doorway. Just inside the room, Culpepper watched her with hooded eyes.

"My lord," Cat said, skipping to the king to hug him from behind. He faced the fire, so we could not see his reaction, but he lifted his hand to touch her face. She removed it and kissed his knuckles perfunctorily.

In the closeness of the room, I smelled the wet clothes of the men, their unwashed bodies, and the crisp fir resin of the fire.

"I wondered if we could borrow some of your gentlemen," Cat said, and sneaked a glance at me. "And perhaps one of your yeomen of the chamber as well."

"What sort of mischief are you planning today?"

"Well," Cat said. "My ladies grow bored and restless, closed in all the time."

"Don't we all?"

"And I thought a game of hide-and-seek would dispel some of it."

"A children's game?" he asked.

"Yes," Cat said. "I thought perhaps the ladies could hide, pursued by the men. One man each."

"Don't you think the men already do enough pursuing?" the king asked with a hint of a smile in his voice.

"Ah, but my maids are too chaste to allow themselves to be caught," Cat said. "In a children's game, the seeker may finally achieve his goal."

"If only they should be so lucky as I," the king said softly, stroking her again.

"I shall sit here with you," Cat said. "And wait for the couples to come back. We will have wine and sweetmeats after they're caught."

"The rest of us can wager on who will be the last girl found," the king said, and looked up at Cat. "So you must hide as well, because you have a cunning about you that I cannot see any of my men matching."

"I shall do my best to win you a fortune," she said.

We established the rules that each man would hunt only his partner, but if he found someone else's partner, he could disclose her location to her hunter.

"However," Cat said. "If another man finds you, you may move. Find another hiding spot. But only if you have been discovered."

"I told you she was cunning," the king said.

We paired up, the men choosing their quarry. Edmund Standebanke chose me.

"I relish the hunt," he said. I enjoyed the warmth of his whisper on my face.

"And what do you do when your quarry eludes you?" I asked, looking at him directly, knowing my eyes would give me away. That they anticipated the plunge of another of his kisses.

"Oh," he said, his lips brushing my temple. "I never give up. Surrender is the only option."

"You're very confident of your success," I managed. His words, his breath, his very nearness were making me excruciatingly aware of my own body.

"Sometimes, the quarry *wants* to be caught," he said.

His words wrapped briery and cold around my spine, so closely did they echo those I'd heard in the forest.

"Not all," I said quietly.

"Are all of you prepared?" the king asked, breaking the spell.

I pushed away the illogical fear caused by Edmund's meaningless banter and smiled up at him.

"Are you?" I asked.

But my eye was drawn to the other side of the room. Cat twitched a filmy kerchief enticingly from the grasp of Thomas Culpepper. He cringed in mock despair. Cat kissed the kerchief and laid it gently in his hand. Culpepper raised it to his own face, almost to his lips, his eyes never wavering from hers.

"Have you a favor for me?" Edmund asked.

I turned to look at him, tilted my chin. A delicious thought came to me.

"Perhaps a kiss," I said with a smile.

"Perhaps more," he replied, his eyes fervent. "I will not let you be until I've had you. Remember, surrender is the only option."

The heat his words generated in me threatened combustion. But it was tempered by a heady dose of trepidation. The word surrender implied forced submission.

"Ready!" the king cried before I could speak. He grimaced as he stretched his leg out in front of him. "Begin!"

Edmund nudged me, his palm on my lower back, his fingers sliding lower.

I ran.

"Count to one hundred!" I heard the king call to the men. "In Latin!"

My height put me at a disadvantage. I couldn't hide in a cupboard or beneath a chair, not without pain. But I didn't want to be found, not for a good long time. I needed some time to think.

I slipped through the great hall. Knots of older men ignored me, busy discussing matters of state. I darted across a courtyard and headed for the kitchen. The boys who turned the spits giggled at me, and the cooks gave me dirty looks. As I stepped into the alley behind it, I breathed deeply, and then regretted it, as the mud and slops from the kitchen mixed below my feet, despite the king's declaration that all parts of the palace must

be kept scrupulously clean. I found a recess in the wall, half hidden behind a trio of spits hanging with the tattered remains of the previous night's meal.

I waited, straining to hear the sound of boots on the cobblestones or the giggling of another girl being found. And I thought about Edmund Standebanke.

I thought about his sultry smile and the way his kiss flashed through me like a cataract. And how he walked away afterward, as if he knew he was being watched. How he looked when he laughed with Thomas Culpepper. And how his words echoed Culpepper's demand for submission from the woman in the forest.

I thought about how my body reacted to him. Like a craving. How I could imagine his hands on me. But not his arms around me.

And with a pain like acute infection, my mind turned to William Gibbon, off in the wilds of the north. I wondered if he missed Alice, and I wished that he missed me. I wished it were he who would discover me in the kitchen alley.

I stood, alone, my toes growing numb in my thin slippers on the wet ground. Edmund couldn't have been looking for me very hard, no matter what he said. I wondered if the others had been found. If Cat had been found.

And I suddenly felt knocked down by a gush of insight.

The king was right. Cat's cunning surpassed all others. She was hidden. For once, she was by herself—something completely

unheard of at court. About to be found by Thomas Culpepper. *In a children's game, the seeker may finally achieve his goal.*

I needed to stop her. Before she ruined herself. Before she ruined her marriage. Before she ruined us all.

I slipped from my hiding place to search for Cat and ran straight into Edmund Standebanke.

"Wanted to be found that badly, did you?" he asked.

"No," I said, unable to shake the feeling of dread from my stomach. I couldn't think clearly, and the sight of Edmund, his lips turned up in a teasing grin, didn't help at all.

"I would never have seen you there," he said. "Why else would you jump straight into my arms unless you wanted to be found?"

"I have to go," I said.

"I believe you promised to bestow a favor."

He gripped my arms and kissed me. Urgently. As if his life depended on it. I was almost able to forget Cat. Forget the possibilities. Except for those that his kiss implied.

"We must claim our reward from the king," he said, pulling away, wiping his mouth on his sleeve. "The only girl not yet found is the queen. And he placed a wager on her, so she was sure to be the last one caught."

"The queen has not been found?" I asked. "How do you know she'll be last?"

"You've been at court long enough to realize we allow the king to win at everything that matters," Edmund said. "She

and Culpepper are probably hiding somewhere near the king's chambers, waiting for all of us to return."

The dread came back and doused me with a chill.

"We have to find them."

"I told you," he said, "they're hiding. Come with me to drink the king's health."

"We need to go to the queen's rooms first."

"No we don't, kitten," Edmund said, his voice a yard of tease and an inch of threat. "We need to go to the king's apartments and collect our prize."

"You go," I said. "I need to find Cat."

"I can't go alone, you silly girl," Edmund said, his grip and tone now equally steely.

I was a silly girl. I had walked right into a trap. My vigilance was down. The constant observance of the court was distracted. It was the perfect moment for Cat to find some privacy.

And I was too late to do anything about it.

I FOLLOWED EDMUND INTO THE KING'S CHAMBERS. THE OTHERS WERE already eating an extravagant indoor picnic of meat pies and good wine and cheeses. The king looked up when we burst into the room.

"Ah!" he said. "Mistress Tylney! You must have hidden well to have given Master Standebanke such a merry chase."

"Yes, Your Majesty," I said, and curtseyed. The bodies of others pressed in too closely. The fire burned too high. The greasy smell of the cheese mingled with those of sweat and wet shoes, conspiring to make me feel ill.

"But my wife is cleverest of all," the king said. "She has not yet been found. I doubt young Culpepper will ever find her. For when my wife sets her mind to something, she makes sure she does it properly."

"Yes, Your Majesty," I said, the words like dust in my mouth because he spoke the unknowing truth.

"Here is your reward, Mistress Tylney," the king said, and gestured to a servant to bring something forward to me. It was a small box, inlaid with shell and silver.

"Thank you, Your Majesty," I said, curtseying again. I didn't want the box. It was like payment for keeping quiet.

"No, no, Kitty!" the king said. "What is within the box is what counts!"

His use of my pet name startled me. I looked up at him, his eyes merry behind fat cheeks flushed with pleasure. He looked like a child, eager for praise.

The servant thrust the box into my hands and I opened it slowly. Lying on a scrap of blue velvet was a chain of gold from which hung a single pendant of startling emerald.

I nearly dropped the box, and the king laughed at my clumsy juggling.

"Thank you, Your Majesty," I said when I held it tight in my hand, and again I curtseyed. It seemed I spent all my days in obeisance.

"Stand up, Kitty," the king said, irritably. "Let young Standebanke here put it around your pretty neck."

I blushed at the king's use of the word *pretty*. Of course, it was only my neck about which he spoke.

Edmund reached around me for the necklace, his forearm just grazing my breast. He gently lifted the fabric of my snood to clasp the chain. His breath raised the hairs of the nape of my neck.

"There," he whispered in my ear, and allowed my snood to fall back, warming the gooseflesh.

"It's beautiful," I said, looking down.

"Come here, Kitty," the king said, and I knelt before him.

"I saved it for you," he whispered, and I looked up at him in shock. "Because your eyes are the same color green. I would have given it to you no matter if you were the first or the last girl found.

"You are my wife's closest friend," the king continued. "She told me this when you arrived at court. I have never forgotten."

"Thank you, Your Majesty," I breathed.

"Remain a friend to her, Kitty," the king finished. "She has many enemies at court."

He no longer looked delighted, just old. Haggard.

"I will, Your Majesty," I said. Knowing, as I said it, it would mean betraying him.

I bowed once more and caught a whiff of an odor, like meat gone bad. Like the rot at the bottom of the Thames. My nose wrinkled involuntarily.

The king moved his legs with effort, a grimace. He scowled at me.

His ulcers. Despite the bandages soaked in lavender, the king knew I smelled them. A tide of remorse swept through me, and an agony of sympathy for the man who had everything, but truly held nothing. Not the honesty of his court. Not the fidelity of his wife. Not the perfection of a true immortal.

I lowered my head and composed my face into a smile.

"Thank you, Your Majesty. For the generous gift. And the generous words."

I wanted him to believe me. To believe that the smell didn't matter to me any more than my plainness mattered to him or

the truth mattered to Cat. But he turned away. I knew that all the other ladies and courtiers noticed. I had the king's favor for an instant and lost it.

Edmund guided me to the trestle laden with culinary delights. It all tasted of soil and smut, and I gagged on the secrets in the back of my throat.

When Cat burst triumphantly into the room, rosy and fresh in her pink gown, her hair a little disheveled, but her face composed, everyone turned and cheered.

"He can't have been looking very hard," Cat told the king. "I was in my rooms the entire time!"

"I couldn't have guessed you would go back to your apartments," Culpepper said coolly. "I searched the most unusual nooks and crannies, delving into the very depths of the palace."

I squeezed my eyes shut, unable to bear the buttery innuendoes issuing from Culpepper's mouth. He was so glib, so smarmy, and so horrible. I didn't know how Cat could stand to be near him.

"Sometimes it is as if my queen is a friend of the fairy folk," King Henry said. "She can be as light as gossamer, ethereal. It is no wonder to me that you could not find her. It has taken my entire life to find one like her."

The courtiers smiled, and the ladies tittered about romance. I wanted to cry.

"But I am real, my lord," Cat said. "Firm flesh and bone. Certainly not transparent."

"No, my love," the king murmured, and held out a hand to

her. She stood by him, and he wrapped a giant arm around her tiny waist. He was almost as tall sitting down as she was standing up. He laid his head upon her breast.

"I am famished, my lord," she said, and extricated herself.

She came to the table and picked delicately at the food laid out there. She glanced up at me, taking no notice of the pain in my face. But she stopped, staring, eyes upon my pendant.

"Where did you get that?"

"From the king," I said. "For the hide-and-seek game."

"What about your reward, Your Majesty?" Alice asked Cat. "Surely yours will be the greatest, as you were the last one found."

"Oh, my prize!" Cat cried.

If she had been anyone else, she would have left it. She would have had the grace to win the game, however dishonestly, and let it go. But not Cat. She returned to the king and perched on his lap, ignoring his wince.

"Your prize, my love, is to be married to me," he said quietly, lovingly.

"The most handsome man in the world," Cat said. She said it as if she had repeated these words a thousand times already.

"I do have a gift for you," the king said. He gestured to a servant who brought forward a plain wooden box, perfectly square, with a hinged lid. It fit perfectly in her lap. Just the right size for a crown. She stared at it, one finger on the catch.

"Open it," the king said.

Cat threw one look out into the room. One minute glance

that hit its mark without question. Culpepper. I felt faint with relief. If Cat got her crown, Culpepper would be history.

The box opened silently, revealing its sumptuous lining of crimson silk. On which sat a wreath fashioned from the blooms of a pink rose.

"My rose without a thorn," the king said. He picked up the wreath and placed it on her still unruly curls.

Cat attempted a smile, her eyes on the lining of the box.

"Kitty got an emerald," she whispered.

"There is more," the king said. "But you shall have to wait for it until we get to York."

"York!" Cat cried. "But that will be forever!"

The king smiled. It didn't seem to bother him that his wife was just a child. And a deceitful one at that.

"But wait you must," he said. His smile faltered as he shifted again in his chair.

"We will leave you now, my lord," Cat said.

"Yes," the king agreed. "We begin our journey as soon as possible."

As one, we turned to look out of the window, expecting to see the rain still churning from the sky. But we saw only white clouds and green hills and just the faintest hint of sunshine.

"We cannot have you tired on the first day of the progress," the king added.

"Of course not," Cat said.

We all knew that the king meant that *he* could not be tired for the first day of the progress. He already looked exhausted. Like he wanted to be alone. I left the room with the rest of the ladies, leaving the king behind with his devious favorites and his uxorious oblivion.

35

We lost ourselves in the chaos of moving the extensive household and all of its contents through the English countryside. Each day's embarkation took the entire morning. By the time the last horses left a place, the king and queen, at the head of the procession, had already stopped for lunch. Which took hours.

We moved from London to Dunstable, Ampthill to Collyweston, stopping at royal residences and the houses of the great and the good along the way. No single palace could contain us all, so additional housing had to be found, tents erected, beasts slaughtered, bread requisitioned, beds made, and every comfort supplied.

I often rode pillion behind Edmund. I told myself it was to enjoy the fresh air. But really I found myself enjoying the feel of my arms around him, the rumble of his voice against me. It ignited something deep inside me that I recognized with acute embarrassment as lust. Cat would be gratified to know that if we ever formed an attachment, it would be driven solely by sex. There seemed little chance we would ever form a bond through conversation, as he didn't say much.

Everywhere we went, the populace thronged to watch our passage. Our entourage clogged the roads and paths, trampled the fields, left trash and excrement in its wake, and yet everyone seemed happy to see us.

"Long live King Henry!" they shouted.

They wore baggy clothing of coarse materials, sometimes patched and torn, their beards untrimmed. They smelled different, too. Like fields and mud, something I found not altogether unpleasant.

They cheered for Cat, too. They called for her blessing. But I don't think I was the only one who saw the determination and concentration it cost her to keep from drawing back from the filthy hands of the toothless peasant women and men cowed by life. She couldn't bear for their want, their need, to be transferred to her. She couldn't stand to be in their presence. And they grew wary and sullen in hers.

I watched her closely, constantly. I watched her work hard to ignore Culpepper.

But I couldn't ignore him. He flirted with all the girls, jested with the king and his men. He and Edmund Standebanke lived in each other's pockets. He went hawking and hunting when we stopped somewhere for more than a few hours. He went nowhere near the queen.

I almost began to believe that Cat had changed her mind. That perhaps one taste was all she needed.

She spent more time in the company of Jane Boleyn, who appeared younger every day. I saw her reach into her pocket

less and less, and wondered if the memory of Anne Boleyn was being erased by the reality of Catherine Howard.

Then we crossed into Lincolnshire, the wellspring of the rebellion five years before. The Lincolnshire Uprising began as a protest of the suppression of the monasteries. But it got out of hand, demanding tax reforms and the repeal of property laws, and lead to riots and the forcible occupation of Lincoln Cathedral. It spurred the Pilgrimage of Grace in Yorkshire and everything ended in a round of bloody executions.

We had a picnic a few miles outside of Lincoln, the region's capital. I fancied I could see the cathedral high on Lincoln Cliff in the distance. We stopped again just outside the city for the king and queen to change their clothes. The king, dressed head to foot in cloth of gold, glowed as if he were Apollo himself. And by his side, Cat was Diana, her gown a tissue of cloth of silver, studded with jewels and embroidered in gold. She wore her hair bound in a caul of white silk studded with sapphires and rode a white horse.

At the gates of the city, the mayor and town gentry approached and made speeches. Groveling supplication for forgiveness. They knelt and cried, "Jesus save your Grace!" And all was forgiven. That easily.

We walked on aching feet through the gates and up to the cathedral. The building shone in the waning summer light, blinding over the brick edifices surrounding it. Inflated on sanctity, it towered over the town and all the people in it. The king claimed it as the tallest building in the world. He

insisted that he and Cat take communion there. I couldn't imagine that Cat had confessed her sins. She was too wary of the wagging tongues of priests. Though truly, entering that great space, the light coming in kaleidoscopically through the stained glass, and the pigeons flying high overhead like angels amongst the ribs, would make anyone want to fall on her knees and confess.

The city was full of exhausted and drunken revelers by the time we exited the cathedral into the darkened streets. I wanted nothing more than to roll onto my pallet and fall asleep. We had a few days in Lincoln. Perhaps we could rest. Really rest.

The Bishops' Palace stood close by the cathedral, renovated and decorated, made warm and comforting by the Duke of Norfolk, who stood at the gate to welcome the king and queen. I carefully avoided looking for William. I didn't need the pain of seeing him look for Alice. I didn't need the pain of seeing him, period. The loss of him still felt like a hole in my chest the size of a fist.

The rooms sat tight on top of each other, accessed by dark stairwells and interconnecting doors. The queen's apartments were surrounded by the rooms of her ladies, separated from the king by the centuries' old west hall, dark and cavernous compared to the gaudy-bright great hall of Hampton Court. Cat kissed the king lightly and he hobbled off to bed, followed by his men.

The city pressed in against the towers of the palace. Torchlight marked revelers in the streets below us, visible from

the squat, narrow windows. Cat turned to her ladies as soon as we reached her bedchamber.

"I require only Mistress Tylney and Lady Rochford," she said "The rest of you should get some sleep."

Groans of appreciation rose, and the room emptied within seconds.

Jane and I helped Cat to take off the glowing silver-white gown. Despite Cat's vow never to wear the same gown twice, I folded it carefully and packed it away. It seemed sacrilege to dispose of it.

I felt toilworn and depleted, and Jane looked like a ghost, her skin pale as thin parchment and her eyes sunken into black sockets. When Cat's hair had been brushed and her nightgown straightened, I removed my slippers and sighed at the freedom of it.

"Do not undress yet," Cat said.

"Why?" I asked, unable to prevent the peevishness in my voice. "Cat, I'm exhausted. We've spent eight days on the road and I've worked my fingers off, and I just want four hours of sleep before you have to get up tomorrow."

"Well, I'm sorry, Kitty, but you'll just have to attend to your queen for a change instead of to your own selfish desires. You are here under my auspices. You are here to do my bidding. You are not here for your own pleasure."

I knew that only too well.

She stared at me for a long moment. Jane stood frozen, her breath held.

"Well?" Cat snapped. "Do you not know how to curtsey? Do you not know how to pay me proper respect?"

Her voice rose ever higher until it became an indignant screech.

I dipped into a curtsey and refused to look at her.

Before she could say more, a knock came at the outer door of her chamber. She looked up, her eyes ringed white and wide with fear. Her expression caused my heart to judder.

"Who is it?" she said. "Kitty, go see."

I stepped tentatively to the door, unsure whether I should expect a cabal of Lincolnshire rebels or the wrath of the king himself. A single guard stood there, the scent of the night and smoke outside still clinging to his garments.

"I wish to tell the queen . . ." he paused as if considering his words. "I would like to make sure she feels protected."

"Oh," I said, my alarm increasing, but he didn't wait for my response.

"I found the back stairs door unlocked and standing open," he reported, his words tumbling over each other. "The stairs lead directly to the queen's apartments. I searched the stairs and the surrounding area, but found no one. I secured the door and locked it myself. She is in no danger."

My mind raced back to the cheering people at the gates of the city that afternoon. The faces all blended in my memory, mouths agape with what I had thought was joy but could easily have been rage. I wondered if the noise and crowds had hidden an assassin. I shuddered at the thought of the hordes still in

the streets, massing beneath the overhanging buildings, drinking and cursing into the night.

"Please, dear lady," the guard said, "be not afraid. I secured the door myself. No one can get in."

"Thank you," I tried to say, but a pebble of fear clogged my throat. I cleared it and said, "Thank you very much. I shall let the queen know."

He bowed.

"I must return to my rounds. You are all safe with me."

"I'm sure," I said, and smiled at him. I did not know the man but had seen him before. His presence was understated and unobtrusive, but ever-present. And indeed, I did feel safe with him on duty.

I returned to the bedchamber and Cat's questioning eyes.

"It was a guard." I wondered how I could tell her without making it sound too terrifying. Danger had been averted. She need not fear for her life.

"What did he want?" Cat said. "What reason could he possibly have for knocking on my door at such a late hour?"

I decided just to tell her straight and hope she could sleep that night.

"He said the back stairs door was left unlocked and hanging open. He said he locked the door and checked the area and believes that there is no danger."

Cat punched a tiny fist into her goose-down mattress.

"Oh, by the Mass, thwarted at every turn!" she cried. "That stupid man!"

I stared.

"Kitty, you must go down the back stairs at once," she said. "Wait there. Listen. Take the key with you."

"But I don't want to, Cat," I whispered. "The guard said there was no danger."

"Danger be damned!" she shouted. "Do as I say!"

Jane scurried to get me a taper.

"And Kitty, when you hear someone outside the door, let him in."

"Let him in?" The guard had just averted one assassination attempt and I was requested to expedite the next?

"Yes!"

"But Cat, are you sure?" I looked at Jane, hoping she would recognize Cat's lunacy. Jane wouldn't meet my eye.

"It is not your job to question me!" Cat said, her voice lowering to that dangerous growl. "It is your job to do as I wish. Now go."

In a daze, I stumbled barefoot down the rough-cut stone stairs, hardly able to see my feet in the weak light of the candle. I was glad I hadn't changed into my linen shift, because the walls exuded the chill of three hundred years of northern winters.

I came to the door and listened against it. The taper guttered, and I prayed I would not be left in that tomblike space in the dark. I thought I heard the whispers of ghosts. I imagined the vagrants and rebels and drunks of the town amassing outside the walls. I envisioned spiders and crawling bugs and the slithering of worms and snakes.

I was so caught up with the terror in my head that a scuffling outside the door made me shriek.

The noise stopped, and even through the thick oak door, I suspected I could hear a man breathing. Or an angry mob quietly discussing how to dissect a maid.

The latch snapped with a metallic echo up the cold dark stairs. I watched it, horrified. The door creaked almost imperceptibly followed by an angry grunt outside when it held fast.

I slipped the key in the lock with trembling fingers and turned it slowly. As soon as it clicked the latch snapped again and the door flew open.

Thomas Culpepper stood before me. In one swift movement, he pinched the flame of my candle out.

"Jesus, Kitty," he hissed. "Do you want everyone to see us?"

He slipped through the door, and in the reflected light of stars, Edmund emerged behind him.

"Stay outside, Standebanke," Culpepper ordered. "If you see anyone, knock, and Kitty here will come and warn us."

"Can I not keep Kitty company?" Edmund asked.

Oh, yes, please, I thought, though I told myself it was because I was afraid of the dark.

"No, you fool. One man standing outside will raise no questions. You're a yeoman of the chamber. You're guarding the queen. If you're with a girl, inside or out, you will be in dereliction of duty."

He pulled the door closed on Edmund's disappointed face,

Father's gaze never wavers. "How could it become known before it was sealed?"

Father doesn't know that I did seal it.

"I didn't—" I start, but Father raises a hand. Not to strike, but I flinch anyway.

"Do. Not. Speak," he hisses.

George is unmoving beside me. I feel his tension run through the room like a whirlpool.

"I return from Spain to find all of York Place in an uproar." Father returns to his chair. He leaves us standing side by side. Not touching. "The cardinal was in the gallery with only his chamber servants but could be heard from every corner, including the door of the council chamber."

So of course Father stopped to listen.

"The cardinal's voice was audible from every corner of the inner courtyard. 'How dare you defile your good name!'" Father shouts in a good imitation of the cardinal's tenor.

"'I marvel at your peevish folly!'" Father continues. "'And to tangle yourself to that foolish girl in the court. You are due to inherit the greatest earldom in England and yet you ally yourself with the daughter of merchants. Of little wealth and no name. One of the king's minions.'"

George sucks in a breath, and Father glares at him.

"So I listen. Wondering who this boy is and with whom he has entangled himself."

Wondering whom he can use the gossip as leverage against.

"'I am a man,' says Henry Percy." Father slams his fist into

less kiss, hard and anxious, and then he pushed me away.

"Culpepper is right," he said. "I can't be seen with you. Now, stay."

He shut the door.

I locked it.

I sank down and pulled my skirts around my feet to trap the warmth. I wrapped my arms around my knees to stop their trembling. When I closed my eyes, finding comfort in a more familiar darkness, I felt a tear slide down my cheek.

I was aiding and abetting treason. I had allowed a man into the queen's chambers in the middle of the night. Not just any man, but Thomas Culpepper.

The man I chose to protect me was Culpepper's best friend. A man who made my blood race but my heart fail. A man who left me in the darkness that terrified me.

I crushed my palms against my eyes to press the thoughts away, sending shooting sparks through the writhing blackness. I stayed there, huddled beside the door, until I fell asleep against the wall.

36

A BOOT IN MY RIBS STARTLED ME BACK INTO THE WAKING DARKNESS.

"Your queen needs you," came Culpepper's voice. The sound of the key in the lock. A line of charcoal gray as the door opened. Whispers.

I sat up, rubbing my side, my arm and face cold from the damp stone. I didn't want to return to the bedroom. To the tumbled sheets. To the smell of him.

I didn't want to talk to Cat.

My bones creaked when I stood, the rough floor painful beneath my chilled feet. I reached out to close the door, but was stopped by Culpepper's voice.

"Well, now you have no choice, Standebanke."

Edmund was still out there.

"It's not like I had any to begin with," he muttered.

"My thoughts exactly," Culpepper said, and I saw his shadow slap Edmund's on the back. With a laugh, he sauntered away.

"Kitty?" Edmund whispered.

"I'm still here."

Edmund wedged himself through the crack in the door and

put his arms around me. His cloak and doublet carried the cold mist from outside and offered little warmth, but I leaned into him anyway.

"What did he mean?" I asked. "That you had no choice?"

"What does Thomas Culpepper ever mean?" he said. "His way is the only way and the rest of us have no say in the matter."

"Shouldn't we all have a choice?" I asked. Knowing that I didn't. I'd pledged my choice away when I had sworn my loyalty to Cat.

Edmund pulled away and kissed me on the forehead.

"Get to bed, kitten," he said, and then moved his lips closer to my ear. "I wish I could go with you."

But I was glad he couldn't. Despite his tentative sympathy, I couldn't forget his coldness in the dark. When I needed him.

I felt my way back up the stairs and into the blinding light of a single candle in Cat's room. Joan turned at the sound of my footsteps, took in my appearance in one glance, and shook her head. She drew the velvet curtain around the bed.

"Shhhh."

"Is the queen not asleep yet?" I asked.

"Yes, even now," she said. "I hope he was worth it."

She pushed me gently out the door and shut it in my face. Joan thought I was the one having an affair.

Jane Boleyn stood alone in the withdrawing room. Haggard. Pale.

"Good morning, Kitty," she said.

I gazed at her for a long moment. Had she already been through this once? With Anne Boleyn? Or was that all a fabrication to rid Henry of his second queen? And even if Jane hadn't been through it before, why was she doing it now?

"How do you do it, Jane?" I asked her.

"Do what?"

"Do what you're doing? Why do you allow this sort of thing to go on?"

"I'm not sure what you're talking about," Jane said.

"My friend is ruining her life," I said.

Jane moved to the outer door and checked behind it. She pulled me to the far corner of the room. Away from the windows. Away from the fire. Away from anything that could conduct our voices.

"Perhaps not."

"She's killing herself!" I said.

Jane made a *tsk* and I realized how dramatic and hysterical I sounded. Like a little girl throwing a tantrum. I took a breath.

"If word gets out, she could be executed," I said. "So could we."

"So we will not allow word to get out," Jane said. She placed a hand on my shoulder. Like a friend. Like a mother. Dispensing wisdom.

"She can't keep doing this!"

"But she will. No matter what we do or say. Look at it this way, Kitty. It's serving a purpose. One that cannot help but strengthen her position here at court. Strengthen the country as a whole. An heir to the throne, especially one from the conservative, Catholic-leaning Howard faction, would stabilize everything."

"You're letting this happen so she can get *pregnant*?"

"It is my duty to make her path smooth."

"That's not smooth, Jane, that's treason."

"No, Kitty, it's the way of the monarchy. Bastards have come to the throne before and will come to the throne again. The Duke of Richmond would have grown to be king had he not died and Prince Edward not been born. The king himself may be descended from the son of an archer and not the royal line at all. If the king cannot do what is necessary to produce children, then we must pursue other lines of possibility."

"So this is your idea?" I asked. "This doomed, ridiculous romance?"

"No!" Jane looked aghast. "I would never suggest such a thing."

"But you would promote it."

"I will do whatever the queen asks."

"Well, isn't that noble of you."

"It is my duty, Kitty," she said, and fixed me with her feline eyes. "And it is yours. You would do well to remember that."

"My duty is to my friend, not to the monarchy."

"Right now, the needs of both are one and the same, and that is your silence," Jane said. "At court, a word spoken is a word disseminated. Even if you think you are alone, you are not. Trust me on this."

I did. I had to. Because if anyone knew how secrets got out at court, Jane did.

37

WE CONTINUED SLOWLY THROUGH GAINSBOROUGH AND SCOOBY AND on to Hatfield, where we paused to spend a few days hunting. Every time we had new quarters, Cat sent Jane to search the castle or the house or the outskirts of the tent-laden field for secret hideaways and hidden entrances. I never questioned her. I knew why she sought them.

I watched. I felt that my very observation could somehow prevent Cat from doing anything more. Anything foolish. Anything obvious.

At Hatfield, I saw Jane shake her head after touring the four narrow wings and dim central courtyard. Nowhere to hide. Not enough space. Cat stayed quiet in her chambers, enclosed by the Coven, listening to music and tired gossip.

More than anything, I wanted to leave. I imagined going back to Lambeth, back to my parents, but knew that even there, people were always watching. Always finding fault. I wanted to go somewhere else. Somewhere I could breathe.

I would even marry Lord Poxy if it would get me out.

Jesus, I must be desperate.

I wished I could tell Cat, laugh with her about it. But the Coven, clucking and tutting, surrounded her.

Gossiping that perhaps she was pregnant.

"It must be why she doesn't ride," Cat's stepmother said quietly when the queen moved to look out the window. "What else could it be?"

"It's about time," Cat's sister muttered. "All his other wives were pregnant within three months."

"Not Anne of Cleves," the Countess of Bridgewater reminded them.

I moved restlessly away. I felt confined, all of us piled into the queen's apartments, waiting for the hunt to return. The closed square of the palace allowed contemplation of the surrounding countryside but cut off escape. I couldn't think straight breathing other people's air, their skirts touching mine, every rustle and whisper setting my teeth on edge.

"What are you thinking?"

The voice sounded calm. Comforting. Familiar.

It belonged to Alice Restwold.

"Nothing," I said. I almost wanted to confide in her. To open the circle again to Joan and Alice and Cat, our friendship like a bulwark against the gossip and the scheming. But Alice had William. And I couldn't break that wall.

"Is it true she's pregnant?" she asked.

"Aren't you the one who's supposed to know everything? How should I know if she's pregnant?"

"Or by whom?" Alice asked.

"I didn't say that."

"You didn't have to."

"She's married," I said firmly. "She's the queen of England. Whose child could she possibly have?"

"Whose indeed," Alice murmured. But she had that sly look about her. The look that carried secrets and used them as currency. Used them as weapons.

"Listen to me, Alice Restwold," I said, and gripped her by both arms. I topped her by at least a head and carried more weight on me, too. She was thin and pallid like a sickly child, and my fingers reached right around her upper arms and nearly met my thumbs.

"Listen to what, Katherine Tylney?" she said, her chin tilted to look me in the eye.

"You will not go spreading idle gossip in this place," I hissed. "You are one of the queen's ladies and as such you should be loyal only to her."

"Whoever said I wasn't?"

I itched to clout the smirk off her.

"You and I both know that you are loyal only to yourself," I said. "But if you breathe one word of gossip about Cat to anyone—*anyone*—I will come down on you like the sword of Damocles. I shall be watching you, the sword held by a hair, waiting to drop." A sudden anger lent force to my words and my fingers tightened involuntarily. I wanted to squeeze until

the blood stopped running to her hands. Maybe that would stop her mouth.

For a second, her eyes grew wide with fear. Then she shook me off.

"You can't threaten me, Kitty Tylney," she said. "I know too much about you. About Cat. About Lambeth."

"We all do, Alice," I reminded her.

A ghost of her smirk reappeared, but she leaned back into the shadows and all expression blurred.

"It's not like Cat was ever particularly discreet when she lived there," she said. "After all, she used to meet Francis Dereham in the back of the chapel."

"So we must be discreet for her," I said, panicked at her indifference to the danger we could all be in.

"For the love of God, Kitty," she said. "Grow up. I'm not likely to breathe a word, because I'm quite happy where I am. I'm in this for me, as you said. But Kitty, you should know better than anyone that your loyalty will get you nowhere."

"What do you mean by that?" I asked, taken off guard. My loyalty to Cat got me everything. It saved me from my parents' neglect. It bought my way out of Lambeth. It rescued me from Lord Poxy.

"I mean that you've been friends with Cat Howard for as long as I've known you. She can make all the promises in the world, swear enduring friendship, insist on her virtue and make everyone believe her. But it all comes down to Cat making Cat

happy. Nothing and no one else matters. At the end of the day, your loyalty means little to her, except for what it can make you do. But you're better than that. You're worth more than that. Surely by now you've begun to think for yourself."

"I've always thought for myself, thank you very much," I said, but the sharpness of my words couldn't keep tears of recognition from my eyes.

"Well, you've certainly never shown it."

The words stung. More so because she was right.

I looked over to Cat, staring vacantly out the window, and saw the way the sun played across her face and the blankness in her eyes. The formal garden outside appeared cramped and precise in contrast to the spread of the fields beyond. She didn't seem to notice any of it.

Then she changed. She stood taller, with her shoulders pulled back, and her bosom heaved like that of a balladeer's heroine.

I followed Cat's gaze and caught sight of Culpepper out the window. He sat on his horse, positioned for full view from Cat's window. He threw a glance over his shoulder and she caught it like a kiss on the wind.

I searched the room to see if anyone else had noticed. The Coven stooped over their endless tapestry silks. The other ladies hovered over a tray of delicacies. Jane Boleyn stood stark and brittle as a frozen sapling, her eyes darting from Cat to Culpepper and finally resting on Joan, who stood at Cat's elbow, ready with a selection of jewels for her hair, one hand raised in

immobile supplication. She stared at Cat openmouthed, blue-eyed and bewildered.

And the secret spread, held by another keeper.

I looked again out the window and caught sight of Edmund on a gray charger, his hair as flowing as the horse's mane. He saw me staring and flashed a knowing grin.

"That man could teach a girl a thing or two," Alice said quietly.

Her eyes were on Edmund. But she could very well have meant Culpepper.

"Maybe there are some things I don't want to learn," I said, and walked away. As if she hadn't already stolen the one man I'd ever wanted. As if Alice Restwold, purveyor of secrets, might not be collecting clues to treason.

I felt the sword myself, hanging by a thread above us all. And only our silence could save us.

38

Rumors of Cat's pregnancy hastened and expanded until the entire court, from the king to the cooks, watched her every move and studied every morsel she ate. She never said a word, did nothing to increase or dispel the rumors.

We moved on to Pontefract, the last days of August turning to autumn in the northern climate. In London, it would still be summer. But here in the northern wilds, the wind whipped across the jagged rocks of the hills and in through the shuttered windows. The timeworn castle stood isolated on a hill, proud and solitary, undulating fields and forests splayed below it.

"They say this was the favorite castle of Richard III," Alice told me. A king who, stories said, usurped his crown from his brother and murdered his nephews in the Tower of London.

"And King Richard II died here," she continued. "Imprisoned and starved to death. The local cook said both Richards might haunt the towers."

The wind sounded enough like ghosts as it was.

"Shut up, Alice," I muttered, unwilling to ponder treason and its shades.

Cat swept into the room, a furious bundle of energy, her face pale, hands clenched in fists so tight I could see the white of bone.

"I wish to speak with Mistress Tylney alone," she said.

The ladies moved gracefully, laying aside embroidery, casting lazy, disgruntled glances my way.

"I wish you all to leave me!" Cat shouted. The ladies jumped and scattered, leaving behind the detritus of court life: needles and thread, paper and chess pieces.

"Joan, Alice!" Cat said. "You stay here, also."

The Countess narrowed her eyes and stalked out the door, her lips twitching. Jane Boleyn paused, cast a quick look around the room, suddenly stark and colorless without its occupants, and closed the door behind her.

"What is it?" I asked.

"It's my grandmother."

"Is she not well?" I hadn't seen the duchess that morning, and it seemed a little disingenuous for Cat to be so concerned about her health.

"She wants me to employ a new secretary."

I failed to see the connection between this piece of information and Cat's agitated state.

"But you hate writing," Joan said. "A secretary would be a good thing."

"She wants me to appoint Francis Dereham."

"Francis!" I gasped. The duchess must have gone mad. There was no way a logical person would think placing Francis

in Cat's household would be a good idea. The endless odious possibilities flooded my mind.

"What the hell does she think she's doing?" Cat demanded.

"What did she say?"

"That he wants to better himself, the little weasel."

"Maybe he does just want a more advantageous position," I said lamely.

"He wants to take advantage of *my* position," Cat said hotly. "Like the rest of you. Even that horrible Mary Lascelles tried to worm her way in. As if I'd ever let her near me again, the miserable tattletale. But you lot I couldn't keep away."

A shocked silence overtook us. Rain flung itself against the shutters and sputtered in the fire.

"We just wanted to be with you, Cat," Joan said.

"So that's why you wrote me that letter?" Cat sneered. "Because you were in 'utmost misery' without me? Because of your love for me? Because of the 'perfect honesty' you have always found in me?" She said the words *utmost misery* and *perfect honesty* in a simpering mockery of Joan's childish lilt.

Joan gaped, open-mouthed.

"It's true, Cat," she said. "I *was* in misery without you. You'd promised Kitty. Alice had her family connections. And I had nothing."

I felt a quick, tight guilt. I would have left Joan behind. Sure as Cat left Francis when the light of something better shone.

"But you didn't have to resort to blackmail!" Cat wailed.

"I didn't blackmail you, Cat," Joan blubbered. "What are you talking about?"

"Perfect honesty?" Cat said. "What else could it mean? That you know the truth about Francis! That perhaps I am not honest, but your own conscience would behoove you to tell the truth if I didn't put you out of your misery."

Joan's rosebud mouth formed a perfect circle and her eyes brimmed with horrified tears.

"Oh!" she gasped, shook her head. "Oh, no!"

Cat stared at her. Narrowed her eyes. Then her face cleared.

"You mean you actually meant just what you said?" she said, still quick with doubt.

"Yes!" Joan protested. "I was miserable! You had promised Kitty. I just thought if I prompted you, I could be included in the promise. You believe me, don't you?"

She looked around at all of us, desperately. Wanting reassurance. I certainly couldn't imagine Joan Bulmer attempting anything so devious.

"Of course, Joan," I said. I snapped a quick smile at Cat.

"And all this time, you thought I would do that to you?" Joan asked, horrified.

Cat shrugged. Mystery solved. Matter forgotten.

"At least having you here has kept you quiet. It might work with Francis, too."

"The duchess is discreet," Alice reasoned. "She knows the

court. She wouldn't bring him here if it weren't safe. And the duke is here to keep an eye on things."

"And you know the duke so well," Cat snapped.

Alice looked taken aback.

"I suppose Francis is harmless," Cat said, waving away any concerns with her beringed hand.

I pictured Francis. The jaunty tilt of his cap when he swept into the maidens' chamber. The hangdog look on his face when Cat had dismissed him. How, when I saw him again at Lambeth, he made a show of appearing more dashing and important than he really was. The spite and jealousy in his voice when he told me about Cat and Culpepper.

"Are you sure?" I asked.

"Silly Kitty," she said. "He's safer here than out there." She flung her arm to the windows and the world beyond. "God only knows what he would say or who he would say it to out there, especially if I turned away his suit. If he's here, he'll know what's at stake. And stay quiet."

So I stayed quiet, too. I suppressed my doubts about Francis. And I suppressed my fears that Cat had brought me to court only to keep me quiet, not to keep me close.

39

FRANCIS STRUTTED INTO THE QUEEN'S CHAMBERS A FEW DAYS LATER, flaunting his chin dimple. His shoulders looked broader, his smile more determined.

"Your Majesty," he said, and bowed low before Cat, just as he had done in the maidens' dormitory.

"Master Dereham," Cat said. She clipped her words. They held as little warmth as that wind-chilled room.

"Lovely to see you again," Francis said, and gazed unflinchingly into her eyes. The Coven, nesting by the fire, rustled and whispered at this flagrant bravado.

"You were in my grandmother's household, were you not?" Cat asked.

I held my breath, willing Francis to play along.

"I was," he said.

I breathed again. He was coy, but perhaps he wouldn't endanger us. Yet.

"You work well with a quill?" Cat asked. "You are discreet?"

Questions that anyone would ask of a new secretary. Discretion was essential. Even if the secretary wasn't your ex-lover.

"I have been told that my handwriting flows like the Thames," Francis said.

I snorted. What a prat.

"And I can be as quiet as a mouse. At sea, we hold many secrets. What are a few more?"

"Well, you will not be keeper to any secrets, sir," Cat said. "My life is an open book. Anyone here can tell you of my love for my husband, my appreciation of music and dance, and my fondness for clothes and jewels and occasional lighthearted mischief. I'm afraid I consist of not much more than that."

"Of course." Francis grinned. "The Queen of Misrule."

"You mistake me, sir," Cat said, and I swore the temperature lowered around her. "And you mistake your place."

"Forgive me." Francis bowed low, eyes closed, face red. Fists clenched.

"I will call you when I have need of you," Cat said.

She leaned close to him and I heard her whisper icily, "Take heed what words you speak."

WE PROCESSED TO YORK, THE CENTER OF THE PILGRIMAGE OF GRACE, where the king bestowed his beneficence on abject city officials, who called out blessings and gratitude. And yet, we did not feel welcomed. The city walls hunched dark and foreboding—resistant to invasion and impending weather. The gates funneled us into the narrow streets, overhung with half-timbered buildings leaning fat and heavy like the rigging of a ship in full sail. The ancient minster perched at the north end of the city like a raven, black and looming against the heavy gray sky.

The people bowed grudgingly when we passed. They didn't care that their city was graced by the presence of the king and queen. All they knew was that the houses and inns and every courtyard were full of strangers who required rich foods, meat, wine, and ale, who would fill the gutters with waste and deplete the surrounding fields of the crops that should sustain the city through the winter and now wouldn't.

In their eyes, I saw that they hated us.

I understood better when I saw the sun-bleached skeleton of

the Abbey of St. Mary. The abbot's house had been renovated and richly furnished for our arrival. But the abbey itself looked beyond repair. Destroyed by the king's reformation.

The weather turned colder, and a miserable, mizzling rain fell. Cat kept me constantly by her side. Me and Joan and often Jane Boleyn. And when Jane wasn't with us, Cat sent me to her with cryptic messages. Promises. Accounts paid. And little gifts. "Two bracelets, to warm the arms." I noticed she didn't say whose arms.

Alice crept around the outskirts of our little quartet, disappearing for hours at a time. To the company of the Duke of Norfolk and his entourage. To William Gibbon. My heart twisted at the thought, so I turned my mind to Edmund instead.

He worked in shifts, guarding the king's chamber, and would find me at odd hours, stealing moments in dark corners and dim courtyards that left me breathless and confused. But wanted.

In September, at the end of a dreary day spent indoors with the Coven, Cat sent me to Jane's rooms at the opposite end of the abbey gardens. I slipped through the deepening shadows of the splintered church on my way back to Cat's apartments, carrying in my mind Jane's cryptic words, "If she sits up for it, I will the next day bring her word myself."

One shadow unhitched itself from the wall and spoke.

"Where have you been?"

"Edmund," I said. My voice betrayed the fact that he had frightened me. "I've been . . . out."

"Alone?" he asked. "Or perhaps sneaking about?"

"I wasn't sneaking," I said. But I couldn't tell him the truth.

"Oh, so it is habitual for you to wander?"

"I needed the air." My excuse sounded lame even to me.

"You needed nothing of the sort," he said, his voice hard. "You planned to meet someone."

"Now who would I be planning to meet?" I asked. My blood fizzled. Edmund's jealousy was shockingly misplaced and unfounded.

"Perhaps a lover?" he said, sinewy and sly. "That's why you shun me, why you play hard to get. There is someone else. A servant? A lord? A married earl?"

"I'm meeting no one," I said. "And I don't shun you." It wasn't as if he had expressed undying devotion.

"Then stop playing games with me, Kitty."

"I don't play games."

"You flirt with me," he said, ticking items off on his fingers. "Kiss me. Arouse me. And yet you make no effort to sleep with me."

I thought back. He always advanced, not I. I didn't want to appear too eager. Too wanton. But there was something else.

"I don't love you."

Edmund threw back his head and laughed.

"Love?" he said. "Who needs love?"

I do, I thought, but knew the answer would elicit more laughter.

"Courtly love is something else entirely," he said, stepping closer. "It's not the treacle of romantic ballads, the knight who dies in defense of his lady."

He put his arms around me.

"Courtly love is a dance," he said, his lips brushing the tender skin just below my ear. "A dance of flirtation. A dance of give . . ." he pushed ever so gently against me . . . "and take." He turned his head and kissed me.

And I let him. Lost myself and my fears in the solid reality of his body.

"I wonder about the appointment of the queen's secretary," he said, casually, breaking away from me. "Dereham. You knew him before, did you not? At Norfolk House."

"He . . . he was in the dowager duchess's employ," I said, my thoughts thrown into disorder by his rapid changes of topic and mood.

"He knew the queen, too, yes? I believe they used to go to chapel together."

"Everyone in Lambeth went to chapel together." Just not the same way Cat and Francis did. Edmund's knowledge struck too close to the truth, and it made me nervous.

"He got into an argument at the dinner table the other night. As a mere secretary, he is not entitled to stay at table with the queen's privy council after everyone else has risen. When Mr. Johns reprimanded him, Dereham replied, 'I was of

the Queen's Council before you knew her and shall be when she has forgotten you.' Now what do you suppose he meant by that?"

Oh, Francis, I thought, *your vanity always did get away with you.*

"He's just a popinjay," I said. "A loud-mouthed braggart. You shouldn't listen to anything that man says." My attempt at a laugh came out a sad bark.

"I could keep him quiet," Edmund said. "I could ensure his bragging goes no further."

"The queen would appreciate her secretary being held accountable."

"But little kitten," Edmund said. "Would you? What would you do to stem the tide of gossip in this court?"

"Gossip is a snake, ready to strike the innocent indiscriminately," I said. "It isn't worth the breath used to vocalize it."

"Then it is probably best to say nothing," he said, his lips against mine. "To seal the lips and speak no more."

He kissed me again. But it wasn't the tenderness I wished for. His hand squeezed the back of my neck, possessive, his lips hot and hard and tasting of charred meat and the malt-and-porridge tang of small beer.

This time, I couldn't kiss him back.

He stepped away.

"Not still thinking of that skinny coxcomb in the duke's employ?"

William. How did this man know everything?

"You didn't really believe he was interested, did you?" he asked. "In you?"

His question bridled me. What else did Edmund know? What did he know that I didn't?

"That creature is out for one thing only," Edmund persisted. "Advancement. He'll get it from the duke. He'll get it from Mistress Restwold. He thought he could get it from you."

"That's not true," I said. I knew it wasn't. But my voice betrayed me.

"The closest companion to the queen," Edmund continued. "That's quite a political connection."

I wanted to strangle him. To stop the words any way I could.

"You'd be foolish to think he'd want you for any other reason."

"Do you mean that I would be foolish to hope that someone would find me attractive? Would care for me?" I asked, my voice shaking. Because I had to hold onto that one piece of truth. That someone had cared about me for me.

"That's exactly what I mean."

The words staggered me backward. He was playing with me. Like a cat with its prey. Pawing at me. Digging in a claw and releasing. Watching the panic rise. Enjoying it.

"And I should think you my savior because you offer to take me to bed?" I managed to spit at him. "What a sacrifice you've made!"

"I've profited from our liaison, as well," he said. "It's not

been unpleasant. And it seemed to me I was giving you exactly what you wanted."

I shuddered at the thought of my own body's betrayal, because in a way, he was right. I tried to find the words to cut him, to make him as small and ashamed as I, but they were obstructed by the tears that threatened to engulf me.

Edmund turned and walked away and let me cry alone.

WE WAITED. FOR THE RAIN TO STOP. FOR THE KING'S NEPHEW, THE King of Scotland, to come for a royal confabulation. For an announcement of a coronation or a forthcoming heir for the throne. The buzzing swarm of gossip over Cat's possible pregnancy grew and intensified.

Francis Dereham lurked on the outskirts of Cat's entourage, ever present, like a toothache. Culpepper appeared occasionally, like the stabbing pain of a recurring injury. When they were in a room together, the very air fizzed like the aura of an impending lightning strike.

I told Cat about Edmund. And what he'd said of Francis's indiscretion.

"I can handle Francis Dereham," she said. "Make sure you handle Edmund Standebanke."

She winked suggestively. But where once that suggestion would have made me quiver with anticipation, it now just left me feeling more alone than ever. Isolated and confined by the court, by its occupants and its suffocating requirements.

I wondered if we would stay trapped in York, prisoners of the impending northern winter.

"Why doesn't he crown me and just be done with it?" Cat grumbled one day while Joan and Alice helped her dress, and I tended the fretful little fire in the grate.

"Did he say he would?" Joan asked, lacing Cat's bodice.

"I suppose it's no secret," Cat continued. "He certainly hinted hard enough. Remember our game of hide-and-seek?"

"What about it?" Joan asked.

"Tighter, Joan," Cat said. "Remember the king gave me a crown of roses? And said I should wait for the rest of my prize until we got to York? What else could it have been?"

So what was he waiting for?

"This is just as tight as it was yesterday, Cat," Joan said. "The edges of your bodice overlap."

"So?" Cat said. "Just tie the damned thing and be done with it. I'm sick of you two flapping around me."

"But Cat," Joan said as she knotted the stays, "if you're pregnant, you should be getting bigger."

Cat whirled and slapped Joan across her cheek. Joan reeled backward and tripped over me, sending the pan of ash flying from my hands.

"It doesn't matter if my belly grows yet," Cat snarled. "I'm young and I'm fit and perhaps the baby won't show at all!"

We all stared at her. It was the first time Cat had spoken of a baby. A bubble of foreboding formed in my stomach, thinking of all the things that could go wrong in childbearing. The baby catching its neck in a noose of umbilical cord. The mother bleeding to death minutes after birth. Childbed fever.

Then the dread burst like an abscess when I wondered whose baby it might be.

"Are you really pregnant, Cat?" Joan asked from the floor, a cloud of ash settling upon her.

"I haven't had my monthly courses yet," Cat said.

"When was your last one?" Alice asked.

"As if you don't know, Alice Restwold," Cat said. "You're probably keeping a daily diary of every time I bleed, pee, or fart."

Joan giggled.

"Oh, so a queen can't use rude words?" Cat said, a grin spreading across her face. "Just because I made an oath to be bonny and buxom in bed and at board doesn't mean I've signed away my tongue."

"Ah, but Cat, you wouldn't use those words at the table," Joan said.

"Certainly not!" Cat said. "But I am here with my dearest friends and you have no reason to divulge my secrets. Except for Alice, of course."

"I have no reason . . ." Alice began and then stopped, turning helpless eyes to Cat.

"Go, Alice," Cat said tiredly. "Go and tell the duke that I said 'fart.' Tell him I haven't started my cycle and I was supposed to seven days ago. Go and tell him all. And then tell him to go stuff himself and to stay off my back or I'll never produce an heir, just to spite him. Go and tell him to hang for all I care."

"I—I don't know what you mean," Alice said.

"You've been feeding the duke information about me since the moment you arrived in my apartments."

"No," she said. She stood, small and quiet, by the door. Not looking at any of us. She had always been one of us, but not part of us, and her separation now felt palpable.

"Yes, you have."

"Maybe you have it wrong, Cat," Joan said, "Like with me and my letter."

"Call me Your Majesty!" Cat shouted, and Joan cringed against the hearth. "And I don't have it wrong. What do you think brought her here?"

"Her family connections," I said quietly. Wanting things to stay the same. Wanting to depend on the family of girls. Wanting the circle to remain unbroken.

"Alice's family connection was the duke," Cat said. "You're the one who told me he was looking for a spy, Kitty. He's the one who asked me to take on Alice. I didn't need any great intellect to decipher that puzzle."

"Is it true, Alice?" I asked her. If anything, she appeared smaller than before. About to disappear.

She nodded. Looked up at me, desperately.

"I tell him what he wants to know and nothing more. When she sleeps. When the king visits."

"Intimate details of my life!" Cat shouted.

Joan whimpered.

"This is the royal court!" Alice cried. "The courtiers know the consistency of the king's shit. If the duke didn't hear about

it from me, he would hear it from someone else. He just wanted a reliable source."

"It's still spying, Alice," I said. "No matter how you dress it up."

"It's what got me here," she said. "And Joan got here through blackmail."

"I didn't do it!" Joan said. Tears were streaming down her face.

"It's still why you're here," Alice said. "Without secrets, none of us would be here. Not me, not you. Not Francis."

"You're right, Alice," Cat said in a low growl. "Without secrets, none of us would be here. Not even me."

She approached Alice steadily, primed for an attack.

"I know that, Cat," Alice said. "We all know that. I only tell him what he needs to know. He has to know first, or he'll send me back to my husband. I can't go back, Cat."

"Call me Your Majesty."

"Yes, Your Majesty," Alice whispered.

Cat smiled.

"Go on, then," she said. "Get out. All of you."

Alice was out the door almost before she threw the latch. Joan wiped her face with ash-covered hands, smearing streaks of tears and soot. She looked broken, walking out the door. I picked up the discarded clothes from the floor and stuffed them in an already overflowing chest before turning to leave.

"I'm so tired, Kitty," Cat said, quietly enough that I almost missed it.

"You need to rest," I said.

"Tired of everything," she said. "The gossip and lies and secrets and truth."

"Are you really pregnant, Cat?" I asked, unable to stop myself.

"How should I know? I've never been pregnant before. I don't know what it feels like."

She sounded shrill. Evasive.

"Because," I said, running my words together in my haste to begin the argument so it would be over sooner, "If you are, I think you should stop."

I left *seeing Culpepper* off the end of the sentence. But Cat heard it anyway.

"All we do is talk," she said.

"He's not a good person, Cat."

"This discussion is concluded."

If I told her, maybe she would put an end to it, and it would all be forgotten. No one would ever know how close we came to treason. Even I would never need know the baby's parentage. One more piece of information I could let go. One more secret none of us would have to keep.

"No!" I said. "No, it isn't."

"Kitty," she said, "You don't want to do this."

"I have to tell you. I saw him. I saw him . . ."

I couldn't say it. After so much time, I couldn't say the words.

"I don't want to know," Cat said. She stood, ready to leave.

"But you must." I found my voice. "I saw him raping a girl in the park. In Lambeth."

The words themselves caused me to shake. A blind veil of horror passed down over my eyes as the images flashed back through my mind.

"The King pardoned him," Cat said. "I don't know why you bring it up."

"What?" She knew? I shook my head. She couldn't know.

"He was pardoned. That must mean what he did was pardonable."

"He raped her!"

"That's what she said. She's a peasant! He's a gentleman usher. Emphasis on the word gentleman."

"But he did it, Cat. Don't you hear what I'm telling you? I saw him."

The woman on the ground, her hair tangled in the fallen branches and crumbling leaves. Culpepper's determined smile. The growl of his voice. Telling her she wanted it.

And suddenly it all came clear. That's what he told the king, too. What he told Cat. And they believed him. I had kept the truth hidden for so long it distorted, gave the appearance of falsehood.

"You don't believe me," I said.

"Kitty," she said pleasantly. "You're just jealous."

I could think of no response. No justifiable reaction to the queen of England telling me a deliberate falsehood.

"You should be happy for me," she said. "Because I have

everything I've ever wanted. Everything I need to make me happy. Pretty clothes. Beautiful jewels. And the company of a man my own age who understands *exactly* what I want."

"But do you love him?" I asked.

"No!" she replied. "And the sooner you realize you don't need love, Kitty, the happier you'll be. I'll tell you what you need. You need firm, strong thighs, hot lips, and hands that know what they're doing."

"And all you do is talk."

Her mouth hardened and she twisted one of her many rings.

"It happens in all friendships," she said. "When one girl gets a man. The others feel left out. Abandoned. Left behind.

"And now you've ruined things with your own lover. You've lost him. And you want me to do the same. You're lying to make Thomas Culpepper look bad. And that's just ugly."

She studied me critically. My clothes. My hair. My face.

"It makes you ugly."

Each word landed like a blow. I flinched. And I thought I saw her smile.

42

I WENT OUT INTO THE RAIN-SLICK COBBLED STREETS OF YORK. Corpulent clouds hung over the inns and merchants' shops. Carcasses dangled from hooks outside the butchers', headless and dripping blood. Living quarters crowded over the shops, open windows allowing waste, words, and laughter to spill out and over me.

I walked blindly. I wanted to walk forever, rain or no rain. I wanted to go home. But I had no home to go to.

"How did I get into this mess?" I asked myself aloud. A woman dressed in an unwashed skirt and tattered cap stepped around me and hurried away.

Not only was I feeling crazy, but I looked crazy, too. Like someone not to be believed.

I listened to Cat, I followed her, because it was easier than standing up to her. I let her tell me what to do. What to think. What to want.

But what did I want? Not this. Not a partial existence of lies and deceit and relationships so hollow they cracked like empty eggshells. I had thought that I wanted to be at court, like the games we played as children. But the reality was a life of doing

Cat's bidding. To her it was still just a game. And all of us Cat's pawns to play as she pleased.

I stumbled to my knees on the cobbles. The blow allowed a sob to escape me. The pain felt good, sharp and distracting.

"Let me help."

William Gibbon leaned over me, a hand outstretched to assist me to my feet. As always, he was dressed in the Duke of Norfolk's livery, his boots shiny beneath the mud spattered there. One eye was hidden by a shock of hair, the other wary. His touch sent a flutter of gooseflesh up my arm. And perhaps he held my hand just a little longer than necessary. But not long enough.

I looked around, like a person waking from a very real dream, and saw that I had walked three quarters of a circle and was now headed back to the queen's lodging.

William thought I was Cat's shadow. Her stooge. William was keeping company with Alice Restwold. But the sight of him felt like the first good thing to happen in this drenched and unhappy city on this long and arduous progress.

"Why so melancholy?" he asked. Then he looked at me. Really looked at me. Not the challenging gaze of Edmund, daring me to give in to him. Not the skeptical gaze of Cat, suspecting that I would turn her in. Not the prying gaze of Alice or the ingenuous gaze of Joan. The searching, concerned gaze of a real friend. A friend I couldn't have.

"I'm afraid I tend to think too much when I'm alone," I said. There was no way I could tell him the truth.

"Ah, but at court, you are never alone."

"So I never think, is that what you're saying?" I asked. I meant to sound flippant, teasing, but the words came out sniping and pinched.

"That isn't what I intended," he said, looking away, twin splotches of pink on his cheeks. "I've always known you could think for yourself."

"But that's not what you said," I blurted. "You said I was Cat's shadow."

"I said too much," he murmured.

So did I.

I didn't know how to tell him. How to fight my way around the lies and the hurt and the secrets and my own betrayal. How to stop the tyrannical compression of emotion in my chest.

"I just never imagined court would make you happy," he said. "Court and all that goes with it."

"Pretty clothes," I said, echoing Cat's words. "Beautiful jewels." The words crumbled and dissolved like wafers on my tongue, with none of the sweetness. Dust.

"Pretty clothes?" he asked. "I believe that is what the queen wants. Or at least that is what she believes she wants. I don't know about every girl."

"You're wrong," I said. "Every girl wants to feel pretty. Every girl wants to *be* pretty."

"I know a girl who used to wear hand-me-down gowns so unbecoming they would make the angels ugly, and yet she wore them with grace and beauty because of who she was."

I couldn't reply. Just over a year ago, that girl had been me. I suddenly, desperately wanted her back. Shabby clothes and all. The livery of the unloved. Except, maybe I had been loved. I wanted to believe that. Despite what Edmund had said.

"What happened, William?" I blurted. "To us?"

"Us?" The look of hope that crossed William's face bordered on desperation.

I wanted to reach for him. But I didn't know how. There was so much in the way. Cat. Edmund. Alice. Me.

"You said . . ." he didn't finish. His hand went to his cheek where I had slapped him, and something crushed the hope from his eyes.

"I didn't mean it," I spoke so quickly my words garbled in my mouth. "You told the truth. About so much."

The crooked smile stoppered me as effectively as a cork in a bottle. A sad smile.

"I was wrong to tell you what to do," he said.

"But since then I've made so many bad choices. I don't know what's right anymore. I hold so many secrets."

"Secrets just get in the way," he said. He'd said it before.

It wasn't by choice. It was by necessity. I waited on the queen. Living the lie that was life as a courtier. Living the dream. That had become a nightmare.

The membrane that held the rain at bay finally snapped and water fell from the sky like a bucket of slops thrown from an overhanging window. It shook us awake and back to reality. Back to the lie.

William tried to shield me from the rain with his cloak. Ever the gentleman. The action brought him close enough for me to feel the warmth of his body and breathe in his fragrance of pine resin and autumn leaves.

"Allow me to escort you," he said. "Before we become as waterlogged as the city of York itself."

We walked together, matching strides on the cobbles, not speaking. I didn't want to break the magic spell that had somehow brought us together under that cloak.

We arrived too soon at the abbey, the unroofed nave and cloister crowded with tents dragged low and heavy by the rain. We stood beneath the arch in the great north wall, sheltered from the worst of the weather.

"I'm glad you came out today," he said, and leaned closer. I thought, for a brilliant, glowing instant, that he might kiss me.

"Well met, Mistress Tylney," he said, the hope in his face masked. And with a quick bow, he was gone. Back to the duke. And his other responsibilities.

And I had to return to mine.

43

THE KING PROWLED THE GALLERIES AND COBBLED STREETS LIKE SOME kind of cornered predator, like the lions he kept in the Tower of London. Dukes and earls and ladies and council ministers fed off his agitated energy and spread it through the entire court like the plague.

I watched Cat's enemies gather in the darkness. The Seymours who had been displaced when the Howards came to power. Elizabeth Cromwell, her father-in-law beheaded the day Cat was married. The families of mistresses past and future.

We spent yet another rainy day endlessly sewing. I wondered at all the shirts we sewed. For the poor. For Cat's husband. How many shirts did he need? Or was it like the fairy tales, and the things unsewed themselves every night? Was she forever sewing the same shirt, like Sisyphus pushing the rock up a mountain for all eternity?

I sat in the corner of the too-hot room, unobtrusive and unnoticed. Weary of the false gaiety of the wall-hangings and draperies brought from London. Knowing that when we left, the dark paneling, the tiny windows, the yawning hearth would echo empty and ugly as the gossip of the Coven.

"The duke will never return to his wife," the countess said shrilly, speaking of her half-brother, the Duke of Norfolk. "She has become too shrill. Too demanding."

I wondered that her own husband didn't desert her.

"But I don't indulge in gossip," she continued, pretending integrity. "It harms the bearer as much as the subject."

The irony was lost on her audience.

Suddenly, Cat cringed and gasped. Everyone stopped mid-stitch and mid-sentence.

"Are you well, Your Majesty?" Jane asked.

"Quite well," Cat said, and sat up straighter, her face pale.

But seconds later she gasped again and curled up into herself.

I knew immediately what it was.

Her courses.

I jumped up to go to her, but she stilled me with a look.

"I have no need of you, Mistress Tylney," she said.

Someone tittered. The others bent their heads over their sewing, but their eyes flickered up to Cat every other heartbeat. Cat bit her lip and poked her needle at the hem of the shirt she worked.

Cat cringed again and a sound escaped her, the kind a wild animal makes when injured and afraid.

"You are not well, Your Majesty," Jane said, rising and going to her. "Let me help you to bed."

Cat said not a word but allowed Jane to assist her to the bedchamber.

"Something warm," Jane said over her shoulder to Joan. "And a cloth, please, Kitty?" she asked. "She will need only her chamberers."

I found the stash of special cloths and bundled one, moving swiftly. Joan pulled a hot stone from beside the fire and wrapped it in fur to place behind Cat's back.

Alice disappeared.

Cat curled up and tears slipped from the corners of her eyes.

"I thought I might be . . ."

She didn't finish. We all knew what she thought.

"God's blood!" A shout and the bang of the door to the outer chamber made us jump. "Where is my niece?"

The cackling of the Coven preceded a heavy knock at the bedchamber door. It flew open before I could reach it. The duke, red in the face, his small body swollen with self-importance and righteous vitriol, pushed past me.

"She is in bed, Your Grace," I said, falling into a curtsey.

"In the middle of the day?" he asked.

"She is unwell, Your Grace." Jane Boleyn stepped in. She, too, curtseyed, and then stood to face him. The duke, in his black velvet doublet with gold piping, looked like something the devil dragged in. Jane, in pale blue and yellow, stood placid and unmoving. He looked as shocked as I felt by her defiance.

"She is not so unwell that she cannot receive her uncle." The duke shouldered his way past Jane. Unable to cow her with his anger, he had to resort to physical bullying.

"It is a ladies' ailment, Your Grace," Jane said.

"I don't care if it's the plague itself."

Cat lay cocooned in crimson velvet. The bed, transported by cart all the way from Greenwich, stood high and wide, but the duke looked ready to drag her from it bodily.

"Do you not bow before your queen?" she said, her voice edged.

"You are menstruating," the duke said by way of reply.

"It is none of your business," Cat snapped.

"I make it my business."

"Then unmake it."

"You stupid girl!" he shouted. As if Cat had any choice to control it.

"Go away, uncle," Cat muttered and turned from him.

"If you don't get yourself with child, we will all be thrown out!" the duke blasted.

"It's not entirely up to me, you know," Cat said.

The duke leaned so close to her face that Cat turned away, corners of her mouth down and nose pinched.

"If you so much as breathe that in less loyal company, we will all lose our heads," he hissed, ignoring her expression. "And you will do what is required of you, or you will not have my loyalty much longer."

Cat laughed to the closed curtains on the other side of the bed.

"I'm a Howard," she said. "The Howards stick together."

"I helped put your cousins' heads on the block," the duke sneered. "If you think I will come to your rescue or welcome

you back to the fold after disgrace, you are very much mistaken. But you will earn the loyalty of every man at court if you put an heir in a royal cradle."

"By any means necessary?" Cat asked.

The duke's head snapped back. He gazed at her for a long moment. And stalked out of the room.

"Go away." Cat waved at us dismissively, as if shooing flies. "Leave me alone. All of you."

Jane followed me from the bedchamber in time to see the Coven still swirling and stirring in the wake of the duke. I took advantage of the confusion to pull her aside.

"She's going to use this as an excuse!" I said. The whole country wanted Cat to get pregnant to provide an heir for the king. I wanted her pregnant to provide protection from Culpepper.

Jane looked at me. She didn't nod or blink or speak. But I heard the faint tremolo of pearls in her pocket.

"How can you of all people just stand by? How can you actively participate?"

"What do you mean, me of all people?" she asked.

She was being purposefully obtuse, and it made me want to hurt her.

"You," I said, allowing my words to come out sharp as a new blade, "who watched your husband and his sister lose their heads over the exact same issue that you now facilitate."

"My husband was accused of incest," Jane said, casting a flickering glance about her. "I see nothing of that sort happening here."

"I thought you were a grown-up," I spat. "I thought you were a mentor."

Jane's expression changed for a fraction of an instant. Sadness. Pain. My words had done their work. Then the courtier was back.

"You have no call to be so blunt, Kitty," she said. "I have done nothing to you."

"No, and you've done nothing for Cat, either," I retorted. "Nothing good, anyway."

Jane stared at me with eyes the color of the withering fields beyond the city walls. The eyes of a woman who had seen great sorrow. Who saw terror and possibly madness in the future. It filled me with remorse.

"I'm sorry, Jane."

"Don't feel sorry for me, Kitty," she said, her voice so cold I almost flinched. "I'm not worth it."

As the ladies of the court nibbled over the gossip that Cat's pregnancy had come to naught, the king and his councilors plotted our journey south.

"Oh, Kitty, we're finally going home!" Joan pulled me into a little dance.

"Home?" I muttered. How could you have a home if all you did was move from place to place? Hampton Court to Windsor to Greenwich to Whitehall to every godforsaken castle in the North. York certainly wasn't home. But neither was London.

Cat recovered from her cramps, and her smile returned.

"There is still time for a coronation," she said. "I always wanted to be crowned in Westminster, anyway, not some hell-hole like York."

A huge final banquet was scheduled to see us off. The Court illustrating extravagance and power with one last hurrah. The people of York celebrating our impending absence.

Cat dithered endlessly over jewelry. She barked at the Coven for wearing hoods that hinted at a peak of gable. She chose and discarded five gowns.

"I've worn that one," she said. "That one has too high a neckline. That color orange makes me look ill."

The ladies clustered and twittered around her, their skirts brushing the floor in a rhythm like waves on a riverbank.

"I shall dress in my most girlish pink," Cat said finally. "All hope and innocence and freshness. He will forget the baby never happened, and remember why he married me."

When she had secured her hair with jeweled pins, she weighted her neck with the diamond collar—the C glittering at her throat.

"You are beautiful, Your Majesty," the members of the Coven cooed, and Joan nodded with eager abasement.

"Attend me," Cat said when she was ready, and the others followed her into the gallery, the flock that moved as one. I closed the door behind them.

I couldn't face the crowd. The press of flesh and fabric. The stink of meat and men. I wanted the scent of ripe apples, and a round, river breeze. Being alone in Cat's chambers would have to do.

I picked up Cat's gowns and folded them carefully, wondering why I bothered. She would just take them out again the next day. Or never wear them at all. But I stroked the soft fabrics and laid them gently to rest.

I cleaned the ash from around the fireplace, my hands stinging from the lye. I washed my hands in the basin and fetched fresh water for Cat to use when she returned.

I picked up Cat's discarded nightdress and hung it on a peg

on the wall near the window. The sunlight shone through the fine linen, bright white as if created from the sky itself. Not like we used to be, in our nightclothes worn ragged, stained yellow by sisters we rarely saw.

I twitched open the bed curtains, chasing dust and ash. I straightened the tangled furs and smoothed the linens. The bed was so large that even I had to stretch to reach the middle of it. I heard the door creak behind me.

"Ah, now that's how I like my ladies," Edmund Standebanke said. "Bent over and exposing the arse."

I spun around and backed up to the bed, wanting to hide the area mentioned. I didn't want him thinking proprietarily of my backside or anything else.

"You have not been invited," I said.

"That looked like an invitation to me."

I held my ground. But the room, with its crowded tapestries and heavy velvet curtains suddenly felt very small and close, and the heavy oak door, shut tight against the empty sitting room, looked very far away.

"Please leave the queen's bedchamber," I said. "It isn't seemly for a man to be in here."

"But I am not the first," he said. "However, I can be discreet. I *have* been discreet, and will continue to be so. Given the right enticements."

"I'm sure the queen could find you a better position," I stalled.

"I am happy where I am," he said.

"You wouldn't say anything." I faked a bravado I didn't feel.

"Not about Culpepper," he said with a grin. "No, he'd kill me. But I've heard that you have a penchant for late nights. For stolen wine and spiced wafers."

Someone had told. Someone had let slip the stories of our midnight revels.

"Who told you that?"

"A little bird."

"What else did you hear?"

"That you were not the only one to share Catherine Howard's bed."

He knew everything. As yet, Edmund Standebanke had kept quiet about his friend and the queen. But would he keep quiet about her past? And this was not only Edmund endangering us. This was someone else. Someone who had already proven to have a loose tongue. I had to dispel the rumor before it grew more legs.

"Did Alice tell you that?"

"No, Mistress Restwold has been too busy with the Duke of Norfolk's entourage, hasn't she?"

"Well," I said, trying to keep my voice from shaking, "gossip isn't the word of God."

"It came from a very reliable source."

"Then it didn't come from any of the girls who lived with us in Lambeth!" I laughed, but had to rub my palms on my skirt to stop them trembling and sweating.

"Oh, a disreputable lot, then?" he leered. "And your reputation as tattered as the rest of them."

"You can say nothing about me that anyone would mind," I said. "I am a mere servant here." I gestured at the room, showing the work I had done.

"It may not be you who needs my protection, but it is you who desires it."

"I don't know what you're talking about."

"The queen has been indiscreet," he stated.

"It is treason to speak ill of the queen," I reminded him, but my warning had little effect.

"Perhaps when Anne Boleyn first came to the throne," Edmund said. "But she proved that a queen can be ruined by injudicious actions and immodest gossip."

A chill ran through me.

"You wouldn't," I whispered.

He stepped closer still, so that I had to bend backward to avoid his barrel chest and prominent codpiece. He smelled of soot and stale sweat.

"What wouldn't I do?" he asked, his voice a purr. "Tell on your little friend? No. Probably not. The court is so boring without a queen and her ladies. But you don't really want to find out."

"You don't care about me. I don't think you even find me attractive." I immediately wanted to snatch back my words. As if I cared what this man thought.

"I never said that."

He just implied it.

"Why are you doing this?" I asked.

"Because I have no choice in the matter." He bent to kiss me.

That was what Culpepper had said, back in Lincoln. Edmund did whatever Thomas Culpepper asked. They were two sides to the same coin.

Repulsed, I wriggled myself backward and away from him, up onto the bed. But he followed, matching my movements. Covering my body with his.

"No!" I cried, my voice cut off as his weight pressed the air from my lungs.

"You cannot refuse," he said quietly, nuzzling me. "Not to save your reputation. Nor to save yourself for your fiancé, for he can give you no pleasure, of that I am sure."

I struggled, but he held me tighter.

"You know you want me," he said and lifted himself to stroke the embroidery where the neck of my bodice met my skin. I had. But I didn't anymore.

When he kissed me, I no longer felt the feverish rush that had overwhelmed my senses. His tongue forced its way between my teeth, wet and abhorrent. I pushed at him, but it only seemed to make him heavier.

So I bit him, the metallic taste of his blood following swift upon the grease of his lips. He cursed and moved to strike, but I rolled out from under him and slid off the bed to my knees, my skirts pulling up to expose my legs.

He reached for me, but seized only my snood, which ripped

290

at my hair as it came off. I cried out at the pain, the tiny hairs at my temples pulling tears to my eyes. I stumbled to my feet, but his other hand was too quick and snagged me around my waist.

"Let go!" I cried, and reached blindly for the door handle. He pulled me toward him, arms tightening. I laid my fingers upon the latch and pulled with all my might.

The door swung open with a lurch and slammed into the wall behind us. The movement sent us reeling backward, and Edmund dropped me to the floor, panting. Running footsteps approached.

"How dare you use the queen's rooms in such a disrespectful manner?"

Edmund pushed away from me, leaving me quaking at his feet.

"It was not without provocation, sir," he said.

"Hussy," the voice growled. I looked up to see one of the duke's gentleman pensioners. Next to him, Edmund stood nose-to-nose with William Gibbon.

Fear kicked me in the chest.

"It's not what it looks like," I said. Edmund's codpiece was askew. My skirts were hiked above my knees, sleeves coming loose, snood thrown to the floor and my hair tumbling around my face. I stood and tried to straighten the disarray. Miserable tears blinded me.

"She invited me." Edmund smirked.

"I did not!" I cried, anger replacing misery.

"She's been trying it on with me for weeks now," he continued.

I risked another glance at William and his gaze slid off mine like oil from water. If only I could speak to him alone. If only Edmund Standebanke had a modicum of honor.

"I did not invite this man to this room," I insisted.

The other man snorted. But I didn't care if he believed me.

"I stayed behind to tend to the queen's affairs," I said to William, my words tumbling over each other in their haste to be heard. "To tidy the room and straighten the bed."

"You are always at the queen's side," William replied, his voice even. "You would never be left behind."

"She stayed behind for me," Edmund declared. Enjoying himself. No matter what, he came out of the situation looking great. He was a man.

He was believable.

And what could I say? I hadn't told anyone I would stay behind. I doubted that anyone even noticed I was missing. It looked exactly as Edmund made it out.

"I wished to be alone," I admitted, looking William directly in the eye, willing him to believe me.

"With me," Edmund agreed. Smug bastard. I couldn't even look at him. I couldn't let him see the irreparable damage he was doing. He would consider it a triumph.

"A word of advice," the other man said, winking at Edmund. "Keep out of the queen's rooms when you're looking for romance."

I could have screamed with fury.

"And what are you doing here?" Edmund puffed up his chest as if intending to push William over with it.

"We heard a disturbance," William said. "And thought we should investigate."

I risked a glance at him, but his face was as blank as a new piece of parchment. Doing his duty. Blocking me out. Forgetting about me.

"Well, heaven forbid I interfere with the men of the Duke of Norfolk," Edmund said, his voice dripping with sarcasm. He slithered out of the door with a flourish as if bowing to William and the other man, though the move was more show than substance.

"There is obviously nothing for me here," he added, throwing me a look of contempt, and strode away up the gallery to the banquet.

I struggled for breath in relief of his absence, grasping the bedpost for support.

"Are you well, Mistress Tylney?" William asked, hollow courtesy emptying his words of meaning.

"I am innocent." I tried not to sob. But was I? Guilt, like secrets, multiplied at court. I *had* wanted Edmund. Once.

"Any maid who allows a man into her bedchamber cannot be as innocent as you wish us to think," the other man laughed.

William turned scarlet.

"From what I hear, the queen's chamberers are not as pure as Christmas snow," the man continued. His eyes traveled down my bodice.

"Cease, man," William said. I turned to him but he did not acknowledge me. "Let us escort the lady to the banquet."

I didn't want to go to the banquet. I didn't want to have anything to do with the court anymore. I hated the drudgery and the tedium. I hated the people and their superficiality. Most of all, I hated the lies. But I shoved my hair into place and brushed down my skirts. I was not going to let Edmund Standebanke win.

"Lady," the other man muttered under his breath, but I ignored him and left the room. I walked with my head up, looking neither right nor left and they both fell into step behind me. I quailed at the thought of all the eyes that would be upon me when I entered the hall. Eyes that would take in my dishevelment. Ears that would already have heard the rumors of my illicit misdeeds in the queen's chambers.

But when I entered the banqueting hall, all eyes were focused on Cat. And though she pretended to pay them no heed, the attention made her more radiant. She glowed like a candle flame, and all the men in the room were moths drawn to it.

So even Cat didn't notice me as I stood in the grand entranceway. Cat, who had known my thoughts and feelings and secrets for almost ten years. Even Cat didn't know that the man she chose had just forced himself on me in her bed. I stared, my wide eyes dry. Even as my world fell apart, she remained its focus, and that of everyone in the room.

A cough at my elbow reminded me of William and the other

liveried man behind me. I turned and William lowered his eyes. He had been watching me.

And I'd missed it.

"We will leave you now," the other man said and they walked away.

William didn't speak a word.

It was a much more subdued court that followed the rather convoluted path back to London. Autumn clouds hung low in the sky, tinting everything drab. Mud-colored leaves drooped on the trees and the harvested fields looked like the stubble of a man's unshaven face. The people no longer clamored on the roads to see us but kept to their houses, battening down for the winter, as if they knew a storm was coming.

Alice practically lived with the duke's traveling entourage. Cat put up a bright façade, shrouded in jewels. Jane maintained her quiet steadfastness. Joan scampered around the outskirts like a lost lapdog. I did my job and kept my mouth shut. I avoided Edmund. And William. And everyone. I was alone in the middle of the most crowded court in Christendom.

At Hull, Culpepper sported a new jeweled cap. An expensive one.

"What's that for?" I heard Francis growl at him in a corner of the banqueting hall.

"To keep my head warm." Culpepper grinned. "Reward for services rendered."

I had seen Jane with it the day before.

And then one night in early October, in some castle that seemed as much of a blur as the rest—it could have been Ampthill, it could have been Kettleby—Jane came back from one of her reconnaissance missions and cornered me.

"The queen needs help this evening."

"With what?" I asked, unable to control my insolence.

"She needs you."

Cat always needed me. To steal a key for her. Lie for her. Keep her secrets.

"What if I don't want to help?"

"I'm afraid it has nothing to do with what you want, Katherine Tylney," Jane said. "You have no choice in the matter. You are here as the queen's servant, and as her servant you will comply with her wishes. Not your own."

I couldn't walk away from this. Life with the queen was like the marriage I'd always feared. My time, my thoughts, my life were not my own. I was completely beholden to another. A possession.

"Fine."

"You will invite Edmund Standebanke to the outer rooms," Jane began.

The very thought made me want to run. How dare Cat ask this of me? But of course, Cat didn't know. She had never asked. She had never noticed.

"No."

"It is your duty."

"It is my duty to make the queen's bed. It is my duty to take charge of her gowns and shifts and laces. It is my duty to clean up after her and tend to her needs. It is *not* my duty to consort with that man."

"You say it is your duty to tend to the needs of the queen," Jane said reasonably. "This evening she needs someone to provide a distraction."

"No," I said. "And I will talk to Cat about it."

I barged my way into her bedchamber and slammed the door behind me.

"You can't make me do this," I said without preamble. "I won't do it."

Cat looked up. She sat by the fire. Alone, for once.

"I provide a perfectly respectable, devilishly handsome man to you at your disposal and you do nothing," Cat said coolly.

Devilish, indeed. My skin burned with anger at the injustice. But I remained silent. I had no need, no wish for my story to become gossip. Or a weapon to be used against me.

"Why is that?" she asked.

"He is not respectable," I said. "He is not honorable."

"Perhaps you are not that way inclined," Cat said, her face as pinched as her words. "Perhaps you miss the evenings in the maidens' dormitory. Perhaps you miss sharing a bed with me, with Joan. You prefer the company of women. The bodies of

women. Perhaps *that* is why Standebanke hasn't got you into bed yet."

I stared at her. If Cat's words escaped that room, I would be thrown from court, my engagement nullified, my prospects eradicated, my future corrupted.

"You shouldn't say things that aren't true, Cat."

"It doesn't matter if it's true," Cat sneered. "Once it's uttered, people believe it. Just like they believe that Archbishop Cranmer has a wife, or Anne Boleyn had sex with her brother, or Catherine of Aragon consummated her marriage to her first husband. Once it's said, you can never shake it."

She let her words hang in the air. Everything stopped moving, trapped in the amber of fear.

"You never had a boy visit you in the maidens' chamber, did you?" she asked.

She knew I hadn't.

"I never met the right one," I said. Thinking of William. I met him too late.

"The *right* one?" she repeated. "*Any* one would do. I for one didn't want to go into a marriage not knowing what to expect. And finding someone handsome enough, with decent *equipment*, wasn't difficult."

Her statement brought to mind a long-past conversation.

"What about rich?" I asked. "And powerful?"

"That came later," she said. "The maidens' chamber was all about *fun*. I didn't want to die without ever having lived."

I toyed for a moment with the idea of telling everything I knew. Of being the one in power for once. Extricating myself from the web Cat had spun around us. I could go to the king with the information *I* had. Or maybe not the king, for the thought of his towering rage made me shiver. But a priest, perhaps. Or Archbishop Cranmer.

"You couldn't get away with it, Kitty," Cat said confidently. "Once I got through with you, no one would believe a word you said." She still had an uncanny knack for reading my thoughts. When it suited her.

"You and Joan will sleep in my chambers tonight," she instructed, as if knowing I could no longer argue. "The other ladies will be excused. Joan and Jane will be in the withdrawing room. And you will remain with Edmund Standebanke in the outer chamber as a decoy. From what I've heard, you two have already caused quite a commotion. Another public display cannot hurt you too much."

She knew. The entire court knew. Edmund's version. I would never be able to tell the truth. Because it is human nature to believe the first story heard, and not its rebuttal.

"I could pretend to stay up sewing," I said feebly.

"You're meeting your lover," Cat said. "It must appear authentic."

I didn't know why they were creating such an elaborate ruse over this particular meeting. They never had before. It seemed to me that Cat had been positively reckless for previous meetings.

But I followed the plans. I didn't ask how Culpepper would enter the narrow bedchamber, high in the castle wall. I didn't want to know. Cat locked the door behind her and I remained in the fusty antechamber, alone and anxious. I would tolerate Edmund's presence. I would sit with him. It would be the last time.

But when the knock came, I opened the door to Anthony Denny, who stood, fully dressed, in the doorframe. He had the grace to avert his eyes from sight of me in my nightclothes.

"The queen is abed," I said.

"And why aren't you?" he asked.

"I came to answer the door," I stuttered, my blush sure to give everything away.

"She stayed up to meet with me, sir," Edmund said from the gallery behind Denny, and emerged, grinning like a gargoyle into the light.

"Well, the king wishes the queen's company," Denny said with a cough.

"She is asleep," I murmured.

Denny strode through to the withdrawing room door and turned the latch, but it didn't open. I held my breath.

"It is locked," he said quietly, one eyebrow raised. "Does that not seem odd?"

He knocked softly, and not a sound emerged from room beyond. Sweat ran hot and icy down my back and between my breasts.

Then the door opened a pinch, and Jane peeked out. If

she was surprised to see Denny there, her eyes gave nothing away.

"The queen is indisposed," she told him.

"Then I shall wait." Denny went to a stool by the fire and sat down. No one said no to the king. Not even Cat.

"Why don't we give Denny a show while the others sort out the queen?" Edmund whispered in my ear. His words slid down my neck and nipped bitterness down my spine.

"For the sake of this farce, I will tolerate your company." I made sure my tone implied I would tolerate nothing more.

"I promise I won't bite." Edmund reached up to stroke my mouth with his thumb.

"I don't."

His thumb stopped moving as he tried to stare me down, but I somehow found the steel to keep from looking away. He moved his hand to my waist.

"Still," he said, "I suppose we should act as friends."

"Acting is a skill every courtier learns early."

"Why have you become so harsh?" he asked. "Why are you no longer the pliable little girl I met when you first arrived? The one overwhelmed by the gaudiness of the dresses and the extravagance of flirtation?"

"I have lived at court for a year," I answered. "And now know that the doublets and bodices hide moral disfigurement. That flirtation is merely a warped sense of possessiveness. That love and truth have no place here. You and your friend have taught me well."

"Perhaps," he said with a little smile, his hand on my waist pulling me to him. "But you still have more to learn. Come closer."

His eyes left mine to check on Denny. Looking for an audience.

"Get off," I said, sickened by it all. By being forced to spend time with Edmund. By having it be a show for the entertainment and titillation of others. By losing William. I pushed on Edmund's chest and he rocked backward, nearly losing his balance.

"Feisty," he said, with an unctuous grin at Denny.

I hit him again. I suddenly didn't care for duty, for friendship.

"Shut up!" I shouted. "Why can you not see that my desire to be rid of you has nothing to do with feistiness or women's problems or fear of being caught, but has everything to do with you!"

Denny stifled a laugh in the corner, turning it into a discreet courtier's cough.

At that moment, the bedchamber door opened, and Jane stepped out.

"The queen," she announced, and the men bowed low.

"Are you to escort me to my husband?" Cat asked Denny.

"At your service," Denny said. "Standebanke, leave your paramour, we have an important duty to perform."

I smiled at Denny gratefully, and he nodded in return. A real gentleman. Probably the only one I'd met at court.

After they left, Jane rushed back into the bedchamber and threw open the door to the garderobe.

"Get out!" she hissed. "Get out and leave this place at once."

Culpepper slunk like a hound from the little room. Not with his tail between his legs, but like a dog who had just picked a choice bone from the table.

"I cannot leave now," he remarked. "Surely there are guards at the door who will note my departure."

"Then you shall have to exit through the only available portal," Jane said, and indicated the garderobe.

"Far too mucky," Culpepper sniffed. "I could hide beneath the bed until my lady returns."

"No, Master Culpepper," Jane declared. "You must leave at once. I insist."

"Oh, you insist, do you, Lady Rochford?" Culpepper swaggered up to her. "And what will you do if I don't comply? Call the guards? How will you explain my presence to them? In the queen's bedroom, smelling of the queen?" He smiled wolfishly—hungry, lean, and carnivorous.

"Yes, she insists," I said, surprising myself as much as the others. Joy and horror rose within me in equal measure. I stilled my quaking limbs and felt a surge of strength.

"Ah, the whipped kitten speaks," Culpepper scoffed.

"The kitten has grown claws," I said, and stepped between him and Jane. We stood eye-to-eye, exactly the same height, though his build was much more masculine, heavy and tight

in the shoulders. I was no match for him, but I didn't care. I was tired of being bullied.

"I quake in my boots."

"So you should," I replied. "You've made my life hell, from the very first second I laid eyes on you. But no more. Get out."

He shrugged noncommittally and threw a conspicuous grin at Joan, who stood in the corner. She smiled hesitantly, and he turned back to me.

"Edmund told me you were a servile mollycoddle," he said. "He said you may not be beautiful but would make a nice auxiliary, available as necessary."

Each word stung but didn't surprise. I stood still as stone and didn't react. I couldn't let him see that he hurt me. I couldn't back down.

"But I think, on closer inspection," he continued, salivating for the kill, "that perhaps he was wrong. You have not the queen's vivacity or elegance, but you certainly have her spark. And therein lies passion. Perhaps not beautiful, but hardly frigid."

He stepped closer. One hand reached up, and I willed myself not to recoil. He rested it on the back of my head, firm and unyielding as a wall.

"And those eyes," he said. "That see all and judge accordingly."

I held my breath, unable to bear the carrion stink of his words. But I stared him down, letting him see my judgment of him.

"Perhaps you should be *my* auxiliary." He brought his face so close to mine his features blurred and shadowed, and all I saw were his hooded eyes. His lips moved on mine like the feathers of a vulture. "For when the queen is unavailable."

I blinked, and a malicious glee entered his eyes. Suddenly, he stepped away, and I nearly fell, like a tree on an undercut riverbank, my footing lost and nothing before me but rushing water.

"But then again," Culpepper announced to the room. "Perhaps you'd rather *watch*."

He strode to Joan in the corner, pulled her whimpering into his arms and mashed his mouth to hers.

He knew that I saw. Edmund must have told him what I'd seen. He knew I'd done nothing. That I would continue to do nothing. He kneaded Joan's bodice and her hands fluttered weakly, her face screwed up in revulsion and shame.

"Stop," I pleaded weakly.

"Yes," Culpepper dropped Joan unceremoniously on the floor amongst the rushes. "Perhaps I will. The company grows wearing, and I think I shall seek more stimulating acquaintances."

He disappeared into the garderobe, and with a thunk, he was gone.

"Back with his own kind," Jane said. "The shit."

Joan began to cry, and I sat down beside her. She put her

head in my lap and I leaned back against the bed that smelled of the ancients, and I stroked her hair.

"Why does she do it?" Joan asked. "How can she?"

Allow Culpepper to touch her. Commit treason. Put us all in danger. Treat us as though we're worthless.

"I don't know."

WE RETURNED TO HAMPTON COURT AT THE END OF OCTOBER, exhausted and out of sorts. It wasn't home. I wasn't even sure what home felt like. Or if I'd ever had one. But after weeks of sleeping in other people's rooms, returning to the palace by the Thames felt almost comfortable. The chambers had been scrubbed in our absence, the windows opened to let the river breezes through. New rushes were scattered on the floors, and the bed linens all smelled of rosewater and lavender.

Everything felt fresh. There were no secret passageways to the queen's apartments. There were no reasons for Edmund to visit. Even the HA HA in Anne Boleyn's gateway looked more scarred and worn. The past was past.

On the first of November, King Henry demanded that a prayer of thanksgiving be said in the churches throughout the country. We heard it in the chapel royal near the king's apartments. The rising sun slanted through the stained glass window, the ghostly figures of Katherine of Aragon and Cardinal Wolsey pale beside the golden glassy monarch in his early years. And the present king himself spoke words of benediction that rang off the vaulted ceiling, painted blue and studded with gold stars.

I render thanks to Thee, O Lord, that after so many strange accidents have befallen my marriages, Thou hast been pleased to give me a wife so entirely conformed to my inclinations as her I now have.

He turned to smile at her, the light from the window reflecting dramatically off the silver that striated his hair. She kissed her wedding ring and beamed at him.

I stood against the wall, wedged between Alice and Joan. By craning my neck, I could just see the king in the royal pew, elevated above us all. I watched him throughout the ceremony. An old man, the excesses of his youth catching up to him. But totally assured that everything would always go his way. In that, at least, he and Cat were a perfect match.

The service ended and the king rose slowly, lifting himself with his arms, shoulders straining with the weight. He stumbled and dropped his prayer book, which an usher retrieved for him, as well as the piece of parchment that had fallen from its leaves. The king scoured the room to see if anyone acknowledged his weakness. I looked away and watched the tide of courtiers hustling through the doors below the balcony, all of them eager to catch the king as he exited through his private door.

Above them, the king hadn't moved. He stood in the same place, one hand on the back of his chair, reading a letter, his face the same color as the parchment. His eyes, wild with some unconcealed emotion, looked up and this time caught me. For an instant, he searched my face as if looking for an answer to a desperate question, but I lowered my gaze as any courtier would. And when I raised my eyes again, he was gone.

A week went by, the palace surprisingly quiet. Everyone was exhausted from the progress. The Coven picked up where they had left off, sewing and gossiping, though the gossip remained tired and stale, tongues as idle as our hands.

"There is word of the Protestants in Germany," Lady Howard began.

"Don't make me yawn." Cat rolled her eyes. "Next!"

"There are accusations of piracy in Ireland," Isabel Baynton said.

"Piracy?" Cat asked. "Sounds daring."

"You have an interest in pirates, Your Majesty?" Elizabeth Seymour, Lady Cromwell, said quietly.

"Only on an intellectual level," Cat explained. "What drives a man to do such a thing?"

"The dowager duchess might know," Lady Cromwell said. "I believe one of her gentlemen pensioners left her service to try his hand at it."

Francis.

Cat and I exchanged a look, and she shook her head ever so slightly.

"Actually, I think pirates are dull, too," she said. "What else is there to talk about? Perhaps we should plan a banquet. A celebration."

"The king may not be up for any festivities," Jane Wriothesley said. She was normally quiet—or absent—so her words came as a bit of a shock.

"Why?" Cat said. "Is he ill?"

The ladies all shook their heads, but none of them spoke. Most of their husbands or lovers were in the constant presence of the king. If anyone knew, they would.

Their silence was worse than their words.

"Kitty," Cat said, turning to me, her face pale, "would you please go down to the king's apartments and ask after his health?"

I stepped out into the long gallery. Courtiers studded the room at intervals, some clustered by the windows, others huddled in shadows. Whispering stopped as I passed.

I moved between the knots of people, skirts swishing against me, swords knocking in their scabbards. I had just cleared a thicket of clergymen when I encountered William. We stood so close we almost touched.

"What are you doing here?" I asked.

The courtier's mask fell away and I easily read the expression that replaced it. Hurt. Betrayal.

"Business of the duke's," he said, securing the mask firmly back in place.

"I thought the duke was at home." He had left us during the progress back to London. Alice had been moping. I had felt a mixture of pain at William's absence and relief that I didn't have to relive that night in York on a daily basis.

"He was recalled to London," William said. "On . . . important business."

His manner stopped me. Businesslike, dissembling, his every emotion obscured. It was so unlike him that my heart

broke for what felt to be the thousandth time. Clearly he didn't want to have anything to do with me.

"You come only for the duke's business."

"I work for him."

"And I serve the queen," I said. "So it is my duty to go to the king's apartments."

He moved to allow me safe passage between him and a group of pages. My stomach twisted.

"You might reconsider your misplaced loyalty," he said quietly. So quietly no one around us could have heard.

"Misplaced?" I said. "Who are you to be telling me my loyalty is misplaced? You who live in the pocket of the most self-serving man at court?"

He looked as if I had slapped him again.

"I'm just saying," he murmured, his voice broken and pitched so low I had to lean close to hear him, his breath on my cheek, "take care of yourself, Kitty."

He laid a hand on my shoulder. He looked directly into my eyes, his own pleading, not hidden, for once, behind the shock of sandy hair.

"I have to," I said, suddenly angry. "No one else will."

William hadn't taken my side with Edmund. He'd assumed the worst.

I hurried away, seething, and didn't look back. Take care, indeed.

The gallery ended in the king's apartments, and another stretched away to the chapel royal. Clusters of petitioners and

hangers-on crowded the processional gallery the king would take to his evening prayers. Anthony Denny answered the outer door and gave me a tight smile.

"I've come to inquire about the king's health," I said.

"The king is indisposed."

"The queen is concerned," I said. "She has not seen him these four days."

"The king will send word."

He wouldn't even look at me.

"What should I tell the queen?" I asked.

"Tell her . . . to be patient."

He looked at me finally. Into my eyes.

"The king," he said, "will leave Hampton Court shortly."

He waited a beat, nodded, and then shut the door in my face.

A cold, thick feeling came over me like quicksilver in my veins. I wanted desperately to run away. Everyone was acting so strangely: the most indiscreet ladies silent; the most silent, speaking; the duke recalled on important business; William speaking of my "misplaced loyalty"; the king departing without even a word to Cat.

My heart raced, but I ignored its pounding. I couldn't give in to the fear that had lain dormant for so many months. I couldn't make a slip, because the very thing I had been afraid of might be coming true.

I tried to affect Jane's smooth, gliding walk back to the queen's rooms. I tried to remain calm. But as I wove my way between cardinals and cupbearers, I became aware that I

passed through the rooms no longer unnoticed. Rather, I felt everyone's eyes upon me.

I hastened to the queen's withdrawing room and sketched a halfhearted curtsey, causing the Coven to twitter and cluck. I didn't care.

"Sir Anthony says to be patient," I told Cat, knowing every ear waited to twist my words.

I willed her to understand, to read my mind as she always had, but she just nodded. I waited, gripping my own fingers with knuckles so pale they yellowed. She looked up.

"He leaves this afternoon," I said.

"The king?" Dawning understanding drained her face of color. I nodded helplessly.

"Where is he going?" she asked the room. The ladies appeared not to listen, intent on their stilled needles and silent gossip.

"I want to know what's going on!" Cat shouted. "I want to know when I can expect things to get back to normal!"

She pushed past me and out the door. The Coven all stood, staring. Lady Howard rocked from one foot to the other, looking for all the world like a heron feeling along the bottom of a muddy pond. I followed Cat to the door.

"Your Majesty," one of the guards said, standing in her way.

"I go to see my husband." She stepped around him.

The guard reached out and laid a hand on her arm.

"How dare you?" She rounded on him.

The guard's visage opened wide. He couldn't speak, but he

didn't let go. The room fell silent, all its occupants shuffling against the walls like drifts from the river.

Cat wrenched her arm from his grasp and turned to run down the gallery.

"Henry!" she cried, a note of hysteria rising like waves of heat in summer. "Henry!"

Her voice broke as two of the guards began to run after her. She turned her head, her hair streaming across her face. She stumbled.

"Cat!" I cried and started forward. Another guard pushed me back.

"Henry!"

The shriek raised the hackles on my neck. Two guards had her by the arms, pulling her backward. She struggled, kicking, looking like a prisoner, not a queen. No one moved to help her. Gawkers and gossipers melted into the sharply carved paneling.

The guards dragged her to the apartments, the ladies shrinking back as though retreating from contagion.

Jane Boleyn stood rigid by the bedchamber door, eyes wide like those of a mouse about to be pounced upon.

"Kitty?" she gasped, grabbing my arm, paper-thin skin covering a vise-like hand. The other clicked the pearls in her pocket.

"Lady Rochford," I said. "See if you can get the kitchen to send up a posset. The queen is unwell."

She nodded, the bland courtier's façade restored, and hus-

tled the rest of the ladies out of the bedchamber. I closed the door behind them.

Cat curled up into a ball at the foot of the bed, knees to chest and elbows to ankles. Her body shook with sobs. I sat down near her and watched her cry. There was nothing I could say.

"Oh, Kitty!" she cried. "Why doesn't he give me a crown? Why doesn't he visit? What have I done?"

I could think of several things, but she looked so small in that big bed, like a child hiding from a thunderstorm. I couldn't say them.

"Cat?" I whispered.

"I never wanted to be queen," she sobbed.

I almost laughed. Cat had always wanted to be queen. Queen of the maidens' chamber. Queen of Misrule. But she hadn't wanted this.

I let her cry until no more tears came.

"I couldn't stop," she finally whispered. "He wouldn't let me."

Her words hung in the silence that followed them like spiders suspended from the ceiling. They could creep away unobserved or continue down their silken strings and bite the unwary.

"Culpepper?" I asked, inviting the spiders down.

She turned away from me and curled up again. I waited for her to tell me that Culpepper had seduced her once and black-mailed her into further meetings. I waited for her to say she

wanted to extricate herself from him, but that he forced her, held her prisoner.

"He didn't force me," she said. "But I couldn't say no."

Trapped. By herself. Not by blackmail.

"Don't tell," she said, so quietly the words could have come from the very air around us. "Deception is my only defense."

"I won't."

"It was all him," Cat said, and paused. "And Jane."

"Jane Boleyn?" I asked, incredulous. The woman who did nothing but what was asked of her?

"Yes," Cat said slowly. "Yes, see, she pushed me into it. She suggested it. To get me pregnant. She carried messages for us."

"No, Cat," I said.

"But she did," Cat said. "Even you saw. She carried messages. She found hiding places."

"She did it because you *asked*." A shudder of revulsion ran through me. Cat couldn't really be thinking of blaming Jane for all of it.

"No one has to know that."

"*You* know it!" I cried. "How could you do something like that to another person?"

"Because she didn't stop him. She could have stopped him."

"It wasn't *him* she couldn't stop, Cat, it was *you*. You were so set on this doomed romance that you wouldn't listen to reason. I tried to stop you. Maybe Jane did, too."

"She didn't," Cat interrupted. But I wasn't finished.

"So because she couldn't stop you it's her fault? That is the ultimate injustice!"

Cat bolted up from the bed, a tiny tower of fury and self-aggrandizement.

"You know what injustice is, Kitty? It's a seventeen-year-old girl being bound to a fifty-year-old dying man!"

"We knew that all along, Cat."

"That didn't make it any easier," she said, desperate tears clinging to her eyelashes. "I can't die for this."

But we both knew she could.

"We don't know what it is yet," I assured her hollowly. "We don't know why the king is leaving. Perhaps he *is* ill."

"He's not ill, Kitty," Cat said. "And we're dead."

THE PALACE TOOK ON AN AIR OF SILENT EXPECTANCY FOR THE NEXT twenty-four hours.

The king left with his entourage for dinner. In Westminster. The entire Privy Council went with him. And stayed all night.

Francis Dereham was missing. Rumors of his involvement in Irish piracy continued to circulate. Culpepper disappeared as well. Someone said he had gone hawking. But I didn't know if I dared believe it.

Cat's apartments quietly emptied as well. Lady Cromwell grew ill. Some of the others were called away on urgent business.

The Coven stayed.

"The Howards stick together," Cat said with a tight smile, nodding her head in the direction of the older ladies in the corner. Sitting like statues. Not sewing. Not gossiping. Just staring into the fire.

"The rest are like rats," I muttered.

"This ship is not sinking!" Cat shouted, causing everyone to jump. "Kitty, Joan, Jane. Come with me."

I searched the room for Alice—the last piece of the circle—but she was missing.

Cat led us into the more public receiving room. It was usually crowded with councilors and servants but now disturbingly empty, as if we had woken in the middle of the night.

"Dance!" Cat commanded.

"There isn't any music, Cat," Joan said, bemused.

Cat made a strangled shriek of frustration.

"When will you stop calling me by that name?" she cried, making Joan wince and stammer an apology.

"We never had music in the maidens' chamber," Cat said. "And we danced all the time."

Her voice fell to a whisper. As if the effort to speak was too great. The weight of memories too much.

I took Jane's hands.

"Something lively, yes?" I asked.

Jane nodded. I started a country dance. One that didn't involve intricate foot work or careful interaction. One that didn't require courtly etiquette. Jane tried to keep up, but her face remained vacant, as if something had pulled away inside her.

Cat grabbed Joan and kept pace. Joan began to hum, off-key as always, stomping her right foot to keep time, the tune growing breathy as they whirled about the empty room.

I turned once more, skirts swinging, and there before me stood Archbishop Cranmer.

He filled the door, tall and wide. The white sleeves of his cassock billowed from his shoulders. His face was bottom-heavy, with small eyes holding little humor. The dust settled around

us as the others froze. I thought I heard Jane whimper.

Behind the Archbishop stood the Duke of Norfolk, more menacing than I had ever seen him. The duke wasn't shouting. He wasn't purple in the face or sweating anger. He was silent, his forehead creased with choler.

Trouble had arrived at our door.

"We have come with some questions to put to the queen," Cranmer said.

Behind him, the duke rolled his eyes up to the ceiling and then closed them tightly, as if sending a silent prayer to the heavens.

"You may enter, Archbishop," Cat replied. Her voice raised a notch in pitch. "We were just dancing."

The men stepped in, and Cranmer motioned for me to close the door behind them. I did so, and stood against the crack, feeling the whistle of wind from the cold gallery up my back.

"The time for dancing is over," said Cranmer.

The duke made a strangled sound like a dog choking on a fish bone.

"I have some questions about your secretary," Cranmer continued.

Cat looked up at him, her expression betraying nothing. Cranmer went on.

"One Francis Dereham, I am told?"

"Is he in some sort of trouble?" Cat asked. "I have not seen him for a number of days."

"He is in London."

"Well if you have any communication with him, I should like you to tell him I resent his disappearance and neglect of his duty."

"Yes," Cranmer said, more cough than speech.

The duke clenched his fists.

"It has come to my attention," said Cranmer, "that perhaps you knew Master Dereham prior to his post here."

The duke shuffled his feet. The rest of us remained as still and silent as the furniture.

"Yes." Cat lifted her chin and smiled engagingly. "He was a retainer in my grandmother's employ. At Norfolk House." The last words pointed. Directed at her uncle. Claiming kinship. Claiming support.

The duke ignored her.

"Is that all?" Cranmer asked.

"Yes, of course," said Cat. "Though I believe he went to sea before I came to court."

"You knew him in no other capacity?"

"How many times do I have to say it?" Cat snapped. "I didn't know the man well. My grandmother employed him. My grandmother asked me to find him a place in my household." She paused. "The Dowager Duchess of Norfolk asked for my patronage as queen." Playing her trump card.

"My source says you knew him quite well," Cranmer's face showed not an inkling of suspicion, not a symptom of sympathy. Not a fragment of consideration for Cat's rank and influence.

"And who is this source?" Cat said imperiously. "Have you spoken with the man in question?"

"At length."

Those two words knocked the life out of her. She disappeared into herself; her eyes remained open and clear, but completely absent of any human intelligence or emotion.

"I see," she breathed.

And then she collapsed. Her skirts flumed around her in a cloud of silk. Her hood tilted to one side, pulling with it streamers of auburn hair. Jane knelt down beside her and drew Cat into her lap. Cat clung to her like a sailor to a piece of wreckage.

The Archbishop stared, horrified, at the cluster of human arms and legs on the floor before him. The duke cringed and then arranged his face to a look of horror and surprise. I couldn't move. Not out the door, nor to the knot of loyalty on the floor.

Cranmer waited for an eternity before turning and approaching me.

"The queen may keep her privy keys," he said.

A candle of hope lit the back of my mind.

"Her ladies are dismissed," he said, extinguishing it. "I suggest she keep to her rooms. I shall send some men to inventory and remove all her jewels."

At this, Cat set to sobbing and wailing more loudly still, her voice high and keening, as if at the death of a loved one.

Cranmer didn't move.

"Please allow me to exit," he said quietly.

I realized I still stood at the gap where the door met the wall. The handle pressed into the small of my back, my hand gripping it so tightly I could no longer feel my fingers.

"Get out of the way, you stupid girl," the duke blustered, and pushed me aside. He ripped the door open himself and swept from the room in a lather of petulance and fear. Cranmer nodded once to me and followed.

THE COVEN WENT QUICKLY. THE SHIP WAS OBVIOUSLY SINKING NOW. They must have heard everything through the withdrawing chamber door. They gathered nothing but their skirts and fled Cat's rooms for their own.

"Oh, mercy," I heard the duchess mutter. "There will be a divorce and she will be sent back to me."

Cat remained on the floor, buffeted by the ebbing tide of retreat, half hidden in Jane's skirts. Joan watched the others leave, panic corroding her soft features. But then resolve hardened them, and she turned back to stroke Cat's hair.

"What did he say?" Cat said after I had closed the door.

"Cranmer?" I asked.

"No, you idiot, Francis. What could he tell them?"

We stared at her. The remnants of her tears still streaked her face. Her hood still lay askew on her head, giving her the look of a demented patient of Bedlam. But her eyes were hard and calculating.

"Well?"

"I guess he could tell them everything," Joan said slowly.

"Everything?" Cat shouted. She pushed Joan away and stood up.

Francis knew a great deal. Knew Cat's past. Knew of her prior interest in Culpepper. How much more did he know?

"Well, he could, Cat," Joan protested.

"But would he?" asked Cat. She turned to me. "Kitty, would he tell them everything?"

"He has to, Cat," I replied. "They are the king's men."

"No, he doesn't *have* to, Kitty Tylney," she mocked me. "He could *lie*, inconceivable as that may seem to you."

"How will you ever know?"

"They'll ask me to confirm what he's said."

"No, they're smarter than that." Jane spoke for the first time since the men had left. "They will ask open-ended questions that require specific answers." Her voice shook. "They will ask them again. And again. And again. Until you answer."

"They can't be that smart," Cat muttered. "They didn't ask me anything before."

"They had no reason to," Jane pointed out. "You were brought to the king as a virgin. Why should they ask any questions? The dowager duchess vouched for you. They had no reason to be suspicious. Now they do."

"We need to find out what they know," Cat declared. "Where is Alice? Alice hears everything. Go find her, Kitty. The queen requires her presence."

I hurried from the room, retracing my steps from the day before. All I'd needed to do then was ask after the king's health. Now, our lives hung in the balance.

I hurried through the eerily quiet palace in search of the

Duke of Norfolk's rooms. I had no desire to see him again; his anger would impale me. But I went, through the galleries, the Great Watching Chamber, Anne Boleyn's gate, the HA HA mocking me. All emptier than I had ever seen them, deserted by those loyal to the king.

William stood outside the duke's door.

"William!" I said. "I need to find Alice."

"Alice left for Kenninghall this morning."

The duke's estate in Norfolk. The duke must have wrung as much information out of her as he could in return for safe passage. Alice got out. I slumped back against the wall.

"Kitty?" William asked. "Are you well?"

"No, William," I said. "I am not well at all."

"Do you need a place to go?" he whispered.

I looked at him. The mask was gone, his features mobile with concern. His eyes flashed over my face, checked the gallery, and returned to me.

"My family's house in Cheapside is rundown and crowded," he explained. "But with a message from me, you would be welcome. And you wouldn't be found."

The implication of this struck me hard in the center of my chest. Leave court. Leave Cat. Save myself.

"Go into hiding?" I asked. "Is it really that bad?"

He nodded. "They're questioning everyone about the queen's activities before she married. Any secrets . . . could be damning."

"Secrets just get in the way."

"And worse."

We stood in the empty gallery, listening to the bustle of the duke's servants packing his things, preparing for flight.

I could leave Cat and all of her secrets behind. Go where no one knew me. Where no one told me what to do or what I wanted. The question was, what did I want?

William stood before me, waiting for an answer, and only one came to mind. *Him.* I only wanted him. The one thing I couldn't have.

Alice was out already. William would surely soon make his way to Kenninghall to be with her. And I, who knew the most, but also knew how to say nothing, was indentured to the queen. Her sister of the soul.

I couldn't abandon her.

"Thank you, William," I said, "for the offer. But I can't take it."

Those words appeared to hurt him more than anything had before. He closed his eyes and let go a great shuddering sigh.

"Go well, Mistress Tylney."

I returned to the queen's rooms. Three men in the scarlet and gold of the king's livery busied themselves, taking stock of all the jewels and valuables in the apartments. They packed everything away in boxes lined with velvet. Pearls. Brooches. An enameled coronet garnished with rubies. The diamond collar.

Cat sat silently weeping by the fire while the men moved about the room.

"My lady," one of the men said to Cat. "Could you please remove your rings?"

"My rings?" she asked, her voice hollow as if traveling a great distance.

"Yes."

Three from the left hand and five from the right. She handed them to him one by one. When finished, she sank back, defeated.

"And the last one," he pressed.

"But that's my wedding ring."

"We were told to take everything." His voice betrayed a perverted joy in her sorrow.

Cat handed him the ring and removed her jeweled hood. Her hair tumbled down her back and she buried her face in her pale, naked hands.

But as soon as the men had left and the door closed behind them, she lifted her face and wiped it with her sleeve.

"Where is Alice?"

"Gone," I said. "To Kenninghall."

"The duke's protection," Cat muttered. "Damn that girl. She knew I would need her, and she only saved herself."

I felt a sudden desire to justify Alice's actions. They so closely resembled what could have been my own. But I stayed silent.

"We're here for you," Joan said, kneeling down to put an arm around Cat. "Aren't we, Kitty?"

"And a damn lot of good you'll do me."

Joan looked stricken.

"And Jane," she attempted.

"Jane?" Cat cried and looked around. Caught Jane by the window. "Jane Boleyn? The woman who has served five queens and survived them all?"

I thought of Jane's fingers on Anne Boleyn's pearls, the beads tapping quietly. The darkness in her eyes as she spoke of Cranmer's questions. And I wondered if that survival was worth the cost.

"No, four," Cat said. "Because Jane won't survive this queen. No one will."

"Don't talk like that, Your Majesty," Joan argued.

"You've finally remembered to call me by my title," said Cat, patting Joan's hand.

I shivered at the coldness, the blankness in her voice.

"We'll all survive," Joan said. "Together. We're family. Right?"

CRANMER RETURNED THE NEXT DAY, ARMED WITH QUESTIONS, PEN AND ink. He sat down at Cat's little writing desk and looked at her inquisitively.

Cat sat mute by the fire. Joan sat next to her. I waited by the door, still fighting the urge to flee. Jane stood by the window, still and silent. The perfect, invisible courtier.

"My lady," Cranmer pronounced, "We can do this one of two ways. Based on the extensive information I have already gathered, I could give a full account of the punishment you will reap for your past misconduct. Or you could tell me your side of the story, and I will be content to listen and draw my conclusions."

Judge and jury, all in one cassock.

He sat back and waited. If there was one thing Cat couldn't stand, it was silence when she was expected to fill it. She tried valiantly. I watched her jaw moving as she chewed her lower lip. She stared into the fire with what I'm sure she hoped was a tragic expression for a good five minutes and then she broke down.

"I knew Francis Dereham when I lived with my grandmother in Lambeth," she began.

"In what way?" Cranmer inquired.

"As a friend."

Cranmer waited. Again, Cat failed to wait him out. She began to sob.

"More than a friend."

"So you knew him . . ." Cranmer let his question trail off, obviously expecting her to continue.

"We kissed in the gallery," Cat said with an impatient shrug. "And in chapel. You can ask any of my friends." And with a single gesture, implicated all of us with an airy insouciance that took my breath away.

"Was there no talk of marriage?" Cranmer asked.

"No."

"Surely, in a household of girls, there would be some mention of marriage?" he pursued.

"No."

Cat met his eye and held firm.

"You never talked to your friends about it. Forgive me if I do not understand, but don't girls discuss these things? Carry locks of hair like holy artifacts?" His mouth turned down in a sneer of distaste. "There was no gossip? No girlish, fanciful discussions of dresses and flowers and the future?"

"No," Cat insisted. "None. We never spoke of those sorts of things because we knew our families would find the best husbands for us."

Her attempt at ingenuousness failed and she just looked desperate.

"All of you?" Cranmer asked. "You, Mistress Tylney? Did you trust your parents to find you a husband?"

"Of course," I forced myself to say. "And I am betrothed to Lord Graves."

Cranmer made a note.

"None of you attempted to make a match on your own?" Cranmer pursued. He sounded so mild, so kindly, like a priest. A father confessor. None of us responded.

"But you, my lady," he turned back to Cat, "chose your own husband in the end. Or he chose you. It wasn't your family's doing at all. It was a love match, is that right?"

Cat swallowed. I saw her Adam's apple swell delicately at her throat.

Cat didn't believe in love. Her match with the king had nothing to do with it. And everybody knew it.

"Yes," she said.

"So I can infer that perhaps it was always in the back of your mind to do so. Then what did you think of this dalliance with Francis Dereham?"

"I thought nothing!" Cat cried and broke into fresh sobs. "I was young, impressionable. He was older and I thought him handsome. I thought he would know better than I. I had been brought up to trust my elders, to listen and obey."

"Listen and obey," Cranmer repeated, making a note.

"My will is not my own," Cat said.

"So you believed that Dereham would think of your best interests."

"He said he would."

"It is my information that he shared your bed." Cranmer fixed Cat with a beady eye. No longer grandfatherly, he now looked like a hawk going in for a kill.

Cat crumpled like the sail of a ship that has turned against the wind. She lost her voice in her skirts. Cranmer leaned forward to catch a whisper of confession. But the fabric muted Cat so thoroughly that the sounds she made could just have been sobs. I couldn't bear it. I couldn't stand to see Catherine Howard debased. Despite her treatment of me, she was still my friend.

"Can't you ask her later?" I pleaded. "She isn't well."

"Fine," Cranmer made a note. Turned to me.

"Did he share your bed, Mistress Tylney? The one you occupied with Mistress Howard?"

I could have cried, too. My intention was for him to leave, not turn his interrogation on me. But he posed the question in such a way that I could tell the truth and yet not all of it. Yes, Francis Dereham shared my bed. It just so happened that he also shared it with Cat. I didn't have to distinguish with whom he *chose* to share it.

"He did," I said.

I thought that perhaps Cat had stopped breathing, as the sounds coming from her skirt suddenly diminished. But she looked up at me, a flash of hate in her eyes. She thought I con-

demned her. A stab of guilt rent through me, though my intention hadn't been to indict her. She dissolved again in pathetic tears.

Cranmer calmly made a note.

"Did you ever share a bed with Francis Dereham when he was naked?" he asked.

Yes. Though I wished to forget that particular night.

"No."

"Did Mistress Howard?"

The room fell silent.

"No," I whispered.

"No, no more did I!" Cat sobbed. "He came to our rooms and . . . and . . ."

"He used to grab my breast beneath the covers," I said over the noise of Cat's renewed sobbing. It had been an accident. The last time I'd tried to pretend he wasn't there. After that, I'd always found another place to sleep. Cat let up slightly, to be better able to hear my confession.

"Dereham?"

"Yes."

"Was he naked at the time? Were you?"

"No!" Cat cried. "Never! How can you keep asking?"

"Because he said he was. He said he came to your bed without his doublet. Without his hose."

We stared. At Cranmer. At Cat. As if watching a silent, frozen tennis game.

"Sometimes he came without his doublet," Cat admitted.

"And once . . . maybe twice, he came without his hose. But not fully naked. Never like that."

"And you never called him husband. He never called you wife."

"No," Cat said in a throaty whisper. "He forced me."

I could have throttled her. Because that one question could be her salvation. Perhaps salvation for all of us. Commitment, consent, and consummation amounted to a legal marriage. It would make her marriage to the king invalid. Give him a reason to divorce her, like the duchess said. To let her go. To let her live. But if Cat had not been betrothed to Francis, then she was a slut and possibly an adulterer. A calculating, manipulative harlot who used her wiles and abilities to dupe the aging, romantic King and then bring her lover into her household, committing high treason just like her cousin, Anne Boleyn. Bigamy was preferable to the alternative.

"But how?" Cranmer asked. "The doors to the maidens' dormitory were locked, were they not?"

"Not in the beginning," Cat said, casting a fleeting look my way. I held my breath. It was one thing knowing about Cat's affairs. It was something else entirely to facilitate them. I looked at Cranmer, who flicked his glance back to his notes.

"I see."

Cranmer packed up his pen and ink and stood.

"You would be best advised to stay in your rooms," he declared, pointedly scanning each face in turn. "All of you."

We bowed our heads in assent. What else could we do?

Cranmer paused at the door.

"Don't think this is the end of the matter," he said. "The truth will out. In the end. And the end is nigh, my lady."

And he didn't know the half of it. Yet.

50

"That bastard!" Cat shrieked when Cranmer was out of earshot.

"Your Majesty!" Joan gasped.

"Not Cranmer," Cat said scornfully. "No, not the perfect image of God on earth. Dereham! The bloody waste of a pirate!"

She slammed the door to her bedchamber and started throwing everything that came to hand. A half-sewn shirt. A wooden box full of embroidery silks. A small mirror of Venetian glass that shattered, sending fragments like raindrops all over the hearth.

Joan ducked out of the way and tried to hide behind the bed. I leaned back up against the door.

"It wasn't my fault!" Cat screamed. "He forced me! And now he's ruined me!"

I was staggered by the strength of her adherence to a falsehood that would be her ruin.

Cat picked up an inkpot from the desk and made to hurl it into the fire. Jane stepped smartly up to her, grabbed her wrist and held the inkpot still.

"Oh, no you don't," Jane said.

"How dare you manhandle me!" Cat roared. "As if I were a common wench!"

"Did you not hear Cranmer?" Jane demanded. "You *are* a common wench, Mistress Howard."

"Until the king says otherwise, I am queen," Cat said imperiously.

"Fine," said Jane, letting go. "But you throw that ink to your own hazard."

Cat set it down carefully.

"Why do you say so, Lady Rochford?" she asked.

"Because now is the time to write your letter of confession to the king. Beg his mercy. You have said more than once that the king loves you, perhaps to the point of delusion. If he still loves you—and he must still love you—then you can appeal to his feelings. Tell him everything."

"Everything?"

Jane paused. "Perhaps not. But everything about Dereham." She made a moue of distaste.

"You judge me, Lady Rochford?" Cat said. "You, who sent your husband to the gallows without a breath of hesitation? You, who let it be believed that he and Queen Anne committed the unnatural sin of incest? You dare judge me for a childish infatuation?"

"No," Jane muttered. I saw her fingers close around the pocket that hung from her waist.

The room lapsed into silence.

"So what do you think?" Cat turned to me. "When I give it

339

to him, should I go down on my knees and kiss the hem of his cloak?"

"Cranmer?" I asked. "He doesn't strike me as the sort of man who would respond well to such a thing."

"The king," she scoffed, as if I were the stupid one.

"The king has left Hampton Court, Cat. I don't think he's coming back."

"He must come back," Cat said. "I have to see him. Make my confession. Beg for his mercy. He'll come back."

"No, he won't," Jane assured her. "He let Catherine of Aragon suffer illness and death alone in Kimbolton. He left Anne Boleyn at a tournament, and never saw her again. He sent Anne of Cleves to Richmond, only allowing her to return when she was his beloved sister and no longer his wife. He will not see you again."

"But he has to," Cat insisted.

"He won't." Jane's voice sliced like a sword through the still room. "You must make your confession and beg for mercy on paper."

"But that's not fair!" Cat cried. "My writing is chaos! I need to see him in person. I need to practice. I must see him."

"You won't."

"But I've done nothing wrong."

Her brazen denial stupefied me. Despite knowing her, sleeping with her, being her mirror for most of my life, I couldn't understand her now.

"I'll just have to beg forgiveness of Archbishop Cranmer,"

she said. "Kitty, come here and pretend to be him. Should I face him with my head bowed? Or clasp him around the knees?"

She knelt before me and reached for my skirts.

I stepped aside, disgusted by her desire to practice. To find a way to tug the heartstrings of Archbishop Cranmer instead of face up to the truth. Terror rose within me. If Cat didn't clutch at the one possibility that might save her—that she was betrothed before she married the king—she could face worse than the loss of her throne.

"You should tell him to his face that you were married to Francis."

"I wasn't," Cat replied stonily. "He forced me."

"It would render your marriage to the king invalid," Jane interjected.

"It would render me a nobody! Mistress Dereham instead of Queen Catherine! I will not consider it. I will not even participate in a conversation about it."

She turned her back on us, arms folded across her chest. I knew there would be no way to persuade her, and the tiny hope I had harbored died.

"Then you should find a way to explain why you brought Francis Dereham into your household."

"Because the dowager duchess told me to."

"Which she may deny!" I cried. "Besides, you're the queen. You don't have to do what she says anymore."

"You mean people will think I brought him here because I

loved him?" Cat asked, incredulous. "People will think that I would actually prefer *him* to the king? I care *nothing* for Francis. I never did."

I almost laughed, but choked on a sob instead.

"It doesn't matter," I said. "Once a rumor gets started, everyone believes it. You of all people should realize that."

It was what she had threatened me with: a rumor that would ruin my life. But now it was the truth that would ruin us all.

"Francis will tell the truth," Cat predicted, ignoring all that I implied. Ignoring the fact that Francis had already told the truth.

"It only takes a little torture to make a man say only what his inquisitors wish to hear," Jane said, her eyes glittering dangerously. No doubt she was remembering the musician Mark Smeaton, tortured to confession of adultery with Anne Boleyn.

We paused to consider this. Francis on the rack, his bones popping, chin dimple receding into his screams.

"Very well," Cat sniffed. "So what should I say in this letter? God, I hate writing! Can't someone else do it for me?"

"Who?" I asked, finally giving in to my frustration. "Your secretary? Oh, maybe not, as he's locked up in the Tower spilling his guts to the king's men."

"You watch your step, Kitty Tylney," Cat growled. "I can still take you down."

"But you already are!" I cried. I wanted to force some sense

into her. To make her see that her games and diversions and petty preferences were no longer of any use to her.

"You show no regard for others and none for the future!" I exploded, each word a catharsis.

"You dare to attack me?" Cat gaped.

"I do! You wasted every moment at court on clothes and baubles and silly games. You wasted your friendships on petty rivalries and manipulation. You've wasted your own life and you've wasted ours, and you will have to suffer that for the rest of your days, however few they might be!"

I stopped when the tears sprang to my eyes, a searing pain rising just beneath my ribs.

Cat stared at me. The others hardly seemed to breathe.

"You *wanted* to be here," she accused. "You wanted the baubles and silly games. You wanted it as much as I."

It was true. I had wanted to be at court. Because it was what Cat wanted. I hadn't thought for myself since I was eight years old. And when I did, I spoke too late. Too late to change her, or to accomplish anything but the infliction of pain.

We might have stood there for eternity, but for another knock at the door and the entrance of Sir Thomas Wriothesley, one of the king's secretaries and most trusted servants. The one Jane had warned me to stay away from on my first day at court.

He wore unfashionable clothes, but well-fitted and startlingly white against his thick neck and russet beard. His face might once have been genial, but had long been marred by antipathy.

"You will pack your things," he said, addressing the room.

"You're taking my ladies in waiting?" Cat asked, looking even more shocked than she had after my outburst.

"Just these particular ones," Wriothesley explained. "You shall have others. Of my choosing. Your days with your clan of friends are over. From now on, none of you shall hear what the others have to say. You will tell only the truth. There will be no connivance."

Joan and I looked at each other, at Cat, unable to move. We might never see each other again. I might never get a chance to tell Cat that I loved her as much as I hated her.

"Come now," Wriothesley snapped. "I have other places to be."

"Can we not say good-bye?" Cat asked, batting wet eyelashes.

Wriothesley hesitated. For the first time, he looked remotely human.

Cat took advantage of this and turned to Joan and hugged her. Tears streamed down Joan's face. Cat hugged me, too, a tight, strangling embrace, her fists balled into the knobs of my spine. I sensed a reprieve in that embrace—a truce in our war of words. "Don't forget your family, girls," Cat said tightly, then added in a whisper, "Do not betray me."

I got the message. Without each other, we were nothing. Without Cat, I was nothing. Our fates were inextricably tied. Cat would still need me. And I would continue to do her bidding.

I saw Jane, over Cat's shoulder, face so white as to be translucent, arms gripped to her sides. Left out of the circle.

"Come now," Wriothesley said again.

"Are we being arrested?" I asked.

"Not yet," Wriothesley said, then narrowed his eyes. "But undoubtedly you will be."

That's when Jane Boleyn began to scream.

I SAT ALONE FOR FIVE DAYS IN A ROOM AT THE FAR END OF THE PALACE. A room with bare walls and a shuttered window that let in little light but all the reek of the river at low tide. A room I filled with too many memories and a fear that smelled far worse than anything outside.

Wriothesley came daily. He assaulted me with the same questions, as if he hoped I would crack and he could pull me apart, layer by layer. But on the sixth day, he brought news.

"You are to be taken to the Tower of London."

I willed myself not to show a reaction while he waited for me to digest the information. It eddied in my stomach like Thames-water.

"The king may be convinced to be merciful," he advised. "He must be given good reason. I don't suspect he will be so toward Mistress Howard. When the facts were presented to him, he grabbed the sword of the nearest usher and shouted, *I'll kill her myself!*' But you are no one. He can afford to be merciful to you. If you help us."

I remained silent.

"Your family has responded to none of our attempts to elicit information from them," he told me. "They say they have had little contact with you since you moved to the dowager duchess's household."

"That is true." I ignored the pinpricks of hurt that came from hearing of their indifference from a stranger.

"And the man to whom you were betrothed?"

"I have not heard from him."

"He tells me the betrothal has been broken," Wriothesley reported. "That your actions in the queen's household—and before—are enough to break any promise he may have made to you."

Abandoned by my parents. Abandoned by Lord Poxy. I really had nothing but my family of girls.

"How fares the queen?"

Wriothesley looked askance at my question.

"Mistress Howard is cheerful," he said. "And demanding. And peevish when her demands are not met, despite the fact she does not deserve to ask for anything."

That sounded like Cat. Still thinking only of herself.

"And Jane?" I asked, afraid of the answer. I didn't know if the screams in my nightmares were real or imagined.

"Lady Rochford is no business of yours."

"What of the others?" I persisted. "They're my friends!" They were the only family I'd ever known.

"Not anymore." Wriothesley's legs creaked in their leather as he leaned closer to intimidate me. He succeeded, despite the fact that he was shorter than I.

"What can you tell us of your life at Norfolk House?" he asked yet again. "How well did the duchess keep an eye on you?"

"Oh, the duchess had an eagle eye, sir," I told him, neglecting to mention the duchess's eye was also blind to what didn't affect her personally.

"So how then did Mistress Howard manage an affair with a servant in her household?"

"Francis Dereham wasn't a servant."

Wriothesley took a deep breath, beard quivering, leaned back and changed tactics.

"What happened when the duchess locked the door?"

"Locked the door?"

"We have it on good authority that when the duchess found out about Francis Dereham, she ordered that the door to the maidens' dormitory be locked. What happened then?" He sounded irritable.

"Francis tried to come in a window."

"And failed. We know this, too."

I shrugged.

"Did the queen steal the key?"

"She wasn't the queen then," I said.

"You equivocate to avoid the question," Wriothesley retorted. "You have truly learned the art of being a courtier. But your answer is clearer than you think. She may not have been queen, but you did not say she didn't do it.

"And you have told me" he continued, "that Dereham could

not have forced his attentions on a girl who went to such lengths to be with him."

Oh, God. I had just told him that Cat stole the key. If she stuck with her story of *not* being engaged to Francis, to the story of him forcing her, my response would prove her a liar. Because no girl would steal a key to unlock the door to unwanted advances.

"I see by your face that you understand," Wriothesley said with a slender, knowing grin.

One more lie, throbbing like a sliver beneath a fingernail.

"Mistress Howard stole the key," Wriothesley declared and waited for affirmation. Again the smile that made his lips disappear beneath the fur of his beard.

I couldn't let him condemn Cat for my misbegotten cleverness. My attempts to say nothing, to give away nothing, only served Wriothesley's purposes. Not mine.

"No, she didn't," I admitted. "I did. I replaced it with a chess piece wrapped in lace."

The truth swung between us, glinting in the light from the windows. It hung by a single thread. Ready to set me free or send me to the gallows.

"To unlock the door of the maidens' chamber," Wriothesley said, the smile so thin he could hardly speak. "To allow entrance to the young men of the house. To encourage relations between your friends and the men they admired. Because that was what you wanted. You wanted to be the arbiter of that affair."

My stomach roiled. I dropped my head into my hands, my

mouth filling with the foretaste of vomit. I would be blamed. The madam of the maidens' chamber.

"And when Catherine Howard married and became queen, she brought you and your friends and Francis Dereham with her because she saw no reason to give up her wicked ways."

"What?" I lifted my head, my hair sticking to the sweat that coated my brow.

"A den of iniquity." He stood and sneered. "Right under the *eagle eye* of the dowager duchess herself. A seething mass of corruption and falsehood. Brought whole to court by the queen herself like a festering wound. Did she think the stench would not give her away?"

I stared at him.

"You cannot prove that," I breathed. He was using me not as a scapegoat but as surety.

"You are the proof," he said, pointing a bony finger at my face. "You are all the evidence I need."

52

I WAS TAKEN FROM HAMPTON COURT BY BOAT, FORCED TO WALK IN CAP-
tivity around London Bridge to avoid shooting the wickedly fast
water flowing between the piers. The skulls of traitors, stripped
of titles, names, and faces, dangled from pikes above the bridge
gatehouse. Thomas Cromwell's must have been there, but was
indistinguishable from the rest.

I could see the White Tower—the castle keep—glowing
eerily from the river as we rowed the second leg of the journey.
Around it, double-walled and multi-turreted, huddled the
battlements. A single crescent broke the wall at water level,
dark and dripping like a dragon's mouth. The Water Gate.
Traitor's Gate.

The portcullis raised and I stumbled up the stairs behind
my guard, across a cobbled alley and up a spiral staircase to my
cell. I hid behind my hair to avoid the curious glances of the
people who populated the castle. The people who were free to
come and go.

I was locked in a room with a tiny window that overlooked
the Tower Green, where Anne Boleyn had lost her head. I had
a hard wooden bench, a straw pallet, and a pathetic excuse for

a fire that sputtered and singed. I lay awake at night, listening to the ghosts of the many prisoners who had lost their lives to Henry VIII's reign. Thomas More. Anne and George Boleyn. Thomas Cromwell. Margaret Pole.

I couldn't bring myself to look long out the window. The scaffold stood there, stained dark by the rain. People laughed and walked, and once I saw a stolen kiss against the wall to the inmost ward. But what hurt most was the tiny portion of sky, cut close between window and wall, crowded by towers.

December arrived on feet waterlogged by rain. The light faded from the lowering sky and the castle walls took on the dampness of winter. But Wriothesley arrived looking positively cheerful.

"I wonder what you know about a certain member of the king's privy chamber of the name Thomas Culpepper."

I sucked in a whistle of air and then ducked my eyes to avoid the shot of Wriothesley's glance.

"Culpepper?" I asked, looking at my slippers.

"Yes. The prisoner, Dereham, said that he is completely innocent of any carnal knowledge of the queen since her marriage to the king. He said that he had been replaced in her affections by one Thomas Culpepper."

"I believe he danced with the queen on occasion," I said.

"Anything else?"

"No," I said, and this time looked him right in the eye. Daring him to believe me.

He gazed back, implacable.

"I will find the truth, Mistress Tylney. No matter how deeply it is buried. You can trust me on that."

I did. I trusted that this man with his leather breeches and his whip-smart questioning could find any truth he wished. But I was set on another course of lies.

"Were you aware of Mistress Howard's activities in the evening while the court was on progress to the north?" Wriothesley asked.

"Of course," I said. "I was her chamberer. It was my duty to know what she was doing, when she went to bed, and to ensure her comfort."

"Did her comfort include Culpepper?"

"No."

"What happened in Lincoln?"

"Lincoln?" How did he know these things?

"Yes. It's a cathedral city on the River Witham in Lincolnshire. The King's progress spent some days in the Bishops' Palace there."

I nodded, pondering, hoping I looked as if I was struggling to place the city amongst the many we visited.

"The guard said he had to lock the back stairs to the queen's apartments that night. That anyone might have entered."

I allowed my face to lighten.

"I remember!" I said. "I answered the door. He told me and I thanked him for keeping us safe."

"Yes," Wriothesley coughed.

"The queen." I hesitated. "She sent me down the stairs to check. I was afraid."

His dark eyes glowed keen with interest.

"And when I returned, I remember asking Joan Bulmer, 'Is the queen asleep yet?' And she answered, 'Yes, even now.'"

The absolute truth.

Wriothesley stood up and moved behind my chair. He gripped my shoulder with one hand, and my hair beneath my hood with the other. He tugged, the tension pulling my head back and to the side so that I looked up at the ceiling. His pallid and heavy eyelids appeared in the corner of my vision.

"Don't play games with me, Mistress Tylney," he said, his wine-soaked breath slippery on my cheek. "I know more games than you have ever considered. I know the games of the king's master inquisitors. I know how to get answers."

I didn't doubt him.

"But are those answers the truth, my lord?" I asked, feeling the fear convulse in my throat. "Because answers called forth by torture are expedient, but often false."

He pulled harder, my neck wrenched painfully, and stars burst across the ceiling.

"You know better than that, Kitty," he said, and let go.

I rubbed my neck. I had no script, no way of knowing what I would say or when. Perhaps the closeness and sureness of death really did addle a person's judgment.

"Did you ever carry messages to Culpepper from the queen?"

"No."

"Between the queen and Lady Rochford?"

I hesitated.

"I often relayed messages between the queen and her ladies," I said carefully. "I was her chamberer. It was my duty."

"Do you remember any in particular?"

"She once asked Lady Rochford for something that was promised her," I said. "That's all I know."

"You never sought out secret hiding places."

"No."

"Not even for a game?" he asked, a slyness to his question.

Hide-and-seek.

"Only for myself."

"Did Lady Rochford?"

"Have you asked her?" I regretted the question as soon as I asked it, and shrank from the fury on his thin lips.

"Jane Boleyn is not in a fit state to answer questions at the moment. In fact, she appears to be quite mad. You may have heard her screaming from the Wakefield Tower."

I thought it was only my dreams. But if she was insane, she could not be executed. It was the king's law.

"It may be real. She may be pretending," he said. It was as if he, too, could read my mind. "The king's own physicians are attending her. And his councilors are attending to the law.

355

"Thomas Culpepper says the affair was Jane Boleyn's idea," he continued. "Mistress Howard confirms this."

Oh, Cat. I sagged, no longer able to fight the implications of his words.

"For this, Jane Boleyn faces the scaffold. And she knows it. It is her guilt that sends her into madness. But you don't face the same fate.

"At *best*, Mistress Tylney," he said, reverting to my last name and striding across the floor to the tiny window, "you will be charged with misprision of treason." He turned, practically snapping his heels together. "Do you know what that means?"

I shook my head.

"It means that you had knowledge of treason in the form of the queen's former relationship with Francis Dereham. You didn't bring it to the king's attention, when he thought he was marrying an innocent girl with no marital entanglements."

He had had annulments from three of his wives for "marital entanglements." Only Queen Jane escaped that by dying before he was ready to get rid of her.

"You had no part in the act of concealment," he went on. "You were not present when the king was courting. This is a feeble way of saying that you knew and did nothing, and you walked away from responsibility.

"However," he continued, "at worst you will be convicted of treason. You had knowledge of the affair with Dereham and promoted it. You had knowledge of the affair with Culpepper and purposefully concealed it."

I stayed silent. He waited for me to admit to one or the other. But I could do neither. Did he expect the young to be stupid as well?

"Would you like to know what sentence you may expect?" he asked with the air of a man asking which sweet I would like from the tray at a banquet. "In both cases, you will be attainted and stripped any titles, land, or money you possess or stand to inherit. I gather that none of this applies to you?"

He looked at me from under his eyelashes, a cunning smile splaying his lips. He knew very well that being attainted would have no effect on my status.

"Misprision can garner a sentence of death or perpetual imprisonment. Treason is punishable by death, unless the king extends his mercy. Either way, you're looking at the end of your career at court, the end of your youth, and the end of your life as you know it."

He waited for this information to register in my mind and trigger an emotional outburst or tearful confession. I struggled with the tears, but kept them at bay. I wanted nothing to do with his manipulation.

"Thank you for telling me," I managed.

"My pleasure."

I'm sure it was.

"Culpepper and Dereham have confessed. They have already been tried and found guilty of high treason. Sentenced to death. Do you know what this means?"

I couldn't move. Not to speak. Not even to nod my head.

"It means that unless the king grants their pleas for clemency, they will be hanged by the neck, cut down alive, their members removed."

My body found its ability for motion and shuddered violently. Wriothesley stepped closer and whispered in my ear like a lover.

"Their members will be removed before their very eyes," he said softly. "Their bowels will be removed as well. They will still be alive when this happens. They will see their innards trailing on the ground and burned before them."

I couldn't beg him to stop. My tongue cleaved to the roof of my mouth.

"Their still beating hearts will be removed. Their heads will be stricken off, their bodies cut into quarters and the pieces hung high on the London Bridge so all may see the fate of traitors to the king. They will be left there until the gulls and ravens have feasted on every morsel of flesh. And there, their bones shall remain, bleached by the sun, buffeted by the wind, until they fall into the Thames or into the road and are trampled to dust and forgotten."

I wanted to cover my ears. I pictured Francis, his cocky swagger, faced with the gallows. I saw Culpepper, his blond good looks shrouded in blood. Even after all he had done, I could not wish such a fate on him, or anyone.

"Their only hope is for the king's leniency," Wriothesley murmured. "To be merely decapitated. I imagine the king's past

fondness for Culpepper may lead him to mercy, but Dereham? Dereham has no hope.

"Women, however, do not attract such a punishment." Wriothesley spoke casually, as if discussing the difference between boning a goose and roasting it whole.

"Queens and nobility like Jane Boleyn are dispatched by the ax. Common women convicted of treason are burned at the stake. Their skirts erupt into flames around them. On a windy day, it could take hours to die as the flames lick and char the delicate skin only to be teased away by the breeze carrying ash throughout the city."

I feared I would remain mute until that day, when at last I would find my voice as it screamed over the cheering of the bloodthirsty crowd. And the tears finally won.

Wriothesley smiled again.

"I shall leave you now."

53

IN THE NEXT FEW WEEKS THE TOWER GREW GLUTTONOUS ON THE INCARceration of traitors.

They brought in the dowager duchess after she burned a coffer full of papers said to belong to Francis Dereham. The rest of the Coven came, too. The number of prisoners soon exceeded Tower capacity. Lower-ranking and obviously innocent members of the duchess's household were shipped off to other prisons. But not I.

The duke stood outside the Tower gates, outside the prison, outside the very law itself and exclaimed loudly and constantly that he knew nothing of his slatternly niece's dubious conduct. He vilified her. Condemned her. Stood free upon the back of her guilt.

The Howard men groveled at the feet of the king, swearing loyalty. And were allowed to go free.

And Edmund Standebanke continued in the king's service.

Men, I thought. *Even guilt can't shackle them.*

But then Francis and Culpepper were executed. Pulled from the Tower by an ox-drawn cart, met with the jeers and silent judgment of Londoners. Culpepper's sentence was commuted to decapitation. Francis was not so lucky.

1542

54

WITH CULPEPPER'S DEATH, MY HORRIFYING DREAMS ENDED. BUT THE long winter nights loomed black and empty. I woke each morning, my muscles cramped from cold, shocked anew at my situation. At the mistakes and betrayals that got me there.

Gossip moved even faster in the Tower than it had at Norfolk House. I got snippets of news from the guards, from the charwoman, from the gardener who fixed a loose stone in the corner outside my door. Cat was imprisoned in Syon House, a monastery suppressed by the reformation, the nuns dispersed and the property relinquished to the crown. Joan languished somewhere in the Tower, far distant from me. Alice remained outside the prison, a star witness. Traitor to our family of girls. The circle broken.

We saw each other briefly at our indictment. Each of us was brought singly through the crowded room, through the press of bodies to the bar. Each of us pled guilty. Lady Margaret Howard. Edward Waldegrave. Alice. Joan. Me. Condemned to perpetual imprisonment. Goods and titles forfeit. The room rocked with weeping—from grief for a future behind stone walls or relief for keeping our heads, I knew not which. I sat on the bench, my head bent, and looked at no one. Utterly isolated in a place where the walls dripped with the moisture of collective breath. Alone.

Christmas came and went, bringing with it nothing but more rain and endless dark days. It seemed nobody kept Christmas that year. The king, they said, too heartbroken for festivities, brooded and wept, and the entire country followed suit.

My family sent me no word, no message, no hope. I was nothing, no one, forgotten in a world so dark that even the shadows got lost. I suffered no longer from the fear of my fate but from the knowledge that nobody cared, not even me.

Early in the New Year, a knock at my door admitted the guard, followed by a tall, thin man with shorn hair and a velvet cap. He wore the king's livery. I retreated involuntarily. Even without the mane of golden hair, without the air of snide superiority, I recognized Edmund Standebanke. My movement brought a flicker of emotion across his face. Understanding? Or humility?

"What do you want?" I asked.

"To help."

I almost laughed. "Nothing can help me."

"I am still the king's yeoman of the chamber," he said.

"And how did you manage that?" I asked. "How did you come to know every contemptible aspect of our lives and still remain employed by the very man you sought to dupe?"

He didn't move. Just stood there in that tiny room, looking

lost. Like he didn't know how he had got there, or how he had escaped.

"They believed me," he said finally.

As I once had. I believed he spoke the truth. I believed he might have cared for me.

"Well, aren't you just the lucky one?"

"Don't, Kitty," he said. "I feel horrible."

"*You* feel horrible?" Bitterness laced my words with poison and I wanted to press them into his flesh. To make him suffer. "You, who stand there, well-dressed and well-fed, not cowering beneath the sword of execution? How *dare* you?"

"He was my friend."

"Cat is my friend! And Joan and Jane and all the rest. Oh, boo hoo, Edmund, one of your friends cheated and despoiled everyone and suffered for it. You helped him! You are free. And here you stand trying to elicit sympathy."

"Just so you know, I have not been well-fed. I cannot eat."

It looked to be true. He was thin. His broad chest collapsed in upon itself. I willed myself to feel nothing.

"And I am not free," he continued. "I am imprisoned by my own remorse. I do feel horrible. I wish things were different."

"Then you will have to learn to live with your guilt," I told him. "Do not bring it to me. Wishing is a pointless exercise. There can be no other outcome to this."

I stood and stared him down. At last, I was stronger than he, because I had nothing to lose.

"I could save you," he said.

With those four words he crushed me. I wanted to be saved. To be protected. From pain. From fear. From heartache. I wanted someone to wipe away the past. To wrap me in something sane and normal and safe.

"Come," he said, "You cannot stay here. You cannot survive on your own. Be mine. Let me . . . Let me make amends."

His words struck bone. *You cannot survive* and *be mine*. He wanted to own me. He did not think I could own myself.

"There is nothing to mend," I said. "There was no structure to begin with."

"But kitten, listen. I can . . . we could marry."

Marriage. My parents, Lord Poxy, everyone had abandoned me. Except Edmund. I turned to the smudged window. To the green where Anne Boleyn had lost her head. Where private executions took place. I would not be so lucky, should it come to that. As it was, it seemed I would sit forgotten in this cell while life and death took place without me.

"Why?" I asked, before I could stop myself. I turned to face him. I wanted to know his answer.

Edmund rubbed his forehead, priming a crease between his brows.

"I could lose my position," he said. "Tying myself to you. The king has no desire to be reminded of . . . her."

"That's not much of a reason," I said. In fact, it sounded like a good reason for him to leave me to rot.

"I'm trying to do the right thing, Kitty," he said, an edge

creeping into his voice. The same edge that told me I was stupid. The same edge that told me I was ugly. "Come, I know you want to."

An echo from far away. From the miserable, aching past. Culpepper's low growl in the park that day, *I know you want this.*

And I saw very clearly that saying yes to Edmund was as sure a prison as saying no.

"Don't presume to tell me what I want."

"Now is not the time for semantics, Kitty. Come with me."

He held out his hand. Reached for me. I jerked away from him.

"No."

"I don't want to live with your death on my conscience."

I flinched. But I couldn't retreat. The room was too small. The past and his part in it were too great.

"Then consider your conscience relieved by my choice. But I do not relieve you of the burden that should be there from the pain you inflicted.

"If you want to make amends, Edmund, go and find that girl from the woods. Find a way to help *her.* Tell her it wasn't her fault. It wasn't her choice. It wasn't what she wanted. No matter what Culpepper said."

"I did nothing wrong," he said, and took a step away, as if to distance himself.

"No, Edmund," I said. "You did *nothing.* And that's not the same thing. It was your fault and it was mine. For not telling the truth. You enabled him to ruin the lives of so many. You

assisted him with a firm grip here, a saucy word there, a little manipulation. You *helped* him rape that woman in the park. And I think you would have done the same to me."

"No, Kitty," he said.

"You assumed, like he did, that you knew what I wanted."

"Because you never said."

"And you never asked."

"I never would have started this if I knew it would hurt you," he said.

"Forgive me if I don't believe you," I replied. "Our entire association was built on lies."

"I never lied to you."

He never told me he cared about me. He never said I was beautiful. He just said he wouldn't let me be until he'd had me.

And that he'd kept my secret.

"You told Culpepper you saw me. That I was in the park that day. Watching."

"I never told him." Edmund looked stricken. Those wide brown eyes smudged and haunted. "I never told anyone I saw you there."

"Then who did?" I asked.

But suddenly I knew. I knew that in this, he wasn't lying. It wasn't Edmund who told Culpepper I had seen him in the woods.

It was Cat.

The betrayal pushed me to the stone floor and pinned me there.

"I am sorry, Kitty," Edmund said quietly.

"Good."

When he left, wordless and wraithlike, I couldn't stop trembling. My chances of survival had slipped from slim to nil. Edmund wasn't much of a savior, but I knew his was the only offer I'd get.

55

Parliament passed a bill of attainder against Cat in February. It stripped her of her worldly goods, her title, her claims to land and property.

And then they stripped her of her right to live. She was condemned to death, without hearing or trial, unable to defend herself or entreat anyone else to do so for her. Her fall brought mine, for a shadow ever falls with its mistress.

And Jane fell, too. Blamed for corrupting the young queen, for abetting the traitorous lovers, for doing her duty, Jane would face the ax as well, one already bloodied by the neck of her young charge. Insanity would not save her. The King reversed that law.

And a new law was created. It declared that if any woman presumed to marry the king without first admitting if she had been unchaste, she would be guilty of high treason, punishable by death. Cat would leave a legacy.

The day they brought Cat to the Tower, I heard weeping. It was cold, the sky heavy and thick as curdled cream. I smelled the river from my room. Not the bright, green scent of a river cleaned by rains and rushes, but the corrupt stench of a river stagnant with blood and offal, death and decay.

Cat came by barge from Syon House, shooting the rapids under London Bridge, where the heads of Francis and Culpepper still hung, impaled on the weather-bleached pikes. She came through Traitor's Gate, just opposite my own cell, out of my line of sight. But I heard her crying.

Silence accompanied her. Not a cheer of support or an offer of prayers. Anne Boleyn had had her supporters. Catherine of Aragon had most of the country behind her. Even poor Anne of Cleves had people who defended her right to remain queen.

Not Cat.

An expectant hush hung over the Tower for two full days, waiting for the ax to fall. The nights were agony.

Then the guard brought me a gown of rich green brocade. I recognized it immediately.

"The queen . . . I mean, Mistress Howard, entreated the king to give her gowns to her waiting women. Being attainted, she had nothing else to give."

I took it and held it up. It looked out of place in that bare room, against my pale skin and frayed slippers. But it felt warm and comforting beneath my chapped hands. It smelled of cedar and better times. I hugged it to me.

"Thank you," I whispered.

"I have also come to escort you . . ." he trailed off. Fear froze me. It was late. Dark. Surely they didn't burn people at night.

An image of a bonfire, shooting sparks into the gloom, blurred my vision.

"But . . ." I gestured helplessly with the gown. How cruel to give a girl such a piece of luxury to burn her in it.

"Leave it here," he said. "You will return to it." His eyes rolled in disdain. He thought I couldn't leave the gown. He thought a scrap of fabric made me stutter and weep. He was right.

I followed him down the spiral staircase and along a muddy track to the queen's rooms. The apartments had been built and renovated for Anne Boleyn's coronation, where she stayed before her day of triumph, carried into the cheering streets of London. They were also where she stayed the night before her execution.

Two guards, dressed in the king's livery, stood before a locked door. They stared straight at the wall opposite them, not even glancing at me or my escort.

"This is the one," my guard said.

I followed him into a dark gallery. At the end, more guards opened another door to a blaze of light and a rush of heat. I stepped into a room furnished with a trestle table and two chairs with velvet cushions. Two goblets sat on the table, a jug of wine beside them. I nearly wept with the relief my hands felt from the constant, cracking cold.

"Kitty!"

Dressed all in black velvet fitted to each curve, Cat looked as beautiful as ever, with her pale skin and dark eyes, her mahogany hair tied up in a simple black hood. She looked sober, quiet.

"Cat," I whispered.

"I can't believe they let me see you," Cat said. "I've been so lonely. So bored. No music. No dancing. No one to talk to. No one to commiserate with. No one to make me laugh."

She didn't offer apologies for landing me and Joan and all of her ladies and family in waters infested by sharks intent to kill. But her eyes retreated into sockets smudged by fear and sleeplessness.

"I heard you had servants," I said stiffly.

"The most boring girls you can imagine. Dull as ditchwater. And so tiresome." She put on a pewling, high-pitched whine. "Don't you want to pray now, my lady? You should ask for God's forgiveness. I pray for your soul every minute of every day."

Cat made vomiting noises and mimed putting her finger down her throat.

"I'm sure they do pray for me constantly," she said. "They certainly do nothing of interest." She walked to the table and picked up the jug.

"Wine?" she asked, waving it over the goblets.

"And the gossip they pass on is frightful," she went on, pouring. "Apparently the king has been seen flirting with Elizabeth Brooke. Thomas Wyatt's wife, the one he left because of her adultery. At least the king knows in advance that she has been *unchaste*."

I nodded, dumbly. Cat was about to die and she was acting like . . . Cat.

"Come and sit," she said, patting a chair. I sank onto it.

Stretched my toes to the fire. It conjured a visceral memory of the duchess's private room in Lambeth. The first time I'd ever dared to sit in a chair with a velvet cushion.

Cat handed me a goblet of wine. Catherine Howard—Queen of England—served me.

"I need your help," she said. "I have to ask you a favor. Something only a sister could do for me. It will take a stout heart. And more than a modicum of affection for me."

I searched my heart for affection and found that I came up lacking. Cat had used me my entire life. Made me do things I didn't want to do—lie, steal, spend time in the company of Edmund Standebanke. She had taken away the things I loved. Convinced me to do things I knew were wrong. But I always came back for more. So who was at fault?

Cat stood up and walked toward a leaded window that over-looked the green. Before it, on the floor, about the height of a stool, was a massive piece of wood, supported on two sides, with a shallow indent hewn from the center.

"Is that . . . ?" I couldn't ask.

"The block," Cat sounded cheerful. "My block. I had them bring it to me. Tomorrow morning, I will lay my neck here," she touched the depression, worn smooth by scrubbing the blood from it, "and the executioner will swing his ax."

"Don't, Cat," I said. The fire did nothing to warm the cold lump of lead that filled my chest.

"I need you, Kitty," she said. "I want to make sure I do this properly."

She wanted me to help her practice. She wanted me to watch her put her head on the block. My every sinew and muscle ached to run away. To pound on the door and be returned to my cold, lonely cell.

Cat knelt down. She untied the hood from her hair, the mass of curls frothing down her back. She swung it once, a full, sweeping motion to clear every strand from her neck, and laid her head upon the wood.

"Is this right?" she asked.

"I don't know," I said. It wasn't like practicing a curtsey or a flirtatious look. All I could see was the ax beginning to fall. I had to look away.

"Then come over here," she said.

Despite my muscles' desire to escape, I found that I could not stand.

"Kitty," she said in the voice that brooked no argument. "Come. Over. Here."

I moved stiffly like a knight in heavy armor with the joints rusted shut. I hated myself for going. I hated her more for asking.

I could see each hair delineated, the thin, vulnerable swirl of down at the nape of her neck. Her great sweep of curls tumbled toward me like a red tide. The curve of her cheek hid her eyes from me. Her jaw tightened.

"They say my cousin laughed before her execution," she said so quietly she could have been speaking love whispers to the block itself. "She said, 'I only have a little neck.' As do I."

I looked at her neck, stretched like that of a swan.

"But that could not stop it from hurting," she continued. "Do you think it hurts, Kitty? When the blow comes? The slice of the blade? When the lips continue to pray or the fingers to twitch? When the blood spurts and the staring eyes lose their vision? Does it hurt?"

"I don't know."

"I think it does," she whispered, and clambered again to her feet, this time her limbs shaking. "I think it hurts a great deal. How could it not?"

I shook my head.

"Why me, Kitty?" she asked. "Why did he choose me? Why not any of the other girls who filled the maidens' chamber or the apartments of Anne of Cleves?"

I thought of all the forces that came together to create Henry's fifth queen: ambition, family advancement, lost youth, vanity, lust. Again I said nothing.

"*Why?*" The scream tore from her throat. Her hands clenched beneath her elbows, her body rigid. For one quavering moment she appeared to hold herself together by sheer force of will.

"Because you're Catherine Howard," I said finally. It could have been no one else.

She turned around and stalked back to the wooden block below the window.

Again, Cat flung her hair to one side. She used to do that when she laughed. Her hair would hit me in the face if I stood

too close. Its trajectory used to catch the eye of the nearest man. But his gaze never followed it to me. It always followed the hair back to her.

She let her head rest as if she could no longer hold it up, and a single tear stained the wood.

"That's not right," I said.

She sat back on her heels. I took in her tiny face, the low-slung collar of her gown exposing her throat, her hands in her lap, clutching at the fabric of her skirts. She looked up at me like a child waiting for a whipping. Like when we were eight and the duchess caught us drinking wine from her golden goblets, Cat with a daisy-chain crown upon her head.

"You should use a hand to pull your hair to one side," I found myself saying. "Gently. It's not so impetuous. So . . . shameless."

Cat nodded, taking my criticism.

"Like this?"

Carefully, she gathered all of her curls in one hand. She bent down and pulled the hair to the left, exposing the tiny bones at the top of her spine.

My breath caught in my throat. Cat, who gave in to her emotions on every whim, wouldn't die a traitor's death, but the death of a queen. I gave in, wanting to mourn for her.

"Yes," I whispered.

Cat put her hands in her lap. She moved them behind her back. They fluttered like lost birds.

"Hold onto the block," I said, kneeling down next to her.

I took her right hand and stretched the arm so she held the rough wood at the side. She did the same with her left. Almost hugging it.

"That's good," she said, her voice muffled. Her fingers tightened, her knuckles white. "I don't have to work so hard to keep them still."

She sat up and stroked the wood.

"Do you think this is the same block they used for my cousin?" she asked. "The king allowed her a swordsman. Brought from Calais. He loved her that much."

Thinking of the heads that had rolled from that block—by ax or by sword—made me want to be sick into the fireplace. More than that, it made me fear the fire, which still might be my own fate. Then guilt enveloped me, as Cat faced her fate so much sooner.

"It looks to have seen a lot of use," she said, as if in conversation about a dish or a goblet. "Perhaps they used it for Margaret Pole. Her executioner didn't know what he was doing. They say he trembled with each swing of the ax."

My stomach began to ferment like old wine, strong and sour.

"I don't want that kind of death," Cat said. "That's why I'm practicing. I have practiced my speech already; would you like to hear it?"

I shook my head.

"No, I suppose not. But I can practice all I want, and I still have no control over the man with the ax. I hope he's practicing tonight."

I fervently hoped the same.

"I wonder what he practices on?" Cat mused. "A cabbage per-haps? Or maybe something more mobile, like a pig. I wonder what happens after it's killed. Perhaps his wife cooks it. If he can afford it. I'd be happy to provide the man with a decent meal if he gets my head with one blow."

I walked blindly to the door. I couldn't listen anymore. I couldn't comfort her. I wished Cat could find the words that would make me love her again. That would make me feel for her, and not just feel sorry for her. But she didn't say another word. It was like I had ceased to exist. As I had told Edmund, wishing was a pointless exercise.

I knocked softly on the door and it was opened into the empty space beyond. I stepped through, fighting the panic that threatened tears. Fighting the anguish of losing my best friend, not to the ax but to the actions that led to its fall.

"Kitty?"

The voice was so quiet I almost didn't hear. Like she wanted me not to hear. I stopped.

"Will you watch?"

"No," I turned. "God. No."

She nodded but didn't look at me, still curled up before the block like a pilgrim at an altar.

"I understand," she said and her voice shook. "Truly, I do. But I would like to know . . . I would like to think that at least one person with a little bit of sympathy watched me die. Wishing me peace. I fear that everyone else will be wishing me ill."

"Why me?" I asked, unable to stop the question.

She faced me then, pale and serene, her eyes untarnished by artifice.

"Because I know you will forgive me."

I nodded.

56

THE SUN HAD NOT YET RISEN WHEN THEY TOOK CAT TO THE SCAF-fold. But there was enough light for me to see the people gathered there. Henry Howard, the duke's son, his face like granite, stood shoulder-to-shoulder with the French ambassador. The small crowd huddled against the drizzling and freezing rain.

Cat walked between two guards, followed by three ladies, one her own sister, Isabel Baynton, their faces emotionless. Women of Wriothesley's choosing.

Cat stumbled at the first stair of the scaffold and the guards had to seize her arms. She collapsed into them, her tiny body tugging them off-balance, as if the knowledge of death added an emotional weight that could wrestle them to the earth. They waited and then, when it became obvious she couldn't do it herself, pulled her to her feet.

They carried her up the stairs, her limbs appearing useless. But when they reached the block, she shrugged them off, and they stepped back.

She stood, alone. I heard nothing of the voice that had shaped my childhood. Every word was pressed down to the earth by the rain, and none reached me, so far from the green, in my icy little tower room.

I watched as she removed her hood and handed it to one of the ladies. She smoothed her dress and then knelt. She pulled her hair to one side, just as she had practiced.

When the executioner raised his ax, I had to look away. I forgave Cat. I wished her peace. But I couldn't watch. In the end, I couldn't do her bidding.

It seemed to take the ax forever to fall. The thump of steel on wood came muffled to my window. Just once. I sank to the floor, wrapped myself in green brocade.

I heard no cheers. I heard no weeping.

An age passed during which I knew Jane went to the scaffold and gave her speech. I covered my head with my arms, unable to offer to Jane Boleyn even half of what I had done for Cat.

But still I heard the second thunk of heavy metal meeting little resistance before burying itself firmly in the block.

 And then all went quiet. The guards delivered food and drink, but little news. The king seemed to have forgotten me. Forgotten all of us. Or perhaps he was just trying to forget. My eighteenth birthday approached, and I finally wept. For myself. Without Cat, no one remembered my birthday. And I wept for Cat, who would never see hers.

In the end, Cat kept our secrets. She blamed Culpepper. She blamed Jane. But she didn't blame me. She protected me. Enough to keep me in prison for the rest of my life, the shadow of a shadow.

I watched the sun rise earlier and set later. I watched the light of day fade and vanish. I watched the little corner of sky that pierced my window and made my life unbearable. I watched as the scaffold was dismembered piece by piece and finally taken away, leaving the spot where it stood an empty hole of memory.

Spring approached, visible only in the reappearance of the grass on the green and the winking blue eye of the sky from my window. One bitter cold morning a knock woke me from my

Stygian sleep. The room was dark, but the window frame was lit by a slant of the rising sun.

The door opened and there the guard stood. With Alice Restwold.

She hesitated in the doorway, searching my face, my demeanor, for welcome or disgust.

"Visitor," the guard said.

Another shade from my past, again wanting something from me. Did they not know I had nothing to give?

"Hello, Kitty," Alice said.

"Alice."

"You look . . . well."

"Considering I'm in prison. Considering I've been abandoned by my family. Considering my best friend is dead."

"It wasn't my fault."

"No," I said. "I suppose it wasn't. You just stood by and let it happen. You just told whatever was asked of you and got away with it."

"I was imprisoned, too!" she cried.

"You?"

"Yes, they held me against my will."

"Not very tightly." I indicated her apparent liberty.

"I've been pardoned."

"Good for you. What did you give them for that?"

"I have little freedom. I've gained nothing."

"Oh?" I climbed to my feet, limbs creaking in dissention.

"Did *you* watch your best friend get beheaded from your chamber window? Did you have to watch her practice putting her head on the block the night before?"

"No, Kitty," she said, a thin line of tears against her lashes. We lapsed into a silence so profound I heard the guard shuffle his feet outside the door.

"Why have you come here?"

"Because you have no one else."

"Thank you for reminding me."

"It's true. Joan has been pardoned as well. She swears she'll never speak to any of us again. She's left for the country already."

"Lucky Joan."

"Cat always said that we only have each other."

I looked at her. She appeared to mean it. I nodded.

"I know you don't like me."

I nodded again. It felt good to acknowledge it.

"I know you don't trust me," she added.

"You've never given me reason to."

"Except that I never said a word about your connection," she said. "Or Joan's."

"You told on Cat, but not on the rest of us? Bully for you."

"Only after they found her out."

"So who told, Alice?" I asked. "I've had plenty of time to think about this and I can figure no one else. None of us but you escaped." I wanted so badly for her to confess. I wanted someone to blame.

387

"You really think that of me?"

"Who else could it be?"

"Mary Lascelles," Alice said, and waited for it to sink in.

Mary Lascelles. The girl who slept in the corner of the maidens' chamber. The one who suffered when Cat raged over being cut off from Francis. The one who hated us from the beginning.

"How?"

"She told her brother. He told his reformist friends. Friends who resented the Howards. They took the information to Archbishop Cranmer."

Cranmer, who always acted on his conscience.

"Lord Maltravers made sure my husband told me every detail. About how the archbishop left a note for the king in his prayer book. About the investigations that took place before we even knew what was happening."

"But you knew," I challenged her. "Because of the duke. Because of William."

"They sent me away before I could warn you."

"I see," I said, and then turned the full weight of my accusing, judgmental eyes on Alice Restwold. "But Mary Lascelles didn't know about Culpepper."

"It was impossible to hide, Kitty," Alice said. "I knew. You and Joan and Jane Boleyn knew. Francis knew. The true miracle was that no one said a word beforehand. Even Cat knew she was living on borrowed time."

Borrowed time. Isn't that what we all lived on? Every moment

we breathed was borrowed from the person who took the fall.

"They knew that they would be found guilty. We all did. They had no escape when the rumors got out."

"But Jane . . ."

"Will always be blamed."

She hid behind madness and made it that much easier for them. After that, no one would believe a word she said.

I nodded. There was no escape. They were dead.

Alice took a deep breath.

"Kitty, the king wants to forget the past. He wants the whole episode with Cat put from memory. He wants all the prisoners gone, and for no one to remind him of what once was."

"So I'm not even wanted in prison," I said bitterly.

As bad as prison was, the thought of getting out was even more frightening. I had nowhere to go. No one to go to. I could step out of the gates of the Tower onto the London streets and into a life of squalor and pain and premature death. No one in my class wanted me and no one else knew me. A woman alone was a woman fallen. And there was only one thing for a fallen woman to do.

"You're released, Kitty," Alice said, smiling tentatively. "You're free."

I could see that she wanted me to be happy, but all I felt was the cold clench of fear. Fear that turned quickly into anger.

"So you've come here to gloat?" I asked. "You have a position with some household somewhere, you have an understanding

with William Gibbon, you have it all. And you've come to let me know I have nothing?"

"No, Kitty," she said, stepping away from my vitriol. "It's nothing like that. It's just that Joan has decided to cut us off completely. And with Cat gone . . ."

"What?" I raged. "You think we can be friends? Why would you want that? I can't give you anything. All I can do is bring you down."

I turned away from her. Avoided looking out the window. The cell grew so silent I wondered if she had left.

"You're lucky, you know."

Alice's voice came from the far side of the room. I wheeled on her.

"Lucky? Oh yes, being friendless, without family or money, trained for nothing and proficient at little is really an enviable position."

"Yes," Alice said, the word a finality. "You are lucky. You have no ties. I'm stuck. Dependent. My husband was questioned. They thought he knew about my involvement. And now . . . he keeps very tight reins. We are both indebted to Lord Maltravers. I cannot leave. I have nowhere to go. I'm nineteen years old and I am little better than a slave.

"You, Kitty, have freedom. You can walk out of this room and disappear into London. No one will admonish you for being part of Cat's household. No one will tell you every day that you are *nothing* because of who you knew. You could change your name. You could live a real life."

"But Alice, all I'm fit for is life in a whorehouse." I nearly wept at how little she understood. "The streets of the city are dangerous. I have nowhere to live and nowhere to go. At least you have a roof over your head."

"I would trade with you in an instant."

I snorted bitter laughter.

"The grass is always greener, I suppose." I replied.

"I wish you all the best," said Alice quietly. She stepped forward and grabbed my hand, tightly enough that I couldn't pull away, though I tried. She glanced once over her shoulder to the firmly closed door.

"I saved this for you," she whispered. She pulled something out of her pocket and pressed it into my hand. I tried to drop it, but she wrapped my fingers around it and held firm. I felt the soft nubbins of embroidered cutwork.

"Lace?" I asked her, my hand still in hers. "Do you mock me, Alice?"

"No," she said, looking a little shocked.

"Lace is where this all started," I reminded her. "The lace wrapped around the key to the dormitory."

"The lace *you made*."

"So?" I asked. "It means nothing."

"No, Kitty," she said, letting go of me, "it means everything."

She walked back to the door, and turned.

"I'm still married, Kitty," she said, almost as an afterthought. "My husband doesn't love me. But I am still married. I have no understanding. Definitely not with William Gibbon."

"Alice," I began, but didn't know where my words would lead. I didn't want her to continue. And I wanted to hear everything.

"He was ordered by the duke to keep company with me, so I could send messages. He would have lost his job, his reputation, if he didn't. I hate to admit that I enjoyed it, even though it wasn't real. Even though it hurt you. William Gibbon is kind and generous, even to a talebearer like me. In the end, he couldn't take the duke's orders anymore, and he left. I believe he's somewhere in London. He had eyes for only one of the queen's ladies. He always spoke only of you."

She knocked and when the door opened, she turned.

"Good-bye, Kitty."

"Word just came," the guard said, allowing her just enough room to pass. "You've received the king's pardon. You're to be released."

Alice always had the news before anyone else.

The guard opened the door wider and it yawned significantly. I could step through. I could go.

"Give me a moment," I said, turning away to hide the panic on my face.

The guard nodded and allowed the door to close, giving me the privacy I might need to use the chamber pot or straighten my skirts.

I opened my hand and looked at the roll of lace. I wondered if I could sell it, make enough money to afford something to eat and drink. It was worn, browned with age and use. It could have been the same piece used to wrap that fateful key,

three years before. Alice was like a squirrel, hiding things away after they'd been discarded. Giving them significance. Keeping things as well as secrets. It felt heavy. Full of memory. Too heavy to be just lace.

I unrolled it slowly, half expecting the key to fall out. I wanted to cry, because Alice had done this to spite me after all. She had a place and a marriage and I had nothing. All because of a foolish childhood friendship and the stupid need to belong. And that bloody, wretched key.

The lace began to spin and an object fell from it, into my left hand. It glowed dully.

The emerald. Set in gold. The one given to me by the king after the game of hide-and-seek, when he asked me to remain her friend. At the very least I had managed to keep that promise.

Alice had rescued the jewel before the men came to take Cat's. I hadn't even looked for it, knowing that my claim to anything precious would come to naught. But Alice, with her forethought and understanding of the importance of objects, had saved it.

And given it back. A river of forgiveness swept through me.

"Alice!" I cried, running through the door, clinging to the stone, the piece of lace trailing behind me like a banner. I passed the stunned guard, stumbled down the spiral staircase and slipped out the door to the forecourt, but Alice was nowhere to be found.

I ran around the tower in which I had been housed, avoid-

ing the sight of the green. I barreled down the small slope to the gate that opened onto the Water Lane and out to Traitor's Gate, now closed to the river by the heavy portcullis.

"Stop!" One of the king's yeomen stepped in front of me.

"You're a prisoner, aren't you?" he said gruffly, gripping my shoulders.

"I've been released," I panted, the short sprint having taken my breath away. I had not moved more than five feet at a time for four months. My words came out as tiny clouds in the cold air.

He looked over my shoulder. I glanced back in time to see the guard from my cell nod.

"Very well," the yeoman said, letting go of me and standing aside. "But a little more dignity, if you please. There's no rush. You have your whole life ahead of you still."

I looked at him. He was shorter than I, though his hat gave the appearance of height. He was old, maybe as old as the king, the gray hair curling on his temples, wrinkles cornering his eyes. He had seen many prisoners in his time.

"Shall I accompany you to the gate?" he asked, as if concerned that I would bolt before someone announced that a mistake had been made.

I nodded, still breathless.

"A friend visited me," I gasped. "I'm looking for her. Did she pass this way?"

He looked at me sideways, walking down the Water Lane. The battlement walls rose on either side of us, creating a canyon of shadow, though the sun brightened the octagonal Bell Tower ahead of us.

"A girl?" he asked.

"Yes. Short, blonde, quite thin. She wore . . ." I couldn't think of what Alice wore. All I could picture was the russet gown Cat had given her.

"I have seen few ladies in the Water Lane today," the yeoman told me. Alice, with her ability to slip in and out of a place unnoticed, had disappeared. "Could she be in the household of someone who resides here?"

"I don't know," I said. "She didn't say. May I look for her?"

"I should think you'd want to be out of the Tower quickly," he said with a grin. "I thought that was why you were running."

"I want to find Alice," I said, stopping to look back over my shoulder. We stood on the bridge that crossed the stagnant moat, the water gleaming and oily around us. Could I have passed her? But there were no ladies to be seen. A milkmaid. A laundry maid. And men. Crowding the bridge, the gates, the Water Lane.

"You won't find her," he said. "The Tower is the size of a village. More people come in and out of these gates than I could count. Visitors. Victuallers. And if you don't know who she's with, the chances are slim."

"The Duke of Norfolk, perhaps?" I tried.

"Not likely," the yeoman laughed. "He hasn't set foot in the Tower. Afraid he'll be forced to stay."

True. The duke wouldn't come near the Tower ever again.

A roar interrupted my thoughts. We passed the animal dens in the Lion Tower, where the road turned sharply to the right to cross the moat one last time. I was leaving. I was walking out. I faced Tower Hill, outside the Tower proper, where George Boleyn and Thomas Cromwell and dozens of others who didn't merit a "private" execution had been put to death. The posts of the scaffold were clearly visible. London lay beyond them.

I stopped walking. "I can't."

"You must," the yeoman said. He must have seen it all before. Prisoners who tried to escape. Prisoners who were executed on Tower Hill. Prisoners released after thirty-five years. Prisoners who had nowhere to go.

He walked me across the bridge. Past the lions' cages where the animals paced in cells smaller than mine, looking balefully through the bars. The lions would never be set free. They would die in the Tower.

I didn't want to do that. Die in the Tower. Even though the thought of being alone on the streets of London terrified me, the thought of dying slowly in that tiny room frightened me more.

"That's the girl," the yeoman murmured.

"Pardon?" I asked.

"You're ready," he said as we came to the Bulwark Gate, the portal to the chaos of the city. "It shows in the tilt of the head, the set of the shoulders. I can see it in your eyes."

He smiled at me again.

"That's a lovely bit of lace," he said, indicating the piece that still fluttered from my hand. "If you cleaned it up, it might fetch a price."

"Thank you," I said. He was being nice. Trying to help me. Giving me possibilities.

"I think the embroiderer's guild makes its home in Cheapside."

Cheapside. William's family once owned a house there.

"My cousin is there. They'll know where to send you. But keep to this side of the river and stay away from Southwark," he added. "Someone might get the wrong impression."

Someone might think me a whore.

"Thank you," I said again, and stepped away from the bridge.

"Good luck," he said. "Keep the spire of St. Paul's in sight, and you'll make your way."

The cathedral jabbed at the sky, clearly visible. Not far. I smiled at him and dipped a tiny curtsey. That made him blush. Though I was no better than he. And thankfully, no worse. No longer a prisoner, I could hold my head a little higher.

He turned and walked back across the bridge. He didn't look back.

I gripped the emerald in my hand and said one more thank you to Alice. She had not only given me a gift, she had given me a push. I didn't need to sell the lace. That I would keep, and I would keep it with me always. It would remind me of who I

used to be. But the emerald I didn't need. I could sell it with no remorse. And for much more money. It represented the secrets I had been forced to keep. The silence.

With the money, I could purchase the materials to make more lace. Make my own way. My own choices. My own life.

The walls of London rose around me, the crushing weight of alleys and crowds. The assaulting odors of hundreds of strangers. The liberating painlessness of anonymity. And above it all, the finger of St. Paul's, beckoning me to my future.

Author's Note

Ask anyone and they'll tell you I'm a little obsessed with English history—particularly Henry VIII and his six wives. Dates and statistics create a framework but to me aren't the appeal of history—the characters are, their motivations, strengths, weaknesses, loves, and beliefs. And the places—Hampton Court, Windsor, the Tower of London. I have always been able to picture the scenes and characters in my mind, the gowns and jewels, the crowded rooms and even the smells (though I'm sure my imagination doesn't come close to the reality).

Because I find history riveting in its own right, I'm dedicated to maintaining historical accuracy in my novels. I spend hours reading histories and biographies. I visit castles and houses and even fields and street corners where palaces once stood, just to get a sense of place. But I have to admit I've taken poetic license when it suits the story.

The facts are these: Catherine Howard was born sometime

between 1521 and 1525. For my purposes, I settled on 1524 for her birth year, her age suiting the character I envisioned.

Little is known about Katherine Tylney. I couldn't discover where she came from or where she went. I don't even know how old she was. I invented her age, her character, her family. I gave her the same birthday as my father.

Wherever possible, I used Katherine Tylney's documented testimony to illustrate her role in Catherine Howard's life—they shared a bed in the maidens' chamber, she carried messages between the queen and Jane Boleyn, she admitted that one night on the progress she came into the queen's chamber and blurted, "Jesu, is the queen not abed yet?" She appeared to be a witness and not a participant. I chose to make her appear more.

Because we know so little about Kitty, we don't know anything about her romantic life. I discovered a T. Gibbon in the Duke of Norfolk's entourage, but changed his name to William because of the multitude of other Thomas names in the story (Culpepper, Wriothesley, Cromwell, Howard). And Ed. Standebanke is mentioned once as a member of the king's guard. I dubbed him Edmund and chose to make him young and handsome, as well.

The two boys are the only fictional characters in the novel. Others are fictionalized—we don't know if Alice Restwold was a "spy" for the Duke of Norfolk or why Jane Boleyn chose to facilitate the queen's affair. Part of the joy of writing historical

fiction is the license to take what we do know and ignite it with the question *what if?*

One historical figure I chose to cut entirely. Henry Manox was the music teacher in the dowager duchess's household, and Catherine Howard's love interest before Francis Dereham. History tells us that it was he who informed the duchess of the midnight revels in the maidens' chamber. But to avoid complicating the story further, and in an effort to shorten the first third of the book, I took him out of the picture. Because Mary Lascelles tattled about Catherine Howard's affair with Manox, I chose to make her the informant on Francis and just cut out the middleman. It tied neatly into the plot because Mary actually did start the snowball of information that eventually brought Catherine Howard down.

There are a couple of other instances where I fudged the truth. Joan Bulmer was in Yorkshire when she wrote the "blackmail" letter to the queen, yet I keep her placed firmly in Norfolk House. I neglect to mention that after the king's illness, the court went on a mini-progress around the south of England before stopping in Greenwich for three weeks—I made it look like they were in Greenwich the entire time. I did this to avoid tangents and explanations that got in the way of the story itself.

While researching this novel, I read the related works of Julia Fox, Antonia Fraser, Karen Lindsey, Lacey Baldwin Smith, David Starkey, and Alison Weir, amongst others. They

write brilliantly and their ability to express the minutiae of historical detail in a profound and engrossing way never ceases to astound me. I am also forever in debt to the encyclopedic knowledge and dedication to detail of my copyeditor, Janet Pascal. Any historical mistakes and all poetic license are entirely down to me.

Acknowledgments

Like Cat, I wouldn't be anywhere without my friends and mentors. I just hope I have made better use of their advice and am able to show the extent of my gratitude.

My brilliant agent, Catherine Drayton, saw the potential in me and in Kitty and launched us further than I ever imagined. Thank you for believing. And my thanks to the rest of the InkWell team who are behind this book: Richard Pine, Lyndsey Blessing, Alexis Hurley, and Nathaniel Jacks.

I couldn't have asked for a more honest or sympathetic editor, but more than that, Kendra Levin's comments and suggestions are always spot on, and for that I am more than grateful. I am also indebted to Regina Hayes for ensuring the book lived up to the title and vice versa. I am eternally beholden to Irene Vandervoort for adorning this book with a sumptuous cover and to Kate Renner for equally embellishing the interior.

From the beginning, I've had the YA Muses to help keep me

sane, to keep me on track, and to keep me going. Novels are not written in a vacuum, and I am thankful for the insight and friendship of Bret Ballou, Donna Cooner, Veronica Rossi, and Talia Vance.

I have also enjoyed the support and encouragement of writers and illustrators I have met personally and those I've only met online. My local critique group, the Apocalypsies, the Class of 2k12, and countless members of the SCBWI, were all kind enough to share their thoughts and wisdom on this rollercoaster, especially Susan Hart Lindquist, who gave me the tools I needed to write this book.

I wouldn't have made it through my crazy life without the friends who populated my childhood and shaped my adolescence, and those I've encountered along my journey through adulthood. You are too many to name, the greatest riches a girl could want. But for this particular book, I must mention Mona Dougherty specifically, because she reads everything I send her.

Lastly, all the words in the world can't express my thanks to my family: Graham Neate, my father-in-law, who never fails to ask how the writing is going; Judy and John Longshore, my parents, who let me find my way; Martha Longshore, my sister and sister of my soul, my first reader and biggest role model; my sons, Freddie and Charlie, who help me believe that anything is possible.

And Gary, who lifts me up and keeps me grounded.

Tarnish

SPEAK

Published by the Penguin Group

Penguin Group (USA) LLC

375 Hudson Street

New York, New York 10014

USA * Canada * UK * Ireland * Australia

New Zealand * India * South Africa * China

penguin.com

A Penguin Random House Company

First published in the United States of America by Viking,
an imprint of Penguin Group (USA) Inc., 2013
Omnibus edition published by Speak, an imprint of Penguin Group (USA) Inc., 2014

THE LIBRARY OF CONGRESS HAS CATALOGED THE VIKING EDITION AS FOLLOWS:

Longshore, Katherine.

Tarnish / by Katherine Longshore.

p. cm.

Summary: "At the English court, King Henry VIII's interest in Anne Boleyn could give her an
opportunity to make a real impact in a world with few choices for women, but when poet Thomas
Wyatt reveals he's fallen for her, Anne must choose between true love and the chance to make
history"—Provided by publisher.

ISBN 978-0-670-01400-2 (hardcover)

1. Anne Boleyn, Queen, consort of Henry VIII, King of England, 1509–1547—Juvenile fiction.
2. Great Britain—History—Henry VIII, 1509–1547—Juvenile fiction.
[1. Anne Boleyn, Queen, consort of Henry VIII, King of England, 1509–1547—Fiction.
2. Great Britain—History—Henry VIII, 1509–1547—Fiction. 3. Kings, queens, rulers, etc.—Fiction.
4. Sex role—Fiction. 5. Love—Fiction.]

I. Title.

PZ7.L864Tar2013 [Fic]—dc23 2012032988

Speak ISBN 978-0-14-751368-7

Printed in the United States of America

1 3 5 7 9 10 8 6 4 2

To my sister, Martha, because the Longshores stick together. Thank you for being the one to pick up the phone.

Tarnish

Greenwich Palace
1523

1

A DEEP BREATH IS ALL IT TAKES TO ENTER A ROOM.

Or to scream.

Or both.

I stand against a wall, five strides from the great oak door of the queen's apartments. The guard watches me sideways, pretending he's not. Pretending he's focused on the stairwell. The pretense fails to deceive me.

I haven't asked to enter. Nor can I turn and walk away. Before reentering the queen's service, I must solicit her welcome. And he knows it. I know he's looking at my risqué French hood. At the black hair it exposes. At my misshapen little finger. I shake my sleeve to cover it.

I know he's thinking about my family. My sister.

We stand like effigies, pretending not to stare at each other.

The walls loom, gray as the rain outside. Like the sky of England itself. Everything seems colorless and humbled, despite the layers of velvets and tapestries, the peacock plumage of courtiers and ladies. Greenwich Palace feels like my father's disappointment made tangible.

I take another deep breath and straighten my shoulders, just as Father taught me when he marched me into the presence of Margaret of Austria, the Duchess of Savoy. I was seven years old and terrified to be left in her care. Father offered only one piece of advice before abandoning me and returning to England. "When you're afraid," he said then, "you need to put an iron rod in your spine. Look your enemy in the eye. Take a deep breath and perform."

The prodigal daughter, he calls me now. Or he would if he were here.

I wipe the sweat from my palms on my skirt and approach the guard, who leers as if he knows all about me and opens the door. I blow him a kiss as I pass by, accompanied by a rude gesture. He pretends not to notice, and again fails to deceive me.

There is something of the dragon's lair in the royal chambers of a palace. And Queen Katherine's chambers don't shatter that illusion. Smoke from the candles congeals at the ceiling in a swirling, palpable mass. And the place swarms with courtiers ready to eviscerate you socially and politically.

Another breath, and I step into the presence of the queen. I have a feeling she won't be happy to see me return. My first duty is to kneel before her until she acknowledges me, and thank her. I worry that she will ignore me—more punishment for my indiscretions. And my sister's.

The room quiets as I enter. I bow my head and approach the queen. She is sewing tiny stitches around the cuffs of a shirt, embroidering a pomegranate motif of white on white. I watch her hands from beneath my lowered brow. They don't pause.

I kneel. She doesn't speak.

But behind me, I hear the whispers.

"Who is that?"

"What's she wearing?"

"She's one of *them*."

"That's the sister? They don't even look related."

"Perhaps they're not."

I struggle not to turn around and give the speaker the sharp edge of my tongue. Protocol demands that I not even look up until the queen acknowledges me.

Then I hear a giggle. Followed by another. And another. Like ripples on a pond.

I'm the stone that caused them and I'm sinking.

I curl my hands into fists under the folds of my sleeves. I know why they belittle me. They see me as the daughter of one of the king's minions—as the youngest of a family of parvenu graspers. They saw me return from France a year ago, only to leave three months later, dressed in humility and veiled in disrepute. Exiled by my expansively critical father. And now returned, supposedly reformed, though yet to be redeemed in Father's eyes.

"Mistress Boleyn."

I look up at the queen. The year has not been kind to her. Her face has fallen into soft folds, like a discarded piece of velvet. Still rich and soft, but a touch careworn. She's five years older than the king and she wears those years like eons. Her eyes reveal nothing to me—not malice, not kindness, not curiosity, not forgiveness. Queen Katherine has lived a lifetime at court and has mastered the art of giving nothing away. Her hands go still.

"I welcome you."

I hear a *tut* and a titter, as if one of her ladies questions the sincerity of that statement. The queen presses her lips together, but before anyone can speak, the door bangs open behind me, followed by a roomful of gasps and a trill of hysterical laughter.

I turn before the queen can grant me permission and see, there in the doorway, five men dressed in silks and scimitars, each with a turban wrapped around his head. Their eyes are white and wild.

Ottoman corsairs.

In England?

I steal a glance at the queen. She stifles a yawn behind a look of artful surprise.

King Henry is famous for his disguisings. For bursting into the queen's rooms in all manner of dress and disarray. For fooling no one, but delighting everyone. Except, it seems, the queen.

"We have come from Gallipoli and the coasts of Spain, searching for plunder." The voice—despite its rolling, guttural accent—starts a hum in my mind, a buzz of recognition at the top of my head.

"And women," another man mutters, his Kentish lilt completely at odds with his appearance.

The others laugh.

I risk a glance at the corsairs. The shorter man by the door is somewhat disheveled, and would be familiar to me even if he actually had traveled from the other side of the world. My brother. Next to him is the Kentishman, his blond hair curling from beneath his turban. He carries himself with the effortless ease of a dancer, and his eyes are the exact color blue that makes me wish he'd look at me.

But it's the man nearest me whose attention I'd do anything to have. He is tall and broad, his hand ridged with rings. His face—a little long, losing its narrowness, a hint of a cleft to his chin, and a mouth with a smile like a kiss—is so etched in my memory, I hardly know if he's real or a fevered imagining. The hum in my head increases, as if my entire body is tuned to his presence.

I remember the first time I saw him, gilded like a church icon, fashioned for worship. And the last time I saw him, shock transfiguring his face. I lower my eyes and stare at his broad-toed velvet shoes, decorated in pearls and gold embroidery. Breathe.

He walks boldly to the queen. He doesn't bow or acknowledge her rank and gentility. A moment unfurls between them during which no one moves or speaks. No one is allowed into the presence of the queen without obeisance. Except the king. He turns, his movements swift and decisive.

"Which one shall we take?" His voice is surprisingly high for a man so large, a presence so Herculean. The others reply with a roar and rattle of scimitars.

The feet turn again, toes pointed directly at my skirts.

"What about this one?"

He's dropped the accent. His words are full of tones round and rich like butter.

He reaches for my hand, his touch like a blinding jolt of sunlight. The fingers feel rougher than I expected, hardened by hunting and jousting and wielding a sword and lance. They carry the scent of orange flowers, cloves, and leather. I do not require his hand to lift me up. I could fly.

I do not look at him, but stare at my hand in his. He twists the ring on my index finger, the single pearl disappearing into my palm. I will my heart—my tongue—not to make a fool of me. Again.

The queen puts a hand on my shoulder, her grip like a tenterhook, fastening me to the spot. I'm stretched between the two of them.

"I cannot permit you to spirit away my maids of honor, Master Turk," the queen says, with no hint of humoring the corsair. And perhaps a touch of disdain. "It is an affront to Spain and an affront to God, what you do."

Her soft voice with its strong Spanish lilt hisses across the room, and four of the men nod their heads in shame. The real corsairs have been raiding the Spanish coast. Stealing women. Some say the king does the same thing from the queen's chambers.

"This one belongs to me." The queen pats my shoulder once.

He drops my hand. I watch his eyes, fixed on the queen. There is a spark of anger there. And a deep burn of petulance.

I want to reach out. To take back his hand. To tell him, *I will be anything you want! I'll play your game!*

I tilt my chin to see the queen. She smiles at me benignly. Motherly.

"On the contrary, Your Majesty," I blurt. "I am not a possession and belong to no one."

The hush that follows mantles the room like deafness after cannon fire. The queen swells, and I'm sure the shock on her face is no match for the shock on mine. I fall into a curtsy, ready to grovel an apology, but I'm cut off by a laugh like wine in a fountain—singular and intoxicating.

Followed by the laughter of every person in the room—except the queen.

I risk looking up to see her hard-edged gaze returned to the man before her.

"Possession or not, I will not take her from you, my lady," he says, sweeping a bow over her hand and kissing it. "Because my heart belongs to you."

He removes his turban, revealing sun-bright auburn hair. The ladies gasp in false astonishment and curtsy low before him.

The queen just smiles tightly.

"My dear husband."

The other men remove their ridiculous headgear, revealing the king's companions. Henry Norris, his black hair brushed back from his wide forehead, mouth twisted in an ironic grin. My brother, George, his hair mussed as if he's just risen from his bed, eyes lighting on every girl in the room. My cousin Francis Bryan, with eyes like a fox and a grin like a badger. And the man by the door, all golden-blond curls and startling blue eyes.

The king flicks a single finger, and the musicians in the corner begin to play a volta. The queen sits back down on her cushioned chair, the motion as overt a signal as her husband's. She will not be dancing.

The king bends at the waist to speak to me, still on my knees before the queen. He exudes cedar, velvet, and élan. The hum traverses to my fingers and toes, followed by a frisson of terror that my incontinent speech will get me flogged or pilloried. Or worse, exiled from court. Again.

"Mistress Boleyn."

I bow my head further, unable to look at him. Unable to utter another word.

"Welcome back."

2

THE DUCHESS OF SUFFOLK AIMS A LAYERED LOOK AT ME FROM beneath her gabled hood as she steps between me and the king. One side of her mouth twists upward, the other down. Then she turns her back on me. She is the king's younger sister, and despite the death of Louis XII eight years ago, still styles herself Queen of France. In a court ruled by tradition as much as royalty, she has precedence of rank over everyone but Queen Katherine herself, so the king will dance with her first.

My own brother is lounging against the doorframe, mouth open in a laugh, but his face is bitter. The blond man next to him echoes the laugh, but not the bitterness, and it sparks a flicker of memory. It's like a glimpse of something caught at the corner of the eye: a golden boy reaching for the sun against the shadowed gray stone of what used to be my home. The image slides away, taking any hint of the man's name with it. He nudges George, nods his head at me.

My brother's eyes are the same color as mine—dark. So dark that sometimes you can't tell if they have a color at all. His face quickly loses any trace of mirth, but I can see the hesitation in his frame.

Our childhood friendship has been lost in the depths of the

English Channel and in the mire of the years I spent in France, growing up and away from him. But he is the closest thing I have to an anchor here in the English court, so I smile, and his hesitation breaks, propelling him forward. Toward me.

I notice little Jane Parker in the corner, watching George. She twists her knuckles into her teeth, her expression screaming her every emotion. She's besotted.

"Welcome back, Anne."

George leads me into the improvisational dance steps we used to practice in the apple orchards of our childhood, back when he would drop me accidentally on purpose and collapse on top of me, shouting that I'd broken his back with my weight, and then giggling uncontrollably.

Now he holds me firmly. And doesn't laugh.

As we circle the room in the precisely measured steps of the dance, I see faces turn away from me. The ladies study their hands or the windows or the other dancers. The men don't even pretend. They just don't look.

"Why do they hate me, George?" I ask. I keep my voice quiet, so he can pretend not to hear me.

"They don't hate you, Anne. Not yet. They just choose to ignore you. And your indiscretions. You're like the green castle in the middle of the room that nobody wants to see." His lips twitch as he tries not to smile at his own joke.

"*The Château Vert* was a year ago, George."

"Yes, and everyone remembers it as a triumph and a gorgeous display. The castle! The costumes! The pageant!" George twirls me once, out of step, causing me to stumble.

"The dancing." He catches me and holds me tightly, his grip as hard as his voice, fingers pinching the tender skin over the bone.

My dance with the king. One stupid mistake. One mindless, improvident action based on a ridiculous infatuation. It got me exiled.

"Am I never going to be allowed to forget it?"

"Certainly not if you controvert the queen. Or throw yourself at the feet of the king, though it certainly saved your skin today."

I say nothing. Just as he wishes.

"You are here to be useful. Not a hindrance. Your only purpose is to advance our family. If you can't do that, you might as well have stayed at home."

"*Home?*"

Home for George is Hever, where I was born. The place from which I've just escaped exile. Home for me is France, where I grew up. I would love to be sent home. Away from England. Away from the eyes that stare but don't look at me.

"Or been married off to James Butler and both of you sent to Ireland with the uncivilized ruffians. You'll fit right in."

"That betrothal hasn't been agreed upon." I don't react to his criticism.

"Close enough," George mutters.

"James Butler is like a bear, only less sophisticated."

This teases a smile from George, and I want more. I want to feel closer to him, as though, somehow, the time and distance between us can be breached.

"I'd marry a bear to get my birthright." The smile disappears. "And you're set to steal it from me."

"I'm not stealing it, George! The earldom of Ormond is Father's. It's yours."

"Father would happily give it to your fiancé if it means pleasing Cardinal Wolsey."

"James Butler isn't my fiancé. It's not my fault Wolsey wants to appease the Irish lords by giving Grandmother's inheritance to the Butlers. I don't want your birthright."

"You don't want to be a countess?"

"Not if it means marrying James Butler."

"You should take what you can get, Anne. The only way a woman can advance in this world is through marriage. And the only way anyone can get ahead in this court is through peerage. Without a titled husband, you are nothing."

"Like Mother?" I slather those two words with all my bitterness.

As we begin a turn, I catch a glimpse of pain on his countenance, but it is gone when he faces me again.

"Mother is a Howard. Descended from dukes."

"That hasn't secured her a place in their hearts." I fling out a hand, indicating the queen, the Duchess of Suffolk, the king. Mother is no longer at court. Not exiled, just not invited.

"You don't need a place in their hearts, Anne. You need a place in their circle." He pauses. "Unlike Mother."

"And how am I to accomplish that?"

"Marry well."

"And until then?"

"Stop saying whatever comes into your head."

I laugh hollowly. "You know me too well to think—"

"Then at least make an effort to look the same as everyone else," he says, exasperated. "Any circle is broken by an odd piece."

"Is that how you see me?" My tone is teasing, but I extract the words like splinters from my throat. "As an odd piece?"

George takes my question seriously.

"You have to be more like the others if you want to be accepted at court. Your sleeves are too long and your bodice too square. Your hood and your accent are too French. You are too different."

"I'll take that as a compliment."

"It wasn't intended as one."

"Different isn't synonymous with defective," I tell him. Though George has managed to make me feel that way.

"But conformity is synonymous with success."

"Baa-a-a," I bleat.

We separate in the dance and I turn to the room, confronted by quickly averted suspicious glances. I've just been caught making barnyard noises in the queen's chambers. I lower my eyes and come back to George, who laughs at me.

"Just like sheep," he says. "Act like the others. Join in the conversations. Fit in. This isn't France, you know."

"Yes, I know that all too well."

"They are our enemies now." He lowers his voice.

I don't. "Not mine."

"Don't say that too loudly, Anne."

"Friendship is not dictated by the whims of kings and Parliament, George, but by the heart. I spent seven years of my life in France. I know nothing else."

I turn away, rubbing my hands against my skirts, ready to leave the room. But George takes my wrist, spins me back into the dance.

"You are English. You are a Boleyn. Act like one."

"You can't tell me what to do." I cringe at my childish rejoinder.

"But Father can."

Yes. Father can tell all of us what to do. And we will do it.

"Father isn't here."

"And I must take his place."

I can't help but laugh. "You'd make a great father figure, George, with your gambling and your unsavory activities."

"I keep my activities discreet." He has the grace to look affronted. But I see past the mask and catch the hint of a smile, the one he used to have when we spent hours compiling inventive insults until we struggled to breathe through our laughter.

"No, George, you just run with a flock of black sheep."

"Yes. And the king finds us charming. But what is charming in a man is despicable in a lady, so don't go getting any ideas."

There is real warmth in his voice now, the hint of a tease. I look into his face, the sharp features and steeply arched eyebrows. We are so much alike.

"Your point is taken, Brother."

The music ends and he snaps a quick bow. He reaches to tuck a stray hair back beneath my hood, his fingers soft. I want to lean into his hand, feel the comfort of it. Feel the welcome of family.

He sighs and looks at me keenly.

"You know, if you tried harder, you would almost be pretty."

I arrange my features to mask how deeply the wound cuts, right along the rift of our broken friendship.

"High praise, indeed."

And I walk away, cradling the pain like deadweight in my arms.

3

I KEENLY FEEL MY DIFFERENCE AFTER MY DANCE WITH GEORGE. I settle into my duties to the queen. Try to remember to hold my tongue. But I feel uncomfortable in my own skin. In my clothes.

After the travesty of *The Château Vert*, that bilious green castle, I spent the days of my incarceration at Hever elaborating all of my gowns. I adapted the French off-the-shoulder look of the sleeves, and turned the oversleeves up to my elbows, showing off the tightly cuffed undersleeves, a dramatic effect. King François had been in ecstasies over the look when his mistress wore it. I modified the tight-fitting bodice, curving the square neckline up over the bust to disguise the insignificance of my breasts. I edged everything in dark velvet and the embroidery of my favorite emblems.

I made my clothing more French, a link to my chosen homeland. Everyone knows the English courtiers have no style of their own and so copy that of France with a passion close to mania. I wanted to set the fashion. Be admired for my innovation.

But the new war with France has changed attitudes. Changed sensibilities. Changed allegiances.

So all I get is laughter. Or worse, pity.

From a few, I sense undiluted animosity. Apparently, English opposition to the French is not limited to political rivalry.

I am a failure. George is right. I am too different. Perhaps it is time to reinvent my appearance.

I study the Duchess of Suffolk, the standard around which all the ladies rally. She wears her clothes like someone expecting to be watched, to be copied. And everyone does, because if they don't, they suffer a slow social death.

The ladies of the court are like a flock of sheep led by a wolf.

The duchess's entire ensemble falls like water in drapes and curves, from the slight peak of her hood—showing a discreet and modest shock of coppery hair—to the twice-fitted sleeves with draping cuffs, to the long cascade of train behind her.

I know what I look like, standing isolated in the center of the queen's watching chamber. My French hood sits so smoothly and so far back off my forehead that it has to be held by pins to my black hair. My skirts are bunched over my flat hips with copious organ pleats. The duchess does not need them.

No wonder they all laugh at me.

I leave the queen's apartments without permission, though I doubt my absence is noticed. Or regretted. I go to the maids' dormitory and dig through my cedar chest tucked behind the bed I share with Jane Parker. We face the wall farthest from the door. Farthest from the center of the court.

I pick up a bodice of gray silk trimmed in blue velvet that was made just before I left France. It is my least favorite color and getting too tight in the bust. It doesn't matter if I ruin it.

I take it to the only one of the ladies of the court I know will help me.

My sister.

Mary sleeps in a single room in the lodgings of the inner court. Theoretically, it is assigned to her husband, a gentleman of the king's Privy Chamber, but he generally makes himself scarce.

I'm glad to find her alone.

"Nan!" Mary looks up from her sewing when I knock and enter her little room. Her voice is round and delicate, though tuneless.

But Mary is beautiful.

Her skin is naturally pale with just a touch of pink. She has wide eyes, smooth hair the color of freshly cut oak, both of which she got from our mother. I once heard my father remark that I must be a changeling child, as all the beauty on both sides bypassed me.

Jealousy rises in me like a twist of smoke from a snuffed candle.

"So nice of you to visit."

Mary reaches to embrace me, but I thrust the bodice at her before she makes contact. I don't need my big sister to mother me.

"I need to change," I blurt. "This. I need to change this. Everyone is laughing at me."

Mary's gabled hood makes her face appear even rounder, like a moon, pale and glowing. The only thing not pale about Mary is her eyes, deep brown and kind, but often strangely vacant, as if she has left her body and wanders different landscapes.

Right now, she's looking at me as if she's never met me before.

She turns her gaze and runs her hand along the stitching at the neckline.

"Lilies," she murmurs.

I almost snatch the bodice back from her. I spent days on those stitches. Weeks. Each one took me farther from Hever, reminding me of the lilies around Fontainebleau. Of fleurs-de-lis. Of France.

"Lilies symbolize chastity and virtue." Mary lifts her eyes to mine and gives a wicked smile. "A bit prim, don't you think?"

I shake my head. That wasn't my intention.

"We could alter the shape." She studies the curve of silk and buckram. "Display your assets."

"What assets?" I reach for the garment, but Mary pulls it away from me, holding it aloft in her right hand.

"I've changed my mind." I reach again, but her body is in my way. "I don't want to change." Not for Mary. Not for George.

Mary giggles and dances away from me.

"Give me a minute to work some Boleyn magic on your bust. You'll be impressed." She grins. "So will James Butler."

I scowl. Mary understands nothing.

"Go play your lute." She waves me dismissively away.

Go play your lute. Go change your clothes. Go become a sycophant and a sheep.

I cannot wreak my words on Mary. She doesn't deserve it. So I pick up my instrument, to lose myself in the music.

I keep my lute in her room because she has more privacy. Stuffed amongst the maids in our dormitory, I never know who's riffling through my things or listening to my music or reading over my shoulder. Yet Mary's quiet and nearly empty room is the place I go so I won't feel so alone. Two outcasts together.

The room is little more than a closet, with poky windows and an inadequate fire. An aging tapestry lines the wall, threads fraying loose and the left half bleached by the sun. But the bed is draped in new velvet, with a feather mattress and real pillows.

Occasionally the lesser ladies of the court visit her. Never the duchess and her confederacy. No, the room is kept quiet for the visits from the king—thus the attention paid to the bed trappings.

I keep my lute in the corner farthest from the window. I like knowing I can find it there. A friend. A reminder. A refuge.

I take my time to tune each course of strings, two to a course. They grow taut, twanging. The body of the lute feels like a belly pressed against me. The wood is smooth beneath my fingers, the strings almost sticky. I pluck them individually, like a conversation.

I love the lute for the dual tone of its strings, for the echo of its notes along my limbs. I love the delicate knots carved into the soundboard and the whiskery feel of the frayed frets beneath my fingers.

I pull the music into my mind. I can feel the vibration of the strings like breathing, like a heartbeat. It's a song I heard the king perform two nights ago, during one of his impromptu entertainments, trying out new material on the girls of the queen's household. His voice rich and his eyes roaming.

They never landed on me.

Mary hums along, and I grit my teeth to keep from telling her to stop.

The tune breaks and stutters in my mind and I have to go back, close my eyes, concentrate. I'm getting two notes wrong. The highest ones. Either the lute is out of tune, or I am. I bear down a little harder, my anxiety growing to get just this one thing right.

"The king used your lute to play that song to me last night."

With a *spang* the chanterelle, the highest-pitched string, snaps and whips out, clattering in the quiet.

"Shit."

I sit in a pinprick of silence. The music is still in me, in my fingers, but I can no longer let it out.

"Nan. Watch your tongue."

She's not my mother. And George is not Father.

"Not you, too!"

There she sits, all placid by the fireplace, enjoying her un-demanding life of leisure and prestige. All the queen's ladies treat her as an abomination, but she has all she needs, all any-one would need. She has the king. And all of Father's praise.

She looks at me with her big, brown doe eyes, and I suddenly want to pluck them out.

"First George and now you, Mary? Reminding me how much I humiliate the rest of the family. How mortifying to have a sister who doesn't fit in!"

"It's not you, Nan, it's your choice of words."

"My choice of words. To whom I choose to speak them. The way in which I string them together. The timing. No, Mary, it's not that. It's you and George wanting me to fade into nothingness because no one at the court wants to befriend me or hear what I say, and you find that embarrassing."

"You're hardly embarrassing, Nan." Mary speaks almost absently. For her, the argument is forgotten before it has even begun. But I'm not ready to let it go. I want to take it all out on someone. The pain and the loneliness. The humiliation. The desperation.

"Stop calling me Nan. I'm not a baby."

"Then don't act like one."

Mary is so easy. I clench the pleats of my skirts in my hands.

"At least I don't play the whore."

I watch her face. Watch the hurt first dawn in her eyes and then drain the color from her cheeks. I expect to feel triumphant. Powerful.

But I have never felt so worthless.

Silently, she hands me the bodice, the seam at the neckline half unpicked. And silently I leave.

4

LITTLE SLIVERS OF RAIN WORK THEIR WAY IN THROUGH THE chinks in the withdrawing-room window, like the little slivers of gossip that work their way under the skin. The room is wet and suffocating with it. Everyone is crowded and close, avoiding the weather.

I wear the gray bodice, which I have unbecomingly refashioned to a more English style, the lilies covered with appliqués meant to be the Boleyn bull, but looking more like marauding boar. I intended to show solidarity: the Boleyns sticking together. But Father is in Spain; Mother, silent and invisible in the country—endlessly visiting Howard relatives.

Mary won't speak to me. Not that I blame her.

George says only a good marriage will help me get ahead. The entrée to the circle of nobility, or perhaps the circle of patronage. They are not necessarily the same. George's friend Henry Norris has no title, yet he's one of the men the king trusts most. And influential friends of the king often are gifted with titles of their own—like Charles Brandon. He was once just the son of the old king's standard-bearer, but now he's married to a princess of the blood and carries the title Duke of Suffolk.

His duchess—the king's trendsetting sister—now sits in the center of the room. She holds her own court, glowing in golden attention, as if she is queen, not Katherine. I study her face, her gray eyes so like the king's, but harder. Her waterfall of tastefully pink skirts flows around her.

The duchess looks up and catches me staring. Her gaze slides rapidly from my hood to my hem. Her lip curls, her eyebrow raises, and she opens her mouth to speak. I am unable to move, dreading what she has to say. I dread even more what I might reply. But before she can say a word, a voice behind me cuts across the room.

"Well, if it isn't George's little sister."

The duchess jerks her gaze to find the speaker at the table of gamblers who have been slapping down cards and groats and boasts and bets at the far end of the room. And I whisper a blessing before I turn as well.

George looks how I feel, surprise glimmering for an instant on his face and then vanishing behind welcome. His hair is expertly tousled, his inky velvet doublet smooth and clean, his soft hands no indication of the dirt he gets into. He sits with Henry Norris, who appears to be paying more attention to my bustline than to the conversation around him. James Butler, my future spouse, is next to him, glowering, his hair thick and coarse over his beetling eyebrows. And at the far end of the table sits the speaker, dressed in green like a modern-day Robin Hood, his gold curls sporting a hint of red at the temples—the Kentishman from the king's disguising.

He leaps from behind the table to approach me, moving

with the hidden strength and lissome grace of a cat. I get the feeling this man will always land on his feet.

"Haven't seen you since I broke my toe climbing the courtyard wall at Hever."

I swallow a knot of vanity, and it sticks in my throat. Because he has seen me. At the disguising. He just doesn't remember.

Or perhaps I just made no impression.

He stops and crosses his arms. Leans back and appraises me with his devastatingly blue eyes. He is still several strides from me, so we face each other like players on a stage, our audience all around us.

I glance at my brother, who expects my silence, and then back at this Robin Hood, who expects my response. He expects me to know him.

"Forgive me, sir. But I do not recognize you."

He laughs.

"Thomas Wyatt."

I do know him, or of him. His exploits are infamous in the maids' chambers. Word is, he's incomparable in bed. And he's shared many. He's a poet. An athlete. A miscreant.

"Your neighbor, from your days in Kent? We used to play naked in the fountain at my father's castle at Allington. Without our parents' knowledge, of course."

He winks at me.

The other men laugh, and I hear a rustle of skirts and whispers from the duchess's confederacy. I twitch a glance at George, who is glaring at me as if this man's innuendos are somehow my fault. Wyatt smiles like a gambler who has laid down a hand full of hearts. I can't let him get the better of me. I can't let this man win.

"It's no wonder that I don't remember you, Master Wyatt, for we must have been much smaller." I pause, blink once, and then open my eyes into blank innocence. "Though for all I know, some things might still be quite small."

The table roars with laughter. The corner of Wyatt's mouth twitches, but his gaze never wavers from my own. When he speaks, his voice is silvery with seduction and wickedness.

"That is a matter which one day you might take in hand to establish the truth."

The devil I will. The men draw out one long, rising murmur and turn to me expectantly. Like they are watching a tennis match.

"Then I shall have to weigh this great matter very carefully," I say, before I can even think, "extracting from it only that truth which I can swallow."

Wyatt's eyes widen. I realize what I've just offered and bite my lip to stifle a retraction. Norris is pounding on the table with glee, and Butler looks as if he's swallowed a toad.

George jumps to his feet, unbalancing a wine goblet with his elbow. He grabs for it and catches it just before it topples, sweeping it up into a gesture to honor me, baptizing me with tiny drops of claret.

"My clever sister," he declares.

George's friends tip their drinks to me, and I flounce a little curtsy.

"Clever?" The coldness in James Butler's voice creates an

awed hush at the gaming table as he lumbers around it and out into the room.

Butler stands half a hand shorter than Thomas Wyatt, but must outweigh him by several stone, his chest and shoulders hard and bulky beneath the velvet of his doublet. He looks like a bear ready to take on a fox.

"Yes, clever," Wyatt says to him. "It means ingenious. Witty. Showing intelligence and skill."

It's only a repetition of George's comment, but the reflection of praise warms me.

"I know what it means, Wyatt. And wouldn't use it here."

A titter behind me indicates that the duchess and her confederacy are still listening. Why should they not be? Not only am I tarnishing my own reputation, but the men are about to come to fisticuffs. Fighting is not allowed within the confines of the court, making it doubly entertaining when it happens.

"You are a man of few words, Butler, and limited speech. Pray tell, what word would you use?"

Wyatt seems completely unconcerned by the palpable menace coming off the man my father intends me to marry. In fact, he seems determined to incite more. Butler turns and stares at me, his face emotionless, his eyes like stone.

"Wanton."

Butler drops the word into the quiet room, ready to combust.

"How dare you?" My hands ball into fists. I might flout the laws of the court myself.

George makes a move as if to shield me. Or perhaps to shield Butler. George and I used to fight as children, and I usually got the best of him. But we are cut short by a laugh. A low, rolling burble that douses the smoldering tempers.

Wyatt claps Butler on his shoulder. Butler doesn't seem to feel a thing.

"Ah, my dear James, you have spent too much time in Cardinal Wolsey's household with the likes of Henry Percy. The game of courtly love and the sometimes . . . ribald banter that accompanies it always catches the witless and sanctimonious unawares. It is nothing but *talk*, my friend, and talk is meaningless at court. Meaningless and soporific."

He says this with such ease and cordiality that Butler doesn't realize he's being insulted. He seems entirely under Wyatt's spell.

I wish I could do that. Turn tragedy to comedy in a moment. Cover indiscretions with poetry. Be accepted despite being unacceptable.

I could learn a thing or two from Thomas Wyatt.

"Witless?" The gray light of understanding begins to dawn on Butler's face. He is not as stupid as he appears.

"As meaningless a word as *wanton*, I am sure," I say. Again all eyes turn to me. Again all ears listen. I apply what I've gleaned so far from Thomas Wyatt's demonstration of his abilities. Say what you want to say, as well as what the listener wants to hear. "For the future Earl of Ormond could never be witless. Nor would he ever marry a wanton." My father contends that the earldom truly belongs to the Boleyns. And I will never marry James Butler.

If I can help it.

Butler narrows his eyes, but Wyatt proffers a devastating grin.

"Nor would he ever call his lady so," he says. "For earls are gentlemen and accord their ladies naught but the tenderest of words and devotion of heart, soul, and body."

For an instant, he holds me in his gaze, and I am as trapped as an insect in amber, the corner of my mouth pitched in admiration at his finesse. Then George throws an arm around my shoulders, as if to claim me. So I take the goblet from his other hand, raise it in salute to Wyatt, and drain it in a single motion.

Then I turn on my heel and leave the room before I say something I may later regret.

5

THICK, WET ENGLISH AIR GREETS ME AS I PUSH THROUGH THE outer doors into the base court. At least it's not raining. I breathe in deeply, the water chasing the smoke from my lungs and the heat from my face. My senses fizz with exhilaration at what I just experienced. A war of words. At the very least a battle. Words to which people *listened*. I glance around the courtyard, eager for more, but the clusters of courtiers just ignore me. The door behind me bangs, and I turn to face Thomas Wyatt once more.

"Headed to the mews?" he asks. Such a casual, unimaginative question.

"And why would I do that?"

"You go every day. To visit your little falcon."

"Have you been watching me?" The compulsion to spar is eclipsed by curiosity.

"I watch all the queen's ladies. Especially the new ones."

Of course.

"The ones you haven't slept with."

A flash of a wicked half smile.

"Yet."

He knows he's appealing, but I will not let him charm

me. I learned early on that my virginity is the only treasure I carry in a royal court. Everything else about me is worthless. Or belongs to my father.

"Watch all you want, Wyatt, but you're not getting anywhere near my bed. I saw in France what happens to girls who fall for men like you." I saw what happened to my sister there.

"I am a respectably married man."

"It doesn't seem your respectability prevents you from extramarital amusements. I know the people with whom you choose to associate."

He takes another step toward me, too close by far.

"Watch what you say, Anne; your brother is one of them."

"That's how I know." I turn and walk toward the mews, uncomfortably pleased when he falls into step beside me. "All you do is play games—jousting and cards, hunting and women. You build a reputation for seduction and pretty words, but show little discrimination."

"Ah," he says, leaning so close to me that I smell sugared almonds on his breath. "Have you been watching me?"

Really. The man is insufferable, and doesn't deserve a response. But I can't help myself.

"I suppose you're here with an offer I can't refuse."

Again the quirky uptick, creating a dimple to the right side of his mouth. Just one.

"Perhaps I'm here to take you up on yours."

I turn at the door of the mews to look him in the eye. Perhaps George is right. Perhaps my incontinent speech will get me into trouble one day. Just not today.

"I had thought you more perceptive than to take me seriously," I say. "But then, the game of courtly love always catches the witless unawares."

Wyatt throws back his head and laughs, a great burbling roar that draws the attention of the courtiers clustered against the walls.

His breath tickles the hair that has escaped my hood at the temple as he leans ever closer.

"I always take such offers seriously."

"Well, you can sing for it, Thomas Wyatt." I'm tired of his drivel and innuendos. "I saw what happened to my sister when she was my age. She succumbed to King François and the other golden boys of the French court. To their sweet words, their grins and dimples. They laughed at her behind her back. They talked about her like she was chattel. A mare to be ridden and passed on. She was forcibly removed from France by my father and married in shame."

"She came to our court and enchanted our king."

That is unlikely to happen twice in one family.

"You think you know everything, don't you?"

"And you know nothing."

I square up and itch to strike the look of amusement off his face.

"For your information, I can speak French better than anyone in this court. I know Latin and some Greek. I have read the works of Erasmus and the poetry of Clément Marot. I've met Leonardo da Vinci!"

34

My words tumble over one another and I sound breathless. I pause to collect myself.

"But you don't know anything about how to get along in the English court."

"I know perfectly well how to get along in this court."

"So you choose to be segregated. A pariah. The one person in the room with whom no one will speak or even make eye contact."

No, I didn't. It was chosen for me. By the court. By my clothes. By my tongue. The pain of having this pointed out to me by a stranger settles hard into my chest. Maybe life would be easier if I just fit in.

"A loss for words." He smiles. "I'm sure that doesn't happen very often."

"Why are you speaking to me?"

"Because I want to help you."

I gaze at Thomas Wyatt without reaction, the courtier's smile on my lips but not reaching my eyes. I can't trust him—a man for whom words are playthings and women little better.

"And what do you get out of this?" I ask. "You offer your assistance, but it's nothing that will line your pockets."

"Perhaps I only wish to promote the advancement of a former neighbor."

Even I can see that Thomas Wyatt would run down his neighbor with a rabid horse without a second thought. I make a noise halfway between disbelief and laughter.

"Would you believe I seek to further my own reputation?"

I am instantly wary.

"And tarnish mine."

"But yours is already tarnished, Anne. Perhaps it needs a little poetic shine."

"What do you know about it?"

"I heard a rumor about the Shrovetide pageant last year."

I hesitate. He wasn't there. Yet the gossip chases me.

"Oh?" I affect nonchalance. "What do you hear?"

"That you had too much to drink. That you stumbled out of the Château Vert and threw yourself at the king."

"I *danced* with him." Or tried to.

"But he didn't dance with *you*. It embarrassed your entire family. Humiliated your sister."

My sister wasn't the only one humiliated. A sharp jab of guilt in the back of my throat prevents me from swallowing. No matter what I do, no matter what my intention, I'm always hurting Mary, who least deserves it.

Wyatt doesn't know what it was like. The candles. The richness. The wine.

The king. The king was dressed in gold and crimson, like a god, with the emblem "Amorous" embroidered across his chest. We were masked. I was new at court, and everything seemed possible. For a single, glittering instant, I dreamed he could be mine.

How was I to know that he'd already slept with Mary?

"I'm trying to forget," I mumble.

"Everyone else already has." Wyatt reaches for my chin and

won't let go when I try to twitch out of his grasp. "It's time to give them something to remember.

"What do I get out of this? I get the admiration of every man here. At this very moment, I'm with a lovely girl who is melting at my touch after a little tiff. It only furthers my reputation."

"But that's not what happened." I fight the urge to see if anyone is watching. "And I'm not melting."

But I don't shake him off.

"Ah, but Anne, in this court, it doesn't matter what really happens. What matters is how it's perceived."

"So you get a little boost to your own self-worth," I prompt. "And you're not looking for anything else?"

"I'm always looking for something else, my dear," he says, his voice rolling low into an octave of seduction. "And you have offered a challenge I can't bear to pass up."

"And what is that?"

"You say I won't get anywhere near your bed. But I challenge you back, Anne Boleyn. I say that if I help you—that if the two of us gain your acceptance to this most unaccepting of courts—before long in this pretty, showy dance, you will want me in your bed."

I laugh right in his face. "Would you like to place a wager on that outcome?"

A glimmer of shock crosses his face—quick, like a sun shadow.

"I never pass up a bet."

"And if you lose—which you undoubtedly will—you will not press me further?"

"As long as if I win, you follow through."

We stand, motionless, the flow of barbs and banter stanched by his proposition.

Wyatt's smile vanishes. I feel something constrict beneath my lungs—something like fear.

"My maidenhead survived the French court intact, Wyatt." I somehow keep my voice even. "I think it can survive you."

His expression changes—a flash of understanding—and I realize I've just told him I'm still a virgin. Something unexpected in a French courtier. Or a Boleyn girl.

"You present me with high stakes," I say to cover up my discomfort. "And yet you forfeit nothing to me if you lose."

"If I lose, I will trouble you no more. I pledge to leave you to your happy life amongst the social elite and always mourn the conquest that never was. I will swear there was nothing between us but courtly banter, and bear the burden of the mocking laughter of my peers."

"You speak in riddles."

"I speak in poetry.

> *"If it be yea, I shall be fain;*
> *If it be nay, friends as before;*
> *Ye shall another man obtain,*
> *And I mine own and yours no more."*

I hold his gaze so that I don't roll my eyes at his doggerel. But one word strikes a reverberating chord in my mind—*friends.* I could use a friend here. Even one like Thomas Wyatt.

"If I lose"—Wyatt holds a hand to his heart—"I will write a poem about you that will be passed down through the ages as a masterpiece of all time. And I will always remain your humble servant."

He bows to me with a flourish, and I am able to affix a mask of nonchalance before he rises. I can't let him see that he's already charmed me. I can't let him see how much I need him.

"So what is your strategy?" I ask.

"I will pursue you. And you will encourage it."

"And what will that gain me?"

"The attention of all the other men at court. At least the ones that count."

"Like Henry Norris? No thank you."

"Norris can get you places. He's a favorite of the king."

"So is my sister."

Wyatt looks at me as one would an idiot child.

"But women don't matter at this court, Anne. In our world, women have no influence, carry no interest."

Have no voice. Have no lives of our own.

"It's the men that matter," he continues. "And most men are too stupid to see what's right in front of their faces. The only time they want something is when they can't have it, a jewel in someone else's bonnet. They take notice of something when it flashes a signal—like the white tail of a deer. The signal for pursuit."

"So you intend to be the flag on my ass?"

His grin broadens to double dimples.

"I intend to hold you up so that you catch the light."

A jewel. The image delights me. Wyatt cocks an eyebrow as if he's scored a point, and I start to turn away.

"Thank you for your offer," I say coldly.

"Thank you for your promise."

I pause. Look back. Narrow my eyes at him.

"It was a bet, Wyatt, not a promise. And I intend to win."

"Shall we kiss on that to seal the deal?"

He steps forward, and my partially turned shoulder brushes his chest, the fabric of his cloak sweeping against my skirts. I can see the stitches in his doublet and feel the heat of his breath on my forehead.

I look up into his face. He is so much taller than I am that I have to tilt my chin to see his eyes, which are focused not on mine but on my lips.

I take a step back.

"I have not yet agreed."

"And what will it take for you to agree?" Wyatt doesn't seem at all put off by my rebuff. Rather, he crosses his arms and leans back lazily, his body completely absent of tension, like a purring cat.

"Time."

"Don't take too much, Anne, or you may find yourself supplanted in my affections."

"Don't follow too closely, Wyatt, or you may be caught in the hunter's net yourself."

Richmond Palace
1523

6

I AM ALONE. AGAIN. THE SETTING HAS CHANGED, BUT THE REALITY has not. The court moved to Richmond because Greenwich was desperately lacking in air, but the crowded conditions grow even more stifling. I share a bed with Jane and two other girls, sleeping in rotation, the linens always damp and smelling of sleep and perfume. And once, I swear, the acrid sweat of a man.

Which makes me think of Wyatt's proposition. I admit, I'm a little afraid he might win our bet. He's charming and handsome and . . . persuasive. But I refuse to let that happen. Virginity is my trump card.

I can't help looking for him in the crowds at court. I tell myself it has nothing to do with his voice or his casual grace or his eyes.

No, it's his words that draw me to him. And the fact that he listens to mine.

But the burgeoning crowds of Richmond conspire to isolate me. To make matters worse, we are now less than an hour by barge from London, which means Cardinal Wolsey and his entourage of hangers-on fill the rooms by day more often than his regular Sunday visit.

The cardinal is the king's lord chancellor and most trusted

adviser, and his arrival always causes a bit of an uproar. I stand in a window of the queen's watching chamber and monitor his progress. The barge, decorated in gold and silk and tinsel and landing at the water bridge, becomes the focal point of anyone wishing access to the king. Men kneel before Wolsey, kiss his ring, whisper in his ear.

One wouldn't think to look at him that Wolsey wields the kingdom's power. He comes from nowhere, a family of merchants and butchers. *He* didn't need to marry well to join the circle. He just used his brains and spoke accordingly. The droopy skin of his cheeks reminds me of a loose-skinned dog, and his chin recedes into the folds of his cassock. But his eyes—shrewd and calculating—tell a different story.

I watch as he moves through the throng. He appears serene, despite the press of bodies and clamor of requests and complaints. His face is serene, but his eyes—shaded by his brow—are triumphant. They are those of a man who can change lives with a single, well-placed word. A man to whom people listen.

Wolsey is followed from the barge by a trail of courtiers. His own. For he holds court at least as well as the king. He collects his courtiers from the best families in the country—young men keen for position but perhaps not vibrant enough to engage the king. And others—like James Butler—are virtual prisoners, hostages to the political machinations that keep their fathers in line. There are no women in Wolsey's household. The boys come to the king's court to learn the rules of flirtation while their master changes the rules that govern us all.

The cavalcade disappears from view, but I continue to watch

the place just vacated. So much power in a butcher's son. The rain returns, and the flat, cloudy light hammers the river into pewter and erases the shadows from the wall. It is as if Wolsey's very passing has caused the sun to cease shining.

The door rattles, and I turn to see the duchess and her confederacy enter. She carries herself imperially, looking left and right to make sure that everyone is watching—and that everyone is bowing.

"Little Boleyn." The duchess's voice resonates high in her mouth, giving it a nasal quality. An ever-present sharpness.

"Your Grace." I keep my eyes on my hands. Deferential. Sheepish.

"Like a little sparrow, aren't you?" she asks. "Drab. And rather . . . disheveled."

Her confederacy titters, the sound rippling away into the room.

I bite my lip and think of George's words: *Be quiet. Be the same. Be accepted.*

I look up. The duchess's head is tipped to one side, her expression one of schooled amusement.

"Many creatures are not as they first appear, Your Grace." I cannot stop the words. "A falcon at rest may be drab and disheveled. And a cuckoo hides its ignobility by insinuating its offspring into a superior bird's nest."

As insults go, mine is thinly veiled, casting aspersions on the duchess's children—the cuckoos in the royal nest, placed there by Charles Brandon, whose ancestry is even more questionable than my own.

45

Her expression freezes. She turns without speaking, followed by a tide of skirts and gabled hoods. Jane Parker glances back at me—the last girl to follow—but quickly scuttles after.

I've done it again. I stand alone in the center of the room, wrap my misshapen finger in a pleat of my skirt, and twist the pearl ring with my thumb. The duchess and all her followers whisper together. The room begins to feel like one gigantic eye—staring, but not seeing. They will never accept me. I need to get out.

I move to the door just as it opens again.

"We have come to entertain the ladies," Henry Norris says as he enters. His gaze slides across my brow and finds the duchess and her confederacy behind me. He is followed by George, who studiously ignores my existence, and Wolsey's men, who crowd up behind him, eager and wriggling like puppies.

I stand to one side, barely observed and highly invisible, as more seductive prey is spotted within the room.

Finally, I can no longer stand it and push my way through the door, running nose first into a russet doublet. I look up into the face of a boy my age. His eyes are strange. Like chalcedony—more blue than gray but almost colorless. His hair is the color of fox fur, and just as thick, a swatch at the back of his head giving the impression of a feather in a cap. His face is cut at angles like stone, creating broad planes, sharp edges, and deep shadows. But when he smiles, the shadows melt away and I feel something warm and delicate rising within me.

He's looking at me. He sees me.

The man behind him gives him a push, and he stumbles forward into the room, breaking our gaze, but my eyes follow him. Until someone grabs my hand and yanks me from the room.

"You flirt with Henry Percy?" James Butler's voice is all rough edges like uncut granite.

"I'm doing no such thing." I wrench my hand from his and turn, but he's whip quick and his grip bites into my elbow.

"Good. His fate is decided. Like ours."

He manages to hide all but a hint of brogue by clipping his sentences and swallowing words. But he can't disguise his coarseness. His shirt is rumpled and his hair cropped roughly, as though trimmed with a scythe.

"Our fates are not decided, James Butler. There is no marriage until it is written and signed."

"And sealed," he leers, exposing the gap of a missing tooth next to an overly sharp canine. I suppress a shudder at the thought of his suggestion. Consummation.

"That will never happen."

"Wolsey and the king want this. It will happen."

The thought that the king is part of the execution of this contract makes me ill.

I allow Butler to walk me through Richmond's crowded rooms and to the covered gallery around the garden. Weak spring sunshine slants over the walls, igniting the gold flame of the cockerels that top the donjon's cupolas. They point north, into the wind, and for a moment I'm reminded of the Louvre, the striped towers swept clean by rain. And I ache to go back. To be anywhere but here.

I'm shaken by my desperation to get out of this predicament. To get my arm out of his grasp. To unlink my life from his.

I stop. Square my shoulders. Take a deep breath.

"The marriage rests on the settlement of the earldom of Ormond," I say evenly. "That is yet to be decided."

I know George wants the earldom. So does Father. I am nothing but a bargaining chip, a sacrifice to the pretense of capitulation. They'll fight Butler. Won't they?

"The earl had only one son. My father." Butler's smile is mocking.

"His illegitimate son."

Butler scowls, but I continue.

"My grandmother was named as coheiress in the earl's will."

"Women," Butler says in a voice most people reserve for the stupid and the Irish, "cannot inherit. They don't know money. Don't know rules. They squander every groat on baubles."

He flicks the *A* pendant that hangs from a ribbon around my neck.

"Women," I counter, grabbing his hand and squeezing it to make a point, "are in every way men's intellectual equals."

He laughs, showing off his teeth.

"We can grasp languages and texts as easily," I continue. "Women translate Latin, compose music, even orchestrate war, as Queen Katherine did in Scotland when the king was away playing games in France."

"A fluke. Desperation. Look at her now. She can't produce an heir."

"She has a daughter."

"Just my point."

I could strangle him.

"Mary will be queen!" I cry. "As the king's only legitimate child, it's her birthright. I'm sure she'll do better than most men, who have lost entire peerages to depravity and gluttony."

"And to the wantonness of women."

"Wars are waged and death unleashed by men who follow without thought their own ambition and misplaced loyalty," I pursue.

"Like your grandfather."

My mother's father, the second Duke of Norfolk, was attainted after fighting on the wrong side of the battle of Bosworth that knocked the crown from Richard III's head and rolled it to Henry Tudor. The Howards have been weaseling their way back into Tudor court life ever since.

I'm embarrassed to be related to them.

"Traitors and pretenders," Butler growls. "I'm doing you a favor."

"How romantic," I say, wrenching my hand from his.

"Romance is only in books and music," he says. "You won't find any of that in Ireland."

I feel myself grow pale. I can't face a future with no music. All we hear of Ireland are stories of barbaric lords and fiefdoms, as if they continue to live in the Dark Ages. No music. No poetry. No court.

"Are you threatening me?" I demand, my voice stronger than my heart.

Butler's face lights up with wicked mirth and he laughs. I smell the meat on his breath.

"Yes. With me, you'll be a countess. Without me, you are nothing."

He snaps a smart bow and turns away before I can even curtsy back. Not that I plan to.

The walls of Richmond press in around me. Ladies whisper as I pass. I keep my face still and pleasant. I don't rush. I don't fly through the rooms as my limbs are desperate to do.

I move slowly, almost regally, to a quiet, disused antechamber at the far end of the palace, just beyond my sister's ill-attended room. It is musty and dirty, with a single, cracked window and no tapestries, and I believe everyone has forgotten about it.

It is the perfect place to cry.

And when the tears are spent, it is the perfect place to plan.

7

"WHAT DO I NEED TO DO?" I ASK WYATT WHEN I FIND HIM IN the long gallery.

"... is exactly the right thing to say."

I struggle not to roll my eyes. It's hard to take the man seriously when he says things like that. But if I'm going to rid myself of James Butler, I need to attract the attention of someone else. Someone better. Wyatt just might be able to help me with that. So I will suffer his foolishness.

I turn to the maps that line the walls of the gallery. England. The Channel. The Low Countries. France. I run my fingers along the shadowy outline of what they call the New World.

"I wish I could go there."

He takes my hand in his and says, "Why would you want to leave England when everything you need is right here?"

He presses my palm to his heart, and I bite back a laugh.

"A little overdone, don't you think?"

"I've been pining for days." He leans in close, and I can see the rim of black around the blue of his eye. A tiny dark speckle, like a grain of onyx, glints in the right one. "It took you long enough to come and find me."

"You were supposed to be pursuing me." I feel his heartbeat beneath my fingers. His breath on my lips.

"You said you needed time. I do little pursuing unless I'm going to get something out of it."

"Your seduction techniques are not going to work on me, Wyatt."

"Do you want to bet on that?" The laughter in his voice is evident—a musical bass note that makes me want to laugh, too.

"I shall choose to ignore them, then," I say lightly. And repeat myself. "What do I need to do?"

"Flirt with me."

"Now?" I glance quickly around the room. It's full of maps and tapestries and quiet conversation. Courtiers plotting advancement. Ladies making assignations. Henry Percy. Norris. George.

Wyatt brushes a stray hair from my cheek to draw my eyes back to his.

"Constantly."

"Wouldn't that be a little obvious?"

"I believe I've said before that most people at this court can't see what's in front of them until you beat them with it. So, yes. It has to be obvious."

"And nothing else?"

"Nothing until you want it, Anne."

His gaze moves from my eyes to my mouth and back. Almost without my wanting to, I look at his mouth, the full lower lip and the hint of reddish stubble on the upper one.

"If you do as I say," he continues so quietly that I find myself unable to stop watching his mouth, "I can guarantee the entire court will fall swooning at your feet."

I force myself to look back into his eyes.

"Think a lot of yourself, don't you?"

"I have to. Or no one else will."

"So what do we do first?"

"First we get their attention."

"And how do we do that?"

"It's already done. We have the entire room watching our intimate little scene."

I realize how we must look to all the others. Standing so close, gazing intently into each other's eyes. Like lovers.

"We have their attention. Now we need to capture their imaginations. Display your assets."

"That's what my sister says." I pull away and cross my arms over my chest. "I don't want lechery."

This isn't why I came to him.

"I meant your eyes. Dark. Mysterious. Alluring. And your face. So haughty, but such promises in those lips."

"My lips have promised you nothing."

"But the point is to look as if they might. You look like someone who has something to say. Something important."

"I do." I take his hand in mine again, hoping he's really listening. "I have ideas. I'm more than breasts and eyes and lips, Thomas Wyatt."

I pause for breath. I've said too much. But I can't stop.

"I deserve to be heard."

He studies me as one would a new species. We are separated

by space and silence, no longer the portrait of young love. This will never work.

"You're right," he says quietly. "You do."

He closes the gap between us, bends over me to whisper directly into my ear.

"Let's make sure you're heard. If you do as I say, if we work together on this, the most important ears at court will listen."

I snap my eyes up to his. *The king?* Our lips are inches apart.

"Good. Now, you must follow my directions exactly. Lower your gaze."

I continue to keep my eyes on his face. To show him that he cannot order me like a servant. Or a wife.

"They all see us. The men will watch your every move."

I hesitate. If he's right, my life at court could turn completely. Perhaps even the king himself will notice. Will hear.

I follow Wyatt's instructions and look to the floor at the center of the room. To the cluster of leather shoes pointed just slightly in our direction. I do not bow my head. I merely lower my gaze.

"Perfect."

The praise is like a strand of melody in my heart.

"Think in terms of music," Wyatt whispers, as if listening to the same tune, "of poetry. Because flirtation is a dance. Count the time in your head."

He taps it out along the pulse at my wrist.

"Now wait for a count of four. Count it in your mind. Then raise your eyes. Tilt your head. And smile. Just a half smile.

Don't look away. Another count of four. Then turn. And walk away."

I picture it, as if I am the one watching. The measured way it operates, like a crescendo, or an unfinished chord, leaving the listener breathless for completion. If he keeps his eyes on me no matter what I do, I will look as if I've captured him. As if I have the power.

"But wait," he says, just before I lift my eyes, his words like a caress on my cheek. "And this is the most important part."

He pauses. And then he does trace the line of my jaw, almost, but not quite, touching my lips.

"When you walk away—and every time you walk away from me—*don't look back*."

Like Orpheus. Like Lot's wife. Looking back would break the spell.

He strokes one finger down the center of my upper lip, as if asking me to hush, then releases me.

"Now go."

I do exactly as he says. The look. The smile. The turn.

I feel him watching me. I feel everyone watching me. I consider emulating Queen Katherine, fingers pressed around each other like a gift, head bent in humble piety. But I am not a queen. Never will be.

So I straighten my spine, elongate my neck. I look down and to the left, not back at Thomas Wyatt. Showing just a hint of my face—an enigmatic glimpse—before I straighten again and walk through the door to the gallery and out of their view.

I hear a rising tide behind me, as if the room has released a collectively held breath.

A sense of power swirls through me like a draft of potent wine, and I have to steady myself, one hand on the cool stone wall. I long to lay my forehead against it but hear the returning murmur behind me and walk away.

8

For four days, nothing happens. Then, at Wolsey's next visit, Henry Percy smiles at me again. One of the king's men asks me to dance. And I hear, in the ripple of whispers around the duchess's confederacy, "What do men *see* in her, anyway?"

It's not much, but it's something.

I try to carry on my normal routine. Serving the queen. Avoiding Mary because I still do not know what to say to her. Practicing my music on strange lutes because I left mine in her room, at the mercy of the king. When I need to escape the castle walls, I visit my falcon.

The mews at Richmond is smaller and more cramped than the one at Greenwich. But I believe the falcons are treated better here, because Simnel, a falconer from the Royal Mews at Charing Cross, has come to care for them.

I carry sugar comfits in my pocket, stolen from the kitchen, nod a good morning to Simnel. Make my way to the dark corner of the back of the mews.

My merlin, Fortune, is smaller than an average female, but persistent. And tenacious. Once she gets hold of something, she will not let it go. This makes her a less than ideal hunting companion, but I find her character faults appealing.

Fortune emits a piercing cry when I run out of comfits.

"Shhh, little one." She dives at my empty hand. Her sharp beak pinches the skin of my finger, raising a welt. I shake my hand and laugh at her.

"What's the matter, little one, don't you love me anymore?"

"Actually, falcons are incapable of love."

I turn to see Henry Norris haloed by the light around the door. Everyone knows Norris. He tilts in the lists and wins accolades in every tournament. He is a gentleman of the bedchamber, and therefore assists the king in his most private moments. Helps him dress.

Every time I see Norris, I think of the king's bare back.

"Sir Henry," I stutter as I dip a little curtsy. "You startled me."

Fortune pipes her agreement.

"That certainly wasn't my intention," Norris says smoothly, and moves over as if to examine Fortune. This is the closest he's ever been to me. And the most he's ever said to me.

Even in the dim light of the mews, I can see the wear of weather on Norris's skin. Days spent hunting have tanned his cheeks and chin and chiseled creases around his eyes. He is the same age as the king but appears older. And he is not nearly as alluring, though he would like to think he is. I can feel his presence, and his intention, in the way he breathes, the manner of his stance. Too close. Too encompassing.

I fight the urge to step away. This is what I wanted. The attention. Someone important who might—just might—listen. Norris is married. And libidinous. But powerful.

I turn my head to look at Fortune, who ruffles a bit. Nervous.

"I wonder, sometimes," I say, stretching my words as if searching for them, "if the court isn't a bit like a mews."

When I look back, Norris appears a little perplexed.

I finish my thought looking him directly in the eye. "Full of separately caged individuals incapable of love."

"Incapable?" His expression is one of mock offense. "All of us? By what reasoning do you come to this conclusion?"

I think of King François in France. Of the words he spoke to Mary that she shared with me, the eight-year-old confidante of a fifteen-year-old naïf. How he loved her. Worshipped her. Adored her. How Mary believed him. Believed in love.

How François passed her on to his friends when he was done with her. And each one took a piece of her until finally she was sent away and I was left alone in a foreign land. Again.

"Evidence of the opposite has yet to present itself to me," I answer.

"Wyatt seems . . . suitably passionate."

So it's working. "Oh?" I ask, wanting to know more. "What makes you say this?"

Norris's eyes drift down my face to my lips. And lower, to my bodice. Mentally, I shake off my revulsion.

"I've seen the way he looks at you," Norris answers. "And at cards last night, he . . . mentioned it."

Now Wyatt is talking about me?

"What did he say?"

Norris grins. "That the passion isn't one-sided."

I narrow my eyes. This wasn't part of the plan.

"Passion and love are not the same thing."

"Too true," says a voice behind us.

We both turn to see George stride in, twirling an empty goblet.

"Passion is easy to show," he says, "love, sometimes impossible."

I wipe my hands on my skirt to keep them from shaking.

"Though some of us could try a little harder," George finishes.

Norris takes a step backward, eyes twitching between my brother and me. George doesn't look at him.

Fortune cries, the tension too much for her. Or perhaps she is just looking for more comfits.

"Sir Henry, I would speak to my sister alone."

Norris doesn't move, stunned, perhaps, by George's bluntness and lack of courtly protocol. The Boleyns are like that. It remains to be seen if we are forgiven for it. Norris tips a bow to me and stalks out.

"Jesus, George," I hiss, "what do you think you're doing?"

"I just thought you should know that Father's going to be recalled. He's coming back." George heaves himself up from the doorframe as if his melancholy has weighted him down.

I feel as if the earth has shifted beneath my feet. We eye each other warily, the rustle of wings around us. Fortune flaps awkwardly on her post. Tethered to it.

Then George turns and walks stiffly through the door and into the wide, open courtyard beyond. I follow, leaving Fortune behind.

"When?" I call, trying to catch up to him, stumbling over the cobblestones.

"Soon. Summer." George waves a hand bleakly, as if trying to brush me away.

"He's coming here?"

George spins. "Of course he's coming here. Or Windsor. Or wherever the court happens to be located. To wherever he can keep me under his eye. And his thumb."

His *r*'s and *s*'s are overlong. His articulation is blurry, the music of his voice down tempo.

"Not just you." I offer an ironic smile that feels more like a grimace. "There's room beneath that thumb for both of us. Because we stick together, George, remember?"

My voice is from my childhood. The one where silence reigned at the dinner table, Father's palpable disappointment an unwanted guest. A childhood where George could creep into my room at night and I would pretend not to notice when the pillow was wet in the morning. A childhood where we could escape to the orchards and climb the trees and make a pact: that we would always stick together. We would always be friends.

A pact Father broke by sending me to the Low Countries and then to France. By turning George into a stranger.

"Do we, Anne?" George looks at me, his eyes dark with agony or anger—I can't tell behind the red-rimmed haze of the wine.

"We're Boleyns. Boleyns always stick together." I reach for him, but he twists away from me.

"We just present a united front. Unless it suits us otherwise."

"No, George," I tell him, wanting desperately to believe it myself.

"You are set to steal my inheritance from under my nose. Wolsey and our Howard uncle are pushing for a resolution of the Ormond inheritance. Their problems will be solved, and Father can't complain if Boleyn blood inherits the earldom eventually. So they want to give it to Butler—to you." He spits. "And you flaunt your unworthiness by throwing yourself at every married man at court." He flings his arm in the direction Norris traveled.

"I don't *want* your inheritance, George! I want nothing to do with James Butler or the earldom of Ormond."

"Well, Father will make sure you have it," George snarls. "To keep it in the family one way or another. Whether or not he finds you in Henry Norris's bed."

I bristle. "I'm not—"

"Or Thomas Wyatt's." George actually leers at me. "So I suppose you had better enjoy him while you can. I hear his tastes run a little . . . wild."

"I don't think I know you anymore, George Boleyn." I struggle to keep my voice from shaking. Rage and humiliation burn in my throat.

George sags and lifts the empty goblet—turning it entirely upside down—and peers into the void, trying to catch a drop. Then he levels his gaze at me, unswaying, and when he speaks, his words are unslurred.

"When Father returns, Anne, you will be the one who disappoints him. You will be the one who suffers his displeasure. Not me, this time." His face twists into a horrific smile that doesn't meet his eyes. "Not me. You're the one with the court chasing your tail. You're the one everyone's talking about. You're the one who called Mary a whore, Anne. To her face."

I step back—slapped by my own words.

"One day"—George pursues me and whispers closely, his breath reeking of wine and malice—"someone will call you the same thing, and you'll know how it feels."

"I think I already do, George. Because I think you just did."

"Clever girl."

George lifts his goblet in an empty toast and walks away.

9

I go straight to Wyatt. I've lost my family. I have no friends. I don't know where else to go.

I find him in the gardens, amongst the lions and dragons, the knots and heraldic emblems.

"Can't stay away from me?"

Wyatt slips an arm around my waist and kisses me quickly. It's so English. So foreign. And far too intimate. My lips taste like sugared almonds when he pulls away.

"What's wrong?" he asks.

"What have you been saying about me?" I ask. "What have you been telling everyone about . . . about this?" I wave my hands through the little space left between us, fingers brushing the velvet on his chest.

He grabs my wrists and lowers my hands.

"You are shrill and agitated," he says tightly. "And this is not part of our plan." He grins. "We cannot have a lovers' quarrel until we are lovers."

"And we are not lovers!" I hiss at him. "So why is Henry Norris talking to me about passion?"

"Henry Norris will talk passion to any girl who listens."

"Why did it sound as if he'd heard about my passion from you?"

Wyatt pauses.

"Did you tell him something?"

"I may have . . . implied."

I set my jaw and ball my fists, tendons flexing against Wyatt's grip.

"You will not talk about me that way," I say, my voice low and dangerous. "I will flirt and pretend with you all you like, but I will not be the subject of lies."

"The small-minded interpret what they see and hear only as they wish to."

I scowl at him. "You are the one who told me the court is filled with small-minded people. Am I to assume everyone will interpret things this way? That they will think as my brother does—that I'm your whore?"

A look of shock crosses Wyatt's face, but he chases it with a wry smile.

"You're scowling," he says, and releases me to brush the strain at my brow.

"There's no one around! No one can see!" I slap his hand away. The man doesn't even argue properly.

"Makes no difference. You have to practice your art in private as well as public venues, my dear. You cannot let down your mask for anyone. Court is a game played in every corner and at every moment. Even while you sleep."

"Even when I'm married?"

"Especially with your spouse." Wyatt's face darkens, and I feel a distinct cooling in the air between us.

"It sounds exhausting." I feel exhausted. "Having to wear the mask for everyone. Even family."

Wyatt lets go of my other wrist, and we stand in the wan April sunlight, arms at our sides, unmoving.

"You and George were always close," he says quietly. "Always together as children. He told me once you slept in the same bed."

I glance up at him. Is he jealous?

"A closeness forged in the iron of my father's will."

"Your father doted on you."

I manage to suppress a snort.

"When I was six."

"No more doting?"

I have to look away from the sympathy in his eyes.

"When I was six, I was his clever little girl," I say, studying the light on the topiary leaves, concentrating hard to keep the pain from my voice. "But I grew up away from him. I came home from France thin and unnoticed, certainly unbeautiful, surpassed in my father's affections by my pretty, easy sister and her capacity to earn him accolades."

"Your voice is sweet, but your words are bitter."

"My words. Everyone tells me my words are wrong. Aren't you really saying it's me?"

He tilts my chin back to face him and gazes at me unspeaking, his narrow features serious.

"It is just something I think you should mind, Anne," he says softly. "Your words will be your downfall."

66

I take a deep breath, straighten my spine, and brush my hands on my skirt.

"Well, thank you for taking the time to make that assessment."

I turn to go, but he grabs my hand to stop me.

"You came to me for a reason, Anne."

My heart lurches. George. Father. Mary. Why did I think Wyatt could help?

Because he said he would be my friend. In a foolish poem. But even a pretend friend is better than no friend at all.

"My father's coming home."

Wyatt hesitates. "With his iron will."

I nod. I don't want to need him. But I do.

"He'll force my marriage to James Butler."

"And you want to prevent that."

"I want to find an alternative."

If I think I see a flash of sadness in those blue eyes, it vanishes quickly into skepticism.

"You don't have much time."

"Then you'll have to work your magic quickly." I try to keep my voice light, and offer a weak smile. But truly, Wyatt is my only hope. If he can do what he claims.

He slips an arm around my waist and, in what I'm sure he thinks is a seductive way, whispers, "You could succumb to my potent and innumerable charms and become my mistress."

"And tarnish myself so much that not even James Butler will want me? I don't think so."

Wyatt laughs. "I could spirit you away to the country, and no one would ever find you. Not even your father."

I manage not to pull a face.

"The country? That might be a fate worse than Butler. Try again."

"Then we'll have to find you someone with more influence. Norris?"

I turn to him full on. He needs to understand this.

"I will not be a mistress. I've seen what it did to my sister and her reputation. She may be a favorite of the king, but I've seen how mistresses are treated by everyone else. I know how they are vilified. I never want to be called a concubine." Or a whore.

"Ah." Wyatt guides me by the elbow along the path. He pulls a leaf from a shrub trimmed into the shape of a stag and twirls it. Speaks quietly from the corner of his mouth. "We have to keep moving. We are being watched." He nods toward the donjon—the palace's central tower—where the windows stare like blank faces from its façade.

"Being a mistress can be a noble pursuit," he says. "Your sister has done well."

"I would not wish for a life like my sister's, or any mistress's. Hidden away in poky rooms or country houses. Disguised as serving women. Even Bessie Blount, mother of the king's son, is not at court. All mistresses are confined to prisons because the men who 'love' them cannot allow them to be seen. Not a noble pursuit at all."

Then again, if King Henry asked, I might find it hard to say no.

"I'll take that as a refusal," Wyatt says, laughter in his voice. "So what you want is a husband."

I consider this for a moment, and Wyatt is silent. The only sound is the scratch of gravel beneath our feet. A marriage would save me from James Butler. It would nullify the influence of my father, placate my brother, put me on equal footing with my sister. Of course, it would also make me subject to the whims and words of yet another man's will. Someone else to silence me.

If only I could find a place where my own whims and words matter.

Ridiculous notion.

"Marriage seems my only option."

Wyatt stops and studies me. Unlike the king, who always seems to be in motion, Wyatt holds his stillness within him, as if it is an integral part of his being.

"There are always choices."

I shake my head. "Not in this case. I need to be rid of Butler before my father arrives. So I need a proposal. A betrothal. Something." I close my eyes and try desperately to think of someone who might listen to me, but the image that presents itself is of Thomas Wyatt, so I open my eyes to the real thing. "Preferably from someone *not* pursuing the earldom that rightfully belongs to my father. Someone at court."

We walk again, side by side beneath the gaze of the donjon.

"Then we shall have to get you into the center of attention—the attention of the royal circle—using much more . . . dramatic means."

"Dramatic?"

"A masque, my dear. An interlude. We'll stage a little play, with you as the focus. We'll invite the king and Wolsey and pretend it's just a little nothing, the whim of a poet. But you will be seen and admired by everyone of influence."

I will be seen by the king. Wyatt is wearing a smirk of supreme self-satisfaction.

"And so will you," I prompt. He has obviously already thought this through.

"My motives are never entirely unselfish."

I have a flashing memory of *The Château Vert*. I tremble at the thought that others will remember, too.

"But won't it take months to prepare? The costumes? The set?"

"It will be simple," he says. "No elaborate costumes. No enormous sets created to give the appearance of false castles. No gilded chariots. As if it's the spur of the moment. Improvisational. And starring whomever I please."

I'm quiet for a moment.

"Not to your liking?" There's an edge to Wyatt's voice.

"It's a wonderful idea."

"But?"

I glance at him. His knuckle brushes mine. It looks accidental, but I think I know Wyatt well enough now to believe it's contrived. It calls attention to our close proximity to each other.

I know him. But can I trust him?

I take a deep breath.

"Will this . . . interlude . . . not merely call attention to my former transgressions?"

Wyatt raises an eyebrow.

"You mean *The Château Vert?*"

I nod.

"No one remembers it, Anne."

"Yes, they do." My heart warps at the thought that the king remembers. That he thinks me a fool. If that's the case, I don't wish to remind him.

"No." Wyatt stops. "They don't. No one remarked on it. No one remembers it. No one cares."

"You knew about it, and you weren't even there!"

"Because your brother told me. No one remembers but the Boleyns."

"It got me sent away. Exiled to the country."

Wyatt sighs. Rubs his forehead. And continues up the path.

"The king's interest in your sister was just beginning then, wasn't it?"

I nod miserably.

I'd been at court for just a few weeks. I was homesick for France, mourning the escalating hostilities. Lonely. Father got me a position in the queen's household, a part in the Shrovetide pageant—a chance to shine. I wondered secretly at the time if the part of "Perseverance" was mine by design. More fool me.

Mary played "Kindness" and positively glowed in the white gown and gold bonnet. I stood beside her, flushed in the sunlight of the king's smile. When the dancing started, I leaped into the king's arms when he held out his hand. To her.

I can still picture the shock and astonishment on the king's face. The bewilderment on Mary's. Until he sidestepped me neatly and swept her away, leaving me alone in the center of the room, rigid with humiliation.

No one challenged Father's decision to exile me to the country. Not George. Certainly not Mary.

"The court doesn't care, Anne," Wyatt says. "Just your family."

A weight lifts from me. If the court doesn't care—if the king doesn't—perhaps there's hope for me yet.

"So what will be the theme of this masque?"

"Why, love, of course, my dear. Nothing but love."

"Sounds inspiring," I tease. "Tell me what I need to do."

". . . is exactly the right thing to say."

I laugh and squeeze his arm, his elbow brushing against my breast. The shadows from the slanting sunlight flicker like a frown across his face, then his dimple reappears in full sun.

"First, we must invite our cast to join us."

My footsteps slow of their own accord. I have no friends.

"Who did you have in mind?"

"Norris. Bryan. Your brother."

I start to interrupt—to argue—but he carries on.

"Your sister."

"She'll never agree."

"And Jane Parker."

I think of the look in Jane's eyes as she gazed at George. "A matchmaker now, are you?"

"Jane's infatuation is obvious to everyone. I'm just creating opportunity. She might be a good influence on him."

I think of George's red-rimmed eyes and empty wine goblet, and I certainly hope so.

"Unlike you."

"Balance in everything, Anne." He leaps onto the ground-trailing branch of an ancient yew tree and runs along it—arms outstretched—and turns without wobbling. "As for your sister, she will agree to it."

"How do you know?"

Wyatt walks back along the branch and returns to earth without a sound.

"Because you are going to go and ask her."

"And apologize." It's been so long, will Mary accept it? Will she even see me?

"Anne," he says, and takes me by the shoulders. He stares hard into my eyes and won't let me look away. "Listen to me. Are you listening?"

His intensity is frightening, as are his fingers, pressing firmly into my flesh.

"Yes."

"Never apologize. It doesn't suit you."

I look at him for a long moment, to decipher the meaning behind his words, and realize he means them exactly as spoken. "Never?"

I try to imagine a life like that. And can't.

"I speak too quickly," I explain. "Let my temper take the lead. Even the queen apologizes."

"Only to God or her confessor."

"She never speaks out of turn, or says anything hurtful."

Wyatt chuckles, a deep rumble in his chest accompanied by his voice's tenor overtone.

"It doesn't mean you'll never have anything to apologize for. It just means you'll never do it."

"People will call me a bitch."

"Who cares? They'll think you're better than they are. More important. Worth more."

I ponder that. I think about the women of the French court. Queen Claude, the woman who should have had the most power, the most respect, received instead the most pity. Not because she was lame. Not because she was always ill with one pregnancy or another. Not because her husband slept more vigorously and more passionately with other women.

But because she was meek.

And Françoise de Foix, the French king's mistress, who roamed the halls of Amboise with a voice like a barking dog, who demanded the high table and shunned the queen's maids, had all the courtiers on their knees in worshipful awe.

Françoise never apologized. I had hated her.

"But—"

"There will be no *buts* in this instruction. You either take my advice or you make your own way. I promise to pursue you. To put you in the path of as many influential courtiers as there are codpieces at court. To do my best to free you from the clutches of James Butler."

"And I appreciate that."

"So never say you're sorry. Do exactly as I ask, and within the month, everyone will want you."

He steps back like a painter admiring his own masterpiece.

"No one will be able to stem the tide of Anne Boleyn."

10

I don't see how I can speak to Mary without asking for forgiveness. Because I want it desperately. I want to erase the entire episode and be a family again, the Boleyns united.

Until Father arrives.

I drag myself to Mary's door, take a deep breath, straighten my spine, and knock.

There is no sound from the other side, and I begin to wonder if Mary has gone out. But then the door swings open, and she stands staring at me, her eyes registering surprise and fear.

My heart breaks a little.

"Nan." Her voice is a whisper. She glances into the empty gallery behind me.

She doesn't want me here. She doesn't want to be seen with me. My entire body tenses with remorse, and I open my mouth to break Wyatt's rule, when Mary grabs my arm, pulls me into the room, and wraps me in a tight hug.

"Nan, I'm so glad you're here."

The corners of my eyes sting, and my apology rises to the back of my throat. The Boleyns do stick together.

"Did you come to play? Your lute is ready." She points to where it lies on a stool by the fire.

My fingers itch to pick it up, to slide right back into how we were before. But I can't yet.

"I came to ask if you'd be in a masque with me."

Mary hesitates. "Like *The Château Vert*?"

"Nothing so grand. An interlude. A little frivolity written by Thomas Wyatt."

"Wyatt?" Mary doesn't smile. "He's a married man."

"And you know what that implies." I bite my tongue at the bitterness of my retort and rush on to cover it. To prevent an apology. "He's a poet. He's asked me to take part. And . . . and I'd like you to join me."

"You're not entangled with him in any way."

"He seems . . . interested." I think of how Wyatt looks at me when pretending to be smitten, and almost laugh. "But I'm not."

"Well, anyone can be interested. It's whom you encourage that matters."

"Thank you for the sisterly advice, Mary."

The hurt look returns, so I reach for her hand.

"I appreciate your concern, truly. And your advice."

She smiles weakly.

"I hope you take it."

She sits on the empty stool by the fire. I stare hungrily at my lute. Mary follows my gaze and laughs.

"Come and play."

I carefully tune the strings of the lute, wondering if the king has played it lately. I imagine his fingers on the strings, the back of the lute pressed tight to his body, his heartbeat in the vibration of the deep voice of the bass strings.

When I first saw him, I was thirteen years old. A maid in the household of Queen Claude, freshly promoted from the nursery and freshly initiated into the court by an unpalatably deep kiss from King François.

François and Henry had agreed to meet in the Field of Cloth of Gold, just beyond the English Pale of Calais. And it truly became a valley swathed in gold, the countless tents radiant with it and glittering with jewels. King Henry had a temporary palace built of wood and canvas with real glazed windows that reflected the sun. A gilt fountain ran with two kinds of wine, at which courtiers from both countries drowned their sorrows at being bankrupted by the expense of clothing themselves.

Carefully, I pick out a French tune on the lute. One written to describe the extravagance and pageantry. As the music flows from my fingers, it carries with it the detritus of memory.

I stayed in Ardres, on the French side, with Queen Claude and her ladies. The two kings met on the field on the first day, like armies, it was said, to the boom of cannon. Three days later, François rode out to Guînes to meet (and probably grope) the English queen and ladies. And King Henry came to visit Queen Claude.

The red of his hair shone against his black velvet cap, echoed in a more subdued shade by his beard. He was dressed all in crimson and cloth of gold, with jewels at his throat and crossing his chest, on his cap and encrusting his fingers.

But it wasn't the gold that dazzled me. And it wasn't the jewels.

It was the way he wore them. The way they fit the body

beneath. Broad chest. Narrow waist. The hard edge of the muscles in his leg beneath the stockings. And he towered above us, especially the lame and stocky Claude, who glowed round and sweet like a gilded pudding.

My limbs weakened at the sight of him, trembling with the hum I felt in his presence.

And then he spoke. Smooth. Delicate. Rich. As though his voice could melt in your mouth.

I should like to create a sound like that.

I reach for the middle strings, the little finger on my left hand, misshapen from a childhood accident, unable to stretch as far as the others. I feel the vibration of the tenor strings as I strum the rhythmic music of the king's speech.

I'm just getting the fingering right—just finding the balance between the tenor and the bright, high notes of the glitter of gold in the June sunlight—when I'm interrupted.

"Mistress Carey."

The voice—rich, smooth, and sweet—sends me immediately to my knees. It's as if I have conjured his presence with the notes themselves. The vibration in the lute continues long after I stop playing.

I hear the king stride into the room, each footstep like the beat of a drum, the rhythm at a slightly higher pace than the rest of us live by. And though my face is lowered, I envision him, dressed head to foot in red and gold, his fingers gilded in rings that he rotates with his thumb, one after the other, when he is thinking.

"Your Majesty." Mary's voice sounds like tin by comparison.

I bury my judgment in my skirts. Mary doesn't deserve it. Or my jealousy.

"Your Majesty, my sister, Nan—Anne—is here."

"Of course." His briskness betrays no discomposure at finding me there when he assumed he had a private audience with my sister. "You are well met, Mistress Boleyn."

I rise from my curtsy, but keep my head down. My face feels hot. Hotter than the rest of me.

"The lute!" he cries, and arrives in front of me in two beats. "Is this one yours?"

"Yes, Your Majesty." I still can't look at him. I may never look at him again. He must have heard me playing. Did he recognize himself in the notes?

"I played it last night. It is a fine instrument. You play well."

"Moderately, Your Majesty."

"Well, you must play better than your sister." There is a rise of laughter in his voice. "For she is completely useless on the strings."

But not in other things. I manage to hold my tongue. George would be proud.

"Anne plays exquisitely, Your Majesty," Mary interjects. "And sings."

"A girl after my own heart."

He raises his hand. I can see it, beringed and bedazzling. His fingers touch my chin and lift delicately. He forces me to look him in the eye.

He is wondrous. His hair blazes and his gray eyes are like

sun behind a cloud, the animated features almost seeming to blur because nothing about him is ever still.

"I greet you like a sister," he says. But there is a hint of mischief in his half smile.

He keeps his fingers on my chin and lowers his mouth to mine. When our lips touch, it is like the alignment of stars. The hint of stubble on his upper lip tickles mine, and I realize, hysterically, that my mouth is bigger than his. The scents of cloves and orange water fill me to drowning, and for one incomparable, darting instant, I taste the sweetness of his tongue.

He laughs and breaks away and I am left breathless, dropping to another curtsy as he turns to my sister.

Mary's laughter echoes his, the sound high above me, thin and wispy like clouds on a summer day. I feel my blood surge within my skull, drowning out their voices with rush and roar. Blindly, my senses reach for him, the scent of cloves and the caress of gold.

I look up from my curtsy, sure that he will be watching me. As moved by our contact as I was.

But he stands with Mary, a full head taller, his neck bent at an angle to kiss her, his hair reflecting the flames in the hearth. She is almost completely hidden, engulfed by his embrace.

I stagger to my feet, my joints barely able to take my weight, my fingers and lips suddenly devoid of all feeling, jealousy tangling my skirts, and elation still racing in my blood.

Because etiquette demands that no courtier turn away from the king, I get to see his every move as I shuffle to the door. He removes Mary's hood, smooths her hair away from his lips as he trails kisses down her jaw and neck.

I manage to slip through the door before his lips drift lower. And I sink backward against it, resting one hand above my heart.

Wishing. Imagining it's me dissolving beneath his touch.

11

I KNOW IT MEANS NOTHING. A JOKE. A TEASE. *I GREET YOU LIKE A sister.* But I touch one finger to my lips, almost able to feel his again.

I stumble through the outer court and into the darkness of the tower gate, across the moat and up the stairs to the queen's rooms.

Where reality hits me. I kissed the queen's husband. Coveted my sister's lover. Ridiculously pictured myself in the arms of the king.

The watching chamber ripples with gossip as I enter. Wyatt says they don't remember *The Château Vert.* I should stop assuming that gossip is all about me.

I avoid the queen's eye as I curtsy before her. I'm sure she can somehow discern what I've done. And how much I liked it.

I search for a place to settle, and Jane Parker smiles at me, then covers her mouth with her hand. Her cuticles are ragged. She glances over to where George is ensconced with the gamblers, his wine close by his hand. Tentatively, she pats the window seat beside her.

"Jane." I sit cautiously.

"Mistress Boleyn."

"Oh, please, call me Anne." I'm irritated by her formality. She may be of the duchess's confederacy, but we sleep in the same bed, for pity's sake. She lifts her hand to bite the cuticles, but I put out my own to stop it.

"Has Wyatt spoken to you?" I ask.

Jane's hand freezes beneath mine, and she looks at me like a startled rabbit.

"No." She casts a glance around the room to see who's watching, who's listening. Frowns. "Why would Thomas Wyatt want to speak to me?" Her upper lip twitches at the corner, and she peeks at me from beneath her lashes. "Not that I'm not delighted at the thought, of course. He's rather gorgeous. And highly beddable."

I fight back the irritation that continues to grow.

"I don't think that was going to be his topic of conversation." Though it might have been, knowing Wyatt. The irritation threatens to ignite and engulf me.

"Oh!" Jane's other hand flies to her mouth, and I can barely understand the words around it. "I'm sorry. Truly. I meant no offense. And no presumption. I forgot, I mean, I didn't think . . . I'm sorry."

She bites the curve of her knuckle and I wince because she doesn't.

"Nothing to be sorry for," I say, thinking of Wyatt's rule. *Never apologize.* Especially when you have nothing to apologize for. And I add, "Stop doing that. You'll hurt yourself."

"It doesn't really hurt anymore." But she puts her hand in her lap and covers it with the other.

"Well, it will make your hands ugly."

"That's what the duchess says."

"Probably the only time we'll ever be in agreement."

Jane laughs out loud and then ducks her head, her hands bouncing in her lap as she struggles not to move them.

"However, the reason I asked if Wyatt has talked to you is because he's planning a masque. An interlude. An entertainment for the king."

"And he wants me to join?" She sounds surprised.

"You were in *The Château Vert*." I manage to say the name without cringing. "It's not like you're no one here. Your father is Lord Morley, a gentleman of the chamber."

"But no one ever notices me."

"That's because you never speak."

"I'm sorry." Jane shrugs.

Again the unneeded apology. I had never thought about the useless, ineffectual habit of offering an expression of regret. Like bandaging a healed wound.

"But we're going to change that," I whisper to her. "Wyatt is penning his own script. For you and me and Mary."

Jane's expression is one of delighted awe. "Me and the Boleyn girls."

I save the best for last. "And George."

Jane's smile completely consumes her, and I hope her joy can make a difference in George's life. Perhaps with Lord Morley's influence, he can get out from beneath Father's thumb.

"When do we start?" Jane leans forward—childlike in her eagerness—and I feel a flutter of jealousy.

"I'll let you know."

Jane tilts her head at me.

"Are you his muse?"

"Whose?" My mind is full of the king. Of how I would feel if he were participating in—and not just viewing—the performance.

"Thomas Wyatt's."

My laugh carries an edge of embarrassment. Jane must think I can't follow a conversation. I contemplate Wyatt's inspirations, and his promised poem about me. One that will be passed down through the ages, he said.

But only if I win the bet.

"Hardly," I tell Jane. "I think women in general are his muse, so he doesn't need a lot of prompting."

"Oh." Jane appears to ponder this. "Well, he certainly seems . . . interested."

"As I said, Wyatt is interested in anything in a skirt. And I know where my boundaries are."

"You must admit it though. He is delicious."

Her face is lit with mischief. But her expression alters in an instant as she spies something over my shoulder. I have to force myself not to look.

"Mind you, that one is striking as well."

I turn. Henry Percy. His stillness is the complete opposite of Wyatt's and seems to emanate from a deep discomfort. But Jane is right. Definitely striking. I look away before I can be accused of staring.

"The duchess says that he's supposed to marry the Earl of

Shrewsbury's daughter," Jane whispers. "But they hate each other."

"Poor boy," I mutter. The court is full of such stories. My own included.

"Hardly," Jane scoffs. "He'll be the Earl of Northumberland soon and will run the Scottish borders and half the country."

I glance up again at Henry Percy—destined to be one of the most powerful nobles in the country. Destined from birth to be a member of the royal circle. A captive in Cardinal Wolsey's household. So free, and yet still tethered.

He is an enigma.

And he's watching me.

12

I ALMOST ASK WYATT TO INVITE PERCY TO PARTICIPATE IN HIS poetic interlude. But then I look at Wyatt's profile, head bent over parchment and ink. The set of his jaw, the intensity of his eyes. And somehow, I can't.

So instead, I stake everything on one night. On the hope that someone watching will see me and save me from my fate, like in a romantic ballad. Because I can't think of another way to save myself.

The interlude is a lovely little joke of a play based on the myth of Atalanta. No set. Simple Greek-inspired costumes wrapped over pale gowns and doublets. We will be the only entertainment of the evening. Except for the dancing.

Wyatt casts me as Atalanta and Jane as my companion. Mary is Aphrodite. I can't complain, because Mary does nothing but stand on a dais and look beautiful. I get to lead the chase.

Wyatt will play Hippomenes—the man who catches Atalanta through cunning rather than fleetness of foot. He dresses in golden sandals and a sky-blue tunic that reflects the periwinkle of my gown, giving the appearance that we are meant to be together. George, Norris, and my cousin Bryan round out the cast of men who lust after Atalanta enough to risk death for a chance at her. I find it a bit perverse that George plays a potential lover, but say not a word. This is Wyatt's show, and I'm following instructions.

I'm grateful for the distraction, because the king has decided to call Parliament to raise funds for the war against France. The galleries and gardens of Richmond are full of the news. Full of men bloated on the thought of war. There is more tension in the court. More rivalry. Less chivalry. And the endless clamor of backslapping and chest-thumping.

The afternoon before the performance, I go to the orchards to smell the blossoms and avoid the heady musk of martial fervor. Unfortunately, the Duchess of Suffolk has had the same idea. I see her gown of deep lake blue, the red of her hair beneath her gable, and realize we are on an intersecting course that I cannot avoid.

She is followed by her confederacy. I'm disappointed to see Jane among them.

"Mistress Boleyn." The duchess's voice carries the same tenor as her brother's.

"Your Grace." She rarely speaks to me. It is rumored that her husband will lead the English troops into France in the summer, and I can't help thinking of it as she slips her arm through mine and turns me to walk with her.

People shuffle and bow out of her way. It is as if she has a giant bubble around her, one that cannot be punctured. One that I, miraculously, find myself inhabiting with her. It's a nice place to be. Watched, but protected.

I pretend I don't hear the whispers and titters behind me as the other ladies follow. I do glance back once. Only Jane looks at me and flashes an almost-smile.

"I must ask you," the duchess says, the corner of her hood's gable preventing truly confidential whispers, "are the women in France very beautiful?"

"Do you not remember, Your Grace? You were the most beautiful woman in the court when you were there." Flattery will surely get me somewhere with the sister of the king.

The duchess caused a fuss in both countries when she married the aging King Louis. After a year in the Low Countries, I was uprooted and sent to serve her. Until she caused an international incident when Louis died suddenly and she ran away with the up-and-coming and entirely unsuitable Charles Brandon. Despite his title, he had no royal blood and no connections and the match brought the king's wrath down on them both.

I had to admire her for marrying for love—and against the king's wishes. But the Brandons were both soon welcomed back to his circle and have been there ever since. We can all pretend the discord never happened.

"I have certainly not forgotten the kindness of a little girl I knew there," the duchess says sweetly. "I spoke French so poorly, and Louis had just dismissed my great friend and translator Lady Guildford. I was eighteen and terrified. And heartbroken."

"Yes, Your Grace," I say. Though she hadn't cared a whit when she left behind almost her entire entourage. Including a lonely eight-year-old girl and her dangerously pretty older sister.

"You are all grown up now, though," she continues. "And looking for a husband of your own."

"Yes, Your Grace."

"And not that spiteful savage James Butler."

I jerk to stare at her, startled.

"No, Your Grace."

I can't see her entire face, hidden as it is by her hood, but I think I see her smile.

"I understand being forced into an unsavory marriage, Mistress Boleyn. And I haven't forgotten your kindness. I'll keep my eye out for a lovely young man for you."

"Thank you, Your Grace."

Why is she being so nice?

I hear a ripple behind me. I try to catch the ladies giggling, but their faces are impassive. Jane won't look at me at all, her eyes only on the ragged skin around her fingers.

"In the meantime," the duchess continues, entering the donjon through a door that opens without her even having to touch it, and flicking a wrist at the usher behind it, "you might consider some other forms of assistance."

We enter her private rooms, and the duchess picks up a little gilded pot of Venetian ceruse, a paint used by some to lighten their skin. She, of course, doesn't need it. She's so pale I can see the blue blood at her temple. She's offering the ceruse to me.

I hesitate. It's said that wearing ceruse can cause teeth to fall out and hair to thin to near baldness. It's said it can kill. Slowly.

"It will make you look less . . ." The duchess turns a pretty pink.

"Swarthy."

I hear the word, sniped from behind me, but the duchess pretends not to.

"Pale skin against your dark hair will make you look more dramatic," she says. "It will accentuate the blackness of your eyes. It will be like a siren's call to the eligible men of the court."

My eyes are not *black*.

But tentatively, I stick a finger in the paste. It smells of beeswax and feels like clay on my fingers.

"Let me help."

The duchess delicately smooths some across my cheeks, over my brow, right up to my hairline. She rubs it across the skin of my neck and where my jaw meets my ear. She even covers my lips and dabs it around the thin skin of my eyelids. A prickling burn in the corners of my eyes makes me squint and blink.

"There."

The duchess stands back to scrutinize me.

"Now you need red."

She finds another paste and daubs my lips and smears my cheeks. My skin feels cold and heavy.

It's like a death mask, the white lead burrowing into my face and freezing my smile.

"Beautiful."

One of her ladies holds up a little mirror of Venetian glass so we can see ourselves, side by side. I see a girl, her face as pale as white linen, her lips red as blood, her eyes wide and dark and starting to spiderweb with reddened irritation, next to a clear-skinned, gray-eyed beauty, unmarred and unpainted.

"How do I get it off?" I ask.

The duchess freezes, staring at my reflection. Her eyes harden and narrow slightly.

"Don't you like it?"

I glance at Jane Parker, who meets my eye briefly, terrified. But then she looks down again, picking at the ragged cuticles of her left hand.

"Of course I do," I say, gagging back the truth. "I mean for later."

"You don't take it off," the duchess says. "You just apply more."

She waves the mirror away.

"You're beautiful, little Boleyn."

I want to believe her. No one has ever called me beautiful before. Different. But never beautiful.

She presses the pot into my hand. "Use it. And everyone else will think so, too."

Not only has the duchess given me a gift, she's also given me a sentence: to wear this death mask until I need a real one. Which, if the physicians are to be believed, will be all the sooner because of it.

A finger pokes me in the ribs.

I sink into a curtsy, barely able to frame my face into a smile.

"Thank you, Your Grace."

"Enjoy it," the duchess says dismissively. "You may go."

Again the rustle of suppressed giggles. A jostling of sleeves and gowns around me, and I am shuffled to the back of the group. Propelled out the door. And deposited outside, like refuse.

A peal of laughter rings through the door before it closes.

13

"WHAT THE HELL HAVE YOU DONE TO YOURSELF?"

I've never seen Wyatt angry before. I touch my face. I can hardly feel my fingers through the mask.

"You look like a fool."

He grabs my chin in his hand, fingers digging in. I try to pull away, but find I can't move. We are in the pages' chamber, where our costumes and properties are stored. No one else is around to see, but the great watching chamber is just the other side of the door, full of people.

"Aren't you the one who tells me we should always be making eyes at each other?" I ask him, setting my jaw and looking at him directly. "Even in private? What happened to your grand façade, Thomas Wyatt?"

He throws his hand from my chin and stumbles away.

"Perhaps it's time for a lovers' quarrel," he says to the wall beyond. His voice is tight, the set of his shoulders rigid.

"We can't have one if we're not lovers."

My eyes, already burning from the ceruse, feel pinched with the onset of tears, and my throat constricts. I can't lose my only friend. My only almost-friend.

"That's good, because I wouldn't want a painted doll in my bed. All show and no substance."

I don't understand why he's so furious. Or why it shatters me.

"The duchess said I was beautiful."

I hate the sound of my voice. Like a child begging for sufferance. I press my palms on my skirts to still them.

Wyatt turns like a cat on the prowl.

"The Duchess of Suffolk?" He stalks back to me, and I flinch. At the sight of it, the predation in him melts away.

"Watch out for her, Anne. She will not be a true friend."

"But she is part of the royal circle—that inner sanctum of status and nobility. Shouldn't I be cultivating that?"

"Not with her. Not with them. No one in that family can be trusted. I advise you to stay away."

It is well known that Wyatt and the Duke of Suffolk don't get along. Some long-standing dispute. The stories make them both sound like infatuated girls, jealous over the king's attention.

"They can only bring you misery."

I'm suddenly tired of instruction. Tired of always getting it wrong, always seeking improvement and never seeming to achieve it.

"Your point is taken, sir."

I rub my hands on my skirts and turn to walk away.

"Don't do that."

More?

"Don't do what, Wyatt?" I don't even turn to look at him.

I can no longer muster the energy to keep up the pretense.

"That."

He takes my left hand—turning me to face him—and flattens it to his. It requires every bit of my resolve not to pull away, my crooked little finger awkward in his palm. He doesn't seem to notice—at least, he doesn't react. Someone must be watching.

"Rubbing your skirts. It's a habit, Anne. And a nasty one at that. It's as bad as Jane Parker biting the skin at her fingernails. But at least that brings attention to her face. Your compulsion makes your face invisible."

"You don't even like my face at the moment," I mutter. Like a sullen toddler.

"Try this." He reaches out to stroke a strand of hair loose from my hood. He winds it along the length of his finger, slowly. "You want to attract the eye." His hand releases mine and drops to my skirts.

"Not here." He draws the backs of his fingers slowly upward, like a man's gaze. "But here. To your breasts, your neck, your hair."

I feel a shiver of heat and hold my breath.

"Your eyes."

His own eyes find mine, and there is something in them I've never seen before. He rests his palm on the side of my face. I smell the ink, metallic on his fingers. I tilt my head slightly, his hand taking a little of the weight from my shoulders.

I want to rub my hands on something, but one is caught up against the velvet of his chest. And the other I find covering the hand that cradles my face.

I swallow, and his gaze trails the action at my throat and comes to rest on my lips.

"We're putting on quite a show," I murmur, and his eyes snap back to meet mine.

"You're learning well." A compliment. But his smile is tight. So after all his criticism, I'm not sure he means it.

"Let's hope it pays off tonight," I say.

Wyatt takes a step back, dropping my right hand from his chest and pulling my left to his lips in a showy, chivalric kiss. But he continues to hold it tightly.

"Absolutely." He nods. "Now go and get ready."

But he doesn't let me. He holds on. And I want him to.

"One more thing, Anne. Before you leave."

I suddenly wonder if he'll ask me to kiss him. I wonder if maybe I'll say yes.

"Yes?"

"Take that rubbish off your face before I see you again."

He bows, drops my hand, and walks past me to the watching chamber. I take a deep breath, avoid touching my skirts, and turn around to leave, assuming I'll meet the half-averted gaze of an inveterate gossipmonger.

No one is there.

14

I scrub my face, the paste leaving white streaks over red skin. The rough linen and cold water scour and burn. The cloth drags at my eyelids and plucks at the lashes. My eyes are as red as my lips—inflamed—my entire face mottled and puffy.

Not exactly the image I had in mind for my bid to conquer the court.

Mary and Jane say nothing when we meet to dress for the play. My face feels raw and my eyes ache. Even without a mirror, I know I look a fright. Jane won't look at me, and Mary just purses her lips together. I dawdle while they dress, helping Mary with her stays while she helps Jane with her skirts. They are beautiful, their faces unmarred.

I'm still in my chemise and bodice, my gown thrown across a cedar chest. Mary shakes out my sleeves before coming to me to lace them on.

"Stop," I say, and she freezes, a sleeve held out before her like a peace offering. "I can't. I can't face them. The crowd. The chorus. The cardinal." The king. "Not like this."

Mary lowers her arms, looks at me sternly.

"Yes, you can."

"Look at me! They will hate me. For my face. My dress.

Because I'm a Boleyn. No matter what Wyatt says, they will hate me. The duchess hates me."

"The duchess hates everyone, Anne."

"You can take over my role, Mary."

"No, I can't. I'm Aphrodite."

"Then Jane . . ."

But Jane is no longer in the room. Mary drops the sleeves and takes my face in both of her hands. Gently. Like a mother.

"Nan, you can't let a little animosity stop you. If I had, I would be pulverized by now. Don't you think I feel this every day?"

"You have the king."

"Yes. And that's part of the problem. I'm the king's mistress." Mary pauses. "But for how long?"

Before I have a chance to respond, the door bangs open and Wyatt strides into the room, fierce and feline. Jane pauses behind him, closing the door with her foot.

"What does Jane mean, you're not going on?"

Wyatt grabs me by the shoulders, then realizes he's touched bare skin at the neck of my chemise. He leaps away, shaking his fingers as if he's been scalded.

I'm so ugly even Thomas Wyatt can't bear to touch me.

I take a deep breath. Hold my hands still. "I can't go on like this."

He studies my face, and his tone softens.

"Good God, what has she done to you?"

Somehow this hurts more than his anger when he called me a fool.

"It will go away," Mary says quickly. "It already looks better."

When Wyatt reaches out to touch my face, I duck and step aside.

"Right," I say. "Let's just put it off for a couple of hours. It's only the king and the cardinal waiting."

Wyatt coughs a laugh, and while his back is turned, I grab a cloak to cover myself, then tie my hair into a knot.

"Actually," he says, "I already have a solution. One that won't require our notoriously impatient monarch to wait."

He turns to Jane, who brings her hands out from behind her back, and with them, three decorative masks. All in white, trimmed in gold. One simple, trimmed with braid. One plumed in peacock feathers—Aphrodite. And one edged around the eyes with black and gold, wings of gold-dusted feathers at the temples. Mine.

I look at Wyatt.

"When did you plan this?"

"When I decided the whole production would be more fun as a masque. Lends an air of mystery."

"And allows the men to choose their dancing partners," I add. He's thought of everything. If only the roles were reversed and I could be the one to make a choice.

Wyatt's dimple disappears when he catches a glimpse of my chemise beneath the open cloak.

"Get dressed." He turns back to the door. Pauses. Looks back. "You'll be wonderful. A jewel held to the light."

He disappears, and I find myself wondering what it would be like to dance with him.

Mary and Jane each fasten a sleeve, and we tuck my hair into the gold caul of my cap before tying on the mask. I feel hidden. Mysterious. Sheltered.

Beautiful.

I silently thank Thomas Wyatt for that.

15

THE GREAT WATCHING CHAMBER IS LIT WITH TORCHES AND candles, their dragon's breath swirling in the rafters along the gilded battens and Tudor roses. The walls are covered in tapestries shining with pigment and gold thread. But even they are unmatched by the riot of color presented by the audience. Mary, Jane, and I stand together in the pages' chamber, peering out at the assembled masses.

Wolsey is a beacon in his cardinal red—a great, round hump of velvet and fur, beaming with self-satisfaction. Behind him run layers of courtiers and sycophants, ladies with faces etched in envy. Percy is near the door, a pillar around which a tide of courtiers flows, bringing with them James Butler, ursine and unruly.

The queen sits on a dais, dressed in lustrous gray that tinges her skin green, and a Spanish hood that cloaks her face in shadow, the soft folds veiled and saddened.

The musicians in the minstrels' gallery start up a galliard, and a group of finely dressed ladies dance with the king's men. I see several of the duchess's confederacy amongst them. A well-cast prologue. Wyatt is quite a diplomat.

The dance is athletic and breathless, and the audience shouts and applauds when the dancers are done.

The person I wish to see most, however, is not here. When he enters a room, he infuses it with light like the moon and the sun all at once—drawing the eye to him, then searing the vision. But he isn't here.

The king isn't coming.

A sharp whistle from the audience wakes me, and I hear Wyatt, already narrating. Mary puts a hand on my shoulder.

"Remember, you're better than they are, Nan." She gives me a little push. "You're a Boleyn."

I adjust my mask and step into the chamber. The light from the torches blinds me. The colors of the doublets and gowns and the brilliance of the jewels and gold dazzle me.

"Smile."

Mary's disembodied voice comes from the shadows at my elbow.

I smile.

Mary moves past me, circling the great hall past all the courtiers, the brush of her skirts sighing over the floorboards and rushes.

I hear a muffled yelp as she passes the duchess.

"Excuse me, Your Grace." A carrying whisper.

I smile and look up. Wyatt is watching me. I imagine he has been the entire time, acting the part of the besotted lover.

"Atalanta," he says, raising a cheer from the men in the audience. "The most beautiful girl in Athens."

He turns to include the audience.

"But also the swiftest, my friends. She is quick as a doe and loath to be caught. Only one man will suit her: the only man who can catch her."

A boom of cannon sounds from outside, and the doors at the end of the chamber burst open. Four men enter, dressed in white and silver and cloth of gold, burning like flame and carrying with them the odors of night and saltpeter.

Four?

They, too, are masked, but easily recognized. Norris with his ink-black hair. Bryan, his dark-red tunic pulled tight around his wiry frame. George, his shambling gait giving him away.

And the fourth . . .

The fourth is the king.

He looks to me, his gray eyes clear and hot and knowing. A prickle at my neck quickly becomes a hum at the top of my head. I hardly know what to do with myself. I glare at Wyatt, who offers a minute shrug as if to say, *How could I refuse the king when he asked?* And then I feel a rush of warmth through me and turn back to the king. He must have asked to join in. I raise a hand to my lips, remembering the press of his there.

The king winks at me.

Wyatt stumbles over a couplet rhyme, and I glance at him in shock. Thomas Wyatt never drops a rhyme. He ignores me.

When I look back at the king, he has turned to Aphrodite, and my stomach roils with an unpalatable mix of jealousy, self-recrimination, and shame.

Fortunately, the play is a carefully choreographed dance and I know the steps well. Pursuit and escape. I can't actually

run about the room—it would look ridiculous. But the dance allows me to skip ahead of the men. Always in front. Always pursued. Never caught.

Mary sets up the final race, giving Wyatt the golden apples one by one. He rolls the gilded fruit before me to slow me down. Part of me wants to ignore them. To win the race. Lead the pack. But that isn't how the story goes.

So I pick them up as he races past me, toss them to the audience. All eyes are on me, faces upturned.

Wyatt, victorious, takes me as his prize, and Mary blesses the union to the applause of the audience. But just as we are about to move into the final dance, he stops us with an upraised hand. The court quiets.

"We come to you disguised, my lords and ladies. Is this who we are? Or merely who we wish to be? Beautiful." He indicates Mary.

"Loyal." He bows to Jane.

"And unobtainable." He turns toward me and hesitates.

His eyes are unquiet. The room falls into silence.

"Unmask!" a voice shouts from the audience.

"Let us be the judges!"

"Dance." Butler's growl is unmistakable.

"Let me set you a riddle." Wyatt turns from me to face the audience. "Solve it, and you tell me who is our Atalanta."

All eyes are on us as he approaches me with the measured steps of the verse.

> "What word is that, that changeth not
> Though it be turned and made in twain?"

I struggle to follow the riddle myself. A-N and N-A. It doesn't change, however it is turned. Unlike me.

> *"It is mine answer, God it wot,*
> *And eke the causer of my pain—"*

Wyatt cannot see my eyebrow raised behind my mask. He's laying it on a little thick.

> *"A love rewardeth with disdain*
> *Yet it is loved. What would ye more?*
> *It is my health, eke and my sore."*

Loved?

He stops in front of me, catches my hands before I rub them on my skirts, and holds them both to his heart. I take a step forward, wanting to taste the almonds on his breath, but his grip tightens and I stop. I study his face, but his true intention is hidden behind mask and make-believe.

"What word is it?" The voice is to my left. A mellifluous tenor. "Why, dear troubadour, the answer is simple."

Wyatt lets go of me and steps back, leaving me impoverished. So I turn to the speaker. The king is facing me, his hand extended, his gray eyes shining behind his mask.

"Anna."

16

BECAUSE HE IS STILL MASKED, I CAN DANCE WITH THE KING.

Because he asks.

I dance with the king.

The eyes of the entire room are on me. Still. Me. Anne Boleyn. I am nobody. And yet I am everything. I will not waste this chance. This time, my dance with the king will propel me forward, not send me home.

The top of my hood barely reaches his chin. I find myself facing the elaborately embroidered doublet—layered and appliquéd in damask and satin, blue, gold, yellow, and bronze. And the heat coming from it is intense.

Or perhaps that heat is coming from me.

This is my moment. This is my chance. I can be what I am. Only better. I know I can dance. In France, I was praised for the lightness of my feet, for the effortlessness of my movements. For the way I seem to feel the music in my limbs.

I feel the same rhythm in his.

The king lifts me with what seems to be so little effort, I feel like I am flying. Floating. His hands at the base of my ribs are like a tether to the sky. His touch sets my sinews vibrating like lute strings, all playing the same note.

My entire world is nothing but silk and velvet, fur and damask and the scent of cloves.

Until the dance ends.

He bows to me and turns, without a backward glance, to the audience, and we all unmask to gasps of practiced astonishment and wild applause. I manage a curtsy, though the note thrumming through my body conspires to unbalance me.

When the dancing continues, the king partners the duchess. It's only fair, because she is the lady of greatest precedence after the queen, who again refuses to dance. Norris—looking delighted—partners Mary, who gracefully adjusts his roaming hands. Jane looks at George, who turns on his heel and strides to the far end of the room, plucking up a wine goblet on his way.

"You didn't look out into the audience."

Wyatt steps me into a turn and I lose sight of Jane, who seems about to cry. The players are all supposed to dance together. I quell a stab of anger at my brother, but Wyatt doesn't miss it.

"Smile. You're supposed to be enjoying this."

I think of the one thing that can restore my good humor.

"Did you see, Wyatt? The king danced with me."

"It's all part of the performance, Anne. He answered the riddle."

Defeated, I search for Jane as we come out of the turn. She is in the arms of Henry Percy, who is smiling. But not at her.

"Was everyone watching?" I ask Wyatt, wanting to taste once more the heady excitement of being part of the most intimate layer of the royal circle. I look up at him. "Did you see?"

"Everyone was watching, Anne. And yes, I saw. You could have shown more deference to your sister."

"But he asked me, Wyatt!"

We execute a turn, and I spin away from him.

"During the play. She was Aphrodite. A goddess. And you treated her like . . . your sister."

"She is my sister, Wyatt."

"Still, deference is due."

We chassé four steps, only our fingertips touching.

"And you missed a line at the beginning."

"Because the king had joined us and I was a little bit surprised! Jesus, Wyatt, can I do nothing right?"

The dance brings us together again. Close. Pressed against each other, my hands in his.

"You dance rather well."

"A compliment."

I give him a hard stare until the dance requires me to move away from him, walking in a broad circle, before returning.

"You do," he says. "You flow with the music. It's very . . . sensual."

The word runs like water down my spine. But then I remind myself who it is I'm speaking to.

"You're still not winning the bet, Wyatt."

He looks away. I follow his gaze to George, who stands leaning against an embroidered silk wall hanging. George raises his goblet to us. We turn, and I don't see him drink. But I see Jane, watching his every move.

"Young Lord Percy can't take his eyes off you."

I meet Percy's gaze, his oddly colored eyes. Jane says something to him, and he answers. But his eyes never leave mine.

"You know"—Wyatt's voice is a little strained, but when I turn to look at him, his face is placid—"Percy could be the entrée into that circle of nobility whose acceptance you so desperately seek. Heir to the earldom of Northumberland. One of the highest—and oldest—noble families in the land."

There is no mistaking the sardonic edge to his voice.

"That's why we're doing this, right?"

He looks at me sharply. "So you can marry Henry Percy?"

"So I can gain acceptance. So I don't have to marry James Butler."

"You could always become my mistress."

The laughter is back in his voice.

"That would only solve one of my problems."

"Oh, I'm sure James Butler wouldn't consider marrying a poet's tarnished mistress."

"I would be the court darling, and the duchess would invite me to be her most trusted friend." I lace my words with sarcasm.

"I said before, Anne, she's not a friend you want to have."

"I think I've figured that out, Wyatt. But you know what I mean."

"Yes," he says quietly. "Yes, I do."

The dance ends and Wyatt takes me by the hand.

"Let's go see what the night will bring."

He leads me to Jane and Percy, who are standing silently, as if completely unsure of how to part.

"Mistress Parker," Wyatt says smoothly. "I hope to have the pleasure of your company in a dance."

Jane's face lights up, and I think about her words that first day we really talked. How she described Wyatt as "beddable." I shoot him a look that's meant to say, *Don't try anything with her.* He flickers a frown back at me.

"Mistress Boleyn," he says, snapping a quick bow. "Lord Percy."

Percy inclines his head as I curtsy. As the son of an earl, he doesn't need to offer much deference to the daughter of a nobody.

"Dance?" Uttering one word brings a flush of color to Percy's face, and I am instantly charmed by his self-consciousness.

But when the music begins, he promptly steps on my white satin slipper.

He doesn't apologize.

And I wonder if Wyatt has been training him, too.

Percy's gaze intensifies as he follows the rhythms of the music. His eyes—a blue so pale they're like sunlight—keep flicking from my face to his feet to the other dancers and back again. Perhaps he's just nervous.

Of dancing? Or of being with me?

We execute a turn and when we face each other again, he clears his throat.

"The masque was very . . . entertaining."

His voice is musical. Like the bass notes of a lute. Thrumming. Resonant.

"Thomas Wyatt is quite a poet." I try to sound noncommittal, but it is obviously the wrong thing to say. Percy's face falls into craggy shadows and he glances over to where Wyatt is making Jane laugh so hard she can't find the steps. I miss one, too, but Percy catches me.

He clears his throat again. A judgment. He thinks I've complimented Wyatt because of an attachment.

"You dance very well," I tell him. Men need flattery. Especially noblemen.

"Thank you." He turns. Frowns at me. "So do you."

No comments on my sensuality from Henry Percy.

I watch him from the corner of my eye as we promenade away from each other. He is watching Wyatt's catlike grace. Comparatively, Percy is a bit stiff. A bit unsure of the steps. I find his insecurity appealing, a nice change from Wyatt's relentless self-confidence.

"I hear that you play the lute," Percy says when he returns to me, all of his attention focused through that penetrating gaze.

"I enjoy music."

"And I hear around the court that your voice could rival Orpheus. That it charms all the animals of the forest and entices the birds to dance."

I laugh. "You shouldn't believe everything you hear at court."

"There is much loose talk," he replies, and narrows his eyes once more at Wyatt.

He's trying to make sense of what he has heard. And I hope he is not one of the small-minded people who believe Wyatt's hints and implications.

"The court is full of stories told by perjurers and poets," I say a little more loudly than I had intended. As we turn again, I take a deep breath and when I come back to him, I murmur warmly. "And one can only believe the things experienced in the flesh."

113

My timing is just right. As I say the word *"flesh,"* his hand is at my waist. I feel a squeeze of pressure before the flush starts at his ears and floods his face and throat.

Wyatt will be delighted. I risk a glance at him, expecting a nod or a wink or a single dimple at the very least. But his back is turned.

"Then I should like to hear you sing one day," Percy croaks, and I look up into his face. Vulnerability softens his features.

I lower my gaze, the steps of flirtation taught to me by Thomas Wyatt as measured as the steps of the dance as it comes to an end. Just as I begin to sense Percy's concern at offending me, I look up and smile.

"One day I will," I tell him. "For I would like to see what it entices you to do."

17

"You certainly made a spectacle of yourself last night."

George enters the maids' chamber at Richmond as if he's been here a hundred times before. He probably has. I shudder at the thought that he could have been the man I smelled on my bedclothes.

"You certainly made yourself scarce," I reply. I'm all alone—for once—looking for the little pot of ceruse. Wanting to give it back to the duchess. I find it and twist it in my hands as I sit down on the bed.

George sits next to me with a flourish and then lies down, his head in my lap, looking up into my eyes. Like a lover. He grins.

"The best girl was already taken by the king."

I stroke his hair, trying to tame it.

"Hardly," I say, the glow from last night still lodged in my chest. And the glow of George's praise.

When we were children Father sneeringly called George a girl when he cried. So we played a betting game to soothe the sting. *Who's the best girl?* The winner got all three desserts at dinner. Mary peed herself laughing the day George came into our room dressed in bodice and skirts, singing a love song in falsetto and salting it liberally with profanity and counterfeit flatulence.

He got all our sweets for a week for that stunt. Made himself sick on them.

"You deny the fact that our sister was the prettiest girl there?"

I sigh and drop my hand to the bed. Of course George wasn't complimenting me. Or renewing our childhood friendship. I surreptitiously wipe my hand on my skirts—George's hair is a little greasy.

"No need to be jealous. Mary's success benefits us all."

"What good has it done me?" I snap. I'm sick of George. Sick of his backhanded compliments and sly criticisms. I want so badly for him to sit here with me, reveling in our success. Not cutting it to pieces.

"It brought you to court, my dear. And won the king's support of your marriage to my legacy."

"I don't want your bloody legacy!"

"Well, you should, you know. If not for yourself, then for the family. A title is the only way ahead. Money. Influence." He looks up at me, his eyes savage. "Having a sister to sell. It's the only thing you're useful for, after all."

I push him off my lap, and he lands in the rushes with a thump and a laugh.

"Get out."

I kick at him and he grabs my ankle and pulls. I cling to the counterpane, but it does nothing to slow my descent and raises a cloud of dust as it falls to cover us.

George laughs again, an almost childish giggle, and I can't help but feel my anger diminish. We are tented beneath the counterpane. Just the two of us. Like it used to be.

"Girls are good for more than that, you know." I prepare to give him the same speech I gave James Butler.

"They certainly are, dear sister." George waggles his eyebrows. "Though I don't expect you to understand."

"Don't be disgusting."

I scramble with the counterpane to pull it off. Before it suffocates me.

"Don't make yourself more than you are." George stands and brushes his doublet. Checks his fingernails. "As a woman, you have no choice. You have to do what your father says. And eventually what your husband says. You can use your feminine wiles to encourage certain outcomes, but at the end of the day, their will is the only will that matters."

I think of Queen Claude: lame, pious, meek. She should have been a queen in her own right. As the daughter of a king she should have ruled. But French Salic law prevented it, so her debauched and warlike husband, François, rules instead.

Even royalty can be rendered impotent.

"I'll just have to put my feminine wiles to work then."

"You already are, dear sister. You have half the men at court panting after you. Just make sure you sell to a higher bidder than Thomas Wyatt."

"I'm not selling anything to Wyatt." I stand and put my bed back together. "Our friendship is strictly that: friendship."

"Anne." George's voice is full of pity, as if I've just admitted to believing in true love. "Men and women cannot be friends. It's impossible. It's like the lion and the lamb. Oil and water. Grain and grape."

I turn to face him. "And why is that?"

"There are far too many reasons to count. Incompatibility. Dissimilarity." He leans toward me. "Sex."

I step back. "That's not an issue."

"Of course it isn't, dear sister. Wyatt has much better taste."

George raises a smirking eyebrow, but I refuse to rise to the bait.

"The real reason that men and women cannot be friends," George continues, "is that women don't know how to have fun."

I stare at him.

"That is wrong on so many levels, George."

"All you do is sit around and sew. Gossip. Maybe play a few boring tunes on the lute."

"Friendship is not based on fun."

"It is in my book."

"If we were given the chance to go out to London and roam the streets and attend a bearbaiting, we might do more than sew."

"You would drink in the taverns and get in a brawl and maybe go whoring afterward?" George laughs.

I scowl at him.

"There," he says, and pats my cheek gently. "See? No fun at all."

He kisses me sloppily.

"Be not afeard, my darling. Friendship has no place between a man and a woman. But fun?" He smiles a sly smile. "Fun certainly does—especially when it comes to sex. And occasionally serves a purpose, as well."

He walks to the door, creaking it open.

"Fun for whom, George? And to what purpose?"

He turns back to look at me. "Why, fun for the man of course. And for the woman, it serves all kinds of purposes, from hooking the man to providing him an heir."

"But no fun for the woman?"

"You just have to learn how to have fun with it, Anne. And you will, with the right guidance. I suppose Wyatt would serve you well in that capacity."

I make a rude gesture that he doesn't see because he has already turned and walked away. I can hear him whistling.

"Bastard," I mutter under my breath. I feel my hair to make sure it's tucked under the edge of my hood, straighten my sleeves, and follow George's footsteps through the doorway, clenching the pot of ceruse in my hand. I might as well have another confrontation. It seems to be the day for it.

But when I round the corner and see James Butler at the end of the gallery, I slow my steps until he disappears into the warren of rooms.

Better not to have more confrontations than absolutely necessary.

18

I NAVIGATE THE CHAOS OF RICHMOND TO THE ROOM RESERVED for the Duchess of Suffolk. I take a deep breath, knock, and am allowed entrance. Her confederacy is there, fussing and bootlicking, except for Jane Parker, who sits in the corner, silent and unobserved.

"Your Grace," I say by way of announcement, and curtsy deeply. It doesn't hurt to soften a slight with deference.

"Mistress Boleyn."

I hear the coldness in her voice. And I believe Wyatt is right. She never really meant to be my friend, just wanted to use me as a doll for a day.

"I have come to return this, Your Grace."

I cup the little pot in my upturned hand and raise my gaze.

My eyes take in Mary Brandon, Duchess of Suffolk, sister to the king, with her perfect skin and silky auburn hair. Her damask sleeves are the color of a weathered rose, her bodice covered in pearls and gold. She doesn't need the ceruse. I should have just thrown it away.

I meet her gray eyes. They hold none of the merriment that the king's do. Still, the similarity stuns me.

"You have no use for it?"

Silence. Jane's hands twist in her lap, and I can see the effort it takes for her not to bite her nails. She catches my eye briefly, and I think I see her shake her head.

"No, Your Grace."

"You have no use for a token of friendship."

It's a statement. Not a question. She is equating her friendship with the ceruse. If I refuse it, if I refuse to wear it, I refuse her.

I think of Wyatt. The ripple of his laughter when I make a joke. The way he actually listens to me when I speak.

"No, Your Grace."

She draws herself up to her full height. She is tall, like the king. She looks down on me, eyes trailing the cut of my hood. My gown.

"You think because you inspire the lust of the men of the court that you have become someone. Someone risen. But you are nothing. And will always be nothing. No matter whom you dance with.

"You will never be one of the inner circle of nobility, Anne Boleyn. A Stafford. A Talbot. A Percy. No matter how many masques you do. Or heads you turn. You should accept the hand of friendship when it is offered."

"I am a Howard."

"I'm afraid often that is more of a hindrance than a help."

Someone in the room titters, but I don't look away from those gray Tudor eyes.

"One piece more of advice, little Boleyn," the duchess adds, affecting a generous smile. "You should stay away from that ras-

cal poet, Thomas Wyatt. He has no honor. He can't be trusted."

I think about the laughter I heard follow me from the room after she slathered me in ceruse. The way that muck felt when I scrubbed it off. The way she looks at me now as if I'm something she found stuck to the bottom of her slipper.

"That is interesting, Your Grace," I say, "because he says the same thing about you."

I know I will regret these words later, but they taste like sugared almonds and I savor them.

Bridewell Palace
1523

19

THE MEN OF THE COURT ARE ITCHING FOR WAR. FOR BLOOD AND pain and death and victory. They are like animals, caged. We move to Bridewell, hemmed in by the City, and tensions rise. Trapped between rivers and walls, squeezed by monasteries on either side, the men's restiveness only partially assuaged by flirtation, cards, and the talk of war.

It doesn't help that Bridewell was built for beauty and not for strength, with elaborately stacked brick that creates a winding effect up the façade and chimneys. The entire building is striped with windows to rooms two stories high. This palace isn't a place to attack or defend. It's a place to see and be seen.

A covered gallery reaches all the way to the monastery of Blackfriars beyond the wall, over the Fleet, slow and sluggish, more of a ditch than a river. Wyatt walks me across on the way to the queen's rooms, and we stop on the bank of the river to watch the noisome water meandering around a knot of grass and a downed tree.

"Not exactly the Loire," I say.

Wyatt chuckles. "Nothing lives up to France with you, does it?"

I sigh and look around me.

"Well. Bridewell has its charms. But Greenwich has poky

rooms. And Westminster is in desperate need of repair. And Richmond just feels . . . choked. None of them is like Wolsey's palaces. York Place. Or Hampton Court. And truly, not even those match King François's plans for Fontainebleau. With frescoes in the galleries!"

"Yes, but what about King Henry's tapestries?"

I scowl a little, which only seems to provoke mirth in him.

"I suppose they're beautiful." I pretend to pout.

"Well, I, for one, don't believe there's a place more magnificent than England. The rolling hills. The South Downs. The chalk cliffs of Dover. The forests that cover half of Kent. The river Medway as it flows past Allington. I can't imagine anything better, or ever wanting to leave it."

"But you have never seen France."

"I don't think I want to. Leaving the land of my birth would be exile. Even to see the beauties of François's frescoes."

"Well, you don't know what you're missing, Wyatt, sequestering yourself here, when you have all of Europe to explore."

I find myself staring blankly at Fleet ditch, thinking of all the places I've yet to see. Queen Claude, on the nights she would weep after the birth of her annual baby, would claim she wanted to take me—and all her own children—back to her home country of Brittany. She made it sound wild, magical. When I met Leonardo da Vinci, he claimed Florence was the only city a cultured young woman should ever aspire to visit.

I want to see it all. But my life is limited by more than rivers and walls and monasteries. These men have no idea what being trapped really feels like. Only my words can set me free, and only when the right person hears them.

We continue through the gate and outer court. The royal apartments are accessed by a grand processional stair, facing the courtyard like a dancer ready to perform. There is no hall; instead the stair opens immediately into the watching chamber, and from there we curve to the right to the queen's north-side rooms. The ceilings soar above us, but the structure still feels subdued by the king's rooms above. As if the men are pressing down on us.

Perhaps it is just my imagination.

Their restlessness is catching. I sense it as soon as I enter the room. Even Jane has laid down her needlework and is twisting her hands in her lap. It feels like the court is a pot near the boil.

I think about George's comment that girls are no fun. That we don't know how to do anything. I sneak a look at the men by the door, sitting at the gaming table. The betting is tense and furious.

They're playing primero, a game Father taught us all to play as children. George and I regularly challenged each other, claiming the loser was the "girl." From the look on his face now, he's winning.

Momentarily, I consider not going over. Not intruding. Letting George win alone.

But I want to show him that girls are smarter than he thinks they are.

More than that, I want to do something that makes me feel less powerless.

I walk to the table. George is hunched over his cards, his back curved like a bent bow—taut and ready to spring. Butler sits opposite him, his cards bending in the tension of his grip while he glowers at our approach.

Henry Percy tries to rise, causing the entire table to look up at me.

"Don't bestir yourselves, gentlemen." I wave an airy hand. "I'm just here to watch. Card games are beyond my ken."

I ignore George's snort of blatant suspicion.

"Would you like to learn, Mistress Boleyn?" Henry Percy's eyes are eager.

"Mistress Boleyn has a habit of making ill-advised wagers." Wyatt takes an empty seat next to George.

"So do you, Wyatt." George doesn't look at him.

"Not a game for ladies," Butler growls.

"Then it's a good thing you don't find me very ladylike," I tell him, and cordially thank Percy, who gets me a stool and seats me next to him.

I flash Wyatt a smile, but he doesn't catch it.

"Do you know the game, Mistress Boleyn?" Percy's words tickle my ear. He's sitting very close. His clothes smell of cedar, sharp and sneezy.

"I've played before," I say.

Men like girls to be helpless, I remind myself, noticing the disappointment on his face. They want to instruct. To advise. *To own.*

"But it's been a long time," I add. "I may need assistance."

I bite back my impatience as Percy tells me the point value

of each card, how the hands and combinations are ranked.

"Jesus wept, Percy, are you in or not?"

Wyatt's hiss cuts through the room. The tension in his shoulders has increased. I widen my eyes at him, but he still won't look at me.

"I'll join in the next round."

Percy leans closer, one arm encircling my shoulders so he can use the fingers of that hand to indicate the cards I hold. If I leaned just a little to the right, my cheek would brush his. I settle slightly, my back pressing into the curve of his arm. He drops it abruptly, his face pink.

Too much. Too soon.

I look at Wyatt again, hoping for some instruction. But his face is blank. Unreadable. He's playing his own game. Not mine.

Butler kicks the table leg, startling me so I look at him. He shows his teeth.

"Let's play," he says.

I know the game inside and out, but I am a little rusty. I make a couple of ill-advised moves. Percy corrects me. Gently. I murmur praise at him and he blushes again. Really, he is too easy.

"Sharing secrets?" Butler growls. "Perhaps you should sit next to me. I won't give special treatment."

The edge to his voice is shocking. Like a dousing with cold water.

"I like where I am, thank you," I reply. "Where I can see you."

Wyatt smothers a laugh.

And for a while, we simply play the game. I get lost in the heady feeling of gambling away my savings. Taking risks. Having fun.

When I raise the stakes again, I look at George. And for once, I see that he remembers, too. Remembers our childhood. Remembers that when we played against each other then, it didn't matter who won. What mattered was who made the biggest bet.

"You're as quick as a man," Wyatt says when I throw my next card down.

"There are some women who know how to play," I say, looking between him and George. "We're not only good for sewing and family services."

Norris whistles when I wager again. "You play like the king."

I vibrate with a warm memory of the king's hand on my waist.

"Except that when the stakes are high, she doesn't lose," Wyatt mutters.

"You should be careful what you wager," Percy says quietly, dismay sprawled across his expression. "And not call attention to it. Play only within your means. And your teaching."

"Have I surpassed your instruction?" I ask innocently. "Is there not more you can teach me?" I raise an eyebrow suggestively, giddy from all the attention.

Color deepens the shadows on his face. I'm beginning to enjoy making Henry Percy blush.

"You do need teaching," Butler says. "Maybe a caning will keep you in your place."

The table goes silent. Not one of them looks up from his cards. Not Percy, who has gone so still beside me, it's like he's trying to render himself invisible. Not George, who studiously runs his fingers along the coins in front of him on the table. Not even Wyatt.

Fear and anger well within me, pressing me tight against the stays of my bodice. Do they agree with Butler? That a woman should be seen and not heard? Should sit back and let others win?

Then Wyatt steals a glance at me. Slants his eyes sideways at Butler.

"I say, James"—the quiet humor in his voice freezes the men around us even more—"to whom will go that pleasure?"

George snorts and Norris brays, the lecherous light returning to his eyes when he looks at me. Percy's cards flutter in his hands like a fan.

Butler overturns his stool in his haste to withdraw, and he pushes roughly past Wyatt on his way to the door.

The entire table turns to me. Expectantly.

"I may not know my place . . ." I say quietly. I stand and lay my cards down, face up—a chorus of kings.

The men look from the cards to me.

"But I believe I know when I've won."

I pocket the coins and leave the room.

20

I CROSS THE YARD, HEADING TO THE GARDENS, THE ONLY PATCH of green in this pile of stone and mud. But it is all in shadow, and as the sun goes down, the air turns bitterly cold. English springtime.

I tuck my hands inside my sleeves. The duchess may say what she likes about the awkward length of them, but at least my sleeves keep me warm. Or warmish.

"I don't know what to do," I say when I hear footsteps approach. Without even looking, I know it's Wyatt. I knew he'd come. "He gets more proprietary every day." Every day that brings my father's footsteps closer to court.

"You could poison him."

"What?" I turn.

"It's the only way to remove the possibility permanently. It also sets your father up nicely to claim the earldom of Ormond unchallenged. I'm sure he'd support the scheme."

I wouldn't put anything past my father.

"There is no way I will resort to something so evil, so brutal. . . ."

I see little puffs of breath coming from Wyatt's nostrils as he tries not to laugh out loud.

"Well, if you're not going to take my problems seriously . . ."
I turn away and suppress a giggle of my own. Me, a poisoner.
Ridiculous.

"No, my dear, I absolutely take your problems seriously.
Without you here, my life will be nothing but desolation."

"You're wasting your poetry, Wyatt."

"Oh, but it brings me neatly to my next proposition. The
one that is sure to save you."

The intensity of his gaze matches the wintry sky behind
him. His sudden seriousness halts my breath.

"It may not be your only choice, Anne. But it may well be
your best."

I wait, chin tilted so I can see his face, the shape of his jaw. I
suddenly want to stroke it.

He clears his throat.

"You could become my mistress."

I feel as if a weight has landed on my shoulders, as if the
English sky itself is trying to force me to my knees. I turn and
stride back to the palace.

"I don't know why I bother asking you," I shout back over
my shoulder. "All you do is joke and offer no assistance whatsoever. I thought you were my friend."

It takes him only a moment to catch up with me—his legs
are so much longer. He lays a hand on my shoulder and I spin
left to shrug it off and keep walking. He stops, and I leave him
behind.

"I am your friend!" he calls. "Which is why I didn't want to
suggest . . ."

I stop and wait, but do not face him. I notice he doesn't apologize.

"Well?" I clench my jaw.

"You could marry Percy."

There it is. The idea that has been in the back of my mind. Spoken aloud. I allow myself a vision of a possible future. Me with precedence, a place at court, a name. A position in which someone might come to me for advice. Seek my favor. Ask my opinion. Listen.

The man who might bring me these things is just a shadow in the background.

I turn back to Wyatt, but I can't see his expression in the gathering dark.

"And why didn't you want to suggest this?" I ask, stepping closer to him. I want to *see* what he thinks as much as hear it.

"I don't like him. He's not the sort of man who can love someone like you." His face is a complete blank.

I shrug off his doubt—and my own.

"What's love? I'm not even sure it exists. And if it does, it certainly has no place in my world. The only thing a girl is good for is to give away or sell to the highest bidder. That's what George says. And I'm ready to sell."

Wyatt looks pained. "I think you could do better."

"Better than the Earl of Northumberland? Wyatt, my father is one of the 'new men.' Cardinal Wolsey calls him a *minion*. I am related in the interminably dark and murky past to Edward I, but I have no heritage, no title, no status, despite my sister's position in the king's bed. The Boleyns may be steadfastly loyal, but they don't really engender love and friendship in anyone. Status and preferment mean more to them anyway. And in that light, I hardly think I can do better."

In the silence that follows, I hear the rustle of a thrush in the bushes, and the distant call of boatmen on the Thames.

"Is that really what you care about, Anne? Status and preferment and ambition?"

"That's what I've been taught!" I want to tear his expression of pity straight off his face. "Isn't that why you brought me under your wing? You took me on as a business proposition."

"Well, now I consider you more than that."

"Really, Wyatt? And what do you consider me? What do you want from me?" I want him to say it. Without a joke. Without a tease.

"I want what's best for you." Wyatt looks down at his hands. They are not still. "As my business proposition."

So much for friendship. "You want me to believe that what's best for me is for everyone to continue to think I spend my spare time in your bed."

"No," Wyatt says, his voice a razor edge of controlled calm. "I just don't want you to tarnish your chances."

"You just want to keep me where I am. Because you've got me right where you want me."

"Oh, no, Anne, my dear," he says, the laughter in his voice ringing false. "You're not where I want you yet."

"And where is that?"

"On top, Mistress Boleyn."

My irritation finally burns through me. "Will you just stop with your innuendos, Wyatt!"

He roars his great burbling laugh, throwing me off-balance and bringing me to earth all at once. "Innuendo is all down to the interpretation, Anne." He sweeps me into the air as if we are dancing the volta. "I mean you are destined for great things! You're destined for the greatest gambles. For the kind of legendary love you only hear about in ballads."

He sets me down and turns me like a spinning top. I can't help laughing. The weight has been removed from my shoulders. But an ache is still lodged in my heart.

"Those love affairs end badly, Wyatt," I say seriously. "I think I had rather be well housed and well connected than alone and miserable after losing the love of my life."

"But they don't *all* end badly, Anne."

His left hand is still at my waist. My shoulder presses into his chest. I smell ink and earth and almonds. I have to pull away.

"Oh, really?" I ask, pretending I don't see the hurt in his eyes. "Name me one that didn't."

He strikes a pose of intense concentration. Frowns. He searches the horizon as if it will give him the answers he seeks. Shakes his head.

"No. You're right. They all end badly. You're doomed."

I swipe playfully at his shoulder. He catches my hand, swiftly as a hawk diving for prey.

"I mean it, Anne." His hand tightens. As does his expression. He will not let me go.

"You mean I'm doomed?" I tease.

"I mean you're destined for something better than Henry Percy."

I pull my hand from his.

"I don't want you to limit yourself too soon." He reaches for me again, but I step backward. Away from him.

"It can't happen soon enough, Wyatt. My father is on his way home. If I don't make my own choice and make it swiftly, I really will be doomed. I cannot wait for better things, no matter how much you beg it of me. I don't have time."

21

But time all too often comes screeching to a halt at court. The king and his councillors go to London to open Parliament, leaving the ladies alone with the old, the young, and the reckless. Leaving a void where once there was a constant intoxicating hum.

Because Wolsey is with the king, his men have no reason to visit. I'm grateful to be out from under Butler's resentful glare. But Henry Percy's absence lays waste to all my plans.

The remaining men at Bridewell roam ever more restlessly. Near-fights and arguments break out in the gardens and long galleries. Rumors explode into accusations. Men practice archery and swordplay in the yard, but this doesn't release the lust for blood and war. There is no room for jousts and no park for hunting. Just the quiet regulation of the monasteries that surround us.

George complains of boredom to everyone within hearing distance.

"I feel as if I've been conscripted into holy orders myself," George mumbles after a particularly dull morning spent on backgammon and prayer.

I have to agree with him. With only the queen's influence—

all needlework and hair shirts—we are suffocating on the tar-nished piety of an incarcerated court.

My fear is that my time is slipping away and my father slipping nearer. I imagine him on horseback, heading for the Spanish coast. Or already on a boat bound for England.

It finally affects me so deeply, I go in search of George late one afternoon—unsure if Wyatt in his determination to make me "wait" will help.

I corner my brother just outside the queen's chambers. He is dressed in blue velvet, a gaudy, jeweled cap riding on his undisciplined hair, his boots cleaned and coins jingling in the pocket at his waist. He is far too smartly dressed for an evening playing cards. I forget my purpose in seeking him out as my suspicion overwhelms me.

"Where are you going?" I ask.

"When the cat's away . . . " he says.

I just stare at him. Force him to finish his thought.

"Bridewell is practically at the very heart of London. We've got to take advantage."

"We?" I ask.

"The usual crowd. Bryan. Norris. Wyatt. And I think we're going to corrupt young Henry Percy from the cardinal's house-hold as well."

"Percy? He's here?"

"Yes. Wyatt invited him along. God knows why. The boy stalks the galleries of York Place like he's got a pike stuck up his arse."

I hardly listen to George's assessment. Wyatt invited Percy. *Here.* He is helping me. I could kiss him.

"So, what do you plan to do?"

"Wouldn't you like to know, dear sister?"

He begins to move past me, heading for the door. For the water gate.

"Will you take me with you?" The words come out before I can evaluate them. I hate asking George for anything. But surely this is what Wyatt intended.

He stares at me for a long, drawn-out moment. "To London?"

"Why not?"

"Because you're a girl." George ticks off his reasons on his fingers. "Because you're in the queen's household. Because it's London. And because it's a boys' night. We're going to see if we can lose Percy's virginity. Not something you want to be around for."

George doesn't know that's the very thing I need to be around for. Only after we're married. I can't believe Wyatt intends to take Percy to the brothels. George must have it wrong. George and his limited vision.

I think quickly, forming a plan. "When else can you have the opportunity to show two ladies of the queen's household the entertainments of the town?"

"Two?" George cries. "Now what are you cooking up?"

"Well, of course Jane would come, too. I can't go alone with a group of men. It wouldn't be seemly."

"It won't be seemly no matter how you look at it, Anne. And Jane Parker won't change that."

"But George, you said yourself how boring it is here."

"You're a girl. You're used to it."

"I'm from France. I'm not." I feel the frustration welling up in my throat. My very breath obstructed by the limitations imposed on me by society, by my sex, by George.

We are still standing there, trying to stare each other down, when Wyatt bursts in, talking away, Percy trailing at a cautious distance.

"There you are." Wyatt strides across the empty room, loose-limbed and confident, the complete opposite of the man who follows him. I smile at Percy, trying to shut out the thought of George's description of him, then remember Wyatt's instruction and turn away. Men only want what they think they can't have. So I turn to my instructor. My savior.

"You came looking for me?" I ask Wyatt. I spy a coiled thread of gold hair on the midnight-blue velvet of his doublet. The sight twists something hot and toothy inside me. I pluck the hair up between my thumb and forefinger and hold it out to him.

He pulls it delicately away, kisses it, and blows it toward the windows and the falling night beyond them.

"Mine," he says solemnly.

My laughter sounds a little too relieved, even to my own ears. "You do love yourself then, don't you?"

"More than anyone else," he says, laying a loud, wet kiss on the corner of my mouth. He turns to my brother. "Let's go, George."

"I'll only be a minute," I say. "I'll join you at the water gate."

Wyatt laughs. George doesn't.

"Tell her," he says. "Tell her she can't come. Tell her men and women can't be friends."

Wyatt's eyes don't waver from mine, but he shifts his weight from one foot to the other. His easy posture suddenly seems fabricated.

"He's right."

I feel like I've been struck. Wyatt turns his gaze to the darkened windows and they reflect the gold of his hair back to me. But not his face.

"London is no place for a girl, Anne," he says blandly, as if he hasn't just shattered me.

"Especially not where we're going." George grins. "Just a certain type of girl, eh, Percy?"

Percy's face flames, and George punches him in the shoulder.

Wyatt won't look at me. "Norris and the ferryman are waiting. Time to go."

George turns and walks away, but pauses at the door.

Percy hesitates, as if faced with a dilemma.

What will he choose? The brothels of London? Or me?

I can feel the sticky wetness of Wyatt's kiss on my cheek. I wipe it away and rub it on my skirt. I see Wyatt's eyes linger on my hands, so I clasp both of them together to keep them still. Even silent, he criticizes.

"Surely the court provides better pastime," Percy says.

I meet his eye. Shyly. I will watch only him. I will not turn my gaze to gauge Wyatt's reaction.

"The court provides me nothing." I can hear the contempt dripping from Wyatt's words like blood. "And any chance I have to get away, I do. The question is, Percy, what about you? Are there such enticements at your castle in Northumberland as there are here? And can anything compare to the City?"

"Alnwick has nothing as compared to here," Percy says, keeping his eyes steady on my face. "Nor, I imagine, does the City."

I feel a surge of victory. Take a step closer to him. Look away. Counting the beats in my head—the music of flirtation.

"Then stay," Wyatt growls. "You waste my time with your courtly drivel."

He turns on his heel and leaves without another word. And I finally allow my gaze to follow him.

I watch the tension of Wyatt's shoulders, the quickness of his step. The easy stride and lackadaisical effortlessness are missing, replaced by a ferocity I've never seen before.

When he's gone, he leaves a hollow space behind.

And I'm alone with Henry Percy.

22

Henry Percy. Soon to be Earl of Northumberland. Warden of the east marches, charged with defending the Scottish Borders against the Duke of Albany and the barbarians of the north. Doomed to become a battle-scarred army rat like his father. Like the Earl of Surrey, my uncle.

The trouble is, Percy doesn't look cut out for all that. He looks like a musician. Like a cleric. His features are stark and shadowed in the candlelight, his face so full of feeling, his hands large and strong, but smooth, as if they've never held anything more solid than a quill in his lifetime.

"How do you like court, Mistress Boleyn?"

He presses his lips together. Not the thin lips of a cleric. Full lips. Soft. I return my eyes to his.

"At the moment, it's frightfully boring."

He looks shocked.

Oh, God. I can't believe I just said that. I'm supposed to be using my feminine wiles.

"With the king away," I amend.

Neither does that sound right. As if I look to the king for all my entertainment. Which I can't. But he is the king. Divine. Divinely anointed.

Our conversation stutters to a halt. Stillborn.

"I mean, everyone seems at a loss. Without the usual enter-tainments. Seeking escape."

I look over Percy's shoulder to the doorway through which Wyatt just exited, trying not to think about where he went.

"Thomas Wyatt is not the most faithful of men." Percy looks as cross as I feel.

"I think he and his wife loathe each other. And from what I hear, she isn't necessarily a paragon of virtue."

"It doesn't give him the right to . . ." Percy blushes. And I realize what his original statement meant.

"You think he should be faithful to me?" My heart clenches.

"I heard . . ." Percy cannot finish that thought. "And he kissed you."

I wipe the spot again.

"After a fashion." I shake my head. "Thomas Wyatt is not my lover."

"Oh."

So much meaning in one small sound.

"He claims we've known each other since I was two and we played in the fountains naked," I add, and immediately want to bite my tongue off. Because Percy blushes so hard his finger-tips turn red.

"I mean we're like . . ." We are *not* like brother and sister. Not like George and me. "There is nothing between us." Something about the words sends a shard of ice through me.

"You're engaged to James Butler," he says with strained casualness.

"I am not! Who told you that?"

"All the court."

"Well, all the court is wrong."

"I suppose I shouldn't believe everything I hear at court." He throws my own words back to me.

"Certainly stories have a way of being told." I lace my words with a lightness I don't entirely feel. "Or worse, believed."

He nods, and we lapse into silence.

"For instance," I say to break it, "I hear you've been engaged to the Earl of Shrewsbury's daughter since infancy."

"Mary Talbot is a sour-faced harpy. Full of nothing but complaints and demons. Like her father and her brother and the whole of the English north."

"My Lord Percy," I say, touching his arm lightly with my fingertips. "I do believe that is the most unkind thing I have ever heard you say."

He has the grace to blush again.

"But you haven't denied my statement." I pretend to pout, feeling ridiculous. Pouting isn't my style. More like the duchess's.

"It is my father's choice, not mine. And I have not agreed."

"Fathers," I say knowingly. "Family pride. Alliances."

"You understand," he says, his face brightening. I'm starting to like the look of him when he smiles. The boy takes over, negating the angry young man.

"My father doesn't care that I have no wish to marry James Butler."

"James isn't so bad. He just doesn't know how to interact with people."

"Doesn't bode well for a marriage, does it?"

The seriousness returns.

"Has it been solemnized?" He presses his lips together. "Signed? Your betrothal?"

He looks away suddenly, as if the question was more than he intended to ask.

"Not yet." I plan my pause carefully. "But my father returns from Spain soon. And I think he'll apply himself to the business of alliances when he does."

"I should like more control of my life," Percy says, and I see his fists clenching at his sides. "To do as I see fit."

"You already did tonight," I say, and grasp his hand in mine. He shudders at my touch. Or trembles.

"Tonight?"

"Wyatt and my brother can be quite adamant. And yet you didn't go with them. Why not?"

I can't look away from his eyes.

"Because I'd rather be here with you."

Christ. At least he's direct.

"Well, you know, sir, you won't get the same from me as you would get from the companions my brother would search out for you in London."

He reacts with such shock and horror, one would think I'd handed him a serpent.

"I-I would never ask," he stutters.

He leaves me with an opportunity. One that I can't pass up.

"I hope someday you will."

His eyes widen. The black centers expand to encompass the

whole of the iris. I turn before the surprise leaves his face and lead him back to the queen's apartments. Safety in numbers. I have to move quickly and keep raising the stakes. But I have to play carefully.

Because if I do—if I win—I could be somebody, somewhere. Instead of nobody, noplace.

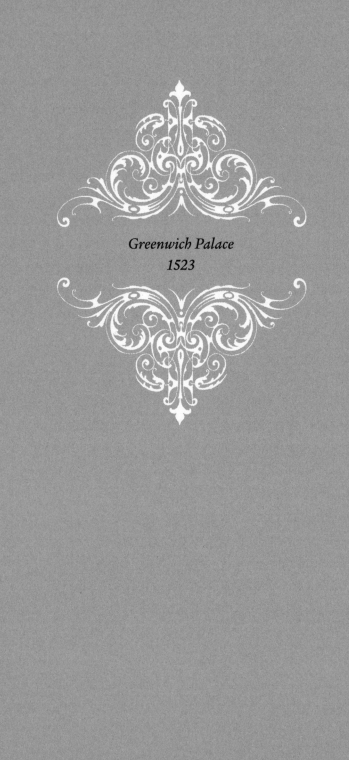

Greenwich Palace
1523

23

Now that war has been decided upon by Parliament, the entire court is out for blood. Mercifully, taxes and armies must be raised, so the inevitable still seems far away. The men must seek satiety at Greenwich, with its expansive deer park and its state-of-the-art tiltyard.

The king rides out every day, leaving before dawn and returning hours later. Wyatt rides with him. The men discuss the hunt far into the night. So singular of purpose. So exclusive.

But then a more general entertainment is planned—with a picnic—and I find myself invited. Not Mary. Me. I'm sure I have Wyatt to thank, though he hasn't spoken to me since that night at Bridewell. And Jane is coming, too.

I rise early that morning and dress in green and brown, my skirts the same color as the forest floor. I include a cap copied from one of the duchess's, but set it farther back from my face. She may be a bitch, but she does have style.

Jane ties my sleeves on securely and I help her tighten the stays of her rust-colored bodice. She can't stop fidgeting, knowing that George will accompany us.

"You should find another occupation for your hands," I tell her. "Or you will tear your fingers ragged."

She nods mutely. She looks as if she is about to be sick.

We make our way to the yards, creeping through the still-sleeping rooms. The palace has been aired and sweetened, fresh rushes laid down and tapestries shaken out. All is muted and shadowed, the subdued domain of the queen.

By contrast, the stable courtyard of the palace is a blaze of color, flickering with laughter and rocking with energy. I stand for a moment, just inside the gate, and take it all in. Courtiers slapping backs and placing bets. Everyone eager to be seen, to be heard. They are drunk on the exhilaration of it, or perhaps merely still drunk from the night before.

My brother, Wyatt, and Norris crowd a corner with the other young men, their chests puffed out like that of the rooster watching them from the wall above. They are falling all over each other with laughter.

"Come." I reach for Jane's hand. "Let us join them. They look as if they could use some maidenly influence."

Jane doesn't move.

"Watch," she says. "I think they've had enough maidenly influence."

Norris is holding up a hand in front of him as if it were a looking glass, shaping his eyebrows and examining the pores of his skin. Then he sticks out his lower lip in a quick pout. George whispers something inaudible, and they fall apart again, slapping Norris on the back and cheering.

"Did he just pretend to be the Duchess of Suffolk?" I ask.

Jane nods. "They already did Mistress Carew and Lady Kildare."

I push a breath through my nostrils. "Children."

I move to march over to then, when George steps forward. He widens his eyes to unseeing roundness, puts a hand up to his mouth, and sets to gnawing at it as if it's a leg of mutton.

Jane sucks in her breath. I turn back to her as the men laugh again. Her face is stricken.

"Jane."

She shakes her head rapidly, as if to dislodge the sight, and points a shaking finger.

"Look."

Wyatt is smoothing his hair as if tucking it into the band of a French hood. Then he elongates his neck and taps Norris playfully on the shoulder. Quickly wipes his hands on his breeches. George guffaws, and my brittle self-image snaps. Wyatt's eyes rise to meet mine and reveal an instant of panicked remorse that is swiftly replaced with a stare of belligerent defiance.

"We'll show them," I say to Jane, squeezing her hand hard enough to make her whimper. "We'll run their asses off."

The king strides into the center of the yard, suddenly the focus of attention. As always, he's like the hub of a wheel around which all other activity turns. The old hum strikes up in my chest when he spies me holding Jane's hand and smiles. He hasn't even noticed me since the masque, yet suddenly I feel I'm the only object of his regard.

"Mistress Boleyn!" he calls. "And Mistress Parker! Mount up, ladies, and get ready for the ride of your life!"

The men bellow, and Jane turns bright as a berry. I see color creeping up the king's face as well, and realize he didn't intend the double meaning. He turns quickly to mount his horse, Governatore. And we are no longer at the center of the wheel.

"Allow me to assist you, ladies."

Wyatt has approached us, dressed in green, the yellow of his hair reflected by a golden feather in his cap. He grins at Jane, who starts to simper. Despite her love for George, Jane unaccountably loses all sense of decorum around Wyatt.

Beddable, I remember her saying, and fury rises in me like a tide, threatening to flood.

"Your assistance is not required, Master Wyatt." I will my voice to remain uncharged. And cold.

"Ah." Wyatt turns the fully dimpled grin on me. "But *required* and *desired* are two different things."

Jane giggles. I want to smack them both.

"The honey of seduction will go nowhere toward catching me, sir," I snap. "We only *desire* assistance from our friends."

Wyatt doesn't move. Doesn't falter. "I am your friend."

I can feel Jane's stillness behind me, the tension in it.

"My friends do not mock me."

"I wasn't mocking you, my dear. I was calling attention to you."

I hear Jane cough behind me. She doesn't believe him any more than I do.

"Calling attention to my . . . habits and affectations is not something I wish a friend to do."

"Perhaps it will convince you to cease them."

We stand glaring at each other like the still leaves at the center of a whirlwind.

I know he will not apologize.

"My friends don't criticize everything I do," I say. "My friends take my side in an argument."

"If you're referring to the London adventure, it definitely wasn't appropriate. Besides"—he finally looks away, and the clamor of the stable yard returns—"it seems to have worked out for you in the end."

"You sound like a jealous lover."

"It was a joke," Wyatt spits. "One you would have recognized as such a few weeks ago. Before you started to think so much of yourself."

"I hardly recognize you anymore, Thomas Wyatt. Much less your jokes."

"Do you know what I think, Anne Boleyn?"

"No. And I don't care, either."

"I think you're angry because I don't support your most recent power play. Your grasp for status. Kick the poet when the aristocracy comes calling. Assuage your doubts by negating all other opinions."

"Don't turn this around."

"Because you need to be angry with me? Is that it? I have a right to be angry with you, too."

"I am not the one in the wrong here!"

"Are you not?" he asks quietly.

Silence balls like a fist between us.

"Mount up!" Nicholas Carew, the Master of the Horse, cries. The stable yard explodes into activity, and the dogs bay from beyond the gate.

"Master Wyatt," Jane says evenly. She has heard it all. "Since you are the only man left unmounted, perhaps we do require your assistance."

Without speaking, Wyatt moves to place his hand beneath Jane's foot. On the back of her bay mare, she is graceful and more at ease. She thanks Wyatt quietly.

"Mistress Boleyn." Wyatt goes to one knee on the cobbles before me.

"Why are you acting this way?" I ask him. "Why are you doing this?"

"Why, Anne"—he looks up at me—"all men want what they can't have. I am only here for the chase."

The expression on his face—one of longing and wickedness and ambition—makes my heart stop and then start again with a bang. Pounding. The rhythm of the hunted.

He looks again at his hands, the fingers entwined. I raise my foot and place it there. His grip is steady and I feel the heat through the leather of my boot. I look at the feather in his cap, the curl of hair at his collar, the stretch of fabric across his shoulders.

The muscles tense to lift me, and I lose my balance. Fall into him, my bust practically pressed against his forehead. We both gasp, and I push away. I steady myself with one hand on the saddle. My horse shuffles nervously.

Wyatt stares at my boot, shoulders tense.

"Ready?" he asks.

I nod. Realize he can't see me. Clear my throat.

"Yes."

In one fluid motion, I am in the saddle, the roan mare shifting beneath me. His hand stays on my foot a moment too long. When he leans forward to speak again, his hair kindles gold in a shaft of dawn.

"I am here for the chase," he repeats. "But not all pleasure is in pursuit, my dear. And there is little pleasure in letting someone else win."

24

THE HUNT BEGINS IN A RUSH OF COLOR AND LIGHT THAT PLUNGES quickly into the darkness of the forest. The shouts of men mingle with the frantic baying of the dogs, the pounding of the hooves, and the crack and blast of twigs and branches breaking. Riding fast takes skill and concentration. I will myself not to think about Wyatt's words. About the look on his face.

Far ahead, I see the flash of white. The tail of the roe deer. With a roar, the company spurs the horses to a froth and we plunge from shadow to light and back again. Horses dodge through the trees, leap fallen branches, vault over streambeds clattering from the spring rain and ditches stagnant with frogs and water.

Does he want me? Or does he just want to win our bet?

We are not bow hunting today, but chasing the deer toward the toils—nets strung yesterday at the other end of the park. This hunt is more of a race.

Wyatt is ahead of me. I can't let him win.

I lean forward over the neck of my horse, her mane flapping against my cheek, ducking branches that come quick-fire at me.

We pass into a blinding splash of morning as the trees thin, and suddenly the king is beside me.

"You ride well, mistress," he says. He is not even winded. Man and horse are like a single creature—a centaur, one rhythm, one heartbeat—beautiful.

"I was taught well, Your Majesty," I reply, trying to suppress the gasp of breath as I suck it in.

"There is nothing like pursuit." The king flashes a grin at me, and we dive back into darkness and suddenly he is gone. Off to the right, dodging another tree. Leaping a ditch. Maneuvering his horse expertly, always with his eye on the quarry.

I turn my horse, her hind foot skidding in a fall of leaves, but she rights herself quickly, shakes her head as if to free herself of the rein, and charges ahead.

We break out into the heathland, and I find myself in the midst of the pack, surrounded on all sides. The king is ahead of me, flashes of gold and red in the spots of new sun, Norris on one side of me, Wyatt on the other. I think I hear George laughing.

I look from one man to the other. Check George. They are watching me. The gorse snags at my skirts, washing me with the stinging scent of sunlit resin. Norris spurs his horse forward, then reins it back again. Keeping pace.

I narrow my eyes at him. "A race?"

He grins and kicks ahead, his wild laugh scaring a raven from its perch high in the trees.

I lean over the neck of my horse and laugh, too. Lost in the motion. In the pace. In the race. Forgetting, for the moment, all the confusion.

When Wyatt pulls ahead, I can't keep up. I spur my horse,

but she stumbles, and I fall a length behind. Norris looks back once, laughs again, and dodges into the trees just ahead of Wyatt. George's horse clears a ditch and he tips his cap as he passes me by.

Wyatt disappears out of sight to the left. Never looks back. Lost in the trees.

"Ha!" Norris shouts again, and they are gone.

Jane catches up to me. Her face is flushed, her cap torn back from it, streamers of chestnut hair following her like a wake upon the river. We slow to a less reckless pace.

"You ride like a man," she says, and I can hear the admiration in her voice.

Ride like a man. Play cards like a man. I seem to fit better in the men's circle than the women's. Of course, the men's circle is wider. More encompassing. With fewer limitations.

"I'll take that as a compliment." We slow to a walk. A girl's pace.

"Oh!" Jane's face gets even rosier. "I meant it as such!"

She shakes her head and glances at her hands. She can't let go of the reins. She presses her lips together.

"I always say the wrong thing. It's the reason I never speak," she says.

"Perhaps I should take lessons from you."

We find the rest of the court surrounding the toils, a clutch of deer lathered and anxious in the nets. One doe keeps breaking away from the others, spinning out into the enclosure, only to stumble back again when faced with the men of the court, who have dismounted, ready for bloodshed.

Norris tips his cap to me and I nod in response. George approaches him, and they clasp hands. George doesn't smile. Norris must have won. George doesn't like to be bested.

Wyatt is nowhere to be seen.

A shout and a cheer herald the arrival of the king. One of the men beside him carries the weapons that will be used for the kill. The doe goes down first in a wash of blood, the courtiers mad with it, and I have to turn away.

Jane turns with me.

"It breaks my heart," Jane says.

"It does feed the court," I manage. Though the sight of all that blood makes me shudder. Death by sword. Why do men seek it out in war? In this respect, I am not like them at all.

"Join us for a feast!" the king cries, and I look at him, blood still on his hands, the blade dripping with it. "I find pursuit whets the appetite."

We follow him to a nearby clearing, a bower of silks and banners already set up, trestle tables laden with food and drink: wine and cheese and strawberries preserved in honey. Strawberries are my favorite, but today, they look too much like clots of blood to be palatable.

The king wanders the knots of courtiers, urging more food and wine and ale on them. He is lit by the sun that is now high and hot over the treetops. It erupts around him like a starburst when he approaches me, and I flatten my hands against my skirts to keep them still.

"And have you enjoyed the pursuit, mistress?" he asks.

"It was certainly invigorating."

He raises an eyebrow at my tone. "You don't like to hunt?"

I wonder at his ability to read me. As if we have known each other all our lives. I feel I can speak the truth to him.

"I prefer hawking." I lower my eyes. I can still feel his gaze upon me.

"Thank you for the excellent entertainment," Jane says.

I'd forgotten she was beside me. I'd forgotten everyone. I felt as though the king and I were the only two present.

I follow her into a curtsy.

"Perhaps we shall go hawking next time," the king says, still watching me. Just me. The bread goes dry in my mouth, and I have to take a sip of wine after curtsying my thanks.

There is a sudden noise from the other side of the meadow. Wyatt finally wanders in on his horse. His cap is gone, his hair tangled with little sticks and leaves.

"Wyatt!" the king calls, and walks away from me. "Someone has led you on a merry chase!"

"Yes, Your Majesty," Wyatt says with a grin, swinging down from his horse and handing over the reins to a servant. I can hardly look at him. He acts as if I don't exist.

"You look utterly weary, my friend."

Wyatt leans heavily with both hands on the trestle table, and nods slowly.

"It can't be the hunt that has exhausted you," the king says. "For I have known you to ride with me for hours and never tire."

"Yes, Your Majesty." Wyatt hangs his head. "It is the hunt. The hunt for hind, the hunt for heart." He scans the group until he finds me.

I want to groan at his overwrought melodrama.

The king raises an eyebrow. "Tell us."

Wyatt strikes a pose. Always ready to share his poetic prowess.

> *"What means this? When I lie alone*
> *I toss, I turn, I sigh, I groan.*
> *My bed me seems as hard as stone.*
> *What means this?"*

Jane squeezes my hand.

"A bad night then, my friend?" the king asks Wyatt.

"Any night alone is a bad one," Norris says.

Someone lets out a low whistle. And suddenly all eyes are upon me. Because of course I am the reason Wyatt lies alone. I feel the heat rise to my face, but I keep my eyes on him. He will not best me.

> *"In slumbers oft for fear I quake.*
> *For heat and cold I burn and shake.*
> *For lack of sleep my head doth ache.*
> *What means this?"*

He leaves the table and walks to the middle of the meadow, the sun on his hair like a torch. His voice is clear and carrying in the morning air. He shines. Even the king, in shadows behind him, is diminished.

> *"And if perchance by me there pass*
> *She unto whom I sue for grace,*
> *The cold blood forsaketh my face.*
> *What means this?"*

"It means you're smitten, friend!" Norris calls.

Wyatt turns to me, the sun on his face washing the shadows from it. His gaze perforates my heart, and I have to remind myself it's all a show. A game. A bet. And I don't want it to be more than that. It can't be more than that. He paces toward me, his voice so low the entire assembly has to lean forward to hear him.

> *"But if I sit near her by"*—

Wyatt falls dramatically to the empty bench beside me.

> *"With loud voice my heart doth cry,*
> *And yet my mouth is numb and dry:*
> *What means this?"*

He falls back against the table, right hand above his heart, the left over his brow with the palm facing outward, the very picture of unrequited love.

The table erupts into cheers and pounding. The women sigh.

Jane looks at me with tears in her eyes and mouths, *"Adorable."*

I wait for the applause to die down, delicately clear my throat.

"It means you need a glass of wine," I say in the driest voice I can muster, and give him my goblet.

My hand doesn't shake at all.

Norris cheers while the others laugh. George turns away. Wyatt raises the goblet to me in a mute toast, apology in his eyes. And something else. Something that sends my heart into a rhythm not my own.

"To friends," he says, so only I can hear.

And something inside me plummets.

25

MY DREAMS ARE HAUNTED BY GREEN AND GOLD. BUT MY DAYS are haunted by other men.

The palace is full to bursting because Christian II, king of Denmark, is coming to visit. Deposed, he is wandering Europe like a minstrel, singing his song of woe, despite having repressed his subjects to the point of riot.

Jousts and banquets and dances are planned. Everyone forgets Thomas Wyatt's silvered poetry in the forest. Except me.

He disappears in the tumult, leaving me to navigate the new court demands on my own. Leaving me to Henry Percy.

Wolsey arrives at Greenwich, perched atop a donkey caparisoned with cloth of gold. The gaudiness of the trappings subverts the impression of the unpretentious cleric the donkey is meant to convey, but Wolsey doesn't acknowledge the irony.

His men come to the queen's rooms. Percy, straight and studied. Butler, unruly and explosive. And the king's men, too, savoring the cover of chaos for illicit flirtation. Norris, especially.

He sits beside me. A little too close. But not close enough for comment.

Butler, obvious in his awkwardness, brays at the card table.

"Mistress Boleyn," Norris says, "I hear you are to marry our friend Butler over there. The match made in York Place."

"Certainly not in heaven."

Norris laughs and allows himself to edge a little closer to me.

"And what about Thomas Wyatt?"

"What about him?"

"Rumor has it that you're his latest conquest."

I look at him archly.

"The term *conquest* suggests submission, Sir Henry."

Norris smiles craftily. "I wonder on which side," he purrs.

"And pray tell what justifies your interest in such a thing?"

"My dear, if anything bad should happen to him, I would look to have you."

He holds my gaze for a long moment, daring me to respond. But I retaliate.

"I would undo you if you tried."

Norris laughs.

"I'm sure you would, Mistress Boleyn."

He stands and walks away, his movements calculated. Exaggerated. He looks once over his shoulder, and grins.

Percy watches him go and moves to take his place. I sneak a sideways glance at him. Percy's clothes are almost camouflaged against the background of the courtiers who swarm the ladies of the queen's chambers like flies on butter. He wears little to distinguish himself—the opposite of Wolsey. Percy doesn't want to be seen or heard but merely exist, unremarked.

Wyatt's words come back to me: *You were meant for some-*

thing better. I shake them away. There is nothing better. There is only worse. Sold to James Butler in Ireland. Lodged beneath my father's shadow. Wasting away as the flirtatious—but unmarriageable—sister of the king's whore. Or the perceived mistress of the court's most notorious philanderer. No, my only escape is this man beside me. Bland, perhaps. But grand, as well.

I glance up to see the duchess studying me. Her gray eyes flick to Percy and back to me. I raise an eyebrow. She glares, and I imagine her face when I join the circle of nobility. So I compose my features and nod my head in deference. Let her think I submit to her superiority. For now.

"Are you friends with the duchess?" Percy asks.

His baritone rumbles through me and settles somewhere south of my heart. I'm used to him being silent.

"Actually, I think she wishes me dead."

"I'm sure you're witty, Mistress Boleyn. But sometimes you speak and act unwisely."

"One of my greatest faults."

"Most faults can be overcome."

"Do you have any faults, Lord Percy?" I tease.

"I am not as brave nor as adamant as my father." He has taken my question seriously.

"I'm sure even our fathers can be overcome." I lay a hand on his.

He twitches it away and I pull mine back into my lap.

"I sincerely hope so," he says. He turns to me, and for an instant I see something spirited in his gaze. But it disappears quickly.

"I need to tread carefully with my father. Someone so"—he looks to the door through which Norris exited—"flamboyant as yourself might make him draw the wrong conclusions."

I wonder what conclusions Percy himself has drawn.

"Are you saying you don't want to be seen with a girl like me?"

"I'm saying I need to ensure my name is not connected to scandal."

The Château Vert. Mary's affair with the king. George's increasingly visible drunkenness. My own flirtatiousness.

"*Your* name."

He nods, not hearing or comprehending the coldness of my voice. "The Percys have been nobility for centuries. We are related to the king."

And have managed to regain lands and titles despite sitting immobile on the wrong side of the battle of Bosworth. The Percys certainly know when to act. And when not to.

"In these days when the king appoints new men to ancient titles," Percy continues, "the old names must persevere. Unblemished."

"And yet here you sit. Next to the daughter of a new man."

Percy suddenly seems to realize my existence.

"Don't get me wrong, Mistress Boleyn," he says, and I see the fervency in his eyes once more. "You are related to Norfolk. To the ancient lines. You are . . ."

He stutters to a halt. Looks at my lips, then down at his hands, clasped in his lap. He exudes the scent of old paper.

". . . extraordinary."

A bubble rises within me, warm and fine and fragile. I spread my fingers on my skirts.

"I don't want my father's choice," Percy says with a cough. As if he feels he's said too much. "I want mine." He looks again into my eyes. "Which is why we must be careful."

The bubble expands at the sound of the word *we*. He looks away. I turn, too, and study the smoke climbing the walls up to the ceiling.

"There can be no indication of a relationship here until it is . . ." Another cough. "Consummated."

I catch his eye just before he looks away again. It is as if we are in the steps of a complicated dance.

"No one can know. Not your brother. Not your sister. Certainly not Thomas Wyatt."

Wyatt already knows. A little. He doesn't approve. He would never set himself up to be a spurned lover. He won't speak of it.

"Not your father."

I finally find my voice. "But when my father returns, he will push my marriage to Butler."

Percy sits so still and so silent, I'm not sure he heard me. The little noises of the room fill the vacant space: the whispers of the duchess and her confederacy in the corner, the soft slip of silk beneath the queen's fingers, the rattle of dice on the table by the door.

Percy turns and looks at me directly. "Then we must find a way to engender a more desirable result."

26

THE UPROAR OVER THE DANISH VISIT REACHES AN INTOLERABLE pitch. The prospect of a tournament makes the men insatiable in the practice of their war games, as evidenced by the constant clangor of metal and shatter of wood from the practice grounds. The women buzz and twaddle over gowns and silks and gossip—the nonessential commodities of court life relegated to the female realm.

The court becomes oppressive, and I begin to reconsider the appeal of Wyatt's teasing offer to hide me away in the country. I laugh at the idea as I slip down the stairs of the donjon and across the inner courtyard, hoping for a moment alone. The conduit burbles, but I still hear the knock of boots on stone behind me.

At the little gallery that leads to the middle courtyard I stop and turn. James Butler is practically on top of me.

"What are you doing?" The brutality in his voice is evident, but I refuse to back down and I won't step away from him.

"Exactly as I please."

My voice wobbles much less than my legs.

"You flirt with the whole damned court." His voice is roupy, ratcheting out of his throat.

"Not with you."

"That's what I mean!" he shouts. I take a step back and glance quickly through the gallery to the empty courtyard beyond. No one else is in sight. "You should not be flirting with anyone. For soon you will be engaged to me. You will be my wife."

"But we are not engaged." Nor will we be. If I can help it.

"Letters crossed Wolsey's desk this morning. Your father will be here any day. The Irish lords are pressing for my return. We will be married by the end of summer."

My fingers grow cold and I rub them hard against my skirts to warm them. Summers in England are short.

"You speak as though you already know the outcome of your life." I clear my throat to steady my voice. "But don't we rely upon God and the king to bring these things about?"

"Wolsey knows the fates of men better than the king."

It's true. Wolsey is a puppet master, pulling all of our strings.

"It *will* happen," Butler says, and I feel his presence as surely as I feel my breath. "And you will change your ways. If you don't, even I won't want to marry you."

"So I should hide myself away like a nun in a convent because your father may agree to this marriage? Or maybe I should just wait until I grow old and undesirable and then truly join a convent."

"You'll never be a nun."

"At least we agree on something."

Butler grabs me by the shoulders. "I will not hear that you are Wyatt's doxy. Or find your brother in your bed!"

I see a flash of memory: Butler outside the maids' room.

"Bed*chamber*," I correct him. "Don't be disgusting."

Butler shakes me so hard my neck hurts.

"You are nothing without me," he shouts, frustration straining his voice into the higher registers. "Nothing!"

I open my mouth to speak, to argue, to contradict, but I'm cut off by a rising shriek that echoes across the cobbles.

"How dare you!"

A tiny ball of deep-blue fury flings itself past me and straight at Butler's chest. Jane Parker beats at his arms with pale fists. Her hood is askew, strands of hair flying like witches' wings.

"How dare you?" she howls again, sounding like a madwoman.

Butler covers his face with crossed arms, releasing me from his grip. I take a step back. Jane looks like a weasel attacking a bear, leaping and stretching, the big beast reduced to terror at the surprise of her onslaught.

It would be laughable under other circumstances.

But fighting in court is forbidden and can cost the instigator a hand—or a head—so I grab Jane from behind, avoiding her flailing elbows, and pull. She steps hard on my slipper, the heel of hers digging into my instep, and I stumble.

The two of us fall backward, a tangle of skirts and pearls, to the damp cobbles of the walkway. She lands on me, heavier than she looks.

My chest collapses and a stopper is put into the bottle of my lungs. Everything tightens. My face strains with the effort to squeeze a tiny bit of air back into my body. Helplessness makes me rigid.

Jane rolls off me and turns, panting. When she sees my face, hers goes pale.

"Butler?" she cries. "What's wrong with her?"

James Butler has disappeared. He left us when we fell. Probably ashamed to be terrorized by a mere girl.

"Anne!" Jane kneels beside me, cradling my head in her hands.

I gasp, a long, low, whining sound. My chest heaves, my stomach with it. I might vomit. I turn to the cobbles, retching.

"I'm so sorry." Jane strokes my hair away from my face. "I didn't mean to hurt you."

I wonder manically if Wyatt would rebuke me for apologizing in a similar situation.

I struggle to draw another breath, and discover that this time, it is a little bit easier. This gives me courage, and I nod faintly at Jane to let her know I understand that she meant only to protect me.

Little, mousy Jane Parker rushing to my rescue.

My third breath gives me enough air to wheeze out a laugh.

"Oh! You're breathing!" She starts to cry.

I push myself into a sitting position and find myself patting her back. Comforting my comforter. The air comes more easily into my lungs and I feel the blood return to my face. Delicately, I touch my ribs, hoping nothing is broken. But the rigidity of my bodice seems to have protected me.

"He just made me so angry!" Jane sobs.

"He has that effect," I croak. "You knocked the breath out of me. I think I'll live."

She wipes her eyes with the heels of her hands.

"I can't believe you have to marry him."

"I won't if I can help it." I reach out to adjust her hood. A French one. "I'll marry someone else."

"Someone you choose?" Jane asks. "A love match?"

I think of Percy and wonder if love enters the equation.

"I would like to have a choice. Or at least some control."

"And your family will honor that?" The hope in Jane's voice is heartbreaking.

"My father only wishes to use me for leverage," I tell her, "and thinks my only goal should be to better my family."

"So . . ." Jane pauses and bites her nail. "What makes you think you can make a difference?"

I think of how a few months before, I had no friends. I was an outcast sitting on the fringes of the court. Now I may not be on top, as Wyatt wants, but I am certainly somewhere in the middle. Closer to the royal circle. I have made a difference already—escaped some of the restraints that bound me—with Wyatt's help.

"I hope we have more control than we are led to believe." I stand up shakily. "Perhaps I can circumvent my father's wishes. Use my own leverage."

I demonstrate by leaning back to pull her up.

"I have to believe that what I want matters, Jane," I tell her. "And what I think."

"And whom you love." Jane's voice is thick with thought. Then she brightens.

"Anne, are you my friend?"

I stare at her. The directness of her question startles me,

because it had never occurred to me to question our friendship. Not like Wyatt's.

"Never mind." Jane shakes her head. "It's ridiculous. I'm too quiet. I never speak. I just watch. That makes people nervous. They can't stand to be watched. It makes them feel judged. Anyone who has done anything remotely wrong always feels judged badly."

"That covers just about everybody at court."

"I know! Which is why no one likes me."

"I like you," I say, giving her arm a squeeze. "Of course we're friends."

She smiles weakly. "I'm nothing like you and George."

"That can be a good thing. We both tend to speak before we think. Not always an ideal quality."

"But you're both so vivacious. And elegant. Everyone follows you. George is the most talked-about man at court. And everyone is madly trying to copy your French hoods." She touches her fingers to the exposed hair at the edge of her own.

"What about the Duchess of Suffolk?"

Jane pulls her mouth down.

"The Duchess of Suffolk is more of an enemy than a friend. She only pretends to be nice to someone if she can laugh at her afterward and then speak against her. They're all like that. That entire crowd."

"At least I know you'll never speak against me."

"How is that?"

"Because, by your own admission, you never speak."

27

Jane's affirmation of our friendship makes me feel lighter. Lessens the burden of my worries. My father is only days away, Henry Percy is nowhere near making his decision, and James Butler is doggedly pressing claims—valid or not. Yet I still feel hope.

Greenwich is tucked into the bottom of a curve of the river Thames, facing water and a wide expanse of marsh on the other side. Behind it is a single, knoblike hill. At the hill's peak is Duke Humphrey's Tower, a pretty little place where King Henry has been said to hide his mistresses.

From the southeast flank of the hill, I can see for miles—all the way to St. Paul's, its spire like a beckoning finger. So I take Fortune up there for a taste of freedom.

I want to roll down the hill like I used to at Hever with George. Mary would stand over us, mothering, until we convinced her to join us by tickling her so hard she couldn't breathe. Then we all rolled together, George and I racing to see who could get dizziest fastest.

Fortune shuffles and cocks her head. She can sense the wind blowing in off the river, carrying odors of the court and the Isle of Dogs beyond it and the rattle and cry of men in the tiltyard.

She flutters again, lets out a high, trilling shriek.

I loosen her hood, untie the jesses, and unblind her. She blinks, squints, flaps, and becomes still.

That is when I release her.

I watch as she glides out over the slope, her cry coming back to me, pitched more like a song.

I lie down in the grass, its scents rising around me like steam. But I don't roll; I sing, my face tilted to the sun. I sing a silly little frottola in Italian by Josquin des Prez about a cricket who needs a drink. A cricket who sings in the sunshine for no other reason than love of the song.

There on the empty hill, I can sing whatever I want, however I want. No one listening. No one watching. On this hill, I am unobserved. Unjudged. I am free.

"*El grillo è buon cantore*, Mistress Boleyn."

I know that voice far too well. The buttery tones. The high-domed warmth. I'm surprised I didn't feel the vibration of his presence before I heard his voice.

I scramble to my feet, the breeze chilling my back where the dew soaked into my bodice and sleeves. I curtsy while surreptitiously trying to brush seeds and stems from my skirts.

"Your Majesty."

"The cricket is a good singer," he translates, obviously delighted to be able to associate me with the song. "And yet I rarely hear you sing."

His eyes meet mine as I stand. Those clear, intense gray eyes that appear to look at me and into the future at the same time. As though anything he sees, he can make happen.

178

"I prefer to play the lute."

He nods as if understanding me perfectly. "The tenor of the strings speaks to me somehow. And the diversity of tones available."

It hits me: *I'm having a conversation with the king. King Henry of England. Alone.*

"I agree!" I cry, and have to stop myself from reaching for him to emphasize how close he's come to speaking my own mind. "The lute is like a chorus! A single voice cannot compete."

"Yours can," he says. And the connection breaks. He's flattering me.

"A king should only speak the truth, Your Majesty."

"You certainly say what you think, Mistress Boleyn." His tone is even, his face immobile. Regret clutches at my throat. I have just called the king a liar. To his face.

Suddenly, he laughs—a fountain of mirth.

"I like that in a woman," he says.

"Others would list it as the most heinous of my many faults."

"I find it difficult to believe you have any faults."

Is the king flirting with me?

"I was taught to hide most of them by King François's sister."

"Marguerite." The king nods. "She was once put forward as a possible bride for me."

I try to imagine the fiery, opinionated Marguerite of Alençon in the place of complacent and pious Queen Katherine.

I fail.

"You are lucky to have known her well," he says.

"She gave me this when I left."

I touch the little gold *A* that rests below the notch at the base of my throat. And then swallow when he looks at it—at the teardrop pearl that hangs from it, resting just above my negligible cleavage.

"Beautiful."

"She is," I say weakly. Pretending he doesn't mean the necklace. Or anything to do with me.

"But she is a dangerous woman. Heretical. She supports her brother in a foolish bid to retain English lands in France."

Despite his assertion that he likes a woman who speaks her mind, I doubt he will countenance my disagreement. Or my opinion that King Henry's own dubious claim to the French throne does not justify his bid to beat France into submission—nor the chaos and death such an action is sure to generate.

No king wants to hear that. Especially from a woman.

"I can see you don't agree."

I look up at him. His face is a guarded question. I don't know how to respond. If it were Wyatt it would be easy. But the king?

"My brother would tell you that agreeableness is not integral to my character."

"Actually, your brother told me you're a very clever girl. Perhaps that's more important."

I stare at him, awestruck. My mouth must be hanging open, thus negating the image painted by George. And the king stares back until my emotions spin from incredulity at George's praise to tingling anticipation of what might happen next.

The king breaks the tension and speaks first.

"You must be wondering why I'm here."

"I was, actually." I find my voice. "It seems unusual for you to be . . . without occupation."

He laughs again. "I'm that transparent, am I? That I am always in need of some pursuit? Music, theology, building projects. If it's not statesmanship, it's hunting. If it's not jousting, it's war."

"You have many interests."

"You are a diplomat like your father. But the truth is, I do have an occupation." He moves closer to me. The braid on his doublet catches on the silk of my sleeve, and I feel the tug like a heartstring.

I wonder wildly if he followed me. If he intends to have two sisters at once. I wonder if Mary is waiting in the tower. I look up again into his mesmerizing gray eyes, knowing that I couldn't say no.

Except I'd rather Mary wasn't there.

"I have come to ponder my responsibilities," he says quietly into my ear, tickling my hair. "It is not easy to send fourteen thousand men to war. Including my best friend."

With a flash like gunpowder, my cheeks begin to burn. He doesn't pursue me.

I turn my head again to look him in the face. He is so close. I can see the stubble of his red beard at his temples, the flecks of gold and umber in his gray eyes.

He does confide in me.

"I believe that the right will win," he says quietly. "But it is not easy."

"How do you know you are right?"

"It is God's will."

"It seems more like a gamble. And a waste."

He steps back and a flash of anger crosses his face. My tongue has taken me too far again.

"You were in France too long. It affects your mind. Your loyalty."

"Not my loyalty, Your Majesty," I say with a deep curtsy, afraid to look him in the eyes again. "I am loyal to you. But my concern is for my friends still in France."

He towers over me, lucent with energy, more like the string of a longbow than of a lute. I feel his gaze rake me up and down, scanning my skirts, bodice, and finally my hood. I am unable to move.

"Your manner is French, madam. And your dress. Even your speech."

"But I am not French, Your Majesty," I say hastily. I try to lengthen my vowels, harden the *j* in *Majesty*. Be English for the first time in my life. I wish I had gabled my hood just a little bit more.

"If, as the Moors say, the enemy of my enemy is my friend," he says, his words barely able to escape his clenched jaw, "then the reverse must also be true."

The friend of my enemy is my enemy.

"You must decide where your true loyalties lie," he declares. "And who your friends are."

He turns quickly and walks away like a storm, blowing the grass into whirlwinds behind him. I watch as he approaches the palace, a great gleaming gold beacon, calling the courtiers to him without sound. And they run to catch up with him like a mass of multicolored ants.

Fortune returns to me silently, and I tether her back to my arm. Back to the earth.

28

THE KING PROBABLY THINKS I'M A SPY. IT'S THE PERFECT disguise—the daughter of a diplomat. He must think I have a network of contacts between here and Paris, all ferreting away information fed to me by my family. By my sister. My father will kill me when he gets back, if the king doesn't do it first. Or George.

I will get us all thrown from court. The Boleyns, exiled back to Hever. Together. A nightmare if there ever was one.

I run straight to Mary's room, and George's presence there, for once, makes me happy. I don't hesitate to tell them the entire devastating tale.

"Nan," Mary says, a ripple of concern on her forehead, "the king doesn't like to be contradicted."

"I know, Mary! Everyone knows that!"

"I can try to smooth things over for you," Mary says uncertainly. "But you have to stop doing this sort of thing. Acting on impulses. Speaking without thinking. It doesn't work here."

She moves toward me, ready to put her arm around me. Comfort me. Be motherly.

I twitch out of her grasp just as George slams his fist down on the table.

"What the *hell* did you think you were doing?" George grabs my arm roughly. "Telling the king you're loyal to France?"

"I didn't say I was loyal to France! I said I was loyal to him!"

"Well, that's not how he heard it."

"I said my friends were in France," I whisper, my anger gone. The choking emotion of it replaced by stifled tears.

"Oh, Nan," Mary sighs. "Don't you see that's just as bad?"

"I do now! But at the time, I thought . . . I thought . . ." I thought I was talking to someone who would listen. I thought, because we shared a love of music, because he understood and spoke exactly what I felt about the lute, that maybe he understood *me*. I thought that maybe—just maybe—the attraction I felt was mutual.

"You didn't think at all, stupid."

It's exactly what Father used to call George when he got his lessons wrong. George lets go of me and stomps over to the little tray by Mary's fire. Pours himself a goblet of wine and drinks most of it in one gulp.

"That's not fair."

"It's completely fair, Mary! Our little sister has been at court for less than a year and she's already jeopardized our position here numerous times! She's an unpredictable hazard. We need to marry her off to Butler and get her out of England as soon as possible if we want to save this family's reputation."

"Status at court isn't everything, George," my sister soothes.

"Yes it is! It is everything and it is the only thing."

"You're talking as if I'm not even here!" I cry.

"It would be better if you weren't," George growls, then

slams his fist down again. "God damn it, Anne! Father will be here in days. Days! You couldn't wait until he was here?"

"What difference would that make?"

"In his absence, he can blame me for your indiscretions. For your stupid mouth."

"That's ridiculous."

"Is it?" He comes close enough to me that I can feel his breath on my face, vinegar-yeasty from the wine. "Is it *ridiculous*, Anne? Do you remember when you ran down to the river and ruined your new frock? Or when you told Father to kiss your ass in French? Or when you broke your finger falling out of the apple tree? All. My. Fault."

The darkness in his eyes threatens to swallow me whole. I curl my misshapen finger into the pleats of my skirt.

"But you weren't even there when I fell out of the tree."

George had said girls couldn't climb trees. So I climbed as high as I could. Just to spite him. I climbed higher than he ever had. I knew it—and he knew it—because I picked the apple he'd coveted the day before and couldn't reach.

"That's why he blamed me." George's gaze is now flat with menace. He turns away from me and takes another drink. "I'm going to send you to Hever."

Hever is nowhere. The country. Far from Percy, who will change my life. Far from court and dance and music. Far from the king.

"You can't send me away." Desperation makes my voice wispy. Inconsequential.

"I can, and I will."

I look to Mary, whose eyes meet mine briefly and then focus elsewhere. She isn't going to stick up for me.

"What about the tournament? The visit from the king of Denmark?"

"What about them?" George sneers. "It's not like you're central to the success of either event."

"But I remember Isabeau from the Low Countries."

"You can't remember the Danish queen. You were seven years old."

I glare at my brother. He stares back, an insolent lift to his eyebrow and his eyes clearly reflecting his words. He doesn't believe me.

"I remember getting the highest apple from that tree," I tell him.

George clenches his jaw. He turns to the tray, refills his goblet, and takes a long drink. A drop of claret glistens on his chin until he wipes it on the back of his sleeve.

"You remember her. What difference should that make?"

"She was kind to me. I could make her visit here more comfortable. A familiar face."

"It's extremely unlikely that she'll remember you."

"I speak French!" I'm grasping at straws.

"Which is exactly why we're talking about this. Besides, her aunt, the queen of England, speaks French fluently. I think Queen Isabeau will be fine without you."

His snide, sarcastic calm boils inside me. I can't let him win.

"You can't make me go," I say, the words tumbling over each other. "I'm going to be a countess!"

George laughs.

"Of *Ormond*. Not exactly the highest rank in the world. And even that isn't guaranteed. Not if I have anything to do with it."

"You can have your piddling little birthright," I hiss at him. "Because I'm going to be the Countess of Northumberland."

Everything in the room stops. Mary is frozen in place, hesitating between us, unsure which side to support. George can't quite seem to alter his expression from one of contempt to one of surprise.

My insides twist, lurch, and plunge. I've just broken Henry Percy's very first "rule."

"How's that?" George asks finally.

"Nothing."

"Henry Percy?"

George is cleverer than he lets on. Latin, he never understood. But politics and manipulation come naturally to him.

I say nothing.

He takes a step closer to me. He reaches up to my face, and I try not to flinch away.

But he strokes my cheek. Places a hand on each shoulder. Leans in close.

"Little Henry Percy?"

Percy is taller than George. George means "little" in the sense that George has a bigger personality. A larger circle of friends. More self-confidence.

I say nothing.

"Are you telling me you have an understanding with Lord

Percy? Future earl of one of the oldest earldoms in England? A family that came over with William the Conqueror?"

Percy's voice is screaming at me to stop. But I can't. It's the first time since we were little children that George has shown anything like admiration toward me.

"Not an understanding," I say. "Exactly."

George's expression dissolves into distrust.

"Well then what, *exactly*, is it?"

His voice is low and rumbling, like the purr of some great cat.

"An . . . interest."

"An interest." The contempt is back. "Like Henry Norris's interest? Like Thomas Wyatt's? That's not the kind of interest that makes you a countess, Sister." He leers.

"It's not like that."

But George sees that he has regained the upper hand.

"And Wyatt's not really interested, anyway. To him, you're more of a . . . challenge."

A piece of truth tears away from my heart, and I feel my resolve begin to break.

"Henry Percy seems like an honorable man," Mary interjects. "If Nan thinks he intends to marry her, then perhaps he does."

Mary has sunk her teeth into the depths of the issue.

"And we should stand by her," she adds. "Because family is blood. And so much more important than these tentative and fleeting connections made here."

"Blood spills easily."

"Not ours, George. Not Boleyn blood."

George looks at me, and for an instant, I see his face across from mine at the dinner table, rigid with pain and determination. Because he blamed himself as much as my father did.

"I will keep Father at bay," he says quietly. "Mary will sweeten the king."

He strides back to the door, suddenly purposeful. He stops, one hand on the latch, and turns.

"And you, Anne, make sure this interest of Percy's becomes enthusiasm. Whatever it takes."

29

I DON'T TELL WYATT ABOUT MY CONVERSATION WITH THE KING. I can't face his criticism as well. We have just started speaking again. So as we walk up Greenwich's apple orchard, I pretend that all is well.

"How many have asked you for a favor to carry in the joust?" he asks, twirling an apple leaf between his fingers.

"Checking up on my progress?"

"I have to know how my protégée fares."

He is all nonchalance and superficial concern. *Protégée*. George's words walk with me—that Wyatt sees me as a challenge. Not a person. Just a girl.

"Henry Norris has asked," I snap. "And my father. Pleased?"

"Your father? Why? He won't even be here."

A shout and the sound of splintering come from the tiltyard beyond the towers and viewing platform. Practice for the tournament has reached a peak of fervid anticipation. Pestilential war games.

"Because he thinks so highly of his youngest daughter that he declared his intention in letter by courier, assuming no one else would offer. Couldn't bear to be embarrassed long-distance."

"Your father's largesse knows no bounds."

"My father's largesse is notoriously negligible."

"You sound bitter."

"Do I?" I want to strangle him. "Why, that was never my intent."

Wyatt stops me and holds my gaze. Will not let me go. I'm itching to slap him. Spit at him. Dare him to criticize me one more time.

"Your father is a commoner. He comes from trade. But you, my dear, are descended from royalty."

"Flattery from Thomas Wyatt?" I ask, my bitterness encompassing everything. "I suppose I should consider myself honored."

"Not flattery. Truth. You're clever. You have poise and beauty and therefore bright prospects. You just have to help your father realize it."

I think of the time I tried to correct my father's French when he was ambassador to the French court. And how he didn't speak to me again until I washed up on England's shores, bedraggled and alone, two years later.

"You don't know my father very well, do you?"

"I know that he has more ambition than the rest of us put together. And that any attachment you make that will bring you closer to the peerage will get his attention."

"So I should just tell him that I'm bound for greatness and that he'd better get out of my way."

Wyatt laughs. "Even I wouldn't tell my father that I'll be better known than he will be. That my name will go down in history, and he will be long forgotten. He would slap me senseless and send me back to Kent, and then where would I be?"

"Kent."

Wyatt throws his head back in that delighted roll of laughter that makes me want to spin with joy. But he grabs me around the waist and does it for me.

"Of course, you're right." He stops, nearly breathless. "But what I mean is that you can know the truth and not tell it. I will be famous. My father will not."

"You certainly think a lot of yourself."

"I have to. No one else will. Certainly not my father. And you are in the same position."

He says it so blithely. Points out with supreme indifference what broke my heart when I was seven. My father abandoned me as soon as he realized Mary was pretty and I never would be.

"So Henry Percy hasn't asked for your favor for the joust?" Wyatt sounds almost too casual.

"No." I keep my voice purposefully neutral.

"And that disappoints you."

It isn't a question.

"It does a bit." I hate to admit it. Especially to Wyatt.

"Your paramour doesn't wish to be connected to you."

"Don't be rude." I'm stung by how close he is to the truth.

"It's true, though. He sits next to you in the queen's chambers, but is never seen with you elsewhere. He doesn't buy you trinkets or ask you for any. He barely looks at you at banquets and dances, when the other men at the court are falling over themselves to accompany you."

My anger layers over itself. At his nerve. At how devastatingly he points out the truth.

"It's not him," I hiss, my voice tight. "It's his father. It's the court. Gossip. He just wants to avoid it."

"There's nothing wrong with having a mistress."

"I don't want to be a mistress! A whore. I don't want to share a bed and not a life."

"And have any of these men asked that of you? Has Percy?" Wyatt's eyes look like a falcon's. Hooded. Unflinching.

"Percy's been nothing but noble. But Norris has made insinuations. And some others."

"And have you said yes to any of them?"

"No!"

"For a favor in the joust," he says, leaning close to my ear. "Not for your maidenhead." The scent of sugared almonds encompasses me. I lick my lips.

"No."

"Good. You shall grant it to me."

"My maidenhead?" I look at him from the corner of my eye, like a teasing flirtation. Two can play at this game.

"God forbid," Wyatt replies tightly.

I suddenly feel like I should cover myself and take a step back.

"Thanks for the compliment."

"My pleasure," he says, his body at ease again. "Your favor is all I ask, my sweet."

"What sort of thing are you looking for?" I think of a colored handkerchief, tied to a jousting lance, fluttering like a helpless maiden.

"This."

Lazily, Wyatt raises the index finger of his right hand and lets it come to rest on the gold *A* that hangs between my collarbones. He leaves his finger there, as if feeling for my pulse, and stares directly into my eyes. His own, glass-blue, reflect the sky.

We are so close. It's unnerving. If I took a step forward, his hand would be flat on my chest, directly over the breakneck rhythm of my heart.

I struggle to move my mouth—to smile or flirt or speak—never letting my eyes waver from his.

"My lady Marguerite of Alençon gave me this before I left France," I manage.

"Perfect." He traces the letter with his finger and then strokes the pearl that hangs from it, never once touching my skin. "Meaningful."

I reach for the knotted ribbon, but Wyatt stops me. There, in the garden, with anyone and everyone watching, Wyatt reaches, his arms encircling me, so close we almost touch. Almost, but not quite. His chin is the same height as the crown of my hood. I suppress the urge to raise my face to his.

His fingers are deft—as if used to managing unseen knots. I picture him unpinning his lover's hood. Untying the sleeves of her gown, the stays of her bodice. Something feral claws inside me.

He pulls the ribbon from around my neck and ties it quickly around his own, the *A* peeking out of his collar. He raises it to his lips with two fingers of his right hand, kisses it.

"Wyatt . . ." I want to ask him to stop. Stop flirting with me.

I want to ask him for more.

"Perhaps it's time you started calling me Thomas."

Yes, I think. *More*.

"Everyone else calls you Wyatt."

"All the men call me Wyatt, Anne. You are supposed to be my lover."

Supposed to be.

"No, *Thomas*, I am the white-assed roe deer you pursue. There's a difference."

"A distinct one."

Silence wraps around us like the summer sunlight—hot and smothering. Another crash from the tiltyard steps me backward, and the spell is broken.

"What will you be wearing?" Wyatt—I cannot call him Thomas because I am not his lover, I am nothing to him—asks, turning to walk me back through the orchard. "To the joust."

"Blue."

"No."

"Now you wish to dictate my clothing choices to me? You tell me where to go, how to walk, to whom I may speak and grant my favors. And now you restrict my choice in gowns?"

"It's for your own good, Anne. The queen will be wearing blue. To match the king. You'd do better to stand out. Wear yellow."

"And it's as easy as that, is it? You can tell me what to wear just like all the rest of them? Like my father, who insists I limit my use of velvet because it is too dear. Like my brother, who tells me I look like a slut in a French hood. Like the Duchess of

Suffolk, who tries to make me up like a halfpenny whore. Like my sister, who claims I should lower the neckline of my bodice to display my assets." Like Henry Percy, who asks that I disappear into the background as he does.

"Well, there's not really that much to display."

"You are full of honeyed words today, aren't you? Just the observations to make a girl feel good about herself."

"My job isn't to make you feel good about the things that are wrong. My job is to ensure you get noticed for the things that are right."

"Your job?" I cry. "You see me as a debt? You claim to be my friend. And I thought you were. Probably the only person who truly knows me. Who knows what I'm afraid of. Who knows what I want, who I am. But you only see me as a challenge."

"No, Anne."

"You may carry my favor, Thomas Wyatt," I say, and walk away from him. Away from the smell of apples. Of almonds. "And I'll wear the yellow gown. But I won't speak to you."

"You'll have to if I win the joust."

I'm forced turn around to look at him because he hasn't followed me. He's grinning. I want to rid him of the grin. Erase the dimples. I want to hurt him.

"Then I shall simply have to hope you lose."

"Only witchcraft can make me lose, Anne."

"That confident, are you?"

"I have to be confident about myself, Anne. No one else is going to do it for me."

"It could earn you the reputation of a braggart." I still want to hurt him. But he deflects all my weapons.

"It seems you're in serious danger of earning a reputation as one who breaks her promises."

A sudden panic overtakes me.

"What do you mean?"

"Well, you swore never to speak to me again," he says with a flourishing bow. "And here you are."

I open my mouth to speak, but he steps close to me, obscuring the sun, and places an ink-stained finger on my lips.

"I listen to every word you say, Anne. You may think no one hears you. You may think no one listens. That you can toss off sentences and condemnations, promises and speeches that will fly into the wind and will never be remembered. But I remember, Anne."

"Because it's your job?" The feel of his touch on my lips nearly takes my breath away.

His hand drops back down to his side. My chest tightens, but my weapons are already unsheathed.

"Because it's a challenge?" I pursue.

For a moment, I think my words have pierced his armor. His eyes flash and flicker over my face.

And he steps back.

"Because someone has to remind you of your promises, my dear."

30

The morning of the joust dawns gray and murky, the sky reflected in the turmoil of the Thames at the incoming tide, as if swirls of sediment fill the very air we breathe.

The queen dons her gown—a deep grayish-blue silk with heavier velvet oversleeves the color of steel reflecting the sky. The bodice is decorated in swirls of seed pearls like wisps of wind, but the whole ensemble makes her look a little dumpy—like a fat cloud on a winter's day.

Nevertheless, the ladies of her chamber—from my step-grandmother, Agnes, the Duchess of Norfolk, all the way down to little Joan Champernowne, who has her sights set on the thin-faced Anthony Denny—all wear similar hues. The entire household is a sea of blue with the occasional flash of green or magenta. The entire flock of sheep obsequiously trying to blend together.

In my yellow gown, I stand out among them. The black sheep. I squared the neckline of my bodice using an ingenious stitch that secures the corners to the lining and fits the bodice flat and smooth. I added chevrons of russet velvet—small enough not to break my father's taut purse strings. Cream-colored sleeves hang to just below the tips of my fingers. And the skirt boasts a train slightly too short so I can move easily and dance quickly at the banquet following the joust.

Each of the alterations on their own would have caused a kerfuffle amongst the ladies. But the combination of all, plus the color of the gown, has created a veritable cacophony of whispers. The French hood I had fashioned from yellow velvet is seeded at the crown with pearls and embroidered with silk of azure blue—my one nod to the monochromatic nature of the other dresses. It sits far enough back on my head to contrast with the black of my hair, but close enough to my face to offset my "sallow" skin.

I feel very, very visible.

Suddenly, all the noise in the rooms ceases. The queen is looking at me, her bright eyes questioning. And a little hurt. I've broken the tacit agreement to prove to our visitors that we are all alike and all agree.

Just before she speaks, a herald comes to the door, ready to announce her at the tiltyard tower. The fun can now begin.

The ladies sigh in disappointment. For now they've been deprived of the fun that had already commenced.

I am free to go, yellow gown, exposed hair, square neckline, and all. For once, fate is with me.

I follow the other ladies from the queen's chambers down the great stair and into the hall. It is already decorated with swags of colored silk, as the lists will be. The forest green of the Tudors, accented with white and gold.

And alternating with swags of blue.

Jane falls back to join me as the ladies make their way to the viewing towers. The duchess casts one scathing look back at her, and I wonder that Jane doesn't combust on the spot.

"Are you sure you want to be seen with me?" I ask. "I'm certainly persona non grata today."

"I'm through with the Duchess of Suffolk and her crowd. I want to be like the Boleyns."

"And what are the Boleyns like?" I ask. We are opinionated. Ambitious. Jealous.

"Different. Exciting."

"No one wants to be a Boleyn."

She looks into my eyes, and the strength of the passion behind hers surprises me.

"I do. More than anything."

We are interrupted by a cheer from the tiltyard. The competitors bow as the queen moves toward the towers, then return to slapping backs and play-wrestling. They know they are being watched. They know they have to show off their strength one way or another.

Percy is not among them.

He is already in the stands, sitting up straight and purposeful. I expect my heart to melt at the sight of him. To feel that pulse of recognition. But there is nothing.

When he sees me, his eyes widen, not with desire, but with shock. I must truly stand out in the sea of blue. Whereas he blends in, a Percy amongst the royal elite.

Queen Isabeau of Denmark enters the stands and curtsies to her aunt, head bowed, deferential. She wears a simple white coif with a short black veil that looks almost like a nun's wimple. She is nothing like the girl I remember from my time with the Archduchess of Austria.

The Isabeau I knew sported bright colors and gaudy embroidery. This one wears gray. The girl I knew fell in love with a portrait, with the idea of being in love. She insisted on marrying this great love of hers at the age of fourteen.

King Christian—on horseback, but not riding in the lists—utterly ignores her.

This girl is pale and meek in her white kerchief and dark furs. Queen Katherine takes both her hands and speaks to her, and Isabeau stands beside her. Two drab sparrows. Fitted tidily into place by rank and preference and then forgotten.

By contrast, the field seethes with a corruption of color and sound. Men and horses are decked in silk and metal. Everywhere, gold braid and silver tissue gleam against the beams of light that shift from the clouds like the fingers of God himself. Gilded metal flashes reflections of the sky, and velvets flutter in the stands in fountains of color.

The horses, dressed in armor that shines like the skins of beetles, stamp with an impatience matched only by that of the men who will ride them. They look like the very devil come to tempt the unlucky into Hades.

The queen moves to a velvet-cushioned chair, shaded by a canopy of state with her initial entwined with the king's as it always has been—almost since my birth. *H* and *K*. Her pomegranate emblem, embroidered in blood-red silks, competes with the white and red of the Tudor rose.

The queen lays her hands primly in her lap, her eyes hidden beneath the gable of her hood. I can just see her chin and jowls. Though I stand some distance from her, amidst the unwashed and unwanted on a hastily constructed viewing platform.

Jane stands with me, squeezing my hand.

"You shouldn't be here," I remind her. "Your family has more status. You should be closer to the queen."

She squeezes my hand again.

"I like the view from here."

She nods to the field. George sits astride his charger, which dances sideways, wild-eyed and ready to run.

George raises an armored fist in salute and spurs his horse toward us.

I think my fingers might break in Jane's grip.

"Sister," George calls, and Jane's hand releases mine. "I have come to ask for a token to bring me luck in the joust."

Father. George does this grudgingly. I can tell by the way his eyes don't rest on me; they scan the crowd.

"I have already given one to another," I call, and his gaze snaps back to me.

"Then perhaps"—his grin is just the right side of contempt—"I must yield to one more exalted than I."

He nods and then turns to the crowd. And raises his fist to Percy in salute.

I can't look.

"Brother," I call. My voice cracks, and I clear my throat. "Mistress Parker needs a competitor to champion her. I can think of no one more suited to the task than yourself."

I sense George's desire to scowl, but he flashes one of his disarming Boleyn grins.

"It would be my honor."

I think a little of Jane's soul escapes in her sigh.

George raises his lance, and I help Jane to tie her pale-blue kerchief to it. She bites her lip, face somewhere between tears and ecstasy. I notice she keeps her hands away from her face.

A roar rises from the crowd. The men on the field roar back, shining in the spurs of sunlight. Nearly all of them, like the queen's ladies, are dressed in blue. The Duke of Suffolk wears the same deep velvet as the duchess and sports his crest of the unicorn against the sun in splendor. Norris is in black with blue slashings in his sleeves.

Even the king, his horse caparisoned in cloth of gold and Tudor green, wears a color like the sea in sunlight. On his chest is embroidered a cluster of forget-me-nots, all in gold. I remember seeing my sister sewing it. I think of her fingers, so close to the skin of his chest. And cough.

"Are you all right, Anne?"

"I was just thinking, Jane." I pause. I shouldn't go on. "Don't you think the king is . . . irresistible?"

"What do you mean?" Jane turns from George to look at me.

"I mean he's . . . luscious."

"Anne Boleyn!" I can tell Jane hasn't fabricated her shock. "It never occurred to me. He's . . . well, he's anointed."

A sense of wickedness makes me blurt, "That doesn't mean he isn't . . . beddable."

Jane turns an unbecoming shade of scarlet and giggles violently into her hand. My gaze lingers on the king as he rides once around the lists, applause following him like a wave. He stops before the queen and lowers his lance. She kisses her fingertips.

As the king rides away, he touches his fingers to the forget-me-nots embroidered over his heart. And casts a sideways glance at my sister.

"Oh," Jane says, the sound like a broken breath. "Oh, my."

I turn quickly. Did she see that? Did everyone? But Jane is staring at the other end of the field.

At Thomas Wyatt.

Wyatt doesn't wear blue. He doesn't wear the red and gold of the Wyatt family. He is wearing yellow. His doublet glows like sunshine, like a beacon, pointing directly at me. The noise of the crowd dips nearly to silence then rises again.

Jane flickers her gaze between us.

"Well." She raises an eyebrow, but a trumpet blast prevents any further remark, and the tournament begins.

George is in the first joust. He charges toward his opponent, who shies away from the oncoming lance and almost unseats himself. The crowd roars with laughter. I cannot see George's face behind his visor, but I can imagine the bitterness in it. As he turns his horse, the kerchief flutters from his lance. Jane bites her fingers when the horse tramples it into the mud. Forgotten.

The king and Duke of Suffolk joust next, and the crowd falls into silence. The men lower their visors, and the horses thunder toward each other—towers of steel and muscle. It takes three passes before the duke is bested, but both are dented and winded when they meet again in the center to shake hands.

Wyatt rides forward on his roan charger. Jane nudges me with her shoulder and giggles. I catch several other ladies glancing at me.

Wyatt rides once around the lists, as the king did, in and out of the patches of sunlight that escape the clouds. He takes his position at the far end of the lists, finds me with his eyes. He bows, deliberately and showily.

In the tower below the queen, Percy stands as though pinned to the wall by his shoulders, his deep-blue doublet and gray sleeves a counterpoint to the queen's costume. He watches Wyatt with an expression of loathing and disbelief.

I hold my breath. Wyatt looks once to the tower, to request permission from the queen, who nods. But his gaze lingers a moment too long on Percy. Then he lifts my gold *A* on its ribbon from beneath his collar. It flashes once when he kisses it. And then he raises his hand to salute me.

Without a backward glance and with barely a show of deference to the queen, Percy leaves the tower entirely. He doesn't look at me at all.

I am left to watch the sickening play at war, gripping Jane's hands so that neither of us shows our reaction to the crack of the lances and the fall of the bodies.

31

The banquet hall adjacent to the tiltyard is lit with countless candles, the shimmer reflecting off the gold plate in the buffet against the far wall. It gleams on the silver goblets on the table—gold is too good for a deposed monarch who tried to rid his country of the nobility.

As everyone is seated, there is a minor confusion at the end of the room. King Henry and Queen Katherine sit at the head on a dais, seen together for the first time in ages. King Christian sits to King Henry's right. But then Mary, Duchess of Suffolk, is given precedence over Isabeau. The duchess, who was once married to the king of France, is seated higher than the queen of Denmark. Isabeau takes a step back from the table, causing a minor blockage in the flow of food and wine being carried from the kitchens. But she doesn't say a word. She melts into her place like a farmer's wife.

The Duchess of Suffolk preens, arranging her black velvet hood—of the French style, I notice—decorated in rubies and pearls. Her gown contains all the colors of a peacock, and seems quite fitting.

"Mutton dressed as lamb," I mutter.

"Watch your tongue, Anne."

I turn to see George beside me. Goblet in hand.

"As well as you watch your lance?" I ask him. "Jane was gutted when you trampled her kerchief."

"She'll recover." George takes a drink and doesn't look at me.

"She fancies you, George."

"All she does is watch and judge. She sees everything and does nothing. It's like being beneath the very gaze of God himself."

"I don't honestly think Jane has the ability to judge you quite so ferociously."

"Oh, you don't know what the judgment of girls can do to a man. You should talk to Wyatt."

The Danish envoy stands to give a speech. His accent is lilting and somewhat soothing. I try to give him my attention. Try to ignore my brother.

"I think it's the reason he moves so quickly from one girl to another." George slings himself up off the wall and practically stands on my toes, leaning into me. "Why they say he is so experimental with his sexual appetites."

Bile rises in my throat, but I keep my eyes fixed on the Danish envoy. Pretend I don't hear. Pretend I don't care.

"So unlike the boring, bland Henry Percy."

George always knows what will hurt most. Like lashing a fresh wound.

"Not everyone can be like you, George. I wouldn't want Percy to be."

"What? Charming, well-dressed, and personable?"

"No. Drunken, womanizing, and rude."

"Oh, Anne, you wound me."

"Not deeply enough, it would seem."

George is quiet for a moment. Takes another drink. Bends his head close to mine, his hair tickling my temples. And whispers.

"Father is coming home tomorrow."

The tension plays out between us like a single, sustained note. The Danish envoy continues to drone on as the noise level rises around him. No one is listening.

No one will notice us.

George takes another drink from his goblet. Refills it from a leather flask he carries in his other hand.

"You'll have to give them up, you know," George says. "Your paramours. Norris."

He pauses.

"Wyatt."

Droplets of wine stand out on the fuzz on his upper lip. He slides his tongue over it to lick them off.

"But that will be a shame. Just when things were progressing so well."

I glare at him. "What do you mean?"

"He knows how to keep you in line."

"Keep me in line?" I barely manage to keep my voice below the volume of the droning Danish emissary.

"Oh, settle down, Anne. Rein yourself in."

"No, I will not settle down. And don't treat me as if I'm a dog or a horse. You have no right to speak to me that way."

"I do if you're a bitch or a nag." George drains his goblet again, the laughter apparent in his eyes.

"You watch yourself, George Boleyn."

"Or you'll do what, Anne? Needlepoint me to death?"

"You're drunk."

"And you're an outspoken harpy."

"How dare you?"

"Father is away."

My fists clench. "So that makes you brave?"

George pales, though I'm sure it's more from anger than from fear. His voice drops a notch.

"It's my job as the man of the family to make sure all the women act as they should."

Another voice cuts in from behind me. "It appears to me you're making her act just the opposite, George."

The banquet returns to my consciousness with a flash, and George's anger and surprise are quickly replaced by a laugh.

"Thank God you're here, Wyatt. See if you can talk some sense into my sister."

I can't even look at Wyatt for thinking about his sexual appetites.

"See if you can put down your goblet for a minute and get yourself something to eat." Wyatt tries to take it away from him.

George shakes him off, splashing wine on the floor and the skirts of the Danish waiting woman next to him. She huffs and moves away, catching my eye. I see something I understand there: a wish to be far, far away, back where she feels most comfortable. She's been exiled from her home because of the political insanity of the men around her.

"Get off me, Wyatt." George stumbles back, nearly knocking me down.

"I'm thinking of your own good."

"I know what you're thinking of," George counters with a sneer. "And it's certainly not my good. More like my arse."

"Don't, George."

"Well, you don't seem to be interested in women anymore. It's the only logical conclusion. You can't sweet-talk me or bully me or inveigle me like you do my sister. Though I have to say that whatever it is you're doing with her finally seems to be working."

Wyatt casts a quick look at me, his eyes wide with shock.

"He's not doing anything with me!"

I step away from them both. Away from George's insinuations and Wyatt's sexual appetites.

"Oh, I don't expect he's *sleeping* with you." George shudders obviously.

"Then what do you expect?"

"George—" Wyatt doesn't move. His eyes are on me. Ashamed. He doesn't want me. No matter what he says.

"I expect a little more deference from my baby sister." George pushes me hard enough that I fall into Wyatt, who wraps his arms around me to keep me upright. The smell of night air and almonds engulfs me.

"Try a little harder, Wyatt."

George turns away with a stumble, narrowly avoiding spilling the entire contents of his goblet over the poor Danish woman, who looks ready to scream or kill him. Or both.

"Excuse me, madam," George says, doffing an invisible cap and bowing gracelessly over his shoes, his wine decorating her hem. She doesn't move, frozen in horror. He raises his face and peers at her closely, only inches away from her nose. Her eyes grow more round and she leans backward, barely able to keep her feet below her.

"Yes," George mutters. "Yes, a female. Despite the mustache. You nearly had me fooled."

He clucks his tongue as if she's been naughty and showily grabs her hand for a kiss. Then, with a flourish that nearly unbalances him, he staggers out the door. The woman sags with relief and wipes her hand furiously on her skirts. I pray she doesn't understand English.

"Don't listen to him," Wyatt murmurs. His arms still encircle me. I want to lean back and rest my head against his chest. Breathe him in.

Instead, I release myself and speak without looking at him.

"He's drunk. And he's my brother. I never listen to him."

"Probably for the best."

I wish I could see his face. Something George said chafes the corner of my mind.

Wyatt takes my elbow and steers me away from the crowd. "He does speak the truth about one thing," he whispers.

"What's that?"

I hold my breath and look at him, his face so close to mine. He's going to tell me his sexual appetites do lean toward men. He's going to tell me I need reining in. He's going to tell me—

"That woman does have quite a mustache."

32

WYATT HUMS A TUNE—HIS VOICE DRAMATICALLY OFF-KEY—AS WE approach the donjon through the middle courtyard. He's looking very pleased with himself. I'm still nauseated over George's insinuations. And something else. Something that has lodged itself deep in my chest.

"Well, that was certainly a success." Wyatt's cockeyed grin tells me he has another plan up his sleeve.

"That, Thomas Wyatt, was a dismal failure." I stop moving. I don't have the energy to face any more.

"Forget George. He'll feel better tomorrow."

"Father's coming home tomorrow. None of us will feel better."

Wyatt hesitates. He takes a deep breath and attempts to guide me to the stairwell. To the queen's rooms.

"No," I say. "No more."

"It's the place to be seen."

"I'm not sure I want to be seen."

"You do, Anne. You can't back out now. Even the king talked about you."

Whatever has settled in my chest flutters a little. Like a living creature stirred by longing.

"What did he say?"

"Just that you had the darkest eyes he'd ever seen. He couldn't keep his own off the little jewel you gave me."

He fingers the black ribbon. My *A* is hidden beneath his collar. Against his skin. I want to touch it. I want to ask for it back. So I say nothing.

"Neither could Percy." Wyatt's voice is wary, and his stillness unnerving. As if he hopes to contradict any expression of joy on my part. Or take the opportunity to point out again that Percy could never love me.

"Oh." I won't give him the satisfaction.

"Did we make him jealous?"

"I don't know. I haven't seen him."

Wyatt doesn't say anything. I can't meet his eyes, his criticism. So I continue talking.

"He walked away. Left the tiltyard. I haven't seen him since."

"It sounds like he's jealous."

"Or maybe he just hates me, Wyatt!" I finally look up at him. "Maybe he just thinks I'm a whore like all the rest do."

Wyatt holds his breath, growing even more still, then says with a sigh, "Jealousy can make a man act in baffling ways, Anne."

"Well, I'm baffled."

"That's why we started this in the first place, is it not? To make the others jealous? To make them want what is between us?"

"There is nothing between us." My throat constricts. I look down to where my hands are pressed against my skirts.

215

"Of course. All I am is the flag on your ass." The bitterness in his voice may be my imagination.

I take a deep breath.

"Maybe this deer is ready to be caught."

Wyatt turns away and walks farther into the darkness of the courtyard.

"A deer ready to be caught is a deer resigned to the slaughter."

I shudder at the thought.

"Don't be morbid, Wyatt."

He stops, the bare specter of a silhouette. "You know how I feel about Percy."

"My father is coming home tomorrow." I catch up to him. I hate the pleading in my voice. "I don't have time to wait. Percy is my best chance. My only choice."

"You do have another choice, Anne."

Wyatt's voice has pitched to that rolling bass he gets when he's trying to be seductive. He lowers his face just inches from mine, one corner of his mouth curved into a dimple.

"Don't say it again, Wyatt," I tell him. He doesn't mean it. All my defenses collapse, and I shrug away from him. "Just don't."

"Fine." He straightens, raises both hands, empty, as if to show he has no hold on me. "You don't need me? You're on your own." He turns and walks away. Leaving me. Letting me go. Abandoning me.

I wait until he's gone. Until I can no longer hear the echo of his footsteps or the dolorous reverberation of my own heart. Only then do I enter the palace, which has become suffocatingly crowded. People are crammed into every corner, Danish courtiers piled into guest quarters and the English relegated to houses and inns round about.

Everyone has eaten too much and had too much wine and lies about, lazy with gluttony and self-satisfaction and war. The tapestries in the queen's rooms are sagging with the moisture of a thousand breaths. The place is full of ladies in heavy gowns and men in padded doublets, throwing dice and fumbling with cards slick with sweat.

I sit down, uncomfortably, next to Jane. Her cerulean gown that looked so vibrant in daylight now matches the shadows beneath her eyes. George has thankfully fallen asleep in the corner, head lolled back against the wall, and she gazes at him, her face full of pain and tenderness. Wyatt sits down to cards with Henry Norris and two Danish men. I don't watch them.

The queen arrives, agitated. Not her usual serene self. After acknowledging everyone's deference, she sits. Fidgeting. She's like Jane. Without her sewing in her lap, she doesn't know what to do with her hands.

She catches my eye and an idea appears in her face.

"Mistress Anne," she calls, over the lolling bodies and lazy voices. "I hear you play the lute and sing."

I don't know who could have told her. Not my sister, certainly.

I wonder, suddenly, if it was the king. And I feel a hum. All the way from his privy chamber where he talks politics and war with the Danish king.

"A little, Your Majesty."

George has woken up and leers at me. Wyatt doesn't even glance my way.

"Will you?"

I move to the foot of the dais on which the queen sits. I pick up a lute and caress the smooth ebony veneer of the neck. I try to get away with just fiddling with the strings and plucking out harmonies that blend into each other. None of the sots listens. None of them matters.

"A tune we recognize, if you will, Mistress Boleyn."

I hear rustling from the duchess's confederacy.

The only song that comes to mind is in French. I hesitate. Surely the court cannot deny the art of the country, even while they are lusting for the blood of its inhabitants.

And this song is perfect.

It reminds me of what Wyatt said. That I am destined to be like the heroine of a ballad.

I sing the first verse. The meeting. Boy. Girl. Love at first sight. It's obvious these two will never be together. I pause and catch Wyatt watching me. I roll my eyes at the ridiculous premise, and he looks away.

The next verse; the girl tells the boy that she is already promised to someone else. The boy tries to convince her to run away. He says how much he loves her—the way she smells and the color of her eyes.

I risk a glance from the strings, and my eyes go to the card table. Wyatt is studying me. Sadly. I look away and see, by the door, Henry Percy. I get the sense he's been watching me the entire time. Ever since I started to sing.

He's wearing a russet doublet and deep-blue sleeves matched in color by the lozenges of lapis lazuli in his heavy double collar. His cap is the same russet velvet, but edged with gold braid. His cheeks look almost hollow in contrast to his sharp cheekbones and raw-edged jaw.

My fingers fumble the first note of the bridge and I feel a compression of panic. I look down at the lute. It isn't mine. I don't recognize it.

I come to the verse in which the heroine of the story tells the boy she will always remain his, and then drowns herself so that her spirit can do so. Then comes the repeating line, *à toi pour toujours*—"yours forever"—the sound trilled like ripples of water on the lowest notes of the lute.

I waver on the high notes, my voice out of practice. Hardly Orpheus. I glance again at Wyatt, afraid he'll be laughing at me, ready to criticize. My gaze meets his like a lock tumbling into place, and there is no laughter in his eyes. I realize I'm singing the song he was humming earlier.

My fingers stumble again, and I look to the door in time to see Percy disappear through it.

I stop, unable to finish the last verse.

"Thank you, Mistress Boleyn," the queen says. There is a hard note of irony in her voice. "That's quite enough."

I hear laughter on the far side of the room. The Duchess of Suffolk has her hand diagonally across her mouth, and her eyes are viciously merry.

George appears to be laughing with her. Wyatt will not look at me.

"Shall I play something on the virginal, Your Majesty?" Jane asks. She has risen and stands next to me, her fingers splayed to keep from biting them.

"Yes, Mistress Parker. Perhaps you can find us something more cheerful."

Jane bites her lip and nods. She grabs my hand, giving it a quick squeeze.

"I'm sorry," she whispers.

I look at the empty doorway.

"Me, too."

I don't rival Orpheus at all. I am unable to recall even the living.

33

I DON'T NEED A WHITE FLAG. THIS TIME, THE DEER SHALL DO THE pursuing. I put the lute beside the dais and make my obeisance to the queen, who nods sleepily. Every line of her age and tiredness shows.

I hear the voices from the card table as I pass by on my way out. The crack and slap of cards. The mutters. It sounds like Wyatt is winning. I don't look.

James Butler steps in front of me.

"Where are you going?"

His grip is surprisingly gentle on my arm. I barely look at his face as I pull away.

"Air."

I step from the room into the crowded stairwell, down through the hall and into a sea of courtiers. I scan the swells of velvet and silk for the russet and gold braid of Percy's cap.

He's leaving.

I follow him out into the night and through the middle court to the lodgings. The noise recedes the farther we get from the hall, and darkness encloses us. It seems everyone is packed into one end of the palace, not wanting to miss anything. Not wanting to miss the chance to shine.

And I am here, walking through the empty rooms and galleries behind Percy. Alone. Dust settles on the floors and tapestries, illuminated by the rising moonlight that shines in fractured pieces through the leaded windows.

"Percy." My voice barely stirs the air. I gather my strength. "Lord Percy!"

He turns, and his eyes are as dark and empty as the gallery. Cold. He takes two steps, and is so close upon me that I can't think to move. I just stand and stare.

His lips barely move when he speaks. "You need to tell me what's happening between you and Wyatt."

Not a question. An order.

"Nothing."

"Nothing?" His voice is quiet and low. And as dark as his eyes. "He seems to think it's something. He's wearing your colors."

Henry Percy flicks the yellow sleeve of my gown. The embroidery on my hood. The collar of my bodice. The movements are quick enough to be violent, to make me flinch, but not hard enough to hurt.

"He carries your favor."

He lays his finger on the spot between my collarbones, where the *A* once rested. His finger feels cold, smooth. Like marble.

"We're friends."

My words—my *excuse*—sound feeble, even to my own ears.

He makes a sound that could be a bark. It could be a laugh— though a forced one.

"It's nothing." I can't face his silence. "It means nothing. He's

Thomas *Wyatt* for pity's sake. The man's soul is made of sugar paste and poetry. You can't believe a thing he says. Or does."

Guilt. Remorse. Sharp as a blade between my ribs.

"It's because he's Thomas Wyatt that people will believe it's true," Percy says. "He's a known rake. A scoundrel. It's assumed that any girl associated with him must also be in his bed."

"I haven't been in *anyone's* bed," I say defiantly. "Ever."

"But you lived in the French court," Percy stutters. "They say no one . . ."

"They say no girl leaves there with her virginity intact," I finish for him.

"And the way you spoke to me . . . The way you flirt . . ."

"It's a game," I tell him, thinking of Wyatt's words to James Butler the first day we met: only the witless and sanctimonious believe the game is real.

"If I . . ." Percy can't seem to keep his thoughts straight. He shakes his head. A rumble of laughter from the courtyard drifts across the darkened cobbles, blurred by the windows.

"Come here," Percy says. He reaches out to catch my hand, but then draws his own back to his chest. Afraid of getting burned.

He dodges suddenly to the right, through a doorway, into an empty room. This one doesn't connect to any others. It has the one door, opposite two tall, narrow leaded windows. These don't allow the rays of moonlight in, but face, instead, the shadow of the lodgings. And the orchards deep in darkness all the way to Duke Humphrey's hill.

Henry Percy steps toward me, and I think for a sudden, terrified moment that he might wrap his arms around me. Tell me he loves me. But he doesn't. He dodges to the right to close the door behind me.

I hear the lock turn.

He faces me. Doesn't touch me. The space between us is like a bulwark.

"If I . . ." He begins again. "If we . . . form a union, you cannot play this . . . game. I won't have you seen with the likes of Thomas Wyatt. I have to know that you're mine."

Union. He will make me a countess. Part of the circle. Elevated. Accepted. At the head of the table. Closer to the king.

But one word rings hollow. *Mine.* I muffle it and push it from my mind.

Percy waits.

"If we form a union," I whisper, taking a step closer. Measured. Choreographed. I see the scene playing out in my head. All a performance. I'm an actor—a dancer—playing a part. "I will be yours."

I tilt my chin up. He is shorter than Wyatt, so I would have to stretch my neck only a little to reach his lips. To press mine to his. Or for him to press his to mine.

He doesn't move.

I do. My body touches his. I smell lavender and smoke. The scent of moonlight infuses his clothes. I lift my lips to his ear.

"Everything will be yours."

Henry Percy steps back and clears his throat. Finally looks at me. The planes of his face are mere shadows amongst the shadows, his pale eyes hidden in darkness.

"I—" The sound catches on something high-pitched and sharp. He clears his throat again.

"I don't want Mary Talbot." Now he is whispering, too. "I want you."

He wants me. He wants me, Anne Boleyn. I know what I'm expected to say. It doesn't have to be rehearsed.

"I want you, too."

"My father is always telling me that a promise is as good as a contract," he says. "That because he promised I would marry Talbot's daughter when we were infants, we are as good as married."

I nod, iron bands around my chest. He wants me to be nothing but a mistress. To be nothing.

"But it is a promise I never made. It was made for me. I have never spoken it. And it has never been . . . consummated."

He coughs. Even in the cold, somber light, I can tell his cheeks are flaming.

I hold my breath and don't speak, daring him to ask for real what Wyatt did in jest. Hoping that he doesn't.

He reaches for my hands, spasmodically, and grips them too tightly.

"If we make a promise, Anne—to each other—and if we bind that promise, no one can break it. Not even the Earl of Northumberland and the Earl of Shrewsbury. You will be mine."

There it is again. That word. I stifle my reluctance to embrace it and turn instead to his other words.

A promise. A promise is as good as a contract.

Because there are no promises in adultery. Henry Percy is asking for more.

He moves a step closer, and I finally see the light in his eyes. The intensity behind them is devastating.

He bows his head, his forehead close to mine. "That is what I will tell my father."

A legitimate vow made through words and actions. A promise. And a consummation.

I will no longer have to face James Butler. I will no longer be held in contempt by my brother. I will no longer be nothing.

"Do you agree?"

He has not said he loves me. I know I cannot say it to him.

"We have to keep it a secret," Percy says. "At least until my father announces it. It must be official."

"The announcement."

"Yes." He nods emphatically. "That has to be done properly. When my father sees there is no way out."

He makes it sound like marriage to me is a trap. I have to clench my jaw to prevent myself from saying this.

"And you must stop any flirting with the other men of the court. I can't have your name associated with any of them. Bryan, Norris, Wyatt. Especially Wyatt. It all has to stop. It will ruin us."

His father is powerful and has powerful friends. If they decide I'm unfit to join the family, they will find some way to get rid of me. Legally, or not.

Surely Wyatt will understand.

"Do you agree?" Percy asks again. "This will break any negotiations made with Butler as well. You will be a countess. You will be mine, forever and always, and no one can deny it."

I will be someone. Belong somewhere. *To someone.*

All I have to do is say yes.

"Yes." And then, to make it more like a marriage, more like we've conducted this in the usual manner, I add, "I do. I will."

Marry you. Be with you.

Be yours.

"Good."

He reaches up and unpins my hood. My hair, set free from the snood, falls loose down to my waist. With his right hand, he smooths it aside, then lowers his mouth to mine and kisses me.

His lips are hard, close to his teeth. He puts one hand on the back of my head, pressing us together. My mind runs wildly. I think of the king's kiss, how it tuned a note deep within me. I think of the taste of sugared almonds.

Percy breaks away to pluck one of my hairs from his mouth. He takes off his cloak and lays it on the bare floor.

He means to do this now.

I want this, I think, as he pulls me down beside him. *I want this.* He kisses me again, and this time I put my arms around his neck. The kiss lengthens and deepens, and he pushes me. Lowers me backward onto the cloak, onto the floor.

It is so dark in the shadows below the windows. I can't see his face anymore. I feel his mouth. His weight. He doesn't speak. Hardly makes a sound.

Before I can move, before I can even think, my skirts are up around my waist, his hose removed, his face above mine, invisible, his breath heavy as sea mist. One hand pushes my left thigh and I feel a sudden dragging, stretching, tearing lurch and a bright, hot stab deep within me.

With a groan, his entire body goes rigid, sending a renewed surge of pain through me. He drops his forehead to my chest, then abruptly lifts it again and pushes my hair away, spitting it out of his mouth. He turns his face away from mine and covers me with his entire weight, my spine pressed hard into the scrubbed wooden floor. Then nothing.

Nothing.

The quiet steals in from the corners of the room.

What have I done?

34

THE COURT TAKES ON A HUSH—WHICH COULD BE CONFUSED with expectancy, but probably has more to do with inebriation— the morning after.

I feel like I am holding my own breath. Waiting. For Father to return. For Percy to acknowledge me.

Except for a dense, aching feeling and a bit of blood, I am not physically different. I am treated no differently. I can act no differently.

But I am different. I am better.

And somehow, I am worse.

Early in the afternoon, Wolsey gathers his cardinal's robes, his papers and seals, and his hangers-on and returns to York Place.

Percy goes with them. My husband.

I watch them leave from one of the towers overlooking the river. I can smell the sweet herbs burning in the barge, but they do little to dispel the stink of the Thames. At least not from where I stand. The choppy tide knocks the men together like tenpins as they step from bridge to boat, and I see Percy look up to the palace. If he sees me, he does not acknowledge it.

I leave the galleries and confining rooms of the donjon and

go into the orchards. The trees are covered in ripening cherries, the thin hips of growing apples, the promise of apricots.

I suddenly want to climb one of the trees. I want to sit on one of the branches, eating unripe fruit the way I used to do with George when we hid from Father. From his disappointment. We claimed we would stay in the trees until we were forgotten. But George always ate too much, stuffing the hard bitter fruits into his mouth until he was sick. Mary would find us hiding in the grass, surrounded by the reeking evidence of our degeneracy. And then George would lean on me as we walked back to the cold and heartless house of our childhood, Mary clucking all the way.

"Worrying about your father's arrival?"

Wyatt is walking toward me. Weaving between the trees as if dancing with them. In and out of sunlight. In and out of shadow.

"You know me too well," I say. My voice catches a little. He's the only one who knows me. And I have to sever that.

"I know you well enough to see that your father's hold on you can't prevent you from achieving greatness."

"Such flattery."

I know him, but I no longer know how to talk to him.

"It's true!" he cries, twirling me straight into an espaliered apple against the garden wall and holding me there. "Look. This tree is bound, pinioned to the wall, but still bears fruit. It still strives for the sun. Can you not do the same?"

My hands are over my head—held in place by his right arm,

his left still around my waist—my senses, like strings, pulled taut to him.

"Dare I not reach and ask for more?" His voice is barely more than a sigh.

The moment spins between us like blossoms on the air. He neither moves away nor kisses me, and I find I want him to do both with equal measure. Until I remember.

"But don't you see?" I slip out from beneath his arm, the summer breeze suddenly chilling. "As a man, you can do what you like. And all the court will admire you. It will not matter if you sleep with your wife or a hundred others. It will be forgiven. For me, it is not the same. Court gossip is a tarnish that cannot be wiped away."

"No, Anne," he says, reaching for my hands. "You will be great, too. Your life will be poetry, the very way you live it. And they will all forgive you because it will be beautiful."

"You have a sugared tongue, Wyatt, and a knack for poetry and flattery. I think you will go far."

"And you, my dear."

"Yes." My throat constricts. "I will be a countess."

He drops my hands.

"What happened?"

I want to tell him everything. About Father. George. How Percy's mouth is so unlike his. My stomach squirms at the thought of telling him about last night.

"He asked me to marry him."

"And he has his papa's approval?"

"Don't be snide."

"I don't have to be, Anne. That whipped puppy can't take a piss without his master's permission."

"He can!" Somewhere in me Wyatt's words strike a chord of truth. I silence it. "He does. And he has."

He waits. Stares.

"Anne," he says hoarsely. "What have you done?"

I hold his gaze, willing him to understand. I can say nothing. There is nothing I can say.

"Jesus." He covers his face in his hands and rubs vigorously. "Shit."

"It's done." My tone is flat. "No one can change it."

He turns and strides up the hill toward Duke Humphrey's Tower. The angle of the morning light sets him ablaze.

"Northumberland can change it," he calls over his shoulder.

"Not even God can change it, Wyatt," I cry as I struggle to catch him up. "Don't you understand?"

"I understand all too well." He stops again, and I nearly run into him. We stand an inch apart, and yet the gap between us feels unbridgeable. "If the earl didn't endorse it, it never happened. A match not made in the circle of power is no match at all."

"It's a love match," I say. "Even the king would honor it. He loved Queen Katherine." Once. "He married her even though his father had broken off the engagement."

Wyatt doesn't speak for a moment, his disbelief carved into the hard lines of his face.

"How can it be a love match if you don't love him?"

I don't want his doubt, and I don't want his pity, so I square up to him, stick out my chin, and let my eyes blaze with challenge.

"Maybe I do."

He looks at me for a moment.

"Then say it."

But I can't. Say it. I'm not even sure I can feel it. I spread my hands on my skirts.

Wyatt watches pointedly and then continues.

"You're just like your father. Scheming and manipulating to get a place as close to the center as you can. All head and no heart."

I will not let him see how much that hurts.

"So which is worse?" I ask. "Being the head that gets to the center? Or being the hand that gets others there?"

"You're a fool."

"No. I'm not foolish. I have chosen my husband. I have made a difference in my life."

"You've traded one tyrant for another—your father for a boy who isn't half the man, despite his lands and titles."

"At least I didn't allow myself to be whipped into a wretched marriage. At least I made my own decision. Not like you."

I spit the last words out and watch them land like poisoned barbs on his face.

"True," he says. So quietly I almost can't hear him over the sough of the trees and the plaintive call of a hawk in the mews.

"Not like me. But because of my own situation, Anne, I know you will never be happy. Not with him."

"Not happy? I'm ecstatic. This is what I'm made for. To be a countess. To escape my family and their limited vision. To be *here*." I stamp my foot on the ground of Greenwich.

"You will not be happy because you don't love him. And he doesn't love you."

"And love is so important?"

Wyatt doesn't hesitate.

"Yes."

"So maybe it can be learned," I say quickly, and look away to where St. Paul's points accusingly at the sky. "And you don't know. Maybe he does. Love me."

I think about Percy's kiss. About how quickly it was all over. Surely that meant something. Surely it meant he at least desired me.

"Love and sex are different things, and should not be confused."

As if he knows what I'm thinking. He always knows what I'm thinking.

"What do you know? You've said yourself that you never loved your wife."

"That's how I know. I have a son with her, but I do not love her and never have. Nor she me. But that doesn't mean I have never loved."

His words grind a hole in my heart so deep I feel I will never again see the sun. So I try to claw my way out.

"Well, I've never had that luxury. My family doesn't beget

love, no matter what they pretend. And I don't know how to love in return. Your concern is misplaced."

I can't stand the pity in his eyes, so I turn away.

"You lost the bet, Wyatt. Your services are no longer needed."

I leave him there. High on the hill, with nothing but the desolate cry of a hawk for company.

35

My father returns. He goes to see the king, the Privy Council. Days go by.

He doesn't ask for me.

He goes to York Place to debrief Wolsey. Matters of state are more important. The war with France is more important. Wolsey is more important.

I am woken in the darkness of predawn. A rough shake. A stumble over a discarded slipper in the maids' chamber. A curse.

"George?" I whisper. I feel Jane stir beside me, feel her arm move. I reach for her hand and hold it down beneath the covers. "George, you can't be in here."

"It's not like I haven't been before," he mutters. Jane stiffens.

"Go away, George. I'll see you in the morning."

"No, Anne." I feel his face near mine, see the almost imperceptible glitter of his eyes. "You'll see me now. And Father's wrath."

"Father? Did he ask for me?"

I release Jane's hand and swing my feet out of the bed. The floor is cold and dusty beneath them. Desolate.

"His very words were, 'Go and get your slut of a sister and bring her to me this instant.'"

Something cold runs up the back of my neck.

"So you came for me?"

"First. I came for you first, Anne. We must go and get Mary, too."

"He doesn't want me."

But I fear he does.

"Please, Anne." The voice is soft and green. "Don't make me go alone."

We creep through the quiet rooms and galleries of the palace, relieved to find only Mary in her room. Then the three of us make our way beyond the palace walls to Father's lodgings at an inn. The Palace is too full to house him. I expect he will somehow add that insult to our perceived transgressions.

As the bleary-eyed innkeeper leads us up the stairs, I number each one in my mind, repeating the refrain, *countess, countess, countess*. I will be a countess, I remind myself. The Countess of Northumberland. Wyatt's words echo back: *no heart, no heart, no heart*.

The three of us stand together but separate as we wait for Father to allow us into his rooms. I do not hold George's hand as I used to do when we were children. But our shoulders touch. Mary takes an audible breath when we hear a voice from within.

"Come."

A single, devastating word.

We enter.

Father is sitting at a little desk. He is still dressed in his court clothes: a doublet that sports more velvet than all my gowns put together; padded shoulders; jeweled cap. His hair is still a bit shaggy from weeks on the road and in war camps.

He doesn't speak.

He waits. Waits for us to stand still, for the door to latch. Waits just long enough for the sweat to stick my linen shift to my skin.

"How could you let this happen?" His voice is like the hiss and rumble of distant thunder, low and menacing. It's inaudible to the innkeeper on the other side of the door, but we hear and understand every word.

He stands up abruptly in one swinging motion, and I'm reminded that my father has always excelled at the joust and the lists, at hunting and hawking and tennis. At war. Despite his age, my father moves like a young man. Like a predator.

We do not move or speak.

Father stops in front of George.

"One of my children creates a false engagement?" he hisses. "Without consent?" A cataract of shame and terror flashes through me. George looks neither left nor right, but straight ahead. Unseeing. Unfeeling.

"Did you know?"

George opens his mouth. No sound comes out.

"Don't." Father and George are face-to-face, and I see how much George has grown. Yet he is diminished by the flare of Father's wrath. George closes his mouth again—the lips a firm, thin line—and lowers his eyes.

Father gaze never wavers. "How could it become known before it was sealed?"

Father doesn't know that I did seal it.

"I didn't—" I start, but Father raises a hand. Not to strike, but I flinch anyway.

"Do. Not. Speak," he hisses.

George is unmoving beside me. I feel his tension run through the room like a whirlpool.

"I return from Spain to find all of York Place in an uproar." Father returns to his chair. He leaves us standing side by side. Not touching. "The cardinal was in the gallery with only his chamber servants but could be heard from every corner, including the door of the council chamber."

So of course Father stopped to listen.

"The cardinal's voice was audible from every corner of the inner courtyard. 'How dare you defile your good name!'" Father shouts in a good imitation of the cardinal's tenor.

"'I marvel at your peevish folly!'" Father continues. "'And to tangle yourself to that foolish girl in the court. You are due to inherit the greatest earldom in England and yet you ally yourself with the daughter of merchants. Of little wealth and no name. One of the king's minions.'"

George sucks in a breath, and Father glares at him.

"So I listen. Wondering who this boy is and with whom he has entangled himself."

Wondering whom he can use the gossip as leverage against.

"'I am a man,' says Henry Percy." Father slams his fist into the desk, making the inkpot jump. "Heir to Northumberland. Sounding like a mouse. 'I am old enough to choose a wife as my fancy serves me best. I cannot go back on my word. My conscience will not allow it. I have committed myself'"—Father pauses, a dramatic master equal to Thomas Wyatt—"'to Anne Boleyn.'"

Father lets the final two words drop into the room like cannonballs. Heavy and indefensible.

I feel as if I am floating. Percy stood up for me. Percy will honor our union. Father's anger comes only from not knowing first.

"You're married, Nan?" Mary whispers. She has turned away from Father and is looking at me. "Betrothed?"

I nod, and she smiles at me. A little tentatively. Unsure.

"No." Father answers for me.

Mary's smile drops, and we turn again to Father. His hands are laid out before him on the desk, gripping the curl of it on the far side.

"No, she is not. Even if some kind of *agreement* was made"—Father manages to make the word sound salacious, indecent—"the boy's father will disown him if he goes through with it." Father looks at George as if he wishes he had a similar excuse. "Wolsey will throw him out. Even the king commands that he never see her again if he intends to avoid the full wrath of his majesty."

The room settles into silence, asphyxiated by Father's vented spleen.

Father glares at George again, and it is as if they are the only two in the room. In the universe.

"This is your fault. She was your responsibility. And now she is a scandal."

He will not look at me. Neither of them will.

"She is not married."

He won't even say my name.

"She is nothing."

36

NONE OF US SPEAKS ON THE RETURN TO THE PALACE. THE muddy streets of Greenwich glimmer, illuminated by a day just beginning to break; then the shine is snuffed by the clouds.

"You did it," George finally mutters as we enter the courtyard through the gate.

I can't even nod. I'm strangled by the knowledge that Percy will be married off to Mary Talbot. And I will be sent—alone—to Hever.

I am devastated by the thought that the king knows what I've done.

"Congratulations—you managed to be more of a disappointment even than I am." George's hair has fallen over one eye. The corner of his mouth is raised.

"She made a mistake," Mary says quietly.

"There are no mistakes in Father's world. There is only failure."

George leaves us on the cold cobblestones, squaring his shoulders before he enters the donjon to go and serve the king.

"If Lord Percy made a promise"—Mary turns to me—"he must honor it. He will have to defy his father."

I wonder if Percy will choose me and disinheritance. I like the idea of a man who would change his life, his status—his whole world—for me. A nobody.

But if he lost everything, I'd still be a nobody. Exiled. Unwanted. Silenced. Besides, no one does that. That's fodder for fairy tales and romantic ballads.

"Would George defy ours?" I ask.

Mary pales a little. No one defies our father.

Then her face softens, and I think I see tears in her eyes.

"Do you love him?"

"I don't think the Boleyns know how to love."

The tears threaten to spill over.

"We love each other."

"Do we, Mary? We don't show it."

"There are different ways to show love. Forgiveness."

Mary doesn't look away, challenging me to contradict her.

"Loyalty is a form of love," she says. "Even in the face of betrayal. And taking the punishment for someone else's mistakes."

"Failure, Mary," I whisper. "There are no mistakes."

"If you love each other, it's not a failure."

I can't reply. Mary studies me. Silently.

"I'm sorry, Anne." She wraps me tightly in her arms and I want to stay there forever. Protected. Safe. Her hair and neck are still scented by sleep. But then I catch the scent of cloves. The king.

I push her away. "Don't feel sorry for me."

My body feels rigid. Solid, but on the verge of splintering.

"Maybe he'll convince his father," she says. "Maybe he'll come for you."

"Maybe Tottenham will turn French," I mutter, so I'm not fooled into believing the fairy tale. "Maybe we'll all become Lutherans. Maybe Father will decide he loves us and let us marry whom we like and we can all live happily to the end of our days."

Mary looks as though she might speak again, so I turn on my heel and go back to the real world. Alone.

I pack. I pay my respects to the queen. I listen for gossip—anything that will give me hope or tear it from me. Father makes arrangements for a few rooms at Hever to be opened and aired, but I hear all this through servants. He will not speak to me and will not suffer me to speak to him.

I haven't seen George. Or Wyatt. Even my sister avoids me.

I want to hope, but Percy never comes.

Instead, the day before my exile begins, I get a visit from a short and spotty youth of imperious demeanor and dubious hygiene.

"Good day to you, Mistress Boleyn," he says, sitting beside me and leaning close. His breath smells like the Thames at low tide.

I edge away.

His face appears as if he were afflicted with the pox, and his eyes do not light on anything for more than an instant. Like flies.

"I am James Melton, and I bring word from a mutual friend."

"Friend?"

I claw through my memories to discover who might be a friend of Melton's. I'm not sure I have any myself.

"A certain lord with whom I believe you are close," he says, angling toward me. He's practically sitting on my lap. My stomach roils.

"Please keep your distance, sir."

"But this is information of a very delicate nature," he breathes. "Something only you should hear."

I turn my head away, as if listening to music. More to avoid the reek of his words than to save my reputation. My reputation is already stained irrevocably.

"It concerns a certain young lord in my lord cardinal's household."

I glance at him quickly, knowing that only one young lord could be sending me word through this cretin. Knowing what it means.

"His father has made an emergency visit to London," Melton continues. "He arrived at York Place and immediately requested an audience with both the young lord in question and the cardinal himself. He spent well nigh an hour berating the young lord, calling him a 'waster' and comparing him to his brothers. Not kindly, mind you. The father threatened to disinherit him."

I bite my lip.

"You see the problem," Melton says, and allows himself a snaggletoothed smile.

I nod curtly, barely inclining my head.

"So the young lord will return to the family lands," Melton says quickly. "The marriage arranged for him is going ahead. He will not lose his inheritance. He will not lose his honor."

All of this is said as if to make me feel better. As if I don't matter. My feelings. My desires. My honor.

Percy left without me to keep his father's promise. To keep his inheritance.

"Thank you for letting me know," I manage.

"But there is more," he says eagerly, his shoulder nudging mine. "The information about the father's visit you could get from anyone. I'm surprised you have not heard the gossip already. No, mistress, I have a private message for you from the young lord himself."

He will escape. He will wait for me. He will convince his father of my suitability.

"He bid me to beg of you," Melton says, and I hold my breath as his words graze my cheek, "that you remember and honor your promise. Which none can break but God himself."

He looks at me meaningfully.

My promise. *My* promise.

I shudder. I cannot believe that Percy has told Melton what occurred between us. After exhorting me never to tell anyone. After making me give up my closest friend for our farce. He has told Melton, who ogles me as if he could be the next in line.

I can't believe that Percy bids of me that I remain unmar-

ried, a spinster, a *widow* to him. Remain his property. While he goes off and marries the Earl of Shrewsbury's daughter. Has children. Becomes an earl. Has a *life*.

He wishes me to be faithful? To a hurriedly whispered oath in a back room in the dark? To a painful, pathetic excuse of a consummation?

He wishes to have my humiliation known by this ridiculous waste of space, who could tell anyone. Could tell everything. Could ruin me. But nothing can touch the future Earl of Northumberland. The English aristocracy will circle their pikes around their own, shutting me out entirely. I could proclaim my virtue before an entire courtroom full of lords, and they wouldn't believe a word I say.

Effervescent wrath sings in my blood and it is all I can do to keep my hands still. "Get out."

"Pardon?" Melton asks, head tilted, an unsure and obsequious smile on his face.

"You know nothing," I say, standing abruptly. "Whatever the 'young lord' told you is a complete fallacy. The vicious lies of a jealous suitor."

He gapes. Unbecomingly. I long to slam his jaw closed.

"Leave," I command. "I never wish to see you again. Or him. I will never speak to him more. *That* is a promise you can tell him I will keep."

Henry Percy has no idea who he's dealing with.

Melton stands reluctantly, looking bewildered. Like a dog whose bone has been stolen by a fox.

He shoulders past James Butler on the way out. But Butler doesn't acknowledge him. Butler is staring at me. Not with the angry, belligerent glare he used when he caught me with Wyatt or Percy or even George. No, Butler is smiling, and it freezes my anger and my blood with it.

Then he blows me a kiss and turns away.

Hever Castle
1523

37

My father calls Hever a castle, and long ago, it was. These days, it is just a fortified and moated house with small windows and freckled walls of golden stone and a garden picturesque in its tidy forms. All of it perfectly represents the Boleyns—the outward show of opulence and strength, the simple lines and calm exterior. Not a hint of what lies inside.

It is hell. Worse, it is purgatory. At least in hell you have something to do. In purgatory, all you do is wait.

Summer fades, and the blue sky is clotted with clouds that change shape like witches from old stories, one moment, a face, and the next, a dragon.

The fruit ripens in the orchard. I avoid going out. Too many memories associated with the scent of apples.

I find myself on long afternoons just staring through the window of the little sitting room. The blue sky crossed with threads of black lead. I let the sky and the lead go in and out of focus, blurring between freedom and prison.

Father's steward makes me jump by entering the room with a bang. He's short and skinny with thin strips of hair stretched across his skull and a permanently sour expression on his pallid lips. A jug of ale totters on his tray and he scowls at it.

"Visitor."

Thomas Wyatt stands at the door like a ray of sunlight too early for spring.

"Well, don't you look pasty," he says, his Kentish drawl like a salve.

"Wyatt!" I leap up and run to him, to throw my arms around him. But the immediate fear in his eyes stops me short. We are no longer on the same footing we once were. And I must tread carefully.

"It is so good to see you."

He's wearing a forest-green doublet that intensifies the color of his eyes. But they flicker around the room. He's purposefully not looking at me.

We stand, unable to speak, for what feels like an eternity. Until the steward coughs and I realize he's still in the room.

"Thank you. You may set it on that table. And tell the cook that Master Wyatt is staying for supper."

The steward scowls again and exits with barely a bow.

"You want me to stay?"

Wyatt sounds forlorn. Again we face a wall of silence.

"I—" I start to speak, but he interrupts me.

"Don't."

I bite my lower lip. "Don't what?"

"Apologize. Isn't that one of the first things I taught you?"

He looks me in the eye and the dimple appears. Finally.

Relief runs through me like a zephyr—a gentle wash from head to foot.

"Thank you."

"Don't thank me, either, Anne. There is little to thank me for."

"Well," I say, bustling to serve us. Trying to hide my confusion in busyness. "I can certainly thank you for coming today. For breaking my boredom. Tell me, what news of court?"

His face falls again, and I rush to continue.

"I hear nothing here. Not even the servants speak to me. I have a maid and a part-time cook. And Father's steward, of course."

I cut my eyes to the closed door and raise my voice.

"Who I think was only returned here to spy on me."

Wyatt grins again. Two dimples. I'm so delighted, I could kiss them.

"I believe," Wyatt says, leaning closer to me, "that I can hear him holding his breath."

I pause for a moment to savor the scent of almonds.

"Show me the house," Wyatt says, stepping back. "Surely he can't spy on you everywhere."

We pass the scowling steward on the way to the entrance hall. He doesn't follow.

"Father had this hall built when he came here," I say. "To make it seem less like a fort and more like a home." I hesitate. "He wasn't very successful."

Wyatt listens as I explain everything. Display everything. In every room. I'm afraid to stop talking. I feel as though only my constant prattle will prevent us from falling back into the inability to speak. To *not* talking about why we're not talking.

"Father had a gallery built upstairs." I point to the ceiling in the dining hall.

Then I stop. The chill of the room overwhelms me.

"I don't eat here," I finally manage.

Wyatt stands close to me. The only warmth in the room. "Why?"

"The table reeks of broken promises and disappointment."

"Then we shall go." Wyatt offers me an arm. Warm. Solid. I finish the tour. The upstairs gallery. The bedrooms.

"This is the guest room," I tell him, showing off the Boleyn bull over the fireplace, the velvet curtains, the bed.

"It has a real feather mattress." I find myself speaking faster. "No straw ticking for our guests." I pause, smothered in silence. "I think sometimes the feathers give me nightmares."

"But you sleep here anyway."

"Shhh," I whisper through a laugh. "It's my one act of rebellion."

"Well, you can notch up another one now. Not only are you sleeping here, but you've invited a man in as well." He steps so close his breath tickles my ear. "And a married man at that."

"You will be the ruin of me, Thomas Wyatt."

Silence washes over us. Because Thomas Wyatt is not the bringer of my ruin. I am.

Without speaking, we return to the sitting room and I order supper. It's simple: cold meats and plain bread. But it had been intended only for me.

"I wasn't expecting company," I say to sidestep apology. "You'll have to warn me next time. And I'll cause more scandal by ordering one of Father's finest wines."

Wyatt glances at me sharply.

"You want me to come back?"

I lean forward to make my point. "You are welcome at any time. I will be offended if you don't visit every time you are at Allington."

He frowns. Swallows.

"My wife is at Allington."

The painful gaps in our conversation are starting to make me tearful. I've been alone too long.

I clear the lump from my throat.

"What news at court?"

Wyatt tells me the gossip. Norris's latest paramour. Wolsey's latest political conquest. I watch him as he speaks, the tautness of his expression dissolving into familiarity, the tension in his body dissipating into that lissome nonchalance. Until he pauses.

"Suffolk has left for France. With fourteen thousand men."

I sag back into my chair.

"He's really doing it, then."

I had thought better of King Henry. And some little part of me—the childish, infatuated girl in me—still thought that we were mystically connected. That he would listen to me, and reconsider. That I meant something. That my words had power.

Wyatt nods soberly. "The duchess has already set herself up as a martyr to the cause."

"I just bet she has."

"And your sister . . ." He hesitates.

"What?" I ask. "What about Mary?"

"You haven't heard? From your family?"

I shake my head.

"My family has cut me off. Now that I'm worthless."

Wyatt looks at me for a moment long enough to become uncomfortable. "You're not worthless, Anne."

I smile wryly. "I am to my family. Now, please, tell me about Mary."

"She's pregnant."

"Oh."

There is no room in our conversation for me to ask the identity of the father.

"I believe she is hoping for a girl."

"If it is a girl," I say slowly, "he won't claim her." I can't say his name. Because of family pride? Or jealousy? "An illegitimate girl is more useless than a legitimate one."

Wyatt nods, his eyes on my hands in my lap. No. His eyes are on my belly.

"The other news at court," he says, and each word sounds as if it is hammered on a forge, constructed with great effort. "The other news is the upcoming union between Shrewsbury and Northumberland."

Percy.

This is why he's watching me. Perhaps this is even why he's come here from court. To find out if I, too, am pregnant.

I stand and turn away from him.

"You are very cruel to remind me of the man who broke my heart."

"He never broke your heart, Anne."

"He broke my ambition, then," I revise. "Because of him I am exiled. So in a sense, my heart is broken."

"You never loved him."

"He didn't love me, either. No one loves me." I cannot get by without pinching the softest parts of my own pain. "Love doesn't matter."

"It does matter, Anne," Wyatt says. He moves to stand beside me. Close enough to touch, but not touching. He looks me steadily in the eyes and repeats himself. "It does matter."

"Maybe for a poet it matters," I tell him bitterly. "Maybe even for a man of some significance, like the king. But for the rest of us, love has no place in our lives. Especially women. If I want to break out of the prison of my birth, I need to have the right person at my side. Whether I love him or not."

"That's awfully cold, Anne."

"It's easy for you; you're a *man*. You can make your own way. Befriend the king, be accepted into his circle." Jealousy stabs me again, and my words crowd my mouth in a bid to escape before I combust. "You can leave your wife and come here and still have friends and lovers. You can still write your poetry and play cards and joust in the tournaments. *You* can have a life."

Wyatt takes a step back, as if he's been slapped. Lightning strikes of anger flash across his expression.

"You know what your trouble is, Anne?"

"That the man who fucked me is marrying someone else?"

The muscles along Wyatt's jaw spasm.

"No."

We are plunged again into a hole of silence that we ourselves excavated.

"What then?" I step toward him, lifting my chin. "What is my trouble, Wyatt? What kind of criticism do you have to offer now?"

We stare at each other, unflinching. Then his jaw relaxes and I see something like sadness—or pity—in his eyes.

"You've never been in love."

"And I'm not likely to be, either," I say, sitting down again. I find I can no longer take my own weight. "It seems a criminal waste of time."

"You sound just like your brother." Wyatt sits on the stool beside me, our shoulders touching.

"That hurts."

Because it is true. It is exactly something my brother would say.

I lay my head on his shoulder, and for the first time that evening, our mutual silence is comfortable. We listen to the chatter of the fire and the shuffling of the steward outside the door.

"I'm not pregnant," I whisper.

"I know."

I raise my head a little to look at him, my lips inches from his.

"How?"

"Because I know you as well as I know myself, remember?"

"Then tell me this." I lay my head back down on his shoulder. "Do you think I am capable of love? Are any of the Boleyns? We're certainly not capable of saying it."

"I think everyone is capable of both." His words stir the hair that escapes from my hood.

"You've been in love, haven't you, Wyatt? Is it really all that wonderful?"

"Yes, Anne," he murmurs. "And yes. It is."

Hever Castle
1524

38

I START TO LOSE THE BATTLE TO RETAIN MY SANITY. SOME DAYS I sit still as stone, unmoved by cold or hunger, and I think I would not flinch if someone were to set me on fire.

Other days, I fling myself at whatever pastime or obstacle I come across—working my tapestry needle until my eyes ache, practicing dance steps until I stumble from exhaustion, or screaming at my maid until she cries.

And all days I wait for Wyatt to return, berating myself for every moment I spend thinking of him. Depending on him. He visits sporadically and always without warning, and my mind and heart are clear for days after.

The summer gave up its fight against the onslaught of the cold English winter. Ash trees gilded the hills, the fields ran rampant with ripe wheat, and I could almost believe I was back in France, so beautiful was the waning light. Then winter arrived on gray, heavy feet. I was not invited back to court for the Christmas celebrations and got little from my family for the New Year. Though Mary sent a book of hours—handwritten and beautifully illuminated and obviously very expensive—with a note that says she misses me.

I find that I miss her, too. I could use a mothering influence, since our own mother has been visiting Howard relatives, despite my residence here. Conspicuously absent. Conspicuously silent.

On Twelfth Night, I get a note from Wyatt saying that he will visit the next day, that he has something important to tell me.

I order manchet bread and meats and spiced wafers for his arrival. I insist that a jar of preserved strawberries be brought from the cool recesses of the buttery and that one of Father's best wines be opened.

After all, I promised. I don't want to earn a reputation as one who breaks her promises.

"I have to send a request to your father," the steward informs me when I tell him about the wine.

"It's for tomorrow," I snap. "You must take the order from me."

"It is my duty to address any unusual requests to Sir Thomas directly."

"This is not an unusual request, but a common one." I stop, considering the true intent behind his words. "You don't take orders from me?"

He offers a thin-lipped grimace.

"No, mistress."

Of course not. Why would Father have the household placed under the command of a disgraced youngest daughter? Who knows what kind of trouble I could get myself into if given too much power?

"Fine. The usual wine will have to suffice."

The steward doesn't even attempt to hide his triumphant grin.

When all is ready, I have the maid bank up the fire and send her away. I sit alone, embroidering a falcon on my yellow bodice. The light fades from the window, gray and lackluster.

As all grows dark outside, the steward enters. Smirking.

"Wine and supper for one, mistress?"

I nod. Wyatt is not coming. The steward has one more piece of news to report to my father.

I take a goblet of the wine to the fire and drink it quickly. The sour tang of it reminds me of George. I drink it all. And then another.

A brisk knock, and the steward reenters. Scowling.

"I'm not finished yet," I say to my goblet. "Go away."

"But I just got here."

"Wyatt." I turn. I want to wrap my arms around him. Keep him here forever. "You're late."

He nods. Cagey. Doesn't leave the doorway.

"You must stay the night."

The steward sucks a breath through his teeth.

"It is far too *dark* to return to Allington on icy roads," I say more loudly, and then turn to speak to the steward. "Food for Master Wyatt, please. And more wine."

He slides past Wyatt, who still stands at the door.

"Come in!" I say finally. "Get warm. Sit down. You're making me nervous."

I pour more wine as he enters. Drink as he sits on the edge of a stool.

The steward brings the food, and when I excuse him for the evening he leaves grudgingly. My father will hear all about this, and I find I don't care.

"Your note said you have something to tell me."

He takes a deep breath.

"I've left Elizabeth."

His wife.

"It's hardly news, Wyatt."

"No. I've said so. It's known in the court. I'm afraid I've upset everyone."

"Well, you didn't have to announce it publicly! You could just go on as you have been."

"I didn't want to."

"So you chose to live outside the norm. Risk being exiled." Like me.

"The king will forgive me."

"Why?" I ask.

"He always does. He finds me charming."

"More fool him," I tease, and realize it's something else the king and I have in common. "However, my question is, why are you leaving her?"

"We are nothing alike."

Like me and Percy.

"But you have a son." I find the words difficult to say. "Surely that means you must have . . . wanted her. Once."

I take another gulp of wine.

Wyatt clears his throat and crumbles his bread between his fingers. The silence in the room rises like heat, stifling.

"Never mind," I say, my words brittle as fallen leaves. More wine.

"No," Wyatt says. "There was a time. I wanted . . ." Again the grinding in his throat. "Everyone. Anyone. I tried hard to be faithful. Elizabeth, she . . . she threw it back at me. Laughed at me. She would get all painted up, like a doll . . . and go and sleep with someone else."

"And you were . . . jealous?"

"No. Humiliated. I never loved her. I think that made her hate me. So we both just . . . lived without regard. Ignored each other. Slept with whomever we wished." He looks away. "Last week she used my bed. With the steward."

I finish another goblet. The room is so warm. Wyatt stares into the fire and his eyes seem consumed by it.

"And when I . . . when the duchess painted me in her ceruse, it reminded you of that humiliation?" I don't want to say it, remembering his anger. But my tongue—which is never tame at the best of times—has been loosened by the wine.

"I reacted badly."

A single statement. No explanation.

"You did," I say lightly. "But our friendship survived."

Wyatt looks at me. Looks like he wants to say more, say something important, but remains mute. I take another gulp of wine.

"You know"—I break the silence—"George says men and women can't be friends."

"You know," Wyatt replies in the same tone, "George doesn't always tell the truth."

I laugh, and Wyatt raises his goblet to me in a toast. I watch him over the rim of mine as I drink, and he does the same. I pause, holding the goblet just level with my lips; the feral creature deep behind my ribs expands and stretches, bringing me to the verge of tears. And laughter.

Wyatt lowers his goblet, leans toward me, ready to speak.

But I jump forward. Spill my wine. Ignore it.

"I need a friend, Wyatt," I say, perching on the edge of my stool. "A true friend. I think so many people wish me ill. So many want me gone."

"We'll stay away from them," Wyatt says quietly. "It will just be you and me. We don't need the court. We don't need your brother or your family or the king. We'll conquer them all. Just the two of us. Together."

"If I see only you"—my voice cracks—"I'll never be married, Wyatt."

"Maybe marriage isn't the pinnacle of success."

I think of Percy in that tiny, dark back room. And I think of Wyatt. Here. Now.

"I'm inclined to believe you're right."

He looks at me for a moment. We are on the verge of something. I feel it like a precipice before me in the dark.

"Why?" Wyatt's voice comes from the other side of that crevasse. I know that if I bridge it, our friendship will never be the same.

I cannot make that leap.

"Well, let me tell you," I say, pulling back from the brink, and begin counting on my fingers. "It makes a woman boring and unattainable, to begin with. No one really flirts with a married woman. Especially one married to a powerful man. Not fun at all."

Wyatt laughs and sits back. His eyes are half closed.

"It's far too much work." I take a swig of wine. I'm beginning to see why George drinks so much. It makes life easier. It makes talking easier. "Not only must a wife run the household and raise the children, but she must also tend to all the needs of her husband."

"Such as?"

Wyatt's eyes are now almost fully closed. But I sense he is watching me.

"Planning his favorite meals, enduring his odious friends." John Melton comes to mind. "Sewing endless hems on endless shirts."

"Don't forget nightly entertainment," Wyatt adds lazily.

I ignore the implication.

"Not only all of that, but marriage completely destroys the equilibrium in the court, taking away all the eligible and interesting men."

"Oh?" His eyes are open now. Guarded. Thinking of Percy. I take another drink and crash on, trying to be humorous.

"Francis Bryan," I begin my list.

"Your cousin from hell," Wyatt snorts.

"Henry Norris."

"You keep going on about him, but I don't think you're really interested."

"Shows how well you know me then!"

He leans forward, over his empty plate.

"I know you better than I know myself, Anne. Henry Norris is not your type."

"Well, he is already taken, anyway," I quip, not ready to give up the banter. "And then there's George."

"He's not married."

"Yet. But poor Jane Parker is ready and willing."

Wyatt makes an appropriately concerned face for her.

"The king."

Wyatt laughs his great burbling roar, more intoxicating than the wine.

"The king belongs to a completely different circle, Anne."

I almost don't say it. But it spews out of me. "And you, taken from the flirting pool long before your prime."

Wyatt coughs on his wine.

"Doesn't seem to have stopped you."

"Nothing can stop me, Wyatt," I say dizzily. "You said it yourself."

"I did," he says, entirely too thoughtfully. Too thoughtful by half for the deliriousness of the wine.

"You must stay the night with me." I stand too quickly and have to grab the table for support. Just one more sip of wine to steady me. I barely taste it. My lips are numb. I press the rim of the goblet to my mouth, awed by the absence of feeling.

Wyatt takes the goblet away. When did he stand, too? He's so close. So close to me. I can taste the velvet of his doublet. Breathe the blue of his eyes.

"Where?" he asks, his voice rough on the skin of my cheek. His mouth so close to mine.

My lips want to kiss him.

"In the guest room," I say, the words troubled on my tongue.

He hesitates. Pauses in the spinning of the room.

"But quiet." I lay one finger on his lips to silence him. Almost like a kiss. "My room is just down the gallery."

"I won't breathe a word." He speaks with a sigh.

"It would ruin your reputation if you did," I scold, shaking the finger under his nose. And I laugh. I try to step away from the table, but my train and skirts turn against me, and I stumble.

"Come, Anne." Wyatt puts an arm around my waist. "Time for bed."

"I bet you say that to all the girls."

I lean into him, my feet happy to be relieved of weight and responsibility. Up the stairs and down the gallery, my hip bumping his, the length of him against me. We stop just inside the door of my great, empty bedroom, and the numbness rolls down my body in a wave, followed by a crash and thunder of sensation. I can feel every point where our bodies touch.

I lift my face to his, sure that he feels it too.

"Undress me," I whisper.

I feel his entire body groan as he takes a step backward, catches me by the shoulders before I fall.

"You're drunk, Anne."

Is that regret I hear I his voice? Or pity?

"My maid," I mumble. "I sent her away. I can't reach my laces."

I turn around and fumble with the knots to demonstrate. Bow my head to hide my face.

I feel his sigh on the back of my neck, his fingers light and quick, unbinding the leather and buckram that hold me together.

"Thank you," I say to the floor. I cannot look at him again.

He turns me around, and I clutch the gaping bodice to my chest. Gently, he pulls the pins from my hood and slides it off. He smooths back my hair, running his fingers through the length of it.

And kisses me.

On the forehead.

He steps out into the gallery and closes the door behind him. I am alone. The moment is lost. I step out of my skirt, drop my bodice to the floor, wrenching the laces out of the last few eyelets. I shed all my layers of protection and crawl beneath the soft, worn counterpane. I press my fingers to my lips. Imagining.

Before succumbing to oblivion.

39

I DREAM OF THE COURT. IT CRACKLES WITH COLOR AND LIGHT, each gown and doublet more vibrant than the last and my head rings with the cacophony of hues. Faces mash and blur and I recognize no one, am recognized by no one. The howl and call of their voices welcome and repulse me.

I dream that the queen has recalled me for a special event. She wants me to play the lute and to sing. I am given a tiny room of my own at the back of the palace, north-facing windows letting in little sunlight but all the smells of the river at low tide. I am told to change my clothes. But I can't find my green damask gown. I can't find the white sleeves shot with gold silk. I can't find my French hood. Everything available for me to wear is red. The color of claret. The color of blood.

Red gown. Red kirtle. Red sleeves. Red hood, gabled so steeply I fear it will block out all light.

And for jewelry, nothing but a string of pearls.

I dress carefully. All in red. Somehow, my fingers manage the laces all on my own. I follow the sounds of laughter and dice down to the queen's rooms, where the men play at cards and the women whisper gossip.

I pick up the lute and stare at the strings. The lute is like an instrument I've never seen before. It feels utterly foreign. I remember the last time I played. *À toi pour toujours*. The look on Percy's face. The look on Wyatt's.

I can't play.

I can't sing.

I don't know how. Silence descends as everyone turns to stare. The string of pearls tightens, like a garrote, and I wake with a start to the pale darkness before dawn. Cold, the air heavy with moisture. My chest heavy with tears. The black bars of the window barely visible against the dark sky.

Then a shadow moves across it.

"Who's there?" I sit up, clutching counterpane and pearls, terror lodged in my throat.

"Anne?"

I recognize his voice. His shape. His weight when he comes to the bed to sit beside me. His breath on the bare skin of my back.

"I had a nightmare."

"I know."

"I was lost," I say. "Dressed in blood. I couldn't remember how to play. I couldn't remember how to sing. They watched me. And I couldn't. I couldn't even sing."

"But you can sing, Anne."

"I wasn't me. I was someone else. Dressed and silenced."

I forgot to remove my pearl necklace before I went to sleep. I fumble to unclasp it and feel Wyatt's warm fingers on mine. Inhale the metallic smell of ink. The pearls cascade from around my neck, and he brushes my hair.

I am painfully aware of my bare skin, like a lute string ready to play music at a single stroke.

"Lie down."

I do.

Wyatt lies down beside me. I freeze, every fiber of my body taut. Remembering how much I wanted his touch outside the door. Remembering the feel of Percy's skin against mine.

"Shhhh," he says. "I promise to stay right here." He tucks the counterpane between us, and I relax. Wyatt is not Percy. He has not come to take anything from me. Even if I want him to.

His weight pulls me into him, the center of the mattress dipping beneath us. His knees are behind mine, his chest against my back. One arm wraps around me, folded over my own, his hand still holding the pearls. He twines his fingers through mine, pearls sliding on my skin.

I close my eyes.

"You still haven't won the bet," I murmur, my words slurred with sleep and the dregs of the wine.

Wyatt tenses. His arm tightens around me.

"Bet?"

"That I'd want you in my bed."

He lies still for a moment.

"I'll go if you wish." Almost a whisper.

"No. Stay. Please." I reach out from under the counterpane to pull his arm closer to me. Don't hesitate at the touch of skin on skin, the warmth of his on my wrist and forearm, cool night air breathing across my shoulder. I retwine my fingers with his. "You win."

I feel his heart beating rapid against me. It slows until my own heart matches the rhythm, and I can no longer decipher whose heart is whose. Whether I can really feel his or just imagine it in my own.

Wyatt moves closer, resting his face against the back of my neck. He doesn't brush my hair away, doesn't push it down as Percy had, trying to tame it. Wyatt buries himself in it, breathing deeply.

I'm closer to sleep than wakefulness when I hear him whisper something, but I can't make out his meaning. His lips brush words over the skin on my neck. I feel them skim across my cheek and down my jaw. They smell of almonds.

When I wake in the morning, head aching and tongue dry from wine, he is already gone.

Back to Allington.

40

He doesn't return.

I want to write to him, but cannot send a letter. Not only could it be opened and read by his wife, by my father, by anyone, but I don't know what to say.

I miss you?

I'm sorry?

I'm jealous that you are at court and I am not. I'm jealous that the court gets you and I do not. I miss his company. Having someone to talk to. Having a friend.

Just a friend.

On a troubled day in early April, one that spits with rain then trembles with a cold north wind, a clatter in the courtyard wakes me from my lonely stupor. I look out of the leaded window and see a big bay horse. A flash of green.

I am suddenly embarrassed by my old gray gown, the high neckline, the simple coif that covers my hair. I am completely unadorned and unbeautiful, and I am suddenly afraid to see him.

"Master Wyatt."

The steward, barely gracious, leaves the room abruptly.

I just stand and stare, tugging at my gown as if I could make it fit better with a pull in the right direction.

"Wyatt."

I flame with embarrassment at how drunk I got the last time he visited. How I practically threw myself at him. How I drove him away with my brazenness and childish fears.

"Anne."

His voice is rough, unused. He is so uncomfortable. We are so uncomfortable.

"Why are you here?" I blurt, and bite my tongue. "I mean . . . welcome."

He doesn't move. I've offended him and yet I can't apologize. I can't face his criticism or his censure. Nor can I face his expression—a combination of fear and sorrow.

"I have news."

"From court?" My voice sounds small—pathetic—even to my own ears.

"Yes. Your sister. She has a daughter. Catherine."

Another Boleyn girl.

"Thank you for bringing such good news." We don't move. He's still at the door, ready to bolt.

"There is more. Not so good. Our mortality is so close to the surface, Anne. It takes only a fleeting event to break the skin of it."

"Is it Mary?" I finally manage to whisper. Images flood my mind. Mary making me a crown of daisy chains. Crying when she left me in France. Wrapping her arms around me like a mother.

"No!" Wyatt takes one step toward me, hand outstretched. "The king . . . it's the king."

My extremities tingle. As if with cold. As if with too much wine. I fall back against the paneling.

"What?"

Wyatt is not the messenger of death. I would have known. I would have felt it. But he is disheveled. Agitated.

"You haven't heard?"

I shake my head, unable to speak.

"There was a tournament. He was . . . showing off."

"What happened?" I croak, my lips barely able to form the words.

"The Duke of Suffolk. His lance struck the king."

Wyatt is visibly shaken. A little wild. He's staring right into my eyes as if his very gaze could keep me from flying apart.

"Unhorsed him?"

"Yes." Wyatt sinks to a bench. "His visor was up."

"It struck him in the face?"

No one could survive that. Not even the king. I start to shake, and clench my skirts to still my trembling hands.

"No." Wyatt has not moved, but somehow seems more distant. "The chest. He fell, heavily. But the lance shattered—splintered in his face."

"He's . . ." I can't say the words. Disfigured? Blinded?

"He's fine. He got up and rode again. More fool him." The last is a whisper. It is treason to speak against the king.

"He had to prove he was well." My words and my small voice cannot encompass the relief I feel. "He has his country to think of. He had to show his strength."

"Our strength comes not from our ability to cheat mortality, Anne, but from our capacity to love. If I were so close to death, I would run. Even if I were called a coward. Run to the one I love and find life there. Life and truth."

He stares at me. Into me. I think of his arms around me, safe in the dark. *Life and truth.* What is he telling me?

"And the king didn't do that," I say quietly.

"No."

I think of Mary and her new baby girl. A familiar twinge of jealousy followed by shame. I'm ashamed of my own relief that he didn't go to her.

Everything I feel is tight in my chest—packed in cotton wool and doused in gunpowder—ready to explode at a single spark.

I rub my hands on my skirts and say the first thing that comes into my head.

"I'm glad the king is well."

Wyatt nods. Stares at his hands. Runs one across his face. Stands quickly.

"I brought something more tangible than news." He retraces his steps to the door. From behind the frame, he retrieves a lute. Its back is a beautiful blond wood that fairly glows, and the rose is carved with intricate knots.

My chest aches.

"Oh," I say. "Oh, Wyatt. It's beautiful."

He hands it to me. Carefully. As if I might bite. The lute has nine courses, and when I pluck at each of the seventeen strings, they're already tuned. He must have done it himself before coming inside.

I can't stop the tears that spring to my eyes.

"Oh, Wyatt. It's the most thoughtful gift anyone has ever given me."

"Perhaps now you can call me Thomas."

"I don't know if I can," I tease. I look up from the lute.

"Try."

"Thomas." The name feels odd on my tongue. Precious. Decadent.

His gaze is so concentrated I have to look away. I pick out a tune, slowly. The notes don't resonate beneath my fingers. The music I make is dull and timorous.

"I haven't played since . . ." I can't tell him. I haven't played since I gambled away my virginity to Henry Percy. "Since the night of the joust."

"I see."

I want to be able to play it. I want to play it for him.

"I think my dream is coming true," I blurt, my fingers stumbling.

"You just need the right music."

He takes the lute from me, plucks a note. He is not an accomplished lutenist. But he makes music. Something I haven't heard in many months.

> "Lucks, my fair falcon, and your fellows all,
>   How well pleasant it were your liberty!
> Ye not forsake me that fair might ye befall.
>   But they that sometime liked my company,

> *Like lice away from dead bodies they crawl.*
> *Lo, what a proof in light adversity!*
> *But ye, my birds, I swear by all your bells,*
> *Ye be my friends, and so be but few else."*

"The story of my life," I say. "None but the birds as my friends."

"I thought you'd like it."

"And you, of course. You are my friend, no matter what George says."

Thomas nods and hands me back the lute. Our fingers touch on the neck of it, and a chord strikes bright and perfect beneath my skin.

He lets go. Pulls away. Walks back toward the fire.

"I'm going to be given the clerkship of the jewels," he says. "My father is vacating the position specifically so I can take it on. Some responsibility."

"Not exactly poetic. Inventory and valuation."

"No. And it means I have less freedom."

"Ah. Your father sounds like mine. The less freedom, the better. And no room for music and poetry when there are numbers to be reckoned."

"The king seems eager to keep me at court, as well. To keep me close."

"That's a good thing," I say, more to remind myself than to remind him. I swallow my jealousy. And my disappointment.

"Isn't it?" I add lamely.

I want him to disagree. But he nods, slowly.

"Yes. Our fathers would agree on that."

I stare at the lute so he can't see my tears. I run my fingers along the knots of the rose, keeping my eyes wide so the tears don't fall.

Thomas kneels in front of me and lifts my chin. He strokes my cheekbone with his thumb, taking a tear with it.

"You *can* sing, Anne. No matter how he tries to silence you."

I nod, and he sits back on his heels.

"Try," he says again.

I pick out a tune. My fingers are unsure and unpracticed. The notes throb against me like an age-old bruise, feeling good and painful all at once.

The tune is one the king wrote, a combination of chords and individually plucked strings. I remember him playing it one night in the queen's chambers. He called it "If Love Now Reigned."

The more I play, the more the music feels a part of me.

"You play like he does."

The thought warms me, warms my fingers. I bend deeper into the notes, forgetting myself, forgetting Hever, living a memory of music and the scent of cloves.

"I'll leave you to it."

Lost in thought and melody, I hardly hear him. But one word spikes through my reverie.

"You're leaving? You just got here."

He stands and strides to the door.

"I must go back to court. Responsibilities."

"Thank you," I call, uncertainty wavering my voice. "For the lute. And for the song."

"I wanted to visit." He turns, but doesn't smile. "I can't come back."

He leaves behind an empty hole of doubt. I fill it with the weight of all my words and play the lute until my fingers bleed. And still the pain doesn't match that of my loneliness.

41

THE SUMMER LOSES SWAY TO THE DESOLATION OF THE COMING winter. The days, such as they are, get shorter. I consider leaving, taking a horse to the wilds of the north and becoming an outlaw. Finding passage back to France, regardless of the war. Running away with the stable boy—the steward's thirteen-year-old nephew, who looks at me like I'm a goddess and laughs at even my blackest jokes.

But all I really want is at the English court. I maintain the fruitless hope that one day I'll return. I am always looking over my shoulder for a pardon without apology.

Then one evening, just after the equinox, Father and George ride in through the portcullis gate at Hever on black horses, looking for all the world like Famine and Conquest having left the other two horsemen behind.

When they dismount, the servants scurry about them like mice, tending their needs and responding with obsequious bows to Father's barked orders. I stand in the doorway of the entrance hall and watch. Waiting.

"You're going back," my father says, with no preamble, and pushes past me.

For a single, shining instant, I feel a cascade of relief, like the rush of water at the breaking of a dam.

"You will need to do exactly as I say and not set a foot out of line."

The stopper goes back in the bottle. I am silenced.

"You should stop talking altogether." George pauses beside me and kisses my temple.

"Heed your own advice, George," Father mutters.

George's smugness at delivering criticism disintegrates. His face, still handsome, is becalmed and wary of Father's contempt.

"Sounds like prison," I blurt.

George cuts me a look that begs me not to speak.

"It will be a prison of your choosing," Father says. "Here or there."

"Or marriage to James Butler."

"That possibility is no longer. You ruined that chance."

"So you need me at court to marry me off to someone else."

"Don't turn this around. I do not need anything, Anne. It is you who needs a husband. You who needs this opportunity. I will not pay forever for you to spend your days here sewing and playing your little melodies."

He turns and walks into the desolate dining hall, engaging the steward immediately in conversation. Leaving me with George.

"You'd do better not to vex him," he says quietly. He is protecting me, like when we were children.

"I can't help it."

"You have to, Anne. Father never should have allowed you an education. It made you think. Thinking makes you speak—something you really shouldn't do."

The memory of our friendship dies, and all I remember is what has happened since. I forget that he protected me from our father's chilling disappointment. And all I see is his.

"Jesus, George, aren't you opinionated today?"

"I'm opinionated every day, little sister. It's the right of an educated man."

"But not an educated woman."

George levels his gaze. "You are clever. You always were."

He leans forward with the grace of a cat, his eyes becoming keen like those of an animal identifying its prey.

"Your cleverness is your greatest defect." Emotions ride across his face like soldiers in retreat. I watch in wonder, because at court, George wears only an expression of amused sarcasm or begrudging sycophancy.

"Father is negotiating for a wife for me," he says quietly.

George is confiding in me. George is asking me to listen. George is here to keep me company.

"Who is it?"

"Jane Parker."

"She might be good for you."

"She's a ninny. A dullard. A skinny, staring, mutton-faced mare. Sleeping with her would be like bedding a sheep."

"You are cruel, George! You don't even know her and yet you judge her." I ball my hands into fists. When we were children, we used to fistfight when we disagreed. I landed a couple of decent blows to his head one day before Father pulled me off him, swinging and snarling like a cat.

It was the only time Father ever slapped me. One of the few times that I was the one who provoked the silence at the dinner table.

George watches me, his gaze flicking to my hands, the tension in my shoulders, my distance from him.

"I don't think you could best me now, Anne, despite your vicious temper."

He takes a step forward that is stunningly swift, and I flinch away from a blow that never comes.

"I didn't come here to fight with you, Anne."

When I look up, his hands hang limp at his sides.

"You could have fooled me."

"You need to curb your temper, Anne. You don't have Wyatt here to discipline you now."

"Leave Thomas out of this."

"Oooh." His voice glides up and down like someone trailing fingers over the keyboard of the virginal. "It's Thomas now, is it?"

I bite my lip, thinking of the warmth of Thomas's breath and heartbeat sending me to sleep.

"Forgive me—I would hate to interfere with your perfect romance," George spits.

"There is no romance." I wonder what he knows of Thomas's visits. I wonder if I'm lying.

"You got one thing right, then."

"What do you mean?"

"Exactly what I say. Thomas Wyatt was never interested in you, Anne. And never will be. You're not his type."

"He doesn't like clever women?" I ask, unable to prevent a trace of bitterness.

"I wouldn't know about that," George sneers. "All I know is that when he visits the stews, he likes the ones that are blonde and busty." He leans closer to whisper in my ear. "The ones that scream with passion. I don't believe cleverness has anything to do with it."

I feel sick.

"Are all men the same?" I ask weakly.

He studies me, and I think I see a trace of contrition or perhaps compassion. Until he speaks again.

"Not, apparently, squirrelly Percy."

He has taken all the fight out of me. Just as he used to when we were children, when he'd describe Father's wrath until the words were more frightening than the reality.

"I'll go pack my things," I say, and my voice is dull and tuneless even to my own ears, "and write a note of thanks to the queen."

"The queen didn't ask for you."

I pause.

"Did Father find me a position?"

"No." George sniffs. "Hardly so. In fact, he tried to place you somewhere else entirely."

"Then why? Why am I to be recalled?"

"It isn't Father or the queen who wants you back," George says. "Mary does."

Windsor Castle
1524

42

A DEEP BREATH IS ALL IT TAKES TO ENTER A ROOM.

This time, I do not pause. I do not wait outside the door, avoiding eye contact with the guard. I have kept my head up and my hands steady as I made my way through the thick battlement gates, across the expanse of the upper ward, the ancient layers that protect the heart of the royal court.

This time, I walk through the door into the queen's presence chamber, allowing my sleeves to cover my fingertips, my too-short train barely skimming the floor behind me. I don't even adjust my hood or smooth the broad expanse of hair it exposes.

It is more than a year since I left. More than a year since the Duke of Suffolk charged his way across the Channel to Calais to wreak havoc on the French. More than a year since I let Henry Percy take from me the only thing that was truly mine to give.

This time, I won't let the whispers get to me.

This time, I have something I didn't have before.

I have Thomas Wyatt.

He is the first person I see when I walk back into the queen's watching chamber. I am drawn to him as if he is a lodestone.

My anchor. When he looks up, a single, perfect note stretches between us. Audible. Visible.

A hiss of whispers ripples through the room, replete with knowing nods and well-timed glances in my direction.

"She's back."

"Again."

"What is she wearing?"

The single note transcends the whispers. I will not let the gossip or the lies deter or defame me. I make my obeisance to Queen Katherine, who smiles tightly and sends me away.

"Anne!"

Jane Parker leaps up from a stool by the window and weaves her way between courtiers and ladies. They watch her, whispering, but she doesn't seem to care, her eyes focused just on me.

There is something different about Jane. The past year has treated her well. She isn't taller, but seems somehow *more*. Better dressed, in a gown of aqua-blue damask split to show a kirtle of pale-blue silk. More vibrant. More beautiful. Her smile lights up her face.

Jane Parker is happier.

"Jane!"

When she hugs me, her arms feel like a steel vise, holding me together.

"You've changed," I murmur.

Jane pulls away, and her gaze flickers over my face.

"So have you." Cautious. Her voice steady.

"You are prettier than ever," I tell her, and slip my arm

through hers. We walk slowly toward the window, knowing that the angle of afternoon light brightens the tawny orange of my gown until I glow like a flame. It sets off the darkness of my eyes and the black of my hair, and only the blind and the stupid will be able to take their eyes off me.

I resist the urge to find out if Thomas is watching.

But Jane clutches my elbow rigidly against the hard edge of her bodice and slows her pace.

"Look." Her voice is strangled.

So I look.

Thomas's eyes are on his cards, and I feel a river of disappointment. But next to him, George is staring, the expression on his face indefinable. As though he can't decide if he's happy to see me or wishes me gone. Probably the latter.

I glance at Jane, who is smiling tentatively, her eyes fixed on George. And I realize that this is one of those situations where she can't tell which of us he's focused on. She thinks he's gazing at her.

When I study George again, I can't really tell, either. He seems to be staring right between us. His expression is unreadable—but . . . yearning.

"Is he looking at me?" Jane whispers, her voice just slightly too loud. I know the tables nearby are listening, the clack of dice not enough to drown her out. I steer her away from him.

I lean my head toward hers, hoping to make the conversation more private. I take in the lavender scent of her sleeves, the point of her gable nudging my own hood farther back on my head.

Out of the corner of my eye, I see George still watching. Now Thomas is, too, and his fierce scrutiny makes me suddenly want to run.

"Because he could be looking at you," Jane continues, doubt creeping into her voice. "But why would he be looking at you like that?"

Like what? I long to ask her. But don't. Whatever Jane saw is not what I saw. I push her quickly out of the chamber and into the next, away from George, away from Thomas.

"Can you keep a secret?" Jane asks. She stops in the middle of the room and glances over each shoulder. Subtle. "I have a secret."

"You, Jane? The most transparent girl in the entire court? You have a secret? It can't be."

"I'm learning to be discreet. I'm learning to be the perfect courtier. No one knows my thoughts anymore."

I imagine even George knows Jane's thoughts.

"I'm sure it will serve you well," I say. "What is your secret? I've been known to hold a few."

Jane lowers her eyes, and a blush tilts up her cheeks.

"My father is talking with your father."

Just as George told me. George was looking at Jane.

"They're discussing a dowry."

What was in George's eye? The same thing I saw in Thomas's?

"We're to be sisters. I'm to marry your brother." Jane lifts up on her toes and bounces.

"Your father agreed?"

She nods and sticks the index finger of her right hand into her mouth and delicately nibbles her cuticle.

"I'm so glad we will be sisters." That, at least, I can say with complete honesty.

"Thank you." She hugs me, limply.

Then she nibbles the cuticle of her little finger.

"Do you think he likes me?"

I consider the truth. How George belittled her. How he has never considered her for one of his conquests.

"George likes all women," I say. I realize how that sounds, so I edit myself. "He must like you. If he has agreed."

"You lack conviction, Anne."

This is the trouble with Jane. The time she has spent studying the people of the court without speaking makes her a keener judge of expression—both facial and vocal. She reads people like some read books.

"One doesn't need affection for marriage." I'm thinking of what happened between Thomas and his wife. But that has not gone well.

"Yes, but one wishes it." Jane's voice is small and ragged. She knows.

I try to look her in the eye. The weak light from the window throws her face into silhouette, her bobbed nose arced upward.

"Affection can grow," I tell her.

"You knew you could never love James Butler."

"That's true. But who could?"

She laughs a little and turns toward me.

"George is nothing like James Butler. But you must know his mind. The two of you are so close. It's like you're more than brother and sister. It's like you're one and the same. The male and female sides of a coin.

"I'm not worried about loving your brother, Anne. He is lithe and funny and handsome and chivalrous. I think . . ." Jane's gaze slides away, and she blushes again. "I think I've loved him from the moment I first saw him."

"What does it feel like, Jane? Love?"

The question comes out before I can stop it.

Jane looks up at the ceiling. Her eyes unfocus as her thoughts turn inward, and a smile like sunrise appears on her face.

"Like music only plays when you're together. Like the very air tastes of strawberries. Like one touch—one look—could send you whirling like a seed on the wind."

Oh, God. My palms begin to sweat and I itch to wipe them on my skirts. My heart feels like a levee about to burst, and my mind is full of green and gold and poetry.

"I hope love is worth the trouble it causes, Jane," I say finally. "For all of us."

43

I can't be in love with Thomas Wyatt.

I make excuses to Jane. Fatigue. Headache.

"You do look shaky," she says. "Do you want me to go with you?"

She glances once over her shoulder. To the watching chamber. To George.

I shake my head.

I have to be alone.

I practically run down the gallery, skirts swishing around my ankles, and into the hall beyond. It is full of the king's courtiers and Wolsey's men. I walk close to the wall, for once not eager to be seen. In fact, desiring the opposite.

I reach the tower—mercifully empty—and breathe my relief. When the door bangs behind me, I turn to see James Butler. My knees threaten to collapse.

I don't have the energy to face him.

"Truth? Or rumor?" His tone is accusatory.

"That I have returned?" I ask. "What do your eyes tell you?"

"My eyes may lie," he says, stepping forward to block my access to the outer door. To the upper ward. To fresh air and freedom.

"My eyes saw you leave the banquet at Greenwich with Henry Percy. You didn't come back. Then he married Mary Talbot. And yet, here you are."

He pauses. "Surely my eyes deceive me."

He looks to where my hands are pressed against my stomacher to still them. "You were gone for nine months. And more."

"If your eyes do not deceive you, your presumption certainly does."

I step sideways to get around him, but he's fast for someone so large. He presses me against the doorframe.

"Did I deceive Wolsey then? Because I only told him what my eyes told me."

"What are you saying? That you told Wolsey what you *think* you saw? It was you?"

Butler presses further. "It was Percy."

"Your eyes aren't the only parts of you that lie." I slip beneath his arm and out the door. My face feels as if it's been slapped, and I welcome the cooling, rain-drenched air. I gulp it, as if to drown.

"He was spouting poetry." Butler follows me. "You like poetry, don't you, Anne?

*"I prayed her heartily that she would come to bed.
She said she was content to do me pleasure."*

I round on him. "Everyone knows that poem! That poem is about a dream!"

"I kissed her,"

he sings.

"I bussed her out of all measure."

"You know nothing, James Butler." I step toward him. To show him that I'm not afraid. That I'm not guilty.

"Oh?" His granite features creak and his teeth appear between flattened lips—a leering grimace.

"He told you nothing," I say quickly. "You have nothing."

"No. *You* have nothing. You are nothing. You will never be a countess."

"That, at least, gives me comfort," I spit at him.

"You could have been," he whispers in my ear, the meatiness of his breath making me want to gag. "You could have been mine, Anne Boleyn. You could have had a man. Not a hasty boy on the floor of some back room."

I do gag, and Butler takes a quick step back.

I square my shoulders and look him in the eye. Swallow.

"One day, I will," I tell him, and remember the feel of Thomas's arm around me. "I will have a man who doesn't think he owns me. A man who tells the truth and doesn't gossip like a laundry maid."

A man who loves me.

Shaking, I turn and leave him.

44

I CREEP THROUGH THE ROOMS OF THE PALACE LODGINGS TO MY sister's door, fear and shame twisting inside me until they spatter like hot oil.

She sits by the fire with her baby on her lap.

"Nan," she says, quiet and meek. "You're back."

Little Catherine has a head full of honey-brown hair and brown eyes like Mary. She looks nothing like either of her possible fathers.

"I have you to thank for it," I say. "I guess the Boleyns do stick together."

"Right." Mary's not wearing a hood. Her hair hangs in strands around her face. She looks like a serving girl, not like the wife of a courtier, or the mistress of a king. But with Catherine in her lap, she looks content.

"I guess it's all over court," I blurt.

"What is?" She finally looks up at me.

"You know what, Mary. Me. Percy."

"The Earl of Northumberland will silence it. And Wolsey. The power of the elite is remarkable. They don't want his name tarnished."

They don't care about mine.

"I suppose that's true." I pause, unsure of how to continue. "I haven't heard anything about . . . about Catherine."

Mary is playing a finger game with the baby. Catherine's eyes follow the finger with avidity, and she burbles with laughter when Mary taps her nose. But Mary's face is grave.

"I don't know," she mumbles.

"You don't know what?"

"I don't know if she's his."

I don't have to ask whose.

"Don't tell me that, Mary."

"But it's true." She closes her eyes.

"If you tell him, he will love her," I say quietly. "He showers affection on little Henry Fitzroy."

"He's looking for another heir. Little Fitzroy is his only son to survive infancy. It doesn't matter who the mother is."

"And your baby is a girl, so it doesn't matter who her father is."

"William will raise her."

"Well, goody for William. He sounds like a real prince. He'll raise her to be passive and browbeaten."

"He may not have the type of personality that you think is the best . . ."

"He has no personality at all!" I cry. "When he leaves the room, I can't even remember what he looks like!"

Mary turns away.

"You shouldn't say such things."

"Well, can you? Can you remember what he looks like with any degree of accuracy? Now, any one of us could describe the

king. His visage is burned onto our eyelids. We could recognize his voice at the end of a pitch-black hall."

I recognized Thomas simply by the weight of his body in my bed.

"Are you trying to pick a fight with me, Nan?"

I stop.

"No. But don't you want more for her? More than boring mediocrity?"

"I certainly don't wish for her to be the butt of jokes," Mary snaps, her face splashed with color. "I don't wish for her to be followed by gossip like dogs after the meat wagon. I don't wish for her to be called a whore." Catherine starts to cry. "Or the daughter of one."

"If he loves you, he should take responsibility. And if you love him, don't you want her to know?"

Mary laughs. Bitterly.

"Oh, Nan, don't be such a child."

"Stop calling me that!"

"Childish? You are a child. For asking such questions." Mary looks up from the crying baby. "I do not love the king. And he does not love me."

"You love William?" I can't keep the derision out of my voice.

"I love my daughter."

"But daughters are worthless," I blurt.

"No, Nan. That's where you're wrong. Daughters are everything. I'll make sure she knows that. No matter who her father is. Or her husband."

She strokes the hair from Catherine's forehead and kisses her there.

I look at Mary and see her probably for the first time. Past her fair skin and beautiful hair. Because of her sex, all she has to give is herself. And she gives it freely. So she is labeled a whore. A concubine. No one else can see past that. Not even our father.

I, too, would want my daughter to feel she was worth more than that.

"The Boleyns always stick together," Mary says, looking directly into my eyes as if she wants to *will* me to agree with her. "Shouldn't the Boleyn girls do the same?"

"I don't know."

She looks at me questioningly, so I continue. "We never have before. When King Louis died and Mary Tudor scampered off back to England with her ill-gotten husband, you left me. Abandoned me. And when you got here, you took it all. You took a place at court. You got a husband. You got the king." I pause, almost unable to continue. "You took Father's love."

"You think I wanted that?" The pain is evident in Mary's voice. "You think I did that on purpose? That I left you on purpose?"

"Maybe you didn't, but Father did. Father sent me to the Low Countries to get a good education. And then to France to cultivate sophistication. Anything to compensate for the fact that I was the ugly one in the family."

"You're not ugly."

"Don't lie to me. Do you see beautiful English skin here? And lovely blonde locks? And pale, limpid eyes that reflect whatever a man wishes? No. You see sallow, swarthy skin. You see the black hair of a witch. You see a girl who should be grateful to get the attention of a waster like James Butler. Or Henry Percy."

"Believe what you like, Nan."

"It's not belief, Mary. It's the truth. I don't have to believe it. I see it every day."

"You don't know what goes on in other people's heads," she mutters. "Nobody knows."

"I can guess."

"Can you?" she asks the wall. "Can you guess that I've been told in confidence that you stir a man so greatly that he hardly dares to breathe around you? Can you guess that he will not tell you so because your opinion is so great and so fixed that he is too terrified of your rapier wit and your unguarded tongue to mention it to you?"

She turns back to me and levels her gaze.

"Can you guess that he would leave his wife for you? If only he could get a word, a look, a touch that would indicate you might feel the same way."

"Who?" And I barely manage to guard my tongue enough not to blurt out, *Thomas?*

A gust of fear pales her cheeks, and she doesn't answer.

"A man is afraid of me?" *Is it Thomas?*

"Most men are. You do tend to speak your mind."

"And they've told you this?"

"No one has to. I've observed their fear of your tongue. I've felt it myself."

A hot needle of regret runs through me, pulling behind it a thread of shame.

"I can speak indiscriminately," I admit, on the verge of apology.

"Yes, you can. But I love you anyway."

"Is it love?" I ask, attempting a tease, but wanting an answer. "Or is it loyalty?"

Mary turns away. "Call it what you will, Anne. It's what holds us together and keeps us here at court. Whether we like it or not."

45

I AVOID WYATT. I CAN'T TALK TO HIM. I CAN HARDLY THINK ABOUT him. But he watches me. I feel it. Guilt sits like a demon on my chest. Because I shut him out for Percy. And even though Percy couldn't kill our friendship, love surely could.

I ponder Mary's revelations. Butler's gossip. George's reluctance for marriage. Jane's belief in love.

I throw my emotions into my music. Only now, I find that people listen. I feel exposed. Naked. As if people are listening to my girlish fancies for the king, my weary disgust of the ongoing war with France, my frustrated affection for my family.

My feelings for the man I can't have.

I seek out quiet places, empty places. Except when Wolsey and his men are visiting. I never want to be alone with James Butler again.

One night, the queen's ladies present a musical entertainment in the king's apartments and Wolsey brings his choir to sing. The bright stars of the court attend in all their glittering sycophancy. I sit in the queen's chambers with the left-behind, the second class, and play for myself.

Quietly.

Norris sits down beside me. He has been standoffish since

my return. Now he sits stiffly. Too close, but not touching me.

"Mistress Boleyn."

"Sir Henry."

I pause.

"Are you not going to the entertainment tonight?"

"I just came from there," he tells me. "Mistress Carew was butchering a song on the virginal. I came in search of someone to distract me while I listen so my ears don't begin to bleed."

I laugh.

"A shared burden is a lesser burden?"

"True enough. Though someone should show Mistress Carew that she needn't mash the keys like a baker's boy kneading dough."

"I'm sure her enthusiasm does her credit." I attempt diplomacy. Elizabeth Carew is, after all, a distant cousin.

"I wonder at the rumors about her."

I angle my chin toward him. "Rumors?"

"That she was the king's mistress."

I arch an eyebrow. "And how does this correlate with her musical ability?" Elizabeth is prettier than I. Paler. Blonder. Kinder.

"I'd hate to think she treated him the same way she treats that instrument."

A vision of Elizabeth's fingers on flesh rather than wood and bone brings a flash of jealousy that settles quickly into a slow burn deep beneath my ribs. I raise a finger to my lips.

Norris grins.

"Will you join me, Mistress Boleyn?" He stands and holds out an arm that I can't begin to refuse.

The king's withdrawing room is crowded and smoky, the windows closed against the gathering cold of the oncoming winter. The noise is great—a bellow of gossip and whispers beating against the glass.

Norris directs me toward the back of the room, while Elizabeth Carew finishes.

"Merciful timing," he whispers, and I feel a shiver of delight. Norris is fun to flirt with. Maybe that's a good thing. Easy. Noncommittal. Not the falconlike swoops and dives of flirting with Thomas. Or the dizzy, escalating vibration of conversing with the king.

The choir launches into an old carol that has been arranged into a sweet harmony. There are twelve boys, and the music they produce is like the voices of the angels. The tallest boy— one who appears to be about to crack, his voice dismissing him from his position—sings with the most passion, as if the music itself has possessed him.

"Who is that?" I ask, pointing to the boy with the neck of my lute.

"Mark Smeaton," Norris says. "He is one of Wolsey's boys. Flemish, I think. He plays the lute, too."

I hope he plays the lute as well as he sings, because he may need it soon. I can see the strain on his face as he pushes his voice to the very edge of its capacity, the knowledge etched across his visage that soon his voice will change, and his life as well.

"I should like to hear him play," I say quietly.

"Then you shall. Come with me." He takes my hand and leads me to the front of the room, where the king sits on a little elevated platform.

"Your Majesty."

Norris bows deeply and I curtsy.

"Norris. Mistress Boleyn."

The two men exchange a look loaded with meaning.

"Mistress Boleyn would like to hear the boy Smeaton play the lute, Your Majesty."

"Have you heard of his prowess, mistress?"

"His voice is extraordinary."

"Let's hope it continues to be so after it breaks."

"Yes, Your Majesty. Even so, I had hoped he had another talent."

"I'm sure he does." Norris winks lasciviously at me over the king's shoulder.

"Sit here." I do as the king commands and I sit just below the dais. A servant brings a goblet of wine, and the king claps his hands, interrupting the choir.

"We should like to hear young Smeaton play," he says. And all the world scurries to do his bidding.

Smeaton pales just slightly—the skin stark against his dark curls—but takes the offered lute with a bow. And I see on his face a glimmer of triumph.

Wolsey stands from his chair on the other side of the king, throws me a look saturated with venom, and moves to re-arrange the choirboys, clouting one on the ear. The boy—the

307

youngest by the looks of him—visibly struggles not to cry.

Then Smeaton begins to play. His fingers move so quickly over the strings that they appear to be vibrating themselves. The music resounds throughout the silent room as the world holds its breath, willing him never to stop. When he does, the audience rises to its feet in unanimous admiration.

"What do you think, mistress?" the king asks.

I feel light-headed, as if I have just looked over the edge of a great height. "I wish I could play half as well as he. I wish I could create such beauty."

He turns to me and smiles, his eyes merry with mischief.

"Perhaps you already have."

"I think you flatter me, Your Majesty, and it doesn't suit you."

"Mistress Boleyn"—the king angles his body to face me, and everything around us disappears—"in all our lives, we hope to come across the beauty of someone who will truly change the world just by being in it. Flattery is superficial. Beauty runs deeper."

I forget all my words and wit and arguments and I look the king in the eye and say nothing. Nothing at all. I don't need to. Because crouching within the recesses of my mind—deep behind the disbelief—is the knowledge that the king is interested. In me.

"A poem!"

The room reappears with the shout, and the king turns back to the musicians with a frown. But it is not the musicians who have interrupted us.

It is Thomas. He takes the lute from Smeaton's uncertain hands and strums a handful of notes that are not a chord. Nor harmonious.

He sweeps a bow to the king and throws a quick smile in my direction. He's wearing a black doublet and sleeves, slashed with green, and he looks diabolical in the torchlight, his narrow chin and arced eyebrows adding to the illusion.

> *"Blame not my lute! For he must sound*
> *Of this or that as liketh me;*
> *For lack of wit the lute is bound*
> *To give such tunes as pleaseth me;*
> *Though my songs be somewhat strange,*
> *And speak such words as touch thy change,*
>   *Blame not my lute."*

"Somewhat strange, indeed," the king murmurs. His expression is a cross between a question and petulance. "What means this?"

> *"My lute, alas, doth not offend,*
> *Though that perforce he must agree*
> *To sound such tunes as I intend,*
> *To sing to them that heareth me—"*

Thomas turns to the entire audience, including everyone in his little oratory, but only one in his little joke.

"Then though my songs be somewhat plain,
And toucheth some that use to feign—"

Thomas pauses, his eyes fixed on me as if I am the only person in the room.

"Blame not my lute."

Thomas bows and hands the lute back to Smeaton, then exits the room.

"I do believe you are blushing, Mistress Boleyn." The coyness in Norris's voice suddenly makes me want to vomit.

I feel the king turn to look at me, feel the smile leave his face, feel the vibration that runs through me lose its hum. I feel the loss keenly.

"Please excuse me, Your Majesty," I whisper, not daring to look him in the eye. "I believe the heat in the room conspires to make me ill."

"Go, mistress."

The voice is cold, no longer flirtatious. All interest withered and gone. I curtsy and stumble from the room.

46

THE NEXT ROOM—FILLED WITH THE HANGERS-ON WHO WISHED
to be invited but instead clamor for attention separately and
alone—is even more stifling. I push through the crowd, through
the rooms and down the stairs, out of the donjon and into
the upper ward. The yard leads to the lodgings of the court.
Courtiers make secret pacts and gossip by the doors. The
cobbles clatter with moonlight. At the far end of the yard, I see
the flash of gold hair, the lightlessness of black velvet.

The moon has risen high and full, casting silver and shadow
over the trees of the great park. I follow Thomas through the
gate and down to the river walk. I gulp at air that smells like
the end of summer, the fall of leaves, and the river taking the
heat from the land.

"What was that?" I call to him.

Thomas turns, the glow of moonlight flashing on his face.

"A poem," he says soberly, walking backward like a player in
a highly choreographed masque. "A trifle. It means nothing. It
says nothing."

"Your poems always mean something, Thomas." I pursue
him, my haste and confusion making my words sharper than
I intended. "You think I don't hear you? Or are you trying to

hint that what we once pretended—what we *feigned* to be—is now real?"

He stops. Only moonlight between us.

"There is so much you don't know, Anne," he murmurs, his voice low and mellow like wine. I feel my heart beat again, as if his is speaking directly to it.

I pause. I could tease him. I could flirt. I could challenge him. But I can't.

"Then tell me."

I speak seriously. Quietly. I ask for him to spill his greatest secrets. I want to hear them. I want to tell my own.

He searches my face as if he could read there my meaning, my intention. As if he could read the future and see my reaction to whatever he might say next. I step forward, ready.

"You're heading into dangerous territory, Anne."

I watch his eyes for a hint of teasing, or a flirtatious wink. There is none.

"I told you to stay away from that family. They can't be trusted."

This I didn't expect. I expected this string—this song— between us to crescendo. But I guess he doesn't hear it, or hears another song entirely.

"What family?" I ask. But I know. He told me to stay away from the duchess. And her *brother*. Not her husband, as I originally thought.

"He holds all the cards, Anne. Cards of life and death. He will have whatever he wants, and you . . ." He stops. As if in agony. "He's your sister's lover."

The song within me ends abruptly with a discordant crash.

"Since when have you become my moral compass, Thomas Wyatt? When did you set yourself up to be my confessor? My father?"

"I'd like to offer some advice."

"No!" My voice pitches higher. "I think you've offered enough. I'm sick of your infuriating rules."

Tears prick at the corners of my eyes. My year at Hever has made me maudlin.

"I'm sick of you," I lie.

Thomas steps between me and the castle gate and any who watch through it, blocking their view of me. Blocking my voice from them, always aware of the ears and eyes of the court.

"You're making a show of yourself," he whispers, his breath quieter than the breeze on my hair.

"I'm always being criticized, Thomas. By you and everyone else. Told who I can or can't speak to. Be with. What I should look like. I need to be more like everyone else. I need to be seen but not heard. I need to marry a man of my father's choosing and disappear into oblivion."

"No!"

Thomas grabs my wrists and squeezes until I look him in the eye. He's staring at me so intensely that the moon appears to be peering out of him.

"No, Anne. You are better than that. You are not meant to be shackled to a man who binds you into his own perfect image. You don't want to be known throughout your days as Anne

Percy. Or Anne Butler. Or Anne the king's concubine. You are Anne! Anne Boleyn."

"I won't be when I marry."

"Then don't."

I laugh then.

"Don't be ridiculous, Thomas. My family won't take care of me forever—no matter how closely the Boleyns stick together. My father looks forward to the day he can foist my expenses off on a rich and profitable husband. Someone who will give back what I've taken for so many years. He'd never pay a living for a single woman forever."

"You can't live your life being somebody else."

"But that's exactly what you asked of me. To do only as you say."

"I thought I had your best interests at heart." He steps closer. "But now I see that I really only followed my own interests."

Still not a tease. Nor a flirtation. This is truth.

"What are your interests, Thomas?"

He doesn't speak, and it's as if we're frozen, our breath stoppered by moonlight. The strand of melody between us singing silently.

"I will not blame your lute," I finally whisper. "I hear the tune, but I do not know the words."

His eyes flicker back and forth between mine. Searching. My hands are still wrapped in his, pressed between us.

One step closer, and our bodies will touch. One word, and I will be his.

"What do you want, Thomas?"

"Money."

Thomas drops my hands and steps away. We both look to see my brother venture out of the shadows.

"George."

There is warning in Thomas's voice. And something else. Something that almost sounds like fear.

George walks toward us, and I can see how hard he concentrates on walking a straight line.

"Why are you here, George?" I ask.

"To stop you from causing more of a scene than you already have, Sister. Flirting with the king. Leaving in a rush after a . . . a . . . *poet*." The mocking twist to his mouth has returned. The look that says he has found a way to triumph. To disburden himself of Father's disappointment because someone else can carry that mantle.

"Thomas is my friend."

But Thomas has taken another step back. The distance feels farther than that between Hever and Allington. Between England and France.

"That's not possible, Anne. I think you know that. Thomas Wyatt is not your friend. He never was."

"When I returned to court, everyone ignored me, even you, George. You claimed I did nothing but embarrass you. Father was away and Mary was otherwise occupied. Thomas was the only one who helped me. He steadied me. Kept me sane. Got me noticed."

"Yes." George nods. "Got you noticed. That was the point."

His wide mouth has grown even wider. The grin bares all of his teeth, like a snarl.

"The point?" I glance at Thomas. His face is closed. I turn back to George, who snarls again. "The point of what?"

"The point of the bet."

The earth falls away beneath me, and the trees along the river close in, looming black and heavy against the sky, spinning like a night full of wine. My lips go numb.

"What bet?"

"George." Thomas speaks in barely a whisper. As if he hasn't the strength to protest.

"The one I made with Wyatt. I said over cards one night that no one could ever make a lady out of my awkward little outspoken sister. Wyatt said he could. So I set him a challenge."

"What kind of a challenge?"

I ask this of Thomas, who seems to be rendered immobile. And speechless, for once.

"That he could make you the court darling," George says. "That men would want to pay you suit."

And he laughs. He's enjoying this.

I have to struggle to make myself heard over the roaring in my ears. "How much did you bet?"

I step closer to Thomas, look him directly in the eye. I cannot read what he's thinking. My heart no longer feels the beat of his.

"And what did you do with the money?"

"He never got it," George scoffs. As if just the two of us are having this discussion. As if Thomas isn't even here.

"Why not?" I don't turn away from Thomas's eyes. I already know the answer.

"Because he didn't win."

47

I AM UNFETTERED. UNBOUND. FLASH-DIVING TOWARD THE earth, which reaches for me with the greedy talons of nightmare. I sway and stop myself against a tree. Even George is quiet. The night is a held breath.

Thomas's expression is creeping off his face, leaving him blank and flat as water beneath the fog, his eyes importunate. Confirming everything.

"Anne . . ."

"No." I straighten and move away from both of them. "No. Neither of you has the right to speak to me. Neither of you has the right to say another word."

I turn and walk down toward the river, blind in the darkness, stumbling over the lifting of roots and stones. Grasses tangle my skirts, and branches tear at my hair. I will sleep in the reeds. I will sleep on the grass of the hillside and drink in the moonlight, be given magical powers to destroy my enemies.

I will lose myself.

I will lose them.

George's laughter follows me. I taste its bitterness on my tongue.

So I turn back. I will not run away. I am not in the wrong. I will not let either of them win.

George stumbles to the courtyard gate, abandoning me. But Thomas watches me. Sees me turn. He strides down the hill toward me. I do not slow down but rush up the hill to meet him.

"Please, Anne. Please let me explain."

I am downslope of him, looking even farther than usual up into his face. But my wrath makes me a giantess. Fearsome.

"There is nothing to explain, Thomas. And nothing you can say that I will believe. Your words are no more meaningful than a castle manufactured from sugar paste. It may look beautiful, it may taste sweet, but in the end, it crumbles and melts and becomes nothing. It cannot sustain a person, and only serves to blacken the teeth and coat the tongue."

"You deserve better."

"*Yes*, I deserve better, Thomas! To you, I am nothing. I am a fabrication. I am nothing but a filthy gamble. And I deserve to be more than that."

"You are more. I didn't know you then, Anne. All I knew was that you had returned from France. You were opinionated and clever and impolitic and different. George wanted you to listen and follow and be discreet and fit in. I thought I could do that. I thought I could . . ."

"You thought to win money off my brother and my virginity off of me. You thought it would be fun."

"Yes."

"You would get me my place at court. You would introduce

me to the most influential men. You would take me to bed. You would move on. Dispose of me like so much refuse."

"Yes. That's what I thought."

"But Percy beat you to it." I fight hard against the tears that threaten to engulf me. "You humiliated me. Made a project of me. A failed project."

"I am sorry."

The apology makes me stutter to a halt. Because I almost think he means it. Because it doesn't make me feel superior to him, not like he said. It makes me feel small and trapped, like a frightened animal.

"It's too late."

He should have told me before. If he truly was my friend, we could have won the bet together. But he is not. I want to throw his apology back in his face, to see if he really means it.

I watch him carefully. "I think you're just sorry that you didn't win."

"I'm sorry for so much more."

"Such as?"

He's holding something back. He's still lying.

"I care about you, Anne."

He won't even look at me. His eyes are raised to the sky and his lips are pushed together in a flat line.

"And you're sorry for that? Thank you, Thomas. That makes me feel better."

"You're making this harder!"

"Good!" I shout, not caring who hears or who looks or who

writes down every bloody word. "I hope I make your life a fraction of the misery mine is. I hope you feel the frustration and
the anger and the agony, Wyatt!"

My voice catches and I gulp back a sob. I will not let him
win. I straighten my shoulders and take a deep breath.

"I thought you were my friend."

The words come without my bidding them. Stupid. I can't
let him think I care. I need him far, far away. It hurts too much.

"I can't be your friend, Anne."

Thomas's voice is barely a whisper. Perhaps I've confused it
with the murmur of the wind in the grass.

"What?" I ask, not wanting to know, not wanting to hear.
"What did you say?"

"I said I can't be your friend."

He still won't look me in the eye.

"Why? Because you believe, as George does, that men and
women can't be friends? That I will try to control you? That I'll
make you into some kind of effeminate fool who can't carry a
lance or drink himself under the table?"

He doesn't answer.

"Or is it because you desire me?" I pursue angrily. "Because
that's the other reason George gives. He says a man and woman
can't really be friends because the man will forever be wondering what she's like in bed. Imagining her naked."

Thomas groans.

"The man will become overwrought with jealousy when the
woman marries. But you, Wyatt. No. You don't feel that way.

You flirt with one half of the queen's maids and fuck the other half, but you only ever saw me as a project. A means to an end. An object. A prize."

"That's not true, Anne."

"Then what am I, Thomas? What am I to you? I'm nothing. So you get nothing from me. No favor to carry into your ridiculous mock battles. No fodder for your overwrought poetry. And certainly no friendship, Thomas. Because I think I finally agree with my brother. It's impossible."

"What can I do, Anne?"

"Just go away."

"I don't want to lose you." The words are ensnared in his doublet as he hangs his head.

"You already have."

He bites his lip. "Anne." His gaze lifts from the grass and roots beneath our feet and he looks right at me. Eyes the color of the sea at sunrise, the color of what used to be friendship.

Thomas squares his shoulders. Straightens his spine. Takes a deep breath. Just like my father taught me. When he exhales, his breath is a silver tissue of brume in air just beginning to frost.

He looks at me steadily. Doesn't say a word. Waits a beat. He is a master of timing. I know it. He taught it to me.

I don't want to wait for what he has to say for himself, what he thinks will make a difference between us. But I can't move.

"I love you."

My heart lurches forward as if reaching for him through my rib cage. I take a step back to prevent it from doing so. For once, the words that form of their own accord and spill from me without thought will not be uttered.

I shake my head.

Thomas closes the gap between us and kisses me. Hard. This is not wet and sloppy like his playful kisses. Or dry and desperate like Percy's. Or teasing like the king's.

No. This kiss is eloquent and alive and speaks directly to my soul. My heart ruptures, and the splinters freeze and tumble all around us with the musical sound of broken glass.

I place my hands on his chest, feeling the pulse of his heart beneath my fingertips.

And I push.

Thomas stumbles back, off-balance.

"Don't," I gasp.

I turn.

And run.

48

The entire court takes on a hue of unreality: the women in their gaudy dresses with their strident voices and overly exaggerated gestures, the men with their dizzying doublets and straight, stuffy gaits. Everything is too clear, too sharp, the movements too jerky.

And it is all so suffocatingly close.

Everything within me pulls in different directions. It's like I'm a piece of linen, washed, boiled, beaten, stretched. Everything happening at once, and everything fighting against itself, threatening to kill me by degrees.

He lied to me.

He loves me.

Mercifully alone, I writhe in my bed from the pain of it all, like some unmade creature shedding its skin. My life is nothing but a game. I am nothing but a single, low-ranked card. Played and spent. A . . . nothing.

I have been defined by others. By my father and his cold disappointment. By my brother and his wily manipulation. By France. By Thomas Wyatt.

Thomas built me in his image. I want to strip away the paint and gilt and discover what is underneath. If anything.

I slide from my bed and stand on shaky legs, a fawn newly born. A fledgling.

I kneel in my room and make a pledge to myself never again to let anyone tell me what to do. Anyone. Not my fiancé. Not my husband. Not my father or my brother. Not society. I will rule myself.

I pull out my book of hours, the book Mary gave me for Christmas. I am more like Mary than I ever thought possible, pleasing others at the expense of being myself. The book's beautiful illuminations glow faintly in the candlelight. I turn the page to the miniature of the Last Judgment.

I will no longer be judged by the standards of others. I will judge myself. I will not live by someone else's rules. I will make my own.

I pick up my quill and write *Le temps viendra*. The time will come.

I sit back on my heels.

"I am not nothing," I say to the empty room. "And I refuse to be nothing. I will become someone, Thomas Wyatt. Without you. I will be more than you. You will not shape me. Because I have a shape of my own."

I pick up the quill again, dip it in the ink. Hesitate. Then I bring it back to the paper.

Je—

I stop.

What am I? I cast my mind into the future. Seeking light. Enlightenment.

I sketch an astrolabe, a tool used predict the movement of

the moon and stars. To predict the future. And I know. I want to be heard. I want to be seen. I want to be remembered. As me.

Anne Boleyn.

The ink seeps into the page. Permanent.

I am me.

I own me.

I will not be held to earth by someone else's tether.

I will let go of the past.

And I will start with Thomas Wyatt.

49

I CANNOT LIVE IN THE SAME HOUSE WITH HIM. EVEN ONE THE size of Windsor Castle. I cannot bear to see him or hear his voice.

I cannot stand the treacherous, feeble thing within me that suffers from his presence. I have to make him go away.

So with a half-formed plan in mind, and a heart full of caustic bitterness, I go to the one person I know who has enough power and enough cunning to do it for me. A person who has no qualms about manipulating the lives of others.

"Father."

Father doesn't look up from his papers. As usual.

One day, I will escape his disappointment. I will find a way for him to respect me—a girl—even if it kills me.

"Father."

"I know you're there, Anne. Allow me to finish."

One day, I will keep him waiting.

"Father."

"Anne!" he barks. "You obviously do not realize how much work goes into being a diplomat during times of war. It actually requires effort. Not sitting around singing and playing cards like a maid-in-waiting. No, being an ambassador means

I have to concentrate and write letters and make decisions. Something you wouldn't understand because you simply follow your whims without regard to the consequences."

He is right. I act and speak before thinking. But I do regard the consequences, because I have to live with them. And I know exactly what it means to be a diplomat in times of war. I am at war within the court itself. A war of attrition.

He throws his quill into the inkpot with a vicious thrust.

"Now. What requires my attention so badly? A new gown? The loss of a slipper? Lute strings?"

I glare at him, but he's too busy shuffling papers to see me.

"All my family ever does is ask for more money," he mutters.

"Father"—I manage to keep my voice calm—"I have no need for extra allowance."

"That's good because I have no extra to share. My family has depleted my treasury. All of my funds. I send money to your mother for gowns and baubles and gifts though it serves no purpose. I never see her. And you! I maintain two households so you can fritter away your time in the country. Your brother spends a fortune on women and wine and is nothing but a joke in the king's service. Worthless. The way you all live is prodigal, even for court. Why, when I first married your mother, we lived on fifty pounds a year. A *year*. And she brought another mouth to feed every six months."

His voice slows down over the course of this speech, and I see that he isn't even thinking about what he's saying, much less conscious of my presence in front of him.

"That's physically impossible, Father."

The words are out before I can stop them. I don't care. I know for a fact there were two years between each of us, including the two baby boys memorialized in the churches at Hever and Penshurst.

"Nine, then." He taps his index finger to a passage on the letter he's reading, his focus fully occupied by it. He doesn't listen even when I point out he's a fool.

I see how I can turn his complaining into a weapon against him. I see the perfect opportunity to present my scheme to him, before the idea fully takes shape.

"Father, I'm concerned about your workload. I wondered if someone else might help carry that burden."

"Are you thinking of becoming a diplomat?" he asks with a curl to his lip. He studies me slowly, taking in my long sleeves and my French hood, then cocks his head to the side with a knowing look. "You have to conform to be a diplomat. Blend in."

"Thank you, Father, for thinking I'm capable enough that only my attire bars me from a post," I say, trying to keep the ice from my voice. "It is not myself I wish to put forward, but a friend." Not a friend. I cross my fingers against the lie.

"Oh?"

"Do you not think our old neighbor, Thomas Wyatt, would make a good diplomat? He definitely knows how to blend in. He speaks excellent French. Everyone likes him." Except me.

Father looks at me. I cross the fingers of my other hand.

"You're right, of course," he says with a nod. "You always were a perceptive girl."

A compliment. Fancy that.

"Thank you, Father."

I offer a little curtsy.

"I shall mention it to the king."

"You know Sir Henry Wyatt, as well. He can be very persuasive." In a harsh, critical, demanding sort of way.

"I shall mention it to Sir Henry, as well," Father says decisively, as if it is his idea. Simple.

"Thomas mentioned he always wanted to go abroad."

I squeeze my fingers so tightly I stop the blood. Thomas loves England.

"Did he now?"

"And he admires you so." I can't feel my fingertips.

Father preens.

It is so simple. Which must be why I feel I am diving off a cliff. Simple—and dangerous.

"I'll see what I can do," Father says.

Father can be very persuasive as well. Thomas Wyatt is as good as gone.

And Thomas certainly won't make Father's life easier.

Two birds. One small stone. But the one time my father hears my words is the one time I wish I could take them back.

I turn to leave, certain that my father has forgotten about me entirely. But his voice cuts the air just as I start through the doorway.

"I know what you're doing."

I almost trip because I stop midstride.

"Seeking preferment for your lovers is commonplace at

court, Anne," he says. I don't turn, but I can hear that he speaks to his papers. He doesn't raise his head. "You just don't want it to ruin you. It's the best thing for you that Thomas Wyatt leave court. That he no longer drag your name through his own muck. That's why I will do this, Anne. Not to lighten my workload."

I don't even attempt to tell him that Thomas is not my lover and never will be. My father believes what he will.

"Just don't mourn his absence." One last piece of fatherly advice.

"I won't." This lie is the hardest to tell.

Because I already am.

Greenwich Palace
1524

50

THE CHRISTMAS SEASON HURTLES TOWARD US WITH PLANS FOR another of King Henry's lavish entertainments. *The Castle of Loyalty—The Château Blanc.* There will be a pageant on the tiltyard. Chivalric oratory and romantic ballads. There will be a tournament of jousting and swordplay and feats of archery. And there will be a great battle over the Château Blanc itself.

In a court obsessed with symbolism, the Château Blanc can stand for many things: Loyalty. Integrity. Trust. Devotion to king and country. Purity.

Virginity.

Unexpectedly, I am one of the four maidens chosen to occupy it. We are given the keeping of the castle, but in reality, we are just ornamentation.

Something over which the men can fight.

The good news is that if I'm meant to represent virginity, perhaps Butler isn't spreading his vicious gossip. Or no one believes him.

The bad news is that Thomas Wyatt is among the men chosen to safeguard the castle. No one else seems to recognize the irony that the man who is rumored to have stolen many a maiden's virginity now rushes to its defense.

And when Henry Percy is selected for the assault, I begin to think I am the butt of an elaborate joke. I would blame George, but he is too busy making merry to conceal his disappointment at not being picked for either side.

I try to console myself with the honor of being chosen at all. And I am determined not to repeat my personal disaster from *The Château Vert*.

The men of the court throw themselves tirelessly into the tactics and technical details of this false war because the real war—the war against the French—has to be suspended due to winter weather.

The king will lead the challengers—symbolically putting to the test the loyalty and integrity of his men. He spends countless hours designing ingenious siege engines that will breach the castle defenses, mechanisms to vault the fifteen-foot ditches and elude the great rollers at every entrance that can unbalance an attacker at the slightest touch.

The strategy and avidity applied to this game only serve to make me hope more fervently that they are never applied against the French.

Even so, I, too, feel the hunger for battle. I wish I could pick up a sword and descend with all my fury into the breach. Wyatt. Percy. George. Father. All of them would feel the power of my wrath.

But no. I sit and sew. While Wyatt helps to oversee the construction of a wooden castle out on the tiltyard, I embroider a thousand tiny gold stitches to create the ridiculous emblems on the pageant banners. The castle could probably withstand an actual assault. I feel my defenses weakening every day, every time I see him.

While he is fitted for new armor, I sew dozens of seed pearls onto a pale-blue bodice. Pearls are a symbol of the feminine, of women. And women are the ones considered to be fragile and mercurial. Weak. But pearls are also a symbol of the never-ending cycle and so represent unending loyalty. The cycle I see in the court is not one of loyalty, but one of distortion. Manipulation. Self-obsession.

I guess I fit in well.

The slippery smoothness of the pearls reminds me of the night Thomas came to my bedchamber in Hever. How his hand held mine, interlaced with pearls. How he soothed away my dream. How I felt that I belonged there.

I think I knew then that he loved me. I just didn't know he had already betrayed me.

The pageant begins on Saint Thomas's Day, a day swamped in symbolism. Thomas the doubter, who would not believe in the resurrection until given physical proof. His saint's day is the shortest of the year, the day that night engulfs the earth.

Countless candles and torches are lit in the great hall to dispel the darkness, belching soot and vapors to the ceiling, the dragons of the court circling below. A clamor of trumpets and the bellow of canon fire from outside announce the commencement of the festivities. A herald enters, carrying a placard painted with the symbols and colors of the castle and its defenders.

I stand to one side, shoulder to shoulder with Jane.

The king is up on a dais, sitting in an intricately carved chair with gilded armrests and a velvet cushion. The cloth of state is canopied over him, gold embroidered with Tudor roses.

Energy radiates off of him like a cataract. He is insatiable. Unstoppable. No effort has been spared in this production. It's like he has something to prove, something to win.

He leans forward slightly, ready to pounce.

He is looking at me.

I reach for Jane's hand, and she squeezes mine.

Before the herald can issue the challenge, the king stands and strides to the edge of the dais. He towers over the throng, and the herald—who is young and visibly intimidated—is rendered speechless.

He is supposed to announce us—the four maidens—so the king can challenge the defenders. It will be a contest over who will be our champions. But if there is no announcement, there is no contest.

I step forward, tugging Jane with me. A rustling murmur rises around us, lapping to the far corners of the room.

"Impudent."

"Presumptuous."

"Brazen."

I ignore the whispers, propelled forward by the eagerness in the king's countenance.

"Before you stand four maidens," I begin.

The herald shudders and steps in front of me. I fight the urge to kick him.

"Before you stand four virgins," he squeaks. Behind the king, Henry Percy looks like he has swallowed a toad.

Jane squeezes my hand. "The king hasn't taken his eyes off of you," she whispers as the herald lays out all the details of the challenge. "What did you call him? Delicious? It looks like he could say the same thing about you."

I raise my eyes back to the king's, and all of my bones vibrate with the hum coming off of him. His expression is volatile. Covetous. Hungry.

"Who defends these maidens?" he asks, glancing at the herald and then about the room. "Their integrity? Their purity?"

He looks back at me. "Their beauty?"

He raises his voice, and it echoes in the silent room. "Who defends the Château Blanc?"

Fifteen men step forward. All of them are young, in their teens or barely out of them. These men—these *boys*—have never been to war. They have never faced a siege. But I can see in their faces that they are ready to. Ready to protect. Ready to prove themselves. Ready to go to war in one way or another.

Thomas strides to the forefront, cutting off Leonard Grey, the captain of their phalanx. I grip Jane's hand to prevent myself from running.

"We will defend the castle and these maidens," Thomas says, and glances once between me and the king.

He pauses. Takes a deep breath.

"And we defend against all comers."

51

THE KING IS LIVID. FOLLOWING THE PAGEANT'S ANNOUNCEMENT, it is discovered that the siege engines he designed have been constructed incompetently. His martial fervor has been quashed by the ineptitude of English carpenters. Everything he hoped for has fallen apart. The carpenters flee before his wrath, and courtiers scramble to fill the void. Jesters. Musical entertainments. Gifts.

Christmas Day is celebrated beneath this cloud—a fog of waiting and desperation.

And then it is announced that the tournament is to go ahead as planned. On the day of another Saint Thomas: December 29, when Thomas Becket was murdered by the knights of a different King Henry for defying royal wishes. The siege of the castle will be postponed.

The morning dawns bright and cold. Frost tinges the trees and runs up the hill all the way to Duke Humphrey's Tower. The cold makes the outlines of everything stark and hard-edged but subdues the colors to a wash—like silks left too long in the rain.

The castle stands to one side. Its walls of wood and fabric and the crenellated battlements, braced and whitewashed, are a simulation of invulnerability. But for today, that conception will remain unchallenged.

George sidles up to me shoulder to shoulder, looking in the same direction. I have not spoken to him. I will not speak to him.

"Ah, the imagery," George sighs. "The Castle of Loyalty cannot be broken by any of the king's devisings."

I keep my silence.

"And the maidens it protects remain unspoiled."

"I wonder, though," he says, quietly enough that only I will hear. And I am lost in the wary darkness of his eyes. "Do its defenders realize the extent of the pretense? For virginity lost needs no protection."

I turn on him, ready to do battle myself. I don't care if the whole court watches. He sees my movement. His eyes go wide, and he takes a swift step back onto Jane.

"Ow!"

George spins and catches Jane before she falls. His grace is barely marred by his early-morning inebriation, and he manages to keep his balance and hers. Her fingers clench on the muscles of his arms and then she goes a little limp.

"I'm sorry," she says, breathless.

"No, forgive me, fair damsel," he says, tugs her upright, and braces her before stepping away.

Jane giggles.

He spins on his toe, back to us, ramrod straight.

"I go to survey your lodgings. Inspect your Castle of Virginity."

Jane presses both hands across her mouth to disguise her giggles as shock.

He waves a dismissive hand at me and walks away. Jane watches every move he makes.

"He's very charming."

"He's maddening."

Jane studies George from beneath the gable of her hood. She looks the very model of the ingenue courtier, the virginal maid-in-waiting watching her knight on the field of battle, just like in a romantic ballad.

I take a deep breath, square my shoulders, and stand next to her. I suppress an inward curl of pain, knowing she loves him, that the marriage agreement is signed. That she is consigned to her romantic fate that cannot—will not—end well. My brother is a lost cause. She says nothing. I say nothing. And we watch, shoulder to shoulder.

Suddenly the field goes silent. The men stop shouting. The women stop gossiping. Even the horses stop clanking their armor. All we can hear is the snap of the banners in the breeze.

The queen enters the viewing tower, and we bow as she makes her way to her gilded chair. She seems even more tired than usual. Stooped. Sad.

A cannon fires and the defenders enter the field fully armed, six of them charging across the drawbridge of the counterfeit castle. The crowd roars its approval. I know which one is Thomas by the way he rides, the way his body moves. I grip the rail of the viewing platform with both hands, caught in the still point between running toward him and running away.

Jane catches my eye, but says nothing.

A sudden silence from the audience turns me back to the field. The defenders have adjourned to one end of the lists. And at the other end, two ladies enter on horseback—ladies I've never met or even seen. Veils hide their faces. Their hair is perfectly coiffed beneath French hoods. They look awkward on their palfreys, shifting in their skirts and sidesaddles.

They lead chargers carrying two old men whose silver hair and beards shine in the shifting light. The men's robes are purple damask. The vibration starts deep in my chest. Even grizzled and disguised, I know him. He is a head taller than the rest of the men at court, his shoulders so broad that even when stooped, he looks majestic.

The queen narrows her eyes.

The two ladies ride directly to the queen and bow as best they can. One nearly topples, and some of the men in the stands laugh. Then the tallest lady hands a rolled parchment up to the queen's usher. As the man unrolls it, I watch the lady. She sits back on her saddle. Scratches under one arm.

That is no lady.

It's Mark Smeaton.

"'Youth has left these ancient knights,'" the usher reads. "'And yet courage and goodwill are with them, obliging them to break spears, if the queen is pleased to give them license.'"

The taller of the "ancient" knights scans the crowd. I follow his gaze as he examines each face quickly and then moves on. He's looking for someone. I straighten my spine, take a deep breath, and wait. When he finds me, I don't look away, nor do I curtsy.

I am not being disrespectful. For the sake of the sham, we both have to pretend he is nothing but an old man. The brim of his shapeless cap dips low over his gray eyes.

But they remain on me.

"You look too old and infirm to challenge the young men of the court." The queen sounds weary, as if she is tired of the games and the pageantry, the disguises and the trickery that can go on behind them. "I should hate to send you to your destruction and humiliation."

"We shall do our best to avoid that, Your Majesty." The knight sounds irritable as he turns and bows to her.

"I praise your courage, sir," the queen says carefully, "and I grant you the right to challenge any and all in the competitions today. May luck be with you."

"Thank you, Your Majesty." The knight pulls away the silver beard. He throws off his robe. Beneath it he wears a gorgeous doublet of white silk and cloth of silver that turns his chest into a broad, shining expanse, upon which shines a gold-embroidered heart, bisected.

The other knight removes his disguise to reveal Charles Brandon, Duke of Suffolk. The duchess rolls her eyes, but raises two fingers, kisses them, and extends them toward him.

Cheers erupt from the stands and the air reverberates with the stamping of feet and pounding of fists. The men already on the field quickly rush to welcome the newcomers.

Wyatt grins and clasps hands with the king—a gesture

of goodwill before the hostilities begin. Eye to eye with the greatest man in the kingdom—possibly in the world—Thomas appears perfectly at ease. I think about his arm around me, about the kiss of his words on my neck.

As if he can hear me thinking about him, Thomas looks up and offers a smile that dives straight to my heart and plucks it from me.

I press my thoughts deep beneath my ribs and pull out the ragged memories of his duplicity. Of every time he hinted seduction. Of every compliment he ever paid me. Lies and betrayal to win a bet.

Then I see the emblem emblazoned on his chest. A heart bisected.

I turn away and lean with my back against the partition. It's like he's still trying to win. But is he trying to win the bet? Or me?

Jane looks me full in the face—her expression an exposed question.

"They wear the same emblem," she murmurs. "The king and Thomas Wyatt. An open heart."

I close my eyes.

"An open heart," I repeat. "Or a broken one."

52

THE KING AND DUKE FIGHT SAVAGELY, AS IF THEY ARE TRULY AT war, and their very lives depend on their winning. During the tourney, the king attacks Anthony Browne with such determination that I'm afraid he'll take Browne's head off.

Needless to say, the defenders of Loyalty don't stand a chance.

After the tournament, the entire court moves indoors, where the ladies must provide the entertainment. The mass of sweaty men and overly perfumed women fills the great hall of the palace with strangling odors and a miasma of smoke and steam rising from damp doublets. The men cannot let go of their bellicosity, and the atmosphere is one of frenzied carousal and blistering self-importance.

The herald enters, leading the defeated defenders, the crowd parting before them, cheering and jeering and making ribald remarks about loyalty, virginity, and sexual prowess.

But when the king is announced, all banter ceases. The men always bridle their vulgarity when he's around. The room sinks to its knees as he walks to the dais and turns to face us.

"Let the defenders of the Château Blanc—the defenders of Loyalty—approach."

The defenders kneel before him. All part of the pageant.

"What say you?" the king asks. "Do you have a spokesman?"

The men hang their heads and glance at one another from the corners of their eyes.

"Thomas Wyatt?"

There is an edge to the king's voice. He is less jovial.

A hush follows. Thomas raises his head, and the two look at each other for a long moment.

"Rise."

Thomas stands, his stillness counterpoint to the king's undeniable energy.

"What say you?" the king asks. "In your defense of Loyalty? Of the maidens?"

"The maidens survived the day with the purity of their characters and persons intact," Thomas says, his eyes never leaving the king's, his expression grave.

The king smiles. Just a little. "Thanks to the decency and rectitude of the challengers."

"As you say, Your Majesty." Thomas pauses. "But the Castle of Loyalty survives intact, undisturbed by any assault. The maidens in question remain ours to defend."

It's a direct challenge, faulting the king for being unable to attack the castle. The king seethes.

Thomas waits a moment more, eyes never leaving the king's face.

"The maidens remain ours to entertain."

I can see the king's jaw working, the spark of ferocity in his eyes. The court holds its breath, waiting for the ax to fall.

"That will remain a subject for debate," the king says tightly. Then he relaxes visibly, as if by great internal effort. "However, as a show of goodwill, I submit that you shall start the dance, Master Wyatt. Whom do you wish to partner?"

Thomas doesn't hesitate.

"Your Majesty, I wish to dance with Mistress Anne Boleyn."

The king stills, just for a moment, then nods his assent.

Thomas turns, his movements loose and graceful. But I can see the calculation in them, the tension in his shoulders, the hesitation in his stride. He's afraid I'll run away. Make fools of us both.

But I can't run away. My body senses his—as if his is the note that will complete a chord, and mine waits for that note to be struck.

The rest of the court melts away. For once, I have no idea what other people are thinking. Whether they see me. If they comment on the fact that I cannot break away from Thomas's gaze.

Behind those eyes, I know a mind is working. I know he is planning, calculating. I know he chooses his words carefully. I know his mind runs to poetry.

And poetry can't be trusted.

"Are you still not speaking to me?"

I find I cannot speak. My mind and heart and body are all at odds. All I can do is shake my head.

His hand touches mine and sends a cascade of sensation all the way down my arm. And I don't know if the music comes from the musicians or from us. But we move to it. With it.

Through it. As if we were formed as two, matched, and became one.

I don't want this. This feeling of completion.

We turn in the dance, my back to him. He takes one step too close, and I feel the length of him against me, like when we were in Hever.

"A man could get lost in you, Anne Boleyn," he whispers, and we are separated by the dance.

I feel as if I have taken flight, as if my body is not my own, as if I have no past. The music pours through me. I want this. This moment. This man.

When we return to each other, palm pressed to palm, he says, "The king is watching you."

It sends me crashing back to earth. And I hear a vivid, reverberating hum shimmer through me. Undeniable. I want that, too.

I look up into Thomas's eyes and see all air and ocean there.

"So are you," I tell him.

The words slip out. A flirtation.

Triumph shines in his two-dimpled smile. I spoke to him. What am I doing? He lied to me. What guarantee do I have that he'll not lie to me again? The only certainty is that we can never be together because even though he left his wife, he's still married. With Thomas Wyatt, all I can ever be is a mistress. Disposable.

But he makes me feel indispensible when he looks at me. When he speaks to me. "Then he's watching both of us."

I have to turn. To look.

The king stands on his dais, looking out over the crush of people. In the dim and smoky light of the hall, his gray eyes are dark and piercing. Directed at me.

His very stillness vibrates.

I break away from Thomas, bow my head, and curtsy.

Thomas's hand slides down my arm and grips my fingers. The king's eyes flicker once to our hands, once to Thomas, and back to me.

The room grows so hot the very walls could melt. Outside, the wind rages, the ice breaks upon the Thames, the beasts cower in their forest lairs, and people die from cold and starvation. But inside Greenwich, men grow fat and red in the face, the ladies grow light-headed, and the music plays on.

"You should go."

Thomas's voice is toneless.

"If you disappear, he'll want you more."

"The king? That's ridiculous." But something tugs at the corner of my mind. The king flirted with me. The king looked for me, challenged the defenders of my castle. His symbol is an open heart.

"Not so ridiculous, Anne," Thomas says soberly. "After all, that was the plan. It's the way the game works. When a deer is spotted, the hunters follow."

"And you're the white flag on my tail."

"I used to be quite crude."

"You are quite crude. No need for past tense."

"Don't tease me, Anne. There is so much I did wrong. The worst was to underestimate you."

I want his words to be enough for me to forgive him. I'm just not sure they are.

"So what next, Thomas?" I ask. "You set yourself up to rival the king? Another challenge? Don't you see how ludicrous that is?"

Even if he is interested, it's impossible. He's married. And I need a friend, not a hunter. Not a man I can't have.

"Why? Because he always wins? Not this time, Anne."

He takes one step closer.

"You love me," he says, so quietly I feel he is lodged within my soul. "I know you do."

"You certainly think a lot of yourself, Thomas Wyatt."

"I know you better than I know myself." He looks up, his expression wary. "He's coming. Go now."

I squeeze Thomas's hand once and let go.

"No."

Because the time has come. Not the time to follow his direction, but for Anne Boleyn to decide her own actions.

53

THE EXPRESSION ON THE KING'S FACE ALMOST SHATTERS MY resolve. I see reflected there my own desires—my childish longings from when I first saw him. In him I see a beginning. Possibility.

Thomas bows beside me and I sink into a curtsy.

"Loyalty has taken a beating this evening," the king says. The edge is there in his voice, his words directed at Thomas.

"Metaphorically speaking, Your Majesty," I say. "The loyalty of your people will never falter."

"Even those who are called more French than the French?"

Looking at him is like trying to look at the sun. Blinding me to everything else in the room. I can't even hear the music anymore. There is nothing but him.

"I appreciate French culture, Your Majesty." I falter, unable to think of anything clever to say.

"As do I, Mistress Boleyn. Grace, beauty, art, and music. I steal as much as I can. Because it's wasted on the French."

He moves closer, bending slightly, immersing me in sensation. The glitter of gold, the scent of cloves, the memory of his lips pressed to mine. The taste of his tongue.

"Beauty, especially, is wasted on them," he murmurs.

"And what makes you say that?" I tilt my chin. The best angle for him to kiss me if he wishes.

"If they appreciated it, they would never have let you go."

For the first time in my life, I feel that I am beautiful. The warmth that cascades through me is not a blush. Guiltily, I recognize it as not embarrassment but a rush of sudden desire.

"Will you dance with me?"

"Of course, Your Majesty."

The distance between us creates a cushion, one that allows me to breathe, to think. Of Mary. Of wounding her yet again. And of Thomas.

But then the king takes my hand in his, and all thought is lost. As we dance, each touch is like a miniature lightning strike, every parting a vacuum.

I hear George start singing in the corner, leading a group of men in an off-key rendition of "Anguished Grief," Gilles Binchois's singularly memorable tune marred only by the joyless lyrics of the Christine de Pisan poem. George stumbles about in mock torment, giddy from laughing at love.

"Interesting that your paramour is not with your brother. For Thomas Wyatt would normally be at the forefront of such a crowd. Perhaps the dart of love has actually pierced his heart."

"I'm not sure anything can pierce his heart." But as I say it, a sliver of doubt pierces mine. And guilt.

The king laughs—a sound like bells. And all else is erased. We turn away from each other in the dance, and when we come back together, the king pulls me just a little bit closer. His touch is so sure, his gaze mesmerizing.

I wonder wildly what perception his fingers could incite on the skin of my back or along the hollows of my ribs. Then shame, in the image of Mary, crashes through me, followed swiftly by jealousy that she has already experienced that touch.

"A woman such as yourself deserves more than a man like Thomas Wyatt."

Another blow of contrition, and a glimmer of anger. My family has never acknowledged that I'm anything more than a child. Not my father, nor my brother. Certainly not Mary. And Thomas treated all our interactions as a game, though not a childish one.

"I shall just have to keep looking, then."

The intensity of his gaze flares, the heat of it reflected beneath my ribs like fire on glass.

"You may not have to look far."

I stumble, and he catches me easily with one hand, pulls me into the crook of his arm.

"No need to be afraid of me, Nan."

I take a deep breath.

"I'm not afraid, Your Majesty."

I look at him directly. Douse the intoxicating heat. Tell myself it's impossible. Remind myself that the Boleyns stick together.

"And no one but my sister calls me Nan."

He stops abruptly—a jolt of surprise and choler.

My breath catches and I look away. I've gone too far, let my words fail me yet again.

"Then I shall have to think of something else to call you."

He swings me back into the dance, but his voice is intimate. "Something private. Just for me. For us."

The flare returns, and I am grateful that the dance requires us to part. I keep my eyes lowered as I execute a turn that bells my skirts around me.

I look up to meet the king's eye as I come out of the turn, and there, behind him, is Thomas. His face is anguished, agonized, like the song. But I only see him for an instant. For as soon as the king returns to his proper position, he blocks everything else from my vision.

The music stops, and the king raises my hand to his lips. Kisses the solitary pearl-studded band that adorns my finger.

Smiles.

"I shall call you Anna."

Greenwich Palace
1525

54

My dance with the king leaves me feeling drunk, and as the year lurches to a close, I suffer the aftereffects. Not headache and nausea, but guilt and jealousy in equal measure.

All I did was dance.

And want.

The new year rides in like the tide, and the court shifts and moves like a house built on the Lambeth marsh. Tottering. Unstable. No one really knows where anyone else is going. No one knows what might happen next. And as the tide retreats toward spring, it leaves everything exposed.

It feels as if everyone is watching me. I am no longer invisible. I hear that some are placing bets on who will share the king's bed next, that the odds are on me. But the men at court will bet on anything.

We relocate, moving from Greenwich to Eltham, Eltham to Bridewell, and Bridewell back to Greenwich like a pack of stray dogs. There is no stability, no promise.

The king watches me. I can feel it. The entire court watches him watching. I no longer know how to act or what to say. I'm not even sure what I want.

And the person I have always asked for advice has disappeared into the columns and tabulations of the clerkship of the jewels. Into his poetry.

I cannot face Mary. I remember too well her desperate heart-break when King François moved on. She claims she doesn't love King Henry. But surely this betrayal will shatter her.

George is lost in his gambling and drinking. George is lost to me, full stop.

And Jane.

Jane comes to me in tears. The hollows of her cheeks are gray, and her wide, catlike eyes are dull and unseeing.

"I can't marry him," she sobs, and throws her arms around my neck. We are in the queen's watching chamber, surrounded by courtiers. All of them watching.

"Why?" I wrap my arms around her, too. Hide her face in my hood and guide her from the chamber and down the stairs to the Middle Court. Here, people can see us as they rush to perform their duties, but at least they do not pause to listen.

"What has he done?" I whisper.

She gasps, shocked, and pulls away to look at me.

"George? He's done nothing. It's my father. He doesn't have the ready cash to pay the dowry."

And my father will never let him get away with anything less than what was originally negotiated.

"But the agreement was signed." I cannot follow my own thoughts, for they move too quickly.

"There are ways around that." Jane's voice is dripping with contempt.

"Maybe it was never meant to be."

"No, Anne! I love him!"

"You don't really even know him."

She sobs again and falls back on my shoulder.

"Without him I will die unmarried!" she sobs afresh.

"Jesus, Jane." I push her away and hold her at arm's length. "You're young and desirable and very pretty. Your father is Lord Morley. You have time."

"No, Anne! I grow old and withered and I will never marry if I don't marry now!"

She's becoming hysterical. I pat her back awkwardly, wondering what I can do for her. What I can do with her.

"Is it someone else, Anne?" Jane asks.

The question startles me, and I'm happy to be able to answer truthfully. "Not that I know of."

Jane's face turns to steel and she clenches her jaw.

"I know he doesn't really want to marry me," she says, "And I know men can't really change, but I'm afraid I'll be a very jealous wife. I'm even jealous of you."

"Of me?"

"Well, not only are you beautiful—"

I cough through my nose.

"You are, Anne. Everyone remarks on it."

Only because Thomas told them so, and they believed the lies of a poet.

"But you also have George's love. He protects you. He advises you. He is the one who told me you're beautiful before I realized it myself. You are so lucky."

"Lucky?" I can't hold it in any longer. "You don't know him,

Jane. You know what he looks like on the outside, but not who he is on the inside. He made a bet." I choke on the truth. "A *bet* with someone that I would *not* be accepted at court no matter what endless sculpting the other man employed. He thinks a woman's worth is only what's between her legs. Not her mind or her virtue or her thoughts or her words. To him, the only thing a woman is good for is as a plaything."

"George isn't like that!"

"He is, Jane. And you need to face it sooner rather than later. You'd be better off not marrying him. Marry someone else. Marry Francis Weston or some other pliable young fool who will think you're clever and feel lucky to have you."

"So only a fool would want me, is that what you're saying?" Jane's tears are frozen on her cheeks. "George wants a clever girl, a pretty girl with a keen mind who he can talk to. Who can make him laugh. A girl like you, is that it? Do you love him yourself, Anne? Do you want him? Is that why you're not married? Is that why Butler won't have you? Why Henry Percy ran away? Is that why you're jealous? Do you think your brother is the only one good enough for you?"

"Jane!" I cry. "That's an evil thing to say!"

"It's an evil thing to do, Anne. But evil doesn't always stop people."

Her words fall on me like a hail of blows. She juts out her chin as if daring me to punch it, and part of me wants to. But I'm terrified that any defense will be seen as acceptance of guilt.

We stand for an eternity. I watch as the color drains from Jane's face, taking the anger with it. Her eyes fill with tears and beg forgiveness, but she says not a word as she turns and walks away.

The perfect courtier, sleek and sinuous in her thinking, cutting in her remarks about others.

Someone who doesn't apologize.

"Walk with me."

I startle at the buttery voice at my elbow. I quickly drop into a curtsy at the king's feet, berating myself for being so unaware.

"Rise, Mistress Boleyn," he says, "and do as I ask."

Walk with him.

We pass through the door and into the long gallery, where all the courtiers and ladies sink before us. It is like watching a multicolored sea dip into the troughs of waves, heads bowed and eyes averted.

As we pass, I hear murmurs and a few singular shouts for attention, but the king merely waves a finger and they are silenced behind him. I catch looks of surprise and suggestive significance as people see my face before they lower their gaze. I hear murmurs of gossip behind me like the sough of a wave on graveled sand.

People are not avoiding me because I'm an embarrassment. They are deferring to me because I am elevated. This is what it feels like to be inside the royal circle, that bubble of protection, the ring of acceptance.

We walk out into the newly manicured gardens, a dozen or so attendants following at an obsequious distance. I can smell the river and see Duke Humphrey's Tower high on the hill beyond, reminding me of the day I incurred the king's wrath.

I look quickly away to the man beside me. His hands are still, his gait even, but I sense his restlessness, his mind working, his eyes roving.

"I wanted to be the first to tell you, mistress. King François was captured at Pavia. The French have lost the war."

With this, the hum of his energy rises a notch. A half step.

"The French have surrendered?" I ask, stunned.

"Soon."

I risk a glance at him. He smiles patronizingly.

"You think his mother and sister will simply hand over the country to you." I can't avoid saying the words.

The king stops and holds my gaze.

"They are women."

I will him not to look away, terrified that I have his attention, that I stand so close to him and cannot touch him. Even more terrified that I am about to argue with him again.

"Women can be formidable when aroused."

A wall of shock crashes down between us, and I take a step back.

"Opposed," I correct myself. "Women can be formidable when opposed."

The king bites his bottom lip and I remember the touch of it on my own. The horror of my verbal flux washes me afresh.

"They can." The king closes the gap I created with my retreat. I am stunned into paralysis by his gaze, like a deer ready for slaughter.

"It appears that you and Mistress Parker had a disagreement."

"You saw that? You heard?" Oh, God. What if he believes it?

"Saw from a distance. Heard nothing."

Relief floods through me.

"You and Mistress Parker have always appeared to be cordial. What was the cause of your disagreement?"

"It wasn't so much of a disagreement." I falter. "She is upset because the plans for her to marry my brother may not come to fruition."

"She loves him?"

I nod, unable to say so in words.

"And you want her to be happy."

"She's my friend." Was.

"I shall speak with Lord Morley," he says abruptly.

"Oh, no!"

I immediately throw my hand over my mouth. I should die. Now. Instantaneously.

He narrows his eyes for a fraction of a moment, then bursts into a full, rolling laugh. I hear a couple of the attendants chuckling sycophantically behind us. They can't help themselves.

I smile weakly.

"Don't do anything on my account, Your Majesty," I say, and sink into a curtsy. I don't want Jane to marry George. I don't want it to be my fault.

"No, Mistress Anna." He offers a hand to lift me up, the vibration buzzing through my fingers, igniting every nerve. "I do it for young Jane. Leave it with me, and I will ensure it comes to fruition. Jane is a sweet girl and deserves to be happy."

"Yes. She does."

I can't tell the king that George may never make Jane happy. I may never speak again, made mute by wanting what I can't have.

"As do you, Mistress Anna."

I stare at his hand, afraid to look in his face. The rings on his fingers have made ridges on his palm. His nails are slightly ragged, as if he chews them. The imperfections only serve to make me want him more.

"You deserve to be happy. The most happy."

I hold my breath and look up. His face is shy. Boyish. As if all the confidence has fled him.

As all of mine has fled me.

The man I fell in love with at the age of thirteen is holding my hand. A man nearly twice my age. But still so handsome it hurts the eyes. And he is looking at me. Really looking. I feel the hum begin to fill me.

He is my sister's lover.

He is married.

And I'm in love with someone else.

The thought hits me like a storm at sea crashing, thundering, blow upon blow. It rocks me over then buoys me up only to plummet me into the next trough. I shake my head to clear it.

"You think you don't deserve happiness?" he asks, mistaking my action. "What would make you happy?"

He looks at me earnestly. As if I can answer that question easily. I would be happy if Thomas wasn't married. If he had never taken that bet. I would be happy if I had never left France. If I weren't tangled in a sticky mess of choices and innuendos and the desires of other people. If I were holding someone else's hand.

"Love."

The word answers for me.

The king smiles. Gorgeously. Dazzlingly. It singes me.

"Perhaps that can be arranged."

As he takes his hands from mine, he slips the ring from my finger, the plain gold band with the single pearl.

"I should like to keep this," he says, and kisses it before sliding it onto his smallest finger. The only one that was bare.

55

THE FIRST RULE OF THE HUNT IS NEVER TO LOOK BACK AT THE hunter.

When I leave the king, my feet take me through the gardens. I don't check behind me to see if he's watching. I pass through the gate, looking ahead into the orchard.

I see a figure dressed in green, conjured from my thoughts and wishes. Vivid. Solid. More. I cannot stop myself from going to him.

"Looking for me?" He cocks his head and grins at me, but his body is still. Stiff. There is tension behind his words.

"No." *Yes.*

"For him." His jaw tightens, and I see the hope diminish.

"What? No!"

"Don't lie to me, Anne," Thomas says, his voice laced with sadness. "I saw you. How you looked at him. How you reacted to him. I know you as well as I know myself. Remember?"

I remember. And say nothing.

"You want the court to fall at your feet."

"I did," I admit. *I do.*

"You want the king, Anne?" His voice cracks. "Is that why you agreed to go along with all of it?"

I did want the king. From the first moment I saw him—gilded and brilliant on the Field of Cloth of Gold. I wanted him more after that foolish, teasing kiss in my sister's room. The one that meant nothing to him and yet everything to me.

Now I don't know what I want.

"Don't be stupid," I croak. "It's ridiculous." *Isn't it?* "A childish fancy. A fairy tale. The influence of too many chivalric ballads."

"The ones that always end badly."

I shiver.

"You should know, Thomas Wyatt. None of your love poems end well."

"I deserve that."

"You do. And more."

"I certainly don't deserve you."

"But you can't have me. Not as a wife. Not as a mistress. Don't you see? This is a chance for me to be heard."

"You want to be heard," he pursues. "But do you know what you want to say?"

"Does it matter as long as someone's listening? I want to say what I think and be taken seriously. I don't want to be nothing. If I have the king's ear," I say, my words slowing upon themselves, "I can be anything."

"It's not his ear he follows you with."

Thomas's voice is low and dangerous. I think of what that implies, and I shiver again.

"I don't want to be the next Mary." I speak without thinking. What I should have said was, *I wouldn't do that to Mary*.

The angles and contours of his face blur beneath the scudding shadows of an early spring sky. His cheekbones stand out against the stubble of his beard, and his eyebrows curve gently above it all like the sharp lines of bare trees.

"Then be with me. Not as a wife . . ." Thomas clears his throat. "Nor as a mistress. Not even as a friend." He smiles warily. "But as the girl I love."

The words stifle him and he doesn't say any more, but his eyes keep asking.

I have no answer.

He reaches out a tentative hand, the fingers a little too knobby, the knuckled bones standing out, the tips blunt, stained with ink. He hesitates, but I don't move away.

His hand catches the side of my face and I lean into it, breathing in the scents of ink and paper, of almonds, of warmth. I close my eyes. There are no words for what I'm feeling. Or perhaps there are too many.

I feel the skim of his breath on my face, the brush of it against my lips.

And he kisses me.

So softly at first, I'm not quite sure he's touching me. The fog of breath. The scent of almonds. The faint roughness of his beard, the flicker of skin on skin.

366

I lean forward, pressing my lips to his, and it breaks me open. His hand leaves my face and traces notes up my arms, strikes chords on my throat and up into my hair. His mouth forms lyrics that expose my soul.

This kiss is like a song played only once. And forever.

And then I remember that Thomas Wyatt has had lots of practice. He knows what he's doing when he kisses a girl. When he touches her.

No wonder it feels so good.

"I can't."

I pull away. My mind is filled with reasons. I open my eyes and look into his. I have the queerest feeling that he's been watching me the entire time.

"Can't what? Kiss me? I think you just did. And rather well, I might add."

A ghost of fear hides behind his eyes. He can't cover it with a joke or bravado, or a single-dimpled smile.

That ghost shadows all my defenses. Because he has lowered his.

"I will never make you do anything you don't want to, Anne," he says.

I think of Percy, how I could want something and not want it all at once. Want it for the wrong reasons. How do I know what are the right reasons?

"I want you to kiss me again," I say without thinking. Always without thinking. Perhaps it's only when I don't think that I say what I really mean.

He traces my hairline with his fingers, following my jaw until he holds my face in his hands, and kisses me again, as if drinking me in. But this kiss is different from the first. It has no melody, just percussion.

I listen to his breath, to his heart. I listen to the words he doesn't say. The three words he said before.

And I believe him.

56

Spring comes in on a cold north wind, fluttering the sprouts of new leaves while the heads of daffodils plunge beneath it. Narcissus bowing before his own reflection.

Thomas is kept even busier. I see him less, now that I want to see him more. And the king . . . keeps watching.

I finally work up the courage to visit my sister. To apologize, no matter what Thomas told me. To tell her . . . what? That nothing happened? Nothing has. But I know that doesn't mean it never will.

I make my way past the courtiers preening in the new sunlight, their feathers and silks bannering in the wind. Pick my way through the crowded lodgings to her door. Take a deep breath. Square my shoulders, as Father taught. And enter.

"Nan!"

Mary doesn't sound angry. If anything, she sounds delighted. She jumps up and holds me at arm's length.

"Nan, are you all right?"

Mary loops her arm through mine and leans close. I can smell her hair—the lavender she uses to rinse it. Her cheeks are slightly flushed, and the skin of her hand is so smooth.

"Do you love him?" I blurt.

She doesn't have to ask who.

"Yes and no. I love Catherine more than anything. More than I ever imagined was possible. So I love whoever gave her to me."

Mary doesn't know who Catherine's father is. It might not be the king. And perhaps, just perhaps, the king's waning interest will not break Mary's heart. I succor myself with that thought, but it's like trying to fill an empty stomach with cherry comfits.

"You look pale, Nan. Like you've seen a ghost."

"I'm fine."

She pulls me through the door and sits me down by the fire. She moves so smoothly. She is so serene.

"Will you play?" she asks. My lute—Thomas's lute—is in the corner.

"I don't think so."

"You're not my Nan." Mary smiles gently. "Give up an opportunity to play? What have you done with my sister?"

She no longer knows me. She knows nothing of what is happening at court. My sister inhabits her own world, and no one can puncture the bubble of it and intrude.

"I'm *nobody's* Nan," I say, and pinch my lip between my teeth to prevent the tears that threaten. "I belong to no one, Mary."

"You will marry soon enough," she soothes, still not understanding. "The Butler marriage would never have made you happy. Shall I ask Father to find someone for you?" She pauses. "Or perhaps the king?"

She says this in a small voice, unsure.

"I think you have asked enough favors of the king."

"Or perhaps given too many."

"I didn't say that, Mary." I stop short of actually asking for forgiveness.

"No, you didn't have to."

"I'm not bemoaning the lack of a husband. I want to belong to myself."

"You do already. Don't you see, Nan? That's why he wants to possess you."

Men only want what they can't have.

Mary knows. We hold the moment, caught tight in the stillness at the center of a storm. I am incapable of apology. And she is incapable of censure. Neither of us is willing to talk about it openly.

"I wish I were more like you." She says it so simply. A statement of fact.

"No one wants to be like me. At least, no one should." Lost. Alone. Hunted.

Broken.

"No, you're wrong, Nan," Mary says softly. "You're strong. You're so sure. You know what you want, and you're not afraid to make it happen. You don't let anyone walk on you or take anything from you."

But I do. I did. Percy took from me.

And Thomas could take everything.

Her eyes slide away from mine. Mary has always had what I wanted. Beauty. Charm. Kindness. The king.

"I'm afraid."

I don't realize the words have come from me until I see Mary's reaction to them. Her eyes widen, and she presses her lips together.

"You?" she asks. "Nan, what are you afraid of?"

This.

I'm afraid I was wrong. Wrong about Mary, who never wanted to be better than anyone else; she just wanted to be herself. Never meant to mother me, just wanted to be a mother. Wrong about Jane, because she never deserved my pity. Wrong about George, who maybe never was my friend, no matter how I remember it. Wrong about Thomas.

I'm afraid all the things I've said and done will hunt me down and haunt me. Because the thing I'm afraid of is the same thing I told the king would make me happy. The thing I've been pursuing through the forest of my own life.

"Love."

57

THREE DAYS BEFORE HIS WEDDING, GEORGE DISAPPEARS. JUST vanishes from the court.

Someone says he saw George on a horse. Someone else says George has taken a hawk and walked out over the hill behind Duke Humphrey's Tower. Another says George clambered aboard a dinghy and headed downstream to London.

Most likely to the stews.

That is the rumor the court believes.

Jane doesn't say a word, and her face betrays no emotion in public.

But when she finally comes to talk to me—trapping me in our little corner of the maids' chamber—all of her fear and love and desperation show.

"Where is he?" she demands.

"I don't know."

I don't need to make it worse.

"Why isn't he here?"

She wrings her hands, and I see that every fingertip is bitten to the quick, the cuticles ragged, one finger freely bleeding.

"I don't know," I say again, and reach out to put a hand over hers in an effort to still them, but she flinches away from me.

"Of *course* you know!" she screeches. "The two of you are like *this*." She shows me two fingers intertwined, a dark scab standing out against the white of her twisted knuckle.

"I tried to tell you," I say. "George and I are not that close."

"Everyone at court knows that's not true. That you and George have been inseparable since birth."

I struggle not to roll my eyes.

"Except for the seven years I spent in France."

"He *pined* for you, Anne. He told me so himself." She says this with such intensity I have to believe her. I don't doubt that Jane remembers with absolute clarity every word she has ever heard George utter.

"What else did he tell you?"

"That he stole apples from the orchard for you when you had a cold."

He did. And ate half of them himself.

"He said he taught you your first word in Latin."

"Shame it was a word that earned me punishment"—the dinnertime disappointment from Father.

Jane stops trembling. Sits down on the bed. Gazes out the far window at the clouds scudding across the sky.

"I thought if I got close to you, I'd get close to him. I thought you'd help me win him."

I feel her confession like a punch in the chest. It knocks me back. The edge of the next bed catches me behind my knees and I collapse onto it.

"You lied to me." Like Wyatt. Like George. Like Father.

I'm a fool.

Jane hangs her head, letting it nod twice.

"I thought you were my friend," I whisper. Feeble. "You fought for me. With James Butler."

She turns to me, her eyes glazed and slightly manic.

"It wasn't you," she says. "He said . . ."

She hesitates as if what she has to say is painful to her.

"He said George was in your bedchamber. He implied . . ."

Oh, God. She was defending George. Not me. I got it all wrong from the beginning. I got everything wrong.

I stumble to my feet. I have to get out.

"Anne." She reaches for me, grabs my hand in hers. I try to shake her off, but her grip is like a vise. I pull again, yank, ready to scream.

"Stop!" she cries. "Wait! That's the day it all changed!"

I stop. My arms drop to my sides. I don't look at her.

"I have loved your brother since the moment I set foot in this court."

I see her hands from the corner of my eye, the nails of the left tearing the skin of the right.

"But the best thing that love brought me is you, Anne. You *are* my friend. It was I who had all the wrong reasons. After what the duchess did to me, perhaps I didn't know what friendship was."

She pauses.

"Butler said those things. And I hated him. I thought it was for George. But then I hurt you. And I couldn't bear it. I realized I . . . I loved you, too. That made me want George even more, so you could be my sister."

Silence envelops us, gently loosening the iron bands around my heart.

"You know, before I told my father about George, he was talking about marrying me to someone else. Some old, fat man with bad breath and a worse temper. Someone who isn't even at court."

"Really?" I ask. "You didn't tell me."

"You didn't give me a chance! You started saying all those bad things about George, trying to make me hate him. But I couldn't face the alternative. I was the one who mentioned George to my father. I was the one who suggested it. Before he could promise me to . . . to . . ." She shudders.

"You changed your own destiny."

"I'm sorry." She winces and puts a finger in her mouth.

I unwind the string of pearls from around my neck and place it over her head. I take her hand and put it to her throat, to feel the rolling beads. They clack gently like the distant chatter of gossips.

"Whenever you want to bite your nails," I tell her. "Whenever you want to hurt yourself, hold on to these. Like rosary beads. Listen to their music, Jane, and let it calm you."

"I can't take these," Jane says. She strokes them with the ragged fingers of one hand. The other hand is still, for once.

"Yes, you can." I press my hand again onto hers. "George will come back. He'll come back to court. He'll come back to you. And then you'll be a Boleyn, and the Boleyns always stick together."

She hugs me.

"I'll be a good Boleyn, Anne."

"I know you will." I hug her back. "Better than the rest of us."

"When I first loved him, Anne, I thought it would just be another infatuation, like all the others that go on here. Something that might be passed along as gossip and then just disappear. Like yours with the king or Norris or Thomas Wyatt."

I flinch at the mention of his name.

Jane stops her soliloquy to study me. And I remember what George once said about her. That she sees everything.

"You love him," she says slowly. "Thomas Wyatt."

I don't have to tell her it's true. She knows.

58

I's not unusual for the king to attend the wedding of one of his courtiers. George is a gentleman of the Privy Chamber, and Father is treasurer of the household.

But I don't believe the king is here for George, or for Father.

I believe he is here to see me.

And so is Thomas.

My emotions pull taut between them, twanging every time either one moves or speaks. I feel visible, exposed. And thoroughly grateful when Jane appears.

She is elegant in pale pink trimmed with coiled crimson satin. Her father is fluffed and preening in the presence of the king. Mine is stuffed with pride. Mary is beside him, quiet, humbled.

George arrives five minutes late. His hair is a mussy nest of spikes and whorls. He looks younger than his twenty years, like a child just out of bed, being dragged unwilling to church.

Jane is smooth and poised, every hair in place. Her smile, clear and bright, breaks my heart. She's marrying the man she loves.

The wedding party moves on to a lavish banquet—Father

for once not caring about the expense, or trying to appear not to care. There is venison and brawn, pigeon and sparrow, lamb and rabbit. The bridecake is demolished and devoured. I linger over strawberries soaked in wine.

I feel Thomas circling. But he doesn't approach.

When everyone has had their fill and the men begin to argue over the bones, the king orders the tables to be taken away and requests music.

The lutenist tunes his instrument, humming over the strings. He wears an expression of detached arrogance. I realize, with a shock, that it's Mark Smeaton, from Wolsey's household. The king has poached him—or his voice has finally changed.

Smeaton knows he's good. He knows he can do this. He feels superior. He smiles, gazes about the room to see who is watching, doesn't watch his own fingers.

And strums.

The noise that vibrates through the room is not the sound he expected. It is discordant and jarring, his fingering all wrong. The look on his face is priceless.

I giggle to myself and then stop. Because the king is looking at me. He is laughing, too. The room is small. He is so very close.

Smeaton recovers himself and dives into a complicated melody that the rest of the musicians do their best to follow. The king and I stare at each other as the music rains down and encapsulates us.

Until Mary brushes by me when she leaves the room, and the king follows her with his eyes. The bubble bursts and I don't look at him again.

The party goes on until nearly dawn, the musicians almost falling asleep over their instruments. The king regales everyone with war stories; my father competes with tales of his diplomatic missions.

George stays awake and away from his chambers, something noticed by all but remarked on by none, until the musicians finally stop.

"I think it's time to bed the bride and groom!" Norris cries.

"One more drink." George's words are nearly unintelligible already. Jane flushes hot by the fireside, one hand gripping the pearls at her throat.

"Nothing more to drink!" Norris declares. "We will carry you bodily to your chamber and listen through the curtains!"

"And don't forget we will check the sheets in the morning," Bryan chimes in.

"It's already morning," George mutters, but allows himself to be removed from his wine and pulled into a mob of backslapping and bawdy remarks.

Jane hides behind her veil and I catch her just before she peels the healing skin from her index finger. I squeeze her hand silently and she squeezes back before she allows herself to be swept through the door by the rowdy throng.

"Come with me." Thomas grabs my hand amid the chaos. He's pulling me back toward the middle court. Away. I glance at the ebb of activity in the room. The king is looking elsewhere.

We cross the court quickly, the May rain saturating us, the castle walls, the chapel and chimneys. Turning the world into a long, wet wash all the way to the Thames.

Thomas plucks at my sleeve and melts into the shadows of a stairwell. I follow him silently, my slippers making no sound on the stone steps.

The clouds hide the moon, and the sun is too afraid to rise.

I kiss him before he speaks. I want to shut it all out. Jane and George. My father. Mary. The rain. The king. I stand on my toes to reach him and twine my fingers in his hair. He tries to hold me back at first. He wants so badly to say what he thinks he needs to say. I silence him with my mouth, steal the words from his tongue.

For a moment, we are lost. His fingers move over the pins and stays in my hood, pulling off the black velvet coronet, dropping the snood to the ground behind me. He tugs my hair from its plait and it falls to my waist. He lifts it with both hands and buries his face in it.

"It smells just like you." He turns to me, and a shy look steals through his expression. "You must think I'm perverted."

"No," I say quickly, thinking again of how Percy treated my hair as a nuisance. And me, too, in the end. "No, it's quite charming."

"Quite charming," he mocks.

"Endearing."

"Would we say endearing?" he asks. "Try enchanting."

Thomas smiles wickedly and pushes me back up against the wall, one arm cradling my neck from the rough, cold brick, the other wrapped tight around my waist. He breathes into my ear.

"Tell me I'm enchanting."

"You're resplendent," I tell him. "Heroic. Majestic."

I tilt my chin for a kiss that doesn't come.

"Ah. There you're wrong, my dear." He takes a step away.

I am unmoored.

"Majestic I am not. And I cannot compete with it, either."

His expression begs me to disagree.

"There's no need to compete."

"Everything at this court is a competition. Especially with the king. Did you think the Castle of Loyalty was just a game?"

Youth versus experience.

Thomas against the king.

He is so far away from me. Watching me. Gauging me. What can I say? My tongue cannot form the three words he needs to hear. No matter how strongly I feel them.

"I am not a prize, Thomas."

"Don't I know it." The tease has a bitter aftertaste. "You are a gamble, Anne Boleyn. One that I won't risk losing."

His words rankle and I move away. Just a little.

"We both know which Boleyn girl he prefers," I argue, the words dusty in my throat.

"We both know that interest is fading." Thomas reaches out a tentative hand to stroke my hair. "I also think he can't help himself."

"From what?"

"From falling in love with you."

The moment freezes, and I with it.

"I don't think the king falls in love," I say finally, awash in the guilty hope that I'm wrong.

"I think he falls in love every day," Thomas replies. "And that's what I'm worried about."

59

THE RAIN HAS DAMPENED THE CHANCE OF ANY SPORT. No tilting, for the mud in the yard is as thick as paste. No hunting, for the season has yet to start. A move to Windsor is discussed for the use of the opulent tennis court alone. As it is, here in Greenwich, the men are irritable and peevish, as if itchy in their own skins.

When it stops raining, I search out Jane and drag her to the orchard with me.

"My hem will get wet," she moans.

"But no one will be able to hear us. And I want to hear everything."

Jane burns red. I can feel the heat from her face.

"Don't be disgusting, Anne. He's your brother." The pearls click beneath her fingers.

"I only meant . . ." I have no explanation. "Are you happy?"

"He doesn't love me."

She says it simply and with no trace of emotion.

"Maybe love can be learned."

A shout from the tiltyard gallery interrupts Jane's response.

"George," she breathes. Plucks at my sleeve, drawing me to the watching towers.

The men have converted the gallery into a bowling alley. A gaggle of them hover at one end, shaking hands and drinking wine. And betting. I am not surprised to see George amongst them.

At the other end of the improvised rink, nearest to us, are the players. The king. And Thomas Wyatt. I step back into the shadows of the tower and pull Jane with me.

They have obviously already played several ends, because the men betting are getting louder and more belligerent. The game must be close.

They did not expect an audience. Thomas has removed his cap and, as I watch, the king sheds his doublet.

"I really must have an alley built here at Greenwich," the king says, stretching, the fabric of his shirt tight across his shoulders. "This gallery is far too small."

"And a tennis court!" Henry Norris calls.

"Perhaps I will." The king laughs. "And a new mews for the falcons while I'm at it. Come, Wyatt. Let me best you."

A fleeting frown crosses Thomas's face, but it vanishes before he clasps the king's hand. He's playing the game. The jack is thrown, going a fair distance down the rink, coming to rest almost at center. The men cheer and drink and bet again.

The king rolls first, and his shot goes wide. He toes the ground in disapproval and turns away—clenching and unclenching his fists. Thomas rubs his hand over his mouth and chin to hide a smile.

I want to grab his hand and drag him away somewhere. Silly

men. Silly competitions. The betting continues, heating up. George is handling the book. Of course.

Thomas takes his shot, which comes much closer to the jack, the bias of the wood making it curve out and then in again in an elegant arc, coming to rest not two feet from the jack.

There is silence. Then a rattle from the onlookers, the exchange of coins.

This goes on until both men have thrown all four woods, a cluster of bowls at the far end, crouched menacingly around the little jack.

"The king's shot is closest!" shouts Norris from the boundary. Another cheer. More drinking. The clink of coins as the winnings are counted.

The king gives a little nod. He reaches for Thomas's hand.

Then Bryan shouts, "I beg to differ, Norris, but Wyatt's first shot lies closer."

Silence.

The king and Thomas exchange a look, and without speaking—like a dance, choreographed—they turn together to stride down to the end of the gallery. I cannot hear their banter, but I see a strange look on Thomas's face. His normal complacency is missing. The casual, assured courtliness has been replaced by rivalry.

They stand for a moment over the jack, the only sound the hiss of rain as it starts up again. The king shines gold, his hair fiery in the dim light. Thomas rubs his hand across the back of his neck, twining in the curls of hair there, his apple-green sleeves fluttering.

He looks up, shoulders set for a challenge.

"I believe Bryan is right, Your Majesty," he says. "Mine is closer."

Time stops.

Everything is a competition at this court, Thomas said. *Especially with the king.*

But the game keeps changing.

The king smiles. A heart-stopping, mischievous smile.

He lifts his right hand, glittering with rings, his eyes never leaving Thomas's face. He points to the cluster of bowls using his smallest finger.

"I tell you, Wyatt," he says. "I am closer than you think."

On his finger is a ring. My ring. One I have obviously worn throughout my time at court. The one he kissed so extravagantly when we danced after the Castle of Loyalty tournament. The one he took from me as "payment" for getting Jane her dowry.

He caresses it. To make his point.

I feel sick. I reach a hand behind me to steady myself on the wall and take a step farther into the shadows. I need to escape.

Thomas stares at the ring for half a moment. Then he straightens, looks the king directly in the eye.

With his right hand, he reaches down inside his blue-green doublet and extracts a worn ribbon.

"If you will allow me, Your Majesty, I should like to measure it," he says; his words carry over the entire rink, where all have frozen silent.

Thomas stretches the ribbon out between the king's bowl and the jack. Then between the jack and his own.

His wood is indeed closer.

With a carefully timed flourish, he opens his hand and something heavy drops to the end of the ribbon and sways there. A golden *A*, a teardrop pearl flashing beneath it.

"I believe that it is mine." Thomas sits back on his heels and flashes a look of triumph at the king. I could kill him.

The king approaches him. There is no sound but the rain. The bettors huddle in the corner as if trying to render themselves invisible.

"It may be so." In the silence the king's voice sounds loud—violent—though he speaks quietly. "Perhaps I am deceived."

He stands facing Thomas, only inches away. The king is taller, broader. Thomas, with his slight build, appears as a willow before an oak.

The king nudges the jack out of place and picks it up to hold between them.

"Perhaps," the king says, "the call is not ours to make."

He spins and strides back the length of the gallery, calling out, "No more games."

He sweeps into the rain-ravaged tiltyard, followed by Norris. The other men swiftly exchange their coins, no longer up for argument, and hasten after their monarch. Except for George, who spreads the coins in his palm, his face conflicted between a frown and a grin.

Thomas watches them go, and then kicks the king's wood, sending it careening after them.

60

I PULL JANE BEHIND ME INTO THE GALLERY, PICKING UP THE still rolling bowl along the way. I hurl it at Thomas, but it is too heavy for me and thunders to the floor. Thomas turns, his smile flickering when he sees me.

"Why did you do that?" I shout.

"Did you see? Fun, wasn't it?" Thomas pauses. "I won."

"It was a stupid, foolish, childish competition! I am not something to be won, Thomas Wyatt. I am not a prize. An object. A possession."

"Now who's being foolish?" Thomas cocks his head, feigning blamelessness. "Nothing was said about you, Anne. It was just a game."

"Nothing is just a game in this court."

George pushes himself between us, and Jane takes a step back. George ignores her and hands Thomas a goblet of wine.

"It looks like I owe you five pounds, Wyatt."

Thomas flicks a glance at me.

"You owe him nothing, George," I say.

"But he did it, Anne. He's made you the queen of the court." George pauses. "Figuratively speaking, of course. Unless circumstances change."

"I don't want your money, Boleyn." Thomas looks at me now. Steadily. "The bet was forfeit a long time ago."

"Excellent news, my friend, because I don't have it." George laughs and pockets his coins with a clatter. "Though it appears my luck may be changing."

"Always looking to your own advantage, George, aren't you?" I bite across his laughter. "Always looking to sell your sisters to the highest bidder." Bought. Sold. Won. Lost. A prize. A jewel. A possession.

"When my sisters attract the highest bidder of all," George crows, dancing around me, "I don't see why not. I don't know how you did it, Wyatt, but you did. You are definitely my hero.

"And you, Anne, you're the rising star. The flying falcon. I wouldn't have thought it possible three years ago, but you've gone higher than any of us would ever have dreamed. You just need to carry the rest of us with you."

He turns back to Thomas. "Right, Wyatt? Surely there's something you want from my sister. You can't let all your hard work go to waste."

Thomas swallows visibly. George is too caught up in his own tide to notice or care that no one else is speaking.

"I need you to work your witchy magic, Anne," he says. "Cardinal Wolsey is planning to purge the king's chambers of anyone unnecessary or undesirable. Heads will roll. And there's a rumor afoot that I've been pilfering the king's wine. I need you, dear sister"—he pokes a bony finger at the center of my stomacher—"to convince our potentate that I am indispensable."

A look of desperation crosses his face at my lack of an answer, and he hurls a genial arm around my shoulder.

"I cannot be thrown from court, Anne. I'm afraid it would kill me."

"No, George," I say quietly. "Your words and the wine will be what kill you."

George loses his bonhomie, his handsome face hard as stone.

"So you just throw me to the wolves, now, is that it? You've surpassed us all, and the rest of us can hang? You've got what you wanted: the king's dick in your pocket. No one else matters."

Thomas coughs and extends an arm to Jane.

"Come, Mistress Par—Boleyn. Let us leave these siblings to their rivalry."

"No." George seizes Jane's wrist. "Stay. You should know what we're really like."

"George—" Jane starts to say, but he silences her with a glance.

"You always wanted everything, Anne. Everything I had. You had to do everything I did."

"I just wanted to be like you!"

"You just wanted to be better than me. You had to be the best. The best at French. Get the best apple. Have the highest reach. And you let me fall and catch all of Father's wrath."

I let him vent and spit. He cannot rouse me. Not like when we were young, and two words would raise my fists to him.

"You know what he said?" George leans in, a gobbet of

spittle on his lips. "The day you broke your finger getting that exasperating apple? He said, 'Your sister is clever and brave, George. More than you'll ever be.'"

"Father said lots of things."

"He *said*," George shouts over me. "He said, 'I wish she was my boy. I wish Anne was my son. I would give her everything. You don't deserve it.'"

George's face is stripped of guile, excoriated, every raw thought and pulsing emotion bleeding and sore.

"But you came back from France and you were nothing. Nothing you did was right. So I made Wyatt here take you on."

I glance once at Thomas, who is watching George with bleak intensity. I level my gaze at my brother.

"Hoping he'd tarnish me beyond redemption."

George chokes and Jane reaches for him, but doesn't touch him. Bites her lip. The rattle of the pearls beneath her fingers is the only sound she makes.

"Hoping he'd win," George whispers.

"Father never . . . " I start, but can't finish.

"He never cared about Mary and me. Just you. He loved only you, his clever, impish princess."

"He didn't love me—"

"He did!" George shouts again, and steps closer, ready to strike. Thomas tries to pull him back, but George yanks away from him. "It was you he loved. I was the failure. The disappointment. When you left, he was only cold. Dead."

"He never loved me!" I scream, everything in me finally tearing loose. "He *left* me!"

392

George is silent. Stunned.

"He took me. Put me on that horrible little boat that shuddered at the hint of a wave. Took me to that gaudy, glittering Habsburg tomb in the Low Countries. A child, George. A child beneath the weight of all that gilt."

I gasp. My words squeeze the breath from me.

"When he took me to meet the duchess, I grabbed his hand and said, 'I love you, Da.' And do you know what he did? He shook me off. Wiped his hand on his doublet, the look on his face like I'd handed him excrement. He said, 'You're sweating, Anne. It's unbecoming.' He left me there."

My gaze briefly meets Thomas's.

"It's the last time I said those words. And now they choke me. Because nothing I did, none of the letters I wrote or the songs I sang or my perfect bloody French, convinced him to bring me home. To love me back. Maybe if I'd failed at my lessons like you did, maybe if I'd fucked King François and half the French court like Mary, maybe then he would have brought me home. Maybe then I would have been more than nothing. But no, my reward was just more punishment."

The world breathes around us, but George and I are no longer breathing. It's the silent moment before armies charge. Or declare a truce.

George takes a deep breath. Squares his shoulders. "You're a Boleyn, Anne. There's no escaping it."

The specter of his cockeyed grin lodges in his expression.

"And the Boleyns always stick together," I say. "There's no escaping that, either."

I want to be like we used to be, when love was simple. When we would sit back to back in the apple orchard, before I climbed to the highest branch to pick the best one. While George sat with the pile in his lap, ready to consume the lot, even if it made him sick. I want to say to him now, *Slow down. Not so much.* I want to make him stop.

"You don't need me to keep you here, George. The only way to stop the rumor that you steal the king's wine is to stop drinking."

"It makes my life tolerable."

I feel more than see Jane stiffen, and reach for her hand, cold and still ragged. George looks from me to Jane and back again, the realization of what he's said etched across his face.

"There is more to life than wine, George. It will be your undoing."

"No, Anne." He sighs. "You will be my undoing."

He takes Jane's hand from me and I see him squeeze it.

It is not a truce. But at least it is not a war.

61

I LOOK PAST THOMAS TO WHERE THE RAIN SLITHERS FROM THE roof tiles and into the deep, wet mud of the tiltyard. George has left, Jane following. I don't know if they'll find a middle ground in their marriage, a compromise between love and ambivalence. I don't know how Jane can face being a Boleyn after what she saw today.

I'm waiting. For Thomas to say something. Do something. Make it right. Kiss me. But he just stares at the bowl—his wood, the one that was closest—as he rolls it in circles beneath his foot.

"I didn't mean to antagonize him," he says.

"Yes, you did."

"You're right, I did."

He isn't joking. The fierceness in his eyes punctures me.

"He has your ring."

"I didn't give it freely."

"He's married, Anne."

I almost laugh.

"So are you."

He looks away, up the steep hill to Duke Humphrey's Tower. He gasps. And when I look, there, in the distant shadows, stands a deer, shrouded in a curtain of rain. It is poised on the impossible points of its narrow legs, eyes wide and dark, still bearing the dappled marks of its youth.

"One of the king's," he murmurs. "Makes me hope I never see it in the chase."

And the deer, as if hearing him, picks its way into the darkness, disappearing like a ghost.

"You're not going to apologize, are you?" I ask him.

"Should I?" He turns to me, his expression an open challenge. "For what?" He pauses. "And to whom?"

"*To me*. For . . ." Confusing me with a thing to be won. For not wanting a doll, but making me into one. "For being married."

Thomas folds himself around me like the wings of a falcon, pressing me into him. I feel the laughter in his chest.

"I can't make things any different from the way they are," he says. "All I can do is love you."

And he kisses me with the deep desperation of a drowning man. This kiss is a song of longing. A ballad that doesn't end well.

I cling to him, digging my fingers into the back of his neck, suddenly, acutely jealous of any girl who has had the chance to know him. To touch his skin. To taste it. Hating his wife, and any future mistress.

"I love you," I whisper into his mouth and into his hair when he kisses my throat.

I cannot say it loud enough for him to hear.

62

THE KING MOVES TO WESTMINSTER AND ON TO WINDSOR, completely caught up in politics and hunting, leaving the queen and her quiet life in Greenwich. He takes a group of favorites with him. And Thomas. He will not leave Thomas behind.

I swallow my guilty conscience and go to see Mary.

Three ladies stand by the door of Mary's private room, huddled like witches over a cauldron.

This does not bode well. My steps slow, and I dread whatever is in that room.

I cough. Once. Then again, louder. The ladies look up and scuttle away like cockroaches in a sudden light, leaving me alone at the door. I knock.

"Mary?"

The only response is a cross between a sob and a moan.

And a splash.

I curse under my breath. All those vexing women flocking to Mary but refusing her any help or solace whatsoever. I curse again.

Another splash. A sudden fear that she might be drowning herself propels me through the door.

The heavy velvet curtains are drawn. The only light comes

through the door. This room is shrouded in darkness and smoke from a single candle. The bed is rumpled, the counterpane flung onto the rush-mat floor.

In the far corner, away from any light, sits a little bath on a stool. Next to it, completely naked, sits my sister.

She has taken a piece of rough linen and is scraping at her body with long, deliberate strokes. The skin of her arms and shoulders and breasts and belly glow red in the dim light.

"Mary?"

She attacks her legs, using both hands to rub the linen down her thigh, the muscles in her shoulders knotting beneath the skin, her head bowed, the hair falling around her face in wet, curling curtains.

I creep up behind her, afraid. She gives no indication that she sees or hears me. She concentrates fully on the long, red marks on her skin.

"Stop."

I put a hand on her shoulder, and she twitches me off. Moves to the other thigh. Determined, purposeful strokes down the thin, sensitive skin on the inside.

"Mary, you'll hurt yourself."

"You think I'm not already hurt?" She rounds on me. A twist of hair is stuck to her cheek, filtering over her upper lip and into her mouth.

"Mary," I say, and a twinge of panic cuts me off. Silence descends until I finally regain my voice.

"What happened?"

"I happened, Nan. Stupid, lazy, selfish me. Ignorant girl

who can't tell the difference between love and sex. Foolishly imagining that if I sell myself, I'll be worth having."

"Mary, you're not—"

"I am. I'm a whore. Everyone says it. You've said it."

"No, Mary!"

But I did. And the guilt of it sends me to my knees. She looks down on me while continuing to ravage her raw skin.

"Never be a mistress, Nan. A mistress is no one. Dispensable. Trash. Dirty."

"Mary, stop!"

"I can't get him off me!" she cries, scraping again at her arms, tears churning down her face. "I can't get rid of him! I can't make him go away."

"Who?" I whisper, knowing the answer.

"The king. My lover."

"But I thought you wanted . . ."

"That's what everyone thought. Because I was getting what everyone else wanted. Father wanted prestige and position for the family. He got that. George wanted a place at court and manor holdings and money. He got those. Even my husband wanted a quiet life, the ability to make a difference in the Privy Chamber, and money. It all comes down to money. And that's what makes me a whore. Selling sex for money and preferment."

I'm shocked by the bitterness in Mary's words. Mary, who has never done anything but agree and look pretty.

"But the king loves you."

Mary laughs. A harsh sound, like gulls crying.

"He never loved me. He doesn't even love his wife anymore."

"He was with you for three years."

She stops, finally. Looks at me. Rests her hands with the twisted and ruined piece of linen on her knees.

"Three years? You speak as if that's a lifetime."

"It's as long as I've been in England," I say. It feels like a lifetime.

"It hardly matters now. He's found someone else."

We stare at each other for a long, slow stretch of time. We have to talk about it now.

"I thought he was just teasing," I finally manage to whisper, knowing it's a lie, after what I saw in the tiltyard gallery.

"That's how it starts."

"I didn't mean for it to happen." Not a lie. "I didn't mean to hurt you. I didn't mean to hurt anyone."

Mary sighs. She picks up the counterpane from the floor and wraps herself in it tightly, despite the heat.

"I know." She sounds weary.

She doesn't look at me. Then she sighs again.

"He was the one who had you recalled, Nan. From Hever."

"The king wanted me back at court?" I can scarcely wrap my mind around it.

"He said he missed your clever repartee." I wonder if Mary makes her voice sound deliberately dull with this sentence. Still she doesn't look at me. She's picking at the threads of her counterpane.

"He missed . . . talking to me?"

"I don't think there are many women who talk to him like you do. I mean, we never talked. For what it's worth, Nan,

I think he likes you. Intellectually. Not just . . . physically."

And it feels like a betrayal to Thomas, but her words send a little thrill through me. This man, this unattainable, golden god of a man, is actually interested in me. Anne Boleyn. In my words.

"Is he . . ." I don't want to ask. I don't want to cause Mary any more pain. But I have to. "Is he the man you said was interested? The one who is afraid of me?"

Mary barks a little laugh. "The king is afraid of no one, Nan."

"Oh."

"No." Mary turns and finally looks at me. "That was Thomas Wyatt."

I sink the rest of the way to the floor, and my skirts belly out around me. Mary rests a hand on my head and strokes my hair. I lower my head onto the folds of velvet covering her.

"I've made such a mess, Mary. It's all such a mess."

Again a little sad bark. "Not as much as I have, Nan."

I tilt my head and look at her. "But now your life can go back to normal."

"Normal? My life has never been normal, Nan. For the past three years, it's like I've been married to two men. Or not really married at all. I don't know my husband. I don't know the father of my child."

"Catherine is well taken care of. You love her. That's what matters."

"I'm having another," she whispers.

I sit farther back.

"Is it his?"

"Wouldn't that be what Father and George want?" she asks. "Wouldn't that just be the making of the Boleyn family? A royal son?"

"Do you know?"

My own treacherous thoughts race to calculate when the king first expressed interest in me. And my calculations tell me an unsavory truth.

"No, Nan. I don't know. I don't remember."

Her voice is hollow, completely empty of emotion. But I think maybe she does know. She just isn't going to say.

"It would be the making of William, too," she says quietly. "He's so far into debt, he can't even see the surface. Right now, it's only me who is keeping us in clothes and candles." She pats my knee. "And I won't be for long."

"I won't let it happen to me, Mary. I won't be his mistress. I won't be easily discarded."

"Don't be anyone's mistress, Nan." She looks at me sadly, and I know what she's saying. *Not even Thomas Wyatt's.*

"Make sure you know what you want," she finishes. "If anyone can achieve it, you will."

"What do *you* want, Mary?"

Her eyes are almost as red as her skin.

"You know, you're the first person to ask me that. Everyone else just thinks I'll do whatever is asked of me. I've spent my entire life being what everyone else wants. An object to be passed around."

"Do you know what you want?" I whisper.

"I want to be loved, Anne."

Mary finally uses my name. My real name. It sounds awkward and makes me strangely sad. She turns, and my arm drops from her shoulders.

"I want to be somebody to someone."

She pauses and gazes at the thin bead of light perched on the edge of the velvet curtain over the window.

"And I want everyone else to leave me alone."

63

THE RAIN TURNS TO SUNLIGHT AND THE SUN SITS UPON THE earth like a blacksmith's anvil, pounding everything to the consistency of iron. There doesn't seem to be a drop of moisture in the air, the sky gleams without a cloud, and even the grass begins to crumble beneath our feet.

The women shed their heavy velvets like snakeskins, opting for silks and damasks, but we still sweat through the light-colored fabrics, chemise, petticoat, kirtle, bodice, gown, and sleeves weighing us down.

I receive a summons.

To see my father.

I try to move serenely through the donjon and down the stairs into the hall. The palace is stiflingly hot and the galleries are haunted by the smell from the river, suffocating and steamy. I may never complain about the rain again.

The palace is quiet and uncrowded, so Father has claimed a double room, with bed, closet, and outer chamber—the latter perfect for meeting with recalcitrant children.

I curtsy when I enter, reminding myself of Thomas's words. *I am clever. I am more. I am loved.*

The last thought helps me smile as I rise to look at him.

"Daughter."

"Father."

"You come to me at a very busy time. Very busy. I suppose you want money. What do you need, girl?"

With that one word—*girl*—he used to be able to render me small and useless. But I am worth more than that now.

"Father, you summoned me."

I no longer want to control my verbal flux. I want to beat him with it.

Father glares at me from under the ridge of his brow, barely taking the time to look up from his correspondence.

"If that's the way you want to play this, Anne, that's the way we'll play. I know what's going on. I know about your activities."

"From George?"

"From everyone."

The silence grows and fills the room.

"Speak!" he barks. "I have other things to worry about. The king is quarrelsome and petulant about the money I'm to collect for his war. Your brother is making a name for himself as a rake. Your sister is about as much use as a decrepit breeding mare. And you"—he points at me—"have yet to earn your keep."

I don't say, *One day you will have to earn yours.* I don't say, *One day you will be a decrepit old warhorse.* I hold my tongue. One day I will say these things, and more. One day, my words will matter. Even to him.

"What say you?"

"Maybe you should have married me off when you could."

Father stops shuffling his papers. I have never spoken to him so directly. None of us has. He stands and walks slowly toward me, leonine. It takes everything I am not to run away.

"That would have cost me not only a dowry but also the earldom of Ormond. Don't be disingenuous, Anne. It doesn't suit you."

I press my lips together and stay silent. My father is playing with me. And I'm still learning the rules of the game.

"However, you have somehow managed to become the delight of the court. At least certain members of it."

"How do you know that?" I ask, my voice rising again and my color with it.

"So it's true, then."

He didn't know. It was a bluff. It's all a game to him. A risky one. One with high stakes. But a game nonetheless. My feelings, desires, and words count nothing to him.

"Your silence is encouraging," he breathes. I feel it on my face. The words smell like pewter. "Well done."

And then my father smiles at me. A smile I haven't seen since I was six years old and began speaking French better than George. A fist of pain clenches in my chest when I smile back. His minimal praise warms something long-concealed inside me. I still *want* to be the one he admires. The one he loves. The one to whom he wants to give everything.

And I hate myself for it.

He turns away abruptly, back to his desk. Lays just the fingers of his left hand upon it and looks over his shoulder to me.

"Did you know I'm to be made a viscount?"

I shake my head. Another elevation. My sister's efforts made him a baron.

"Congratulations."

"The king assures me it is because of my *continued* service to the crown."

I don't like the way he stresses the word *continued*. His first elevation to the peerage was a payment for the prostitution of his oldest daughter. Is this new one because of me? Is the quality of loyalty and service dependent on pandering?

"The Ormond earldom is also likely to be restored to its rightful inheritors."

The Boleyns. I begin to feel I am fetching a high price. I'm not sure I want that on my head.

"The king asked that you attend the creation ceremony at Bridewell next month," Father continues. "He would like to see you there.

"I have already ordered a new gown for you. Slashed with cloth of gold, as befits your status as the daughter of a viscount."

For my father, the deal is already done. Signed, sealed, and delivered in a cloth-of-gold gift wrap.

Father shuffles his papers and brings out a little wooden box, decorated with the Boleyn bull, edged in gilt.

"For you, Daughter," he says, and gives it to me. "Make me proud." He strokes the newly acquired ermine collar of his doublet.

My hands shake as I open it. It is lined with crimson velvet.

With one finger, he pushes aside the folds of velvet to reveal a string of pearls—much like the one I gave to Jane. But this string carries a pendant. A gold *B* from which hang suspended three teardrop pearls.

"So you don't forget where you came from."

He walks back behind his desk, then turns to me with something almost like affection in his eyes.

"My clever girl."

I look at the box and the jewel it contains, the fresh gleam of the gold. For once, I'm the prized possession of Thomas Boleyn. But my rise in value is dependent on the depreciation of my siblings.

"I may be clever, Father," I tell him coldly, "but I am not yours."

I curtsy and leave him there. I will make my own choice, whether or not it elevates my father.

Still, I fasten the chain around my neck. Because the Boleyns will stick together. I can never forget where I came from, whatever choice I make.

Bridewell Palace
1525

64

THE COURT RECONVENES AT THE CONFLUENCE OF THE THAMES and the Fleet beneath the hottest sky I believe I've ever seen. It is white with the height of summer, not even a trace of blue above us. The many-paned windows glitter against the gaudy red and white of the palace façade and fill the rooms with the blanching bright light until the curtains are drawn and the entire palace is cast into manufactured gloom.

I escape to the little hemmed garden between the palace and the wall of Whitefriars. The heat of the sun has flattened everything, pounding the golden grass to the earth, the blossoms from the trees, and the river Fleet to dead, miasmic lifelessness. The sun feels close, heavy. My shadow doesn't appear before me. It's stuck tight to my slippers. I have no advance notice, no rearguard. Only me.

I see him before he sees me. He is a man with direction and purpose. With reason. With choice. I can do nothing but stare as he approaches.

I'm in love with the curls in his hair, with the way he walks. I thrill at the sound of his voice and the thought of how his body moves. I want to know him, touch him, see him, devour him.

As always, Thomas knows my mind as well as I do. He takes

the last three steps to me like a comet drawn to earth. I feel like I did the day Jane knocked the breath from me. He kisses me to the point of collapse, and then follows me down to the long grass at the base of a gnarled apple tree.

I can't let kisses make the choice for me.

"Listen to me." I open my eyes to the grass, the tree, the sky. To him.

"I am," he murmurs, trailing kisses down my throat. "Every move is music." He follows the neck of my bodice to where the skin is so sensitive I forget what I'm thinking.

Almost.

"Stop." I push him away and he sits back, irritable.

"I can't." I can't look at him when I say it. "You're married."

"I've left her."

"It doesn't change the fact."

"Don't be intractable, Anne," he says, desperation graveling his words. "There are plenty of men at court who are in love with women who aren't their wives. Look at my father. Look at your uncle Norfolk. Look at . . ."

I feel the tears burning and itchy against my lashes.

"Look at the king? That's the point, Thomas. I don't want to be Mary."

I don't want to end up weeping on the floor. I don't want to hate myself for my choices. Or my love.

"No, Anne," he says harshly. "Look at me. I'm not him. Don't you see? Can't you see me?"

I see him. I also see the future with him. Hiding away from the eyes and gossip of the court, from whispers. Being with him. My body aches with wanting it. I see the months and years curl away like smoke, my words and possibilities with them. Because no one would speak to me. No one would listen. Not even my family.

"I don't want to be a mistress to anyone."

I feel a tear traverse the sunburned patch of my cheek. And Thomas catches it.

"The king wants to send me away," he says. "Away from England. He thinks I would make an excellent diplomat." He flashes a sardonic smile. "I think what he really wants is to get me away from you."

I stare straight ahead of me, unseeing. The weight of the *B* around my neck presses the breath from me.

"Apparently your father put the idea forward. And my father thought it was a good one." He sighs. "Good riddance, more like."

I force myself to choke out the words. "I'm sorry."

I'm sorry for being the craftsman of that path. I'm sorry I can't tell him I love him. I'm sorry I want so much. I'm sorry I'm me.

He pulls me to him so my head rests over his heart.

"Never apologize. I thought I taught you that long ago."

"But it's my fault. I'm the one who started it. I was so angry with you and I wanted you gone."

"You could do penance, then, and come with me," he says, stroking the path of my hair where it twists beneath my hood. "We could travel the world together. You've always wanted to leave."

"And you've never wanted to."

"It wouldn't matter if I were with you."

I lift my head to look at him. His face is so close to mine, I can see the chips of flint within the blue of his eyes.

"The life of a diplomat is no life for a girl," I say, repeating the words I heard so often from my father. But I know they are true. Long, grueling hours on the road. Rough, primitive sleeping conditions. War camps. The girls who travel with them are not mistresses, but worse.

"What would you do if I asked you to come to Allington? If I could hide you away there? Forever?"

"What are you asking me?"

"To give up the admiration of a thousand people for the love of just one."

We stare at each other for a breath. For a lifetime.

"What would you do, Anne? If I asked you for that?"

"I would . . ."

Love you.

"Would you go if I asked?"

Something about his question rings untrue. I sit up.

"If?" I can hardly speak through the constriction in my throat. Through the doubt and hope. "If you asked? Because right now you're not really asking me that, are you?"

Thomas stops. He is right next to me, but he is so far away.

"The castle belongs to my father."

"And he would never condone such a sordid use of it."

"It wouldn't be sordid to me, Anne. It would be sacred."

He tries to pull me back down, but I resist.

"And Elizabeth—*your wife*—lives there."

"I'll throw her out." He looks at me hopefully.

"Even you wouldn't be so heartless, Thomas Wyatt."

He turns his attention to the grass by his knee. I watch him slide his fingers along one blade at a time. The tips of his fingers are stained with ink and he wears no rings. He plays the lute with little talent and none of the feeling he expresses in his poetry. And yet those fingers make me sing beneath his touch.

"He asked about you and me."

I don't have to ask who *he* is. It is now as if this hum encapsulates the three of us. Like a bubble. Like a web. Emotions crash through me. Delight. Fear. Anticipation. Guilt.

"What did you tell him?"

I ask it casually.

"That we were neighbors. That we share a love of words." Thomas pulls up a strand of grass and examines it. "He laughed at that."

Tension coils like an iron band across his shoulders. He stares at the blade of grass, as if pulling his thoughts from it. He's holding something back.

"What else?"

"He asked . . . he asked about our relationship."

His words are almost lost in the shadows. His fingers pick at another blade of grass, peeling one at a time from the earth.

"And?"

He finally looks at me.

"I told him the truth."

"Which is?" Even I don't know the truth.

"That I'm in love with you."

I wonder if this is my reprieve. There will be no choice. It will be made for me. The king believes in love. The king will let me go. There is a certain amount of serenity in this thought.

"What did he say?"

"He laughed again."

Thomas returns to his study of the grass, wrenching larger clumps out by their roots. The sound is like the shredding of dreams.

"And then he asked if you felt the same."

I remember Jane's words: *Like music only plays when you're together. Like the air tastes of strawberries. Like one touch—one look—could send you whirling like a seed on the wind.*

"I told him I didn't know." Thomas examines the green that stains his fingers. "That you had never told me so."

"Oh."

Terror strikes hot in my chest. I'm going to have to say it. I wipe my hands on my skirts.

"I—"

"He asked," Thomas interrupts, "if I'd ever shared your bed."

My mouth goes dry.

"What did you say?"

"Yes."

"But that's a lie!"

I push him roughly and scramble to my feet. Push him again when he tries to get up. He cowers. Doesn't defend himself. His actions are defenseless. And he doesn't apologize.

"Why would you say that?"

"Because it's the truth; don't you remember?"

The night at Hever. Of course I remember. That night was magical. That night should have been left untarnished.

"Or were you too drunk? Always trying to outdo George."

The accusation flings me backward, and I stagger against the orchard wall.

"That night was mine," I gasp, feeling again that he's knocked the wind out of me. "It wasn't yours to tell."

Thomas sees the damage he has done. Recognizes it. He leaps up, all grace gone. He cannot land on his feet this time.

"I love you, Anne," he says desperately, reaching for me, but I stumble out of reach. "It makes me crazy. Insanely jealous.

"He made me kneel before him. Like a supplicant. We've been friends for ten years, and he made me do that. Treated me like no one. Like nothing. I wanted to hurt him. To stop him from wanting you. Because *I* want you. All of you. All for myself."

I feel like this should make me happy. He loves me that much. But I don't want him to have all of me. I don't want to give that to anyone.

And I don't want all of him. Not the jealousy. Not the possessiveness, the willingness to see me as a gamble, as a prize.

What was it the king said over that game of bowls?

"Perhaps the call is not yours to make."

Even beneath the radiant sky, his eyes have lost their airy lightness and have become dark and deep and vivid.

"So you don't want me," he murmurs.

I want him so badly I feel like glass on the verge of shattering.

"Do you want him, Anne?"

"I don't . . ."

But I do. Or I did. Contrition and despair stanch the flow of words. The time to answer expires, and we are silent.

"You don't what? Want him? Or you don't know?"

Whatever I say, I can't take back. Wherever the next moments take me, I will not be able to alter the course of my life once they are past.

"I don't want to be nobody," I say finally, "locked away in the country while you travel the world in service to your king. You say you want all of me, but how can I give up my family, my friends, my position at court? My self?"

The words come out without me thinking about them. As usual.

"Thomas, if I were to leave—this court, this life—don't you see? I would always wonder what would have happened if I stayed."

I can't abandon the life I was meant to live.

"I don't want to be forgotten."

"But you will not be forgotten, my dear. Remember?" A dash of his bravado returns. "I will make you famous in my poetry. Your name will go down through the ages, rolling from the tongues of strangers."

"I don't want to be remembered because of you, Thomas," I choke. "I want to be remembered because of me."

Thomas wraps his arms around me. Kisses my forehead. I can't move.

"For what it's worth, I don't think he believed me. I must

have looked like I was lying, because what I implied bore no relation to the truth of what I felt."

"Your grip on the truth is tenuous, Thomas."

I feel his smile on my temple. And we stand there in an embrace that isn't.

"He told me never to speak of it again," he says quietly. "He made me promise."

Thomas releases me and rubs his hands over his face. Stares up into the heat of the sky.

"Do you want to be chased all your life, Anne? To run always, trying to stay ahead of the pack?"

"No, Thomas, I don't want to run." I look him straight in the eye, daring my heart to break. "I want to lead."

He closes his eyes, his face twisted like someone recovering from a blow. When he opens them again, they are hollow.

"Then you win, Anne. You win the bet. I will not pursue you."

He stops. Swallows. "But I will follow you anywhere."

He takes my hand and turns it over. Strokes it open. I feel the kiss on my palm all the way up through my arm and into my heart.

Which snaps into ragged halves.

65

BRIDEWELL IS TO BE THE VENUE FOR THE CREATION CEREMONY in which my father will become a viscount. And Henry Fitzroy, the king's six-year-old illegitimate son, will become an earl and a duke in a single day. The men of the court simmer and sweat as some of them strive for elevation and others remain stagnant. It is like living in a stewpot.

The day before the ceremony, I seek out coolness and quiet, my lute newly strung. Instead of playing, I sit and stare at my hands on the strings. They are very pale, nails smooth and short. Calluses on the tips from the lute strings. A single ring. One crooked finger.

I think of Thomas's poem, the one he spoke when I played Atalanta. The riddle over my name—the same backward and forward or even split in two. Anna. I pluck two notes. An-na. Two halves. Incomplete.

An usher approaches me and bows.

"The king requests your company."

A personal request. From the king. For me. All the notes fly from me, my fingers like startled birds. I barely manage to control my tongue.

"I should love to see His Majesty."

"Good. Then he expects you at eight of the clock."

I stand, still and anticipatory in the quiet that follows.

Was that a request? I wonder. *Or an order?*

When I sit, I discover that I can no longer find the music within me.

As the hour approaches, an usher comes to escort me through the guard and presence chambers, the last of the sunlight slanting through the towering expanse of glass on the south wall, the gardens and the Thames splayed out below.

We pass through the closet and into the Privy Chamber, where King Henry stands, alone. The usher bows low, and I kneel into a curtsy.

"Leave us," the king says, and the usher beside me scuttles away. And I am entirely alone with the king. I wonder if he will keep me kneeling, ask the same questions he asked of Thomas.

I can feel his presence in the room, his restless energy. The inaudible hum as though from a constantly vibrating lute string.

"Rise, Mistress Boleyn." He breaks the silence. "There is wine, if you would like some."

I look up, surprised. The king is offering to serve me?

But no. Two glasses have already been poured. Every need anticipated.

"And strawberries."

A dish of them. Red and round and glittering like jewels.

"I saw how much you liked them at George's wedding."

He looks shy. Wanting to please.

"Thank you."

The color of the claret and strawberries reminds me of the dream I had months ago. A dream of red and blood and the inability to sing.

"No, thank you for answering my request. You didn't have to come."

"Didn't I?" I blurt the words, and stutter the next through my hand. "Your Majesty, my greatest fault is my inability to stop my thoughts from becoming spoken words."

The king laughs. He throws his head back, the wash of red-gold hair flashing against the last of the sun's rays. His wine sloshes in the goblet, sending drops scattering across the wooden floorboards like fallen beads.

"Then your greatest fault is one of the things about you that I find most charming." He cocks his head and squints at me a little. "But are you so used to following orders?"

"The men in my family expect subservience."

"I doubt you give it to them."

His gray eyes are childlike despite the fan of sun-worn creases just beginning to show around them.

"I believe," I begin, and look at him again. His posture invites intimacy. "I believe people should have the right to make their own choices. Even women."

"In life? Or in love?"

He studies me, waiting. We are talking around the very issue I want to avoid. I do want a choice. My choice. I just wish it were easier.

"Both."

"Did you choose young Lord Percy yourself?"

He asks this so conversationally. As if speaking to an acquaintance, a friend. Not to a subject. Not to the girl whose very choice was thwarted by the machinations of his own chief minister.

I nod. I chose Percy. More fool me.

"He would never have made you happy, Anna."

I nod again. I won't make that mistake twice.

"Now I have no prospects at all," I say. If the king truly was part of the plot to end the match, to get Percy married to Talbot's daughter, let him feel a little remorse.

"None?"

"Because of the Percy scandal, the man to whom I was betrothed now shuns me. And no one else is interested."

"The poet Wyatt seems to be."

There is nothing childlike in his face now.

"He's married."

"That's hardly an impediment to true affection."

"It seems to me," I say pointedly, "that the outcome is always the same. At the end, the woman is left with a tattered reputation, no self-esteem, and the label of a whore."

He frowns and inspects the contents of his goblet. I stare at his lowered brow, holding my breath.

"You certainly speak your mind. I wonder"—he looks up at me again, and I see shame on his face—"what is your opinion of me?"

"You certainly ask direct questions."

"I wish to know the answer, Anna. I see no reason to beat around the bush. You are the only person who has ever spoken to me as if I am a man as well as a king. Flawed, but by things that can be rectified. I cherish your words even when they run counter to my own thoughts. And I love to hear your voice." He takes a step toward me, and all the air is sucked from the room.

I see the man—my body makes this embarrassingly clear. But I am also painfully aware of the power embodied in him.

"I think you are a great king," I stammer. "A humanist and a patron of the arts."

"Enough flattery." He fixes his gaze on mine. "What do you really think?"

I take a deep breath that fills me with elation and terror in equal measure. He's given me license to speak my mind. Without censure.

"I think you treated my sister as if she were disposable. As if she didn't have feelings of her own. I think you rushed to war with the French over a flimsy excuse, to prove your might and masculinity. I think you wield the fear people have of you like a sword. And that you are blind to the feelings of those around you."

King Henry's face darkens. His eyes narrow. The vibrations of his energy increase in speed as if tuned to a higher pitch. A long, sharp note.

I have gone too far.

He twists a ring on his right hand. My ring. I stare at it, sure he'll take it off. Throw it at me. Send me back to the beginning. To where I came from. To Father. To nothing.

Then he sighs.

"I regret any pain I caused your sister. She is a sweet girl, and beautiful. But not someone who is truly my match. I thought it better to cut our bonds now, rather than extend the pain later."

I say nothing, pegged still by his nearness, by his response, by his confession.

"I have no remorse over my war with the French, for they are a constant threat. But I can tell you now that you were right: women can make formidable foes. And I have ceased my crusade against them."

He looks at me, his gaze clear and direct.

He said I was right. My words made an impact. Or at least an impression. He has stopped the war. Just as I suggested so long ago.

My words have power. My opinions were correct.

"So it was not God's will."

I will push him to the brink of detonation. He doesn't speak, so I press on. If this is the man I am to choose over Thomas Wyatt, he has to know who I am. My heartbreak has made me reckless.

"It was a waste."

His gaze will not let me go.

"This sword of fear you say I wield," he says. "It does not seem to affect you."

I am afraid. Only my tongue is not.

"I have but a little neck," I tell the king. "It will not hurt if the blow comes clean."

He suddenly crosses the distance between us in two strides. His movement makes my heart flutter in panic. His nearness turns it to liquid ready to boil.

The scent of cloves and orange water fills my senses. And something else. Earthy and animal, like ambergris. Wild. I have to lay my hand on the table to steady myself. Everything I ever wanted is right here before me. Everything but one thing.

"I believe I am blind to nothing," he murmurs, the words fragrant and honeyed. "Especially not the feelings of others."

He takes one more step forward and moves to kiss me.

"You already have a wife," I say as fast as I can before his lips touch mine and everything is lost. "And I will not be your mistress."

"You are very sure about that."

He is close. Too close. He doesn't move away. I can almost taste his lips from here.

"All my life I have been shipped and trundled and bought and sold by my father. I want to be mine. I don't want to be a mistress, Your Majesty, because a mistress is not a person, but a thing. Worse than that. Nothing. I don't want to be nothing."

I watch him for a long, slow moment, and he studies me. Cautiously.

"You are not a possession, Anna. Not a *thing*. And you could never be nothing."

"Exactly, Your Majesty," I say. Soaring, untethered by the knowledge that he understands. "I will never be anyone's mistress. Ever."

"Then there is no hope for Thomas Wyatt, is there?"

The sound of his name makes me want to sink to the floor

in defeat. But I manage to keep my limbs stable, to keep my feet under me. I look the king directly in the eye. And shake my head.

"Good." The king erupts into that devastating smile that first caught me at the age of thirteen and refused to let go. "I will ever live in hope, Mistress Boleyn. Hope that you will never be a mistress. But a partner. A friend."

"My brother says that men and women can't be friends."

"Well, let's see if we can prove him wrong, shall we?"

He extends his hand, to escort me back to the door.

"What seems impossible is not always so, I have found," he says slowly. "The sun can turn dark in the sky. The flat earth is actually round." He stops. Turns to me. "A commoner may marry a king." He pauses. "My grandmother was the daughter of a 'new man.'"

A tingling buzz spreads up my arms and into my scalp, sending my thoughts scattering like wisps on the wind. I catch hold of one. "Your grandmother was related to the courts of Europe."

He chuckles. "Distantly. My grandfather married her for love, not connections."

"What are you saying?" I manage to whisper through the howl of my thoughts. I can't take my eyes off of him.

"Only that there are more ways than one around a problem. And that there is always hope."

My mind retraces all the steps of the conversation, lurching from one point to the next, throwing each one down so I don't expect too much. I tell myself all the lies I need to hear. He's flirting with me. Pursuing me. Just like Wyatt used to with his offers to make me his mistress.

The king's eyes are once more like a child's. Buoyant. He's offering friendship. Nothing else.

"A kiss, Anna?" he asks. "Just this once."

I lift my chin, tilt my cheek to offer it. But he kisses me full on the mouth, warm and strong and sweet.

And wild.

It is not a friendly kiss at all.

And I like it.

66

On the morning of the creation ceremony, the sun rises quickly into the white of the sky and the world is drenched in lemon. The flavor of the air changes the higher the sun rises, from citrus to rose to claret, and the sultriness submerges us as the court makes its way to the king's chambers.

My father has had me dressed head to foot in finery—my gown, my sleeves, my hood decked with jewels and gold embroidery. And my *B* strung from its chain of pearls. *B* for *belonging*.

I want this. The elevation. The ceremony. The belonging.

The king.

The sun comes hot through the windows, the room awash in gold and silk. I am surrounded by the press and stench of perfume, the musk of ambition.

"Make way!"

Three ushers abreast, arms interlinked, push their way through the crowd. I am stuffed beside Lady Kildare and Lady Arundel. Pushed back against the men behind us, solid as a wall. I step on a wide-toed boot and turn to its owner.

Henry Percy. My skin threatens to crawl off my bones to escape even the possibility of touch, my spine prickling with revulsion. For him. For myself. One wrong choice. I press down the fear that I might make another.

His face betrays nothing.

A blast of trumpets signals the beginning of the ceremony. The Earl of Northumberland, swathed in superiority and ceremony, enters, carrying a sword before him. A herald bears the new coat of arms. And next comes a little boy, flanked by the earls of Arundel and Oxford, shining like a newly minted coin, cast in the mold of his father.

The Countess of Arundel mutters, "Two earls and a bastard."

I hold myself still. Tell myself I won't react. Won't respond. Won't say a word.

Then I take a deep breath and turn on Lady Arundel.

"Two earls and a *prince*, your ladyship."

She purses her already thin lips until they disappear. "And what right have you to an opinion, *Mistress* Boleyn? What right have you even to be here?"

I look at her, knowing I shouldn't say what I'm about to.

"I received a personal invitation from the king."

The words are just too sweet.

I look to the dais, where he sits. Where the little boy shines, the king is positively radiant. Dressed in red and gold, he is my memory made manifest, the embodiment of all I ever wished for. And I am here at his request.

The cardinal, Wolsey, stands on his right, the two dukes on his left. But he dwarfs them all. For the rest of the ceremony, its parade of pomp and cloth of gold, I can't take my eyes off him.

Little Fitzroy is granted the title of his grandfather, Duke of

Richmond, and the title of the Duke of Somerset, the earldom of which had belonged to the boy's great-great-grandfather, himself the illegitimate son of royalty. Fitzroy's grandfather became Henry VII. I'm sure the entire world wonders if this little boy will become Henry IX. Princess Mary is the king's only legitimate child and therefore his heir. But these men don't want a girl on the throne. Rumor has it that Queen Katherine has gone through the change and will now never have sons. So the court—and the king—may be seeking other options.

He needs a legitimate son. She can no longer have children. He has good reason to wish to replace the queen. *A commoner may marry a king.* I tell myself it's impossible, but his words beat against the back of my mind like the tide: *what seems impossible is not always so.*

The list of elevations grows long, and the number of peers increases. The king honors each new peer with a word, a glance, a smile. Each man takes a turn as the center of attention, the heart around which the world revolves.

I allow myself to imagine, for a moment, what it might be like to be that heart forever.

Finally, my father stands before the king, kneels, and is given a blessing. Raised from nothing. The Boleyns, sons of merchants and mayors, commoners, but not common.

The king looks out at the crowd over my father's head and finds me immediately, following the line of tension between us. It resonates through me. I cannot look away.

When the ceremony is over, the crowd spills out into the garden and courtyards, finally able to move and breathe. I find myself in the outer court, baking and breathless beneath the midday sun.

Face to face with the Duchess of Suffolk.

"You're here," she says, looking me up and down over the bridge of her nose. She knows. Somehow, she knows.

She holds a tiny boy by the hand. Her three-year-old son has been made the Earl of Lincoln today.

"Well?" she snaps. "Do you not honor the new earl?"

I curtsy to the little boy, who looks about to cry.

When I rise, I match the duchess's level gaze.

"Only an earl, Your Grace?" I ask, delirious with the pleasure of watching her pout.

She flounces away, dragging the boy behind her, his thumb in his mouth.

The king and his son enter the courtyard. They greet the new peers one at a time, following courtly rules, following precedence. After each greeting, the king scans the crowd and finds me. Every time. Acknowledging me. Wanting me.

Fitzroy is starting to droop, his face flushed, his eyes heavy. But he maintains an air of strength and control, despite his age, despite the heat.

He might actually make a good king.

"Mistress Boleyn," the king says, as his son arrives at my skirts. "May I introduce the Duke of Richmond and Somerset."

I curtsy deeply, my head almost at the height of the boy himself.

"Your Grace," I murmur, look into his face, and wink.

432

Little Henry Fitzroy grins back, and squinches up his face in an attempt to wink as well. Then we both giggle.

"Will you be attending the banquet and dancing later this evening?" the boy asks, standing to his full height, which is still just level with my midriff.

"Yes, Your Grace."

"Will you do me the honor of a dance?"

I like this boy. Almost as much as his father.

"Yes, of course, Your Grace."

He bows and I curtsy again. When I rise, I risk a glance at the king's face. His smile creases deep into his cheeks, his eyes alive with it. The hum starts to throb within me, and I take a deep breath, catching a whiff of cloves.

"Dare I exploit your generosity by requesting a dance, as well?" the king asks. He watches my every move.

"It would be an honor, Your Majesty."

He leans over his son so he can whisper to me out of the boy's hearing. "The honor to touch you will be all mine."

I am submersed in a premonition of that touch sparking like fireworks on my skin. I fall into a curtsy to hide my expression—or to hide from his. I rise when he moves on to show off his son to yet another group of courtiers. He turns once to look over his shoulder at me.

And to wink.

"You've done it, Anne." George takes my arm, squeezes it, and swiftly kisses my cheek. "You are the clever one."

I look at him over my shoulder. I don't smell wine on his breath.

"Aren't you lucky to be related to me, then?"

He grins, but there is sadness in the corners of his eyes.

"I always have been, Sister."

"As have I."

The white flags are raised. For now.

"I have something for you."

"A gift?"

"Yes, but not from me. Even I don't change that quickly."

He presses a little package into my hand.

"It's from Wyatt."

I look away, across the courtyard to where the glass shines flat like eyes.

"I almost didn't give it to you."

When I turn back to him, George seems vulnerable, beseeching.

"I hope I did the right thing."

I nod, but cannot answer.

I find a corner beneath the all-seeing windows and open the parchment. Inside is my jewel, the bright golden *A*, the single pearl. The ribbon is gone. Instead, around it is a poem:

> *Whoso list to hunt? I know where is an hind!*
> *But as for me, alas! I may no more.*
> *The vain travail hath wearied me so sore;*
> *I am of them that furthest come behind.*
> *Yet may I by no means my wearied mind*
> *Draw from the deer; but as she fleeth afore*
> *Fainting I follow. I leave off therefore*

Since in a net I seek to hold the wind.
Who list her hunt, I put him out of doubt
As well as I, may spend his time in vain.
And graven with diamonds in letters plain,
There is written, her fair neck round about:
    "Noli me tangere; for Caesar's I am,
    And wild for to hold, though I seem tame."

I look for him, to tell him I am no one's but mine. Not his. Not Caesar's. I look to argue with him. To kiss him. To run away with him.

But he's nowhere to be seen.

He left me. My palms begin to sweat and I have to grip the paper between my fingers to keep them still.

No.

I fold the poem deliberately, paying careful attention to every crease until my heart resumes a steady beat.

He let me go.

A trumpet blasts. The king stands at the bottom of the processional stair, his son beside him. The entire court descends into a hot, heavy hush.

"Please accompany me into the great hall," he says. "We will celebrate this day with feasting." His eyes find me. "And dancing."

The crowd murmurs, a sound heavier than the buzzing of bees in the roses.

He extends his hand to the queen but watches me all the while.

Queen Katherine cannot begin to smile. She refuses to look the little duke in the eye when she passes him. She is here under duress.

Owned.

By him.

I hesitate, watching the guests scramble to queue according to precedence. None of them notices when the king winks at me again.

"Come, Sister." George is at my side, offering his hand. "Shall we embark on the future?" In his face, I see a glimmer of my childhood familiar. The one who challenged me to climb the highest, because he knew I could.

I look once more around the emptying courtyard. The shadows from the palace walls have just begun to nip at our feet. I step away from them and slip the poem and my jewel into the little pocket at my waist.

"Together," I say.

Hand in hand, we climb the processional stair, rising in the celebratory uproar of a capricious court. As we enter the palace, we are blinded by the ascent from sunshine into darkness.

Author's Note

A considerable amount of research goes into any work of historical fiction, and I am indebted to the writings of the multitude
of historians who devote their time and their passion to dis-
covering the truths of history and making the past come alive
in the retelling. Particular thanks are due here to Julia Fox,
Antonia Fraser, Eric Ives, David Loades, Claire Ridgway, Nicola
Shulman, David Starkey, Simon Thurley, Retha Warnicke,
Alison Weir, and Josephine Wilkinson.

The facts about Anne Boleyn's early life are sketchy at best.
There isn't consensus among historians even about the year
of her birth. Strong evidence presented by Hugh Paget in 1981
suggests that she was born in 1500 or 1501. Most modern
historians accept this date. However, a marginal comment in
a seventeenth-century biography of Anne's daughter, Elizabeth
I, suggests Anne was born in 1507. This theory is supported in
detail by Retha Warnicke in her biography *The Rise and Fall of
Anne Boleyn*. Because I wanted to write a book about a teenage
girl who returns to a "home" that is patently not her own, I

chose the latter date. I don't necessarily think it is more likely, but it serves my purpose best. I am, after all, a writer of fiction. Though I am committed to historical accuracy in my novels, to me, the story matters most, and I will leave the debate to the experts.

We know that Anne participated in the pageant of *The Château Vert* at Shrovetide in 1522, performing the part of Perseverance—a name that ultimately describes her well. I suggest that Anne is sent to Hever in disgrace after the pageant, but because she disappears from the accurately dated historical record for a while, there is no evidence to support or contradict this.

There is evidence that Anne formed an attachment to Henry Percy, the eldest son of the Earl of Northumberland, during the spring of 1523. In fact, Percy was interrogated twice about this relationship—it would have been an impediment to Henry and Anne's marriage, but it also might have provided grounds for divorce when things went sour. Both times, Percy swore upon the Bible that there had been no precontract, no betrothal, no attachment. Do we believe him?

During the reign of Katherine of Aragon's daughter, Mary I (who temporarily was made illegitimate when Henry declared his marriage to Katherine invalid and subsequently married Anne), several stories were written defaming Anne Boleyn as promiscuous and possibly a poisoner. One story involved Thomas Wyatt and a visit to Hever during which he spent the night in her bedroom. Another tells how Henry interrogated Wyatt, who admitted to a relationship with Anne, which the king told him to keep quiet. These stories could be hearsay—invented by Mary's supporters, who would naturally want to depict Anne and her daughter, Elizabeth, negatively. I have my doubts about the truth of these stories—their intention was slander—but found the concept interesting.

Anne's detractors also made much of any perceived physical imperfections. Though I don't believe the myth that Anne had a sixth finger, I give a basis for the invention of one by creating a minor deformity caused by a childhood accident.

Thomas Wyatt's grandson George wrote a biography of Anne Boleyn as a rebuttal of her detractors. In it, he describes an argument between the king and Wyatt over a game of bowls during which both men produced little trinkets belonging to Anne Boleyn. George Wyatt's tale was written decades after Anne's death and, again, the accuracy is questionable—it was probably passed to him verbally by Thomas himself. If my version is slightly different from his, couldn't it be because a poet would want to present himself in the best possible light—and his rival in the worst?

No one knows the exact timing of the beginning of Henry's interest in Anne. Some place it as early as *The Château Vert* in 1522. Others speculate that Henry's displaying the motto "Declare I Dare Not" at a joust in 1526, proves that was the beginning. And still others trace it to 1527, when they think they can date his first love letters to her. David Starkey, in *Six Wives: The Queens of Henry VIII*, suggested *The Castle of Loyalty* and Christmas 1524, and I have gone with that. I shortened the time line and slightly altered the chronicle of the pageant (which took place over several weeks) in order to preserve the pace of the story. The imagery of that Christmas and the creation ceremony the following summer captured my imagination.

I also took a little poetic license with the card game Anne plays with the men of the court. Primero is a complicated forerunner of poker, with four of a kind being the best hand. However, because of an intricate point-counting strategy, Anne winning with a hand of four kings was not a foregone conclusion, and despite the excellent hand, she still could have lost. I just couldn't give up the delicious image of the four kings on the table signaling her victory.

Most of the poetry quoted is attributed to the real Thomas Wyatt, though they have been transcribed from the originals to be easier on the modern reader and some have been abridged to suit the context. In the Tudor court, poetry was often spoken rather than written down thus making it more fluid and adaptable to circumstances. I like to think of Wyatt revising and adding to each one as suited him best.

Wyatt dated none of his written works, so placement of them in time is difficult. It is generally believed that the poem that begins "Whoso list to hunt" was written after his ambassadorial trip to Italy in 1527, when he would have become much better acquainted with Petrarch's sonnet on which it is based. But I chose to move it up a few years—call it poetic license. There is no record of him creating a play about Atalanta, but a poet and a romantic such as Wyatt could easily have done so.

The poem that James Butler quotes about a man who dreams a girl comes to his bed, "content to do him pleasure," is unattributed, but is known to have circulated the court around this time.

Poetry was extremely useful at court—for saying things that one wouldn't necessarily say out loud in other circumstances. I owe much of my knowledge of Wyatt's poetry to Nicola Shulman and her excellent book—*Graven with Diamonds*—about Thomas Wyatt and his literary canon. However, all allusions and intentions I attribute to the poetry come from my own imagination.

So what happened next?

A simplistic (and not entirely accurate) account is that Henry changed religion—and the Western world—in an effort to terminate his marriage to Katherine because Anne always refused to be his mistress. She finally married him when he succeeded in having his marriage to Katherine annulled— eight years after the events in this book. Again, I leave the comprehensive explanation of this complicated issue to the experts.

George Boleyn rose quickly in the king's service, acquiring appointments, stewardships, and manor holdings—perhaps due to Anne's influence? His story certainly continued to be irretrievably linked with Anne's. Not much is known about his marriage to Jane, and though many assume it was unhappy, the evidence to support that interpretation has been called into question.

Thomas Boleyn became Earl of Ormond in 1529, though

the title fell back to James Butler after Boleyn's death in 1539. He became Earl of Wiltshire the same year, allowing George to become Viscount Rochford. Mary's husband, William Carey, died of the sweating sickness in 1528. Six years later, she married her second husband, William Stafford, secretly. For love.

Thomas Wyatt went on his first ambassadorial mission to France in 1526—one for which he volunteered. Some say he was heartbroken and had to get away. He spent a great deal of time abroad during the next few years (including a short stay in a Bolognese prison). But at court, he was a favorite of both Anne and the king, and followed them everywhere.

And Anne? Most people know what happens to her. I prefer not to include it here, because in this book, at least, she is alive and optimistic, on the verge of love. About to face the biggest adventure of her life.

Acknowledgments

There seems to be an accepted sequence to these things but in the spirit of my main character, I'm going to defy convention and start by thanking my family. My husband, Gary, and my two sons, Freddie and Charlie, have learned and graciously accepted much about living with a writer. I want to thank them for their support and their enthusiasm, and for the boys' weekends without me that turned into boys' *weeks* as I became more and more determined to do Anne justice.

Unlike Anne, in all my life, I can't remember my father being disappointed in me or my mother being absent. I want to thank them both for supporting all my decisions and crazy schemes, even when I made what was obviously an unsuitable choice.

Because we choose our families as well as being born into one, I must thank my friends. The ones who helped define my childhood—Mona Doughterty, Wilathi Weaver, Carrie Ferguson, Abe Crow, Kelly and Karen Moore, the drama geeks and scholarship nerds. And my friends today who form The Village—Brenda Seyk, Eva Bush, Maureen Ladd, Trina Camping, Julia Smith, Jenn Henderson, Amber Robinson-Burmester and their husbands and kids—for their help and support in times of celebration as well as in times of need.

My family of writers made sure I stayed true to my story, did the right thing by my characters, and didn't succumb to the crazy.

Thank you. To Bret Ballou, for well-timed texts and e-mails and for being the closer. To Donna Cooner for seeing the point and offering distraction. To Veronica Rossi for a fabulous title and late-night chats, and for saying you love my "wicked words." To Talia Vance for loving Thomas Wyatt as much as I did, even before there were kissing scenes. And to the rest of my honored and trusted confederacy of beta readers: Jackie Garlick, Kristen Held, and Beth Hull. And thank you to the Class of 2k12 for picking me up when I fell down and for creative curse words that made me wish I wrote contemporary novels so I could use them in my work.

Like people, every book has a family. *Tarnish* wouldn't exist without my agent, Catherine Drayton, who asked if I could write more than one novel set in the court of Henry VIII and then made it happen. Thank you, as well, to Lyndsey Blessing, for taking my books abroad and to Lizzy Kremer for being their advocate in the UK.

From day one, the team at Viking and Penguin Young Readers have been enthusiastic champions of my work. Special thanks go to Joanna Cardenas for perceptive comments at a crucial time, to Theresa Evangelista for a stunning cover and Kate Renner for an equally gorgeous interior. I must thank Janet Pascal and Kathryn Hinds a thousand times for checking my continuity and accuracy and for correcting my punctuation—a vexatious job, I'm sure, but I am ever so grateful. And to Marisa Russell and all of the Penguin marketing and publicity family, thank you for holding *Tarnish* up to catch the light.

Writing a book is a solitary endeavor, but revising it is a team effort. You can't always see how a sibling helps shape your life, but I can see on every page of this book how my editor's gentle touch and keen eye added structure, emotion, and depth. Thank you, Kendra Levin, for everything.

And finally—but most importantly—thank *you*. A novel needs a family of readers to have life, so thank you for being a part of Anne's.

Keep reading for a sample chapter of
Katherine Longshore's next book

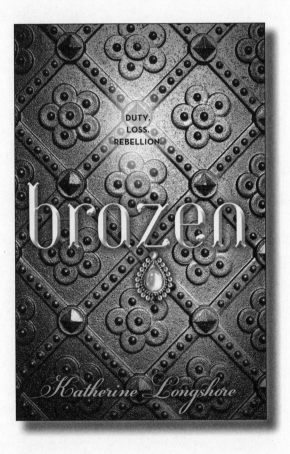

DUTY.
LOSS.
REBELLION.

brazen

Katherine Longshore

Hampton Court Palace
26 November, 1533

MARRIAGE IS A WORD THAT TASTES LIKE METAL—THE STEEL OF armor, the gold of commerce, the iron bite of blood and prison bars.

But also bronze. A bell that rings clear and true and joyously. Like hope.

As my father guides me through the palace rooms to the chapel, I don't know which way the door to my cell will swing. It could ring loud, metal to metal, locking me into a life I never asked for. Or it could open wide, hinges creaking, into a life I never imagined.

I concentrate very hard on not tripping over my own train as we turn the final corner and proceed through the chapel doors. I will never hear the end of it from my mother if I blunder.

Henry FitzRoy is already there. Watching me.

My family has known him for years. When he was a child, Father helped organize his household, his tutors, his finances, his friends. My brother, Hal, was sent to Windsor to be his playmate.

But I don't know him. I don't know who he's become. All I remember is a little boy with golden-red hair and eyebrows that seemed to soar right off the top of his forehead. A little boy with no chin and an air of superiority.

It appears I'm marrying someone quite a bit more attractive.

His eyebrows still arc high into the fringe of hair ready to fall into his eyes at any moment. Eyes the color of a clear winter dawn. His nose is perhaps a little too big for the mouth below it, the full lower lip complementing the now well-defined chin.

The mouth tips into a smile. Of relief? Or of expectation?

As I watch, unmoving, one eyebrow curves even higher.

A question.

An invitation.

A challenge.

Father walks me to the altar. The shallow, barrel-vaulted ceiling looms heavy overhead. The magnificent stained-glass window in front of me filters the light of the wintry sky through depictions of the king and his first queen, Katherine. To either side of me stand witnesses dressed in gaudy blue and green and crimson. My eyes never leave the boy in front of me.

Father squeezes my arm and whispers, "Make me proud."

I say the only thing I can.

"I will."

We turn to face the priest and Father puts my hand in Henry FitzRoy's. His palm is rough beneath my fingers; his sleeve tickles my wrist. He is taller than I am, his presence beside me solid.

His breath comes easily, while mine is trammeled in my throat from fear.

And something else.

I search my heart. It can't be love. I don't even know this boy.

4

And it's not lust, despite his good looks. Besides, I don't really know what either of those is supposed to feel like.

I glance at my father out of the corner of my eye. See the glitter in his as he stares straight ahead, lips pressed against his teeth to suppress a grin. I recognize what I see there reflected in me.

Triumph.

A Howard marrying the son of the king.

"I take thee, Mary, to be my wedded wife."

FitzRoy sounds so assured, saying those words. As though making that promise is as easy as stepping into a role in a masque.

Which is really what we're doing. He wears the mask of husband. I represent wife. We will perform this showy little dance for the pleasure of king and courtiers, fathers and family.

Then we will exit the stage and go our separate ways.

I risk another glance from below my lashes.

FitzRoy catches me looking at him, and I turn quickly back to the priest. Watch the watery blue eyes floating in a sea of creases. Watch his mouth move, the words like vapors.

And then it's my turn.

"I take thee, Henry . . ."

I stumble once. *Till death us depart.* Death is so far away. We're only fourteen—*till death* is a long promise. It's a long time to be imprisoned by our *parents'* actions and not our own.

A breath of cold air brings gooseflesh to my arms and neck.

The priest takes my hand, his skin cool and papery, sliding like the discarded shell of a beetle. He places my right hand in that of my husband and binds us together with a white ribbon. Raises his hands in benediction.

Then it's over. All hands are dropped. FitzRoy and I turn together to face our collective families. My parents stand to my right, not touching, not speaking—in fact, each pretending the other doesn't exist. But together. In the same room. A miracle if there ever was one.

And suddenly, in the doorway, dressed in crimson and cloth of gold and shining like a newly fat sun, there is my husband's father. The king. And his wife, my cousin, Anne Boleyn. They must have been watching from the privy balcony, hidden above us.

The king calls me daughter and kisses me on the mouth. I fight the urge to wipe his spittle off as he claps his son on the shoulder.

"The bride and groom!" he shouts.

I look at my new husband again and find him already watching me. Bride and groom. Husband and wife. Strangers. I don't even know what to call him. Your Grace? Henry? Husband?

"Fitz!" My brother rescues me with a shout that rings off the windows. Hal kneels before the king and queen, then stands to throw his arms around my husband and pummels him.

"A married man, Fitz!" he shouts again, his joy contagious.

"Same as you, Hal."

My brother laughs, but with a little less mirth than before. I'm not sure he likes his wife.

Fear clutches at me and I look down at my hands.

"We're related now," Hal says, sounding overly gracious. "You can call me Surrey."

Mother and Father never called Hal anything but Surrey—making sure the earldom stuck for good. When the two Henrys met as children, they decided that calling each other by their first names was too confusing. And that Richmond and Surrey were too formal. Henry FitzRoy gave Hal his nickname. So Hal dubbed him Fitz in return.

Fitz laughs and wraps his arm around Hal's neck, nearly throwing him to the floor. The rest of the congregation charges forward, uplifting them both, so close there is no space between the bodies and I cannot breathe, my vision limited to the bright chevrons of green and blue on the sleeve in front of me.

I slide out between them all and swallow air like a landed fish.

"You blundered." My mother has dressed in black for the happy occasion, the velvet of her gown sucking the light from the chapel windows while the gold braid of her hood reflects it. Like a halo. The darkness of her eyes negating any semblance of divinity.

I try to still the trembling of my limbs.

"And slouched."

I stand up straight. Shoulders back. Neck elongated.

If my life is a prison, my mother is my jailer. Her words turn the locks of fourteen years of daughterhood, keeping them tightly closed.

The word *daughter* tastes of bitterness. At least in my mother's mouth, it does.

The group beside us bursts into raucous laughter, but we

7

are in our own little circle of misery. My mother's mouth turns down, the lines around it sharply defined.

I hold my breath. I know what that face precedes.

"A feast!" The king's voice breaks us apart and I take advantage of it to move closer to my father. He always takes my side.

That is why I will always take his. Even when it's the wrong one.

"And a celebration," Father says, his narrow face animated, "of the joining of families."

The king takes Queen Anne's arm and strides out the door into the cloister. My mother steps up behind them. She is the Duchess of Norfolk—second only to the king's kin and protective of her own precedence. She hesitates when my father doesn't move to join her. Glares her disapproval.

She opens her mouth and I cringe, waiting for the vitriol sure to spill forth.

"Your Grace." My new husband steps forward, nods his head in a quick bow.

Everyone stops—even the king and queen. They turn, eyeing the flow of people snagged in the doorway behind my mother.

"Your Grace," Fitz says again, quietly. Intimately. Yet his voice, rich and luxurious as velvet, deep and smooth, carries throughout the silent church. "Mother." He smiles, almost shyly. Engaging and embarrassed.

She hesitates.

And then she smiles back. I suppress a gasp.

"I feel I must remind you"—he pauses and leans closer to

her, his tall, supple frame curling slightly over her small, inflex-ible form—"I am the Duke of Richmond and Somerset."

Mother goes pale.

"Your daughter is now my wife."

He cuts a quick sideways glance and a heart-stopping smile my way.

"She is my duchess."

His.

His wife. His duchess. His prisoner, if he so chooses.

For the first time, I really look at him. Try to see the whole and not just the parts. The eyes, brows, nose, mouth, chin encompassed by a face still round with a boyhood completely at odds with his bold self-confidence..

He raises an eyebrow into the flop of hair.

Definitely an invitation.

"She should have precedence." He unfurls his arm and holds out his hand. To me.

I hesitate. I know that if I step in front of my mother, she will never forgive me. But I do it anyway, my train whisper-ing behind me. Or perhaps it is the hiss of Mother's breath as she sucks it in through her teeth. I take Fitz's hand, warm and tight and . . . comforting.

I allow my husband to escort me to the chapel door—behind no one but the king and queen.

In the distance—beyond the great hall—I hear a bell ringing.

2

THE GREAT HALL CLAMORS WITH MUSIC, BOOT FALLS, AND THE collective voices of the hundred or so wedding guests. The mud carried in from the outside lies flat on the floor, leaving slick spots and the smell of earth. The food keeps coming, delivered first to the king and queen, then to my husband at the king's right.

And then to me, where I sit next to my father, just below the queen.

"What do you think of him?" Father asks.

I look down at the table, tracing the edge of it with a crumb of bread.

"He's handsome."

Father puts his fingers beneath my chin and lifts my face to his.

"It would serve you well to notice more than that." His voice is gentle, but carries a hidden steel. Like a dagger swathed in velvet. "He may be a bastard, but at least he's a boy. We expect great things. From both of you. You are the triumph of the Howards, Mary."

He releases me when he sees my mother approaching, and excuses himself quickly, leaving an empty chair and a half-full plate beside me.

My mother, still wearing black and an expression of deeply felt pain, kneels before the king, barely acknowledges the queen, and departs without giving me a first glance, much less a second.

Her absence should alleviate my discomfort, but I feel little relief. She is no longer watching me, but I am still on display.

"Congratulations, Cousin."

My thoughts made me forget that the queen sits beside me. I turn and bow my head, almost falling into her lap.

"Thank you, Your Majesty," I stutter.

She pulls me close and kisses me lightly on the cheek. She is only ten years older than I am, but the kiss is more motherly than anything I've ever received from the Duchess of Norfolk.

"May your marriage make you happy." The queen glances at the door my mother passed through. "And free."

"I don't know that I'll ever be free," I blurt, and immediately regret my words. It isn't my place to contradict the queen. But she laughs.

"You remind me of myself at your age," she says.

There are some people who make an impact as soon as you meet them. Lodge themselves in your mind. Embed themselves in your very soul.

Anne Boleyn is one of those people.

I am not. I can't even keep the attention of my new husband, who has not looked at me since we stepped into the hall.

Queen Anne is dark and poised and beautiful. I am clumsy enough to fall off a chair without moving, and my hair is the color of brass. She says exactly what is on her mind, while for all my love of words, I am afraid to use them at all.

"Thank you," I manage.

I want to smile. I remind her of herself?

The queen angles her body so she can speak to me more intimately. She wears a tight bodice that presses her breasts flat, tapering to a narrow waist. Her skirts are pleated at the hips to give an impression of curves. The peacock-blue damask only serves to make her coloring more striking.

"Your mother." Her voice is barely audible over the clamor of the wedding feast. "Is it true she opposed the match?"

When Mother found out that my father and Anne Boleyn had collaborated to marry me off to the king's son, she liberally employed the words *bastard* for my husband and *whore* for the queen.

She used worse for me when I acquiesced to Father's wishes.

"You will be sucked into the mire of Tudor refuse," she spat. "And if you deliberately defy me, I will be only too happy to watch you drown in your own muck."

I can barely meet the queen's eye.

"My mother . . . has firm opinions."

The queen laughs. "I can read equivocation as easily as I can understand Latin, Mary. Your mother opposes the match." Her dark eyes search my face. "What can she do about it?" She is truly looking for an answer this time. An honest one.

"Nothing, Your Majesty." The wedding is over.

"Nothing? She's the daughter of the Duke of Buckingham. The wife of the most powerful nobleman in the country."

"Forgive me, Your Majesty, but my grandfather is long dead, and my father hasn't spoken to my mother in years."

"A woman without male allies is a woman powerless, is that it?"

Her gaze penetrates me. She's daring me to speak my true mind.

The truth is that my mother has no allies. My brother avoids her. Father keeps a deliberate distance—even going so far as to lock her in her room. And yet the strength of her judgments unbalances us all.

"Power undetected is not the same as power*less*," I tell her.

"Well said, Cousin." The queen sits up again, our conversation open to the public.

"And what are your feelings, Mary?" she asks. "About your marriage."

I feel we have walked out onto a thin pane of ice over the Thames, the frigid blackness waiting to draw me under if I make a misstep. Above, all is blue sunshine and cheery laughter. But the water below moves swiftly.

"It is a great honor," I say finally. "For me and for my family."

"But you do not love him."

The little smile tugs at the corner of her mouth.

"I do not know him, Your Majesty."

That, at the very least, is the truth.

"Do you know who you are?" she asks. "Perhaps that is more important."

"I am a Howard," I say automatically.

"Not anymore," she says steadily. "You're a FitzRoy."

13

As if by the single swing of an ax, I am separated from the one truth that always held me secure. My father's name, my brother's name.

"You are more than a Howard or a FitzRoy or a wife or a daughter," the queen continues.

"My life is defined by those things."

"But *you* are not." The queen looks out over the crowd to where her brother, George, stands with Henry Norris and the poet Thomas Wyatt. The three men must be at least thirty years old—Norris is probably older—yet they maintain the air and attitude of adolescents. "I am a Boleyn. And the Boleyns always stick together." She turns back to me. "But I am also Anne. Able to make my own choices and speak my mind and fall in love, against all odds."

I glance at the king, his lips red from the wine, and back at my cousin, whose face has begun to show the seven years they spent fighting Queen Katherine, the country, and the pope for their right to marry. I wonder if love is worth the fight.

"What does love feel like, Your Majesty?" I ask.

"It's like music only plays when you're together," she says, not even pausing to think. "Like the very air tastes of strawberries. And like one touch—one look—could send you whirling like a seed on the wind. My brother's wife said that once, and I still believe it to be true."

I like the idea of *love* tasting like strawberries, but can't quite find it as I roll the word around on my tongue. So I nod, as if I understand. And wonder at the undercurrent of sadness in her voice.

 14

She smiles at me and adds, "I hope we've stacked the odds in your favor. If Fitz is anything like his father, loving him will be a daily adventure."

Behind her, the king leans back, one hand on his belly, the other resting on the table beside hers. Their little fingers touching. He catches me staring and lifts her hand to kiss it.

I turn to look for Fitz. He has moved to sit with my brother, both of them leaning lazily against the wall, their feet up on stools, boot soles out. As if nothing in their lives has changed.

He doesn't look at me. My husband has not come within ten feet of me since we left the chapel We've never even had a conversation.

The bridecup is passed. When it reaches me, it is slippery from the lips of all the others. The bridecake is consumed. And the evening starts to feel like fantasy—the atmosphere that comes with the overconsumption of celebration and wine and the underconsumption of reality.

Fitz wanders the room, greeting guests. I watch the way he walks, his movements completely uncalculated. The way he stands, his weight resting on one foot, cocked, as if ready to try anything next—running, dancing, riding.

I wonder if he's ready for this marriage.

"We must bed them!" George Boleyn stands by the fire, goblet raised, his dark eyes and narrow face alight with mischief and something not entirely innocent.

I can't move. A wedding—and banquet—is one thing. But the thought of getting into bed with a complete stranger makes me feel as if my skin is creeping with a thousand tiny feet.

Especially when the process is to be done in public.

I look for rescue. My father has already left. Hal is part of the cheering throng around Fitz.

The king frowns

"So be it."

There is no rescue.